THE BROKEN RUNE STAFF

THE BROKEN RUNE STAFF

Roger Whitmore

Copyright © 2022 Roger Whitmore

The moral right of the author has been asserted.

Apart from any fair dealing for the purposes of research or private study, or criticism or review, as permitted under the Copyright, Designs and Patents Act 1988, this publication may only be reproduced, stored or transmitted, in any form or by any means, with the prior permission in writing of the publishers, or in the case of reprographic reproduction in accordance with the terms of licences issued by the Copyright Licensing Agency. Enquiries concerning reproduction outside those terms should be sent to the publishers.

This is a work of fiction. Names, characters, businesses, places, events and incidents are either the products of the author's imagination or used in a fictitious manner. Any resemblance to actual persons, living or dead, or actual events is purely coincidental.

Matador
9 Priory Business Park,
Wistow Road, Kibworth Beauchamp,
Leicestershire. LE8 0RX
Tel: 0116 279 2299
Email: books@troubador.co.uk
Web: www.troubador.co.uk/matador
Twitter: @matadorbooks

ISBN 978 1803130 279

British Library Cataloguing in Publication Data.
A catalogue record for this book is available from the British Library.

Printed and bound in the UK by TJ Books LTD, Padstow, Cornwall
Typeset in 12pt Adobe Jenson Pro by Troubador Publishing Ltd, Leicester, UK

Matador is an imprint of Troubador Publishing Ltd

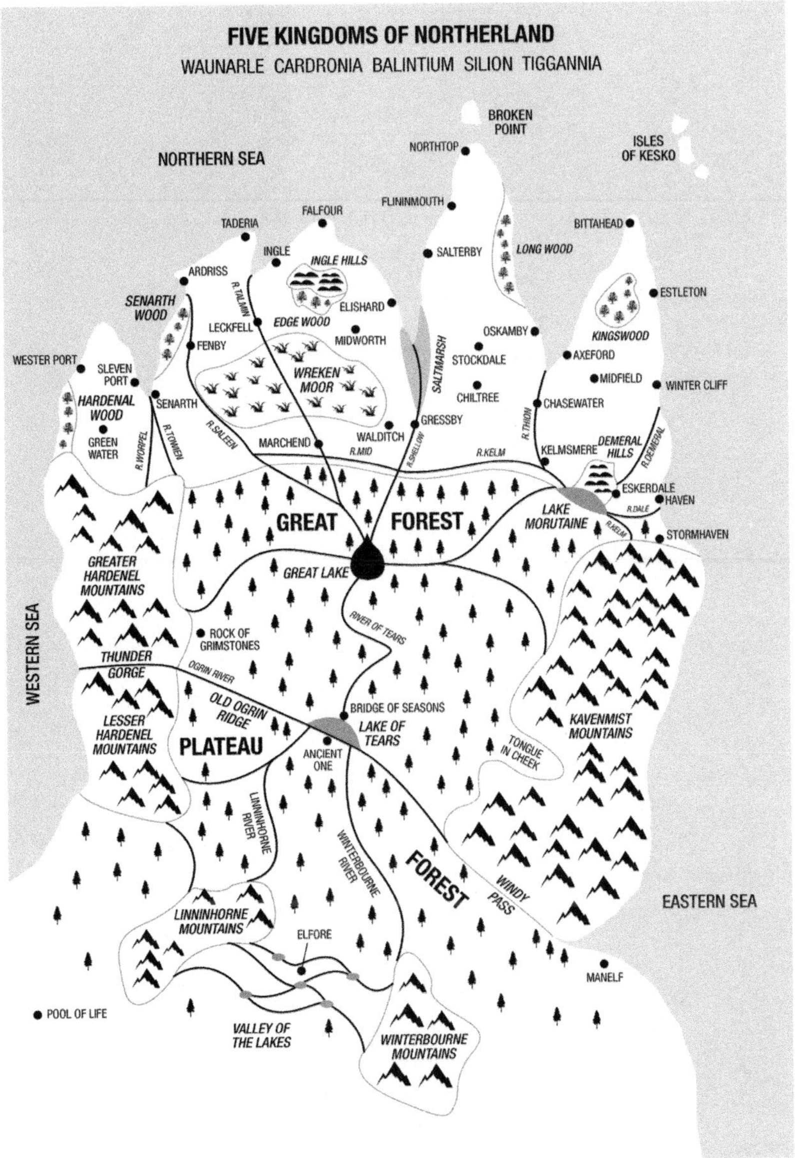
FIVE KINGDOMS OF NORTHERLAND
WAUNARLE CARDRONIA BALINTIUM SILION TIGGANNIA
BROKEN POINT
NORTHTOP
ISLES OF KESKO
NORTHERN SEA
FLININMOUTH
FALFOUR
TADERIA
BITTAHEAD
INGLE
INGLE HILLS
SALTERBY
LONG WOOD
ARDRISS
ESTLETON
SENARTH WOOD
R. TALMIN
ELISHARD
LECKFELL
EDGE WOOD
MIDWORTH
OSKAMBY
KINGSWOOD
FENBY
SALTMARSH
STOCKDALE
AXEFORD
WESTER PORT
SLEVEN PORT
WREKEN MOOR
MIDFIELD
WINTER CLIFF
HARDENAL WOOD
SENARTH
CHILTREE
CHASEWATER
GREEN WATER
R. WORPEL
R. TOWIEN
R. SALEEN
MARCHEND
WALDITCH
GRESSBY
R. THIDN
DEMERAL HILLS
R. DEMERAL
R. MID
R. SHELLOW
R. KELM
KELMSMERE
ESKERDALE
HAVEN
R. DALE
GREAT
FOREST
LAKE MORUTAINE
R. KELM
STORMHAVEN
GREATER HARDENEL MOUNTAINS
GREAT LAKE
WESTERN SEA
RIVER OF TEARS
ROCK OF GRIMSTONES
THUNDER GORGE
OGRIN RIVER
OLD OGRIN RIDGE
BRIDGE OF SEASONS
LESSER HARDENEL MOUNTAINS
PLATEAU
LAKE OF TEARS
ANCIENT ONE
TONGUE IN CHEEK
KAVENMIST MOUNTAINS
LINNINHORNE RIVER
WINTERBOURNE RIVER
FOREST
WINDY PASS
EASTERN SEA
LINNINHORNE MOUNTAINS
ELFORE
MANELF
POOL OF LIFE
VALLEY OF THE LAKES
WINTERBOURNE MOUNTAINS

PART I

KING WIELDER

CHAPTER I

The wind blew from the North, bringing with it a sudden flurry of snow, the first that winter.

King Rolfe of Tiggannia stood atop the battlements of Stormhaven stronghold, and although he had his fur cloak wrapped tightly around him, the winter's chill cut through him like a knife, clawing at his body, making him shudder.

His blond hair and beard started to fill with snow, beginning to give him the appearance of a stone statue, but another bout of shivering gave him away.

Reflected in King Rolfe's eyes was the reason for his early vigil this cold grey dawn. For down below him were the countless campfires of his invaders, the alliance armies of the Kingdoms of Waunarle and Cardronia.

Some of the fires, King Rolfe noted, were still embers from the night, but most had been rekindled, their flames beginning to lick greedily at the snow falling from the cold air. As if with hunger in anticipation of what was surely to come that day, thought King Rolfe distantly.

Staring at the campfires, lost in his thoughts, King Rolfe did not notice Cantell, the King's protector, join him on the battlements.

"You rise early this grey morn, sire," greeted Cantell, his words turning to mist as they met the cold air.

A glimmer of a smile met King Rolfe's lips as he turned to acknowledge his protector. "Ah, faithful friend, I could not rest. I have been watching our enemies stir from their slumbers."

Cantell could hear the weariness in his King's voice. As he looked at his King's face, he could see the strain and sadness etched upon it. A face that was once full of laughter, which now only showed the deep lines of foreboding.

Cantell could see clearly enough what ailed his King as he turned his head towards the campfires. *Our fate will be decided this day*, he thought.

"You see the urgency with which our invaders busy themselves, Cantell," said King Rolfe, interrupting Cantell's thoughts as he kept his eyes cast on the scene below.

"Indeed, sire, they prepare for a final battle," said Cantell, speaking the remainder of his thoughts to King Rolfe's nod.

"Yes, the time has come. The beginning of winter's snow has made up their minds for them."

Cantell could hear the battle of emotions coming from his King as he spoke, and fell quiet as they both watched the scene below. Losing themselves in the memories of what had passed more than two seasons ago.

The alliance armies of Waunarle and Cardronia had situated themselves along the valley that ran between the stronghold and the small fishing village of Haven. Just enough shelter for them from the now cutting winds coming in from over the Eastern Sea. With the River Dale running through it, Haven had always been a picturesque and peaceful place, that is, until the invasion!

King Rolfe could not see what remained of the village, but he knew it was just a burnt-out shell. Most of the villagers had sought hasty refuge within the stronghold's thick walls, while others had fled. Some had remained, mainly the old and the stubborn; after all, it was their home. Taking their chances on the mercy of the invaders, but the only mercy they were shown was at the end of a blade! None were spared. Ransacked for whatever could be found, then burnt to the ground; there was nothing left of the once thriving village.

All this lay heavy on King Rolfe's heart, forever gnawing at his conscience. Though there had been over nineteen summers of peace throughout all of Northernland, he should have taken more notice of what was going on around him. Signs were there in the neighbouring kingdoms, but he had ignored them. Through his ignorance, his people had suffered terribly and were still suffering.

He had not listened to his advisors of the build-up of forces in Waunarle and Cardronia. For all intents and purposes, he thought Cardronia was going to attack Waunarle, or advance into the Kingdom of Balintium, with Waunarle being aware of this and readying itself.

He would have been ready to help if either had happened, but to combine their armies and attack Tiggannia! Never! How wrong he had been, how stupid!

When he was told of King Taliskar of Cardronia's treacherous accusations of him being solely responsible for the deaths of the royal family of Waunarle, he had merely shaken his head, not wanting to hear such tales.

"What would you have me do? Do battle with them on a lie! On hearsay!" he had ranted.

"Is this not final proof enough to suspect him of trying to join forces with Waunarle with the aim of making war against us, sire? We must be ready!" they had warned him. He could still hear his advisors' words of warning being shouted at him, faces turning red at their King's blindness.

King Rolfe turned his head and troubled mind from the campfires to look out along the great arc that was Stormhaven Bay, its sands stretching as far as the eye could see.

Normally, the waves would crash on its sands, chasing each other freely along its length, but through the snow, King Rolfe could see the waves divide and fall as they hit the alliance warships that still littered the bay.

How many had appeared that day? Thirty? Forty? It did not matter now as he thought of that fateful day when Tiggannia's shores became stained with the blood of the fallen.

A shout had gone up and all had looked out towards the Eastern Sea. They must have come around the Isles of Kesko to keep their distance; otherwise, they would have been spotted from Broken Point, he thought for the umpteenth time.

He had decided to meet his foe on the shoreline as they landed. A breeze had sprung up from over the land and so gave favour to his infamous Tiggannian bowmen to launch a hail of fire arrows into the alliance warships before they reached the shore.

So with his army he had readied himself. Rather one decisive battle than suffer a long, slow demise under siege, so he had thought.

Messengers had been sent out to the Kingdoms of Balintium and Silion in the slim hope of help, but he knew in his heart there was small chance of that.

After all, Silion was a kingdom of farmers with no wish to fight, and with his advisors warning him about Taliskar's treacherous remarks about him, Balintium would not risk lives on someone they were unsure of. No, they were on their own.

So he had waited on the shore with only one thought; that by the end of the day, that slime King Taliskar would be resting impaled on the end of his sword!

How strange those last moments were before the battle, where so many would meet their fate. How still it had all felt, his soldiers quiet in silent thought of their loved ones while the waves from the Eastern Sea were gently breaking over the shore, washing the sand.

No birds could be heard singing; they seemed to have sensed what was on the way with the breeze whispering past King Rolfe's ears, seemingly warning him as it did so, *here comes death! Beware!*

Then suddenly they could hear the shouts of defiance from the alliance warships. If King Rolfe had had any doubts about who his enemies were, then this was the time they revealed themselves to him in plain sight.

For there were the two flags of the Kingdoms of Waunarle and Cardronia flying side by side on one of the nearest warships.

The Tiggannian bowmen had let loose their fire arrows to rip through the sky in whistling death. They had some effect, but not what King Rolfe had hoped for, as the warships' sails were lowered and oars taken up.

Another rain of arrows was let loose upon them, and another. The warships had returned fire as soon as they were near enough against the breeze.

The shouts of the alliance soldiers were heard, sounding as if they had worked themselves up into a frenzy, ready for battle.

Then there they were, jumping ship and running headlong into them. Axes and swords held aloft, ready to slice the nearest Tiggannian. Easy pickings to begin with, but they just kept coming and coming. How many there were on those warships King Rolfe had no idea, but the battle was soon in full cry.

Metal on metal mixed with the shouts and cries from both armies had filled the air. King Rolfe's sword swirling like a whirlwind with no time to think, just kill. He knew death, but the sound of ripping flesh and shattered bone made him shudder inside.

The battle had raged on until his attention was drawn to the horizon, where more warships had appeared.

Assessing their losses, bloodstained and exhausted King Rolfe had decided to withdraw, fighting his way back to the stronghold.

Half the garrison had perished that fateful day with many more wounded. Bodies had covered the bay and as the waves had broken gently on the shore, they had washed over the fallen bodies, turning Stormhaven's sands into a carpet of scarlet.

The sad song of that day would be forever engraved in Tiggannian hearts.

No one did come to their aid. The only soldiers to appear were from the alliance army, bringing with them great catapults. Once in place, a constant bombardment of rocks battered the stronghold throughout the siege.

The stronghold walls had withstood the bombardment well, with its stone proving to be much stronger than the hurled rocks that had smashed against it.

Thankfully, the huge gates, somehow, had also held firm, although the battlements and their own catapults, which were placed upon them, had taken a battering. Not that the Tiggannian catapults were much use during the siege, with the alliance army making sure their encampment was out of range.

Starvation and disease had cast its spidery web over the stronghold in the long months that followed, its clinging touch taking its toll to kindle the flames of their fires that had seen their loved ones being burnt.

So here they were awaiting their fate as the alliance army prepared themselves now winter was here.

King Rolfe had not noticed the guard that had appeared on the battlements talking to Cantell, so lost was he in his recollections.

Cantell turned with a smile on his face. *What is there to smile about?* King Rolfe said to himself with a frown.

Cantell brought the guard over, who immediately dropped to one knee. "Sire!" he exclaimed.

"Please stand," said King Rolfe, cupping his hand under the guard's arm to lift him up onto his feet. "The time for such formalities has long since passed," he stated.

"Thank you, sire. It is the Queen, sire, she…"

King Rolfe suddenly came back to reality with a jolt. "She begins!" he exclaimed.

"She does, sire," finished the guard, and quickly withdrew with a bow.

King Rolfe looked at Cantell, half talking, half whispering in sudden emotion. "All this suffering we have endured, Cantell, and through it all, my little Queen Elina is about to have our child, a tiny life in amongst so much death."

King Rolfe shook his head in his emotion as a flurry of snow blew into the eyes of both warriors, to aptly hide the tears that were welling up as they wiped away the snow in excuse.

"I must make haste to the royal chamber, Cantell. Get ready all those that can fight. This day promises to be an eventful one!"

CHAPTER II

"Get that lazy dog to his feet!" shouted the young Captain of the Cardronian horse soldiers to the dozing soldier's comrades. "Do you think you are capable of doing that between you? Or has the ale he drank this past night detached his legs from his body, making it impossible for you to do so?"

One soldier started to laugh but was duly elbowed in the ribs, making him cough instead. The soldier was soon on his feet and staring into the cold stare of his Captain.

"It has been a long wait, tedious perhaps," The young Captain looked at each and every one of them as he spoke; not a word was said.

"I trust then your fighting skills will match your drinking skills, for today we attack the stronghold!" He finished to be met by a yell; they had sat around long enough.

The young Captain looked again at the soldier who had been helped to his feet.

"You will be at the front of the attack. I am sure your taste for ale will be more than equalled by your taste of blood. Go and report there now!"

"Yes, Captain, sir," the soldier replied, bowing a heavy head.

The young Captain's eyes followed the soldier. *They are all good men,* he thought, *but they need a kick up the backside now and again.*

He looked up at the snow, knowing it must have made up his King's mind, but he wondered why they had not waited it out a bit longer. Lives would have been saved by not fighting; capitulation was inevitable. It would only be a matter of days, he thought, by the stench of death that was coming from the stronghold.

He gave one last warning before going to find his King: "Be sure your wits are as keen as your blades. Remember, though they are weak, it is their land they fight for!" All saluted their Captain as he strode off in the direction of the King's tent.

He would not find him there, for King Taliskar stood at the edge of the encampment, looking up at the walls of Stormhaven stronghold.

A tall man whose features held the look of a preying hawk ready to strike, with hair as black as night, a trait of most Cardronians; not that any showed with the snow falling. His hooded cloak saw to that.

His eyes narrowed for an instant as he watched two figures scurry away from the battlements. *Rolfe, your time has come!* he thought, with a scowl written across his face.

"When are we going to attack, Taliskar? We have waited long enough!" This disgruntled deep growl came from Brax, protector of Waunarle. Built like an ox and short of stance, he was ready for battle.

A position as protector of Waunarle he had eventually gained after the loss of the royal family to their people.

They had met their end in a tragic accident after a hunting trip, so it was said at the time. All were lost when their carriage had plunged over the cliffs near Westerport.

A full year had passed by while an heir to the throne had been sought, but all to no avail. Every time a new lead was found, the trail had led nowhere.

King Taliskar, meanwhile, began using his persuasive powers on the governing body of Waunarle, but more importantly on their army, who held the power, that an alliance should be forged with him, and Brax should be their Protector, someone they could trust, until an heir was found.

Alongside this were the rumours that had begun to circulate throughout the Kingdom of Waunarle. Rumours that had become voices to be heard, that the royal family's tragedy was no accident. That King Rolfe was the culprit behind their deaths!

King Taliskar had finally persuaded the governing body of Waunarle that with Cardronia by their side in an alliance, they could seek out vengeance of the murderers of their royal family, or as King Taliskar had pointed out, "That murderer! King Rolfe!"

It had been a long, slow process, but in the end they had listened, for them both to be here at last, seeking King Rolfe's blood in the name of the alliance.

King Taliskar turned to look at Brax's face with a smile, speaking to him like a naughty boy. "You are so impatient for blood Brax."

This only made Brax turn red. "Impatient! Impatient! We have been stuck here now for, for… only the stars know how long, able to do nothing but scratch our own backsides!" Brax almost spat the words out.

"My dear Brax, our waiting is finally at an end. We shall take this place and then Tiggannia will be mine."

"What did you say!" exclaimed Brax, looking sharply at King Taliskar, turning even redder.

King Taliskar watched Brax try to control his emotions; how he loved to see the ugly pig's face writhe.

"Forgive me, Brax, I forget myself. Ours, of course," said King Taliskar, still smiling but staring straight into Brax's eyes.

Though King Taliskar had put Brax in the position of protector, with the further promise of power and riches, he loathed the man. This hold over him, however, meant he could control Brax, but he had promised himself that when his usefulness was over, he would have his throat cut and silence the pig forever.

He heard his beautiful wife, Queen Helistra's, words echo in his mind as he thought about it. How he missed her and longed to look into those deep green eyes once more. He had not seen her since the siege; too long.

How lucky he had been to have found a woman like her, he thought. It was she who had spoken quietly in his ear about forming an alliance. *The deaths of the royal family can be used to your advantage,* he remembered her saying. *By forming an alliance, you will have the power to overthrow King Rolfe. No one will be stronger than you.*

Put Brax in a position where he needs you, then when he is no longer needed, you must do whatever you deem is necessary. Be patient, my love, the throne of Tiggannia awaits.

King Taliskar's smile broadened as he thought of her and her words of counsel while still looking at Brax, but Brax had turned away from his gaze.

He knew what was going on in Taliskar's mind; he could see how he was using him. He was not stupid.

Knowing if he did not watch his back, he was a dead man, but not if he struck first and took the throne of Tiggannia for himself!

But her, she was different, he felt uneasy in her presence. There was something.

Keep them in their little castle, let time weaken them, he remembered her saying in that crystal clear, sweet voice of hers, but one with hidden depths that belied her beauty.

Looking up at Stormhaven stronghold, Brax remembered the day they had invaded; it was not a case of keeping them in their little castle on that day.

They had come in force and found a reception waiting for them on the shore. Only after the fiercest of battles where many lives were lost on both sides had they retreated behind those impregnable walls.

It was true that since that day, time had weakened them. The smell of death coming from the stronghold told him that, but it had been a long wait.

When was it? he thought, the month of Beginning or Growing? And now it was the month of Snow! Six whole months and that weasel says I am impatient! *Calm yourself, Brax,* he told himself, *you will soon be upon the throne of Tiggannia with Taliskar on the end of your axe, and there will be nothing she will be able to do about it.*

They did not notice the flushed face of the young Captain approach them as they looked on at Stormhaven through the snow, mirroring each other's thoughts.

The young Captain should have known King Taliskar would be here and not in his tent where he had just been. Where else would he be but looking up at the Stormhaven stronghold?

"The men are ready, sire," he announced, making them both turn quickly.

"Ah, good, but first we will give them a chance, Captain Tarbor. I want you with whomever you deem fit to ride to the gates and ask for their surrender," ordered King Taliskar to the raised eyebrows of Brax.

"At once, sire," acknowledged Captain Tarbor, and turning, he shouted at the nearest group of soldiers as he moved towards his horse.

"Ask for their surrender? Am I hearing things? Is this Taliskar the merciful speaking?" quipped a surprised Brax.

"I am not without heart, Brax," answered King Taliskar, making Brax nearly choke. "We both know the task ahead is still a formidable one. There is perhaps a slight chance they will surrender, judging from the smell," he added, although he knew, as did Brax, that they would fight to their last breath.

"Why not wait it out then?" Brax found himself asking, even though there was nothing more he wanted to do than fight.

"We do not want to be here in winter," pointed out King Taliskar. "It has been a task in itself to feed our armies in the good months. We will let our armies' hunger be quenched instead by the spilling of Tiggannian blood. They have waited long enough and are ready, as we are. Do not worry. We will be warming our hands on their burning bodies soon enough," King Taliskar said with a smile as both men surveyed their goal once again.

Looking at Stormhaven stronghold, the task did indeed look a formidable one.

Though it had taken a pounding from the alliances' catapults, the outer wall of the stronghold was hardly marked. Whoever had built it, had built it with a hidden inner strength.

Its walls locked into either side of the mighty Kavenmist Mountains that rose majestically behind the stronghold. Semicircle in shape, four turrets could be seen dividing the outer wall into four sections.

The two outer turrets King Taliskar knew held the stronghold guard, along with the two middle turrets, which also held the stronghold's enormous gates, with the gatehouse situated above them.

The gates were believed to be more than double the thickness of a hand. They must be, King Taliskar had thought, to still be there after the amount of rocks they had been hit with.

Adorned on the gates were some strange markings, but nobody knew what they meant. *Once known, but now forever lost*, someone had said.

Waiting behind those gates was an archway laced with arrow slits. Once in there, you could be picked off at will by hidden archers. The archway ended in a solid rock wall, making you turn left or right onto roadways that led up and around to another pair of gates set in an inner wall.

The inner wall loomed in front of you, overlooking the roads in a straight line to meld into the mountains, just as the outer wall.

It stood higher than the outer wall, an ideal vantage point for archers, with only two central turrets holding more soldiers and Middle Gate, as it was simply called.

Not as high or substantial as the outer gates but, nevertheless, it took four men to lift one of the two wooden bars that were there to hold the gates in place.

Behind Middle Gate, a grand courtyard opened out with many buildings within its enclosure. From storerooms to the great hall itself, which was the centrepiece of the courtyard.

Well, not quite, for rising majestically out from the back of the great hall was the magnificent Forest Tower. It had the same bonding of stone and rock as the walls to make it look as if it was as one with the mountains, affectionately known as the old sower of the mountains.

Through the great hall off the base of Forest Tower lay the throne room, a large chamber cut out of the solid rock.

Two stone thrones stood there, hewn in the same way, polished so that they shimmered even in torchlight. On them, as on the gates, more strange markings were to be seen.

Opposite the stone thrones on a simple ledge lay the two golden crowns of Tiggannia, adorned by an array of precious stones.

It was all either man wanted as they looked on, all they could think of, waiting there, the thrones of power and crowns of glory, waiting there for them!

They watched Captain Tarbor with three horse soldiers gallop up towards the gates of Stormhaven stronghold as their minds intertwined with thoughts of so much power.

"The dog Rolfe is mine," said Brax out of nowhere, *then you*, he thought.

"He is yours," replied King Taliskar, *then you are mine*, his mind said with the same thought.

CHAPTER III

Queen Elina lay on the royal bed looking as beautiful as ever, a shock of red hair framing the picture of her petite face.

Her hand servant Charlotte had got everything ready, as best she could under the circumstances, for the impending childbirth, with the ever-faithful Mrs Beeworthy in close attendance.

Her normal duties were that of kitchen cook, but she had been more like a mother to Queen Elina, ever since Queen Elina's mother had died when she was very young.

King Rolfe sat on her bed holding her small hand whilst looking into her sea blue eyes as another tug of pain crossed her face.

"Are you all right, my little one?" he asked with concern in his voice.

Queen Elina observed the concerned face of the man she worshipped and saw how the lines of worry had run deep into his features. She squeezed his hand and smiled. "Soon I will be, my husband," she replied in a drawn breath.

Another bout of pain made her go tense and her squeeze became a grip. King Rolfe looked at Mrs Beeworthy.

"The time is at hand, sire, time for us womenfolk to be getting on," said Mrs Beeworthy in her broad spoken Stockdale accent, whilst releasing Queen Elina's handhold of King Rolfe, shooing him towards the door.

"Not to worry, my treasure, Beeworthy's here. You have been a brave little girl," she said reassuringly. "Those two little devils wriggling around inside you will soon be in your arms," she added with a smile.

King Rolfe stopped in his forced tracks. "Two!" he exclaimed, looking at his Queen. "I… I did not realise… you never said."

Mrs Beeworthy turned red with embarrassment and threw a frown at Queen Elina. "I am sorry, my husband, I should have told you," she apologised.

"At first, I was not sure and then when I was, those tyrants had invaded. You had enough on your mind and I did not want to bother you," she finished, turning her head to one side. She could not look at her King.

"Bother me?" King Rolfe's jaw dropped in astonishment.

"Are you angry with me, my husband?" she uttered.

He was back by her side, stroking her face lovingly. Cupping her small chin in his hand, he gently pulled her face around to look into his. "I could never be angry with you," he said softly.

Then he squeezed her chin a little and shook her head side to side, gently letting out a roar of laughter whilst doing so. Queen Elina laughed with him, setting off another bout of pain, but it did not matter to her. It was good to see her husband laugh again, even in such dark times.

"Two!" He beamed. "Two heirs to the throne of Tiggannia!" Their laughter died down and more serious matters had to be quickly spoken of. As much joy as there was for the new lives soon to be born, King Rolfe knew they would be in jeopardy if he did not act.

King Rolfe squeezed his little Queen's hand. "You know what we must try to do. We have spoken of it before. Though there will be two, it does not alter things," he said quietly, looking squarely into his Queen's eyes to see the anguish she was going through to make such a sacrifice, as she nodded silently.

"Taliskar will end the siege this day and attack." He informed her on what he had witnessed from the battlements.

"We must try and make good their escape for the future of Tiggannia. No matter how slim we feel their chance is of survival. We both know that under Taliskar, they will have no future," he finished, leaving Queen Elina with an empty feeling on hearing such cold reality.

"You are right, my husband, a slim chance is better than none," she replied, trying her best to smile. "They will be the hope of all Northernland. Now, go. I have the future to deliver!" She cried as another bout of pain stopped any more talking.

King Rolfe gave his brave little Queen a parting kiss on the cheek and whispered in her ear, "You never cease to amaze me, only with your strength have I managed to survive these last months. I love you," and with that King Rolfe left, looking back at her with a smile as he walked through the door. Only then did Queen Elina's eyes fill with tears.

Cantell was waiting at the bottom of the spiral steps that wound their way around the inside of Forest Tower, fiddling with the hilt of his sword. Even though death was knocking at the gates, he was no good in situations like this, turning as he heard footfall to see King Rolfe duly appear.

"The Queen, sire, has she…?"

"Not yet, but soon, Cantell, then I will be a father of twins!"

Cantell had to look twice at his King. "Twins, sire? I thought there was only going to be one?" he questioned.

"As did I, my friend, but what do we know about such things?" And both men started to laugh.

"Let us sit and talk," said King Rolfe, leaving the base of Forest Tower between two mighty pillars that showed the way to the open arched doorway of the great hall across a linking corridor.

Sitting at one of the long tables, King Rolfe looked around him. "Do you remember the last time we feasted here?" he asked, catching Cantell a little off guard.

"I do, sire, the day you and Queen Elina became as one," remembered Cantell with a smile.

"That memory will be as nothing if Taliskar finds I have heirs to the throne. We must make good their escape!" came King Rolfe's worried warning.

Cantell looked at his King; he knew he was right. Taliskar would show no mercy to anyone, but how would they escape? he wondered.

Just then, the great hall doors that led to the grand courtyard opened, letting in Kelmar, Captain of the stronghold guard.

"Ah, Kelmar, your timing is excellent as usual," greeted King Rolfe.

Kelmar strode down towards them with determination in his every stride, his fair hair flowing in his wake to put a smile on his old friend Cantell's face.

He was built in the same mould as King Rolfe and Cantell, with the advantage of the odd year or two on his side. Although these past few months had taken their toll on everyone, Kelmar's strong features were as keen and alert as ever.

He stopped short of the two and nodded. "Sire, Cantell," he acknowledged.

"Any news, Kelmar?" queried King Rolfe.

"Four horsemen approach the gates, sire," he announced.

"What? A surrender party from Taliskar? Pah!" scoffed King Rolfe.

They all knew it to be false; even if they surrendered, he would still have them put to the blade.

King Rolfe quickly told Kelmar of the impending births, that Queen Elina was going to have twins!

"Two, sire, that is good news, and the Queen holds well?" Kelmar enquired.

"She is well, Kelmar," King Rolfe said smilingly as he thought about her.

"It does mean I will need someone else to come with me, sire," pointed out Kelmar, looking at Cantell. Cantell looked back at Kelmar then at King Rolfe looking at him, realising what Kelmar was hinting at.

"Kelmar is right, this unexpected news has altered things. Two are needed, who I can trust, to help secure the future of Tiggannia," nodded King Rolfe.

"But what of you, sire, and the Queen?" questioned Cantell immediately.

"You know my place is here, my friend. I cannot leave my people in their time of need. I have already cost them dear in my ignorance, and your Queen has let her views be known to me that even if she was able, she will not leave my side," stated King Rolfe to Cantell's protest.

"As is my place as your protector, sire!"

King Rolfe looked at Cantell, understanding that he was not just his protector, he was his friend.

"No, Cantell, you have done your duty by me, my friend. Now I want you to do your duty as protector of the twins that are to be born. Not just for the future of Tiggannia, but for the whole of Northernland!" said King Rolfe, quoting his Queen to make himself clear.

Cantell looked at Kelmar with mixed emotions at what his King was asking him to do. Kelmar knew what he was going through. His protests had also gone unheard, him with a newborn!

"But, sire, what chance will newly born babies have of surviving in our hands without their mother?" pushed Cantell, with worried feelings of what he wanted him to do.

"Slim, I know, but it is better than none if they fall into Taliskar's hands," King Rolfe was quick to point out.

Cantell knew that to be true, but leaving his King and Queen to their fate without him there rankled, knowing it could be the last time he would ever see them again once Taliskar had his hands on them.

King Rolfe watched his friend's emotions run through him as he waited, for although it was an order, he still wanted to hear his old friend agree.

A silence followed as Cantell got to grips with what his King was asking of him.

"I will protect them with my life, sire," said Cantell finally, to the grin of King Rolfe. "Now, how do we escape from here with the siege blocking us in?" he asked, looking at Kelmar with a strong suspicion as to what the answer was going to be.

"Through the caves under Kavenmist at the back of Forest Tower," came the assured answer from Kelmar.

Cantell knew it and groaned, shaking his head. "You have explored those caves for… well, for how long I do not remember, but each time they have led you nowhere, only to dead ends and roof falls!" said Cantell, feeling exasperated.

"Yes, but you think you have found a way through this time, Kelmar," urged King Rolfe.

"Yes, sire. I do. We all know the Kavenmist Mountains have many caves and tunnels that were worked long ago, with many claimed back by the mountain, but I have always felt that one of them must lead to the edge of the Great Forest," began Kelmar.

"Even before the siege, I was halfway through unblocking one of the tunnels in my quest to find this out." Kelmar stopped to look at Cantell and King Rolfe.

"And?" prompted Cantell.

"I finished unblocking it and explored further to come across another roof fall, but this time, as I began to unblock it, I felt cold air upon my face and the smell of the forest in my nostrils. It can only be the edge of the Great Forest beyond the blockage," said Kelmar, with excitement in his voice.

"It is still blocked then?" queried Cantell.

"Yes, it is, time has been against me, but the rocks are moveable. They are not boulders," urged Kelmar, seeing Cantell's face.

Cantell wished he had Kelmar's spirit, but it still sounded as if their chances were slim to him, but he had not been left with a choice.

"We have dwelt on this matter long enough, my friends. I know the task ahead is a daunting one, but it is our only hope," said King Rolfe, getting to his feet.

"We will be ready, sire, and if the stars are watching over us, we will head for Kelmsmere once we make it through," stated Kelmar.

"Ah yes, your mother lives there," said King Rolfe with a nod.

"She does, sire, she will help us," confirmed Kelmar.

Cantell had forgotten Kelmar's mother lived in Kelmsmere, which would certainly be useful if they made it. He only hoped all was well there and that the alliance armies had not ransacked it as they had Haven, for Kelmar's sake as well as their own.

"Is there anybody else we can turn to for help, sire?" he asked, thinking on it.

King Rolfe thought for a moment. "King Stowlan of Balintium could prove useful," he replied.

"I know he stayed neutral, not knowing what to believe, but his people are more used to wielding hayforks than swords. Their battle is with the land, not their neighbours," he added. Cantell understood, nodding.

Just then the great hall doors opened and a guard appeared. "Sire, there are four horse soldiers at the gate," he announced.

"Very well," answered King Rolfe. "See to it you are ready, my friends," said King Rolfe, looking at his two comrades. They in turn saluted him and watched him leave the great hall.

Outside, the snow had abated a little, but the grey gloom still hung heavy overhead as the wind instantly cut through King Rolfe as he moved across the grand courtyard with an escort of soldiers.

He observed what remained of his people. It saddened him that it had come to this as he did so.

As he passed under Middle Gate, a man shouted words of encouragement to him. "We are with you, sire! Never fear that!"

King Rolfe stopped by the man and put a hand on his shoulder. "They will find out what we Tiggannians are really made of," he said with a grin.

"They shall not pass me without tasting my sword first, sire!" The man grinned back whilst slapping the hilt of his sword.

"Nor mine," replied King Rolfe, and he slapped him on the shoulder. How many good men had he lost like him, he thought as he moved on.

More shouts came to his ears as he walked down the road between the inner and outer walls. An archer from the battlements could be heard above the rest. "Tell them, sire, that we would sooner throw ourselves off old Sower than give into them scum!" A cheer went up from his fellow archers.

King Rolfe looked up and gave them a grin; he could not believe the spirit they all showed.

Captain Tarbor was waiting outside the giant gates, surveying the ground that led up to the outer walls whilst he waited.

The alliance armies had built two large siege towers ready to scale the wall either side of the gates, and he was eying the ground when the huge gates began to open.

Dismounting, Captain Tarbor approached King Rolfe as he appeared. King Rolfe found himself looking at Captain Tarbor twice; he reminded him of someone.

"King Rolfe," acknowledged Captain Tarbor. King Rolfe said nothing and waited for Captain Tarbor to say what he had to say.

"I have been sent here by King Taliskar of Cardronia, sire, to ask you to lay down your arms and surrender, to let death be at an end," he announced, and waited for the reply he knew he would get.

"Taliskar is asking us for our surrender? Is he not feeling well?" came King Rolfe's sarcastic reply. "I presume his lapdog is still by his side?" he continued in the same vein.

"Do you mean Brax the Protector, sire?" said Captain Tarbor adding to King Rolfe's bemusement.

"Brax the Protector! That oaf is nothing but a mercenary out for his own gain!" King Rolfe could see the plotting between them for this day.

"How well he has done with Taliskar's help since King Palitan of Waunarle met his tragic end," noted King Rolfe. "Tell Taliskar and that mercenary," King Rolfe smiled as the words of the archer came into his mind, "I would sooner throw myself off old Sower than give into those two murderers!"

With those words hanging in the cold air, King Rolfe gave Captain Tarbor one last penetrating look before turning heel and heading back through the huge gates, for them to slowly close with a resounding thump.

Captain Tarbor remounted his horse and as he turned round to head off back to the encampment, he turned King Rolfe's last words around in his mind; *murderers of King Palitan.*

Exactly the same as King Taliskar had said about King Rolfe. The whole reason for them being here, but why did King Rolfe's words feel as if they held the truth within them to him?

Shaking his head, he glanced up to see the Tiggannian flag being unfurled and start to ripple in the wind. *I think that will give them their answer*, he thought, and off he rode.

King Rolfe returned to the great hall issuing orders for a score of archers to come to the base of Forest Tower with him.

Reaching the base, he looked around. A good place to defend for a last stand, he thought. His eyes caught sight of the five wide steps at the back of the base that led down to the mountain throne room.

That is all they are after, he thought, *what that room represents, power.* He found himself going down the steps. Opening the door, he took a lingering look. He could see their faces now drooling over what lay in there, for he had no illusions as to how the day would end.

In the middle of the room were the two magnificent stone mountain thrones carved with beautiful flowing pictures, glimmering in the torchlight.

Symbols were etched on each one, as on the huge gates, but what they were there for or meant King Rolfe had no idea.

For some reason, one of the thrones had an uneven hole bored into its arm. It was as much a mystery as to why it was there as the ancient symbols.

King Rolfe had always felt he was just a guardian of the stronghold, that one day someone would come with the key to unlock all of its mysteries, but until then…

His head turned towards the two crowns on the rock ledge. He had only worn his crown twice, he remembered. Once when he was crowned

King and then when he had been joined with his love, Queen Elina. A happy day, he thought.

That all felt a long time ago now and with that last thought, he closed the throne room door behind him to prepare himself for the final assault.

CHAPTER IV

"I will bury him in that flag!" spat Brax as he looked upon the Tigannian flag flying in defiance.

"Your wait is nearly over, my dear Brax," said King Taliskar with a smile.

"Be to your post, Captain, and await my signal," ordered King Taliskar to Captain Tarbor, who had returned.

"Sire," he confirmed, and was gone.

King Taliskar mounted his horse. "Come then, Brax, let us be about this place. The hunt has been a long one, let us enjoy the kill!" And Brax was on his horse without being told twice.

With flared nostrils and eyes wide, the two horses, with their riders, galloped to the east siege tower.

King Taliskar looked over the siege tower as he got there. It was going to be hauled into place by three lines of soldiers who had huge ropes running over their shoulders, whilst round shields were strapped to their arms as protection from arrows.

Giant blocks for the back wheels of the siege towers had been made from tree trunks. Cut so they would wedge under the wheels instantly, they were held ready by two pairs of soldiers to throw into place if the tower was in danger of rolling back.

Soldiers lined up behind each tower ready to scale them, whilst archers waited on top of the towers and on the ground at the sides; all was ready.

King Taliskar drew his sword and looked across to Captain Tarbor, to see him waiting for his signal. He could see the flag of Waunarle flying next to him, whilst hearing his own flag flapping in the breeze behind.

He looked up at Stormhaven stronghold, waiting there in grey silence with the Tigannian flag flying in the breeze. That flag would soon be replaced by his, he thought, and he raised his arm in the air to feel a rush of blood course through him as he dropped it to announce the attack, letting his sword slice through the cold air.

Up went the cry! "Heave!" With a creak from the wheels and a grunt from the men, the siege towers began to slowly move, the ground beneath their feet holding well, considering the snow that had fallen and the fact they were having to gradually go uphill.

Muscle and fear drove the soldiers on, pulling with all their might to the sound of rocks ripping through the air overhead from their own catapults at the stronghold's battlements.

Slowly they pulled the siege towers nearer the outer walls as rocks began crashing through their locked shields, fired from the few catapults that had survived along the stronghold's battlements now their catapults had ceased firing for fear of hitting them.

At the same time, the Tiggannian archers were sending their rain of death over them as they strained to pull the siege towers. Those soldiers who fell from the rocks and arrows were replaced as alliance archers returned fire tenfold onto the battlements especially to see off those hurtling rocks at them.

Captain Tarbor watched as one Tiggannian archer took a moment too long, letting loose his arrow to be hit by no less than three arrows, thudding into his chest to make him reel and disappear backwards.

The siege towers drew nearer, making for bigger targets, with rocks bouncing off the wooden sides that were there to protect those climbing up inside to reach the wooden bridge when it was dropped onto the stronghold's battlements.

Fire arrows joined the rocks with what looked like black bandages tied near the arrowhead, set alight to burn the siege towers. Some blew out as they fizzed through the air; others hit their target with mixed results.

The siege towers were wet from the snow, making the fire arrows hiss as they thudded into the wood, but those that caught burst into flames!

Closer and closer they moved towards the outer wall, until those soldiers pulling the ropes at the front began to peel off and run back to double up on each rope.

"Heave and hold!" shouted Captain Tarbor on his side. "Heave and hold!" *Nearly there to drop the bridge down*, he thought, whilst looking at the front of the tower starting to catch alight as more soldiers peeled off and the blocks were jammed into place under the wheels.

Suddenly the Tiggannians poured hot black liquid down upon them, with rocks pushed over the battlements and fire arrows sent to ignite the black liquid.

Soldiers ran in all directions, screaming in agony, holding their faces; suddenly everything was in the balance!

"Hold!" yelled Captain Tarbor earnestly above it all. "Hold the tower!" Soldiers rushed in, shouting and swearing, with bodies trampled on as they did so. Arrows were fired back at the Tiggannians that showed themselves as nerves and limbs were tested to breaking point to keep the siege tower from rolling backwards; it held!

Captain Tarbor looked up; it was close enough at last to where part of the stronghold's battlements had been flattened by their constant bombardment.

"Block the wheels! Drop the bridge!" he yelled, with the first of the alliance soldiers already climbing up inside the siege tower to the bridge as the flames began to lick more hungrily.

With their shields before them and swords waving in the air, they ran across the wooden bridge, yelling at the top of their lungs. Yells that were cut short by arrows flying in from the inner wall.

Those behind them ran like madmen, jumping over their fallen comrades to be met head-on by the waiting Tiggannians. The battle was soon in full flow, with sparks igniting the air as swords met.

Captain Tarbor was off his horse and up the siege tower with a group of soldiers in his wake. The bridge looked quite narrow at this height when he looked down. No time to think the flames were reaching the bridge! *Just go!* he told himself.

His grip tightened on his sword and shield as he ran across the bridge. The soldier at his side took an arrow in the chest, his momentum sending him headlong over the side. Tarbor saw his body hit the outer wall on the way down before reaching the ground, leaving a trail of blood down the wall, pointing to where his crumpled body lay.

It made Captain Tarbor run harder to make it across onto the battlements, to be met by a Haven man wielding an evil-looking mace.

He ducked just in time to hear the swish of the mace go over his head. Thrusting his sword straight up, Captain Tarbor buried it deep into the Haven man's rib cage, stopping him in his tracks, and with a sideways blow of his shield, he smashed the Haven man across his head, sending him sprawling.

A Tiggannian soldier lunged at him from the side and Captain Tarbor swept his sword across him, managing to deflect the blow, turning to meet his adversary as he did so.

As they clashed swords together, Captain Tarbor could see the soldier was well trained in the use of his sword, but he felt the lack of strength in his strikes as they did so. *His time under our siege has caught up with him*, he thought.

Striking him with added force, Captain Tarbor drove the soldier back, making the soldier stumble as he did so. His guard momentarily dropped and Captain Tarbor did not hesitate as he drove his sword through the side of the Tiggannian's stomach, leaving him clutching the fatal wound.

"Tarbor!" The shout came from Girvan his old friend, who came to his side.

"Girvan, I am glad to see you have survived," said Tarbor with a smile. "How fairs the battle?" Even as he asked the question, he could see the Tiggannians were in retreat from the battlements.

"They fight bravely, Tarbor, but the battlements are ours," Girvan answered, keeping one eye out for arrows as one whistled past their heads.

"We need to move, we are sitting ducks," said Tarbor, warily casting a glance over the scene on the battlements as they moved towards the spiral steps that led down into the west turret.

Tarbor took in all the fallen bodies from the battle, their blood soaking into the stone of the battlements as it ran free. Tarbor had always done his duty, but this time something was not feeling right, something was niggling him, and he looked down at his sword feeling it shaking in his hand. It was his nerves from the battle, he thought dismissing it.

"See to the wounded then follow us," he shouted to the nearest soldiers to him, seeing the siege tower now completely engulfed in flames behind him; they had only just made it.

"The rest of you, follow me," and he disappeared with Girvan down the spiral steps that led into the west turret.

Nothing but wooden beds came into view as they entered the west turret room, with passageways leading out of the room both ways. More spiral steps led down to what he presumed was the same again.

Tarbor could hear fighting echoing from down the passageway ahead of him. "That must be coming from the gatehouse," he stated to Girvan.

"We need to get down there quickly and get those gates open, Tarbor," replied Girvan. Tarbor nodded and moved into the passageway.

No daylight reached the bleak passageway; only torchlight lit the way ahead, casting flickering shadows as they moved cautiously past their flames.

Tarbor reached an arched opening that led into the gatehouse turret and rushed in ready to strike at anyone, anything, but they were too late. Only the aftermath of the fight that had taken place met their advances.

Bodies lay across the floor through into the gatehouse, *and no doubt in the east gatehouse turret*, thought Tarbor.

A Cardronian soldier came over to Tarbor and saluted him. "Captain, sir," he acknowledged.

"Yes, what have you to report?" asked Tarbor.

"We are from the east siege tower, Captain, sir," he began. "After dealing with the resistance we met at the east turret, we saw your siege tower on fire and ran to help. We ran straight into their soldiers waiting in the passageways beyond and behind us, trapping us. Only our numbers still coming from our siege tower swung the balance," concluded the soldier.

"And the Tiggannians?" asked Tarbor.

"They fought to the end, Captain, sir. None are left," he replied.

"I see. And where is Captain Arncote?" enquired Tarbor, looking around him.

"He is dead, sir. Sergeant Borvel took over, but he is wounded." The soldier turned his head sideways and nodded to a soldier resting against a wall.

Tarbor looked and saw the wounded sergeant grimacing in pain, holding a sword wound, blood seeping through his fingers.

Tarbor gripped the soldier's arm. "You have done well. Go now and rest awhile," he urged. The Cardronian soldier was only too glad to as he saluted and turned away.

"Another good man gone, Girvan," said Tarbor, thinking of his fellow Captain.

"He is not the only one," replied Girvan sadly, looking at all the bodies and the wounded sergeant.

Tarbor started to look around him inside the gatehouse turret room. A large wheel with four stout wooden handles protruding from it held itself at one end of the turret.

This operated one of the huge gates by pushing the wooden handles to open it, with the same in the east gatehouse turret.

Walking into the gatehouse, Tarbor saw steps leading down either side of the gatehouse to passages where archers would have been in wait, if the Tiggannians had decided to leave the gates open, to an invitation of certain death in the archway they overlooked.

A great barred gate at the end of the gatehouse had been dropped through the floor into the archway, sealing it, sealing with it the fate of whoever got caught in the archway, thought Tarbor.

Tarbor ordered the barred gate to be pulled up and for men to man the gate wheels to open the huge gates.

Whilst this was being done, Tarbor took a moment to look out at the scene below from one of two narrow arched windows.

He could just see the burning siege tower with bodies laying everywhere in the settling snow as he moved his eyes to below him. The alliance armies were holding themselves by the outer walls, keeping out of sight of the Tiggannian archers on the inner wall. Waiting with them was King Taliskar and Brax, waiting for the huge gates to open.

He pulled away from the narrow arched window with a sudden feeling of nausea. Something was bothering him, but what?

Girvan noticed the look on Tarbor's face. "Is there something amiss, Tarbor?" he asked, seeing his look.

Tarbor shook his head. "No, not really, my friend, just my mind starting to wander, something about this place," added Tarbor a bit vaguely.

"Nothing new then," replied Girvan with a half-smile for Tarbor to smile back at his friend's remark.

"No, nothing new," and Tarbor slapped Girvan's arm as he moved past his friend to the steps that led down into the archway.

A thick barred door at the bottom of the west gatehouse turret steps had to be opened before they could finally get into the archway.

The huge main gates were open and there stood King Taliskar with Brax, having dismounted.

"Is all secure, Captain Tarbor?" asked King Taliskar straightaway.

"It is, sire, the outer wall is ours," reported Tarbor. *At a cost, though*, he thought. "Shall we proceed with the battering ram, sire?" he asked.

King Taliskar did not answer. Instead, he walked to the solid rock that ended the archway and chanced a glance out. He was met by an arrow fizzing past his head. He quickly ducked back in.

King Taliskar stood there with his back towards them, half looking out of the archway without saying anything, as if thinking.

"The battering ram, sire?" repeated Tarbor.

"Let it wait for a while," answered King Taliskar finally, in a voice that was still commanding but had taken on a soft tone.

Brax glanced at Tarbor with suspicion in his eyes. This was not the first time he had known King Taliskar to sound as if he was not there.

Tarbor caught Brax's glance; he knew what he was thinking. He had also heard him talk in that distant tone before; it did not seem like him.

What neither of them could see to confirm their suspicions were King Taliskar's eyes. No white was showing; they were completely black!

"Wait a while? Wait for what?" questioned Brax, moving a step nearer.

"So we can find the secret doorway in the lower eastern passageway," said King Taliskar simply.

Brax and Tarbor looked at each other as Girvan suddenly moved between them to ask what they were all thinking.

"Secret doorway? What secret doorway?" Tarbor thumped him. "Sire," added Girvan quickly.

"A doorway that is connected to another by a passageway," answered King Taliskar, seemingly oblivious to anything, his voice not altering.

"That opens into a storeroom that leads onto the courtyard where Middle Gate will lye before us. We will surprise the enemy from behind and Stormhaven will be ours!" finished King Taliskar, with his voice rising and dying at the same time.

"Where in the name of the Great Forest did you hear such stories!" scoffed Brax. "You have never spoken of these secret doors before," he added.

Both he and Tarbor watched King Taliskar turn back round to them slowly with a blank expression on his face. His eyes seemed to be blinking more than usual, and was that sweat on his brow? Sweat and King Taliskar did not go together, thought Tarbor, half sarcastically.

"Are you all right, sire?" he asked.

"Yes, yes, that arrow was a little too close for comfort," came King Taliskar's lame excuse to Brax's ears.

"Never mind that," *although it would have been better if it had found its mark*, thought Brax. "Who spoke of these secret doors?" asked Brax again, his voice starting to rise.

King Taliskar's face suddenly changed from a blank expression to a knowing smile. "My adorable Queen Helistra."

Tarbor could hear Brax inwardly groan. "Of course she did, I should have known," remarked Brax sarcastically.

King Taliskar began to explain, undeterred by Brax. "Before Queen Helistra and I met, her love was to travel throughout all of Northernland. The knowledge she gained on those travels can only be surmounted by her beauty," he began, to another groan from Brax.

"On one such journey," King Taliskar continued, "she told me how she came across an old wise man whose knowledge knew no boundaries. He spoke to her of many things, one of which was the secret doors within the stronghold. An ancient castle stood here long before the stronghold came to be. When it did, the secrets of the old castle were forever hidden, but those doorways remained," he finished.

Brax looked on in bewilderment; his jaw had physically dropped. "We hold this day where men have lost their lives for this… this story from an old man and you believe it!" said Brax, flabbergasted.

"You dare to doubt the word of my Queen!" challenged King Taliskar, narrowing his eyes and sounding more like himself.

"Who would dare doubt the word of your Queen," threw back Brax in confrontation, "but it is still just a story from an old man!" he countered.

"You will see, you will eat your words when all she has learnt comes to pass!" spat King Taliskar, and he turned away to walk through the archway's eastern turret doorway.

It had all sounded too incredulous to Brax's ears. Taliskar may trust her words, but he did not. His feelings right now were telling him to be more vigilant than ever as he followed King Taliskar through the doorway, but not before shouting to Tarbor to bring a torch.

Girvan looked at Tarbor. "What did you make of it all, Tarbor?"

"I do not know, Girvan. We can only follow and see. Clearly, Brax thinks it is all unbelievable, secret doors, a story from an old man, but if it is true..." Tarbor left it there.

"His Queen, not ours, Tarbor," pointed out Girvan, "and did you see King Taliskar's face when he turned round?" he posed.

"Yes, I did, that blank look and sweating, but his eyes, Girvan, I swear..." Tarbor paused.

"Swear what, Tarbor?" pushed Girvan.

"I am not sure, Girvan, but just for a moment..." Tarbor left it hanging there once more.

Tarbor looked over Girvan's shoulder and saw Sergeant Urchel waiting in the gateway. "Ah, there is Sergeant Urchel, Girvan. Inform him to be ready with the battering ram in here and for them to rest whilst they can. We had better get after them," ordered Tarbor, and Girvan trotted off to convey his message.

Tarbor took the moment to allow himself a chance to clear his head, taking in the cold air deep into his lungs to blow a misty breath back out.

He walked the few steps to where King Taliskar had stood. Even though he had wanted to clear his mind, he could not help but think of what he had just heard.

If these secret doors turned out to be true then there was more to Queen Helistra than even he had realised. She looked so young to have such knowledge, he thought with an involuntary shudder. Was it the cold that had made him do that, or that he had always felt a little on edge in her presence?

Tarbor felt himself gripping the hilt of his sword as he peered out of the archway at the Kavenmist Mountains looming above him, making sure he kept out of sight of the Tiggannian archers.

He bent slightly to take in more of their splendour, resting his hand on the solid rock face that ended the archway as he did so, but as his hand touched the cold rock, something happened that threw his thoughts into further chaos. Words were cascading from it into his mind!

Help me! Help me! She comes! Tarbor recoiled away from the rock as if he had been bitten. His mind was in total confusion. What was that?

He looked around him. Girvan was still talking to Sergeant Urchel. No one else seemed to be looking.

He looked back at the solid rock in disbelief. What in the name of the stars had just happened? He was imagining things; solid rock does not talk!

Tarbor found himself reaching out to touch the rock once more to find out he had not imagined it as words rushed into his mind again.

She will poison the land! Night will fall forever! Evil will reign! Help me! Tarbor dropped his hand away from the solid rock, cutting the voice off in his mind. He could not take any more of its heartache, so full of terror and sadness, yet there was an unmistakable vibrancy to it.

Girvan came back to see his friend's face had gone white. "What is it, Tarbor? You look like you have seen a ghost."

"I… I think I have just heard one, Girvan," uttered Tarbor vaguely.

"What are you on about?" said Girvan with a frown.

"If I tell you what has just happened to me, Girvan, you would think me mad," said Tarbor, clearly shaken up.

"Tell me, Tarbor. What is it? We are friends, are we not?" urged Girvan, seeing the look of shock plainly written all over Tarbor's face. Tarbor quickly told Girvan; he needed to.

Girvan listened to his friend's account of what had just happened to him, only to stare at him when he had finished.

"I told you I would sound mad!" said Tarbor, seeing Girvan's expression.

"No, no, you do not, but it is hard to believe that the rock just spoke to you."

"There you are, I told you!" said Tarbor again, feeling frustrated.

Whilst Tarbor's thoughts were everywhere, Girvan walked up to the rock and put his hand upon it. Tarbor suddenly realised what Girvan was doing and went to pull him away, but Girvan had already taken his hand away, shaking his head.

"I felt nothing, Tarbor," he declared as Brax appeared at the eastern turret doorway.

"Are you coming with that torch so we can get this over with?" Brax shouted, before disappearing again. Sounding as frustrated to Tarbor as he was feeling right now.

"We will talk later, Girvan, about what has just happened to me, but let us find out first if what King Taliskar has been told holds true." Tarbor half smiled at his old friend.

Girvan gripped Tarbor's shoulder assuredly for a moment, nodding. He could not make head nor tale of what was going on, either with his good friend or King Taliskar. He could only wait and watch, he thought.

Tarbor waited in the doorway whilst Girvan fetched a torch. His mind was in turmoil. A thought came into his head to join the many that had suddenly entered it as he waited there. *She comes! She will poison the land and evil will reign!* No, thought Tarbor, *can it be?*

CHAPTER V

Mist hung over the gentle River Thion, making shadows of the trees that dwelt within its grasp. As it slowly wound its way towards the Northern Sea, the river's water flowed softly over a bed of stones, seemingly caressing them, as if not to disturb anything in this tranquil scene.

There on a rock by the riverbank sat a lonely-looking figure shrouded in the mist. For all intents and purposes, it looked as if the person had fallen to sleep, with no movement to be seen in such a peaceful setting.

The figure was covered in a cloak, hiding any features to tell who it was. An inclined head under a hood hid the face from view. Only a pair of hands showed themselves, hands with long smooth fingers, holding what looked like a walking stick in their grip. These alone would begin to tell the story of who this was.

Then, as if coming out of a slumber, the hands momentarily twitched. Then, there again, another; but never once loosening their grip on the walking stick.

Suddenly without warning, the figure's body sat bolt upright, and as it did so, the hood fell back to reveal a shock of chestnut hair that flowed as if in harmony with the river.

Eyes of dark green darted left and right, bringing into focus the peaceful surroundings as they looked around.

A young face of sensual beauty smiling a contented smile at last made it known who it was; there was no mistaking Queen Helistra.

She stood and stretched, her tall frame making an imposing sight on the riverbank. Now you could see that her cloak was a dark crimson, as the mist swirled around her in dance at her movement.

As she moved, she brought the stick she was holding up into the crook of her arm and held it there lovingly. Only now could you see that it was not a walking stick she held at all, but a rune staff, for rune symbols adorned it, carved down its length, but at one end it was broken, with a piece missing.

As Queen Helistra looked around, she stroked the broken rune staff with affection, letting the symbols draw pictures on her fingertips.

"Why do I always pick the stupid ones!" Queen Helistra spoke out loud as if she were in conversation with someone. "The fool needs reminding now and again which path he is to follow."

Each time Queen Helistra finished speaking, an inaudible humming noise followed in her mind.

"Yes, I know I cannot wait to see him. He will think he has unequaled powers!" This thought gave vent to cold, ironic laughter cutting through the stillness, so strange a sound to hear from such a beautiful mouth, as more humming entered her mind.

"It will be over when we get there. A feast should await us…" humming sounded. "No, we have been patient enough. If we wait any longer, spring will make it stronger…" more humming.

"When he is of no use, his time will come…" humming once more. "Yes, so will I!" More cold laughter came from her beautiful mouth, adding further to the winter chill.

Queen Helistra turned away from the gently rippling River Thion. Little did it know of what had just passed before it.

With the broken rune staff held tightly under her arm, she covered the ground to her escort like a breath of wind.

Sergeant Wardine stamped his feet, as did the other four horse soldiers, whilst waiting patiently for Queen Helistra's return. As soon as she appeared, he waved over her horse from the horse soldier holding it. A magnificent white beast given to her by King Taliskar.

"Are you feeling better, my lady?" enquired Sergeant Wardine, bowing his head.

Ah, there he is, another little power-hungry man, she thought as she approached her horse.

"Thank you, Wardine, I feel much better. The air and walk have cleared my head, even in this mist," she said, looking around her. "A pity it is such a beautiful place," she added, mounting her white horse expertly whilst sheathing her rune staff in its leather holder at the same time.

"I fear King Taliskar will not be best pleased, my lady, when we arrive. Travelling without his knowledge and putting yourself at risk," spoke Sergeant Wardine, sounding concerned.

Queen Helistra looked straight at him, watching his eyes, which were in constant motion, flitting everywhere as if he was nervous.

A soft hum whispered in her mind. *Crafty, yes, I know, but I will let him have his moment*, she answered quietly in her mind.

Queen Helistra was about to speak as if to snap Sergeant Wardine's head off, holding herself back just to see him squirm.

"Let me worry about the King," she said smilingly, "I know making this journey will be against his better judgement, but I was worried for his well-being after all this time. You have more than made sure of my safe passage on this journey, Wardine, and I in turn will make sure this is conveyed to your King." She smiled reassuringly.

"Thank you, my lady," said Sergeant Wardine with another bow and a certain amount of relief.

"But if that does not work, Wardine," she paused again and watched Sergeant Wardine hold his breath, "I will just have to win him over with my charm!" Queen Helistra smiled down impudently at Sergeant Wardine as he gave her a timid smile back.

"My lady," was all he could muster at her assurance, with yet another bow.

Queen Helistra watched Sergeant Wardine get onto his horse. *I thought his beady eyes were going to pop out of his head*, spoke her mind to a soft hum answering her. *No, it does not take much to please a mind so small.*

Sergeant Wardine could feel her eyes upon him as he mounted his horse. Not many people unnerved him, but she did, holding that broken staff the way she did all of the time. *Something strange there*, he thought.

Her acknowledgement of him to the King would be worth it, though. He had said the right words at the right time, he thought. Promotion should not be too far behind. He knew who the real power behind the throne of Cardronia was.

Once mounted, Sergeant Wardine looked at Queen Helistra astride her white horse waiting for him, and could not stop a thought coming into his head. Beauty and the beast, but which was which? *A dangerous thought, Wardine*, he told himself.

"When you are ready, Wardine," prompted Queen Helistra, and with a wave of his arm, Sergeant Wardine set the small party off on their way once more for Stormhaven.

CHAPTER VI

A torch blazed in Girvan's hand as he moved down the lower passageway of the eastern outer wall with Tarbor, King Taliskar and Brax close behind him.

Entering the outer turret, they passed the wooden beds that occupied it to go straight into a linking narrow passageway beyond.

Girvan put the torch high in front of him to see his way into the pitch-blackness. "Does this passageway lead to anything?" Girvan found himself quietly asking Tarbor behind him.

"I do not know, Girvan," whispered Tarbor back, thinking the same. "What are we looking for, sire?" he then asked King Taliskar out loud.

"A stone in the shape of an arrowhead, I think," came the reply from King Taliskar, sounding slightly unclear. He was trying to clear his mind and recollect what he had been told by Queen Helistra, but for some reason he was feeling a bit tired.

"You think! Men are waiting to die on what you think," scolded Brax.

King Taliskar gritted his teeth and managed to keep quiet at Brax's remark. He thought again. "It is more in the shape of a small shield," he said, this time sounding more assured.

They began their search of the stone wall, looking high and low for the shield-like stone until they reached the end of the passageway, where an open doorway stood before them.

Girvan held his torch in the opening to reveal a room hewed out of the solid rock of Kavenmist. Inside, there were empty racks, telling them it was where arms were stored. "Nothing in here," reported Girvan.

They turned to look again for the shield-shaped stone. This time, King Taliskar held the torch, but still they could not spot it.

"We are wasting time! This is pointless!" retorted Brax. "It is just a story, nothing more," he added impatiently.

"We will search one more time," replied King Taliskar, handing the torch back to Girvan. His Queen could not be wrong, he told himself.

Screwing his eyes up to see through its light, Girvan brought the torch nearer to the wall to see the stones better. Up and down he moved the torch, moving slowly along the wall's length, trying to take it all in. The narrow passageway did not help him, having to lean his head away from the stone wall to see all of the shapes.

They were all looking alike to him when suddenly he caught sight of a different shape and stopped dead. No one else anticipated him stopping so quickly and consequently they stumbled into the back of him, much to Brax's annoyance.

"What are you doing, Girvan!" he spat, once he had got his footing back. Girvan held the torch aloft and said nothing. Instead, he let the torchlight show them a triangular-shaped stone in the wall above. They all looked.

"It is upside down if it is in the shape of a shield. No wonder we were blind to it, it is more to the arrowhead you first spoke of, sire," remarked Tarbor.

King Taliskar stepped forward. *Is that it?* he questioned himself, as if even he wondered whether it could all be true. "It does resemble an upside-down shield," he found himself saying.

"Well, is it what you have been looking for or not?" questioned Brax, feeling a little apprehensive at seeing the stone.

King Taliskar said nothing. Instead, he moved forward, remembering Queen Helistra's words: *Push the stone firmly twice and a door will reveal itself.*

Raising his hand up, King Taliskar pushed the stone, but nothing happened. Brax smiled.

"It is too high up for me to get any purchase upon it. I need to be higher and have my weight behind it," decided King Taliskar, looking at Girvan.

Girvan inwardly groaned and gave the torch to Tarbor so he could crouch down for King Taliskar to stand on his back.

Climbing onto Girvan's back, King Taliskar found himself holding his breath as he placed his palm on the shield-shaped stone. He pushed hard and felt the stone resist, for Brax to keep smiling.

He tried again, pushing with all of his might, when suddenly the stone gave way, sinking into the wall with King Taliskar nearly falling off Girvan's back. Brax's smile gave way for King Taliskar's to replace it.

The stone came back out and without hesitation King Taliskar pushed it back in again.

As he stepped off Girvan's back, allowing him to get up, they listened as a resounding clunk came from the wall to echo down the passageway, to be followed by the sighing sound of escaping air.

Tarbor and Girvan looked at each other whilst King Taliskar looked at Brax in triumph with eyes that said, *now do you disbelieve!*

Two cracks had appeared, running down the stone wall. Tarbor motioned to Girvan to help him push between them and they put their shoulders to the task, to feel the wall give way, revealing a stone doorway.

"What do you think of my Queen now, Brax?" smirked King Taliskar. "I would like to meet the man who told her about this," he replied, emptily staring at the stone door.

Stepping over a stone, they moved through the doorway to be met by the smell of cold, damp air, finding themselves standing on some steps that led downwards.

Girvan led the way, following the steps until they ended in a passageway whose walls reflected back at them in glistening grey wetness through the torchlight.

Cautiously, they made their way along the passageway, looking at all the cut marks in the walls as they passed through, leaving them in no doubt that the marks were man-made. How old they were they could only wonder as they moved silently along its hewn length.

Onwards they moved, with the passageway beginning to wind its way upward. Then, as the passageway turned to their right, an old wooden door appeared in front of them, set back in the rock.

"A door, sire," said Girvan, standing at the side of it.

King Taliskar moved forward to look at it. "No, this is not the door that leads to the storeroom," frowning as he thought of Queen Helistra's words once more: *At the end, a door set in the rock awaits you.*

"Not told you about this door then," said Brax, whose mood could be compared to his surroundings.

"There is no need when it is not the one," came King Taliskar's curt reply.

Ignoring the old wooden door, they continued to walk down the cold, damp greyness of the passageway until suddenly it came to an abrupt end.

Girvan held his torch up only to see the solid rock of the mountain looking back at him. "We cannot go any further, sire. We must have missed the doorway," announced Girvan.

"There are no stones we can push, sire, it is a solid face," noted Tarbor.

Brax looked also. "There is nothing here. Her knowledge has led us to a dead end!" exclaimed Brax, berating King Taliskar.

King Taliskar ignored Brax's comments and moved to the rock face, closing his eyes to think more clearly as to what his Queen had said to him.

The mere thought of the mountain face in front of him triggered a process in his mind, planted there unbeknown to him.

All thought emptied in his mind as another came into it. His breathing slowed and he stood there motionless, before the waiting looks of the others.

The stillness of his being was only matched by the stillness of the passageway, with only the dancing flames from the torch breaking the silence. A voice in his mind gave a simple command: *Open!*

Brax, Tarbor and Girvan were all watching, waiting, wondering why King Taliskar was just standing there doing nothing.

Then the air around them seemed to be getting heavier, more difficult to breathe. The feeling that somebody was behind them when there was nobody there crept over them all, making the hairs on the back of their necks start to rise.

Suddenly a crunching, grinding sound, that made their hearts lurch, came from the solid rock face in front of them; the mountain wall was slowly opening!

Mouths fell open in disbelief as a mountain doorway revealed itself. No one could say anything; the words were stuck in their throats.

Brax finally gasped his words out with suspicion in every one. "How? What… what sorcery is this she has shown you? How have you made possible the impossible?"

Tarbor was as confused, first a voice from solid rock and now a door? What was going on? What was this place?

Girvan's mind was turning over one word that Brax had said: sorcery!

"Well, what have you to say?" challenged Brax.

King Taliskar was looking at Brax with a blank expression; the mountain doorway opening had left his mind in a whirl.

The realisation of what had just happened was slowly dawning upon him. His Queen had told him what he must do, but it was he who had actually done it! A hidden power within him, he thought, one he never knew existed, but she did! *She could see it in me!* King Taliskar felt a mixture of elation and wariness at the same time as he thought of it.

He pulled himself together and looked at Brax, answering him with confidence. "My Queen simply told me if I concentrated my thoughts and asked the hidden mountain door to open, it would open, which it has, at my command," King Taliskar said with a smile.

"Pah! You must take me for a fool, Taliskar," scoffed Brax. "There is more to this than just a story she heard from an old man. After this day is done, you and I will talk of this sorcery we have just witnessed!" spat Brax, with a promise in the form of a threat in his voice.

King Taliskar did not flinch and moved closer to face Brax. "It is thanks to her and all she has learnt that we will seal victory this day. When victory is ours, I will send for Queen Helistra, then you can confront us both with your accusations of sorcery!" he promised with a snarl.

He dares accuse me and my Queen of sorcery! He confuses it with power! A power I have been blessed with, one I have been guided to through her perception. His end cannot come quickly enough! he thought as he stared at Brax with malice in his eyes.

Brax looked straight back into them and in that moment, even in the flickering torchlight, he thought he saw a madness deep within King Taliskar coming to the fore.

He would have to deal with him, and soon, thought Brax. Then he thought about confronting Queen Helistra. He did not relish it, she was different, but he knew it had to be done. "So be it," he confirmed.

Tarbor and Girvan just listened, not daring to speak. Brax had touched King Taliskar's nerve by speaking of Queen Helistra that way, thought Tarbor, but it was best to take a step back to see what would unfold, even though his mind at this time was in chaos and needed answers just as much he was going to keep quiet, he decided.

He looked at Girvan, but all Girvan could do was shake his head, telling Tarbor that he was just as confused as he was.

"Sire, we keep the army waiting," intervened Tarbor finally, speaking with caution in his voice. Another moment passed before King Taliskar came away from staring at Brax.

"Yes, yes, Captain Tarbor, you are right," replied King Taliskar, and he looked at the mountain door before walking through it. *That was me*, he thought.

As foretold, a storeroom met them on the other side. A few torches came into view, held in place by holders hammered into the rock. Girvan lit a couple from his.

On looking around, they saw the storeroom was quite large, half of it cut out of the mountain, the other half built onto it. It lay empty, apart from one barrel standing on its own in a corner.

"An ideal place for ale if there was any here," remarked Girvan on seeing the barrel.

A wooden door showed up in front of them. Tarbor opened it to reveal another storeroom, with daylight penetrating through its door.

"Put out the flame and see what lays in wait for us beyond," ordered King Taliskar.

Girvan extinguished the torch and moved towards the door. He slowly opened it enough to see a cold scene of grey skies and snow.

He rubbed his eyes at the light and looked out again. A large courtyard opened out before him, joining everything together that stood around it.

Latched onto where he was were more storerooms. Straight opposite stood the great hall, with the imposing sight of Forest Tower looming over its roof. Buildings were built onto the great hall's side, and more showed themselves on the opposite side of the courtyard.

To his right were the stronghold's inner walls, protecting what they were after: Middle Gate. He could see soldiers on top of the battlements and some milling about around the turrets, but otherwise it was fairly empty.

"Well?" came King Taliskar's voice from behind him, for Girvan to close the door quietly.

"Soldiers line the inner wall battlements and some lye outside the gates, sire. Otherwise, all is quiet."

"Good, go and inform…?" King Taliskar looked at Tarbor.

"Sergeant Urchel, sire."

"Inform him to bring sixty men here. That should be enough to get those gates open," he decided.

Girvan disappeared, with his torch relit, back down the passageway whilst King Taliskar, Brax and Tarbor waited for his return in an uneasy silence as each one of them turned over their thoughts on what had just happened in their minds.

It did not take long before the first of the soldiers came through the mountain door.

King Taliskar stood by one of the torches in the first storeroom, its flickering flame playing across his face, casting him in a sinister light.

Soldiers openly stared at him as they passed through. King Taliskar looked back at them, smiling as he thought of the power opening the mountain door had given him.

They are in awe of the mover of mountains, he was thinking. He would be feared throughout the Kingdoms; no one would dare challenge him. King Taliskar and his Queen by his side on the thrones of Tiggannia!

CHAPTER VII

From the balcony at the top of Forest Tower, Cantell and Kelmar commanded an excellent view of the situation below.

Although the weather had taken a turn for the worst for them to take full advantage of it. With the snow falling heavier and a cold grey mist beginning to move in from the sea.

A lull had occurred in the fighting and there was no sign as of yet that the alliance army were about to attack the inner wall.

Cantell looked through the snow over to where the Great Forest lay, *well, on a clear day*, he thought absently.

"Do you think we stand a chance of making it, Kelmar?" he asked, the cold weather not helping his thoughts.

Kelmar looked out at the snow cutting through the grey sky. "I fear a better chance than those we leave behind," came his reply, not making Cantell feel any the better.

"It does not feel right leaving them behind, I am their protector," said Cantell, turning away from the balcony and walking into the ceremony room of Forest Tower.

"We will be protecting the future," pointed out Kelmar, reminding Cantell.

Cantell cast his eye over the provisions Kelmar had placed on the floor of the ceremonial room in readiness as his mind tried to come to terms with what he had been asked to do. "I see you have a sturdy length of rope here, Kelmar," he said, seeing it coiled up on the floor.

"We will be in need…" Kelmar suddenly stopped what he was saying as a yell caught his attention to make him look over the balcony.

"What is it, Kelmar?" Cantell said with a frown, joining him.

Their eyes were immediately drawn directly below them to a trail of figures coming out of a storeroom.

The shout Kelmar had heard was a warning shout from the inner wall battlements as they watched more and more figures running out of the storeroom.

"We are being attacked from within. Where? How did they?" exclaimed Cantell.

"I do not know," said Kelmar, frowning. "Those storerooms back onto the solid rock of Kavenmist itself!" he added with disbelief in his voice.

Both men looked at each other. "Our time has been cut short, Kelmar. We must tell the King!" cried Cantell, and they both scurried down the steps that entered the ceremonial room to disappear through the wooden floor.

Down the spiral steps of Forest Tower they hurried, passing a number of doors before reaching the royal chamber door, and even though their time had been cut short, Cantell still knocked on the door.

"Enter!" came a shout. Cantell and Kelmar rushed in to be confronted by King Rolfe holding a furry bundle.

His eyes glistened with tears of joy and a broad smile beamed across his face. "Behold, my friends, our little boy, Prince Martyn," he announced proudly.

Both warriors fell to one knee, bowing in honour of the newborn Prince, and then immediately got up to tell King Rolfe their news.

"I know the stronghold hides many secrets. It is old and its ways are many. One of which it seems has been found by our enemy and led them into our midst, but still how that has been possible I do not know. That storeroom has the back of Kavenmist upon it!" said King Rolfe, in puzzlement, echoing Kelmar.

"Nevertheless, they have come through it, sire, and we need to move. There is no time left for us," said Kelmar in earnest.

"You are right, Kelmar," answered King Rolfe, looking down at his newly born son. He looked at his little face all screwed up and stroked his tiny cheek. *What chance have you got if they can do that?* he thought. A cry of pain made him look around at Queen Elina. Moving over to her bedside, he knelt down beside her.

Queen Elina's eyes were closed; her face looked pale and sweat covered her brow. Charlotte tended to her on the other side of the bed, holding her hand whilst she wiped her brow.

Mrs Beeworthy was holding herself ready for the delayed event as King Rolfe caught her eye. "A while longer yet, sire, not be in any hurry to come out, this one," she pointed out, with the worry of what was happening written across her face.

King Rolfe knew what he had to do. "Can you hear me, my little one?" he said softly.

A smile came over Queen Elina's face when she heard her husband's voice, holding out her hand for him to clasp tight.

"Our hand has been forced, my love. Our enemies are already within the courtyard, we cannot delay." King Rolfe hesitated at what he was going to have to say next.

"We must make good little Martyn's escape. We cannot wait for our second child to arrive, there is no time."

King Rolfe had made many decisions as King, but making this one as a father also was the worst by far.

Queen Elina flickered open her eyes and saw how the decision had pained her husband. All what they had been through, and now they must endure further heartache by letting their newborn child go, knowing his chances were small, like him.

He could not be in better hands to stand a chance, she knew, but what of their chances? She cast that thought aside only to think of another as a bout of pain brought that thought home to her with a feeling of dread: what chance did her unborn child have?

Queen Elina looked into her husband's pained eyes with love and understanding. "Let me see him one last time," she said finally.

King Rolfe handed the furry bundle over into her arms. She looked down at her son with tears in her eyes. One dripped onto his tiny forehead and she tutted to herself as she gently wiped the tear away with her finger.

She kissed him softly on his little cheek, thinking it may be the one and only time she would ever be able to do that, making herself feel more depressed than ever. She gave the tiny bundle back to King Rolfe with a brave smile as another bout of pain ran through her body, helping to hide away her tears of sorrow.

King Rolfe turned to Cantell, but before he could do anything, Cantell had to ask one question.

"There is but one child to take now, sire. I can stay by your side whilst Kelmar makes good his escape!" Cantell could not help himself; he had to try.

"I can see why I made you the King's protector, but no, Cantell," replied King Rolfe firmly, quelling any more thoughts that Cantell had of staying.

"Call it what you will, this is how it was meant to be," he said smilingly, gripping his old friend's shoulder. "With both of you watching over him, his chances have just doubled. You have been like brothers to me and I know I could not ask for anyone better to watch over our son. So take your future King and then one day right the wrong that has been done here," finished King Rolfe, with steel in his last words.

"We will, sire," answered Kelmar. Cantell could only look at the floor; the sadness of the moment cut deeply into him.

King Rolfe kissed his baby son on the forehead and handed him over to Cantell, who immediately felt awkward.

Mrs Beeworthy suddenly appeared by their side with a pouch, handing it to Kelmar. "This be best I could do for the little one. I hope it helps, but I worry," she said quickly, and resumed her place next to Queen Elina.

"Thank you, Bee," said King Rolfe affectionately. *How Elina will need her*, he thought.

King Rolfe moved to the door and opened it. "May the stars and spirits watch over you both," said Queen Elina suddenly, looking at the two warriors with her baby in their care, trying to sound strong.

"Thank you, my lady," said Kelmar and Cantell, bowing before her.

"Come now, it is time, be ever vigilant. Taliskar's knowledge of this place is worrying," warned King Rolfe.

"We will, sire," answered Kelmar, leading the way. Although he had not said much, his feelings for his King and Queen ran as deep as the mountains. This moment was leaving him with a bitter taste in his mouth as he clasped his King's forearm in a warrior's grip as he got to the door.

"To the death, sire," was all he could say, with eyes that held defiance in them.

"To the death, old friend," King Rolfe said with a nod, and he watched as Kelmar bounded up the spiral steps.

"We will return and avenge this day, sire," promised Cantell, clasping King Rolfe's forearm the same.

"I know you will," King Rolfe said smilingly, gripping Cantell's forearm firmly before he turned to follow Kelmar.

The scene of Queen Elina and his King by her side would be forever imprinted on Cantell's mind. *The stars and spirits! We might need a little bit more help than that*, he was thinking as he trudged despondently up the spiral steps, looking at the little screwed-up face in his arms.

King Rolfe watched Cantell disappear with a, "Be safe, my son, be safe," whisper on his lips as he listened to Cantell's footfall die away.

It was immediately replaced by that of a soldier's footfall running up the spiral steps to announce the enemy was outside the great hall doors!

"Are the men ready?" King Rolfe asked quickly.

"They are ready, sire."

"Good, I will be there shortly, go now!" King Rolfe returned to Queen Elina's bedside.

He knelt down once more, holding her tiny hand, to see her eyes flickering and her teeth clenched together as her pain grew stronger at the impending birth.

"I have to go now, my love. Always remember I love you," he said, squeezing her hand, wishing he could say more, but there was no time.

King Rolfe got up with a heavy heart and moved towards the door. "And I will always love you, my husband."

Queen Elina's words made him stop and look around. Her pale face was looking at him, with tears running down her cheeks. "Be brave, my little one," he said softly.

"Look after her for me, both of you," he said, looking at Mrs Beeworthy and Charlotte.

"We will, sire," they both answered, and King Rolfe left the royal chamber to the sound of Queen Elina's sobs.

As King Rolfe appeared at the bottom of Forest Tower, he drew his sword in readiness and looked at the soldiers with him in this last defiant stand, smiling.

"Your Queen has given birth to the future King of our Kingdom, my friends. He escapes with Cantell and Kelmar from these worms as I speak.

So let us take as many of them with us as we can to help give them time. Our end may be near, but he will be the new beginning for Tiggannia!"

King Rolfe spoke with hope in his voice, and all the soldiers thumped their breasts in salute to their King.

"I shall dance in celebration of his life over the Great Forest, sire," said one.

"We all will, sire," said another as a resounding crash announced the alliance army at the great hall doors.

"Did you hear that!" remarked Cantell, as he and Kelmar made ready.

"Yes, I did. We had better move!"

Picking up the provisions, such as they were, they moved to the back of the ceremonial room into the ceremonial chamber.

"This is where your mother and father were joined," said Cantell, remembering that day as he looked at the little scrunched-up face in his arms.

"You begin his teachings already," said Kelmar whilst pushing at the altar that sat at the back of the ceremonial chamber.

Cantell the teacher and guardian, thought Cantell. He had not thought about his future responsibilities in that way.

Kelmar pushed the altar aside to reveal an opening and with a lit torch he looked at Cantell. "Are you ready?" he asked.

Cantell heard the shouts from the soldiers below as the sound of battle came echoing up the spiral steps. He remembered once more that happy day when his King and Queen were joined here to much different shouts.

He took a deep breath and held the little Prince tight. "As ready as we will ever be," he confirmed. So the two warriors and their little furry bundle disappeared into the network of tunnels under the Kavenmist Mountains.

Below them, the alliance soldiers had stormed into the great hall with a deafening roar. They plunged headlong towards the small force at the base of Forest Tower.

"For Tiggannia!" shouted King Rolfe, and the archers let loose their arrows. One, two, three arrows were fired from their bows in quick succession to strings humming and bodies falling, but the alliance army rushed at them in numbers to force a frantic hand-to-hand battle.

King Rolfe's sword cut through his enemy like slicing an apple; bodies littered the floor. One by one, the brave Tiggannians were cut down as the sheer weight of alliance army numbers soon told, with finally King Rolfe being pinned to the spiral steps by three alliance soldiers ready to run him through.

"HOLD!" came a loud shout from behind them. One soldier glanced behind him and saw it was Brax who had given the order. They slowly withdrew, leaving a grinning Brax facing King Rolfe.

"You are mine, Tiggannian!" Brax said with a grin whilst deliberately wiping his bloodstained axe on the body of a fallen Tiggannian archer.

King Rolfe looked at Brax with contempt, saying nothing, whilst keeping a firm grip on his sword.

"Clear these bodies!" ordered Brax, and soldiers hurriedly cleared the dead bodies out of the way.

"It is going to be a pleasure to kill the murderer of our royal family," scowled Brax, savouring the moment as he began to circle around King Rolfe.

"The people of Waunarle will find out who the real betrayers are here," replied King Rolfe, keeping Brax at sword's length.

"Taliskar will pay for what he has done to Tiggannia! And you lapdog, you will pay now!" challenged King Rolfe.

That did it. Brax gripped his axe firmly, swinging it side to side through the air. "I shall enjoy nailing your head on the gate, Tiggannian!" *Then Taliskar's*, thought Brax.

Brax lunged at King Rolfe, wielding his axe over his shoulder, aiming at King Rolfe's head.

Parrying the oncoming blow with his sword, King Rolfe felt the impact of Brax's strike shudder through his body with the sound of their weapons meeting reverberating around the tower.

For his size, Brax moves swiftly, noted King Rolfe as Brax swirled his axe from side to side once more.

King Rolfe parried and countered each blow Brax struck out at him whilst watching for a moment where he could strike a fatal blow, but then he slipped!

Taking a step back to parry another blow, he trod on some spilt blood and momentarily lost his balance, for Brax to seize his chance.

Wielding his axe around in a full circle, Brax brought it down fiercely into King Rolfe's shoulder. The leather armour he wore proving ineffective to such a smite as Brax's axe drove deep crushing bone along the way to send him crashing into the stone wall.

The pain from the blow shot through King Rolfe's body and screamed in his mind. Brax pulled out his axe with a stomach-churning, sucking sound, grinning.

King Rolfe pushed with his good sword arm against the stone wall to aid him to his feet as Brax sensed the moment and moved in for the kill.

Brax brought his axe to bear down, cutting it through the air in an arc to find King Rolfe's rib cage. He had not been quick enough to his feet and felt his ribs smash agonisingly with the blow.

King Rolfe dropped his sword with a clatter, falling to his knees, holding the fatal wound. Blood oozed over his fingers and he cursed at himself as he waited for Brax's axe to claim him.

Brax should have finished him off there and then but could not resist the accolade he was getting from the onlooking soldiers as he responded to their cheers by raising his blood-soaked axe in the air.

Tarbor was amongst the soldiers looking on and waited for the inevitable with mixed feelings.

King Rolfe's mind was clouding as the cheering resounded in his pounding ears. He saw his sword laying there and looked up, wincing in pain, to see Brax's grinning face.

King Rolfe made one last wish to the stars and spirits to give him the strength to finish this. Breathing in a painful, bloodied breath, he made for his sword.

The soldiers' cheering suddenly stopped at the sight of King Rolfe lunging at Brax, unable to move in their disbelief.

Brax's grin disappeared and instead blood gushed through his mouth as King Rolfe plunged his sword with both hands straight through Brax's side under his raised arm.

Brax turned his head with eyes staring upwards to be met by King Rolfe's bloody grin. His axe fell to the floor with a resounding crash and they followed, falling together, with King Rolfe still holding on to his sword.

As he lay there feeling the Great Forest calling him, King Rolfe heard the distant cry of a baby. "My child," he whispered, with a dying smile and his eyes closed.

Tarbor looked on blankly at the two warriors lying there in an everlasting embrace of death as he listened to the only sound that could be heard in the deafening silence: a baby crying.

King Taliskar's timing was perfect, choosing this moment to walk into the great hall. He wondered why the hall was so quiet as the soldiers parted to let him through. He was sure he had heard cheering not a moment before he had entered. Was it because the mover of mountains had entered? he thought to himself, smiling, for it to be soon broadened.

He reached the base of Forest Tower and saw Tarbor bending over the two bodies. He could not believe his eyes; King Rolfe and Brax! Both of them! King Taliskar's mind soared with the birds in the sky as Tarbor stood up, seeing him arrive.

"What happened here, Captain Tarbor?" questioned King Taliskar, asking the obvious whilst trying not to sound elated. Tarbor started to explain briefly about the battle that had just been fought as King Taliskar eyed the two bodies.

He caught the frozen look of surprise on Brax's bloodstained face and smiled to himself. *Thank you, King Rolfe. Now no one is in my way*, he thought with smug satisfaction.

"The baby still cries," finished Tarbor.

"The baby?" King Taliskar looked at Tarbor with a frown. He had only been half listening to what Tarbor was saying in his elation at seeing Brax dead.

Tarbor did not answer him; he let the crying from above do it for him. "I see," said King Taliskar, listening. "I will look into it later," he said, sounding uninterested.

His interest lay down those steps and behind that door: the mountain throne room! "Make arrangements for them, Captain Tarbor, as befits them both," he said matter-of-factly, and he moved towards the mountain throne room door.

"Yes, sire," answered Tarbor, and he watched King Taliskar open the mountain throne room door to slowly disappear behind it.

Is that what this has been all about, not to bring justice to the people of Waunarle, but for his lust for power? thought Tarbor.

Tarbor looked away from the mountain throne room door, back to the two dead warriors. He tried to reflect on what the day had brought, but his mind soon became confused and unsettled. The only thing clear in his mind was lying there in front of him.

CHAPTER VIII

Cantell soon lost all sense of direction, only knowing that Kelmar was taking them deeper and deeper into the darkness of Kavenmist.

He looked on thankfully at the torchlight showing them the way, revealing as it did the scars and cracks that marked the passageway they were walking down.

"He still sleeps," he remarked as he looked down at the Prince's little face in his arms.

"That is good, there is no telling how far sound would travel down here if he was crying," pointed out Kelmar.

Cantell was just thinking that if it was all like this then it would not be so bad, when Kelmar stopped and raised his torch.

Cantell looked at Kelmar, knowing his thoughts of walking all the way through were about to end.

"Why have we stopped? The passage goes on before us," he queried, squinting in the passageway's direction. Then he saw the narrow opening Kelmar was pointing out to him with the torch. "Ah, through there," he answered aloud to himself; so much for his previous silly thoughts.

"That was the way once, but the roof fell in halfway down, blocking the passage," informed Kelmar, not that Cantell was surprised to hear this.

"If we cannot travel down there because of a rockfall, what makes the one we are heading for so different?" questioned Cantell.

"Your memory is short-lived, my friend," he said with a smile, "I told you I could feel the breath of the Great Forest upon my face. It can only be a small fall for me to have felt that. We will be able to move it, I know we will," recounted Kelmar, sounding assured.

"I remember you saying," acknowledged Cantell, trying not to sound sceptical. He admired Kelmar's self-belief and hoped his friend was right. Otherwise, this blackness would be their end, he was thinking, giving himself a chill at the thought.

Holding the provisions on his other side, Kelmar turned sideways and started to inch his way through the gap. Cantell followed with the sturdy rope over his shoulder and little Prince Martyn tucked underneath his arm.

It seemed to take forever negotiating this natural passage. Turning one way then another, squeezing through a narrow gap one moment and then having to crouch low to avoid hitting their heads.

Handing Prince Martyn over to Kelmar and back again for each of them to get through, until finally coming out the other side to gladly stretch their backs.

Kelmar moved slowly forward with the torch in front of him, looking at the rock floor they had come out onto.

"Where have we come out?" asked Cantell, hearing his words echoing.

"We have come out into a long chamber. There is a split in the rock floor before us that has created a gap that we must cross, but there is an old rope bridge ahead for us to do so," explained Kelmar as he moved steadily forward. "An underground river runs far below us. Can you hear it?"

Cantell stood still and listened. "Yes, I can," he confirmed, hearing the river's rushing waters. "It has made it slippery here, be careful," warned Kelmar.

"The passageway we left comes out further down this chamber some… oh!" Kelmar stopped what he was saying and came to a halt.

"Oh, Kelmar?" questioned Cantell as he looked to see what the problem was. Then in the flickering torchlight he saw the rope bridge Kelmar had just spoken of hanging down from a metal bridge pin on the other side. The rope had somehow broken, leaving shredded pieces hanging from the other bridge pin. "Our way across," said Cantell, staring at it.

"Rocks must have fallen from the chamber ceiling. Ah well, it is no use pondering over what is done," was Kelmar's calm reply, for Cantell to turn round and have the torch thrust into his hand.

"The span is not great, but it is too far to jump," stated Kelmar. "I will loop the rope and throw it over the bridge pin with the loose rope hanging from it. After I have swung across and pulled myself up, I will throw the rope end back over for you to tie the provisions onto with some leather ties that are inside the pack, then between us we can slide the provisions down the rope. Prince Martyn can follow in the same way, then I will hold firm whilst you tie yourself and swing over," finished Kelmar.

Cantell looked at Kelmar, blinking, thinking it was as if he knew that rope bridge was already broken as he listened to the underground river, which had suddenly become much clearer now to his ears.

"How far down is that river?" he found himself asking.

"I did drop a torch down there once. It was like a star in the sky before it became no more," answered Kelmar, making Cantell groan. Why did he have to ask?

Cantell caught sight of the one metal bridge pin that had remained on this side, not making him feel any the better as Kelmar tied a loop in the rope.

He went to inspect it, to see it had held in the rock but was bent. "Have you seen this, Kelmar? This pin is bent. Will the other bridge pin hold?" he queried, giving it a kick to see if it still held firm.

Kelmar moved over to Cantell with the looped rope ready in his hands, to glance at the bridge pin. "It should do, we will soon find out," he said, removing his leather coat. "You had best do the same, the lighter the better. They can be packed into the provisions," he added, and began to twirl the rope above his head.

Setting Prince Martyn down, Cantell stood to the side, holding the torch out enough to see light catching the metal of the bridge pins on the other side.

"I have not done this since we brought in those wild horses," remarked Kelmar, making Cantell smile and frown at the same time.

It showed as Kelmar missed three of four times before finding he had looped the bridge pin. Pulling the rope to see it go taut, Kelmar did not waste any time in tying it around his waist.

One last tug to make sure and Kelmar looked at Cantell. "Now we shall find out," he said and before Cantell could say, *it ends here if you fall*, Kelmar had dropped out of sight to thud against the rock on the other side.

Cantell held his breath and then let it go when to his relief he saw Kelmar inching his way up the rope, to know the bridge pin had held.

Finding a convenient crack in the rock floor, Cantell wedged the torch into it, leaving Prince Martyn lying under its light.

Removing his own leather coat, Cantell packed it into the provisions with Kelmar's and waited for Kelmar to reach the top.

On reaching it, Kelmar took the rope off the bridge pin and threw the end over to Cantell, who tied on the provisions with the leather ties that Kelmar had told him of.

Lifting the rope his end, Cantell watched the provisions slide over to Kelmar with ease.

With two more leather ties, Cantell secured the little bundle of Prince Martyn. He looked at his little face still scrunched up and wondered if he was looking at the King of Tiggannia now instead of the Prince. A thought he had not wanted to think about, but he could not help it entering his head.

"Ready, Cantell?" called Kelmar thankfully, ending Cantell's dark thought of his King and, like the provisions, he held Prince Martyn up in the air.

The rope was pulled taut and down slid the little furry bundle to Kelmar. Now it was Cantell's turn.

First, Cantell threw the torch over to hear it object by spitting and crackling as it travelled through the air. As it landed, Kelmar picked it up and jammed it into another crack on his side.

Cantell tied his end of the rope around his waist and waited for Kelmar's call. Kelmar looped the rope around the bridge pin and tied it around his waist. Sitting down, he managed to find a hole in the rock floor where he could wedge one of his heels in, and holding the rope firmly, he called to Cantell, "Ready when you are!"

Cantell decided to sit down and inch his way to the edge of the gap to push himself off. He looked at Kelmar in the torchlight, who nodded, and Cantell pushed his feet against the rock face.

What a sensation Cantell had felt, going through the air for just those few moments. He hit the rock on the other side with his feet and felt the rope go taut as it took his weight, but then what he had feared could happen happened: the bridge pin came loose!

Though the bridge pin had held strong for Kelmar and he was taking the strain, the sudden tug upon it was enough for it to loosen its hold in the rock floor. Bending over and finally coming out altogether, it pulled Kelmar's heel straight out of the crack it was in, twisting him right around. Before he knew where he was, Kelmar was being pulled along headfirst to plummet straight over the edge!

As Kelmar slid over the edge, what was left of the dangling rope bridge hit him in the face and he instinctively grabbed out at it for his life! Somehow, he caught hold of a piece, feeling it burning through his hands as he held on to it.

His arms immediately felt like they were trying to come out of their sockets, as he clung on with the weight of Cantell hanging from him, for them to both hang there in mid-air from the remaining bridge pin!

Cantell felt the sudden drop and feared the worst. This was it, he thought; they had failed before they had even begun.

Then he realised he was still hanging there in mid-air like a puppet on a string, thumping against the rock face.

Holding his feet against the rock face, he steadied himself and his heartbeat to look up. He could make out Kelmar looking like a silhouette in the torchlight, struggling to hold on to the broken rope bridge for all he was worth.

"Kelmar! Are you all right?" shouted Cantell.

"For now," came Kelmar's strained reply.

Cantell looked at the rock face but could not make out any cracks in the face that would help him climb up.

"Hold on, Kelmar, whilst I climb up the rope," he shouted.

"Do you see me having much choice!" came Kelmar's curt response.

Cantell chose not to reply and started to pull himself slowly up the rope, hoping against all hope that this bridge pin held.

Kelmar held on grimly as Cantell made his way up the rope with every muscle in his body aching from the strain of doing so.

He also looked for footholds in the rock face but thought better of it, instead concentrating on holding on. *The less movement, the better*, he told himself.

Kelmar felt Cantell get nearer and nearer, wondering how much longer he could take this pain, when suddenly there he was, grasping the rope bridge beneath him to feel instant relief on his arms.

"Thank the stars for that!" cried Kelmar in his relief, when suddenly he felt the rope bridge move!

"Stay still, Cantell, I will climb up first," he called, on feeling the movement, and started to climb warily up the rope bridge.

Cantell had felt the movement also and had closed his eyes in silent prayer.

Kelmar wanted to move faster but dared not as he inched his way to the top, with his hands shouting at him that they had had enough.

Finally, he made it to the top, pulling himself onto the ledge, to see the bridge pin bent at an angle. He scrambled quickly to it and summoning what was left of his strength, he held it in place, calling for Cantell to climb up. "Hurry, Cantell!"

Every pull on the bridge pin made Kelmar curse through gritted teeth as Cantell pulled himself up.

Kelmar held on until there in the flickering light appeared Cantell's head peeping over the ledge. All Kelmar could do was laugh in nervous exhaustion at the sight of Cantell's face peering up at him.

Cantell grinned at Kelmar's laughter as he rolled onto the ledge to join him, exhausted and thankful that they were both still alive.

Someone else, though, did not think the same and cried out at the top of his little lungs.

"He does not like this," said Cantell, resting with Prince Martyn, attempting to feed him with some goat's milk that Mrs Beeworthy had given them.

Kelmar looked up from resting his head on his knees to see a look of disgust seemingly crossing Prince Martyn's face as he sucked at a little wooden spoon that Cantell was trying to feed him with.

"What is it?" said Kelmar, getting up.

"Goat's milk, I think. Mrs Bee always kept a couple for their milk," remarked Cantell.

I am surprised they had not been eaten, thought Kelmar, coiling up the rope. "If he does not want it, I could try it on my hands," he quipped, looking at his burn marks.

"I do not think so," said Cantell with a smile, "but he does not want this," he worried.

"You can try later. For now, we need to keep moving. There is a section I want to get through," informed Kelmar, to make Cantell feel wary as Kelmar handed him the coiled rope to put over his shoulder.

With the provisions slung over his shoulder, Kelmar held the torch out in front of him once more to guide the way, whilst Cantell followed, wondering what else lay in wait for them, as he held a disconsolate-sounding Prince in his arms.

Cantell was soon sliding through more twists and turns as Kelmar brought them out into another passageway. It was narrower, but at least they could stand up in it, thought Cantell.

The passageway soon began to go downwards, deeper into the mountains. Its walls glistened back at them, with water seeping through cracks in its structure.

The scars and cracks that showed themselves here began to make it look very unstable to Cantell, as if it was all going to give way at any moment, making him feel uncomfortable.

Kelmar suddenly stopped. "Here is where we go next," he stated.

Cantell looked to where a gaping hole in the passageway wall showed itself. "In there!" he exclaimed. "Do I presume we have to go in there because of another rockfall?" he guessed with raised eyebrows.

"In a way," Kelmar quickly explained. "Rockfalls have led me to here, although this particular passageway leads to a mined chamber, a dead end. The hole before us links up to another part of the underground river," finished Kelmar.

"And then?" Cantell waited.

"We wade through the river to another chamber," answered Kelmar, unperturbed.

Cantell took the torch from Kelmar, shaking his head. *Go into here and then wade a river. Does nothing daunt this man?* thought Cantell as he looked into the hole.

"It is narrow but passable," said Kelmar, already making his coat and provisions into one tight bundle.

"If you put your coat around the Prince, it will help keep the wet at bay," added Kelmar.

It gets better and better, thought Cantell.

Cantell set the torch down to follow Kelmar's instructions with a question on his mind. "Is it far after we wade the river, Kelmar? We will be in dire need of some warmth if we are to get wet. We only have the means to light a torch," he pointed out.

Kelmar nodded his understanding. "Once we are through here, we will rest a short while by the river before crossing it. The chamber beyond is not far, then we travel only a short distance before we smell the air of the Great Forest. That will be enough to give us the strength to cast aside those few rocks that need to be moved for us to light a fire under the branches of the Great Forest's mighty trees."

Cantell could only look at his old friend and smile. "I should have known better than to have asked."

"I will go first, pushing the provisions—" began Kelmar.

"With me behind, pushing the Prince and dragging the rope," interrupted Cantell, looking down at Kelmar tying it around his leg.

"And who will be holding the torch?" worried Cantell, knowing the answer as soon as he had asked the question: no one.

"It will hinder rather than help in the space we are entering," replied Kelmar, confirming Cantell's worries. He knew he was not going to feel comfortable in total darkness.

"Leave it here to die out. There are two more in the provisions for later, enough for our needs," he added.

Kelmar put the provisions into the hole and climbed in after them, soon disappearing from view. Cantell reluctantly left the torch on the floor and followed Kelmar into the hole, bracing himself for what lay ahead. He was already not looking forward to this part of the journey.

Pushing the thankfully sleeping bundle of Prince Martyn before him, Cantell started to pull himself along, feeling the rope pull on his leg behind him as he did so.

Pitch-blackness instantly encircled them as they began to crawl painstakingly along the narrow tunnel-like gap.

Cantell began breathing in deep breaths of cold air, exhaling it slowly to calm his nerves. Darkness was one thing, but this was different.

The dampness of his surroundings soon became apparent as his hands moved over small, wet rocks beneath him, to scrape at his body through his tunic as he moved.

He felt above him and to the sides, only to make him feel even more enclosed in the nothingness they had entered, as the narrow tunnel proved to be only a hand or two away wherever he touched.

Slowly but surely, the cold, damp conditions started to gnaw away at the two warriors as they crawled along.

"How are you doing?" came Kelmar's sudden question out of the dark, making Cantell jump, resulting in him lifting his head and cracking it on the rock above.

A curse later, he answered, "You mean, apart from this bump that is forming upon my head!" Kelmar smiled to himself in the blackness.

"I do not think our encounter with the rope bridge has helped. My body is beginning to ache in places I did not know existed. This dampness penetrating my clothes does not help," moaned Cantell.

"There is only a little way to go," replied Kelmar, and on he moved, with Cantell wishing they had not stopped. He was finding it hard to get going again.

Cantell started to replicate in his mind what he was doing. Even though this in itself was tedious, it somehow helped to take his mind off where he was.

Push the Prince, now pull yourself and drag the rope; a shortened version of how he was really feeling: *Push the ever heavier-feeling Prince, pull your chilled body along in this damp black hole and drag the saturated rope behind you.* It was all beginning to take its toll on his body and his mind.

After what seemed forever to Cantell, Kelmar stopped and called back.

"Nearly there, just this gap to get through. It is a bit tighter, but then it opens out and joins the river," encouraged Kelmar.

"Thank the stars," said a tired Cantell, more to himself than Kelmar.

Kelmar pushed the provisions through the smaller gap and followed. Inching his way through, he could feel the rock bearing down onto his wet tunic, but a twist and a grunt or two later, he was through.

"Take it slowly and ease yourself through, Cantell. It has not helped with our tunics becoming wet," Kelmar warned, as he carried on to get out of Cantell's way.

Cantell pushed Prince Martyn through the gap and followed. He immediately felt the rock close in around his shoulders as he moved forward, trying to twist his way through. He was finding it harder and harder to get through, not realising his tunic was riding up on his back, wedging him into the gap. Before he knew where he was, he was stuck!

Cantell's mind flooded into the realms of panic, making him struggle, only to make it worse. His breathing became erratic as he tried shifting one way then another. He suddenly felt like the whole of the Kavenmist Mountains were bearing down upon him and he immediately began to sweat.

He screwed his eyes shut and gritted his teeth, trying to wipe it all from his mind. He did not want to end his days in this tomb of blackness! Then a horrible feeling of spiders crawling all over his body made him shudder.

"Are you through?" called Kelmar behind him, unaware of Cantell's plight.

Cantell took in a sharp breath. "No, I am stuck!" he replied, trying not to sound hysterical, but not too sure if he had succeeded.

Kelmar knew that voice coming from his old friend. The fear of the dark had always been with him. He had done well not to let it surface so far down here, but there it was now, he thought.

"How are you feeling?" asked Kelmar quietly, waiting a moment before he heard an answer. "Stupid," came the self-critical reply.

"It is not stupid to have fear." More silence for a while, then…

"I am supposed to be the King's protector, not much of one at the moment, stuck here like a stopper in a bottle!" Kelmar could hear Cantell's frustration at himself and tried to think of something that would take Cantell's mind off his situation, to calm him down.

"Lying here, I can feel the breeze the underground river makes as it races past," said Kelmar suddenly. "Do you know what it reminded me of when I felt it on my face?"

It was good to hear Kelmar's voice, Cantell was thinking, but what was he on about?

Kelmar continued when he did not hear an answer. "Riding my horse through Kelmsmere Valley, feeling the fresh spring air hit my face. Do you remember those days?" quizzed Kelmar.

Cantell could see them instantly, picturing them both riding hoof to hoof through the valley until their horses snorted enough. "Good days, my friend," he answered.

Good, he is listening. Kelmar continued: "One day, we will ride there once more with Prince Martyn by our side," he promised.

Cantell nodded to himself, riding together in Kelmsmere Valley, but not like this, he chided himself. What sort of man was he? He had a duty to the child, his King and Queen!

"I will move backwards and try again," said Cantell at long last, for Kelmar to blow a sigh of relief.

He has come round. "Look to your tunic, Cantell. Make sure it has not ridden up somewhere. I will carry on to the river and light a torch," said Kelmar, realising how cold he suddenly felt by not moving for a while.

Cantell closed his eyes and breathed slowly until he felt some semblance of self-control come back to him. He felt a bead of sweat drip from his nose, telling him how far he had gone down the road of sheer panic. *Now ease yourself backwards*, he told himself.

A small twist here, a little push there, and Cantell started to feel some movement towards helping him become unstuck, continuing until finally he was free.

It took some time for him to straighten out his tunic, which he found had become gathered on his back, tutting to himself that something so simple had caused him such anxiety. A last blow of his cheeks with the effort of pulling his tunic straight and he was done, try again!

Arms in front of him, Cantell set about the task once more, keeping more aware of what he was doing this time. *Once your shoulders are through, the rest of your body will follow*, he told himself.

Cantell dug in with his hands whilst pushing with his feet to start easing himself through the gap. Bit by bit, he inched his way through with a little twist side to side, and before he knew it, he was through the narrow gap. His whole body drained in relief at making it, and he thanked the stars for watching over him.

Cantell crawled forward, feeling for the bundle of Prince Martyn. It had gone! In the time it had taken him to get through the gap, Kelmar had been back down the narrow tunnel, fetched the Prince and was waiting by the underground river! Had it taken him that long?

It was not far for him to crawl before seeing the welcoming flickering light of the torch Kelmar had lit. A smile long-needed crossed his face as he saw it.

Then the breeze Kelmar had spoken of touched his face, and he thanked Kelmar in his mind for the picture he had painted for him of them riding together through Kelmsmere Valley. How stupid he felt, but how thankful he was to have a friend like Kelmar by his side.

He emerged onto a ledge to the sound of the rushing river. Kelmar smiled at him and handed over some cold meat for him to chew on, frowning as he looked at Cantell's knee. "You are bleeding." Cantell looked to see; he had gashed it and not even noticed.

"Sit down, Mrs Beeworthy has thought of everything," said Kelmar, rummaging around in the provisions and coming out with a cloth and some dried herbs.

"These will help," and Kelmar dipped the cloth in the river to wipe Cantell's cut before applying the herbs to it.

Cantell let out a yelp. Whatever the herbs were, they certainly stung!

"I am sorry, Kelmar. I am more of a burden to you than a help," spoke Cantell, once they had settled down.

"You are not a burden. You are my friend and comrade. We all have our fears, there is no more to be said," concluded Kelmar, cutting short any misgivings Cantell was feeling.

"You are a true friend," said Cantell, and both men fell quiet for a moment.

"Though I must admit for a moment back there, I thought you had put on weight!" quipped Kelmar, sniggering, and both men laughed out loud.

"He is quiet," remarked Cantell, looking at the little bundle of Prince Martyn.

"He has not woken since he cried himself to sleep," replied Kelmar, trying to chew on his cold meat and finally giving up, throwing it into the river.

"I will be glad when we get to Kelmsmere and have some proper food instead of this excuse for it," said Kelmar, spitting the rest of the meat, half chewed, out of his mouth.

"That is, if the alliance army has not had it all," pointed out Cantell, to Kelmar's thoughtful nods.

"My mother will be there. She will have some and know what to do for the Prince," he said assuredly as he thought of her.

Cantell hoped he was right. Being under siege all of these months, they had no way of knowing.

Neither man spoke anymore; instead; they rested themselves on the rock ledge to lay awhile. Letting the sound of the river relax their weary bodies and minds before setting off once more on their journey under the Kavenmist Mountains.

CHAPTER IX

Nighttime had just drawn its veil over the sky as King Taliskar appeared on the outer wall of Stormhaven stronghold battlements. The mist was slowly clearing, swirling its way back out to sea whilst the snow fell steadily, covering the ground the mist had revealed.

King Taliskar's eyes did not take any of this in; instead, they were looking into the distant places of his mind.

He wandered along the battlements trying to let the cold air clarify his thoughts as to what had happened to him that day. He was still in wonder at how he had opened the mountain door without an understanding of how he had done it, and yet he had!

His Queen had told him to focus his mind and tell it to open, but nothing was clear to him, no matter how he tried to remember. Yet when he opened his eyes, there it was!

He remembered the feeling of power that had washed over him in that moment, but nothing else. Doubts and confusion were beginning to circle together in his mind.

There was no confusion at the feeling of power he had had when he sat upon the mountain throne of Tiggannia. Its cold stone had sent a shiver of exhilaration throughout his body. He could not help but try the crown of Tiggannia upon his head as he sat there with his eyes closed, basking in the glory of it all.

A smile crossed his face as he thought upon it, and broadened all the more as Brax's stunned dead face came into his mind. He would have had King Rolfe killed anyway, he thought idly.

Then his smile disappeared as he thought of the word Brax had challenged him with: sorcery! King Taliskar frowned and shook his head. Surely that was not true; his Queen would know it not to be, he thought.

Then suddenly that was all he wanted to make his day complete, his beautiful Queen Helistra by his side. He had sent a messenger to summon her, but it would be an age before she arrived.

As he thought about her, King Taliskar looked up through the snow at two huge bonfires that had been lit outside the stronghold's walls, to see the snow glow a golden yellow all around them.

The bodies of the fallen, from both sides, were being burnt upon their flames, their souls cast to the four winds to find their final resting place over the Great Forest, a belief that was shared throughout Northernland.

To King Taliskar, though, it was just a matter of clearing up; he wanted them out of the way before his Queen came.

"Party approaching the gate!" came a cry from one of the guards. King Taliskar looked out between the fires and caught sight of some riders coming in.

Probably a patrol, he thought as he reached the spiral steps and started to go down them, then his eyes suddenly widened; one on a white horse!

King Taliskar rushed down to the gatehouse to look out of an arched window. There was no mistaking his Queen Helistra, he thought. She looked so elegant on the white horse he had given her, with her dark crimson cloak flowing over the horse's hindquarters.

He waved through the window to her as she got closer, and seeing him wave, she smiled. That was all he needed. His legs could not keep up with his heart as he ran down the spiral steps to greet her.

"My Queen," he greeted her breathlessly. "I was just thinking about you and here you are!"

"A nice surprise, I hope, my King," she replied, sliding down into his waiting arms.

Whatever King Taliskar was going to say was completely lost in the moment as he looked into her eyes; he was so intoxicated by her beauty.

"Well, my love?" she asked with a knowing smile.

"I... I could not have wished for more," he said with a sigh, hugging her tightly.

Queen Helistra took the broken rune staff out of its sheaf and gave Sergeant Wardine her horse to be tended whilst King Taliskar watched her.

He knew the staff meant a lot to her and even though it was broken, she was never without it. She had chanced upon it on her travels and thought it once belonged to one such as she, another Queen from long ago. An ancient symbol of justice whose symbolic meaning had been lost and forgotten.

All this she had told to King Taliskar, but he still thought of it as just a broken stick with crude markings upon it, but if it made her happy then he was too.

Queen Helistra moved forward to the huge gates and looked out at the two bonfires.

"I see the battle was hard fought, for the fires burn bright," she observed, as two soldiers threw yet another body onto the flames of one of the fires.

"It is true, they fought well and losses were high. I had hoped to…" King Taliskar stopped short of what he was going to say by the simple gesture of Queen Helistra's raised hand saying to him that whatever it was, it did not matter.

Her face was reflected in the glow of the fires, one of sadness and concern, but inside she trembled with anticipation. Her timing could not have been better, for this was just what Queen Helistra needed, more souls!

She had already tasted a host of souls from the battle as she had ridden alongside the River Dale, to whet her appetite. Drawing the souls in with the broken rune staff so they would never reach the Great Forest and rest in peace.

She could feel more in the air for her to feed upon with the fatally wounded dying, and though their hearts were still warm, their souls would flee before the burning pyres consumed their bodies.

Closing her eyes, Queen Helistra touched some of the broken rune staff's symbols, to feel a soft hum respond in her mind. She breathed in deeply and together they welcomed the souls with open arms, tasting like nectar as they drank them in greedily.

Seeing her eyes closed, King Taliskar let her have this moment to herself, thinking she was bidding the fallen a last farewell.

She felt his looks; if only he knew that the ending of life could give someone so much power, power beyond even his wildest dreams, she thought, smiling inside.

Queen Helistra opened her eyes; feeling the strength from the souls invigorating her, replenishing power was delicious! Her mind shouted.

A quiet hum spoke in her mind once more and she let the broken rune staff take over, feeling it tingle in her hands as she did so.

"It is a sad day for many," she said with concern in her voice, turning away from the bonfires.

"It is, my love," answered King Taliskar, looking at her in admiration. *How she feels for everyone*, he thought.

"Now, my King, come and show me this stronghold you have conquered," Queen Helistra said with a smile as she held out her arm for King Taliskar to take hold whilst feeling the warmth of the broken rune staff in her other arm as it entrapped more souls.

"It will be my pleasure," said King Taliskar smilingly, and off they strode up towards Middle Gate, arm in arm.

King Taliskar could not wait to tell her of Brax and King Rolfe's fate as they walked in the shadow of the inner wall.

"There they both were, dead! By each other's hand!" he said, grinning.

"Both of them!" exclaimed Queen Helistra. "How unfortunate," she said, giggling, and they both laughed.

"I see you have not lost your wicked sense of humour, my love," said King Taliskar, still chortling.

As they walked under Middle Gate, Queen Helistra turned to King Taliskar with a question she had been dying to ask.

"You have not told me how surprised the Tiggannians must have been when you appeared from behind them. The knowledge I gained about the doors was true then?" she pushed.

She watched as King Taliskar looked back at her with mixed emotions. The elation of power he had was clear to see, but mixed with it was the unsureness of what had happened.

"You were right, my love. The wise man who told you they were there spoke true. I opened them, just like you said, but the one in the mountain, though, I am not…" King Taliskar faltered suddenly, feeling nervous.

"Not sure how you did it?" finished Queen Helistra, looking into his eyes, her voice purring in his ears. "It does not matter how, my love, but you did as I foretold. You are the mover of mountains!"

King Taliskar's mind drowned in her lyrical tones as she was joined by a soft humming sound.

"By opening the mountain door, you have taken Stormhaven, it is yours! Brax and Rolfe are no more. You are King of all you survey!" Queen Helistra's eyes burnt into King Taliskar's as her words spun in his mind. She let go of his arm and curtsied majestically before him. "My King," she said humbly.

King Taliskar stood still for a moment as her words took hold. No, it did not matter how. He had opened the mountain door and it in turn had opened all before him, he thought. Everything he had wanted he now had! Even Brax and Rolfe were dead!

Stormhaven and the throne of Tigannia were his, and here before him was the most beautiful woman in all of the Kingdoms, bowing before him. What more did he want!

King Taliskar suddenly blinked, to only just realise his Queen was bowing before him! "Please, my love, you do not have to do that!" he said, embarrassed, nearly falling over in the snow as he stooped to lift her back up.

All felt clear to him as he looked at her, to suddenly yawn without warning. "I am sorry, my love, I do not know what has come over me," he apologised.

"I think the day has caught up with you," she suggested.

"Yes, I think you are right."

"Perhaps you should go and rest. I would like to look round for a while. I will not be long in this cold before I join you," she promised, stroking his face.

"I will go to our chamber I have had prepared for us, my love, and wait for you there," and King Taliskar started to walk towards the great hall, thinking, *King of all I survey, I like that.*

"The royal chamber, of course, for the conqueror!" called Queen Helistra behind him, smiling.

King Taliskar stopped and turned around; he had totally forgotten to tell her. *I hope she will not be angry with me,* he thought, walking back towards her.

"We are in Forest Tower, my love, but not in the royal chamber," he began explaining. "Queen Elina still occupies the royal chamber. She is with her newborn, a girl this very day." King Taliskar watched as Queen Helistra's face at first frowned and then smiled back at him.

"You spared them?" she said, sounding surprised.

"I am not the monster people think I am," he defended himself. In truth, he had spent his time daydreaming in the throne room, forgetting all about Queen Elina and her baby.

"I was thinking of you, my love. I knew you would like to see the newborn," he lied. She looked back at him, knowing he was lying, but it could prove interesting, she thought.

"A newborn baby! Of course I would!" she chirped.

"Shall I announce that you will be coming to see them as I pass?" he asked as he turned once more for the great hall.

"No, there is no need, I will announce myself," she replied, and watched him go with an idea hatching in her mind.

Queen Helistra turned and walked back down to the archway as a soft humming entered her head. *Good, we will have more than enough for what we need.* She smiled to more humming.

I know, this place has started to put questions even into his feeble head. The sooner it is quenched, the better.

Entering the archway, Queen Helistra smiled as she saw the solid rock. *Let us see if she is listening,* she mused.

Queen Helistra gently brushed her hand against the rock, to immediately feel a shrill cry of terror flood into her mind, making her grin as she heard it.

I will be with you soon. Do not worry, she promised.

No! No! Stay away! You are evil! Only death walks your path! cried the little frightened voice.

I do hope so, ridiculed Queen Helistra and she let go of the rock, leaving the already frightened voice in tears.

As Queen Helistra turned away from the rock, her eyes rested on the two huge gates that were just being closed. She watched as the old markings upon them disappeared to the outside. *They did not keep me away, Gentian,* she thought. A soft hum reminding her of something made her smile. *That is true. Even if they knew how to, they are useless without one.*

Queen Helistra made her way to the first of the secret doors, wanting to trace the steps she had been told about for herself. As she reached the lower eastern passageway, a soft white light emanated from the broken rune staff, showing her the way.

Reaching the open doorway, she stepped through it to smell the cold, damp air. She made to touch a symbol to close the secret door for a hum to sound. "No, you are right, it might bring suspicion upon myself," she agreed, and left the secret door open.

Walking on, she came to the old wooden door that was set back into the rock. She opened it and walked in. The small room revealed nothing except an old shield lying on a roughly hewn seat that ran all around the room. She moved over and picked it up, rubbing some of the dirt from it that had gathered over time.

A hum sounded as she looked at it. "I thought I would come and look," she responded to more humming. "No, thinking of Gentian did not put it in my mind…" another hum. "Perhaps I should not have, but he has no idea and you know it is useless without the shield…" more humming. "I would have destroyed them all, but we were not strong enough then. As it is, they are scattered well to the four corners of Northernland, they will never be found!"

Queen Helistra grew tired of the constant questions and threw the shield back down with contempt.

Soon she stood in the mountain doorway and thought of King Taliskar's face.

"It must have been one to behold," she smirked as humming spoke to her once more.

"Whatever uncertainty we might have will end this night," she said with cold assurance.

Queen Helistra moved through the mountain doorway into the empty storerooms and out onto the grand courtyard, to let her eyes look up.

Though the skies were grey and full of snow, she could still see Forest Tower soaring above her, blending into the Kavenmist Mountains as snow swirled about its form.

There you are, her mind said, *though you bury yourself into the mountain, there is no hiding from me!*

Entering the great hall, she walked to the base of Forest Tower, stopping to look at the blood-stained floor where the last stand was fought.

Brave fools, she thought, *but thank you for your souls.* She looked at the middle of the stone floor, sensing where Brax and King Rolfe had fallen, ending each other's lives.

A humming sounded. *Brax was a pig, but his soul was strong. We were wise to leave King Rolfe's be. His would have been as strong, but we do not want to spoil the power we have by tainting it.* She grinned sarcastically.

Queen Helistra made her way up the spiral steps and stood outside the royal chamber. *Shall we see who keeps us from here?* She smiled to more humming. *No, I will not do anything silly,* and she walked into the royal chamber to see an exhausted Queen Elina sleeping.

Her hand maiden, Charlotte, was by her side holding her hand, whilst Mrs Beeworthy stood over a little bundle in a cradle.

Charlotte looked wide-eyed at Queen Helistra as she walked into the chamber. In all of her time, she had never seen anyone so beautiful, let alone at this time of death and hardship. Her eyes flitted to the sleeping Queen Elina. *Except for you, my lady*, she quickly thought.

She made to get up in the presence of Queen Helistra, but a hand held up and a shake of a head told her to remain. "It is all right, my child, you have no need," confirmed Queen Helistra softly. *Pitiful girl*, thought Queen Helistra, *her soul would not feed a hair on my head!*

Mrs Beeworthy spun around on hearing another voice, not having heard her come in, and gave a small curtsy when she saw who it was.

"Please do not let me disturb you. I could not help myself when I heard there has been a little one born, a tiny life in so much tragedy," she said, echoing King Rolfe's words.

Mrs Beeworthy and Charlotte could feel the deep sadness in her voice as she spoke.

"Here be Princess Amber," said Mrs Beeworthy, stepping aside for Queen Helistra to walk over and look into the cradle.

Queen Helistra held out her hand and put her little finger into the palm of the Princess, to feel her tiny hand trying to grip it. "Oh, how lovely she is, and what a beautiful name she has been given, so fitting," she said with a smile.

A humming spoke in her mind, seeing what she was thinking. *She is ideal. We can groom her in our ways for the future.*

Suddenly Queen Helistra started to softly hum a tune to the little Princess. Mrs Beeworthy and Charlotte looked at each other, both smiling with the same thought: how nice that is.

What they could not hear was the humming that had joined Queen Helistra. Her other hand held certain symbols on the broken rune staff underneath her crimson cloak. Without getting any louder, the humming deepened in intensity and then suddenly stopped.

Queen Helistra let go of Princess Amber's tiny hand. *You will come to me when the time is right,* her mind said, and she stood upright once more.

Queen Helistra moved over to look at the sleeping Queen Elina. "How does she fare?" she asked, sounding concerned.

"She be frail, but she is strong of heart, my lady. Some good food inside her would not go amiss," answered Mrs Beeworthy, all the time looking at Queen Elina with affection.

"I will see to it that you receive some, and now I will leave you all to rest," and Queen Helistra turned towards the door.

Mrs Beeworthy quickly moved to open it for her with Charlotte by her side.

"Such a lovely child," said Queen Helistra as she passed them.

"He be... she be lovely like her mother." Mrs Beeworthy quickly corrected herself, but not before Queen Helistra had stopped and turned around, looking at Mrs Beeworthy like a snake ready to strike, even though her face did not portray it.

He? Queen Helistra was thinking. *Is this bumbling fool hiding something?* "He?" Queen Helistra said with a smile.

"A slip of the tongue, my lady," said Mrs Beeworthy, shaking her head, smiling back, her reddening face not helping matters.

Have I got to waste power on these pathetic idiots? she thought, still smiling at them. "It is easily done with what you have had to go through these last months, but listen to me, I am walking away from you without even asking your names. How rude you must think me," said Queen Helistra, changing the subject whilst looking into their eyes.

Mrs Beeworthy and Charlotte could only stare back at Queen Helistra, as her voice had taken on soft melodic tones to their ears, caressing their senses as a soft humming joined it.

"I be Mrs Beeworthy, my lady's cook and companion," said Mrs Beeworthy without another thought.

"And I am Charlotte, my lady's hand servant." Both were lost to her as they stared back with unfocused eyes.

"So much you have both been through, and your Queen with child," coaxed Queen Helistra, and she waited for what they were hiding.

Mrs Beeworthy and Charlotte could not talk quickly enough as they told Queen Helistra everything that they meant to keep secret.

"No, not one, but two! She be carrying twins all this time! Not even King Rolfe knew," chortled Mrs Beeworthy.

"Our Queen had a baby boy first," joined in Charlotte. "They named him Prince Martyn and he escaped before Princess Amber was born," she said with a grin.

"Escaped?" came the obvious question from Queen Helistra.

"Yes, my lady, he be gone with Cantell and Kelmar under Kavenmist Mountains. I do not know if he will survive," and Mrs Beeworthy's eyes suddenly flooded with tears.

"Do not alarm yourselves," said Queen Helistra reassuringly. "I will leave you now. I am keeping you from your duties and you must be tired," she announced, leaving Mrs Beeworthy and Charlotte none the wiser as to what had just happened to them, only that they were suddenly feeling very tired.

Queen Helistra thought on what she had just been told as she climbed the spiral stairs. *So she has a brother making his way through Kavenmist, a journey not without its hazards*, she thought. *Wait until he hears this.* She smiled.

Walking into the chamber that had been prepared for her, Queen Helistra was met by the snoring of King Taliskar lying on the bed. Humming immediately entered her mind. *Yes, I know, you do not have to keep reminding me.* She sighed.

"Wake up, I have something to tell you," she said, promptly tapping him on the head with the broken rune staff. King Taliskar woke abruptly, rubbing his forehead, to a smiling Queen Helistra.

"I have some news for you," she began.

"What news is that, my love?" said King Taliskar, looking at the broken rune staff in her hand whilst rubbing his head.

"Queen Elina did not have one child, but two."

"Two? Where is the other child? Has it died?" he questioned, frowning.

"No, the boy has escaped with two soldiers, Cantell and Kelmar. They are making their way through the Kavenmist Mountains as we speak," she informed him, making King Taliskar sit up and get to his feet.

"A boy!" blurted King Taliskar. All he could think was that a King of Tigannia still lived! "Where did you hear this?" he queried.

"From Queen Elina's two attendants. The cook let it slip when she was speaking to me about the baby girl," explained Queen Helistra.

"Through the mountains? Is that possible?" said King Taliskar, in puzzlement.

"I do not know, but if they do make it, the edge of the Great Forest awaits them," surmised Queen Helistra with a hint of knowledge.

"They will have to be dealt with!" stated King Taliskar, starting to pace up and down. "They are the future of this Kingdom, born to lead. They could prove dangerous!" he said, annoyed with himself. He should have dealt with the child straightaway instead of dreaming.

"That is true, but they will be of no threat to us, my love. We have the girl, and the boy will have nothing. We have what would have been theirs. The thrones of Tigannia are ours and always will be," said Queen Helistra, sounding assured.

King Taliskar stopped his pacing and looked at her with expectation. "You sound confident," he observed.

"We can post patrols along the valley where it meets the Great Forest. If they survive and make it through the Kavenmist Mountains, we will be there to capture them. Then you can do as you wish with the boy," she said smilingly.

King Taliskar nodded, thinking. "His death cannot come soon enough for me, but I understand what you are saying. He already has nothing, no army, no Kingdom. It is ours, but that still leaves the girl," he pointed out.

"You could have dealt with her already, but can I hazard a guess as to what you were doing?" she asked, to see King Taliskar turn away from her looks.

"I have seen her, such a sweet child," continued Queen Helistra, "and have thought of having her for my own," she stated to King Taliskar's looks this time.

"She is but a baby. I can bring her up in the ways of a Cardronian, she will never know. You know I have not been blessed with children of my own. Would you deny me this moment?" she added, with a hint of a warning in her voice.

King Taliskar was quick not to upset her. "No, no, of course not, but we have been down this path once before," he recalled.

"You would not let me keep him," she chastised King Taliskar straightaway.

"I know I did not, but it was a dangerous time. We were preparing the ground for this moment. Remember who brought him to us. We could not trust him not to open his mouth," he pointed out. "I had to pretend I had the child killed even though I did not, for your sake, knowing how you felt," he added.

"No, you did not. That is true. He has grown to serve you well, but now there is no one to challenge us as before. Brax is dead, and the murdering King Rolfe is no more," she said with a smile.

"What of the Queen, though?" said King Taliskar.

"The dungeons await her. She will never see the light of day," replied Queen Helistra, with a coldness that made King Taliskar suddenly shiver.

"Very well, it is as you say. Who is there to stop us? I will call the guard to inform Captain Tarbor to organise the patrols," he said, offering her his arm. "Now let us go and see this child that has caught your eye." He smiled, thinking not only was he a King of all he surveyed, but he would soon be a father also.

Queen Helistra took hold of his arm and smiled back as if in gratitude as humming came into her mind. *I know it is painful to keep up this pretence, but when it is set in motion…* more humming. *No, it cannot come soon enough…* humming once more. *If the child does not, then I will kill her!*

CHAPTER X

After a patrol of the stronghold making sure the needs of the men were being seen to, Tarbor and Girvan sat at a table in the warmth of the kitchen tucking into a well-needed meal, with no one there to hear them talk of what they had witnessed that day.

"I am glad we had supplies with us," said Girvan, finishing off another mouthful of food.

"I do not think food will help straighten out this head of mine," replied Tarbor, spearing some meat with his dagger.

"Tell me of the voice again from the rock," probed Girvan.

"It sounded frightened and yet she had a strange… vitality," Tarbor said hesitatingly, trying to think of the right word to describe the voice he heard.

"She, you say, you could tell?" queried Girvan.

"I know a woman's voice when I hear one," Tarbor rebuffed, making Girvan smile.

Tarbor helped himself to another piece of meat as he thought of what it had said. "Help me, she comes, she will poison the land. Evil will reign and night will fall forever," remembered Tarbor.

"That does not sound good," said Girvan, frowning. "The voice never said who this could be?" he asked further.

"No, but is it more than just a coincidence that Queen Helistra has suddenly arrived here?" said Tarbor, finding himself speaking more quietly.

"You cannot accuse her because she has happened to appear. She is King Taliskar's wife after all," pointed out Girvan.

"That may be so, but she is always in the background. Her name comes up each time," said Tarbor thoughtfully.

"Of course it does, she is the Queen," said Girvan, wiping his mouth on his sleeve.

"What about the story of the wise man she met, speaking of secret doors? That came from her," pointed out Tarbor.

"Well, the knowledge she learnt from him proved right," came back Girvan.

Tarbor thought again. "All right, how does a mere man open a door in a mountain?" challenged Tarbor, for Girvan to shake his head, not knowing how but thinking of the word Brax had used: sorcery.

"How did King Taliskar appear to you in the archway and then at the mountain door? Did he not seem, well, strange?" questioned Tarbor eventually. "I know it is not the first time he has been like that, and Brax saw it as sorcery!" added Tarbor, saying what had crossed Girvan's mind.

"We have no proof of anything, though, Tarbor, and Brax is dead," said Girvan, trying to keep Tarbor's emotions under control. "You cannot accuse anyone of anything with hunches. I for one would not want to cross Queen Helistra. Our lives would be forfeited," he warned, making Tarbor think.

"You are right, it would be unwise to," agreed Tarbor, resting his hand on the side of his face, staring aimlessly at nothing, feeling frustrated. "Only the stars know what has happened to me since coming to this place." He sighed.

"Of course!" said Girvan suddenly. "Go to the rock again and ask who the evil one is. Not that you could tell anybody. Who would believe you and who could you trust besides me? But at least it would make things clearer for you, Tarbor," said Girvan with a smile.

Tarbor turned and looked at his comrade. "It is always good to have a friend like you," he said, smiling. "You are right. It might say her name and give me some peace of mind, knowing that I am on the right path. Come then, let us see what happens," and Tarbor was up on his feet.

The two cloaked figures made their way to the archway through the ever-present snow. They were soon standing next to the cold rock that had revealed itself earlier to Tarbor. The gates were shut and all was quiet, but Tarbor still found himself holding the hilt of his sword for reassurance. "Let us see if this is all but a dream," he said softly, and he slowly put his hand on the rock.

How do I speak to a rock? he found himself thinking as he touched the rock, to feel a wave of fear instantly wash over him.

Do not! She will hear! Go, find Speedwell! No sooner had Tarbor put his hand on the rock than he was taking it away again.

"Well, did the voice tell you who it, she, fears?" asked Girvan straight away.

"No, Girvan, she broke off too frightened, saying that she will hear, but that only points to Queen Helistra. Who else has come here to Stormhaven and could hear what is said?" reasoned Tarbor.

"Nothing that we can prove, though, Tarbor," said Girvan, a little disappointed that the voice had not said who.

"No, it is not, but she did say a name, though," added Tarbor, making Girvan's ears prick up.

"What name was that?"

"Speedwell!"

"Who?"

"Speedwell," repeated Tarbor.

"A name I have never come across," said Girvan, scratching his head.

"Well, that is the name the voice said, telling me to go and find him," informed Tarbor.

"He sounds like the wise man Queen Helistra could have met," said Girvan, off the top of his head, making Tarbor frown.

"Surely not! What would be the point in telling me of someone who could have helped Queen Helistra? No, he must be someone who can help shed light on what has happened, the mountain door, the voice," concluded Tarbor.

"Well, could we not look for him? Our time here is done for now," suggested Girvan.

"We can, once we have escorted Queen Elina at King Rolfe's funeral, then I will tell King Taliskar," stated Tarbor.

"Will he not be curious as to why?" queried Girvan.

"No, not when I tell him we are escorting Brax's body back to Waunarle." Tarbor smiled at Girvan, who nodded his approval and then grimaced.

"A dead body on a long ride, Tarbor!"

"But think on, Girvan, we could go and see your father in Slevenport afterwards," said Tarbor, smiling, to see Girvan do the same.

As they began to walk back up the slope to Middle Gate, Girvan stopped and looked at Tarbor with a quizzical look on his face, for Tarbor to look at him enquiringly.

"I wonder if that old wooden door is hiding anything?" he asked in curiosity. Tarbor had forgotten all about it, such was the day.

"We have time. Let us go and look," replied Tarbor.

Relieving a torch from its holder, they retraced their steps from earlier, stepping through the secret door and moving along the glistening passageway until they reached the old wooden door set back in the rock. Girvan opened the door and walked in, to be disappointed at what revealed itself before his eyes. Tarbor followed and shared his friend's disappointment.

"Such a small space, an old storeroom of sorts perhaps," remarked Girvan as Tarbor moved forward, spotting a shield on the floor.

"A shield, Girvan," he said, picking it up to look at it in the torchlight. Girvan immediately pointed to where someone had rubbed some of the dirt from it.

"Someone has been in here, probably one of the soldiers sneaking a look," he assumed, but Tarbor was shaking his head, smelling the air.

"I do not think so, Girvan."

Girvan began to smell the air with him and caught a soft fragrance cutting lightly through the cold dampness. A smell that reminded him of woodland flowers as Tarbor confirmed his suspicions of who had been there: "Queen Helistra has been here!"

It made Girvan want to look at the shield all the more. Giving Tarbor the torch, he started cleaning the shield with his cloak to examine it more closely.

"If only my father were here to see this!" he exclaimed suddenly. "I thought the legend was just a story, but this shield proves otherwise!" said Girvan in awe, making Tarbor wonder what could be so fascinating about an old shield.

"Look at this." Girvan pointed to the top corner of the shield, for Tarbor to see etched onto the back of it a hawk's head, part of the Cardronian crest. Even though it told Tarbor it was a Cardronian shield, it still meant nothing to him.

"Look down its length," urged Girvan, holding it lengthways so Tarbor could look. Tarbor looked and at first saw nothing, only metal shining back at him where Girvan had cleaned it.

He looked again, holding the torch closer, and his eyes began to see the subtle blend of colours along its length, interweaving with each other, making him realise that only workmanship from a master craftsman could have made such a shield.

"It is beautiful, Girvan. I can see why you are excited by such workmanship, being a blacksmith's son, but what story are you on about that your father told you of?" asked Tarbor, puzzled.

"Have you never heard of the legend then, Tarbor?" asked Girvan, only to receive a blank expression from Tarbor.

"My father told me of it more than once when I was young, of five swords and shields forged long ago deep within the realms of the Great Forest. They were called the defenders of the five Kingdoms, entrusted to each King by the children of the forest," remembered Girvan to an open-mouthed Tarbor. What was he on about?

"See how the metals blend within its make-up. This has been caused by the mixture of metals that were used. It was said they melted metal from a rock fallen from the sky to mix with earthly metals, its unique element giving them their strength of earth and sky. My father said they all disappeared without trace long ago and now here is one before us! We talk of sorcery, but there was another word used for these ancient weapons: magic!" finished Girvan to a bewildered Tarbor.

"I am having a hard time taking in what you have just said, Girvan. Are you sure it is not just a bedtime story your father made up?" queried Tarbor.

"I did think so once, that it was a story handed down through time, but the evidence that it is true is here looking at us!" argued Girvan, pointing at the shield.

"A story from an old man and now one from your father, what next?" said Tarbor, finding it all hard to swallow.

"A voice from a rock!" retaliated Girvan, annoyed at Tarbor's comment.

Tarbor stopped himself and looked at his friend then at the shield; he had hurt Girvan's feelings without thinking.

"I am sorry, Girvan. I did not mean to disrespect you or your father, it was wrong of me," he apologised. "This day has tested me," he added.

Girvan smiled in understanding, looking at his friend. "I have only managed to confuse matters even more, I know, but do you not find it strange that she has taken the time to come here and look at this shield?" he questioned.

"You are right. Why would she? Does it hold a fear for her, which is why it is hidden away? Why they have all disappeared?" Tarbor thought further as he held the torch close to the shield once more, to see the intricate patterns of the metals flowing delicately along the shield's length, their strange colours glinting back at him.

"These children of the forest, though, Girvan, who are they?" He had to ask, thinking of the name he had heard, Speedwell.

"My father told me they were a people who lived in the Great Forest long ago, who crafted the defenders," answered Girvan, with the same thought as Tarbor in his mind. "The name you heard, Speedwell, could well be one of them, but if that is so, they have not been heard of or seen for hundreds of years," he added, only to make Tarbor feel a sense of disappointment.

"There is something else that is only going to add to the confusion you already feel," spoke Girvan further as Tarbor laid the shield back down to look at him.

"I did say I thought once upon a time that my father was only telling me a story, only a story, that is, until I saw your sword, Tarbor," revealed Girvan, making Tarbor's forehead furrow all the more.

"What are you on about, Girvan?" asked Tarbor, perplexed.

"Your sword is the same, that of the shield, an ancient defender!" Tarbor nearly dropped the torch; such was his amazement at Girvan's revelation.

"I… I only received this sword from King Taliskar himself in honour of my becoming a Captain this last year," uttered Tarbor, not able to comprehend what Girvan had just said. "What makes you say this, why now?" Tarbor was speechless, his sword the same as the shield?

"I would have, but you would not have believed me. After all, it was only a bedtime story," Girvan said smilingly, for Tarbor to nod in acknowledgement of his doubt.

"It was when we practised once together. As you unsheathed it, sunlight caught the top of the blade, reflecting the colours briefly to me that you saw on the shield," explained Girvan. "You do not exactly keep your sword clean, but seeing this shield now has made me certain in my mind that you are in possession of an ancient defender," finished Girvan.

Tarbor could only look at Girvan as he drew his sword to look at it with him. Only the scars of battle and the grime of not being cleaned met Tarbor's eyes; he could see nothing else.

Girvan held out his hand. "May I?" As he twisted it one way and then the other, Girvan's eyes came to rest on the spine of the blade underneath the hilt. Spitting on it and rubbing it hard with his cloak, he suddenly broke out in a broad smile, with any doubts he might have had disappearing. "There, look, Tarbor!"

Tarbor looked at his friend and then at the sword, with a certain feeling of apprehension running through him. His mouth dropped yet again as he saw the subtle blend of colours shouting back at him like the shield. "By the stars! This gets stranger and stranger," was all he could say.

As Girvan passed back Tarbor's sword, he pointed to its pommel. "Of course, there was one other thing I spotted that told me what you possessed. Have you not seen these?" he queried, for Tarbor to look. Two wavy lines on each side of the pommel met his eyes.

"Yes, I have seen them. They are mere decoration, Girvan, nothing more," replied Tarbor, dismissing them.

"No, Tarbor, they represent the two rivers of Waunarle, the Worpel and Towien, part of the crest of Waunarle. You have been given the defender of the Kingdom of Waunarle!"

Quietness ensued as they walked along the passageway up to the mountain doorway, each warrior trying to understand what was happening in this place.

Tarbor's head was spinning. He had doubted his friend but knew he would not lie to him, but all it had done was put more questions into his head without any answers.

Standing in the shadow of the mountain doorway only made for another question from Girvan. "What of King Taliskar? Is he to be feared?" he asked as they looked at the huge rock that had opened to reveal the doorway.

"I do not think so. He has what he wants, power. I saw the look on his face when he entered the mountain throne room. No, there is more to this than meets the eye, but what it is I am at a loss to say, but she has to be behind it all," Tarbor said thoughtfully as he moved through the mountain doorway into the storeroom.

Tarbor doused the torch and moved through into the other storeroom. Opening the door, he stepped outside into the grand courtyard to be welcomed by a carpet of glistening white snow. It had finally stopped falling to give way to a sky full of stars.

"You were right about King Taliskar's face. It did seem distant in the archway and at the mountain door," said Girvan as he joined Tarbor in thought. "He did not look as if he knew where he was," he added.

Tarbor stared up at the stars, as if for inspiration. "It was his eyes, though, Girvan. Did you not see them? I swear they had turned…" Tarbor hesitated.

"Turned what?" pushed Girvan.

"Just for a moment, I thought they had turned completely black!"

A guard suddenly appeared, trying to run across the grand courtyard towards the two warriors looking at each other.

"Captain Tarbor, sir!" the guard called as he got closer.

"Yes, what is it?" answered Tarbor, without looking at the guard.

"King Taliskar requests your presence, sir, in the great hall," he reported.

"Very well, tell him I will be there shortly," and with that the guard turned away to make haste back to the great hall.

"Black!" exclaimed Girvan, as if the guard had not been there.

"Black, Girvan, and all it does is bring us back to what Brax spoke of: sorcery," replied Tarbor, sounding worried.

"If it is sorcery then perhaps it can be fought back with the magic of the defenders!" said Girvan, more in hope than anything else, for Tarbor to shake his head.

"Sometimes, Girvan, you are beyond hope. If these weapons do possess the power of earth and sky, as you say they do, surely I would have felt something by now," he posed.

They walked across the glistening snow towards the great hall, listening to its crispness under their boots as Girvan thought on what Tarbor had said. "I think you did, I saw you holding the defender's hilt when you touched the rock. It could have helped you hear the voice," responded Girvan, making Tarbor stop and look at him.

"This is getting us nowhere, Girvan. My holding the hilt can only have been a coincidence. You told me they were made for the Kings of each Kingdom, and I am an ordinary Cardronian, not the King of Waunarle, so how could it?" questioned Tarbor.

Girvan had no answer this time as they reached the great hall doors. "Whatever happens, though, Girvan, we must be vigilant and wary of what we say," warned Tarbor whilst Girvan opened the doors.

"I understand, Captain, sir," nodded Girvan, seeing King Taliskar sitting there waiting for them in the great hall as they walked in.

"Ah, Captain Tarbor, you grace me at last with your presence," said King Taliskar, eying them both.

"I am sorry, sire, to keep you waiting. I was seeing to the needs of the men. The battle has been hard, there are many wounded," he answered, whilst trying to put to the back of his mind all the thoughts that were going through it.

King Taliskar nodded his understanding and then started to speak of the escape. "I have been told that Queen Elina had another child, a brother to the girl, before we secured Stormhaven," began King Taliskar.

"The child escapes through the Kavenmist Mountains as we speak, carried by two warriors, a Cantell and Kelmar. I want you to post patrols between the Great Forest and the River Dale. If they survive their journey through the mountains, they will have to negotiate the river. They will not venture into the forest, no one does. They will need shelter, but not from trees," he informed and ordered Tarbor.

"At once, sire," replied Tarbor promptly.

"Make sure you post enough men and when you capture them…" King Taliskar paused whilst he stood up and looked Tarbor squarely in the face, "kill them all! do you understand?"

"Yes, sire, I understand," answered Tarbor straight away, but he felt immediately uneasy in his mind. Killing warriors was one thing, but killing a baby!

"Very well, see to it!" ordered King Taliskar further, and he left them to go to the mountain throne room.

Tarbor and Girvan bowed, watching him. "There he goes. You were right, Tarbor. He has what he wants, but this has altered things," said Girvan. "We have no chance of escorting Brax's body to Waunarle now," he added, disappointed at the thought of not seeing his father.

"Perhaps, we will have to wait and see," said Tarbor, thinking. "So we have to kill the brother, but what of the girl?" said Tarbor thoughtfully.

"I do not know, but the thought of doing so leaves a nasty taste in my mouth," said Girvan, feeling the same as Tarbor.

Leaving the great hall, Tarbor and Girvan walked towards one of Middle Gate's turrets to organise patrols from the men resting there.

Tarbor found himself asking Girvan about the split crests on his sword and the shield as they walked. "They are not complete. The hawk's head has a quarter moon under it and the rivers have a crown over them," he pointed out.

"If the shield had been that of Waunarle, it would have had the crown upon it linking the two together to become one, protector and defender of the Kingdom of Waunarle, linked by magic!" Girvan smiled again as he thought of his father's words.

Tarbor could only groan inside. *There he goes again, but could it be true, could anything?*

CHAPTER XI

Cantell woke with a start, jolting his neck in the process, to immediately feel a stiffness that had begun setting in from laying on the rock. He rubbed it, cursing.

"Ah, I see you are awake," Kelmar smiled at Cantell's cursing.

"My neck still thinks I am not," replied Cantell, standing up and stretching, feeling his gashed knee sting, to make him curse again.

"You do not wake very well," said Kelmar, who was ready to go.

"Being cold and wet before we rested has not helped," remarked Cantell.

"Resting! So that is what the snoring was," jibed Kelmar. Cantell ignored him and made ready.

He picked up the little bundle of Prince Martyn and looked at his tiny face. "Has he made a sound?"

"None," was Kelmar's short worrying reply.

"The sooner we are away from here, the better," said Cantell, concerned as he looked at the river they had to cross.

"The river is running fast, Kelmar," he commented, watching it race past as it moved in and out of the torchlight, making it look even faster.

Kelmar had tied one end of the rope around his waist and had moved to tie the other end around Cantell's as he answered his friend.

"It is fast, it moves much faster when the winter snow melts. That is when it is impossible to get through. As it is, with the precaution of the rope, we will be able to wade through it, but tread carefully, the river floor is strewn with rocks," advised Kelmar.

Kelmar moved forward to some steps that had been hewn out of the rock, making it easy to enter the river. Holding the provisions and a torch, Kelmar braced himself against the cold rushing water as he slowly started to wade across.

Moments later, Cantell followed him into the river holding a quiet baby Prince, letting out another curse as the cold water hit his knee.

As far as Cantell could see through the light of the torch Kelmar was holding, the underground river was not that wide, but wide enough for how he was feeling, he was thinking.

He could see why Kelmar had warned him about the rocks on the river floor; they moved under your feet as soon as you touched them. With the river forever in a hurry, trying to nudge him over, it made for slow progress.

Kelmar reached an opening on the other side and jammed the torch between some rocks. Cantell squinted and saw what looked like more steps in its glow. Kelmar moved onto the bottom of the steps and went to lay down the provisions, but that was as far as he got!

A sudden tug on the rope pulled him off balance, straight back into the river, headfirst!

The provisions flew out of his grasp into the rushing river and out of sight as he held on to the rope, fighting against the force of the river.

The reason he had been pulled back in was struggling at the other end of the rope. As Cantell had spotted the steps, he had stood on a loose rock. His knee had given way, plunging him and the sleeping Prince into the icy cold water.

As hard as they tried, they could not get a foothold on the river floor. Cantell held on to Prince Martyn for dear life, gasping lumps of air as they bobbed up and down in the water.

Neither man saw the head of rock that was ahead of them, dividing the underground river into two in the darkness. Kelmar passed it on one side and Cantell on the other, whilst the rope caught the head of rock to hold fast against it, pulling them both to a jerky stop.

Both men gratefully grabbed the chance they had been given and scrambled to their feet as the rope held. To Cantell's relief, as he regained his feet, the soaking little bundle of Prince Martyn screamed into life in terror above the noise of the river.

"Are you all right?" shouted Kelmar in the pitch-blackness that had engulfed them both. "Yes!" Cantell shouted back, angry with himself at letting his friend down yet again.

"Let us not waste any time then. We must walk against the river until we can see the torchlight again. Ready?" shouted Kelmar once more.

"Ready!"

Slowly and carefully, they waded their way back up the river, which was seemingly taking great delight in trying to knock Cantell over again.

It was with relief that Kelmar spotted the tiny glow coming from the torch. "There it is, just ahead," he called thankfully. Cantell blew out his cheeks, grateful that he was soon to get out of the river's clinging coldness, not that Prince Martyn knew anything about it as he sobbed, frightened and hungry, in Cantell's ears.

Both men finally sat, cold and sodden, on the hewn-out steps, where a passageway awaited behind them.

"I am sorry, Kelmar. I seem to be a walking accident. My knee just gave way when I trod on a loose rock," apologised Cantell.

"Do not reproach yourself, my friend. We are alive. Thankfully, there is not much further to go, but we need to keep going. Otherwise, our bodies will be overtaken by the cold in this wet state," warned Kelmar. "What of the Prince, though? How does he fare?" he asked, more concerned about the Prince than himself.

Cantell felt Prince Martyn's little body under his leather and cloth wraps. He was surprised how much water had been kept at bay by the leather wrap, but he was still cold. The ducking he had received had obviously frightened him more, as his sobs confirmed. "Frightened and cold," replied a worried Cantell.

"Let us keep going then. This torch is not going to last much longer. With our provisions gone, it is all we have got," and Kelmar was up on his feet, the life-saving rope slung over his shoulder, down the passageway behind them.

Cantell followed quickly with the sobbing bundle, hoping the torch would last until they felt the air from the Great Forest on their faces.

"Whoever it was went to great efforts to mine ore all the way down here," remarked Cantell, thinking of the steps that had led in and out of the underground river.

"Well, they did not find any here," remarked Kelmar.

"Oh, why is that?"

Kelmar did not have to answer, as he suddenly emerged from the passageway for the torch to reveal to them a chamber of strange beauty.

Crystal clear water ran away to their left in an arc, with what looked like waxy stone columns dotted along its path. They came out of the water and joined the rock ceiling, like pillars holding up a building.

More showed themselves to their right, reflecting in four individual pools of clear water. Some were not joined together; instead, they just hung there from the rock ceiling, whilst their counterparts protruded from the water.

As they walked between the waxy forms in their pools, another form suddenly appeared in the torchlight before them, cascading itself out of the rock like a frozen waterfall.

"What is this place?" said Cantell in fascination.

"A timeless cavern of beauty, my friend, worked by nature," Kelmar said with a smile. "Whoever found this cavern must have been in wonder, as I was, but we have no time to admire it," he added, and led the way out through the wondrous chamber.

Passing by the arc of clear water, they threaded their way through the pools until the chamber narrowed and was no more as they entered yet another passageway.

"Not long and we will be moving those rocks I spoke of," said Kelmar with anticipation in his voice, for their pace to quicken.

They came to the end of the passageway and into another chamber. A large chamber where two more passageways could be seen, one immediately to their left and one to their right, sloping off by the side of a pool that was glimmering back at them at the back of the chamber. Kelmar turned to head down into the right one.

Downward they travelled, to snake right then left before it levelled out. Then suddenly Kelmar came to an abrupt stop and let out a gasp at what was caught in the torchlight in front of them.

There to his dismay were slabs of rocks strewn across the passageway from ceiling to floor. A rockfall had sealed tight whatever hope Kelmar had had of clearing a way through.

"The mountain has claimed back what was taken away from it," sighed Kelmar, "all these months I have searched in hope and now…" Kelmar trailed off in frustration.

For the first time, Cantell could hear dejection in his friend's voice as the torch decided that this was the time it would spit and fizzle out, leaving them in total blackness, with only Prince Martyn's cries to keep them company.

"What can we do?" asked Cantell, already feeling the blackness pressing in upon him.

"We cannot go back. Only death awaits us there, even if by some miracle we could make it back," answered Kelmar, only to make Cantell feel more desperate at their situation.

The two warriors suddenly felt cold, wet and hopeless as they slowly walked back up the passageway, feeling their way in the pitch-blackness. It was no use staying where they were. Not before Kelmar had thrown the spent torch in the direction of the rockfall in annoyance.

They reached the large chamber and found themselves sitting by the pool. They sat silently in disillusionment; even Prince Martyn's sobs had ceased.

"The river could be our only chance," said Kelmar after a while.

Cantell shuddered at the thought. "That path will lead to our certain deaths, more so than trying to get back to the stronghold," dismissed Cantell with another shudder, but this time it was because he was feeling the cold.

"You are right. It must disappear under the mountain somewhere. Only a watery grave would await us. Even if we had a slim chance, the little one would have none," agreed Kelmar, resting his arm behind him to feel his hand slip into the pool.

One of his fingers began to sting at the water's touch. He must have cut it somehow without realising, he thought.

Kelmar instinctively put his finger to his mouth to suck at the cut, and as he did so, something caught in his mouth to make him frown. *What is that?* It made him take a handful of water from the pool to taste it.

"What are you doing, Kelmar?" asked Cantell as he listened to Kelmar swilling the pool's water around in his mouth and spitting it out.

"This pool has something in it," he answered, but before Cantell could ask what, Kelmar was in the pool and wading through it.

"What do you think you are doing?" quizzed Cantell, listening to Kelmar wading through the pool, only to hear a splash and then silence, telling Cantell that Kelmar had dived into the pool.

Cantell reached down to cup some of the pool's water in his hand and took a sip to see if he could figure out what was in it to have triggered Kelmar's actions.

He found he was chewing on something, but what was it? His senses were dulled with so much cold. Where had Kelmar got to?

A sudden sound of water breaking echoed in the stillness. "Cantell! You will not believe it!" cried a jubilant Kelmar.

"What, Kelmar?" shouted Cantell back immediately, sensing the jubilation in Kelmar's voice.

"This pool is linked to another cave where the breeze blows in from the Great Forest! There is a gap in the rock at the bottom, enough for us to swim through!" Cantell could not believe his ears; the elation he felt almost made him cry.

Kelmar almost fell over Cantell holding Prince Martyn in his haste to tell him, as he fumbled in the dark, getting out of the pool.

"It was the trees I could taste in the pool, the tang of their needles," explained Kelmar in triumph as the two warriors hugged each other in wet celebration.

"Do you think the Prince will survive this ordeal and then the journey to Kelmsmere? He is already cold, wet and hungry," posed Cantell afterwards, "as we are," he added.

"We can only keep moving and hope the stars are watching over us," was all Kelmar could say. "The way through is not far. Wrap him well in my coat. Even though it is wet, it should help," he said thoughtfully, taking it off.

Before doing so, Cantell thought he would give Prince Martyn's little chest a rub in the hope of giving him some warmth before they attempted to swim through the gap.

Cold hands on a cold body in the cold, he thought. It sounded mad, but he hoped to create some friction to give little Prince Martyn's body some warmth.

Taking him out of his leather then cloth wrap, Cantell was met by an instant stink. "By the stars!" he gagged. "You had better hold him whilst I wash him," said Cantell, coughing, handing him in the direction of Kelmar, who had to turn away.

Cantell dipped the cloth wrap into the pool, for Prince Martyn to soon let him know what he thought of his bottom being washed by screaming in his ears.

"We have smelt bloodshed and death before, old friend, but nothing quite like this!" said Kelmar whilst holding Prince Martyn at arm's length, making Cantell wonder why he had to think of giving Prince Martyn's chest a rub.

Feeling his ears ringing, Cantell finally rubbed Prince Martyn's little chest, arms and legs, to wrap him back up in his leather wrap, discarding his dirty cloth wrap.

Folding Kelmar's leather coat around him and tying the sleeves across his tiny body, Cantell hoped it would protect him enough to make it through the pool.

Kelmar tied a shortened rope, thanks to the dagger he kept in his boot, around their waists once more and hopefully, he thought, for the last time.

Stepping into the pool, they both walked forward until the water reached their shoulders. Cantell was surprised how quickly the pool's floor dropped off as he held Prince Martyn above the water.

"Are you ready, my friend?" asked Kelmar.

"I cannot wait to see the sky again," was Cantell's reply. He was not looking forward to this.

Cantell listened to Kelmar as he disappeared underneath the water and took in a lungful of air. Holding Prince Martyn close, he dropped down to disappear into the pool. *Out of one blackness and into another*, he thought, feeling the cold water enclose him.

Cantell focused his mind on the feel of the shortened rope and tried not to let the watery nothingness get to him. Following Kelmar's pull on the rope, he soon found he was touching the rock of the pool floor.

Pushing against it to help him along, Cantell felt the rope give a sudden pull. *Kelmar must be through the gap*, he thought, and followed the rope's pull.

Cantell was right. Kelmar was through the gap, but he was unaware that as Kelmar was making for the surface in the linking pool, the rope was brushing against the top of the gap, for him to hit his head with a crack on the rock, dropping Prince Martyn!

Kelmar felt the rope suddenly holding him back, to immediately warn him that Cantell was in trouble. Without thought, he stopped and swam back down to find a struggling Cantell. Grabbing him, Kelmar pulled Cantell through the gap to the surface of the linked pool, to find out he had not been struggling but had been desperately trying to find Prince Martyn!

A lungful of cold air and Cantell gave vent to his concern. "I dropped him, Kelmar, when I hit my head!"

Kelmar did not need to hear any more; he was diving back into the pool to hit the bottom. Finding the gap, he frantically searched around with his hands to find the little bundle. Then there it was, to his searching touch, lying there! He made for the surface as fast as he could!

Cantell had got out of the pool and was waiting on the cave floor for any sign of Kelmar. It was too dark to see anything, with the cave cast in shadows from a night sky that was thankfully coming in from the cave entrance, but even though Cantell had longed for this moment, none of it interested him; he only had one thing on his mind. Where was Kelmar? Had he found him?

Then there he was, breaking the surface with the wet bundle of Prince Martyn in his grasp.

They both grappled with cold, wet hands at the coat and leather wraps around his little body, undoing them as fast as they could.

"Does he live?" cried Cantell as Kelmar listened for Prince Martyn's breathing. He could not hear anything!

Putting him in the palm of his hand, Kelmar began alternately to rub and pat his back; Cantell could only watch in silent prayer.

Kelmar continued patiently, to begin feeling trickles of water come out of his little mouth as he kept rubbing.

More water came out, he patted his back, yet more water, then suddenly a retch, a cough and a scream, announcing that the most frightened child in all of the Kingdoms was alive!

Neither warrior could hold himself back as they jumped up and down for joy at the sound of his cries. For once, his cries were like those of a songbird to their ears.

"You have brought us through, old friend," said Cantell, grinning.

"We have brought each other through," Kelmar said, grinning back.

If only that were true, thought Cantell, *I have been more trouble than help.*

They began to look around at the cave, their eyes immediately drawn to the cave mouth opening.

As they walked towards it, cold sharp air and a night sky met them. They stood there feeling the biting cold penetrate their wet and chilled bodies.

Cantell tucked the sobbing Prince Martyn into his tunic, hoping his body would help give his little body some warmth.

Standing at the mouth of the cave, they began to take in their surroundings. A canopy of snow-covered trees met their gaze, lit by a night sky full of stars and a shining half-moon, making the snow glisten on the tall fir trees that stood there like sentinels below them.

"Thank you, stars and spirits, for watching over us," said Cantell quietly as he took in the breathtaking sight. Kelmar felt the moment and said the same in his mind.

"We have come out in a small ravine," said Kelmar, looking around, trying to get his bearings.

Cantell looked with him, then something caught his eye. "Look!" he cried, and pointed, "there in the distance!"

Kelmar looked to see a plume of smoke meet his eyes. "They know of our escape and have posted guards!" He cursed.

"There are probably more posted along the edge of the forest," surmised Cantell.

"That is where we will find warmth," Kelmar said, smiling, "once we have overpowered the guards." Cantell nodded; the thought of a warming fire gave his spirits a lift.

"Do you think they heard the Prince's cries?" Cantell said thoughtfully.

"Perhaps, there is only one way to find out," answered Kelmar as he picked his way down the ravine's slope, aided by the starlight.

"It should only be loose rock under the snow," he added, and off he went. Cantell followed. *Loose rocks*, he thought, he knew all about them!

Reaching the bottom of the small ravine without any trouble, Kelmar and Cantell set off through the edge of the Great Forest.

Cantell rubbed Prince Martyn's little body to comfort him as they walked through the touching trees, whilst the snow creaked beneath their feet.

"I think my feet have departed from my body already," remarked Cantell as he tried to tread in Kelmar's footprints.

"That campfire will not be far ahead," said Kelmar quietly, looking left and right into the trees' shadows as he spoke.

Cantell peered into the trees, feeling the stillness that surrounded them, a belief told to him when he was a child coming into his mind as he looked.

Upset the spirits of the Great Forest and you will be cursed forevermore. He had never believed it, it was only superstition, but a shiver went down his spine as he thought about it.

He quickly put the shiver down to how cold he was feeling and how hungry he was. *A warm fire and some hot food will soon put paid to both*, he thought.

They weaved their way through the edge of the Great Forest until suddenly Kelmar stooped low and held an arm out.

"What is it?" whispered Cantell.

"Someone approaches, I can hear them," warned Kelmar, listening. "You carry on, I will surprise them from the side," he proposed, to Cantell's nod.

Drawing his dagger from his boot, Kelmar disappeared into the trees whilst Cantell carried on.

Then Cantell heard not one but two voices ahead of him as Prince Martyn let out a sob.

"There! I told you I heard something," said one voice.

"Quiet then, you fool, you will give us away!" replied the other, annoyed.

Cantell could hear the fear in their voices at being in the Great Forest, albeit only the edge. *They have been told the same stories as me*, he thought.

"Stop where you are!" came a command from in front of Cantell as he brushed past the hanging branches of a tree to be confronted by two cloaked Cardronian soldiers.

Cantell saw the glint from their drawn swords as they moved warily towards him, looking around them as they did so.

"We were told there were two of them," said one to the other as they approached. "Where is the other Tiggannian?" questioned the soldier, holding his sword menacingly at Cantell's throat.

"He… he never made it… only me and the baby survived that awful place," said Cantell, sounding lost and tired.

Cantell's words were still mist in the air when Kelmar struck. He seemed to come out of nowhere to drive his dagger into the neck of the Cardronian soldier holding his blade to Cantell.

His comrade froze momentarily before raising his sword to strike at Kelmar, but his lapse gave Kelmar time to turn his dead comrade towards him to take the thrust of his sword.

In one movement, Kelmar took his dagger from the dead soldier's neck and drove it into his comrade's neck, who was still holding his sword. One push later saw them topple over to lay dead in the snow.

Cantell just stood there, only having had time to blink as he looked down at the two dead Cardronian soldiers, Kelmar's dagger sticking out of one of their necks.

"Something about necks?" he jibed.

"No time to socialise," Kelmar said with a smile, already donning a helmet and taking off their uniforms. "Get these on, they will warm our backs and disguise us well," he added, for Cantell to join him.

They felt all the better in dry clothes, though ill-fitting, and with Prince Martyn wrapped up in one of the cloaks fashioned by Kelmar's dagger, whilst Cantell wore the other, they set off once more.

Branches were nearly touching the floor on some of the forest's trees as they moved through them, laden as they were with snow, whilst others reached for the sky, letting them pass underneath their outstretched limbs.

"There is bound to be at least one more, if not two," said Cantell as they walked through the dense forest.

"We shall soon see," said Kelmar, suddenly stooping down behind a tree and pushing a low branch to one side.

A welcoming campfire met his gaze, with two figures hugging its warmth. "Two it is," he confirmed.

Cantell, though, was looking over his shoulder at what else the campfire revealed in its glow, tucked away as it was by the side of one:

the stumps of trees! "This is where they got their wood. They have dared to desecrate the Great Forest to build their siege towers!" he protested in disgust. "I hope they are all cursed!"

"Those two are about to find out they are," promised Kelmar as they broke cover.

Kelmar walked in front, whilst Cantell tucked in behind him, with his hood firmly pulled over his borrowed Cardronian helmet and a whimpering Prince Martyn hidden under his cloak.

Kelmar could see one soldier sitting down eating, whilst the other was tending to a pot hung over the fire. Beyond them, he could just make out their horses tied up and hoped they would not spook when the time came; they would be needed.

As they drew near, the soldier stirring the pot spotted their shadowy figures. "Well, did you find anyone?" he called, thinking they were his comrades.

"No, nothing," answered Kelmar.

The soldier turned away, not realising who they were, and continued to stir the pot. Cantell's nostrils smelt the food the Cardronian was stirring, for his stomach to respond with a loud growling noise, overshadowing Prince Martyn's whimpering.

"You had better get some of this inside of you before your stomach falls out," said the soldier with a laugh, spooning some of the broth out of the pot into a wooden bowl whilst the other soldier laughed with him.

"Here, you sound like you—!" The Cardronian soldier had lifted his head to hand the bowl of broth to who he thought was his comrade, to find he was looking into the face of Kelmar!

"Thank you," Kelmar said with a smile, taking the bowl, and duly dispatched the open– mouthed Cardronian soldier with his dead comrade's sword.

The other Cardronian soldier dropped his bowl and made to get up, but Cantell was already on him, thrusting his borrowed sword into his side.

They did not take long to drag the dead Cardronian soldiers' bodies out of the way and take their place by the fire. Laying Prince Martyn down near its warmth, Cantell looked into the pot the Cardronian soldier had been stirring and took in a deep breath of its aroma.

"Meat, potato, barley and there is bread!" He drooled and helped himself to a bowlful. Kelmar followed suit and they both proceeded to demolish it, eating ravenously.

Another bowlful followed and they began to feel the food's goodness warm their insides, whilst the glow of the fire thawed their aching bodies.

"Is he having any?" asked Kelmar as Cantell tried to tempt Prince Martyn with some bread dipped in the broth for him to suck.

"He has had a taste, but it is not to his liking," replied Cantell, concerned, seeing a scrunched-up face.

"At least he is warm again," said Kelmar, beginning to stretch and relax.

"That may be so, but we need to get him to Kelmsmere, and quickly. He cannot last on nothing," warned Cantell, worried, to suddenly yawn and feel the sensation of wanting to sleep wash over him.

"Their horses will see us to the River Dale, where we will find a Haven fishing boat to take us to Kelmsmere," answered Kelmar, finding he was talking to himself. Cantell's chin was resting on his chest; he was fast asleep!

Kelmar smiled for his friend; it had been an arduous journey. The wet and cold they had endured had tested their resolve to its limits. He would give him a moment before setting off again under the cover of a night sky.

He looked up at the stars as he thought of it and hoped they were watching over his mother as they had watched over them. Hoping she was still there in Kelmsmere and that nothing had happened to her.

He stared at the fire as he thought of her, seeing her face reflected in its warm glow, making him smile, but as he stared his eyes grew weary and closed with the thought that when they opened again, he would see her.

CHAPTER XII

Stormhaven slept under a clear night sky. All was quiet, nobody stirred, nobody, that is, except for one: Queen Helistra!

Silently closing her chamber door, she glided down Forest Tower's spiral steps without a sound. No torches lit her way; she did not need one. A soft white light from the broken rune staff saw to that.

She paused a moment outside the royal chamber door with a smile. *I hope you are sleeping well, my little one,* she thought, and then carried on down the spiral steps.

Reaching the base of Forest Tower, she walked across to the mountain throne room door with anticipation in her every step. The moment she had waited for all these years was finally here.

Down the five steps and through the door, she walked to behold the mountain thrones, her dark green eyes widening as she beheld them.

Holding the broken rune staff aloft, a thought crossed her mind and the room grew brighter. She sat down on the King's mountain throne, letting her hand run along the smooth rock arm until her fingers touched the uneven hole. Taking the broken rune staff, she gently slid it into the hole.

Her eyes looked around the mountain throne room for a moment and came to rest on the crowns that lay on the rock shelf; a humming spoke to her.

"They are mere trinkets, but little minds like little things," she said, laughing, with the humming joining in.

She sat there a moment longer, relishing the thought of what was to come as she felt the cold ancient throne embrace her. How long she had waited for this moment, she reflected.

Her patience had been sorely tested, having to waste her hard-earned power all of these years. Manipulating people to do her bidding, not too much, but just enough so they, he, did not sense it. Watching the seasons pass her by whilst she planned for this one moment had taken forever, but now at last all of her scheming and deception was finally about to reap its reward!

She looked at the broken rune staff, ready to do her will, remembering how time had known no ending when she had first tried to gain its trust, to unite with it and become as one. Slowly bending it to her ways and gradually gaining control until finally she had it in her power! It did not matter that the broken rune staff could hear her now; evil had bred evil! A humming interrupted her recollections. "Yes, I am ready."

Queen Helistra touched certain symbols on the broken rune staff and watched as the staff slowly glowed a bright yellow before gradually fading again. She touched another symbol; the broken rune staff responded this time with a faint humming sound followed by a click as the broken rune staff turned further into the hole, like a key in a lock.

Queen Helistra touched more symbols and this time the broken rune staff slowly turned bright green before fading again. A touch of a symbol, soft humming and another click saw the broken rune staff turn further into the mountain throne arm.

Once more, the pattern was followed, for a bright white light to shine and fade. One more symbol, a humming and a click for another turn saw Queen Helistra touch one last symbol.

This time, a clunk was heard, followed by a rush of whispering air, and the King's mountain throne started to move forward!

Queen Helistra moved to the back of the King's mountain throne and watched as the throne revealed steps leading downwards into total darkness. She gently retrieved the broken rune staff from the mountain throne arm and proceeded to go down the steps.

The soft white light returned, to show her the way once more as the mountain throne slid back into place above her. Down the steps she went, letting them lead her deeper and deeper beneath the mountain throne room until at last they straightened out.

Then she entered a long passageway that reflected back the soft white light. Finally, she came into the place she had dreamed of all these years: the crystal chamber!

The crystal chamber immediately reacted to the light coming from the broken rune staff, reflecting back its soft white glow. The broken rune staff suddenly began to display the colours it had used to unlock the mountain throne.

Yellow, green and white pulsated from the broken rune staff, the crystal chamber copying its colours without hesitation, as if it were glad to see someone.

Then the broken rune staff displayed a rainbow of colours to set the crystal chamber alight. The crystal chamber answered back in a display that lit its crystals from wall to ceiling, festooned as they were all over the chamber.

The beauty of the moment could not be spoken in words as the crystal chamber became awash with colour, but none of it interested Queen Helistra. Her eyes were fixed on the small insignificant pool of water that lay in the middle of the chamber.

She walked up to the side of the pool and grinned. The broken rune staff stopped its display and returned to a soft white light. The crystal chamber immediately did the same, as if it had become friends and bonded with the broken rune staff.

Queen Helistra knelt before the small pool and dipped the unbroken end of the broken rune staff into it.

A silent scream ran through the little pool, making Queen Helistra grin even more.

"My greetings to you, little pool," chirped Queen Helistra.

Go away, you evil creature! came the petrified reply in her mind from the little pool.

"Oh, such harsh words, you hurt me so," mocked Queen Helistra.

You are poison! Leave me be! I have done nothing to you! pleaded the pool.

"No, that is true, but I have a message for your sister, and only you can send it," teased Queen Helistra.

You will not get away with this! the pool warned.

"Oh, but I will. Who is there to stop me?" taunted Queen Helistra.

Speedwell! He will stop you! challenged the pool.

"You talk too much!" seethed Queen Helistra on hearing that name, and withdrew the broken rune staff from the pool.

Turning the broken rune staff around, Queen Helistra put its broken end into the pool. Holding it with both hands, she closed her eyes whilst touching its symbols.

Controlling her breathing to slow down her heartbeat, Queen Helistra began to channel the slow rhythm of her heart into her fingertips, which were touching the broken rune staff's symbols.

The broken rune staff felt her heartbeat through her throbbing fingertips upon its symbols and began to pulsate in time to them. Slowly, the pulsations of the broken rune staff grew in strength and as Queen Helistra moved her fingers over certain symbols, the broken rune staff slowly started to turn red, blood red!

The crystal chamber responded to the broken rune staff's change of colour by turning all of its crystals crimson red, pulsating in the rhythm of the heartbeat it could feel.

Queen Helistra started to whisper softly to the broken rune staff as the whole of the crystal chamber pulsated around her in blood red. "Let the soul blood flow, let the soul blood flow!"

From the broken rune staff's broken tip beneath the little pool's surface came drops of thick red poisonous blood, its thick venom spreading instantly all over the little pool.

The little pool's essence wailed in agony at the searing pain it felt from the touch of the venomous blood, fleeing from the pain in the hope of finding some refuge deep within its waters.

Queen Helistra stopped whispering and grinned as she opened her eyes, eyes that had turned blood red! Her face looked like a grotesque mask of evil as she knelt there in the pulsating red light of the crystal chamber.

Her tall frame stood up to hold the broken rune staff over the little pool, for it to continue dripping its poisonous blood.

Queen Helistra's mind was purring with elation; it was working! She had turned the souls of the dead into deadly venom that would at last destroy the Great Forest. Cold, bitter laughter rang out in the blood-red crystal chamber in triumph.

Queen Helistra stopped her laughter and spoke in a voice full of loathing. "Go now and give my love to your sister in the forest! Let my love spread to every living thing! From tree root to leaf tip, let them soak in my love!"

Closing her blood-red eyes once more, Queen Helistra breathed in the smell of death she had sent to the Great Plateau Forest, letting her mind and body drown in its fulfilment of her needs. She had waited so long for this moment and now it had begun!

The red poison within the little pool gathered into a thick venomous mass and slowly started to wind its way underground, growing bigger all the time, tainting everything in its path as it began its journey of destruction that was destined for the Great Plateau Forest. The pool of life had become the pool of death!

CHAPTER XIII

Snow had started to fall again in the grey of a new dawn. It fell in quiet whispers, as if not wanting to wake the two sleeping warriors that were huddled around the embers of a fire. Someone else, though, thought differently; hunger was gnawing away in his tiny body and he was letting them know the only way he knew how.

Kelmar's and Cantell's eyes flew open to look at each other then at the crying Prince. "Quick, he will be heard!" warned Kelmar immediately, standing up and looking around him.

Cantell picked up the crying bundle of Prince Martyn and tried to console him. "We have nothing to give him," said Cantell, finding his comforting did not help.

"We have slept when we should have kept going," said Kelmar, annoyed with himself.

"We were cold and hungry, it could not be helped," said Cantell, looking around also.

One of the nearby tied-up horses snorted, getting Kelmar's attention. "The horses, quick, before we are found," he urged, grabbing what supplies he could before he and Cantell with the crying bundle headed for them.

Mounted, they rode out from the edge of the Great Forest into the valley towards the River Dale in its midst.

Neither warrior looked over his shoulder as they rode down the valley's snow-covered slope, to see the river shrouded in mist through the falling snow. "That will give us cover," shouted Kelmar.

A valley road suddenly loomed in front of them, revealing horses' hoofprints in the snow along its path where patrols had come and gone. Kelmar and Cantell rode straight over them, down into the lower valley.

Pulling on his reins as they neared the mist coming off the river, Kelmar let his eyes search the valley around them. Cantell trotted next to him, trying to keep Prince Martyn's cries muffled under his cloak.

"Anything, Kelmar?" asked Cantell, looking around himself.

"Not that I can see through this snow, but we must make haste nevertheless," replied Kelmar, as they kept to the edge of the mist, dodging around bushes and trees that flanked the river as they went along.

The mist, though, had other ideas as its thick greyness descended upon them, spreading ever further from the river, slowing them down to a walking pace.

"We will leave the horses here, we might as well walk along the riverbank," decided Kelmar as they came across a small copse. "I cannot even see the river, let alone a fishing boat, in this mist," he informed Cantell.

"We are open targets if they find us," warned Cantell, looking over his shoulder, only to see mist and snow.

"There is plenty of cover here to hide behind. We stand a better chance on foot in this than astride a horse, if the little one does not give us away, that is," said Kelmar, hearing Prince Martyn sobbing.

"He has worn himself out crying in his hunger," worried Cantell as they walked along a grassy stretch of the riverbank dotted with bushes.

Kelmar suddenly stopped in amongst them, listening. "What is it, Kelmar? Do you hear something?" asked Cantell, also trying to listen.

A familiar noise came to his ears as he listened, a horse snorting, then, "They have to be here somewhere!" could be heard, telling them it was a patrol!

Kelmar and Cantell ran further along the bank, taking cover behind one of the bushes. Crouching, they waited with drawn swords for the Cardronian patrol to get closer, but someone's sobs could not be quelled, however muffled.

"We cannot surprise them whilst he sobs," whispered Kelmar, looking behind him, sensing another noise. "Quick, back here," he gestured suddenly.

Cantell followed Kelmar's lead and found himself following him into a thicket of snow-covered reeds brushing against each other in the river's breeze. Enough for Kelmar to know they were there.

The compacted reeds held firm to begin with, but soon they were treading water. Kelmar suddenly stopped to look and listen.

"Our footprints will lead them straight into here, Kelmar! What possessed you to come into these reeds?" queried Cantell, feeling the river's water seeping into his boots as he peered through the dense snow-covered reeds.

Kelmar, though, was smiling and pointing his finger in amongst the reeds, to make Cantell frown.

Cantell looked to where Kelmar was pointing and saw some reeds lying flat. They were covering something; they were covering a boat!

"How did you know there would be one in here?" he had to ask, whilst attempting to help Kelmar take away the reeds covering the boat.

"I did not. I chanced my arm that one would be hidden in these reeds, knowing how Haven fishermen think," admitted Kelmar.

"You chanced more than your arm!" came Cantell's retort.

Clearing the reeds, Cantell stared at what they had uncovered. A sort of round-ended fishing boat met his eyes, with just enough room for two. *Three of us with you, little Prince*, he thought.

He could see it was made of wooden rods that had been woven tight by its inside and covered in hide. A board ran across the middle of the boat acting as a seat, and a short-handled paddle lay in the bottom.

"What sort of boat is that?" he exclaimed, whispering.

"One that will take us to Kelmsmere," Kelmar said, smiling, and he began pulling it out of the reeds to more open water.

"Climb in here. I will hold it steady," said Kelmar, with water coming over his knees.

As Cantell got unsteadily into the boat, a voice came through the mist loud and clear. "Here! Footprints! They lead into the reeds!"

"Quick, Kelmar! Get in!" urged Cantell, and he held on to two clumps of reeds to keep the boat steady. Kelmar got into the rocking boat, nearly capsizing them all before managing to sit on the seat. Taking the paddle, he trod water quickly to get them out of the reeds.

A sword could be heard hacking its way through the reeds as Kelmar pushed against the last of the reeds to break free and catch the river's flow.

The river's mist immediately embraced the small fishing boat in its arms, concealing it and its occupants from the glare of a Cardronian soldier peering through the reeds.

"There is nothing here," informed the soldier, cursing, his words caught in the mist, for Cantell and Kelmar to look at each other in relief.

"That was close," said Cantell with a sigh, trying to comfort a still upset Prince Martyn.

"Close enough," agreed Kelmar, and he let the river help them go quietly along in its waters, guiding the fishing boat with the paddle within its flow.

Locked in thought, Kelmar paddled on most of the day, not that you could see any daylight with the mist holding firm. Cantell watched him, deep in thought, knowing he was thinking of what lay ahead as he tried to keep an unsettled Prince warm; it was all he could do. How much longer he could survive like this he did not know. It could all be for nothing, he worried.

The snow was falling gently as they made their way along the River Dale, swirling now and again as it got caught in the river's breeze.

As the breeze swirled, it would lift the mist in places to reveal the riverbank, but one such swirl showed Cantell they had reached the Great Forest that bordered one side of the river, telling him they were nearing Lake Morutaine.

He saw its trees overhanging the river, their branches reaching out to touch its waters, giving Cantell a sense of how dense the forest was. Then it was gone, shrouded in mist again.

"It will take them more than several days before they can reach Kelmsmere on horseback, by which time we will be long gone from there," said Kelmar, suddenly coming out of his thoughts.

"If they are not following us," pointed out Cantell.

"Then we will deal with them," countered Kelmar, not helping looking over his shoulder as Cantell brought it up only to see mist.

A sudden sideways motion, making the fishing boat bob up and down all the more, brought Kelmar's attention back to his paddling.

"Nothing to worry about, the River Kelm is joining us." He smiled, steadying the fishing boat with the paddle.

"I always did wonder where you got your name from," jibed Cantell, keeping the smile on Kelmar's face.

Flowing from the Kavenmist Mountains to merge with the River Dale, the River Kelm was announcing its presence, bringing with it a fresh breeze, to finally blow away the mist that had lingered around them all day, only to reveal that night was beginning to fall.

Stars began to light the sky and with them a coldness to penetrate the oncoming night.

"How does he fare?" asked Kelmar, looking up at another half-moon.

"His hunger must be hurting him. His cries are growing weaker, we must keep going," implored Cantell. Kelmar nodded; he was not going to fall asleep this night, he thought.

What time of night it was, Kelmar had no idea. His shoulders were aching and his hands were feeling the cold bite of the night air, but he kept going under the light of the stars, thankful that at least the snow had stopped falling.

Then there it was, glimmering in the night before him: Lake Morutaine! Kelmar knew this huge lake well, with its rivers feeding it. Shadowed by the Demeral Hills that rose over its east side, with the Great Forest skirting its western bank.

His father came straight into his mind, making him smile. The fish they had caught here together, he thought, and feeling his strength inside of him, Kelmar renewed his efforts in paddling the small fishing boat.

The River Dale, having been joined by the River Kelm, now went on its way once more to lose itself in the depths of the Great Forest.

As it departed, so another river joined the huge lake further up. The Demeral River had travelled all the way from the Eastern Sea through Tiggannia, to cut its way down the side of the Demeral Hills until it came to rest in the lake's calm waters.

Kelmar was smiling at the thought of it all as Cantell did an involuntary shiver, to wake up feeling stiff against the weave of the fishing boat. He immediately looked at Prince Martyn, who was whimpering in troubled sleep.

"How far on are we, Kelmar?" he asked, trying to prop himself up more without rocking the fishing boat too much.

"You will be able to see for yourself soon," replied a tired Kelmar, "dawn is on the horizon," and he nodded to the side.

As if on cue, a winter's sun began to rise in the East, to spread its rays over the lake, unveiling the snow-covered Demeral Hills in the distant background as it did so.

"You look tired, Kelmar. Let me take over," suggested Cantell, seeing him yawn. Kelmar was not about to say no, but not here in the middle of the lake.

Keeping away from the road he knew ran between the Demeral Hills and the lake, not wanting to be spotted, Kelmar made for the other side of the lake where the Great Forest bordered it.

Paddling over to the overhanging trees, Kelmar spotted some convenient tree roots sticking out into the lake. Grabbing hold of them, he managed to stop the fishing boat and with Cantell's help pull the boat in between the roots.

Kelmar held on to the roots whilst Cantell stiffly got out of the fishing boat, stretching to feel the gash on his knee once more. Kelmar followed, pulling the boat out of the lake, enough for it to perch over the roots.

The noises of the forest awakening came to their ears, with the sound of animals scurrying through the undergrowth and birds singing in the tree branches to greet the early-morning sun.

Cantell laid Prince Martyn down over some more roots that were closer together, so he could relieve himself as a sudden hush came over the forest.

"I have to go. All this water, I do not know how I have held it!" sighed Cantell, hiding behind a tree.

"Nor I. It has been a long while since the underground river," agreed Kelmar behind another tree.

"Listen, that is strange," remarked Cantell when he had finished.

"What is?" Kelmar frowned, joining him.

"There is no sound to be heard. The birds were singing a moment ago and I heard animals scurrying about, probably rabbits, but now there is not a whisper," he observed.

"Of course not, they have heard us, smelt us. We have probably frightened them," answered Kelmar, smiling.

"That would be it." Cantell smiled and picked up Prince Martyn. As soon as he did so, the birds started singing again and animals could be heard once more in the forest.

Cantell looked into the denseness of the forest with a strange feeling coming over him. He looked at Prince Martyn; he was peacefully fast asleep with not so much as a whimper.

Back in the fishing boat, Cantell paddled out of the Great Forest's shadow into the middle of the lake. He looked over at the Great Forest, finding what he had just felt strange.

"It was if the forest felt him lying there, tired and hungry, giving him the comfort we could not to see him through," said Cantell vaguely to himself.

"What are you on about? Keep your eye out for the return of the Kelm," advised Kelmar, and he tried to settle down as best he could with the sleeping bundle in his arms.

Cantell shook himself out of his distant thoughts and concentrated on paddling.

Slowly, the Demeral Hills grew bigger and bigger. Then there to their right was the Demeral River, rushing into the lake.

Cantell kept going, wondering how long Lake Morutaine really was. Long enough, he thought.

The Demeral Hills began to fade into the background as Cantell paddled on, with another day beginning to pass.

He looked over to his right and there in the shadow of the hills he could just make out fields of snow, which he knew were tilled by the townsfolk of Kelmsmere, with the odd building dotted in between.

Then he felt a pull on the fishing boat. The River Kelm was beckoning them, he thought, as the night sky began glistening once more, but not with stars, with snow; it had started again. Cantell pulled his cloak tighter around him.

Time had seemed endless to Cantell, before they finally departed Lake Morutaine to feel the flow of the River Kelm.

Not that Cantell could see them properly, but more and more dwellings were presenting themselves to his right, announcing that Kelmsmere was becoming ever closer.

Kelmar woke suddenly as if coming out of a dream. He tried to sit up more to get a better view but found it was a waste of time.

"Are we getting nearer?" he asked, trying to see.

"I saw buildings earlier, but this snow is too thick to see anything now," replied Cantell, trying to keep close but not too close to the Kelmsmere side of the river.

Then there before them looming out of the snow was a jetty. Cantell bumped straight into it, for them to be bounced back out into the river. Cantell paddled like mad to get control of the twirling fishing boat.

Now he was having to paddle against the flow. A brow that had been cold before soon turned to sweat as his aching arms dragged the fishing boat back towards the jetty.

A ladder showed itself. Kelmar grabbed hold of it whilst Cantell picked up Prince Martyn with one hand and took hold of the ladder himself with the other.

Climbing out, Kelmar was soon up the ladder and onto the jetty with Cantell following him, letting the small fishing boat go.

It was soon out of sight, to bobble merrily away in the clutches of the river.

"I am glad to see the back of that," said Cantell, blowing his cheeks.

"A horse will be a welcome sight after that," agreed Kelmar, "if there are any here, it looks deserted," he remarked, looking around him.

Cantell looked with him. Not a light could be seen; there was no one in sight. Though it was cold and snowing, there was normally someone around, he remembered, a town that was always bustling with life, even in this.

Kelmsmere itself could not have been more beautifully situated, set as it was at the bottom of a valley whose hills rolled softly away into the distance behind it.

It sat at a junction where the two rivers, the Kelm and the Thion, met. The River Kelm departed to wander off through the Kingdom of Silion, whilst the River Thion arrived from the Eastern Sea, having divided the two Kingdoms of Tigannia and Silion.

But all of Cantell's recollections soon became a distant memory as they walked towards the first buildings and looked up one of the streets to see a sight they both hoped had not happened.

Though it was dark and snow was falling, there was no mistaking what they were looking at. There were tables, chairs, beds, people's belongings of all description strewn all over the place after being thrown into the streets.

"They have ransacked the town!" said Kelmar angrily, immediately worrying about his mother.

"At least it is not gutted like Haven, but they have left nothing unturned," added Cantell, beginning to worry himself.

Everywhere they looked, the same desolation met their eyes; street after street was the same as they walked hurriedly to where Kelmar's mother lived.

They were so busy looking that when they turned a corner they did not see an old man with his head down, walking slowly in front of them, to walk straight into him, nearly knocking him over.

Kelmar gripped his arm and stopped him from falling. "Thank…" The elderly man stopped what he was going to say when he saw they were dressed as Cardronians, and eyed them with contempt.

Then he spotted Cantell was holding the little bundle of Prince Martyn.

"Oh! So there is no one else left for you to kill except old people and babies, is there!" He chastised them in disgust. "You have even taken her child away! Have none of you any heart!" And he made to walk away in disgust.

Kelmar instinctively grabbed the old man's arm to ask him what he was on about. "You are wrong about this child, old man. Who is it you speak of to make you think so?" he asked.

The old man looked at Kelmar's hand holding him back, for Kelmar to let go.

"Do not take me for being stupid, Cardronian. If it is your wish to kill me then get on with it, but to take her baby away after all she has been through! Pah!" The old man spat and turned to walk away again.

"But whose baby?" called Cantell after him.

"Why should you care! Her life is only spared because her father is the blacksmith here," grumbled the old man over his shoulder, and he disappeared around the corner.

Cantell looked at Kelmar, at him looking after the old man. They both thought they were hearing things.

"Druimar! Druimar is here, Kelmar!" exclaimed Cantell, his mind already racing, realising what it could mean for Prince Martyn.

"And if he is here then the old man was talking about Permellar! He thought we had her baby! Do you realise what this means!" Cantell could not contain himself.

"If she is feeding her own child, she could help us with Prince Martyn!" Cantell's hopes were soaring as he spoke for him, to suddenly remember that he was talking about the woman Kelmar was once in love with and should have married. They were all close friends back then, but adventure had called, he remembered.

Realising, he apologised. "I am sorry, Kelmar. I was not thinking."

"Do not be. It was a long time ago. It seems she has found happiness and I am glad for her. I doubt if she has forgiven me for choosing the army over her," a decision he had come to regret, but had realised far too late.

"We were all young and foolish then, Kelmar. Adventure was in our blood," said Cantell in understanding.

"Stupidity too," added Kelmar, and on they walked to find his mother's house.

"I do not like the sound of what the old man said, though, that whilst Druimar's skills are needed, Permellar's life holds good," said Kelmar thoughtfully as they walked through the debris of the town.

"You are right and they have her to keep a hold over Druimar," related Cantell with some concern. "A double-edged sword if ever there was one."

"A visit to the blacksmith's is needed, Kelmar. Permellar could be Prince Martyn's best chance of survival, we need to find her," urged Cantell.

"We will, but we have no idea how many guards there are here to deal with. We will see what the situation is after we have found my mother. We are here, look," pointed Kelmar, who was already holding his breath, seeing his old street full of furniture thrown out of their houses, all covered in snow.

They walked along Kelmar's old street in silence with their eyes constantly looking around them, until there it was: Kelmar's mother's house.

Kelmar took another breath; the door was already open!

Kelmar's blood drained from his body, fearing for his mother as he walked through the open door to find nothing as he remembered, it only an empty room.

No table remained with a candle lamp upon it. No benches to sit upon. Not even the bowls they ate out of remained. Kelmar climbed up the stairs and found it was the same. The house was just a shell; his mother was nowhere to be seen.

Kelmar sat despondently on the step at the bottom of the stairs. "She is not here, Cantell. My mother is…" He could not finish what he was going to say; instead, he buried his face in his hands.

Cantell felt for his friend, but they could not stay here. He looked at the little face of Prince Martyn, wondering how he could still be in such a quiet slumber since laying him down in the Great Forest, but that would change when he awoke, he thought.

"Though your mother is not here, Kelmar, it does not mean she has met her fate. Let us find Permellar. She may know something of her and then hopefully she can help us with this one," pushed Cantell.

Kelmar looked up. "I am sorry, my friend. I have let my personal feelings get in the way of what is important. You are right. Let us find Permellar. She may be able to help us in more ways than one," he apologised, agreeing with Cantell.

"You have no need to be sorry, she is your mother," understood Cantell, and they walked away from Kelmar's empty house to find the blacksmith's.

Moving through the snow-covered belongings that littered the streets everywhere, they kept their eyes alert for anyone else that might be there, especially guards, but they came across no one; the town was deserted. Only a dog barking down one of the streets half caught their attention.

With snow covering everything and mist beginning to hang in the air, it was looking more like a ghost town to the two warriors as they made their way to the north side of the town.

Finally, the two warriors stopped by the side of a building, keeping hidden as they peeked around the corner.

The old North Road ran in front of them and unlike all the streets they had just walked through, it was relatively empty of belongings for what they could see.

This did not come as any surprise to Kelmar and Cantell. It had always been the main road through Kelmsmere, leading north to Chasewater and east to Eskerdale, an ideal place to have a blacksmith's.

There across from where they were looking were the two large wooden doors of the forge, open to let out the heat.

The familiar sounds that Kelmar remembered as a child when he used to play in there came to his ears. A bellow he had always thought sounded like an animal breathing fire, and then there it was, the rhythmical sound of a hammer hitting metal against an anvil.

"Druimar is in there," he whispered.

"Being useful, having to shoe Cardronian and Waunarle horses, no doubt," whispered Cantell back.

Just then, two Cardronian guards appeared at the forge doors for Kelmar and Cantell to duck back behind the building.

"Where is she with that food!" they heard one of them say.

"She will be here," said the other, stretching, as if the cold air had just woke him up from the warmth of the forge.

"Here is our chance, Kelmar. They must be waiting for Permellar to bring them their food," pressed Cantell.

"There may be more inside and Permellar might not be alone," cautioned Kelmar.

"If there is, we will deal with them and then we will see if Permellar brings more than just food," said Cantell, reminding Kelmar of what his words were to him in the fishing boat.

Finding an open door, Cantell sheltered Prince Martyn behind it out of the chill, before he and Kelmar walked boldly out into the street to confront the two Cardronian guards.

The Cardronian guards instantly drew their swords upon seeing them, relaxing a little when they saw the crest of Cardronia on Cantell's cloak.

"You can put those away, comrade. You have nothing to fear from your own kind," Kelmar said, laughing, as they approached.

The two Cardronians looked at each other and sheathed their swords, but kept a wary hand upon their hilts.

"What are you doing here?" questioned one.

"Is this not a blacksmith's!" said Kelmar, laughing, again to see the two guards were not amused. "We have ridden our horses into the ground with the good news we carry for Cardronia and Waunarle. Hence my horse is sore of foot and needs shoeing," replied Kelmar, sounding truthful.

"What news?" questioned the same guard, wondering what it was.

"Stormhaven has fallen, it is ours." Kelmar grinned, to receive grins back.

"We have waited a long time in this forsaken place to hear that. Perhaps at last we can go home," announced the guard.

Kelmar kept grinning, as did Cantell. He needed to see if there were any more guards inside the forge first before dispensing with these two.

"Does the man know what he is doing? I value my horse," asked Kelmar, going into the forge past the two guards, to see a sight that made his blood boil.

There chained to his anvil was Druimar the blacksmith hammering a red-hot shoe. He looked up at them and spat on the floor in contempt at their presence before carrying on.

"I see he has the manners of a Tiggannian," remarked Cantell, making the guards who had followed them in laugh.

"He does as he is told. Otherwise, his wife and daughter will be no more," smirked the other guard.

Kelmar and Cantell managed not to let their faces drop when they heard the guard mention Druimar's wife, knowing she had died many years before. He must have married again, they both thought.

"As it should be," agreed Kelmar, walking right up to Druimar whilst looking into the forge. No one else was there.

Drawing his sword, he pointed it menacingly at Druimar. "You had better shoe my horse well, blacksmith, or you will taste what you forge!"

This brought raucous laughter from the two guards as Kelmar gave Cantell a look. Turning, Kelmar drove his sword straight through the nearest guard, who fell with disbelief written on his face. A quickly drawn sword saw Cantell swoop on his comrade to despatch him with a single thrust, the guard's hand still holding his hilt.

Druimar's hammer had stopped in mid-air; he could not believe what he had just witnessed. He was still open-mouthed as Kelmar and Cantell took off their helmets to reveal who they were.

"You can put your hammer down now, Druimar," Kelmar said with a grin. Druimar had to rub his eyes and look more closely at the two grinning faces in front of him.

"Is that you, Kelmar! And Cantell!" he boomed in his deep voice.

"Shh, quietly does it, Druimar." Cantell grinned at Druimar's expression.

"I cannot believe my eyes. I thought, well, I thought with Stormhaven under siege!" he exclaimed, and before they knew where they were, he was hugging them both, chains as well.

"We managed to escape." Kelmar smiled, dragging the two bodies to the back of the forge after finding the key to Druimar's shackles.

"For now, all we need to know is how many more guards are there and where is Permellar?" asked Cantell as Kelmar undid Druimar's shackles.

"You know she is here?" asked Druimar, surprised.

"We heard from an old man we bumped into that you are a grandfather," Cantell said with a smile.

Druimar nodded. "It is true, little Kayla, barely two weeks old..." Druimar paused as he thought of her, whilst Cantell gave Kelmar a look, "they are being held at the tavern in the square by three guards, there are no more here," informing them finally what they needed to know.

"Of course, where else! We will pay them a visit and free them both," promised Cantell.

"And my wife, she is there also," Druimar informed them further.

"Ah, so we were not hearing things. You have married again. Who is the lucky woman?" asked Kelmar, relieved they had not stumbled into finding out otherwise, but before Druimar could answer, they all heard footfall outside.

Druimar quickly picked up his hammer as Kelmar and Cantell turned to face the back of the forge, quickly putting their helmets back on.

A cloaked figure holding a wooden tray with food on appeared between the two wooden doors of the forge. Druimar smiled, knowing full well who it was, but turned to put heat onto the shoe he was previously hammering so as not to give the game away.

Both Kelmar and Cantell kept their backs turned as the figure put the tray down.

"I have brought you your food," was all the figure said and turned to leave, not looking up to notice the two dead guards in the corner or the fact that Druimar was free of his shackles.

Kelmar's jaw dropped whilst Cantell stared at him as they heard the figure's voice. Kelmar spun round, taking off his helmet.

"Is there any on that tray for me, Mother?" he nearly cried, whilst Cantell could only grin.

Kelmar's mother froze to the spot, nearly falling over as she heard the voice she thought she would never hear again: her son's!

Turning round, she gasped out loud when she saw his face. She ran to him and flung herself into his outstretched arms, crying, hugging him tight, never wanting to let go.

Clasping her hands on his face whilst in his grasp, she stroked it lovingly. "I thought you had been taken from me," she cried, still not believing it was her son.

"I thought I had lost you, Mother, for a moment back there," cried Kelmar, grinning with relief that his mother was safe.

"Well, I hate to interrupt this family get-together, but I hope I get a hug too," Cantell said, laughing.

Kelmar's mother looked across at Cantell and laughed with him through her tears. "Cantell, it is you after all this time." She laughed and proceeded to hug him just as hard.

After all three had hugged each other again, Druimar spoke quietly to Kelmar. "You know I would never presume to take the place of your father, he was a good man," he worried, hoping Kelmar would not be angry with him when he fully realised that he had married his mother, albeit widowed.

"My mother could not be married to a better man." Kelmar grinned, to receive a relieved hearty slap on his back.

"When did you two get married, Oneatha?" quizzed Cantell, smiling, seeing Druimar feeling slightly awkward and to get a look off Kelmar.

"Druimar and I have long been friends. We always spoke of getting married, but never did. Hearing you were under siege and fearing for what might happen, we decided to get married. Days later, Cardronians ransacked the town and if Druimar had not been a blacksmith who would be of use to them, we would all be dead," explained Oneatha, to quiet thankfulness in Kelmar's mind that Druimar was a blacksmith and by being so, had saved his mother's life, leaving Cantell feeling slightly awkward himself for having asked Oneatha in the first place.

"How did you escape from the siege? We thought… well, I thought—"

"We thought you were dead," intervened Oneatha, hearing Druimar mumble.

"We escaped through the caverns of the Kavenmist Mountains and then in a Haven fishing boat," said Kelmar, making it sound simple.

"We escaped with the future of Tiggannia," added Cantell, disappearing out of the forge as he said it, to the frowns of Oneatha and Druimar.

They waited only moments before Cantell reappeared with the little bundle of Prince Martyn.

"This is the reason why we are here, Oneatha," Cantell said, smiling, showing her Prince Martyn's sleeping face, "meet King Rolfe and Queen Elina's son, Prince Martyn."

Oneatha gasped and immediately held out her arms to hold him. "The poor mite, has he eaten?" came the first thought in her mind as she looked at his little face.

"Not really, Mother, that is why we have come here in the hope of finding you to help him," began Kelmar, "but then we bumped into an old man and found Permellar was here with her child, so we thought she could help him with…" He stopped, not quite knowing how to say it in front of his mother.

"With her own milk," Oneatha finished for him.

"Yes, Mother," as forthright as ever. He smiled to himself; how good it was to hear her voice again.

"Well, you had better free her then." She smiled, seeing her son's smiling face.

"But what of the King and Queen?" asked Druimar, already fearing the answer.

Kelmar's smile soon faded as he thought of them. "When we escaped, our King was going to make a last stand. We do not know of his fate, but we fear the worst," he answered sadly.

"And the Queen?" asked Oneatha, hoping to hear better news.

"Prince Martyn was about to have a brother or sister before we escaped, but events did not allow us to wait until the birth," explained Cantell this time.

"He is a twin! By the stars! All this time under siege fearing for their lives whilst waiting to give birth, and then having this one torn away from her! What that poor woman has been through." Oneatha shook her head and stroked the side of Prince Martyn's cheek.

"Their fates are with Taliskar and Brax now," said Cantell, not so much in hope but in sad acceptance of what he had always felt would befall them in their hands.

All fell silent at the thought.

"No matter what has happened to them, our path is clear," spoke Kelmar, breaking the silence as he looked out of the forge, up and down the street, to see the snow still falling.

"Is there a cart or wagon to be found to get away from here with horses?" he asked as he looked.

"Leave that to me, Kelmar. You have already freed up two horses," answered Druimar, nodding at the dead guards.

Oneatha had not even noticed the dead guards lying there in her elation at seeing her son once more. She gave them no more than a cursory glance of contempt.

"Good, what about supplies? Is there anything left?" queried Kelmar further.

"We will find enough. Now, has Druimar told you Permellar is at the tavern in the square, guarded by three guards?" asked Oneatha.

"Yes, he has. Once we have her and Kayla," remembered Kelmar, "we will meet you back here," he informed her.

"Have you thoughts as to where to go next?" asked Druimar.

"King Stowlan at Elishard eventually, but for now I am not sure. Everywhere will be watched," said Cantell in thought.

"You will be coming with us, Mother. I hope you have no thoughts of staying here. It will be far too dangerous for you," worried Kelmar, knowing his mother could be stubborn.

Oneatha smiled at her son's worry for her as she answered him. "Your father would have been looking down upon me already, shaking his head, wondering why I stayed here in the first place, but it was always in the hope of seeing you once more and here you are. I am not about to let you out of my sight just yet." She grinned and they hugged each other once more.

"Now hurry, this little one must be hungry," she urged, "although he sleeps so peacefully," she added, frowning slightly as she looked down at Prince Martyn's contented sleeping face.

"He has been like that since... since we laid him down to rest in the Great Forest on the banks of Lake Morutaine," said Cantell, without giving away why they were really in there.

"The Great Forest? You rested in the Great Forest?" repeated Druimar, sounding surprised. Cantell just gave him a look, for Druimar to smile with a nod.

"Be careful," called Oneatha as she watched them go.

"I hope they bring them back safely," worried Druimar.

"They will, Druimar," she assured him, whilst looking at the little sleeping face in her arms. "The look in my son's eyes told me they will," she added, knowing that look; she had seen it before.

Kelmar and Cantell made their way through the ghost-like streets, seeing the same throughout; every one littered with belongings.

It did not take them long before they reached the town square, to see to their dismay what had once stood in its centre burnt to the ground.

An old oak tree had grown there proudly at the heart of the town and now all that remained of it was a burnt-out stump!

The heat that must have come from it when on fire could be visibly seen on the building they stood next to, scorched as it was.

"Is there nothing sacred!" cursed Cantell upon seeing its snow-covered stump.

Smoke could be seen twisting its way upwards from the tavern's chimney on the other side of the square, with light flickering through a shuttered window.

A last look to see if anyone was around, and two figures moved swiftly over the square to stand next to the window that was throwing light out through its crude shutters.

Kelmar put his ear to the gap between them but heard nothing. "Are you ready with a story?" whispered Kelmar.

"Leave it with me." Cantell smiled and opened the tavern door.

The door creaked as soon as Cantell opened it. Walking in, they entered a large room dotted with tables and chairs, lit sparsely by a couple of candle lanterns.

A roaring fire blazed away at the far end of the room, giving out more light than the candle lanterns.

A pair of boots was resting on a stool in front of it, from a guard relaxing in a chair. His head had dropped and he was clearly asleep by the sound he was making.

The reason why he was fast asleep stood on a table next to him: an ale pot! Kelmar pointed at it, smiling. Cantell nodded enviously, thinking how long it had been since he last had any ale.

"We will deal with him if he wakes," whispered Kelmar, and they proceeded to the stairway by their side, leaving the guard to his slumber.

At the top of the stairs was a simple passageway lit by more candle lanterns. A row of doors on one side of the passageway showed themselves in the dim light; all were shut.

Which one is Permellar in? thought Kelmar. He reasoned that the other two guards would be in the first two rooms, so he made for the last door.

As they moved down the passageway, the floorboards groaned underneath their feet. "If that does not alert them then nothing will," whispered Cantell, looking behind him, but no other sound came to their ears.

Reaching the last door, Kelmar opened it slowly; the room was empty. The next room proved to be the same, but then in the next, sat on a wooden bed, was the woman Kelmar had let go: Permellar.

She had been looking at her sleeping baby daughter in her cradle when she heard the Cardronian guards outside her room, creaking about. The trepidation she always felt in their presence welled up inside her as her door opened to reveal the guards, but she did not recognise these two. She held her breath in fear of what they wanted with her.

Closing the door, Kelmar and Cantell took off their helmets, to see Permellar's face go white with shock. She clasped a hand over her mouth and nearly fell off the bed in her surprise.

She did not know whether to laugh or cry at the sight of them both standing there, smiling at her. She had never thought she would see either of them ever again. Tears flooded into her eyes as she got up and flung her arms around them both.

"Permellar, you are safe," Kelmar said with a sigh, breathing in her beauty, which he had never forgotten.

"You are alive," she cried, unable to contain her sobs of emotion.

"Of course we are," said Cantell, smiling, "now let's get you and little Kayla out of here." Permellar let them go.

"But my father, he—"

"Is waiting for you with my mother," Kelmar said smilingly, to see a smile brighten her tearful face, a face he realised he had missed more than he had admitted to himself.

"Where are the other guards? There is only one downstairs asleep," asked Kelmar whilst Permellar picked up Kayla after donning her cloak.

"One is in the end room, and if there is only one other downstairs, the other guard must be outside somewhere. They are always looking around to see if there is anything left worth stealing," she said bitterly.

"Very well, let us make haste," and together they left the room that had been Permellar's prison.

As they reached the top of the stairs, a voice suddenly boomed out from behind them. "Stop! Where do you think you are going with her?"

They all turned round to be confronted by a stocky-looking Cardronian guard, who had just come out of the last room scratching his stomach.

"And who is it that asks?" said Cantell, smiling, taking two paces forward to confront him. "Someone who is charged with watching her," came a curt reply.

Only a flash of a dagger blade was seen by the guard as it entered his heart. "Not anymore, we are taking her off your hands," spat Cantell, and he pushed the gasping guard over for him to hit the floor with a resounding thump.

They took to the stairs, hearing movement from below. The noise had awoken the other guard from his drinking slumbers. He came running up the stairs with his sword drawn. As he looked up and saw them, he was met by Kelmar's boot right across his jaw. The guard was sent sprawling backwards, hitting his head on the stairs as he toppled over to land in a heap at the bottom.

"I always told you drink dulls your senses, Kelmar," Cantell said, smiling, as they all walked past the crumpled body.

Kelmar opened the door and looked out. "All clear," he half whispered, and moving quickly, they headed back to the forge.

A pair of eyes watched them go. The third Cardronian guard had been rummaging through some nearby houses. He was just about to walk through the tavern door when he heard the clatter of someone falling down the stairs behind the door. His mind told him not to rush in and confront whoever it was. Instead, he quickly hid from view in the next house, behind a broken shuttered window.

Not daring to breathe, he watched with a frown as he saw two Cardronian soldiers run across the square with the blacksmith's daughter and her child, to disappear out of sight on the other side of the square.

As soon as they had disappeared, he quickly ran into the tavern. He knelt down over his comrade's body to see he was still breathing but out cold. Up the stairs, he found his sergeant, clutching the Cardronian dagger that had killed him in his chest.

Cardronian killing Cardronian? That cannot be right, he thought. *Who can they have been?*

He would attend to his comrade first and then check the blacksmith's, he thought. If they had come to rescue her then they could have already been to the forge, stolen his comrades' uniforms and come here, he reasoned.

If so, they would know of his presence, he further thought. He was not going to confront them alone; he did not want to end up like his sergeant, best he kept out of sight.

Druimar looked anxiously down the street for any sign of his daughter and granddaughter. Knowing of a covered wagon, he had worked fast hitching it up with a team of four horses, with two more tied on the back.

Oneatha was still putting supplies in the back of the wagon when Kelmar, Cantell, Permellar and little Kayla all appeared.

Druimar grinned at the sight of his daughter, free at last from those leering guards, he thought.

She approached him and gave him a hug for the first time without those horrible shackles binding him.

"Are you all right, Permellar?" he asked, looking at her fondly.

"I am, Father." She smiled as Druimar looked at his granddaughter.

"Asleep through it all, I see." He laughed, but more out of relief at seeing them both safe.

"Would you like to hold her, Father?" Druimar answered by holding out his arms to take little Kayla and cuddling her up to the side of his face, something he had not been able or allowed to do these last months.

Suddenly a little strained cry went up from inside the wagon; someone was very hungry. Permellar looked away from her father with a frown.

"A baby? Who else is here?" she queried.

"No one, only us, Permellar. We have not told you yet, but when we escaped from Stormhaven we brought someone else with us, Queen Elina's baby son, Prince Martyn," answered Cantell, to see Permellar's mouth fall open.

"Queen Elina's!" she exclaimed. "What, but how—?"

"We will tell you everything once we are on our way," interrupted Kelmar, "but for now will you help him? He is very hungry. We lost what food we had, as much good as it was, and when we heard you had a little one..." tailed off Kelmar, feeling a little awkward.

Permellar understood immediately, noting the concern on their faces.

Smiling at Kelmar's awkwardness, she held out her hand. "Help me up, Kelmar. I will look after the Prince," and with Kelmar's helping hand, she climbed up into the back of the wagon.

They waited for what seemed an age as Prince Martyn's cries continued, worrying that he would not accept Permellar's milk and that all they had been through would be for nothing.

Then relief washed over them as silence ensued; they could breathe again.

"All is ready, Druimar," called Oneatha, sitting in the back of the wagon holding Kayla, whilst Permellar still held Prince Martyn next to her. Cantell sat up front with Druimar, in a thankful change of clothing, whilst Kelmar was on one of the horses at the rear of the wagon, also feeling better in a change of clothing.

"To Silion then, Druimar, if you please," said Cantell with a smile, for Druimar to set them on their way with a snap of the reins and a shout of encouragement.

As they began to disappear up the North Road out of the town, a figure emerged from between the buildings opposite the forge.

The Cardronian guard looked inside the forge and saw his two dead comrades on the floor, still in their uniforms.

He came back out and looked up the road, thinking. *Where had they got those uniforms from then?* A thought came into his head. *No, impossible, it had been under siege for months.*

What should he do? His comrade had been lucky, only being badly bruised, and was resting. A good job he had been drinking that night, he thought; it had helped soften the blow.

Not so lucky, though, were his sergeant and two comrades lying in there. There was only one thing he could do, he decided; he was not about to go after them on his own. No, he would ride to Stormhaven and report what he had seen; someone needed to know of this.

CHAPTER XIV

Queen Elina sat on the side of her bed, holding Princess Amber in her arms. Though she was holding her beautiful daughter, she had never felt so alone at this moment. She was waiting for someone to escort her to her beloved husband's funeral and as the thought came into her mind, so the tears began again.

The thought of him was only replaced by her worry for her son. What perils were waiting for him and if he would survive them.

He was in good hands, she knew, with Cantell and Kelmar, but would they make it through the Kavenmist Mountains, she could not help thinking, let alone escape from Cardronian eyes if they made it? She had been told of the patrols sent out to find them if they did.

All these thoughts weighed heavily on her mind, making her feel helpless as she sat there.

Just then, a knock on the door made Queen Elina instinctively hold Princess Amber tighter, but when it opened, it was only Mrs Beeworthy with a hot drink.

She managed a half-smile seeing her. "There you are, my lovely, drink this whilst it's hot. It be cold out there," said Mrs Beeworthy with a smile, seeing the sorrow in Queen Elina's eyes.

She sat on the bed by her Queen and put a loving arm around her. "He be watching over you all," she said, trying to give Queen Elina some comfort.

Queen Elina looked at her, with tears running down her face. "I know," was all she managed.

Just then, another knock on the door sounded and in walked Charlotte with some blankets for the Princess's cradle. She lay them down and turned to walk out again.

"Wait, Charlotte, come and sit here beside me," beckoned Queen Elina. Charlotte smiled and sat on the opposite side to Mrs Beeworthy.

"Tell me again of our visit from Queen Helistra," she enquired, for Mrs Beeworthy to turn immediately red. They had already talked about what had happened before Queen Elina had woken up to find them both asleep by her side.

"She came in and wanted to see the Princess. She hummed a lullaby to her and then asked how you were," spoke Charlotte first.

"She seemed so nice, so caring of how we all were," continued Mrs Beeworthy, remembering. Queen Elina, though, felt suspicious of her. Taliskar's wife nice?

"Then what happened?" asked Queen Elina, looking straight at Mrs Beeworthy's red face.

"She was leaving and said what a lovely child she be," Mrs Beeworthy hesitated, "I... I said *he is* and stopped myself, realising what I was saying. Then I said, she be lovely like her mother." Mrs Beeworthy looked at the floor, ashamed for being so stupid.

"It is all right, Bee. I am not blaming you." Queen Elina knew she would never do or say anything to hurt her.

"She did stop and turn round, but only to ask us our names," stressed Charlotte, seeing Mrs Beeworthy's distress. "I am sure we never told her anything of the Prince," she whispered.

"No, no, that be right, nothing," agreed Mrs Beeworthy, lifting up her head.

"Then the next we remember is when we woke," finished Charlotte.

Something was not right, thought Queen Elina. She could see Bee's red face now, a certain giveaway if she did it when she slipped up as that woman was leaving, but if they say they did not tell her anything then she believed them. So how did they know of the escape? They did not lie, but no one else knew.

As if on cue, into the royal chamber walked Queen Helistra, unannounced. Queen Elina looked up to see a beautiful face looking down at her, but felt the need to hold on to Princess Amber even tighter.

"Queen Elina, at last we meet. The last time I came you were tired from childbirth, although I must say motherhood becomes you," she said with a smile.

Queen Elina did not know if she was being understanding or sarcastic.

"Thank you, you are kind," she replied as she eyed Queen Helistra's tall frame.

"I trust you are all rested now," Queen Helistra enquired of them all, looking at Mrs Beeworthy and Charlotte as she said it.

They suddenly felt their presence was not wanted and both stood up to leave the royal chamber.

"Oh, please do not leave on my account," she said, smiling.

"No, that be all right, my lady. Chores await in the kitchen," excused Mrs Beeworthy, and they hurriedly left the royal chamber.

In their place, Queen Helistra sat down next to Queen Elina. Queen Elina watched Queen Helistra adjust the strange-looking object she was holding in her lap, as if she was holding a baby.

Their eyes met and as Queen Elina looked into Queen Helistra's dark green eyes, she saw her instantly for what she was: a manipulator.

Queen Helistra looked back at her with a smile, but with a coldness running through it, although it did not show.

A humming entered her head. *You are right, she sees me for what I am. She is not stupid…* to more humming. *Yes, she is strong of spirit, but it will do her no good.*

As Queen Elina looked, she could not help but notice how bloodshot one of Queen Helistra's eyes was. "Have you a cold?" she queried on seeing it, for Queen Helistra to frown. "Your eye is bloodshot," Queen Elina pointed out.

More humming… *not to worry, a short rest and it will be gone. We will have to be careful how many we use next time.* "Oh, when I sneezed, I think it appeared," she answered, matter-of-factly.

"Now the pleasantries are out of the way and we have got to know each other a little, tell me, how did you feel letting your other child go? It must have been heartbreaking for you," said Queen Helistra, grinning, with sarcasm in her every word, catching Queen Elina unawares.

Queen Elina looked at her with disdain. "What are you on about? I only have the child you see before you!" she challenged, feeling her anger rise up inside her.

"Oh, so what your servants told me was made up, but why would they do that?" she questioned, with a look that made Queen Elina go cold.

"It is you that is making it up. My servants did not tell you anything, because there was nothing for them to tell," countered Queen Elina.

"Enough of this, they did, my dear. They told me everything," and Queen Helistra took great pleasure in revealing all they had told her whilst under her hold.

"Prince Martyn, a good name you have given him, with two of your warriors, Cantell and Kelmar, escaped under the Kavenmist Mountains through the back of Forest Tower not an hour before this one was born." She smirked, enjoying the look on Queen Elina's face.

How did she find out? wondered Queen Elina, in puzzlement. There was no point in pretending anymore. She could only pray to the stars and spirits that they would be safe.

"With them, Tiggannia still lives!" she spat in Queen Helistra's face.

"Not for much longer, my dear, when they follow your husband to their deaths," crooned Queen Helistra.

"How can you talk so cruelly?" cried Queen Elina, for Queen Helistra to smile her cold smile.

"If you are so minded, why then do we live?" asked Queen Elina, looking at Princess Amber's little face, feeling the hopelessness of it all.

Queen Helistra merely continued smiling, letting Queen Elina's question hang in the air.

She enjoys playing with my feelings, thought Queen Elina. *Caring, nice, did they say? No, cold and calculating is more like it!* A knock on the door stopped all thoughts for now.

Tarbor had come to the royal chamber to escort Queen Elina to King Rolfe's funeral. As he approached the door, he could not help but overhear Queen Elina's raised voice.

No guards were present, so he chanced listening. *Tiggannia still lives,* he heard. *Not for much longer, something or other, follow your husband to their deaths. Talk so cruelly, why then do we live?* Silence.

He knew who Queen Elina was talking to; it could only be one person. Tarbor thought of a cat playing with a mouse before the cat kills it as he knocked on the door, not daring to listen anymore.

"Enter!" Tarbor breathed in. *Keep your mind clear. Do not let her suspect anything,* he told himself.

Entering the royal chamber, he found himself standing in front of Queen Helistra. Bowing his head, he acknowledged her: "My lady."

"Ah, Captain Tarbor, it seems such a long time since I last saw you," she said, smiling.

She sounds like a kitten now, thought Tarbor, smiling back as he answered. "It has been, my lady. I have come to escort Queen Elina," he informed her, noting Queen Helistra's bloodshot eye as he turned to look at Queen Elina.

Queen Helistra in turn looked at the little Queen. Queen Elina stood up and gave Queen Helistra a look of her own. This only made Queen Helistra inwardly smile all the more.

"I must first find my companion," she said curtly to Tarbor.

"If it is to take care of the child, I will gladly do that for you, my dear," said Queen Helistra with a smile, knowingly antagonising Queen Elina all the more.

"I do not think so!" fumed Queen Elina, and she stormed out of the royal chamber clutching Princess Amber.

Soon, though, my little Queen, very soon, spoke Queen Helistra's mind. "You had better run after her, Captain Tarbor, she is upset. With what she is going through, it is understandable." Queen Helistra's face looked full of concern as she spoke.

How you are enjoying seeing her pain, thought Tarbor, and bowing, turned to leave.

"Oh, Captain Tarbor," called Queen Helistra after Tarbor, giving his heart a lurch.

He turned back. "Yes, my lady?"

"Is there any news for the King on those that escaped?" she asked, for Tarbor to breathe again.

"There is nothing to report yet, my lady."

"Very well," and she dismissed him, for Tarbor to turn away gladly in pursuit of Queen Elina.

Tarbor soon caught up with her and saw the tears running down her small face. He could not help but feel sorry for her. They walked on in silence along the corridor that joined all the various rooms, until they came to the kitchen.

Mrs Beeworthy and Charlotte sat there quietly talking. They stood up as soon as they saw Queen Elina. "Take care of little Amber for me, Bee, whilst I attend my husband's funeral," she asked, with a certain amount of calmness returning to her voice.

Mrs Beeworthy held out her hands to receive the little Princess. "Do not let that woman touch her," she ordered.

"No, she be all right with us. Have no fear, my little one," assured Mrs Beeworthy, but with a doubt in her mind that she dare not show to her Queen.

Queen Elina looked at Tarbor. "I am ready."

Queen Elina donned her fur cloak around her shoulders, ready for her journey to the River Dale. The cold winter's air bit at her face as she and Tarbor stepped into the grand courtyard.

Mist hung all around as the snow fell in large flakes, tickling the horses' noses that Girvan was holding.

Tarbor went to help Queen Elina onto her horse. "I do not need your help, Cardronian," she said dismissively.

Though her strength was low at best, she swung herself ably into the saddle and held the reins, waiting. Tarbor looked at Girvan, who just looked back, expressionless.

No one else was present for King Rolfe's funeral; no one had been allowed. The survivors that could have attended lay in the dungeons, wounded or not. Only Sergeant Wardine and six archers followed Queen Elina, Sergeant Wardine's eyes flitting all around him as ever. To Queen Elina, it all felt as empty as her heart.

Slowly they rode down the valley towards Haven. The two bonfires that had been lit for the dead still smouldered from the hot embers that lay inside.

The outskirts of Haven came into eerie view, with the mist circling around the ruins of what was left. The snow was trying to cover its destruction, but somehow it only added to its sadness.

There tied to the riverbank next to the bridge that joined the divided village lay a small ship with a large sail hoisted upon it. In the middle of the ship resting on a pyre of wood was the body of King Rolfe, draped in a ceremonial cloak of Tiggannia, leaving only his head showing.

Tarbor was off his horse and to Queen Elina's side as she visibly collapsed over her horse, nearly fainting at seeing her husband's body draped on the small ship.

Tarbor helped her down, holding on to her arm, but as soon as she realised, she pulled her arm away.

"Will you be all right, my lady?" he asked, stepping back.

"Thank you, Captain, I am well enough," she answered, giving him a wary glance.

She is strong of mind, but at least I am a Captain again, he thought.

They walked the short distance to the ship's side as it bobbed up and down, as if eager to get away.

Tarbor and Girvan stood back in respect as Queen Elina stood motionless, looking at her husband lying on the ship.

She trembled not with the cold but with her broken heart as she began to speak her words of farewell.

"I call upon you, Great Forest, to accept the soul of this good man I knew as my beloved husband. He tried to do what was right in this life we have been given. Keep him safe in your arms until the day comes when I can join him and be happy again." Queen Elina paused to wipe away her tears. "Go now, my husband, be at rest in the Kingdom of the Great Forest," she finished, and turned away.

The wind suddenly sprung up, blowing in from the sea, making the ship's sail billow. The mist swirled around the ship's frame as if making ready to escort the ship on its journey. Girvan released the ropes that held the small ship to the bank, and they all watched as it sailed away on the swell of an incoming tide.

Fire arrows waited on the end of the archers' bows for the order to fire from Tarbor; he looked at Queen Elina. She gave a tearful nod of her head and in turn Tarbor nodded for the archers to release their fire arrows.

All watched as the fire arrows span through the air to find their mark and set alight the small ship.

Flames began to engulf the ship around King Rolfe's body as it started to disappear down the River Dale, to finally become only a glow in the river's mist before disappearing altogether.

"Farewell, my love, may the river and stars guide you safely to the Kingdom of the Great Forest. Wait for me there," whispered Queen Elina in never-ending tears.

Queen Elina allowed Tarbor to help her onto her horse this time. Just as he had done so, two riders approached him and got off their sweat-laden horses.

Tarbor recognised them as two of the guards that had been posted along the valley. They must be here with news of the two Tiggannians and the Prince. He wondered if they had been captured.

"Captain, sir," one addressed him.

"Yes, what news have you?" he asked as Queen Elina watched and listened in hope at what the guard was going to report.

Girvan joined them to hear the tail end of what the guard had to say. "We did not see them, they had disappeared into the mist. We tried to find another boat to follow them, but our attempts to find one proved fruitless," explained the guard. "They killed two of our comrades and two were still missing when we left to report to you, Captain, sir," he finished.

"I see. Very well, rest yourselves and your horses, I will convey this to King Taliskar," ordered Tarbor, and the two guards left with a salute.

Tarbor turned to Girvan, but before he could speak, Sergeant Wardine was upon them to see what the guard had said.

"Was that about those two that escaped?" he asked bluntly. Tarbor did not like or trust this man whatsoever.

"It was, Sergeant Wardine. Somehow, they have made it through the Kavenmist Mountains and now travel along the River Dale," Tarbor informed him.

Sergeant Wardine grunted in disgust as his flittering eyes caught sight of a broad smile on Queen Elina's face. They had made it through! She was thinking, *My baby boy is alive!*

Sergeant Wardine walked over to her horse. "Make the most of this moment, for as sure as I am standing here, they will all meet their fate!" he promised, to receive a glare from Queen Elina.

"And if I had a dagger in my hand, you would meet yours!" she snarled, not able to contain herself, not that she needed to have said anything as Tarbor stepped in.

"Wardine! Mind your tongue! She is still a Queen!" he berated him.

Sergeant Wardine turned and stared hard at Tarbor. "Sounds like you have become a Tiggannian, Tarbor, and should be dealt with in the same way," threatened Sergeant Wardine.

Tarbor made for his sword, but the hand of Girvan restrained him. Sergeant Wardine grinned and walked away to his horse.

"Thank you, Captain, there was no need," said Queen Elina as Tarbor mounted his horse. "We are not all like that, my lady," he apologised.

Tarbor caught himself looking into Queen Elina's sea blue eyes a moment longer than he should have as he spoke.

What are you doing? She has only just said goodbye to her husband, he thought, and he looked away quickly.

Queen Elina caught his look but saw another look in his eyes; that of someone who was not at ease with himself.

Tarbor's mind half wanted not to report back what the guard had told him. Knowing that this gentle woman riding next to him was the mother did not help matters.

It did not matter how he felt. King Taliskar would find out soon enough, he thought as he watched Sergeant Wardine riding off in front of them.

Tarbor rode on in silent thought next to Queen Elina whilst Girvan rode on the other side of her when suddenly Queen Elina turned to speak to Tarbor.

Seeing the unrest in Tarbor's eyes, she was going to take a chance on him and appeal to the inner voice that she felt was going around in his head.

"Captain, you do not seem like a soldier that could let barbarians like that man kill my son." Tarbor looked across at Girvan, who quickly glanced behind him and then back at Tarbor.

Tarbor looked at Queen Elina with the same helplessness she had felt earlier. "But, my lady, it is out of my hands. What could I do?" he put, proving to her he had mixed feelings about it all.

"Go find my son before that creature does, and save him from her! It is Taliskar that craved power, but it is her that controls it!" she pleaded.

Tarbor looked at her. She was right, he thought, he had been blind to it all until he came to this place.

"You will not see a new dawn, my lady, if they hear you talk like that," he warned her. Queen Elina ignored him; this was her son she was trying to save.

"Only my servants knew of his birth, yet she knew my son's name and the names of those who escaped with him, but we never spoke a word of them. There is more to her than meets the eye!" warned Queen Elina, making Tarbor think of Taliskar's eyes and the voice from the rock in his mind: *She comes, she is evil.*

"She wants my son dead but has designs on my daughter, I am sure of it," she worried further as they reached Stormhaven and entered the grand courtyard.

Tarbor helped Queen Elina from her horse as she pleaded with him one more time. "If you do it for no other reason then do it for me," she implored him, appealing to the other look she saw in his eyes, making Tarbor feel guilty for looking at her the way he did.

Queen Elina made her way back to the kitchen, with Tarbor and Girvan following.

"Did I hear right?" whispered Girvan.

"She echoes our thoughts, Girvan, with a woman's intuition, but with a mother's worries. I overheard her talking, if you can call it that, to Queen Helistra," he whispered back.

Tarbor quickly told Girvan what he had heard as they followed Queen Elina, how Queen Helistra had taunted her with the death of her son.

"You are right. She enjoys playing with us all," said Girvan thoughtfully, after listening to Tarbor.

Queen Elina managed a smile when she saw Mrs Beeworthy with Princess Amber in her arms. She took her daughter from her and made for the kitchen door, stopping in front of Tarbor and Girvan.

"You are soldiers, not murderers, are you not? Could either of you kill a little baby such as this?" posed Queen Elina, showing them Princess Amber's little face.

"She already has Tiggannia. What is there to gain from the death of my son?" She looked at Tarbor once more with desperation in her eyes, before going back to the royal chamber, leaving him and Girvan feeling empty.

They followed at a distance until she reached the base of Forest Tower, where she disappeared from view up the spiral steps. The door that led to the mountain throne room opened in that moment and out walked a smiling King Taliskar. His smile did not fade when he saw Tarbor and Girvan standing before him; he had been enjoying the feeling of power.

With a bow of their heads, they greeted him: "Sire."

"Captain Tarbor, have you any news for me?" he enquired straight away.

"I have, sire, the two warriors and the Prince have made it through the Kavenmist Mountains," reported Tarbor.

"And where are they now?" came a voice from behind King Taliskar.

Tarbor and Girvan looked on uneasily to see Queen Helistra elegantly appear from the mountain throne room as King Taliskar stood aside to let her pass.

"They have broken through our patrols and are somewhere along the River Dale, my lady. Most likely heading for Kelmsmere," replied Tarbor, trying to keep composed.

"That is exactly what Sergeant Wardine has just told us," she said with a smile.

I was right, he could not wait, thought Tarbor.

"He also told me that you were ready to strike him, if it had not been for your comrade here holding you back," queried Queen Helistra, moving to stand in front of Tarbor as he answered her, for him to see her bloodshot eye again.

"That is true, my lady. We have never liked each other," he admitted.

"Are you sure it is that and not because you have developed feelings for these Tiggannians, especially Queen Elina?" quizzed Queen Helistra, speaking coldly as she spoke Queen Elina's name.

King Taliskar was looking on in amusement whilst Girvan groaned inside, wondering what Tarbor would say.

Queen Helistra glanced down at Tarbor,s hand that was nervously fiddling with the hilt of his sword. *Hmm, what ails you so? is there something going on in that mind of yours?* she thought as a humming came into hers.

I know my eye is a warning, but he is hiding something, it will not hurt me for what I want. She smiled and looked into Tarbor's eyes. "Well?" She smiled as she looked.

Let me see what it is that troubles you, and she began to reach into Tarbor's mind, only for a pain to shoot straight through her bloodshot eye into her mind. The pain blocked her senses from seeing and she swayed backwards, for the humming to strike up again.

Yes, it is hindering my inner sight. I should have heeded the warning you gave me... to more humming... No, he is not as important as the demise of the Great Forest, I was not thinking. I will go and rest until it is gone.

Tarbor had found himself caught in Queen Helistra's stare as he was about to reply. For a moment, he had a carefree light-headed feeling as if floating in the air. Then suddenly her bloodshot eye had filled with blood, covering her whole eye, making her sway back from him. Blinking, he began to reply, none the wiser.

"I will not lie, my lady. It is not a fondness I have towards the Tiggannians. It is the thought of killing a baby. It does not rest well with me. I am a soldier and have always obeyed your command, but in this I cannot," answered Tarbor, not helping, but look at her blood filled eye.

Girvan was looking at the floor; he could see his friend in shackles, or worse.

King Taliskar, though, was looking at Queen Helistra with some concern.

"Are you all right, my love?" he asked, holding her arm. "Your eye looks worse. You should rest," he advised her, worried.

"I am all right. It is just something I must have caught. I will go and rest," she assured him.

Queen Helistra looked back at Tarbor, wondering if what he had just said was true as humming sounded in her mind again.

And how would he know? Anyway, it is useless without the shield! Queen Helistra was feeling agitated enough as it was at not being able to use her powers properly, and the broken rune staff was not helping.

"I will leave my husband to decide what is to become of you, Captain Tarbor," and with a swirl of her cloak, she left abruptly.

King Taliskar watched her go and then turned to Tarbor. "Guard!" he shouted immediately.

Two guards ran through the great hall and stood to attention.

"Put Captain Tarbor in irons and throw him into the dungeons!" he ordered, to see Girvan step between them.

King Taliskar looked him up and down. "What is the meaning of this!" he challenged.

"Sire, Captain Tarbor has served you without question, risked his life in doing so. He is a Captain who is respected by both his own men and those of Waunarle. I too would find it hard to take the life of a child as a soldier," spoke up Girvan in Tarbor's defence.

King Taliskar stared at Girvan before answering him. "I understand your loyalty towards your Captain, but he is refusing to obey my order, his King's order!" And King Taliskar nodded to the two guards to take Tarbor away.

Girvan risked himself again. "We understand why you want to end the child's life, sire. You see him as a threat to you in the future if he lives." King Taliskar kept staring at Girvan. Girvan knew he was getting in deeper, but carried on. "But Tiggannia is no more. Who would help him if he lived? No one," pointed out Girvan, holding King Taliskar's attention.

"King Rolfe never had anyone help him whilst he was alive, so why would anyone help his child?" pointed out Girvan further.

Tarbor stood there, held by the two guards; none of them were taking their eyes off Girvan.

Girvan swallowed; he was dry. *Here goes nothing*, he thought, thinking of what Queen Elina had said, but he had to be careful not to quote her.

"I have just seen Queen Elina holding her baby daughter. Is she to be killed as well, sire?" questioned Girvan to total silence, putting King Taliskar on the spot.

Girvan felt in that moment he had pushed his luck too far and would be joining Tarbor to await his fate.

Tarbor closed his eyes. King Taliskar will have them both thrown into the dungeons now, if not worse, he thought.

King Taliskar looked at Girvan, weighing him up. If he had not known better, he would have thought that Girvan had been listening to him talking to his Queen.

Queen Helistra's words came into his head as he thought of her: *You are King of all you survey*. He had everything he ever wanted, nothing had stopped him and nothing was going to, he thought.

If this Girvan was right about anything, it was about Tarbor; he was well liked by his men, he had just proved it by speaking up for him, but they would have to be dealt with, but not here, thought King Taliskar, thinking of Tarbor's popularity.

The words he spoke were true enough, *but I am their King*, he told himself, *the mover of mountains! My word is to be obeyed!*

Asking about the boy's sister like that, he thought, *I cannot allow anyone to talk to me in that way, to make me feel awkward, knowing as I do my Queen has a liking for her.*

"I have listened to your comrade, Captain Tarbor, and it is he who you must thank for the decision I am going to make," began King Taliskar, instantly making Tarbor and Girvan think they would never see the light of day again.

"Let me make it clear the matter of the child Prince will still be dealt with. Sergeant Wardine will finish what you cannot, as Captain Wardine from this moment on. He will take your place, as I am stripping you of that position. You are a Captain no longer," decided King Taliskar, making Tarbor grimace. Wardine a Captain!

"I do not have to answer you about the child Princess, but I will. Queen Helistra asked me if she could not be spared, and to show her I am not without heart, I agreed," said King Taliskar, making Tarbor and Girvan look at each other.

"Your friend is right. You have served me well, Tarbor, and for that reason alone I am going to spare you from the dungeons," and King Taliskar nodded to the two guards to let Tarbor go.

"Instead, you can carry out the arrangements you yourself have organised by escorting Brax's body back to Waunarle under Sergeant Urchel's command," he informed them, to their surprise.

"Now report to him, the pair of you, and do not let me hear of anything else. Otherwise, shackles will be the least of your worries!" warned King Taliskar.

"At once, sire," they both replied, and bowing their heads, not quite believing their luck, they turned and left him.

"We will be able to go and see my father after all," Girvan said with a smile, whispering as they made their way through the great hall.

"It does not feel right, though, Girvan, letting us go. He could have thrown us into the dungeons and thrown away the key," whispered Tarbor back.

"Well, we will have to watch our backs as we go on our way then," replied Girvan to the nod of Tarbor.

King Taliskar called to the guards to fetch Sergeant Wardine as he watched Tarbor and Girvan go.

Wardine would see to it that he would never see his face again, he thought, smiling, then he would be finally out of his way.

His Queen with her motherly instincts, he thought, and now she was doing it again, but this time he was King of all he surveyed. He smiled.

Just then, Sergeant Wardine entered the great hall and walked up to King Taliskar. "You wished to see me, sire?"

King Taliskar smiled. "Yes, I do, Captain Wardine!"

CHAPTER XV

Not a grey cloud could be seen in the sharp winter blue sky that held out its arms over the Great Plateau Forest. The sun's rays sparkled and glistened off the fall of snow that had covered the forest like a blanket; a breeze springing up now and again to blow the snow from the trees' branches, creating its own spray of clouds as it did so.

Birds sang in the warmth of the sun, happy that the winter's night had passed them by, whilst animals scurried down trails of old, hoping to find a morsel of some kind somewhere on the forest floor.

They were not alone in their scurrying, as they were joined by a lone figure walking hurriedly down one such trail.

A cloak of many furs covered the figure as it moved towards a ridge that overlooked a vast valley. The figure stopped at the top of the ridge and pulled back a hood that had been covering a head of long, matted white hair. Speedwell, Keeper of the North, was here at last.

He was a long way from his domain here in the west plateau. A warning had come to him that the mountain throne had been opened from the Ancient One in his dreams. That and the sad songs of foreboding from his rune staff.

She had surfaced once more and was on the move with the broken rune staff of Grimstone's. Her evil threatening the forests and all that lived in them. Speedwell was here to stop her.

Steel blue eyes looked out over the valley below from a face set in stone. To the north far behind him lay Thunder Gorge rumbling its discontent, closed off on this side by the Lesser Hardenel Mountains.

To his east lay the sharp-rising mountains of Linninhorne, unseen in the distance. Both ranges overlooked where he stood on the west side of the Great Plateau Forest that reached out as far as the sea.

Speedwell looked out over the valley with apprehension. He knew this day had long since been coming, but in his heart he had hoped it never would.

The beauty of the valley below glowed in the winter's sun, reflecting in Speedwell's eyes, but all Speedwell could see was darkness and destruction if he did not stop the threat of death he felt coursing its way through the earth.

With a furrowed brow and a tighter grip on his rune staff, Speedwell started to make his way down to the valley floor.

By following a snow-covered path imprinted with deer hooves, Speedwell made quick progress into the heart of the valley.

Twists and turns through the trees brought him to a trickling stream. He followed the stream until he came upon some rocks that showed themselves above the ground, and there nestling in amongst them was a little pool; he had arrived.

Speedwell brushed one of the convenient rocks next to the pool of its snow and sat down. Not wasting any time, Speedwell touched some of the symbols upon his rune staff and dipped its end into the pool.

Closing his eyes, Speedwell joined with his rune staff in search of the life force that lived within it.

Where is she? his mind asked as he searched the pool for humming in his mind to answer him.

She has good reason to hide, for what we have felt, replied Speedwell.

Then suddenly in front of his probing mind, tiny dense bubbles appeared. It was the essence of the little pool, come to greet him.

Speedwell! Speedwell! Thank the forest! You are here!

Yes, I am here, Speedwell answered, sensing how frightened the pool's essence was.

I knew you would come. My sister is in danger, I can feel it. I am sure something horrible has happened to her, but I dare not go and see. I am too afraid.

The tiny bubbles of the little pool's essence swayed back and forth through the water in worry as she spoke in Speedwell's mind.

Do not worry, I will go forward and find out what is amiss. I am sure nothing has happened to her, spoke Speedwell's mind, calmly trying to sound reassuring.

Be careful then, Speedwell. Evil is at work here, warned the essence of the little pool, and made to go.

Can I ask you for some of your tiny droplets of life before you go? It would be wise of me to have some of their life force inside of me first.

They are yours, Speedwell, and without hesitation, the little pool's essence cast some of her tiny bubbles aside. Speedwell thanked her as she left, whilst the tiny bubbles attached themselves to his rune staff.

Lying his rune staff down carefully so as not to dislodge the tiny bubbles, Speedwell produced a wooden bowl from his pouch that he carried.

He began putting a mixture of herbs into the bowl and then added some strange-looking dried berries. He then dipped the bowl into the pool to collect a little water to mix it all with.

Taking his rune staff, he touched certain symbols upon it and let the tiny bubbles drop into the mixture.

Closing his eyes, Speedwell began to chant softly, with the humming of his rune staff joining him. The rune staff began to gently vibrate and Speedwell lowered its tip into the mixture. Moving one of his fingers onto another symbol, he stopped chanting as a hiss sounded in the mixture.

Speedwell opened his eyes to a horrible-looking warm green mixture, and swallowed at the thought of having to consume it.

Using his fingers, Speedwell ate half the mixture and drank some of its liquid residue. His face contorted at the foul taste, even when he could feel the potion start to revitalise his body.

The herbal mixture was cleansing him, whilst the tiny bubbles of the essence would explode inside of him with life-giving energy if needed. He left the other half of the mixture by the little pool, just in case.

Dipping his rune staff into the little pool once more, Speedwell touched different symbols upon it and held it steadfast.

Closing his eyes, Speedwell wondered what awaited him as he let his mind join as one with his rune staff, to send their presence down through the little pool, underground to the essence's sister pool under Stormhaven.

Speedwell pushed his presence forward in his rune staff's protective embrace, deep into the earth. Twisting and turning along the waterway, his presence sped ever onwards, forever keeping alert for what may lay ahead.

He started to sense the passage of water going back up when suddenly a warning hum telling him to be careful brought his presence to a stop.

Speedwell moved his presence slowly forward as he searched cautiously in front of him and then suddenly there it was. Though he could not see it, he could feel it: evil!

Moving forward slowly, Speedwell's presence began to see a dense cloud of blood-red poison emanating evil from its every being. Its denseness made it move slowly, but its power was unmistakable.

Within the blood-red cloud, Speedwell could see small explosions happening, making the cloud become bigger all of the time. The explosions were the poisonous venom within the cloud, becoming more volatile with each passing moment.

All that the Ancient One had felt and feared was happening right in front of him, thought Speedwell.

He sensed he would need more than just his cleansing potion to protect him if he was to enter the poisonous cloud. He needed to stop whoever was casting its evil, but first he had to find out for sure who was doing this, even though he knew it could only be one person.

Back at the little pool, Speedwell's fingers suddenly began moving over his rune staff, to summon a spell of protection as his body started to sweat in reaction to the presence of the blood-red cloud.

Speedwell's rune staff suddenly turned ice-blue. His finger moved to another symbol and an ice-blue flame shot into the little pool, joining Speedwell's presence in an instant, covering him in an ice-blue protective shield of flame.

He held fast, ready to enter the poisonous blood-red cloud. He would have to be quick, he thought, already beginning to feel how powerful the poisonous cloud was.

His mind said now, and his presence immediately shot into the blood-red cloud. The poison within it tried to claw and penetrate his protective shield as he sped through, but the ice-blue flame repelled any such attempts, burning the venomous poison.

Speedwell suddenly stopped. He was there in the home of the sister pool's essence under Stormhaven. He tried to see if he could sense anything of her, but he could feel nothing, only the loathing of the blood-red cloud.

His presence pushed on whilst all the time being attacked by the poison, until there above him was the crystal chamber. He saw sadly how the crystals were reflecting back into the little sister pool the colour of blood-red. All had been tainted, he thought sadly.

But even worse for him was who was causing it all, as a movement made Speedwell look over to the side of the little pool, where all his fears were confirmed.

Oozing drops of red poison into the sister pool was the broken rune staff of Grimstone's! But who was holding it made Speedwell become overwhelmed with sadness; it was Helistra, his daughter!

A cold half-grin showed itself across Queen Helistra's face as she sensed Speedwell's presence in the little pool.

Well, well, look who's come to visit! came her cold voice into Speedwell's mind, *my so-called pathetic father!*

All Speedwell could feel in that coldness was her hatred for him. *Have you come to try and stop me, Father!* Her cold laughter rang out around the crystal chamber, making the surface of the little pool vibrate as if shaking in terror.

You will not get away with this evil you have wrought, my daughter, he promised.

She growled in anger at hearing him call her his daughter, any such thought of her being so had long since ended.

Taking the broken rune staff out of the little pool, she exposed its broken end dripping with poisonous blood and held it over the little pool. Touching some symbols upon it, she blew along its length and sent a bolt of red poison straight at Speedwell's presence. She had blown him a kiss, a kiss of death!

Speedwell was gone, thankful he had covered his presence with the ice-blue flame of protection as he felt the poison within the blood-red cloud increase its efforts to penetrate his protective shield.

The poison was relentless in its attacks as Speedwell's presence sped through the red cloud, despite being burnt continuously, but the poison was doing enough to hold Speedwell's presence back for the bolt of poison to attach itself to the ice-blue flame.

The bolt of poison instantly seared a hole right through the ice-blue flame before it could be burnt, penetrating its venom into Speedwell's presence, making it twist in agony at the searing pain.

Finally clearing the blood-red cloud, Speedwell's presence shot back, screaming through the water like a bolt of lightning.

Speedwell's presence hit his waiting body by the little pool, still screaming as it rejoined it, for the screaming to continue through Speedwell's open mouth.

His rune staff exploded out of his hands, hitting a tree behind him whilst animals scattered all around and birds flew away in fright as the piercing scream reverberated across the valley; Speedwell collapsed!

As he lay there, a battle began in his body as the red poison that had invaded his presence headed straight for his heart. The cleansing potion he had wisely had before entering his presence into the little pool fought back to stop it.

The two clashed together, with the cleansing potion diluting the poison and the tiny life giving bubbles, exploding in amongst it, for both to cleanse the poison from Speedwell's being.

The poison, though, was proving to be more virulent than the cleansing potion could cope with. The potion was being effective, but it was too slow and there was not enough to deal with what poison had invaded Speedwell's body.

Speedwell suddenly came round with a start, catching his breath. His head was spinning and he felt sick. Night was calling and so was the poison inside him as he felt it closing around his heart.

He called to his rune staff, catching it as it flew to him, and with fingers that shook pressed some of its symbols to turn the rune staff ice-blue once more.

He could feel the battle going on in his body and knew he needed something more than the cleansing potion to rid himself of the poison. It was taking too long and he needed something quick.

He gave his rune staff an order as he touched one more symbol upon its length, to release a bolt of ice-blue flame into his body.

The ice-blue flame entered Speedwell's nose and mouth, making his whole body convulse as it swept through him. It knocked the breath out of him as the blue ice crystallised the poison, whilst the cold blue flame seared it through until it was no more.

Speedwell shakily picked up the remainder of his herbal mixture and thankfully drank it, without thinking of how horrible it was.

He coughed as he drank it, gasping in the cold air between gulps as the potion washed through him.

He breathed in deeply as he felt the mixture cleansing him and the droplets announcing themselves by exploding inside his body with their life-giving energy.

Finally, Speedwell was able to stand up. Closing his eyes, he thanked the stars and trees for watching over him in his time of need.

His body was cleansed of the poison, but now he needed to rest, he thought, to restore and replenish his energy fully before tackling the poisonous red cloud.

Lying down, Speedwell pulled his cloak around him as much in comfort as to keep himself warm, to eventually fall into a troubled sleep.

Vivid pictures entered his mind in a nightmare setting, to haunt Speedwell's sleep.

Everything he could see was soaked in blood; trees, bushes, flowers, grass, the very earth itself. Nothing was left untouched; the forests were bleeding to death!

Animals were drinking from a blood-red pool and turning into malevolent beasts; saliva dripping from hanging mouths ready to devour their freshly killed prey, whilst eyes of burning yellow searched for their next victim. All the time he was watching this horror unfold, he could hear cold mocking laughter taunting him from behind.

Speedwell woke with a yelling jolt. "NO!" he cried, wiping his sweating brow with the horrible realisation that his nightmare was going to become reality if he did not stop the poisonous red cloud.

Sitting by the little pool, Speedwell dipped his rune staff into its still waters once more and called to the pool's essence. She came straight away, with worry in her voice.

Speedwell, my sister, is she…?

I did not feel her presence and her song was not to be heard, but in my haste to get out of there my senses were overshadowed by my fear to have felt anything. I am sorry, apologised Speedwell.

Do not be, Speedwell, you are braver than I, admitted the pool's essence, bubbling with tears for her sister.

What did you find there to make you fearful? asked the little pool's essence, not really wanting to know but needing to, for Speedwell to feel almost too ashamed to say.

It was my daughter Helistra. She has returned with the broken rune staff of Grimstone's within her power. The essence felt the same heartache that Speedwell was going through as she was feeling for her sister.

What has she done? An answer she knew she would not like hearing.

Poisoned your sister's pool with a ferociousness I have never seen before, and it is on its way here to destroy the Plateau Forest, unless I stop it, warned Speedwell.

The little pool's essence wailed in anguish at her sister's plight. Speedwell could only bow his head.

I am sorry for the hurt I have caused you, but it will be nothing if I do not stop this abomination that threatens us, worried Speedwell.

It is not your fault, Speedwell, that your daughter's mind has turned evil. It is of her own making, not yours, pointed out the little pool's essence, hearing the blame Speedwell was putting upon himself.

The little pool's essence sadly drifted away to find a safe hiding place, leaving Speedwell with some more of her tiny bubbles of life before she parted.

Speedwell had never felt so empty-hearted, not only in sadness for the essence of the little pool, but with the thought that he was going to have to confront his own daughter. He knew, though, that he could not show any weakness; otherwise, it would be his downfall.

He had not even noticed that daylight was beginning to spread itself across the valley, a grey dawn to match his mood.

Speedwell thought of mixing another cleansing potion, but instead bottled the life-giving bubbles and put them away in his pouch. He was fully rested and could feel the cleansing potion still working inside him.

He would not get caught out again. There was no need to take his presence into the poisonous red cloud this time; he knew what he was up against. He would cast his spell and watch it destroy his daughter's evil. He was the Keeper of the Forest and he was not going to let anything happen to it!.

Speedwell stood over the little pool, breathing in the cold morning air, looking around at the beauty of the snow-covered forest before closing his eyes to concentrate upon his spell.

Speedwell's fingers touched the runes upon his staff as if playing a tune, to instantly set his rune staff humming. Speedwell began chanting and joined his rune staff, creating a rhythmical sound that vibrated through the snow-covered forest.

Suddenly his rune staff turned into blue ice fire and began to form a circle of blue cloud around it. Slowly the blue cloud grew, becoming denser and denser as it did so. Blue ice fire began joining the blue cloud in hissing streaks of blue fire, entwining itself within it.

Speedwell's chant changed, making the blue cloud react. It started to spin faster, with streaks of blue flame shooting out of its sides. The blue cloud grew bigger still, becoming ever denser as the weave of his spell grew in potency.

Speedwell opened his eyes and saw his spell was ready. By now, he was immersed inside the spinning blue cloud, lost to sight as it crackled with power.

Speedwell stopped chanting, for his rune staff to follow as he held it over the little pool. The wind from the swirling blue cloud formed a dip in the little pond as it hovered above it, waiting.

"May the Ancient One give me the strength to finish this!" called Speedwell, and touching another symbol, he cast the blue cloud into the little pool.

The blue cloud shot through the water, with Speedwell's presence following.

As Speedwell's presence approached the sister pool once more, he started to feel uncomfortable; something felt different.

Then there before him, shielding the poisonous red cloud, was a sheer red wall of malice!

Volatile venom crackled and fizzed within it, spitting dense red flames of poison, ready to consume anything that got in its way.

Its ferocity took Speedwell aback; he had never seen anything like it. Whilst he was resting, she had seized the moment and cast this malevolent spell in front of the poisonous red cloud, knowing he would try to stop her. Her evil knew no limit, he thought, but there was no stopping now.

Speedwell threw the cloud of blue ice fire at the red wall of malice, hoping it would punch through it and reach into the poisonous red cloud.

It hurtled into it, causing a shock wave as the two collided, with tremors running through the earth up into the Kavenmist Mountains, but the red wall of malice held firm.

Instead, a solid wall of thick blue ice instantly formed across the path of the red wall of malice as it hit it, freezing the venom it had invaded then searing it with blue flame.

At first, the blue ice fire had the upper hand, such was the intensity with which it had hit the red wall of malice, but the malice began regenerating itself, pushing back the blue ice fire with dense red poison that spat out in flames of red, covering the blue ice fire before it could do anything, consuming it until there was nothing left.

So the battle between the two spells raged throughout the day, with both spells able to renew themselves as they fought each other, whilst the water hissed at the constant freezing and burning.

Speedwell watched the wall of malice holding its ground against his blue ice fire, keeping his spell at bay from the red cloud of poison, for Speedwell to finally withdraw his presence, deciding he needed help.

The malevolence she had cast was proving difficult to break down, making him realise he could not defeat Helistra on his own.

He would cast a spell of containment to block the underground waterway as a precaution, to give him the time he needed to seek out the Ancient One's advice, he thought.

Dipping the tip of his rune staff in the little pool, he called once more to the pool's essence.

I must go and seek help, Speedwell informed the essence as she joined him.

When will you return? she worried.

As soon as I can, but you must stay hidden, warned Speedwell.

Perhaps that is what my sister has done. That is why you could not feel her, spoke the little pool's essence in hope.

I am sure that is what she has done. She would know where to go, replied Speedwell, hoping that was the case also. *Hide well. I am going to cast a spell of containment before I go, to make sure the poison does not get through,* informed Speedwell further, to assure her.

I will. Hurry back, Speedwell, sighed the essence, and she parted for the last time to find a place of safety. Speedwell watched her as she departed, listening to her sobs of loneliness at her not knowing of her sister's plight. He wished he could have done more.

Speedwell closed his eyes once more, to repeat his spell of blue ice fire to contain the poisonous red cloud and its wall of malice, feeling the battle beyond still raging as he began touching the symbols on his rune staff.

This time, when Speedwell had finished chanting and opened his eyes, it was with satisfaction at seeing a much tighter weave within his spell. It was going to be needed, he thought. No loose streaks of blue flame showed themselves as the blue cloud spun around him. It glowed in blue power, ready to seal the underground waterway.

Its touch would freeze the waterway solid with lines of blue flame held ready to sear any poison, but Speedwell already knew it would only last so long.

He had not said anything to the essence, but he had watched how the wall of malice had regenerated itself compared to his spell. It had been slow at first but had gained momentum as the battle wore on. It was only a matter of time before it wore down his spell, making him realise how much stronger his daughter had become, hence him blocking the waterway completely.

Speedwell pointed his rune staff downwards and sent the blue cloud spinning its way into the little pool.

Leaving enough water for the animals to drink, the cloud of blue ice fire formed a continuous barrier of frozen water behind it as it sped through the underground waterway.

Having froze everything in its path with lines of waiting blue flame throughout, Speedwell's spell shot into the red wall of malice, trying to breach it once more.

Spearing itself into the red wall, the blue ice fire found itself closed in upon immediately, to set the underground waterway alight with their colours of burning blue and red as the battle began anew.

Speedwell could do no more and made himself ready to seek counsel with the Ancient One.

Nighttime had started to fall over the valley with snow just beginning to fall as Speedwell took one last lingering look at the little pool that had nearly claimed his life, before pulling his hood over his head and walking away into the night, deep in thought.

All returned to as it was before, to a little pool in the middle of the forest for animals to drink from, as if nothing had ever happened.

Only beneath the little pool could the story be told, as a cold, frightened essence hid in a fissure in the rock, away from the frozen barrier, wondering what fate awaited her.

CHAPTER XVI

"Has the wind changed direction? I can smell him again," said Girvan as he asked his horse to trot forward, with Tarbor doing likewise, to get in front of the wagon that carried Brax's body.

"Is it your turn to take hold of these reins then, Girvan, and put up with the smell for the rest of the day?" chortled Idrig, who sat next to Sergeant Urchel on the wagon.

"Er, I do not think so, Idrig. When it is, then I will," replied Girvan, attempting to tie his kerchief even tighter over his nose.

Tarbor and Girvan had duly reported to Sergeant Urchel to escort Brax's body back to Slevenport the following day, after King Taliskar had stripped Tarbor of his captaincy.

Sergeant Urchel had found out himself much to his surprise from a smirking Captain Wardine that they were going to join him and Idrig on their journey, or as Wardine had told him, "King Taliskar wants them out of his sight!"

Sergeant Urchel was glad they were travelling with him; they were all old friends, but nothing had been mentioned as to why they had been put with him. He had not asked, feeling it was not his place to. He only knew Tarbor and Girvan as men you could trust, so he was puzzled as to what had happened.

As for Idrig, he was another old trusted friend, a farmer before the call, like Urchel himself.

They had first met at Fenby cattle market, bidding for the same herd of cows. It became a natural meeting place for them both, with Idrig's farm being in Cardronia and Urchel's in Waunarle.

Their farms were waiting for them both when this was all over, which they both hoped was soon, now that Tiggannia had fallen with the taking of Stormhaven.

You could see why Urchel had asked for Idrig to be with him not just as a friend, but as someone who even he would not like to meet in battle, towering over them all as he did.

Tarbor looked up at the sky closing in upon them, but not before looking behind him once more for the umpteenth time.

"Will you stop that! You are beginning to make the horses nervous, let alone me," remarked Girvan, seeing his friend.

"I am sorry, Girvan. I keep expecting someone to be behind us. Taliskar only wanted us out of the way so it would look better for him if we happened to meet our fate elsewhere. I should have gone after the baby Prince, not stay here. What had I to lose?" reflected Tarbor, still haunted by the pleading look Queen Elina had given him.

"You have just avoided being in shackles for the rest of your days, Tarbor. You will sign your own death warrant, for sure, and mine at that if you do not forget that path," warned Girvan.

"You know there is only one person whom Taliskar would ask to carry out such a deed against you. Wardine, and he will be a good day or more ahead of us by now after the baby Prince, so forget looking behind you. Instead, let us get this journey over with. Then we can go and ask my father about your sword, the defender," advised Girvan.

"You are right, Girvan, it is too late now to do anything, there is enough to think on. I will deal with Wardine if the time comes," promised Tarbor to himself, and he turned to Urchel.

"We could rest here the night, Urchel," he called, having seen a reasonable piece of flat ground in between the scrub just ahead.

The ground behind it sloped upwards sufficiently to give some shelter from the wind that had been constant that day. Urchel nodded back gladly; the cold was starting to get to him just sitting there on the wagon.

Urchel jumped down and started to stamp his feet on the snow-laden ground, to get some life back into his body.

Idrig reached back into the wagon to get some of the wood they had brought with them for a fire, before jumping down himself. "I will soon get some life back in that body of yours." He smiled at Urchel and began making a fire.

"Three days and the River Dale still travels with us," remarked Urchel, watching the mist coming off the river in the distance, bringing with it more winter chill.

"I think he will be rotted away by the time we get to Slevenport," said Girvan, tying his horse to a nearby bush, away from the smell that had caught his breath once more.

"It is no different from finding cattle dead in the fields," pointed out Idrig, making Girvan's stomach turn at the thought.

"It will be some time before we see Stormhaven again," said Girvan thoughtfully, whilst taking off his horse's saddle.

"I cannot say I will be sorry, the further away the better," said Tarbor as he thought of Queen Helistra.

The small group settled down around the warm fire Idrig had made as the grey sky began turning into nighttime above them.

Idrig was stirring some vegetables to make a broth in a crude pot over the fire when he suddenly looked up. "I hear horses approaching," he informed the others.

Tarbor could not help but think of Wardine as he stood, to stare down the darkening road.

Two horses and their riders could just be seen as they came into view, set against the snow.

"Who rides this road?" called Tarbor.

"Two Cardronian guards from Kelmsmere, Tarbor," came a knowing and familiar voice to Tarbor's ears, making him try to think who it was.

"You do not recognise me after all this time?" said one of the riders as he dismounted his horse, to stand in front of Tarbor with a broad grin.

"Tarril! I cannot believe it, how long has it been?" Tarbor grinned and gave Tarril a soldier's embrace.

"We trained together at Ardriss... is it four years ago now, Tarril?" Tarbor tried to recollect.

"No, five, your memory was never that good," quipped Tarril to laughter. "This is my comrade Cillan." Tarril introduced his companion, to Tarbor's nodded acknowledgement.

"Come, warm yourselves around our fire," Tarbor said with a smile, and after they had tied up their horses they gratefully joined them all to thaw out cold bodies.

"What brings you down this road?" Tarbor said, smiling, as they all tucked into Idrig's warming broth.

"We are riding to Stormhaven from Kelmsmere," said Tarril, getting Tarbor's attention at hearing Kelmsmere mentioned.

"From Kelmsmere, you say, Tarril?" asked Tarbor, wondering if he had seen or heard anything. He was to hear more than he expected as Tarril explained what had happened back in Kelmsmere.

All listened to what Tarril had to say: "I was not about to show myself. I had no idea as to what had happened to my comrades, so I thought it best to report what I had witnessed at Stormhaven," he finished.

"You could have tracked them to see where they were headed for then reported back," suggested Girvan.

"There was no need, I already know where they will be heading," replied Tarril assuredly as he finished off his broth.

"You do!" said Tarbor and Girvan together.

"Yes, Permellar has a small farm in Marchend's East Valley, they will go there." Tarril smiled confidently.

"How do you know she has?" asked Girvan.

"I have ears for listening," Tarril replied as he looked at Tarbor and Girvan looking at him. "Is there something I should know?" he asked, seeing their expressions.

Tarbor explained about the final day of the siege, how the two Tiggannians had escaped with the baby Prince, whilst not revealing his experience when he touched the mountain rock, and the thoughts of Girvan about his sword.

Tarril and Cillan listened to Tarbor in fascination. Urchel and Idrig listened just as intently, even though they had heard it from Tarbor already, along with his feelings about it all.

"He opened a mountain door, Tarbor! How is that possible?" questioned Tarril straight away, after Tarbor had finished.

"I do not know, Tarril. Even Brax who lyes in that wagon thought it was sorcery. King Taliskar told us Queen Helistra had gained the knowledge of it from a wise man on her travels and when he asked in his mind for it to open, it did! We were there and still cannot believe it!" Tarbor admitted, to receive looks of disbelief.

"I do not like the sound of sorcery," remarked Cillan, to no one in particular.

"And I thought they were freeing Druimar because he was a blacksmith helping us, when all the time they needed Permellar," said Tarril, able now to understand what he had seen.

"So you are no longer a Captain because you refused to kill the baby Prince, and that is why you are here," said Cillan, for Tarbor to look at him twice.

He had a leather-like face, with eyes that had seen hardship. "It is, Cillan," he answered.

"I would have done the same," he stated without hesitation.

"Are you sure it is not the bump on your head you received that is talking!" mocked Tarril.

Cillan smiled; he was used to Tarril by now. "I was the lucky one. They were protecting their future King," he said simply.

"Have you seen Wardine and his men on the road to tell them what you have told us, Tarril?" asked Tarbor, wondering.

"Oh, I remember him, shifty-looking, his eyes never stayed still. Ah, he is doing what you refused to do," understood Tarril.

"No, Tarbor, we have come across no one, only you," replied Tarril, for Tarbor to frown.

"There are two roads out of Kelmsmere to get to Stormhaven, both are as long," said Tarril, seeing Tarbor's expression. "We came around the Demeral Hills, past Lake Morutaine," he added.

Tarbor had forgotten with all that was going on in his head. "Of course, round or over the Demeral Hills," he remembered.

"Going back over the hills, you come to a fork in the road to go to either Kelmsmere or Chasewater," pointed out Cillan.

"Wardine must be heading for Chiltree or Gressby. He would consider Kelmsmere a waste of time and try to get in front of them, trying to make up ground," said Girvan thoughtfully.

"How would he know where to go? He does not have my knowledge," pointed out Tarril.

"That is true, but he could gamble on them going to Elishard for help. We have heard talk that King Stowlan is not without feelings for

Tiggannia," said Tarbor, thinking it through.

"And Gressby is the junction where you can go to Elishard or Marchend," added Girvan, for them both to get a frown from Tarril.

"Why should any of this concern you? It has been taken out of your hands. You are escorting Brax's body back to Waunarle," queried Tarril.

"I… I have my reasons, but now is not the time. I have already said more than enough, enough to put you all at peril. Besides, you would think of me as being mad if I told you," explained Tarbor, trying to smile it away as Tarril gave him an enquiring look.

"Try me," was all Tarril said as all eyes were on Tarbor, waiting.

"I know you, Tarbor, whatever it is has been on your mind ever since we began this journey. You are our friend. If something is troubling you then we want to help," said Urchel, to Idrig's nod.

Tarbor looked at Girvan, who shrugged his shoulders, leaving it up to him.

Putting his empty bowl down, Tarbor looked into the fire and began telling them what he had felt at Stormhaven, about his sword and finally what Queen Elina had told him, but not what she had asked of him.

"She is keeping the Princess alive for her own ends, of that there is no doubt in my mind, and I think her brother could be the answer to saving her from Queen Helistra's evil," said Tarbor, revealing his thoughts. "She is a darkness looming over all of the Kingdoms," finished Tarbor, to see bewildered faces once more looking back at him.

"Well, you said it, Tarbor, mad! I have never heard anything like it in all of my days," blew Tarril.

"I know how I sound. Nothing makes sense to me, but I feel there is a connection to it all in there somewhere, but what it is I do not know," admitted Tarbor.

"This voice you heard telling you to find Speedwell, if it is true, where would you begin?" asked Urchel.

"It is true as I am here before you, Urchel, but where to begin, I do not know," Tarbor admitted.

"If your sword, that you say is a defender, was made in the Great Forest then that is where I would start," answered Cillan, to the blinks of everyone else, except Tarbor and Girvan.

"You are right, it was made by the children of the forest, but that was hundreds of years ago. No one lives that long," said Girvan, to get further looks himself.

"That will present no problem then, to go into the vastness of the Great Forest, where no one dares roam, and look for a man called Speedwell who is hundreds of years old, because a voice from a rock spoke to you!" scoffed Tarril in disbelief at the nonsense he was hearing.

"You are right to ridicule me, Tarril. I would feel the same way, but if you take anything with you from what I have said then be wary when you report to King Taliskar or Queen Helistra!" warned Tarbor.

Idrig had been quiet whilst trying to think before he spoke. "You mean to go after the child?" he asked, simply for Girvan to reply, not helping himself.

"I have told him not to, Idrig. If the Tiggannians do not kill him then he will have opened the door for Wardine to do so."

"You would be playing straight into King Taliskar's hands if you did!" added Urchel, agreeing.

"I already have, Urchel, by refusing to kill the Prince in the first place," Tarbor half smiled in frustration at how he felt, "but he is part of a puzzle in my mind that I cannot put together, and if I have any hope of doing so then he needs to be alive," stated Tarbor, trying to convince himself more than the others.

"Can I look at your sword?" asked Idrig, suddenly holding out his hand.

Tarbor gave Idrig his sword for him to look at its blade in the light of the fire. He looked at the two wavy lines on each side of the pommel and then gave the sword back to Tarbor.

"It is a sword of quality unlike any I have seen before. Were you going to see your father, Girvan? He is a blacksmith in Slevenport, where we are going, if I remember," enquired Idrig.

"We were, it is my father who told me the story about the defenders, but Tarbor, I think, has made up his mind as to what is more important, although I have to admit when I heard Queen Elina—" Before he could say anything more, Girvan was cut dead by Tarril.

"Ah, now we come to it. Here is the real reason why you could not go through with it: Queen Elina. I might have known. All this rubbish you are talking when really all you want to do is rescue the child because you are taken with her!" exploded Tarril. He had heard enough and got up to lay under the wagon, despite the smell.

Tarbor did not know where to put himself; part of it, he knew, was true. "I am sorry, Tarbor, me and my mouth," apologised Girvan.

"It is not your fault, Girvan," said Tarbor, sighing.

"What I was going to say was," continued Idrig, ignoring Tarril, "it is going to take us well into the month of winds before we reach Slevenport. By then, you could have rescued the Prince and met back up with us in Fenby, where we can wait for you. We were going to stop there for a couple of days anyway," said Idrig, making it all sound so simple.

"One other thing that has crossed my mind is that Druimar is also a blacksmith, like your father, Girvan. Perhaps he has heard of these swords of old and can help you, not that you could not see your father afterwards," said Idrig, smiling.

Tarbor had to look twice at Idrig; he made it sound all so straightforward. If only his mind was like that right now, he thought.

"What of the blacksmith, Idrig? His wife, daughter and granddaughter, they have to be considered," pointed out Urchel.

Idrig just looked at his friend, shaking his head. "Urchel, are you not listening? They have a farm on the other side of Marchend Valley to me. As his daughter seems to be looking after the Prince already with her child, what better place could there be to hide him? They are already a family. Who would know? Cillan and Tarril are not going to say anything, are you, Tarril?" boomed Idrig suddenly, over his shoulder.

"No, Idrig, nothing will pass my lips. He is still my friend, no matter what I think," came a quiet reply from under the wagon.

"We will take heed of your warning of Queen Helistra and be on our guard when we get to Stormhaven," promised Cillan.

"Only the Tiggannians to worry about then. I had better come with you," said Girvan with a smile, resigned to the fact that this was what Tabor wanted to do all along, no matter what he thought.

Tarbor could only slap his good friend on the back and smile at Idrig. He had sorted it all out without so much as a worry in his voice.

"I will not forget this, risking yourselves for a madman." Tarbor smiled and looked around at Tarril, who could only shake his head, thinking Tarbor was a good man but his head was full of rubbish.

Pulling his cloak around him to ward off the cold, Tarbor settled down by the fire with the defender by his side, resting his arm over its blade and hilt, ready for any surprises.

He drifted into a sleep of troubled dreams that began to disturb him. He dreamt that he was floating in the air, drifting aimlessly with darkness all around him.

Then through the darkness a pool of crystal clear water shone out to him. A whispered name was coming from it, but he could not catch what it was.

Suddenly the crystal clear pool started turning cloudy and reached up towards him, swallowing him into its depths.

He could only watch as the cloudy water became the colour of blood-red all around him. He tried to swim for the surface to break free of its hold, but he was somehow being held down. He struggled to breathe as he felt the breath of life being squeezed out of him.

Then out of nowhere came a bolt of blue flame piercing through the red water, releasing him, throwing him out of the pool.

Tarbor woke, gasping for air as the ground suddenly shook beneath him.

The dawn was still in the making as all were stirred from their sleep by the tremors beneath them. Idrig managed to stir some life back into the fire from its embers, catching everyone's faces looking full of foreboding in the grey of the dawn.

"What is that?" said Girvan, trying to get to his feet as the ground shook.

"The mountains are displeased," said Cillan, looking around him.

"What makes you say that?" asked Urchel, frowning.

"Blood has been spilt in their presence and has seeped through the rock down into their midst. It is their way of telling us it was wrong," worried Cillan.

"You run deep sometimes," said Tarril, whilst Tarbor could only see a pool full of blood from his dream as Cillan said it.

Not dwelling on what had just happened, it was not long before all were ready to travel and go their separate ways.

"I must admit you have been beyond me, Tarbor, with all that goes on in that mind of yours, but I would trust you with my life," Urchel said with a smile.

"Thank you, Urchel," Tarbor said, smiling, gripping Urchel's hand in farewell.

"We will meet in Fenby in the month of winds, and if by chance you travel through Marchend to the Western Valley, drop in to see my brother Vartig. There will always be a good meal there waiting for you," Idrig said, grinning.

"What would I do without friends like you, Idrig?" said Tarbor, thanking Idrig for his understanding. "Is Vartig like you?" He had to ask.

"He is my twin!" said Idrig, laughing.

"I will recognise him then!" Tarbor laughed with him.

"I am sorry, Tarbor. I should not have lost my patience with you. You did always tell the truth, but what you have told us this last night is hard for me to digest. Nevertheless, I will keep my wits about me," promised Tarril.

"That is all I can ask for," said Tarbor, smiling.

"Quite a first meeting." Cillan smiled, gripping Tarbor's wrist in a soldier's farewell.

"To think only a week or so ago, I was like you, Cillan, just an ordinary soldier doing his duty, and then I entered Stormhaven, for it all to change," recollected Tarbor as he looked at Cillan.

"Watch him in there, Cillan. I remember how he used to always be the inquisitive one. Mind what you say and do, you cannot trust her," warned Tarbor once again.

"Do not worry. I will watch him, and you are right. He has not changed," said Cillan with a nod.

Goodbyes said, Tarbor and Girvan mounted their horses to wave farewell as they urged their horses into motion. The small company watched them go before they parted their ways as the breeze brought a familiar odour to their noses.

"I hope that is not a sign of what is to come," said Cillan with a shudder, as if the earth's tremble had only just reached him.

CHAPTER XVII

"That old man has stopped me from reaching the forest!" cursed Queen Helistra, for humming to enter her head. "He may have only delayed the poison, but till when!" she shouted, irritated.

She stood tapping her fingers in frustration on the balcony of the ceremonial room as she watched two riders enter Middle Gate through the snowfall.

Her annoyance had lasted for days since Speedwell's presence had confronted her when she was adding to the poison in the crystal chamber.

She had been annoyed enough when her powers were interfered with from a simple bloodshot eye, but this!

Her poison spell was much slower than she had hoped for, as it built up its venom journeying to the Plateau Forest, but now it was almost at a standstill as it battled against his spell of blue ice fire, even though she had released a wall of malice to drive the blue ice fire back.

"He has sealed the pool right through to the forest," she raged, "now is the time whilst it is winter that the forests are at their weakest. It will be spring if not summer by the time my venom gets through!" she spat, still shouting, as the humming tried once more to calm her down and get her to listen to what it had to say.

"What? What is it? I do listen! What is it then you wish to say?" she asked in her anger, to hear the humming's own frustrations at her for not controlling her emotions, telling her in no uncertain terms.

Queen Helistra heard an anger and impatience in the tone of the humming that she had not heard before. Her own emotions seemed to be having an effect upon it, she thought. She needed to heed its warning and refocus her mind.

"I know my impatience and vanity will be my undoing if I do not keep it under control. You are right, we need to keep the bond strong and my anger is not helping. It is together that we can achieve everything. I am sorry, I bow to your greater wisdom," she apologised.

Clearing the anger that was clouding her mind, she paid attention to what the humming had to say. The humming then spoke to her of a way they could penetrate the blue ice fire more quickly.

"They will? You have? No, I did not feel it, but with fresh soul blood you say it will break, but whose?" An obvious answer came from the humming. "Of course, who else!" She grinned. The time for her games was over… it hummed… it was time for her to rule all that she surveyed!

Tarril and Cillan dismounted their horses without taking their eyes off Forest Tower.

"It loses itself into the mountain," said Cillan as they looked up. Tarril thought he saw someone disappear from a balcony right at the top, but was not sure through the falling snow.

"I think we will report after finding the kitchen, Cillan!" said Tarril with a smile,

"A good idea." Cillan smiled back, his stomach rumbling in agreement.

King Taliskar sat in front of the fire with a cup of wine in his hand. He had taken to a small room off the main corridor and was sitting there with thoughts of further conquests. King of the five Kingdoms, he was thinking, then his Queen would be right: he would be King of all he surveyed! A knock on the door interrupted his smile.

"Enter!" A guard opened the door and in walked Cillan and a full-bellied Tarril, from Mrs Beeworthy's cooking.

King Taliskar looked at them both with a frown. "Two guards reporting from Kelmsmere, sire," announced the guard, for King Taliskar to wave him away with a nod.

He stood up and poured himself another cup of wine. "Well, what is it you wish to see me about?" he asked as they stood there.

"We come from Kelmsmere, sire," began Tarril.

"I think that is what my guard has just said, get on with it," said King Taliskar, sounding tired as he slumped back down in the chair.

Tarril quickly explained what he had seen in Kelmsmere. "That was seven days ago, sire," said Tarril, finishing his account.

"I see. Do you have any idea as to their destination?" asked King Taliskar, finishing his wine as Cillan glanced at Tarril.

"No, sire," lied Tarril.

"And have you?" asked King Taliskar, seeing Cillan's glance.

"No, sire, I confronted them, but they rendered me unconscious," answered Cillan truthfully.

King Taliskar looked at him and Tarril. Two guards of little intelligence, he thought, guard duty was about right for them. He was feeling lenient after a cup or two of wine. There was no point in punishing them for letting them slip through their fingers, he thought, and poured himself some more wine.

Not that he was worried about the baby Prince anymore; he had his spies everywhere and Wardine had his orders, he thought. They would be easier to catch now they were in a wagon, and the women would slow them down, he thought with a smile, straight into Wardine's eager hands.

"Is there anything else?" asked King Taliskar, gulping down another mouthful of wine. Tarril was going to say that they had come across Tarbor escorting Brax's body, but thought better of it. There was no need; he could see what interested King Taliskar. Was this really a mover of mountains? he thought.

"No, sire."

"Very well, you are dismissed," gestured King Taliskar, waving his hand, and with a bow they left King Taliskar to his wine.

"You decided to keep your word to Tarbor then, Tarril," whispered Cillan as they walked down the corridor.

"His life hangs by a piece of string for what he is about to try and do. He does not need me to add to it," answered Tarril. "I still remain sceptical as to what he told us, but it does not surprise me that he refused to kill the child, after seeing King Taliskar like that. How he opened a door in the mountain is beyond me," he pondered.

"No, but Tarbor did talk of sorcery and that it was Queen Helistra we should be wary of," Cillan reminded Tarril, to hear him utter a "hmm," sufficient for Cillan to know his comrade's inquisitive nature was going to take over once more.

King Taliskar's thoughts returned to being King of the five Kingdoms as he sat there in the warm glow of the fire. With the added glow of wine inside him, he was soon asleep in the chair.

The night drew in and Stormhaven watched silently as the snow continued to fall.

The door opened to the small room where King Taliskar still dozed, and in walked Queen Helistra. She looked at him sleeping there, to a humming in her mind. "I know, I have wasted too much time on him," and she shook him awake.

King Taliskar struggled to open his eyes and smiled sillily when he realised who it was. Standing up clumsily, to nearly fall over, he felt the wine lying heavy in his head.

"My love, you caught me resting," he said whimsically, with his silly smile.

"I do seem to have caught you at an inopportune moment, but there is something I would like to show you, come," and she held out her hand for his with a smile.

Holding his hand, Queen Helistra led him to his favourite place: the mountain throne room.

She sat on the mountain throne with the odd-shaped hole in its arm and watched King Taliskar fall into the other mountain throne, to look at her with his silly smile.

"Drink seems to have overcome you these last days, my love," she mused, seeing the future he was shaping for himself.

"There is not much else to do, my love, with winter all around us," he said with a smile.

No, there is nothing more for you to do, she thought.

"Why have you brought me here anyway, my love?" he asked, sitting back, closing his eyes, picturing the crown on his head as he did so.

"The power you have now is nothing compared to what you are going to see. It is a power beyond your wildest dreams. This place hides a secret and I am going to show you what it is." She smiled, luring King Taliskar's eyes open at her words, catching his attention.

"What do you mean, my love? What secret?" he asked with interest, managing to sit more upright.

Without replying, Queen Helistra put the broken rune staff into the hole in the arm of the mountain throne, to see an instant frown from King Taliskar.

She smiled at the look on his face as his eyes nearly popped out when the different colours displayed themselves all around the mountain throne room, but when the sound of clicks came to his ears and the mountain throne she was sitting on began to move forward, revealing steps, his face dropped.

His eyes widened as he looked at her looking at him, and suddenly the mountain door came into his mind.

"Come," she said with a smile, and King Taliskar got up unsteadily onto his feet, but it was not the drink this time.

Down the steps into the darkness they descended, guided by a pale white light.

For the first time, King Taliskar realised all was not as it seemed with his Queen. "What is that you have always carried so close to you?" he asked, seeing the pale light emanating from the broken rune staff. "It is not just an ancient symbol of justice, is it?"

"What, this? My broken stick with crude markings upon it," she chided, for King Taliskar to wince at hearing what he had thought about it.

"No, you are right, my love. It is much more, the key to everything," she said with a smile, "it is a rune staff, an ancient symbol of power that is held by the Keepers of the forests, the Forestalls, except for this one that has come into my possession," she answered, letting her fingers stroke its symbols.

King Taliskar detected a bitterness in her voice as she spoke of the Forestalls. "Is that because it is broken?" he said thoughtfully, thinking that was how she had come by it.

"In a way, yes," *and you are going to find out how it broke.* She smiled to herself.

King Taliskar was none the wiser as a cold inevitable feeling started to come over him as they continued to go down the steps that seemed to go on forever under Stormhaven.

By the time they had reached a long, dark passageway, his heart was in his mouth and sweat was stinging his eyes.

Then there in front of him was a strange red glow, and as he came to its source, he could only stand and stare.

He stood there open-mouthed, looking at the crystals that adorned the chamber, which were vibrating in happiness at feeling the presence of the broken rune staff once more, glowing pure red.

"What is this place?" he asked with a voice that nearly croaked at seeing the red crystals glittering back at him, whilst their power vibrated through his body.

"An ancient power, one of legend," said Queen Helistra with a smile, moving forward, "but this is what I wanted to show you, the life force that flows to the forest."

Queen Helistra stood next to the little pool with her hand outstretched as King Taliskar hesitantly moved forward to where she was and looked.

A little pool whose water ran red, blood-red, he thought, to make him shudder. He saw how it shimmered and moved to the vibration of the crystals as he stared into the pool, but what was that? He thought he caught a glimpse of red and blue flashes coming from deeper within the pool. What were they?

"A battle rages within the pool," she answered, as if she could read his mind, "one that I am winning, but I need to hurry things along," she said matter-of-factly, moving close to his side. "That is where you come in," she whispered in his ear, for King Taliskar to hear his heart beat faster.

"This little pool runs all the way to the Great Plateau Forest where its sister pool lies. Once I have won the battle, my poison will lay it to waste! The Great Forest will follow and then, well, I will see if it pleases me or not to leave the five Kingdoms be," she said with a grin. "It will all be destroyed. The Ancient One, its Keepers, nothing will be in my way and then I… I alone will have the power to rule all!" she crowed, looking coldly straight into King Taliskar's eyes as she did so.

Though King Taliskar did not know what she was on about, it did not matter; he saw his life was at an end in that moment.

As she looked at him, he blinked, and suddenly his mind became clear, seeing it all. A sudden realisation of how his lust for power had been used to her advantage to get to this place. He had been so blinded by her beauty and charm that he had not seen her cunningness, but she had far more than that at her disposal, he was realising all too late.

Brax had been right all along, he thought. It was sorcery, and he had had no idea it was happening to him; such was her power.

He was no mover of mountains; it had been her all along, reaching into his mind in some way without him knowing.

He closed his eyes at his own pretentiousness. What a fool he had been. He sighed and opened them again to see her cold grin mocking him.

"I see now how you have played me for the fool with your sorcery, but all this deception to destroy the forests, why?" he queried, puzzled, even though death was literally staring him in the face and it did not matter.

Queen Helistra looked at him without any sense of emotion and drove the broken rune staff straight into his chest, making him scream in agony. "You will never know, you stupid little man!" She grinned and twisted the broken rune staff right through him.

Lifting him up as if he were lighter than a feather, Queen Helistra hung King Taliskar over the little pool like a toy doll.

He hung there barely conscious, with blood seeping through pain-ridden eyes. She smiled as humming entered her head. "Yes, tears of joy at being able to help us, how touching," she said with a smirk.

The broken rune staff dripped with King Taliskar's blood into the little pool as Queen Helistra began to chant, touching some of the exposed symbols along its length at the same time.

Humming joined her and together they began to make the crystals resonate in a deep droning sound, making the already blood-red crystals become even darker.

A finger moved to another symbol, releasing the soul blood from within the broken rune staff, for it to combine with King Taliskar's as they fell into the little pool, twisting around each other to bind tightly, creating a woven ball of venomous poison!

It rose to the surface of the little pool and began spinning in mid-air, for Queen Helistra to see concentrated globules of poison soaked into its weave.

A wind started to stir around the crystal chamber from the spinning poisonous ball as it span faster and faster.

As she felt it, Queen Helistra touched another symbol, for the crystals to react by reverberating even more to create a constant wall of sound.

The wind built from the poisonous ball and blew across the droning sound coming from the crystals to make a continuous threaded coil of energy.

Queen Helistra stopped chanting and stood firm, ready for the impending force that was about to surge through the broken rune staff; the spell was ready.

Before sending the poisonous ball into the little pool, she looked at King Taliskar's pain- stricken face with a grin; he was barely alive. "Goodbye, my love," she chirped, and with one cruel twist of the broken rune staff, she ended his pain, letting his body slide sickeningly off the broken rune staff into the little pool.

As his body sank to be no more, Queen Helistra touched one more symbol, sucking the combined power of sound and wind into the broken rune staff.

The combined energy flowed endlessly through the broken rune staff, testing it to its fullest as it condensed it into a dark mass before sending it into the poisonous ball.

As soon as the dark mass entered the poisonous ball, it crackled and glowed with power, before hurtling into the water like a whirlwind, to spin out of sight.

Queen Helistra's hair looked as if it was trying to follow as it was pulled by the force of the spell as she waited for the crystal chamber to return to normal, although it would never do so again, she thought with a smile.

Finally, all became still and her hair settled back into place as humming re-entered her mind. "I know. I felt its reaction also. We have misjudged how much power the crystal chamber holds. A fresh soul released in here must be worth thirty or more we have stored. Now let us see our spell at work," she urged in anticipation.

With that thought, Queen Helistra's presence watched the progress of the poisonous ball through the broken rune staff.

Immediately she saw how the venomous ball had smashed its way through the blue ice fire, leaving a gaping hole behind it as it spun through Speedwell's spell unperturbed.

The wall of malice and poisonous red cloud had been pulled into its wake by the power emanating from the poisonous ball's dark mass.

The blue ice fire was being shattered under the relentless force coming from the poisonous ball. The drone of the crystals that had been captured in the spell cracked and splintered the blue ice fire, whilst the wind within it drove the poisonous ball forward.

Poison shot into every fissure created by the poisonous ball, drowning the blue ice fire in venom, for the wall of malice to simply come along and mop up, searing all in red poisonous flames with a blood-quenching thirst, leaving the poisonous red cloud free to deliver its death call to the Plateau Forest.

Queen Helistra watched in silent rapture as her spell went through Speedwell's spell of containment as if it never existed.

Then the moment came for which she had waited all these years as the poisonous ball announced its arrival in the Great Plateau Forest as it flew out of the sister pool high into the sky to make its dark mass explode, with deadly globules of poison all over the nearby trees and bushes.

A deadly poisonous slime bled out from the globules in search of destruction, whilst the blood-red cloud turned the sister pool instantly red before soaking into the earth that surrounded it.

Snow began melting under the spreading blood-red poison, whilst trees and bushes began to feel the death grip of the thick poisonous slime as it started to eat away at their very being whilst they lay dormant in the grip of winter.

But then as the blood-red poison spread out further, it ran into the thick slime, to transform into a different death for the forest.

A mist began forming over the poison-soaked ground and from it grew strange-looking pods. They slowly opened to reveal spores inside that shot out everywhere, to inject poison into whatever they had attached themselves to.

Only the rocks were left untouched by the poison's destruction that had begun all around them.

A terrified essence was thankful that whatever evil it was had not touched the rock fissure she was in as it hissed past her, after smashing through the blue ice fire and then turning her pool blood– red.

She knew she could not stay here now for fear of her life, and reducing herself into minute bubbles, she left through the fissure she was in, along cracks that permeated the earth that only she knew about.

Queen Helistra's spirit was soaring when she returned her mind back to the crystal chamber. At last, her dream was coming true!

Her poisonous ball had gone through the blue ice fire like a firestorm burning through a forest! Making her smile at the thought of it.

She could not believe how much the crystals had increased the power of her spell. Her wall of malice and poisonous red cloud had been drawn into the path of her poisonous ball in the blink of her eye, delivering their death sting with results she had not foreseen, leaving her in a wave of euphoric bliss.

A humming brought her back from her elation. "Yes, it has begun at last," she said with a laugh, "there is no stopping it this time! By confronting us, he has played into our hands without even knowing it. We have gained knowledge of the crystal chamber to make us stronger, more so than even we realised could be possible, all because of him." She laughed like a child at it all.

"It is the beginning of the end for the forests!" She crooned for more humming to come to her. "We should rest, you are right, but let us not wait too long before we bring another!" She laughed in exhilaration.

Tarril had not been able to settle for the night. He was walking across the grand courtyard, looking up at Forest Tower.

Although it was late at night and the snow was bringing with it the cold chill of winter, Tarril's curiosity to explore had got the better of him once more. This was Stormhaven, the Keeper of the mountain thrones, something he had always wanted to see.

He could hear Tarbor's words of warning in his mind: *Be careful of what you say and do.* Well, he had been careful in what he had said and now all he was going to do was look around.

Now surely there was no harm in that, he thought; after all, it had saved his life in Kelmsmere!

As he had pointed out to Cillan, whom he had left snoring away in the soldiers' quarters. A boot across the face and a bang on the head had made no difference to him. Tarril smiled to himself as he entered the storeroom, where Tarbor said he had emerged coming through the mountain door.

Tarril found two guards fast asleep on the floor next to a brazier, whose fire was nothing more than an ember with torches blazing on the wall, showing the storeroom to be well stocked with goods. He found the back storeroom was the same once he had crept past the sleeping guards.

Then there it was in the corner, still open, the huge rock doorway that Tarbor had told him of! Tarril shook his head at such a thing happening, but he was looking at it!

He had asked the question when Tarbor had told him of its existence, and now standing here right next to it, he asked it again; how could this be possible?

Tarril put out his hand to touch it, hearing Tarbor's words of sorcery ring in his ears.

He looked beyond the mountain door but found himself not wanting to go any further, even for him. A grunt from one of the sleeping guards made his excuse for him. He had better not wake them, he thought.

He soon found himself walking along the corridor next to the great hall thinking there was a distinct lack of guards when suddenly the door opened to the room where he and Cillan had reported to.

He ducked from view into the recess of another doorway. Holding himself still, he chanced a glimpse to see King Taliskar being led by his hand by Queen Helistra. Only going to their chamber, he thought, but best keep out of sight.

As they disappeared around the corner, he thought of sneaking into the small room to chance a drink of wine and a quick warm, but the pull of seeing the mountain thrones was much stronger, and he crept up to the corner.

Peeking around the corner, he saw them disappear around one of the huge stone pillars at the base of Forest Tower and then heard a door being shut.

There was only one place they could have gone: where he wanted to go, the mountain throne room, he thought irritably.

He moved quietly towards the huge pillar and looked around it at the base of Forest Tower. There was the door to the mountain throne room, the spiral steps that led to the chambers and as his eyes looked back at the mountain throne room door, he saw the bloodstains on the stone floor.

Cillan's thoughts about the mountains not being pleased came into his mind, then Tarbor's account of the Tiggannians' last stand here, ending in the deaths of both Brax and King Rolfe.

He ought to get out of here, he thought, but how long would they be in there? Not that long, he thought. There were no guards to be seen; he would hide a few moments and wait for them to come out, he decided.

Tarril quickly looked around to see where he could hide without them spotting him but where he would be able to see them come out. Only the two huge fireplaces either side of the great hall offered any cover, and Tarril made a beeline for the far one.

No welcoming fire was lit; there was just cold grey stone as he hid in the shadow cast by one of the tall elaborate columns that enclosed the fire hearth.

As he waited, peeking now and again to see if they were coming out, he had the strangest of sensations. The whole of his body tingled and goosebumps ran through him from his toes to his fingertips.

He shook his body, thinking he was getting cold standing here. How long had he been waiting? He should go, he was being stupid, but wanting to see what was behind that door had got the better of him. When would he ever get an opportunity like this again? He thought and he waited.

Then, finally, Tarril heard the throne room door being opened and he slowly cast an eye around the fireplace column to see Queen Helistra come out on her own.

To Tarril, it looked as if she was giggling to herself as she suddenly looked into the great hall.

Tarril pressed hard against the stone wall, feeling she was looking straight in his direction. Where was King Taliskar? Still in there, he thought, cursing.

Hearing her footfall on the spiral steps, Tarril breathed easier and waited a moment longer for King Taliskar to come out.

When he did not appear, Tarril took a chance and made for the mountain throne room door to listen for him, but he could hear nothing. Was he just sitting in there?

Before Tarril had thought it through, he was turning the great wrought metal ring and opening the door to find no one was in there.

He stepped inside; there were the two mountain thrones looking back at him, making him go wide-eyed at their splendour.

Out of the corner of his eye, he caught something glittering in the torchlight, to make him look up and see the two golden crowns of Tiggannia lying on a rock shelf, but where was King Taliskar? He had come through the only way in or out of here; that was when something told him to get out of there! He should not have risked it!

He turned to go and nearly yelped in fright at who was standing there blocking his way out: Queen Helistra!

He had not heard a thing for her to be there as she stared at him, grinning. "Well, well, who have we here?" She kept grinning whilst closing the mountain throne room door.

Tarril could not speak; his mind emptied and his body drained of all feeling as his eyes fell upon the broken rune staff she was holding; its end was covered in blood!

CHAPTER XVIII

Screwing up his eyes, Kelmar looked out over to the other side of the snow-laden valley. They had reached the tip of Marchend's vast East Valley at last, where Permellar's small farm lay.

She had suggested they could all stay there, at least to see out winter, but Kelmar was not comfortable with the idea.

The guards they had left alive in Kelmsmere would have reported what had happened by now, and the first place they would come would be there, he had thought, although Permellar had been adamant that she had not given anything away about her farm whilst being held.

Kelmar had not doubted her word, but he knew that ears would have been listening, even if Permellar thought they were not.

So he had agreed they could go there, but only for a couple of days; they had to keep moving for the Prince's sake.

They had stopped in Walditch that morning for some much-needed supplies. Permellar had done the bargaining, whilst Druimar had supplied the labour.

Kelmar and Cantell had kept close to the wagon with their heads covered, whilst their eyes watched those around them. Though in the Kingdom of Balintium, they knew there would be certain eyes watching.

Now Kelmar's eyes were scanning the south side of the valley where another road ran as he drove the wagon, sitting next to Cantell, on the North Road.

Between the two roads ran the River Mid, shallow at this point at the beginning of the valley. Not that he could see much of the river, or the road for that matter, but with the sky a clear blue and not a cloud in sight, it held the valley in a serene stillness, helping him to see any movement there might be.

High above him and the valley, stretching as far as the eye could see, was the Great Forest, skirting the length of the southern hilltops like a guardian.

As he looked, Kelmar's thoughts wandered through the conversations they had all been having.

With time to sit around a campfire each night on their long journey, they had been telling each other their own stories.

Kelmar looked around into the back of the covered wagon, where his mother was having a rest with the two babies, who for the moment were quiet.

He could hear her exclamations in his mind when he had told of how he and Cantell had escaped with the baby Prince through the Kavenmist Mountains, Oh dear! Kelmar! Never! Cantell!

Looking back in front of him, he smiled to see Permellar and her father enjoying a rare ride together, remembering her story that was full of sadness.

She had told them of how news had been brought to her of her father being ill. So with her husband of only a year, Edwin, she had travelled to Kelmsmere to see him, bringing with her glad tidings of the impending birth.

It had been less than a month since they had arrived when a rider came into Kelmsmere announcing the news of the invasion at Stormhaven by the alliance force.

Panic had emptied half the town within a week, with some riding to Stormhaven never to return, but they had decided they would stay and look after her father.

That was when his mother and Druimar were married, just before the raiding parties started. Constantly, the alliance forces came looking for food and supplies, with any resistance met by force.

Until one day there was no more to give. They had taken all they had; there was barely enough to survive on for themselves. That was when they went house-to-house and laid everything to ruin.

Druimar had continued the story for Permellar, as the memory of it all became too painful for her, remembered Kelmar.

They had come to the forge and finding Druimar was the town's blacksmith, they had wanted him to start working the forge straight away, even though he had not fully recovered.

Edwin had tried to tell them this and received the hilt end of a sword in his face for his troubles, warning him to keep his nose out.

Permellar had gone to his aid, only to be manhandled away by one of them. Edwin had seen red and had pushed the soldier aside, but in doing so had paid the ultimate price.

Then it was as Kelmar and Cantell had found them: Druimar chained to his anvil whilst his mother and Permellar were servants to the Cardronian guards.

The birth of little Kayla being the only good thing to happen, but when Druimar had spoken of it, Permellar had broken down in tears with the thought that Edwin would never see his child.

"I think we have company, Kelmar," said Cantell, suddenly breaking Kelmar's recollections.

Kelmar looked to the south side of the valley and made out two horsemen, looking like dots against the snow.

"Keep your eye on them, Cantell. The valley is looking to widen here. We will see if they keep to their side." Cantell nodded.

"Druimar! Permellar!" They both looked around as Kelmar shouted to them, seeing a pointed finger telling them why.

A few moments later and Druimar was driving the wagon with Permellar inside; Kelmar and Cantell trading places to ride in front of the wagon.

"There is only the two of them, Kelmar. Nothing for us to fear," said Cantell, not really worried by the horsemen's appearance.

"You are right, but it is best we stay alert. It could be a scouting party," replied Kelmar.

"I do not think so, Kelmar, they are heading towards the river," answered Cantell, seeing the horsemen turn towards them.

Tarbor and Girvan had pushed their horses on as much as they dare. Riding and walking with them whilst resting in between. Days and nights blurring into one, to find the small party before Wardine did.

Tarbor drew in a deep breath when he saw the single covered wagon on the other side of the valley. "I hope that is them," said Girvan, scratching himself, "these cloaks we purchased in Gressby I swear are full of fleas. No wonder they were eager to sell them to us," he moaned, scratching himself once more.

"The sight of us dressed like this will go down better if we are to be deserters," put Tarbor, for Girvan to look at him. He had not given it a thought, but he supposed that is what they were by their actions.

The two of them rode down into the valley and across a shallow stony part of the River Mid up the other side through trees, until they eventually came across the valley's North Road.

They had come out further up the road to the small party, so they waited with bated breath until the two cloaked riders and covered wagon pulled up before them.

"Who are you that stops us from our journey?" spoke Kelmar first, his hand gripping the hilt of his sword, as did Cantell's.

"We are deserters from the Cardronian army meaning you no harm. I am Tarbor and this is Girvan," replied Tarbor calmly.

"Is that so? What has that got to do with you standing in our way?" questioned Kelmar, with a warning in his voice.

"We are not here to cross swords with you," continued Tarbor, unperturbed, "but to add ours to yours to help protect the baby Prince you carry," spoke up Tarbor, for Kelmar to look at him with mistrust in his eyes then at Cantell with a frown.

"There are soldiers on their way looking for you, to kill the child, and we wish to help you fight against them," Tarbor informed them, to looks of suspicion.

"How did you know where to find us?" asked Cantell, not hiding the fact of who they were. This Cardronian looked no fool, he thought.

"We met two of the guards on the road who had guarded the blacksmith and his daughter at Kelmsmere. They told us," replied Tarbor.

Kelmar heard his thoughts come true; a guard had heard Permellar.

"If you were already on the road, how do we know you are not part of those you speak of who hunt us?" challenged Cantell.

"You do not, you only have my word as a soldier, but we were escorting Brax's body to Slevenport at the time when we met them," Tarbor told them, to receive smiles.

"Are you saying Brax is dead?"

"Yes, he is," said Tarbor, but not saying how.

"The pig got what he deserved," said Kelmar, scowling and looked at Cantell.

"Best thing that could have happened to him, like those guards at Kelmsmere," added Cantell, to watch how Tarbor and Girvan would react.

Neither Tarbor nor Girvan rose to the bait. They had chosen their path by being here, no matter how strange a calling it had been; there was no turning back now.

"If what you say is true, why would you want to help a Tiggannian Prince?" asked Cantell, curious as to what Tarbor was about.

"There is more than one reason why we wish to safeguard the Prince, but you will not believe me even if I tell you," said Tarbor plainly, to see Kelmar and Cantell waiting for him to say anyway.

"Queen Elina herself asked me to help save her child," revealed Tarbor, to get immediate looks of disbelief.

"Queen Elina would sooner throw herself from the battlements of Stormhaven than ask such a thing from a Cardronian!" scoffed Kelmar.

"I witnessed her asking," backed up Girvan.

"Of course you did!" retorted Kelmar.

"Tarbor does not lie!" countered Girvan.

"She asked me because she was afraid, afraid of the unseen, the unknown, the darkness that had entered Stormhaven," continued Tarbor, getting lost in his own feelings as he spoke, only coming round when he saw Kelmar and Cantell looking at him.

"Have you not wondered how our soldiers suddenly appeared inside Stormhaven from out of the storeroom?" asked Tarbor, for them to look at each other this time. They had not forgotten; they could see the alliance soldiers running from the storerooms, not knowing how, but their plight to escape had taken over.

"We were there because of what King Taliskar did in front of our eyes," said Tarbor hesitatingly.

"Which was what?" said Cantell with a frown, knowing the storerooms backed onto the rock of Kavenmist.

"Open a doorway in the solid rock of the mountain," finished Tarbor, to see their faces drop.

"King Rolfe said the stronghold held many old secrets, but…" In his disbelief, Cantell did not finish.

"Some it seems that could be unlocked, but only two words came into our minds, to see such a thing happen: magic and sorcery!" put forward Tarbor, to meet utter silence.

"Are we to stay here all day whilst you decide what to do? Darkness will be upon us soon and we are in need of a fire!" shouted Kelmar's mother from the wagon.

Kelmar looked up to the skies. His mother was ever the practical one, but she was right; they had sat here long enough.

"Very well, we will find somewhere to camp for the night and listen to more of what you have to say, but first you will hand us your swords as a gesture of your good intent," said Kelmar, holding out his hand for their swords. With a warning smile of what would happen to them if they did not.

Tarbor did not argue as he looked at Girvan and nodded; he had their attention. Unsheathing their swords; they handed them over hilt-first, for Kelmar to hand them to Druimar, who put them into the wagon.

"Do not misjudge us, Cardronians. By Queen Elina's bidding or not, if you make one wrong move it will be your last," warned Kelmar as he nodded for them to go in front.

"We understand," acknowledged Tarbor and, with Girvan, trotted off in front of them.

"We have made it, Girvan, and found their ear," said Tarbor thankfully.

"No sign of Wardine either," replied Girvan, looking around.

"Not yet," was Tarbor's warning reply.

"Well, what did you make of that? Is he telling the truth? Do you think Queen Elina did ask him?" came the torrent of questions from Kelmar.

"I am not sure, but he has put his life on the line either way to have sought us out. We will listen to more of what he has to say and then decide. He seems to have much on his mind. His eyes tell of nights of uneasy sleep," replied Cantell quietly, in thought.

Another hour on the road saw the clear day start to fade away as a cattle shelter came into view at the bottom of a rocky hill across a field of snow.

"Do you think you can get the wagon across to that shelter, Druimar, without getting stuck?" said Kelmar, looking over the white field. Druimar's answer was to turn the four horses into the field, for Kelmar to smile. *Same old Druimar*, he thought.

Kelmar took one last look around, to see the edge of the Great Forest starting to merge into the oncoming shadow of the night.

The valley itself was starting to bend gradually to his left, with the River Mid no longer shallow as it coursed its way snake-like down the centre of the valley, whilst mist started to hide its passage and spread through the trees that made up a narrow wood further along this side of its bank.

Kelmar did not like the closeness of the wood to the road. *A good place to ambush us*, he thought, and having two Cardronians in their midst was not helping his thoughts.

The cattle shelter turned out to be of a decent size but in a state of disrepair. The rocky hill behind it had been dug out partly to form its back. Stone walls that were full of holes made up the sides and front, with an opening that had been made wider where the stones had fallen away, on one corner.

A small tree trunk had been wedged in the corner where the missing stones were to help hold up the crude roof of timber and earth, which was somehow holding together under the extra weight of the fallen snow.

"It will do," observed Oneatha, and she tucked herself next to the stone wall with the least holes, holding Prince Martyn in her arms.

Permellar sat down by Oneatha's side to feed Kayla as she announced her hunger by crying out into the cold air, setting Prince Martyn into motion at the same time, whilst Druimar tried to ignore the crying as he set about kindling a fire.

With the horses settled and tied to the fence that ran out in front of the cattle shelter and the wagon stationed further beyond them, the four warriors joined the crying after relieving their horses of their saddles.

"There will do, whilst we eat," pointed Cantell, to the broken wall by the opening where there was enough room for Tarbor and Girvan to sit, pulling their cloaks tight around them as they did so.

All the warriors sat quietly as the fire began to crackle and Oneatha conjured up a wonderful- smelling broth whilst trying to comfort an annoyed Prince Martyn at having to wait.

When she was satisfied, she gave Druimar bowls of the delicious-smelling food to hand around to everyone.

Prince Martyn's cries finally quietened after his wait for Kayla, who was now fast asleep, as Kelmar and Cantell waited to hear what Tarbor had to say to them.

Tarbor was gratefully slurping down the last contents of his bowl and saw them looking at him.

"Now you are fed, what is this about magic and sorcery?" spoke Cantell, straight to the point, for Druimar, Oneatha and Permellar to look up at Tarbor as well.

"I would speak first of your King Rolfe," began Tarbor, for Cantell and Kelmar to wait for the inevitable. They knew what he was going to say.

"A last stand at the bottom of Forest Tower saw him fighting Brax. They died by each other's hand," explained Tarbor, for Cantell and Kelmar to bend their heads in sadness.

To the death! they heard in their minds.

"So it was our King that put an end to that mercenary you were escorting," Cantell said with a nod, wishing it would give him some sort of satisfaction, but it did not.

"King Rolfe's funeral was dignified, as befits a King. His body was sent on its way by Queen Elina to the Great Forest upon the River Dale on a ship of fire," added Tarbor.

"It is good to know he will be watching over us, and Queen Elina then is well? The little Prince here was only half the story as we left," enquired Cantell.

"She is strong of will and gave the Prince a sister, Princess Amber," informed Tarbor, to nods and sighs of mixed emotions.

"But her worry is Queen Helistra, that she will take the Princess for her own," warned Tarbor. "She is the one we have come to warn you about, the one to fear, King Taliskar to her is but a puppet. If she does take the Princess as her own then there is only one path she will show her: the path of evil!" warned Tarbor further, with a foreboding in his voice that everyone felt.

This statement did not go down well with Cantell and Kelmar; *Brought up as a Cardronian,* they were thinking! But what could they do? They were safeguarding Prince Martyn!

Tarbor did not stop there; he moved on to King Taliskar and the mountain door. About how distant he became and how more than once he was sure his eyes had turned completely black!

"Even Brax challenged him, saying it must be sorcery!" explained Tarbor, and then he told them that it was Queen Helistra who had told King Taliskar of its existence, a knowledge she had gained from an old wise man she had met on her travels.

Tarbor paused; he had thought about it long and hard. It was clear to him who it was, but how she had achieved it was beyond him. Even though they talked about magic or sorcery, they had been just words to him, but then he had heard the voice speak to him.

"However it works, somehow, through magic or sorcery, she used King Taliskar to open that mountain door. He could not have opened it by himself," concluded Tarbor, to get the looks he expected.

"Queen Helistra met what man on her travels who knows of such things?" queried Cantell, stupefied by it all.

"I do not know, although we have come across a name that might be him." Tarbor looked at Girvan as he spoke his name. "Speedwell."

"Who?" queried Cantell.

"That is what I said after Tarbor heard the voice from the rock," blurted Girvan without thinking, for everyone to look at each other.

"What are you on about? Voice from a rock!" scoffed Kelmar, wondering what in the name of the stars he was listening to.

"It is true," continued Tarbor, "when I was in the archway behind the giant gates of Stormhaven, I chanced to put my hand on the rock that ends it and heard a small frightened voice speak to me in my mind."

"This is insane," pleaded Kelmar to Cantell. He had had enough. "We should finish it!"

"Those soldiers came through solid rock, Kelmar. Something is not right. Look into his eyes, they are not lying," spoke up Oneatha, seeing how troubled Tarbor was as he spoke, for him to carry on.

"The voice warned me of an evil that will poison the land and cast it forever into darkness. *She comes! Evil will reign!* it told me. Then after Queen Helistra had entered Stormhaven, I tried again. This time, the voice warned me, *Stop! She will hear! Find Speedwell!*" finished Tarbor, to the exclamations of Kelmar.

"This is nonsense! I have heard enough! Let us be done with this!" And Kelmar reached for his sword.

"Kelmar! You attack a man who has given you his sword!" shouted Permellar. "You would spill blood here in front of the babies!" She chastised Kelmar, to hold him back from drawing his sword.

"We have already done so, Permellar, when we rescued you, and they were no different to these two," pointed out Kelmar, to feel a restraining arm holding his back in the form of Druimar.

"You wore this when you touched the rock?" he asked, holding up Tarbor's sword.

"Yes, I did," answered Tarbor, wondering what Druimar was going to say.

"I have heard the tales of these swords from long ago. Five swords and shields made to defend evil from the five Kingdoms by a people called the Elfore, who lived deep within the Great Forest," he stated, to see Tarbor and Girvan smile.

"Not you as well, Druimar!" groaned Kelmar. He could not believe it, what was all this? And he walked out of the cattle shelter, not wanting to hear any more, hoping the night air would clear his head.

"The Elfore, Druimar? Swords and shields made to ward off evil?" questioned Cantell, more perplexed than ever.

"They were called the children of the forest," answered Druimar, for Tarbor and Girvan to smile at each other.

"Something happened between man and the Elfore long ago, what it was is a mystery. Superstitions have grown over the years of what lays in wait for us if we enter the depths of the Great Forest, making it become a forbidden place for man to this day for fear of his life," explained Druimar, as best he could.

Cantell found himself looking out to where the Great Forest lay at the top of the hills as Druimar spoke, only able to see their shadow against the starlit sky. He was remembering how quiet the forest had gone when he had laid Prince Martyn down and then when he had picked him back up, how that peacefulness had comforted him.

He thought again of what his mother had told him when he was young. Upset the spirits of the Great Forest and you will be cursed for evermore. *Are the Elfore those spirits?* he thought.

"To hold such a sword as this that was only a story handed down through the ages is beyond belief," continued Druimar, "yet here it is, an ancient defender, three metals fused into one: earth, sky and mountain. Only the Elfore were said to be able to forge such a blade. It was beyond our skills," spoke Druimar in appreciation as he looked down at the sword in his hand.

"What of the name Speedwell? Did his name ever come to your ears?" asked Girvan hopefully.

"No, but the stories tell of Keepers who once looked after the well-being of the forest," replied Druimar thoughtfully.

"You have never told me of these stories, Father," said Permellar, feeling somewhat left out.

"Ah, but I did, Permellar, when you were a small child. You would not go to sleep if I did not tell you a bedtime story," said Druimar with a smile, remembering.

Permellar tried to recollect, but nothing would come to her; so much sadness had happened to her these last months that any happy memories had been wiped away.

"How did you come by such a sword?" asked Cantell, taking it from Druimar to look at it.

"King Taliskar gave it to me when I was made Captain, but it is not that of Cardronia. It has the royal half crest of Waunarle upon its pommel," pointed out Tarbor truthfully.

Druimar looked at Tarbor as if to speak but said nothing when Kelmar appeared, taking the sword from Cantell to look at the pommel and then at Tarbor. He had still been listening to what they were saying, despite not wanting to.

"Does this not prove it! That you Cardronians killed King Palitan and blamed King Rolfe for his death to start a war!" he challenged.

"It proves nothing," spoke up Druimar, "these weapons have not been seen for hundreds of years. King Palitan would not have known of its existence," claimed Druimar.

"There is only one person who could have known," intervened Tarbor before Kelmar could say anything.

"Queen Helistra," finished Cantell, for Kelmar to look at him open-mouthed.

"I know, Kelmar, I am as confused as you about it all, but one fact remains. We were taken by surprise by something we have not come across before: magic, sorcery. I am at a loss as to what to say, but I agree with the Cardronian. King Taliskar could not have opened a door in the mountain on his own," decided Cantell, much to the relief of Tarbor and Girvan.

Kelmar fumed inside, but he would never go against the word of his friend. Instead, he looked at Tarbor and to Tarbor's surprise, handed him back the defender.

"You are lucky, Cardronian, that I have a friend such as this to listen to you, but remember, if you are playing us as fools, it will be the last thing you ever do," he warned.

"I assure you, Kelmar, it is not me that plays you, but Queen Helistra. She plays with us all," warned Tarbor back as he took the defender from Kelmar, who looked him square in the eye.

"Was that how Queen Elina felt?" asked Permellar, curious but trying to ease the tension she could feel at the same time.

"She thought of her as a woman who wanted her own way, no matter what or who she used," replied Tarbor, making him remember Queen Elina's small face pleading with him.

"We have talked enough, we all need to rest," decided Cantell, giving Girvan his sword back as he spoke.

"I think the wagon will give you enough shelter," suggested Cantell, to see Tarbor and Girvan take their leave.

"I hope you are right trusting them," worried Kelmar, watching Tarbor and Girvan make their way to the wagon.

"Something does not add up about a door in a mountain, Kelmar. Even you must admit that. As for what else was said, I do not know what to think. We will wait and watch them for now. Now go, get some rest whilst I take first watch," said Cantell, smiling, and he watched his friend settle next to Permellar before walking out into the night air, drawing his cloak around him, wondering if he had done the right thing.

Tarbor and Girvan had picked up their saddles to use them as headrests as they settled down between the wagon's wheels when Druimar appeared, peeking under the wagon at them. "Druimar, are you under here as well?" said Tarbor with a smile.

"No, I came to speak to you more about the legend," replied Druimar, crouching down.

"You saved us from Kelmar, speaking out as you did, we owe you our thanks. Not that I can blame him. I thought my friend here just as mad when he told me of it," said Tarbor, understanding how Kelmar was feeling.

"My grandfather told me of the stories a long time ago. He was a blacksmith in East Marchend, so I know why Permellar chose to come here. I spoke of it often enough, though it is sad to see her mind clouded by grief not to remember," remembered Druimar with a sigh.

Tarbor and Girvan stayed quiet as Druimar recollected his grandfather, but by now they knew there was something else on his mind, for him to be here.

"My father had no time for Grandfather's rubbish, as he called it," he continued. "I was just a boy when my mother died. That was when my father decided to go to Falfour and become a fisherman. How did you come to hear of the legend?" asked Druimar, catching Tarbor and Girvan out with his sudden change of tack.

"Er, my father is also a blacksmith in Slevenport. He used to tell me the stories," said Girvan, smiling.

"Ah, I see, so you were going to escort Brax's body to Slevenport and then show your father the sword," said Druimar, nodding.

"Well, we were, but it has not quite turned out that way," Girvan smiled, "I wish we had taken the shield to show him also," revealed Girvan, thinking back, for Druimar's eyes to light up.

"You mean you have seen a shield too!" Druimar then listened to Girvan as he told him how they had come across the shield's existence and how it had been visited by Queen Helistra secretly.

"How many secret doors can there be in Stormhaven!" exclaimed Druimar, after hearing of their exploits. *If Grandfather were here now*, he thought.

Druimar then came to the issue he had wanted to confront Tarbor with: "If as you say you felt the voice from the rock wearing that sword, you cannot be a Cardronian, Tarbor, but a Waunarle, and not just any Waunarle, but the King!" Druimar informed Tarbor, for him to hear

Girvan's words telling him the same. He could only answer Druimar the same as he did then.

"How can I be, Druimar? I am a soldier of Cardronia, raised in Ardriss," protested Tarbor.

"All that I have heard, albeit from my grandfather, says you must be of the blood, and not just any blood. Being that it is the sword of Waunarle and King Palitan is no more, it could only respond to the next rightful heir, which must be you, or have you been lying all along!" posed Druimar, putting Tarbor on the spot.

No matter how he tried, Tarbor could not get his head around it. Me the rightful King of Waunarle, impossible! "It cannot be, Druimar, how could it?" exclaimed Tarbor in exasperation. His mind was everywhere as it was, and now this again.

"I wonder why King Taliskar gave you that sword in the first place and where he got it from," pondered Druimar.

"That is obvious. She is behind it, Queen Helistra. It is one of her games she likes to play," suspected Girvan.

One that could have gone wrong with you hearing the voice, thought Druimar. "There is a story that would join you and the sword together," said Druimar, making Tarbor think what in the name of the stars could that be?

"When the tragedy of the royal family of Waunarle happened, it was said that they were on their way back to Westerport from a day's hunting in the Hardenel Woods. They were travelling along the coastal road in a carriage when it careered off the road straight over the cliff's edge, for them to meet their deaths. No one knew how or why it happened. The King and Queen were found days later washed up further down the coast, but their child, the baby Prince, was never found," finished Druimar, looking at Tarbor.

"What are you trying to say? That I… that I could be that child!" protested Tarbor once more, finding it all too incredible to believe.

"Was there no one else with them to see? What of their escort?" intervened Girvan.

"Both dead, a driver and a guard, that is all. It was a time of peace in Waunarle and they were loved by everyone," answered Druimar to Girvan's exclamation: "Huh! Not all, it seemed."

"It was presumed that the Prince had been swept out to sea. One so small would not stand a chance, it was thought. What would he be now if he was still alive? Twenty-two or three? About your age, I am guessing, Tarbor, and here you are with the ancient sword of Waunarle in your possession, feeling things you have never felt before. Given to you by King Taliskar as if he knew, as if they both knew, who you really were. A cruel game being played on you without you knowing," concluded Druimar to a bewildered Tarbor.

"Of course, you know who found the bodies?" asked Druimar suddenly, not quite finished as he paused to receive blank looks. "Brax!" He smiled to see a look of astonishment on Tarbor's face.

"But if that is true, Druimar, you are implying that Brax actually spared the child's life? That does not sound like him," argued Tarbor.

"He was not the man you know back then, Tarbor, but power in itself can corrupt even good men. He had a good teacher in King Taliskar and from what you have told me, an evil one in Queen Helistra. It could have been to keep him quiet, and that is when he became the Protector of Waunarle," explained Druimar.

"And so the plot had begun," voiced Girvan in thought.

Druimar decided it was time to go; enough had been said to think on and he got up to make his way.

"We will speak again tomorrow. I think it will be my turn on watch soon, we have talked long enough for it to be," he said with a smile, to leave Tarbor and Girvan looking at each other with more than enough to reflect on.

A misty grey dawn had already revealed itself as Cantell half dozed, sitting by the doorway of the cattle shelter.

He had drawn the short straw and was on his second watch as everyone slept; nobody was stirring.

Kelmar, Druimar, Oneatha and baby Prince Martyn all rested under the cover of the cattle shelter.

Permellar, though, had decided she felt more comfortable in the back of the covered wagon with little Kayla, whilst Tarbor and Girvan still lay under the wagon after talking half the night.

Druimar had kept Cantell from his sleep when he exchanged places with him to go on watch, telling him what he and the Cardronians had been talking about. Hence, Cantell was barely able to keep his eyes open.

Cantell's head was beginning to drop once more when a rumbling sound made him jolt back to awareness.

Standing up, he instinctively drew his sword and looked around him to see nothing but snow— covered fields through the misty greyness.

Then his hearing told him to turn round and as he turned, he looked up. There above him tumbling down the hill through the snow were boulders of all sizes, heading straight for the cattle shelter!

"What? Kelmar! Druimar! Oneatha! Wake up! Get out of there!" Cantell yelled at the top of his voice.

With the sound of the boulders and his own voice shouting, Cantell never heard the first arrow zip pass him, but he felt the second! It torn through his arm and pinned it to his side under his ribs, making him drop to the ground in agony.

The boulders smashed through the roof of the cattle shelter, sending it crashing onto the half-awake company.

Boulders crashed around the horses, making them frightened, pulling frantically at their ties around the fence, for some to break loose and bolt.

The wagon luckily being further away was untouched by the boulders as Tarbor and Girvan awoke to their noise, to see the horses trying to break free.

They rushed out from underneath the wagon with their swords, to see the cattle shelter totally demolished.

Girvan saw Cantell was hit and in agony on his knees. He ran to his aid in front of Tarbor, only to be met by two arrows, one entering his hip and one finding its mark straight into his chest. He fell headlong, snapping the arrow in his chest as he hit the ground, only to push the arrow further into him.

"GIRVAN!" Tarbor was at his side in an instant. "Girvan!" Tarbor whispered hoarsely as he saw nothing but Girvan's blood pouring from his wounds; he was barely alive.

Horses' hooves thundering over the ground made Tarbor look up. Three horse soldiers were crossing the field, coming towards them brandishing their swords; it could only be Wardine. He seethed, and rage took over him as he ran headlong at them with the defender in both hands.

Arrows whistled past him as he ran. He sneaked a look and caught sight of two archers crouched down in the next field.

The first horse soldier was upon him, slashing out with his sword. Tarbor met the blade, deflecting it away as the next horse soldier came at him on his other side. Tarbor twisted the defender in his hands and brought it round to cut straight through the rider's leg, sending him sideways off his horse, but by doing so Tarbor had left himself open to the third horse soldier's sword as its blade cut right through his shoulder.

Tarbor stayed on his feet despite the pain, but an arrow into his leg saw him drop onto one knee, luckily for him, as the first horse soldier had come around again to see his sword swish over Tarbor's head.

As he rode past him, the first horse soldier dropped off his horse but ignored Tarbor's plight, to run onto the collapsed cattle shelter's roof.

Pulling back his hood, Tarbor saw a grinning Wardine. "Hold him there, I want to savour the moment!" he shouted, for Tarbor to feel a sword digging into his neck from the dismounted third horse soldier. He dropped the defender in front of him.

Tarbor looked around to see Cantell had the two archers standing over him with their swords drawn, whilst the other horse soldier lay sprawled on the ground in agony, holding his blood-soaked leg.

Still grinning, Wardine moved to where he could hear the clear cries of Prince Martyn through the collapsed roof.

Oneatha had half covered Prince Martyn with her body in protection as the roof had come down. A sword thrust through the rubble from Wardine into her shoulder made her scream and let go.

Wardine reached down through the rubble and dragged the screaming little Prince Martyn out of her grasp.

Walking back towards Tarbor over the rubble, he held the screaming Prince high in the air, upside down, in triumph, for Tarbor to look at him with hate in his eyes.

He looked at what was left of the cattle shelter behind Wardine to sense no movement coming from there, only the cries of pain from Oneatha.

Tarbor was beside himself at his own failure; his friend Girvan was lying there dying in his own blood! He had failed him and those he had come to help.

All his talk about everything that had happened to him was worth nothing compared to their lives at this moment. He looked up at the distraught baby Prince, who Wardine was now holding a dagger to, and cursed at his failure.

"What a bonus, Tarbor. You and the brat together. I thought a good hunt for you was ahead of me, but here you are!" Wardine said, grinning, enjoying every moment whilst he teased the blade of his dagger at the crying Prince.

"Take me, not the child! I thought you were a soldier!" shouted Tarbor, with all the venom he felt inside for Wardine.

Wardine glanced at the fallen body of Girvan. "Your friend does not look like he will be able to help you, Tarbor. I think his time is over, as yours soon will be! But first you can watch the brat die that you have so painstakingly come to save!" sneered Wardine, ignoring Tarbor's plea.

"You are scum, Wardine! You always have been and always will be!" spat Tarbor.

"Captain Wardine, Tarbor. Where are your manners?" Wardine could not help but laugh.

As Wardine's laughter subsided, little Kayla's crying suddenly took over as she burst into tears.

Although Kayla had been woken by the noise of the boulders, Permellar managed to comfort her back to sleep and kept her close in the wagon, not daring to move, having witnessed Cantell, Girvan then Tarbor being wounded, but now she had awoken again, frightened.

Kayla's cry's caught Wardine by surprise as he held his dagger at the little body of Prince Martyn. His face dropped as he looked over Tarbor towards the cries from the wagon.

Another brat? he thought, as a moment of doubt entered his head. Had he the right one? *To make sure, they both must die!* he thought.

As Wardine paused in his moment of doubt, Tarbor saw his chance. If he had thought a moment longer on what he was going to do, the moment would have been lost.

In one movement, Tarbor suddenly produced his dagger and without looking where to strike the horse soldier that was guarding him, he lifted himself off the ground, bringing the dagger's blade straight across the horse soldier's throat.

As he rose to slit the horse soldier's throat, Tarbor grabbed the defender with his other hand. Gripping it by the hilt, he threw the ancient sword through the air with a silent prayer in his head: *Let my aim be true, ancient sword of Waunarle.*

The defender spun through the air, silent and deadly, to find its mark straight through Wardine's forehead with a blood-curdling sound, sending him backwards with its force to pin him to the ground like a stake! For little Prince Martyn to fall on the ground crying, unharmed.

Cantell took Tarbor's lead whilst his captors were still open-mouthed. Breaking the arrow that had pinned his arm to his body, Cantell ignored the pain as he grasped out for his sword that they had kicked away.

One of the archers reacted more quickly than the other and lunged down at Cantell with his sword, but Cantell rolled to his side to avoid his blade whilst swinging his sword at the same time, to slice through the archer's legs down to the bone.

The second archer went to fling himself at Cantell, but Tarbor was on him, crashing into him, to send them both sprawling onto the ground.

Tarbor got up unsteadily onto his feet, leaving the horse soldier lying there, his dagger sticking out of his neck and blood gushing onto the snow from the fatal blow.

Tarbor turned to see Cantell finish off the horse soldier he had sliced, and saw the other horse soldier had passed out with his loss of blood.

Tarbor limped back to kneel painfully by Girvan's side. Touching his hair, Tarbor wept; he was gone.

"Girvan, my friend, I am sorry." Tarbor's words caught in his throat as he knelt there.

Cantell held his side as he watched Tarbor, feeling for him at the lost of his friend. "He was a brave warrior," was all he could say as he moved to pick up Prince Martyn, finding Permellar was already doing so.

Tarbor choked in remorse as he stood back up. "This is all my fault," he cried to himself as Cantell wondered how many more there were; that rockfall did not start on its own.

As Cantell thought it, the answer came rolling down the hill in the shape of two bloodstained soldiers' bodies, one thumping on top of the smashed cattle shelter to give rise to groaning underneath.

"Come, they live!" shouted Cantell to Tarbor, who reluctantly left Girvan's side to try and move some of the smashed cattle shelter with him, though neither he nor Cantell were in any fit state to move anything, but the sound of more horses stopped them from trying any further.

Both warriors looked on at the riders closing in upon them. "I am not sure I have the strength to fight off any more," remarked Tarbor, peering at the four horsemen, who had come clearly into view.

Cantell, however, was in relief as he recognised one of the riders, who was wearing an eye patch. "You will not have to. There is only one person who wears one of those," he said thankfully, "it is Kraven of Balintium, an old friend!"

Coming to a standstill, the four horsemen dismounted and looked around them. Kraven came up to Cantell and saw his bloody arm with the arrow shaft sticking out either side of it.

"You do not look as good as the last time we met, Cantell, old friend," he chided.

"Whereas you, Kraven, look as ugly as ever," Cantell managed to smile back.

"What has happened here? We saw you in need and despatched those two." Kraven nodded at the two crumpled bodies.

"For that we are thankful, Kraven, and I will explain later, but for now there is no time to lose. Kelmar is underneath that rubble with his mother and Druimar the blacksmith from Kelmsmere," he explained quickly.

Hands soon got to work removing what was left of the cattle shelter roof. Boulders were hauled away or moved, whilst timber and earth were thrown aside.

Permellar had taken a sobbing Prince Martyn back to the wagon and sat watching in silent worry as the soldiers started to uncover Kelmar, Oneatha and her father.

With the weight of rubble pinning him down, Kelmar was the first to surface, with a leg that was found to be broken. Not that it concerned him; he was more worried by the scream he had heard from his mother, frustrated he had not been able to move to help her.

Helped out and having sat down with some pain next to Cantell, Kelmar saw the state of Cantell's shattered arm as to his relief his mother was pulled out, crying with the pain coming from her shoulder.

"Thank the stars," he blew at seeing her as a worried Permellar came with some water for them all.

"Is the Prince safe?" Kelmar asked as his mother was brought to them.

"He rests quietly now with Kayla in the wagon," answered Permellar as she watched for her father.

"I could hear the Cardronian. I thought the Prince's time was up," admitted Kelmar.

"You had better thank him then that it is not." Cantell nodded at Tarbor.

Kelmar looked at his friend and then followed his eyes to see Tarbor bent over Girvan's body.

"He meant what he said, Kelmar, and has paid for it with his friend's life. Trust is something you have to gain, and I think he has just done that, no matter what we think of his stories," pointed out Cantell.

Kelmar did not reply as he looked at Tarbor and then at the prostrate body of the Cardronian who had come to kill Prince Martyn, with Tarbor's sword sticking out of his head.

Kraven suddenly appeared before Cantell, Kelmar, Oneatha and Permellar with a disconcerted look upon his face.

"What is it, Kraven?" Cantell frowned on seeing his look.

"The one you say is Druimar has not survived. A rock has gone clean through the roof and killed him," reported Kraven, for Cantell and Kelmar to look back at him blankly, not believing it.

Oneatha broke down, crying, whilst Permellar ran into the rubble, shouting, "No! No! No! Father, no! Please, not you!"

Tears flowed as Permellar reached her father's side, lying there with his face covered in blood from a nasty-looking gash on the side of his head. The rock that had hit him had driven deep into his head, killing him instantly.

She held his hand, crying in despair. First her husband and now her father; her world had collapsed.

Oneatha felt Kelmar hold her hand. "I am sorry, Mother." She could only squeeze his hand as her tears flowed down her cheeks.

"Now what will we do?" she finally managed to ask, for Kraven to answer, "You can all come with me to Walditch where we can see to your wounds. Then as you are in no fit state to be on your own, Elishard awaits you if you wish, where you can rest until those wounds are healed at least," suggested Kraven.

"Thank you, Kraven. Then we will be able to do something about Queen Elina and the Princess before Queen Helistra gets her hands on her," prompted Kelmar, looking at Cantell.

"Think on what you are saying, Kelmar. We already have our duty to perform with the Prince," Cantell reminded him, "and it will be some time before we go anywhere with these wounds," he added.

Tarbor had stood up from the body of Girvan and limped over to where Wardine lay. "The Prince will stand a better chance at Elishard, as long as he is kept hidden," he said more to himself than anyone, as he stood over Wardine's body. "Then I will go and look for this Speedwell," and putting his foot across Wardine's face, Tarbor pulled out the ancient sword and held it steady before him, "and find him with this!"

CHAPTER XVIV

Speedwell stretched his aching feet as he sat down. Closing his eyes, he let the rich earth smell that lay deep beneath his tired feet fill his lungs.

All was quiet; no light was to be seen here, no breeze playing upon his face or cold trying to bite through him as he sat there. Speedwell was taking great comfort at being in the Ancient One's domain after his long journey.

Opening his mind, Speedwell felt the Ancient One's presence enter it with soft whispery tones greeting him as it did so.

How fare you, Speedwell?

I am well, Ancient One, if not a little tired.

What news do you bring from the West Plateau?

Not good, Ancient One. It was as you feared. Helistra has surfaced once more. She has opened the mountain throne and entered the crystal chamber to cast evil upon the forest through the pool of life, informed Speedwell.

We have underestimated her evil intent. She has grown in power beyond our expectations since last she showed herself. I have left a spell of containment there, but it will not hold indefinitely. That is why I am here to seek your advice, informed Speedwell further.

Your spell has already been broken, Speedwell, for as we speak, the earth soaks in blood and quivers in fear. She has unleashed spores of death into the Plateau Forest, enhancing the power of the crystal chamber to do so.

Speedwell groaned to hear his spell of containment had failed already.

We should have stopped her long ago in man's domain, Ancient One. Gentian knew it would come to this and we did not listen to him. We were wrong to withdraw from Northernland to safeguard the forests only, regretted Speedwell.

That was my decision, Speedwell, not yours. With Grimstone and Gentian no more, the forests were my first concern. Though it was broken, I did not think she would be able to bond with Grimstone's rune staff, let alone be in harmony with it so as to enter the crystal chamber, but I was wrong, completely wrong. My senses were blinded by my thinking it could not happen. When Grimstone's rune staff broke, something must have changed within its very fabric and I did not become aware of it in my blindness, admitted the Ancient One.

And now she has groomed it in evil all these years, staying hidden from us, using her cunning to get where she wanted. Only then using Grimstone's broken rune staff's power subtly so as not to alert us. I only became aware of those subtle changes in the earth and sky when it was all too late, reflected the Ancient One.

You are too harsh upon yourself, Ancient One. I agreed with you it was what we had to do, but what are we going to do now to stop her, now she has used the crystal chamber? worried Speedwell.

First, you must go and make recompense with your brother, Ringwold, then together our weave will be strong enough to hold her poison back indefinitely.

Ringwold has not spoken to me since Grimstone's death. He still blames me for Helistra's actions, thought Speedwell.

Then it is long past the time when you should have talked to him. Our needs are great and time is not on our side. I sense the poison she has unleashed is spreading fast.

Where would you have us hold her back? Though our weaves may be strong together, we cannot protect everywhere, asked Speedwell, trying to think where himself.

You are right, Speedwell, we cannot. That is why I want you to send Ringwold here whilst you fetch Tomin and Gentian's rune staff. He can help us, though putting him on that island has had its disadvantages with the learning of the ways, ordered the Ancient One, thinking.

It will be good to see my grandson once more. Speedwell smiled to himself.

It is obvious to me that Helistra will stay where her power is at its most potent whilst she poisons the Plateau Forest: the crystal chamber. That gives you the chance to bring him here with Gentian's rune staff for him to bond better with it under the cover of the barrier we shall create. Then when he has retrieved the broken piece from Grimstone's solid form, we can confront her and mend Grimstone's broken rune staff to end her evil.

Easier said than done, Ancient One, worried Speedwell.

We will meet that barrier when all is in place, Speedwell.

And of barriers, Ancient One. You have not yet said where.

I have decided that we will make our stand here along the Old Ogrin Ridge. The Plateau Forest cliffs form a natural barrier in themselves and we can reinforce them with our own barrier, conveyed the Ancient One.

To sacrifice so much by sealing the Plateau Forest off from the Great Forest grieves me so, carried on the Ancient One before Speedwell could protest, *but I see no other way. By the time Ringwold gets here, I fear she will have already poisoned a great part of the Plateau Forest.*

From Thunder Gorge to the Windward Pass is a long way, I know, but here I rest in the middle, and with Ringwold here with me, whilst you bring Tomin, we will be strong, finished the Ancient One assuredly.

But you are inviting the poison onto your very being, Ancient One! You are the heart of the forests! protested Speedwell immediately.

Where I am at my strongest, Speedwell. There is no better place. Speedwell could sense the Ancient One was not going to be swayed, though he did not like the thought of it.

What of the Elfore and the Manelf? They will lose everything, thought Speedwell further.

They must both begin again in the Great Forest behind the barrier we will create. You must send someone to warn the Elfore of the danger that approaches them when you speak with Ringwold.

The Elfore will not be easily persuaded to leave their homes, Ancient One, knew Speedwell.

Then they must be made to understand that their very existence is under threat, for if they do not leave, a darkness like never before will overshadow them and cast them into oblivion, warned the Ancient One, to make Speedwell suddenly feel cold.

When I retrieve Tomin, what of the spell that conceals him? As I use my rune staff to break it, she will sense the spell of undoing to know he still lives, thought Speedwell, not able to hide his worry that if she found out before they had retrieved the broken piece, all could be lost.

Something came to me that I have not felt for a long time, Speedwell, to overcome it: a defender.

A defender, Ancient One? One that Gentian had made by the Elfore? I thought she had scattered those to the four winds when she battled with him under Stormhaven.

So did I, but I felt it. But why would one of those surface now? I do not know, but nevertheless one has. Its presence was strong when it came to me as it touched the essence beneath Stormhaven.

Gentian had more put into those swords than any of us were aware of, thought Speedwell.

The sword has somehow found its way to the rightful King for me to have sensed it. My hope is that the shield will make itself known to him now the sword has come to light. Then together they will hide Tomin whilst you break the spell without her feeling his presence.

I do not doubt your word, Ancient One, but that is filled with ifs and buts. Surely it is more of a risk going to Stormhaven under the nose of my daughter to find this King wielder than getting Tomin in the first place? pointed out Speedwell.

I understand your worry, Speedwell, though Helistra will have enough to occupy her mind when the barrier goes up. There is another reason why I wish you to pursue the defender. I have not spoken of it until now in fear of it being just a hope.

Speedwell heard something in the Ancient One's tones, a sense of anticipation. He waited to hear what he was going to say.

When I sensed the defender, two spirits came through to me in a whisper from the essence. Two new lives whose spirits we have waited for, for a long time. Their strength dared me to think that after all this time we could be complete again, revealed the Ancient One.

I hear the hope within you, Ancient One, but if you have felt them then Helistra must have, They could be already in her grip.

That is true, Speedwell, but if I did not see what was right in front of me then she could well have done the same. Her lust to destroy the forests blinds her, and the power she has gained from the crystal chamber could have blocked them from her mind. It is but a hope, I know, Speedwell, but see if you can seek them out whilst you find the King wielder.

Speedwell was silent whilst he thought on what the Ancient One had asked of him before he spoke.

You are of the belief then that these newborn that came through to you from the essence could be future Forestalls to help us confront Helistra? That they will need protecting also, not just Tomin? If they have not already fallen into her hands, which will make matters worse for us, queried Speedwell.

It is what I have felt, Speedwell. But for how long will we have to sustain the barrier if it is true before they can help? Twenty… thirty more winters? Can we hold such malice at bay for all that time with Helistra having the power of the crystal chamber? Their minds would have to grow quickly if they are to do what is needed.

I hear your doubts and worries, Speedwell, but I need to know one way or the other. If I am wrong then there is no need to worry. We must prepare with Tomin and make ourselves stronger to defeat her. If I am right then let us hope you are the one to find them first and not her. *Now go, Speedwell, we have spoken of much and you have much to do. Speak with Ringwold, and may the stars watch over you on your journey.*

I will, Ancient One, and may the earth always embrace you.

And with the Ancient One's words fresh in his mind, Speedwell left his domain to start his journey to the Windward Pass, with mixed feelings keeping him company.

CHAPTER XX

The month of snow had come and gone, although the Windward Pass did not show it, covered as it was in a white blanket as the month of frosts began to freeze it over, stopping the easterly winds having their way by blowing it everywhere.

Two figures peered over a rocky outcrop high on a hill that overlooked the Windward Pass. Way below them to their right was the mouth of the River Ogrin, beginning its journey into the forests with the majestic Kavenmist Mountains seemingly touching the sky whilst at the same time keeping the river company as it ran alongside.

A winding path led away from the two figures all the way down to the river, weaving its way through the trees that covered this side of the pass.

"We are the only ones who tread this path today, Piper," observed Ludbright.

"You are right, my arrows will not leave their quiver this day," replied Piper as both Manelf hunters continued to watch in the hope of any sign of an animal that could later be served as food on their table.

As they crouched behind the rocky outcrop, their brown cloaks kept covered the slim form of their leather-clad bodies. Hoods blown against their heads by the wind hid long brown hair, whilst boots tied tightly over leggings could just be seen keeping out the winter's cold.

A bow slung over each of their backs with strings taut against their chests helped stop their cloaks from flapping in the wind as a quiver full of arrows waited, bristling on their shoulders.

Finally, the two hunters gave up and stood, giving their position away. "It is no use. We will have to move further into the forest," pointed Piper, revealing her leather wrist strap, "no animal is going to come out here in this wind. It is too fierce."

As Piper looked around, the wind immediately blew off her hood to whip her plaited hair into her face, revealing her telltale pointed ears, a trait from the union of Elfore and man long ago.

The Manelf were a slowly dying people, but not through any fault of their own. Helistra killing Grimstone and then Gentian had seen to that. They had been the chosen Forestalls of the Elfore and were now dead by her hand, the hand of man. Even though they had their blood in them, the Elfore had made the Manelves outcasts, never to be seen or spoken to again. Any that dare come near the domain of the Elfore would be killed on sight. So here they were, pushed out onto the eastern side of the Great Plateau Forest, forgotten and left to die.

"Where is Tintwist? Is he lost again?" asked Piper, sounding annoyed as her eyes of mottled brown searched through the trees as she spoke.

"He is already deeper in the forest," said Ludbright. "Why? Has he teased you again?"

"He can irritate me sometimes," said Piper, sounding a bit distant, "though I sometimes think we have been in each other's company for too long. We make out the little things in our lives to be big, when really they are meaningless."

Ludbright never answered; instead, he pulled Piper back down behind the rocky outcrop. Piper frowned and looked to where Ludbright nodded.

A figure could be seen appearing and disappearing in amongst the trees at the bottom of the hill. "Who can it be out here?" queried Piper, as two arrows were notched, ready to take flight.

The figure suddenly stopped and looked up to where they were crouched. "Whoever it is, he is looking right at us," said Ludbright softly.

They watched as the figure's hands slowly and deliberately moved to its fur hood to pull it down, revealing long matted white hair, to make the two hunters lower their bows.

"It cannot be, can it? There is only one person that can look like Ringwold and hold such a staff: his brother Speedwell!" exclaimed Piper.

"But they have not seen or spoken to each other for years," said Ludbright in quiet shock at hearing Piper say Speedwell's name.

"Just like us and the Elfore then," remarked Piper, "but to be here cannot be a good sign," she worried, and they began to walk towards him.

As the two hunters drew near to Speedwell, they stopped and bowed, acknowledging him. "Forestall."

"There is no need to greet me so," professed Speedwell, feeling somewhat awkward at such things.

"It is only right we do so. You are a Keeper of the forest, our protector," Piper reminded him.

Speedwell smiled at Piper's honesty and decided to bow back. "I bow to you then, hunters of the Manelves, archers without equal," said Speedwell in respect, making Piper and Ludbright feel taller still.

"Who of the Manelf hunters are you?" enquired Speedwell.

"I am Piper and this is Ludbright, Forestall," answered Piper, just as a figure came bounding out of the forest with a broad grin on his face and a brace of rabbits on his shoulder, oblivious to everything.

"Look what I…!" Tintwist stopped short in his tracks and sentence when he saw Speedwell. Dropping the rabbits onto the ground, he bowed deeply.

"And this is Tintwist!" Piper said with a glare.

"Forgive my ignorance, Forestall," apologised Tintwist, looking up sideways to see Piper staring down at him.

"And my apologies to you, Piper, for startling you earlier," he said with a smile, as she continued to glare back at him but could not help inwardly smiling.

Speedwell smiled to see them so. *At least there is still spirit within them,* he thought, *they will need it.*

Speedwell began walking with them to their village, where they lived with Ringwold, as Piper could not hold back her curiosity.

"What brings you to this part of the forest, Forestall?" she asked, feeling it had to be important for Speedwell to have suddenly turned up after all this time.

"A story awaits you all, and deeds that must be done," replied Speedwell seriously, making the three look at each other.

Onwards in silence they walked through the driving wind, with the three Manelves wondering what deeds they could be that was wanted of them.

They walked across a valley in and out of the trees until they came to a coastal path. As they revealed themselves to the open sea, the wind tried to whip them away from the clifftop, whilst waves hurled themselves onto the rocky cliffs far below, pounding them, to send white spray high in the air.

Trees shaped by the constant onslaught of the wind saw them safely leave the coastal path as they thankfully dropped into a sheltered wooded valley.

Smoke could now be seen in the distance, caught by the wind and sent swirling its way through the treetops into the winter sky.

Speedwell looked around him as they walked along the valley floor through the trees. Simple little wooden huts had begun appearing, scattered between the trees to mark the beginning of the Manelf settlement.

Their occupants were standing outside their homes, looking at him. Speedwell saw how different some of their faces were, some leaning more to man, whilst others leant more to Elfore. All, though, had the same look of worry as to why he was there.

Walking on until they had nearly reached the other side of the valley, Speedwell looked up in front of him to see its tallest trees standing on the valley's slopes.

Their giant roots showed through the earth, intertwining with each other, and had been taken advantage of by the Manelf.

Hollowed out beneath them, blocked off and fronted by crude doorways, the roots had become a dwelling place for the Manelf, but in particular for one person, Ringwold, Speedwell's brother.

He stood outside one of the doorways, a grey cloak wrapped around him matching his grey eyes, which looked on unemotionally at Speedwell.

"Brother, it has been a long time," spoke Speedwell, first attempting to break the icy look he was getting.

"Brother," replied Ringwold, his look not altering.

"I bring news from the Ancient One."

"I know, bad news, like you always have," returned Ringwold, and he disappeared through his doorway.

Speedwell closed his eyes with an inward groan. *Still the same*, he thought, and he followed him in under the twisted root doorway, leaving his escort outside.

A fire was set in the middle of a large hewn-out chamber, with a hole in its roof seemingly sucking out the smoke.

A large semi-circle table fitted snugly into one corner of the chamber, its top littered with items strewn across it.

Roots came and went as they pleased, all around the hollowed-out chamber, forming strange patterns. It was all just as Speedwell remembered it.

Speedwell sat on a log in front of the fire, opposite Ringwold, and looked at his brother.

"You know why I am here then," began Speedwell.

"The Ancient One has whispered to me of your daughter showing herself again to spread evil into the forest," scathed Ringwold.

"Yes, she has. I tried to hold her back, but her powers have grown. She has unlocked the mountain throne and found out how to use the crystal chamber to enhance her spells," explained Speedwell quickly, to see a look from his brother, and he waited for the backlash he knew was going to come.

"If you had fully taught her the ways of the forest before she met Grimstone, none of this would have happened!" scolded Ringwold.

"How was I to know Helistra would be jealous of her own son being taught the ways?" said Speedwell, defending himself.

"That is as may be, but you were her father, her teacher in the life of the forest, brother! Your daughter! Your responsibility! Not Grimstone's!" shouted Ringwold.

Speedwell was silent for a while, feeling the depth of his brother's anger at him, but he was right; he should have taught her everything before her being as one with Grimstone, he thought, but there was one question that had played on his mind: would it have made any difference? Stopped what lurked inside of her, waiting for the day when it could show itself? He would never know now.

"You are right, Ringwold. I should have taught her more. I suppose I just wanted her to be the same carefree happy child who used to run through the forest making the birds sing with her laughter," reminisced Speedwell, "do you remember those happy days?"

"I remember them," reflected Ringwold.

"And now my little girl only wants me dead! She poisoned me, Ringwold, when I tried to stop her. I was lucky to have had the essence's droplets of life to hold it back, or she would have got what she desired!" Speedwell was close to tears as he recollected that moment.

Ringwold clearly heard the hurt and sadness in his brother's voice. The pain he must be going through, he thought, a daughter wanting to kill her own father, who he knew had always adored her. He decided he had said enough; too many years had gone past like this. They needed each other more than ever right now, from the foreboding he had felt from the Ancient One. It was time for him to be his brother again and not a stranger.

"What is it the Ancient One wishes us to do?" he said simply, for Speedwell to look up and see the brother he loved looking back at him with a smile.

Just then, Piper and Tintwist appeared with some much-needed food.

"Ah, I am glad you have come when you did. I believe what my brother has to say concerns us all." Ringwold gestured for Piper and Tintwist to sit down with them, after giving them their food.

Speedwell tucked in, not realising how hungry he was. As he ate, another Manelf entered the chamber, or so he thought, for there stood Fleck, an old Elfore friend, his sharp features smiling at him.

Speedwell grinned at the sight of him and stood up to give him a hug.

"Fleck, you are a sight to behold. You are still here," he greeted him.

"Where else would I be, Speedwell? This is my home." Fleck smiled with his wry old grin.

"Your home is something I have to talk to you all about, but seeing you, Fleck, has sorted out one problem for me." Speedwell smiled, for Fleck to look at him with eyes that were still as sharp as Speedwell remembered, along with that same wry look that told its own story.

Fleck had rebelled against his own kind, the Elfore. He could not blame a people for one person's actions, no matter where they had come from, so here he was living in exile with the Manelf, as an outcast, like them.

Speedwell began speaking whilst finishing his food. "I have spoken with the Ancient One. He has told me of what we must do, because of what Helistra has done. She has used the broken rune staff of Grimstone to spread evil over the Plateau Forest by poisoning it," informed Speedwell, to open-eyed silence.

"Because her poison is spreading fast, the Ancient One has decided to put a barrier between the Plateau and Great Forests along the Old Ogrin Ridge to hold the poison back whilst we ready ourselves to defeat her," explained Speedwell, to Fleck's immediate alarm.

"But that will mean the Elfore and Manelf will lose their homes, Speedwell! Must it be there?"

"The Ancient One did not want it to be this way, Fleck, but he has decided it is the best place. He sees no other choice. That is why I need you to inform your kindred of what comes their way. The Ancient One wants them to move to the Great Forest," said Speedwell.

"You ask for the impossible, Speedwell, not that I will not go, but to get them to leave their homes!" stated Fleck, shaking his head.

"You must make them listen, Fleck. Tell them if they do not leave, they will all die, or worse," replied Speedwell bluntly.

"What form does this poison take for you to say something worse could happen than dying, Forestall?" asked a puzzled Piper.

Speedwell looked at her and felt cold inside as he thought of it. "It is more than just a poison. I felt it in my dreams and when it entered me," began Speedwell. "A malevolence runs through it that I have not felt before. Whatever it touches will turn rotten and die. Trees, bushes, flowers, all will perish. The sky above will turn black as the evil rises from the forest, turning day into night. Poisonous spores await in its midst to inject deadly venom, to turn innocent animals into malevolent beasts."

Speedwell paused for a moment as he thought of the darkness that had always been in his daughter. "If the poison should enter any of you, it will attack whatever darkness it finds hiding inside of you and feed upon it, making you become the beast that lyes within. Do not be fooled. There is darkness in all of us, no matter what we choose to think," finished Speedwell, seeing the horrifying picture he had just given them in their eyes and a look of understanding from Ringwold at how Speedwell was feeling.

"Who is Helistra?" asked Tintwist suddenly, not really understanding why someone would do such a horrible thing.

"She is my daughter," replied Speedwell, sadly seeing the shock on Tintwist's face as he told him.

"Your own daughter is doing this to the forests?" Piper could not believe it, but knowing now why Ringwold had not spoken to his brother in all of this time, nor mentioned it to them.

"She is, but why is for another day," said Speedwell, dismissing it, turning instead to what had been asked of him.

"The Ancient One has set me the task of finding a King wielder so that I can protect Tomin without Helistra knowing, for one has come to him," revealed Speedwell, for Ringwold's and Fleck's eyes to widen.

"A King of Northernland in possession of a defender? But they are no more, Speedwell. We both know that," said Ringwold, frowning.

Speedwell told them of the Ancient One sensing the defender through the essence.

"So I have to find him and the shield, if he has not already," finished Speedwell.

"Whilst I and the Ancient One create a barrier and hold the binding tight," understood Ringwold.

"There is one other thing the Ancient One sensed at the same time through the essence of the pool that he wants me to seek out: two spirits," said Speedwell, looking straight at Ringwold.

"Two spirits, Speedwell?" Speedwell nodded. "Could they be what we have waited for all these years?" posed Ringwold.

Speedwell could only shrug. "It is the Ancient One's hope."

Fleck, Piper and Tintwist could only look at each other, not really understanding what they had just heard but sensing it could be important.

"We must part now. Fleck, you must make haste whilst we gather the Manelf together and tell them they must journey to the Great Forest. I will walk with you, brother, to the Ancient One and then make for Northernland," said Speedwell, going over it all in his mind, to see Piper and Tintwist looking at him.

Ringwold nodded. "It has been too long since I have been in the Ancient One's presence," he said, smiling.

Fleck gave his wry smile as he thought of seeing his kindred once more. "It will be nice to see the Valley of the Lakes as an outcast," he mused.

Piper and Tintwist had not taken their eyes off Speedwell; how they longed for adventure.

Speedwell finally looked at them both, knowing what they were after, and smiled. "You two can come with me. You will be my guardians, but keep those ears covered!" Piper and Tintwist grinned.

CHAPTER XXI

Fleck clung on to the top of a tree as the month of winds lived up to its reputation. A grey cloudy day had met his eyes when he got up there, casting a gloomy haze across the vast canopy of the Plateau Forest.

He was thinking that perhaps he should not have bothered as the tree swayed back and forth. It was dominant over the other trees, which is why he chose it, but it had not given him the view he had been hoping for, a glimpse of one of the lakes in the valley.

He should have bided his time and been patient, although seeing the Winterborne Mountains rising before him to his left had made up for it to a degree.

Fleck climbed down out of the wind to the shelter of the trees. Snow still covered most of the ground, hardened by the many frosts.

Fleck continued his journey through the forest, wondering how he would be greeted, if at all. He listened to the noises of the forest that followed him along his trail as he thought on it.

Despite the cold, birds were singing to each other in the treetops, as branches brushed together in the wind.

Somewhere, an animal was moving in the undergrowth of the forest floor, trying to find something tasty, thought Fleck, wishing the animal luck.

A squirrel suddenly ran up a tree trunk in front of him in a stop-start, nervous sort of way, for Fleck to think sadly that all this will be gone.

Then there was silence with only the wind in the trees to be heard; Fleck instinctively hid behind a tree on one knee.

He smelt the air; there was no mistaking that smell: blood. He would have smelt it earlier if he had not been daydreaming, he thought.

Then the crunching of snow underfoot could be heard, soft but clear to his ears. How many? Two? No, three. Elfore, a hunting party. Fleck stayed still and suddenly caught sight of them moving past him further on.

The Elfore hunter at the back had a small deer slung across his back. The two in front were carrying the long Elfore bows on their backs. All were in brown leather from head to toe.

There is my escort to the King. Fleck smiled and he let his hand rub against the bark on the tree.

Lightning reflexes revealed themselves as the two Elfore hunters spun round, taking their bows lightly from their backs and with arrows notched, aimed at Fleck's head. Only the sight of another Elfore had stopped them from killing him.

Fleck wondered if his own reflexes would have been just as quick to avert those arrows if he had needed to.

"My apologies to you, fellow Elfore. I did not mean to startle you," said Fleck, smiling.

"Who are you that hides in amongst the trees?" questioned the Elfore carrying the deer.

"I am Fleck, I have journeyed from the Eastern Sea to talk to the King," replied Fleck, seeing just a hint of surprise on their faces. "You have heard of me?"

"We have heard of you, the one who lives with the Manelf."

Fleck could not discern if that was contempt or knowledge in the Elfore's reply.

"Why do you wish to speak to our King?" questioned the Elfore further.

"I bring grave news of imminent danger to all who dwell in the forest," said Fleck with a warning in his voice.

"Why would our King want to listen to you, an outcast?" came back the sarcastic reply.

Now that was contempt, thought Fleck. "Because the Keeper of the North, Speedwell, has sent me," stated Fleck, making the Elfore hunting party glance at each other.

"So you would do well not to question me any further in such a manner when I bring word from a Forestall. I may be an outcast, but I am still an Elfore. I suggest you treat me as such." Fleck's tone told them they were stepping onto dangerous ground, and he watched as their faces took in his words.

"I apologise, Fleck. I should not question a messenger from a Forestall," heeded the hunter, "we will take you to King Vedland, come."

Fleck waited whilst they shouldered their bows before joining them. He watched their long bows rise above their heads as they did so, making him remember how deadly they could be. The Manelf were a match, he knew, but these bows could make an arrow travel twice as far and with an accuracy only an Elfore could master.

He looked down at their boots and leggings as he joined them, to see how similar their dress was to the Manelf, after being apart for all these years.

Two of the hunters wore leather helmets to only show their faces, whereas the third had his long hair deliberately parted so as to proudly show his pointed ears.

The trees began to rise high in the sky as they journeyed deeper into the Valley of the Lakes. Then the first of the outpost villages appeared, sheltered in the spreading arms of their grandeur.

Further in, dwellings of all sorts met Fleck's eyes in and around the trees. Fleck took them all in as if seeing them for the first time.

Some were simple stone buildings, whilst others took on a more elaborate form with funny twists and turns to them.

Above him were those of the Elfore, who wanted to be as one with the trees, their tree homes seemingly knitting into the branches of the trees, whilst others seemed to hang from them. Walkways could be seen linking them all together, spreading from tree to tree.

None of the folk took much notice of them; it was only another hunting party after all, although Fleck felt the odd curious look come his way.

"We will rest here the night," decided the hunter who had had the deer slung across his back and was now giving it to one of the Elfore folk who lived there. Fleck presumed he was the leader.

Fleck looked where they had stopped to find he was looking up some wooden steps that spiralled upwards around a huge tree, for the leader to gesture to Fleck to climb them.

Climbing them, Fleck felt all his senses being flooded with the smells he once knew so well. He breathed them in deeply until he reached a wooden dwelling woven into the branches.

He entered a surprisingly long room, to eventually find himself sitting before a fire that was in the process of being made in a large grated metal container standing on a tray to catch any embers.

The Elfore were always careful around the use of fire, wary of the damage it could do to the forest they lived in.

Immediately two more Elfore appeared as the fire took hold, with food for the hunting party, which Fleck heartily accepted.

"Does no one live here?" asked Fleck, looking around at the bareness of the long room.

"No, it is always left empty for any hunter who may pass through," replied the leader, who had sat down next to Fleck.

"You are indeed held in high esteem," remarked Fleck. "Tell me, who do I travel with to be held so?"

"I am known as Sleap, this is Levan and Bannel. We have all come from the settlement around the Lake of Tranquillity," replied Sleap, for each of them to nod their acknowledgement of each other.

No one spoke as they ate their food, but Fleck could feel Sleap wanted to ask him something.

"Tell me, Fleck, you have met the Forestall Speedwell then?" Sleap finally asked, to no surprise of Fleck's.

"Yes, I live in the same valley as his brother Ringwold and the… well, you already know," answered Fleck.

"You live with Ringwold, the Keeper of the East, and have met Speedwell!" repeated Sleap, sounding in awe to Fleck's ears.

"My words earlier were uncalled for, I spoke in haste without thinking," apologised Sleap once more.

"It is forgotten," said Fleck with a smile.

"What are the Forestall brothers like?" Sleap asked further, not helping himself. The thought that Fleck, an outcast to his kind, had spoken to them, whilst he could only imagine what they were like had aroused his curiosity.

"They are both gentle, humble men who have become haunted by the evil of Helistra," answered Fleck sadly. Eyes looked at each other as Helistra's name was mentioned.

"I too have a daughter. I cannot imagine what his mind must be going through," spoke Sleap quietly at the thought of it.

"None of us can," agreed Fleck.

The hunting party set off early the next day to a misty morning. Sunshine had tried to break through but was getting nowhere with the hanging mist that lay between the trees. No wind either, thought Fleck, to blow it away.

Only as the day wore on did the mist begin to slowly lift and let the rays of sunlight penetrate the forest's frozen floor.

Fleck was just thinking how strange it all seemed to be back amongst his own kind when there before him lay one of the lakes of the valley, revealing itself from between the trees.

Ever-present mist that the sunlight had not dispersed hovered over its calm waters. Fleck smiled as he remembered swimming in the Lake of Sorrow's cool waters once upon a time.

In truth, when he thought about it, he had swum in all of the lakes at one time or another, except the Lake of Tranquillity; no one was allowed to swim there.

It was a lake revered by the Elfore, where they believed all the souls from the departed ended their journey. Cleansed by its pure waters, their souls would return back to the earth.

The forest around the hunting party started to bustle with Elfore as they travelled towards the middle of the Valley of the Lakes, whilst the path they trod became wider and intersected by other paths.

Dwellings began showing themselves again, but in greater numbers amongst trees that stood tall and proud as Fleck remembered them. He looked up to see more walkways linking treehouses together, looking like spiders' webs in the sky, with Elfren running along them, laughing. He saw them stop to stare at who they were and then run off again.

Fleck started to notice the odd Elfore pointing at him, the deeper they walked into the Valley of the Lakes. He could guess what they were saying: "That is the Elfore outcast who lives with the Manelf!"

Night drew in upon them to rest again, this time in a cabin on the forest floor, to Fleck's disappointment.

After he had eaten, Fleck stood at the cabin doorway breathing in the cold night air. He was joined by Sleap and they both took a moment gazing at the torches that lined themselves along the path they were to take the next day, not that there were that many to see, with the Elfores' wariness of fire.

"You have travelled far to hunt, Sleap," remarked Fleck, having thought about it as he looked out.

"We are one of many hunting parties sent out to see where the best game lyes," replied Sleap. "We were lucky to have seen the one we caught. The deer herds were nowhere to be seen," replied Sleap, thinking nothing of it, and he returned back inside the cabin.

Fleck reflected upon Sleap's answer as he looked at the dwellings flickering in the light given by the torch flames, remembering Speedwell's words of what destruction was on its way if the Elfore did not leave.

"Perhaps the deer have left already," he said to himself and he turned, shutting the door behind him, leaving his words to fade in the cold night air.

Another misty day met the hunting party as they set off once more. It did not seem long before Elfore began lining the way, pointing and talking behind their hands to each other.

As the day wore on, and the closer they came to the Lake of Tranquillity, so his presence had started to bring everyone out to line the way.

The word of mouth is quicker than an arrow, thought Fleck with a wry smile to himself as suddenly two guards appeared before them.

"Sleap, you are back. Who is this who travels with you?" asked one of the guards, not taking his eyes off Fleck.

"This is Fleck, he—" began Sleap, to be interrupted by the other guard.

"Fleck? Fleck is the outcast who lives with the Manelf!"

"The very same," replied Fleck, feeling he should bow.

"He brings urgent news from Speedwell the Forestall for our King Vedland," finished Sleap.

The first guard's eyes left Fleck to look at his comrade as Sleap said Speedwell; a moment passed as he thought. "Very well, I will ask the King if he will give an audience to the outcast Elfore."

Fleck looked at the guard with some amusement. "The outcast Elfore. I suppose that is better than the traitor at least, when I was last here. Tell King Vedland if he does not give me an audience then the deaths of everyone here will be upon his conscience," warned Fleck, for the guards to look at him then Sleap, wondering what he meant by his remark before leaving them to see the King.

The hunting party moved on, whilst Fleck thought of how he was going to persuade the King to leave here on the word of a Forestall he did not trust. But he had to!

The vastness of the Lake of Tranquillity opened up before Fleck and as if on cue a shaft of sunlight broke through the grey clouds to reflect off its surface. How Fleck had missed seeing the lakes like this.

He let his eyes wander slowly over everything before taking in what he had sacrificed for all these years.

A giant tree towered in front of him, standing proud of the lake, with steps on one side of it leading upwards into its branches to a dwelling that overlooked the lake.

A stepped wooden platform stretched out either side of the giant tree along the lake's banks, where Elfore could come to enjoy the lake's beauty.

Fleck had to go and look. Stepping up onto the platform, he breathed in the lake's beauty with a sigh. She would destroy this, he thought.

He then heard footsteps behind him. Looking around, he saw Sleap and his two comrades bowing, to realise the person who was climbing the steps was King Vedland.

Fleck bowed and then took in King Vedland before he spoke. He was dressed no differently to any other Elfore, that of simple cloth seen underneath a cloak of leather. Only a wide metal belt of woven intricacy showing the craftsmanship of the Elfore stood him out from the rest.

"Sire, I am honoured with your presence," spoke Fleck as he met King Vedland's eyes.

"I never thought to see you, Fleck. My father told me of you. I am told you have urgent news from the Forestall Speedwell, the one you sided with rather than your own, but I am here to listen to what he has to say, and what is this about my conscience?" queried King Vedland, letting Fleck know he was not happy with him being there.

"I apologise for such language, King Vedland, but I needed to get your attention," began Fleck, "Helistra is amongst us once more. She has sent poison to the Plateau Forest to destroy it and all who live in its shelter," warned Fleck.

"What can I do? Is that not up to Speedwell to stop her, her father?" replied King Vedland with some disdain in his voice, not grasping the enormity of what Fleck was trying to tell him.

"It is, sire, but her powers have grown tenfold. Her evil spreads rapidly in the West at this very moment, poisoning the forest. The Ancient One has spoken to Speedwell with the intention of creating a barrier across the Old Ogrin Ridge to hold her poison back. Ringwold is already on his way there to help them. That is why I am here, to warn you! You must leave here and go to the Great Forest behind the barrier, before it is too late!" implored Fleck.

King Vedland looked at Fleck whilst he tried to take in what he had just said to him.

"The Old Ogrin Ridge? The Ancient One is prepared to surrender all of the Plateau Forest! All of our homes!" King Vedland was incredulous, gesturing with his hand all around him as he spoke.

"There must be somewhere else other than the Old Ogrin Ridge to hold this poison back before it gets here? What poison has she cursed upon the forest for such action? Do Speedwell and the Ancient One know what they are doing?" gasped King Vedland, questioning Fleck as he realised what was being asked of him.

"They know, sire. The Ancient One has felt the potency of Helistra's poison and Speedwell has seen its malevolence, for them to take these drastic steps. Time is needed so they can organise themselves to defeat her, sire," answered Fleck.

"How much time do they need to allow this to happen?"

"I do not know, sire, but you must leave here," warned Fleck again, seeing the turmoil King Vedland was going through.

King Vedland turned to look along the forest path, where Elfore stood watching them talk.

"You expect my people to leave their homes where generations have lived before them?"

Fleck heard his own thoughts in King Vedland's words; he could only repeat what Speedwell had said to him. "Leave here or die, sire, or worse."

King Vedland looked at Fleck with a frown to then echo Piper's thoughts. "Is not death enough in itself? What could be worse than that?"

"Death in itself is peace, but this poison will not allow that," warned Fleck, and he told him of what Speedwell had said would happen if the poison should ever touch anyone.

Fleck did not have to look at the faces around him to see the reaction of the horror he had just described; he had felt the same.

"How can I trust the word of Speedwell when it is his own daughter's hand that plagues us?" challenged King Vedland.

"It is not Speedwell's fault, sire, that she has turned evil. If you do not trust him then you are saying that the Ancient One is not to be trusted either. Your father turned his back on me because of my trust in Speedwell, but I would advise you not to do the same now. It would be the end of the Elfore!" came Fleck's stern warning.

King Vedland looked at Fleck, hearing the hurt in his voice that still lay deep inside of him from his father's decision. Though he would not normally tolerate such conduct, he heard Fleck clearly enough. He should not question a Forestall, let alone the Ancient One.

"You are right. The evil that Helistra does is not of his making, but I will need proof of this happening before I speak of leaving here, proof that her evil is spreading poison throughout the forest," decided King Vedland, to Fleck's alarm.

"Proof, sire! How am I going to do that? If I try to bring something back that is poisoned, it would poison me!" exclaimed Fleck.

"Would my word be proof enough, sire?" intervened Sleap, "if I go with Fleck and see the poison for myself?"

King Vedland looked at Sleap and nodded. "I will trust what your eyes see, hunter," he agreed.

"I have spoken of trust, sire, but I can see you need more than just the word of a Forestall or the Ancient One. You do not turn your back on them, but you still question if they are right!" said Fleck, annoyed by King Vedland's decision.

"I have to have some sort of proof, Fleck. I cannot tell my people to leave their homes at the bequest of someone whose very name we do not speak of," insisted King Vedland.

"There is one other thing that I have not mentioned," remembered Fleck.

"Which is?"

"The Ancient One has felt the call of a defender," declared Fleck, to see the look of surprise on King Vedland's face.

"A defender! The call of Gentian after all this time!" King Vedland could not believe it. "That is where Speedwell goes now, to find it and the shield, as we speak," informed Fleck.

"To help protect him in his fight against Helistra?" said King Vedland thoughtfully.

"To help protect his grandson from his mother's hand!" stated Fleck, to the shock of King Vedland.

"Once Speedwell has found the King wielder, he is going to secure his grandson from his hiding place under cover of the defender to help with the barrier. All will be needed if we are to defeat Helistra," informed Fleck further, to the shake of King Vedland's head.

"He is in hiding from his own mother because she would see him dead!" King Vedland could not believe what he was hearing.

"The call of a defender does not just happen. It is always for a reason," said King Vedland thoughtfully, "but no matter what is happening, I will still need you to seek out proof, Fleck, and report back to me," ordered King Vedland, for Fleck to resign himself to the task asked of him.

"Very well, sire, if it is your wish then I can only obey," acknowledged Fleck and he bowed, to leave King Vedland to his own thoughts of how he was going to tell his people to leave their homes. He hoped that time would never happen, but the call of a defender and the evil intent of Helistra told him otherwise.

Fleck walked away with Sleap, Levan and Bannel, with a worried feeling of what could be waiting for them.

"We only have to see that something is wrong, Fleck, and report back," said Sleap, reading Fleck's mind.

"That is true, Sleap, but you were not there when Speedwell told us of the poison she has cast upon the forest," recollected Fleck.

"But you have told us, Fleck."

"I know, but what you did not hear from me was the cold fear I heard in Speedwell's voice," remembered Fleck, to look into Sleap's eyes with nothing but worry etched upon his face.

"We will see it through, Fleck," encouraged Sleap.

"I hope so, Sleap, for the sake of us all."

CHAPTER XXII

How the waves enjoyed the north winds helping them lash into the cliffs where Elishard Castle was perched. Nothing protected the castle from the howling wind that tried relentlessly to find any cracks there might be within its thick walls.

No movement could be seen inside its walls or from the town outside them. Everyone was indoors on such a day, huddled around their fires with hands outstretched to catch their warmth.

Seagulls were normally the masters of the air here, but even they thought better of flying on a day like today.

The stoutly figure of King Stowlan gladly rubbed his backside against the roaring fire of the hall as Cantell and Kelmar recounted the past weeks of what had happened to them. King Stowlan listened to their account with his bushy eyebrows moving up and down to the movement of his leathery face as their story unfolded.

"It is only thanks to Kraven that we sit here today," finished Cantell.

"How you have come through such an ordeal, only the waters of the sea know," said King Stowlan, rubbing one of his eyebrows out of habit.

"It only happened that Kraven was in that part of the Kingdom patrolling our border near Marchend. Feelings are running high in that bridged town, as they are in Leckfell. There is so much unrest," said King Stowlan, sounding unsettled himself.

"There can be no surprise, sire. That is what war does," said Kraven, adjusting his eye patch, which itched in the heat from the fire.

It was at times like these when it irritated him, when he wished he had not been playing with his friend at warriors. He had learnt early on in life the pain of a wounded warrior.

That wooden sword had changed how people looked upon him. Though he was a mild- mannered man at heart, his eye patch had made people wary of him; to their eyes, it gave him a hardness that was not there.

It was thanks to him that they were all there, albeit bandaged, or limping, as in the case of Kelmar and Tarbor.

They had spent a while healing in Walditch before moving to Elishard Castle. Cantell's arm was tied to his side, which he found extremely awkward, but his arm for now had been made useless by that arrow and the less movement the better.

Kelmar cursed at his painful limp, whilst Tarbor was more wounded by the loss of his good friend Girvan.

Oneatha's shoulder ached from her wound, but she was on the mend, whereas Permellar had withdrawn into herself, only able to see the faces of her dead father and husband forever in her mind.

All sat, as best they could, along a large wooden table that had the remains of the food they had just eaten scattered over its top. Oneatha with Permellar had withdrawn to look after Prince Martyn and Kayla whilst the men talked.

"Your help in our hour of need is appreciated, King Stowlan," acknowledged Cantell, "but Tiggannia could have done with your help when it was really needed." Cantell had tried to bite his tongue remembering King Rolfe's words, but he had to say something.

King Stowlan looked at Cantell, knowing he would probably feel the same way if he was him, but he was unwavering in his own decisions as to what he did or did not do.

"I understand your anger, Cantell, but Balintium's army compared to that of Cardronia and Waunarles is but a token force. You were already under siege when news reached me of the invasion. Then when news arrived that your garrisons at Axeford and Estleton had fallen, I had to make a decision. That decision was not to send such an inadequate force as ours to your aid. They would have been slaughtered for a cause that was already lost," explained King Stowlan bluntly.

Cantell could not argue with King Stowlan's reasoning, however hard to take. He could hear King Rolfe in his ear now: *Their battle is with the soil, Cantell.*

Kelmar looked at Tarbor when the garrisons were mentioned; it was news to him. "Why have you never talked about our garrisons falling?" he asked, but knew he was wasting his time when he received a blank expression back. *Why would you?* he thought to himself. *You only hear voices from rocks!*

"I heard the rumours of who was thought to be at fault for the deaths of the royal family of Waunarle," continued King Stowlan, "but as the years passed by, that was all I thought they were, rumours. Just how wrong can someone be? I let that time lull me into a false sense of well-being. Our trade agreements were in place with everyone, the land was good to us. That an invasion of your Kingdom would happen was the last thing on my mind. I am not proud of myself for being so blind to what was always in the wind waiting to happen," admitted King Stowlan, feeling guilty.

"You were not the only one not to see what was unfolding for all those years," revealed Cantell. "King Rolfe chose to ignore his advisors on what was happening in Cardronia until it was all too late," disclosed Cantell.

"Now that pig Taliskar sits on the mountain throne of Stormhaven," cursed Kelmar.

"And the one who pulls the strings sits with him, Queen Helistra," said Tarbor suddenly. "She is the one to be wary of!"

King Stowlan looked quizzically at Tarbor. "Why should we worry about Queen Helistra? Is it not King Taliskar we need to be watchful of? He may not rest now Stormhaven is in his hands, for which I must prepare," put King Stowlan.

"Tarbor is convinced she is a sorceress who has manipulated King Taliskar to her needs, but what they are?" Kelmar shrugged. "He possesses a sword called a defender and believes it will put an end to her," conveyed Kelmar, mocking Tarbor in his tone.

"I do not know if that is the case, Kelmar, and I hope I am wrong about her, but this feeling I have will not go away. You would do well not to keep mocking me. My friend died saving your Prince," Tarbor reminded Kelmar with a warning in his voice.

If Kelmar had not broken his leg and Tarbor's shoulder had not been sliced through, Cantell could have seen their swords crossing each other. He knew Kelmar still mistrusted Tarbor, even though he had saved Prince Martyn.

"Tell King Stowlan about your beliefs and what you have heard, Tarbor. The day is foul and we still must heal before we can do anything," suggested Cantell, already seeing Kelmar getting ready to leave before he had finished speaking.

Cantell held his arm. "He was our enemy, Kelmar, but now we cannot judge him the same. He told us true that he would help protect Prince Martyn, and did so whilst losing his comrade by his own. Remember, Druimar had heard of these ancient weapons. Do not stain his memory by acting in haste."

Kelmar looked at his friend, if it had been anyone else but him, and he resigned himself to listening to Tarbor's story once more.

Tarbor was not really in the mood to talk about anything, but as he started to tell King Stowlan and Kraven of what had happened to him at the beginning when he entered Stormhaven, he found himself caught up in its mystery, revealing his thoughts as he spoke.

"My path is clear to me now. Once I have been to Slevenport to give Girvan's father the news of his son's death, I am going into the Great Forest to seek out the name I heard: Speedwell. He must live there with the Elfore somewhere. Perhaps then I will understand what has happened to me and with his help be able to defeat her evil," finished Tarbor, to utter silence.

The silence was broken only by the crackling fire and King Stowlan scratching his head. He stood there with his mouth open, wondering what in the name of the sea he had just heard.

"So you do believe Queen Helistra to be a sorceress and this ancient sword you carry a defender of the Kingdom, but if I have listened to you correctly, you are saying you have to be the King of Waunarle?"

"I know how it sounds, King Stowlan. I am as much in disbelief as you. I have gone over and over it all in my mind a thousand times, but I am not making any of it up," expressed Tarbor in frustration at it all.

King Stowlan did not know what to make of it. He could see Tarbor had trouble believing it himself, but could also see he meant every word.

Kelmar shook his head, smiling. "I told you, he is disillusioned."

"I am finding a lot of what you have told me hard to digest, and you say you are going to go into the Great Forest to find this Speedwell, because of a voice you heard through a rock?" asked King Stowlan, understanding Kelmar's scepticism.

"Yes, I am, sire, but I am troubled for the safety of Princess Amber. She will be vulnerable to Queen Helistra's control," worried Tarbor.

If Kelmar agreed about anything, it was about that, even if it was with a different understanding. "We should rescue the Queen and Princess," said Kelmar, looking at Cantell, without thinking of the danger it involved.

"That is not what King Rolfe wanted, Kelmar," argued Cantell straight away. "Our duty is to protect the Prince!"

"He will be under our protection, Cantell, whilst you are here. If anyone comes here to harm him then we will have to meet that threat with force," promised King Stowlan. "We have stood by and watched you suffer long enough. The time has come to make a stand."

Cantell half smiled back in thanks to King Stowlan, but it did not change his mind. "It could be certain death. Kelmar! We have our orders!"

"I cannot stay here whilst Queen Elina and the Princess are prisoners! I must try!" pressed Kelmar.

Just then, a guard entered the hall and whispered into Kraven's ear. Kraven looked at the guard with a frown. "Are you sure?" The guard whispered to Kraven again. "Very well, you may go."

All had gone quiet whilst the guard was giving Kraven his message. King Stowlan looked at Kraven expectantly.

"News has just arrived, sire, that King Taliskar is no more at Stormhaven," relayed Kraven vaguely.

"What, has he taken to march upon us?" worried King Stowlan in fear.

"No, sire, he has disappeared!"

"What do you mean disappeared? Explain yourself."

"Cardronian soldiers returning home were overheard in Midworth saying that King Taliskar had disappeared. He had not been seen leaving Stormhaven, but nevertheless he was not to be found anywhere and his disappearance is said not to be the only one! Prisoners who were captured during the siege are lesser in number too!" spoke Kraven, trying to clarify what he had just been told.

"Wounded prisoners put into the dungeons would always be in fear of looking death in the face," remarked Cantell.

"But the soldiers were heard to say there were no bodies to be found, so they could be buried or burnt," replied Kraven.

"What none?" King Stowlan said, frowning.

"That is what the messenger told me."

"As if there is not mystery enough!" said Kelmar, looking at Tarbor. "Your spies are reliable, I trust, not to be wrong in what they heard?" questioned Kelmar.

"Always," confirmed Kraven.

"Then there is no better time than now, with King Taliskar gone, however that might be, to rescue Queen Elina and the Princess," broached Kelmar of Cantell.

"They will be on their guard even more, Kelmar, because of it," pointed out Cantell.

"I am willing to gamble upon the confusion left by his disappearance to rescue them," responded Kelmar to Cantell's groans.

"But, Kelmar, your duty, our duty, is to Prince Martyn!" repeated Cantell. "What if you are caught? You know where we are!" he pointed out.

"Then my blade will send me to meet my King," said Kelmar, without a thought for himself.

He needed to do something; whether his life was at risk or not, the thought of Queen Elina being a prisoner and Princess Amber being under the influence of Queen Helistra did not agree with Kelmar's warrior-like thinking.

"I cannot stop you, but even if I could help with two good arms, I would not be going with you. One of us must stay with Prince Martyn," asserted Cantell, to an understanding nod from Kelmar as to what he was asking of his friend.

"I can help, Kelmar. I know just the thing a soldier needs when his nerves are stretched, it will get us in anywhere," said Kraven unexpectedly, with a knowing smile.

King Stowlan was not going to say anything to his trusted friend Kraven; they had stood back long enough. If he could help, he was not going to stop him.

"Good, we will set off on the morrow. My leg will be mended by the time we get there," said Kelmar with a smile.

Tarbor was lost in thought all this time as he turned over in his mind what he had just heard. The mover of mountains has disappeared? She was not in fear of him, he would have been her foil, he reasoned. So why would he disappear? Was she planning something? But what could that be? Questions tumbled through Tarbor's mind.

"Beware of her, Kelmar. Another pawn in her game has been removed," he warned him, after thinking.

Kelmar looked at Tarbor in total disregard. "Do not worry about me. My path is clear. I would worry about the path you are taking," he advised sarcastically.

Tarbor did not rise to his sarcasm. "If you need help when you are at Stormhaven, seek out Tarril and Cillan, the guards who were at Kelmsmere. They will help you. They are friends who also know of my feelings about Queen Helistra," advised Tarbor, even though he knew he was asking Kelmar to seek out two of the guards that were guarding his mother.

Kelmar nearly fell off his bench. "You must think I am as mad as you! I will not be mentioning your name to anyone if I want to keep my life, let alone to those particular guards! I am sure they would want to help me, friends of yours or not!" Kelmar shook his head in disbelief.

He is right, thought Tarbor, *that was stupid of me.* "You are right, Kelmar. I should not have mentioned them, it was just a thought."

"Well, whilst we remain here, in your absence I will quietly begin organising our Kingdom of farmers into a fighting force, what I should have done in the first place. They will have to learn how to handle a sword as well as a plough from now on," promised King Stowlan. "I will inform King Meldroth of Silion of events, and trust he will take the same action," proposed King Stowlan to the agreeable nods of everyone, except Tarbor.

He worried that it did not matter what they did. Something told him that she had planned all of this a long time ago, and whatever it was, it was already happening.

CHAPTER XXIII

An old cutaway path that led over the corner of the Linninhorne Mountains had come in handy as a shortcut through to the western part of the Plateau Forest for the Elfore party.

Eventually, it had emerged to overlook the forest, which normally could be seen as far as the eye could see, but not today.

Instead, a carpet of whispery mist had gathered over the forest's canopy to greet their eyes as they walked along the old stony path towards its clinging greyness.

A grey sky loomed overhead to keep out the sun and though snow still held on the mountains, only wetness waited to greet them on the forest floor, now it was the month of rain.

The path began to slowly descend as Sleap, Levan and Bannel followed Fleck down its narrow cutaway until finally it merged into the forest.

A breeze played across their faces as they trampled the forest floor, but the mist did not seem to want to move under its coaxing.

"This mist looks like it is going to be with us for the rest of the day," remarked Sleap, looking around him.

"There is little chance of seeing the sun break through that grey sky, if we could see the sky!" added Levan as everyone instinctively looked up to see the mist hanging all around them in the trees.

"The day is set for us," confirmed Bannel, as Fleck looked upon the mist with a different feeling coming over him, hoping it was just the weather and nothing else.

"Do you think we will find anything, Sleap?" asked Bannel from the back.

"If what Fleck has told us about might be out there, then I hope not!" answered Sleap over his shoulder.

Onwards they travelled, ever deeper into the forest, starting to feel it getting decidedly colder. A murky dampness seemed to be permeating the forest air as they walked further on.

Fleck stopped a moment to listen. Sleap listened with him; they could both hear something, but what was it?

"What is that, Fleck?" queried Sleap. "I am not sure," answered Fleck, but as he spoke, something made him look up.

Through the misty gaps of the trees he spotted the silhouette of a bird, then another, then more, all squawking to each other as if in warning as they flew towards the mountains.

"There is your answer," said Fleck, as the others looked up with him to see the mist turn darker with the birds' passage as their numbers increased to become hundreds!

The mist swirled around to the flapping of their wings as they made, to Fleck's mind, their escape, but from what he worried!

Fleck did not want to think of what was ahead of them and when he saw the look in his fellow Elfores' eyes neither did they.

"That is not a good sign," worried Levan.

"Something has scared them," said Sleap warily, and they all looked at each other with the same feeling of dread.

Onwards they walked, with caution entering their every step. Fleck stopped and looked up again, smelling the air.

Birds were still flying above them in lesser numbers, but now he could hear movement in front of them! Before the party knew where they were, animals of every description appeared from between the trees, for them to dive for cover behind them.

The hunters and the hunted ran side by side in the stampede of animals rushing past them.

Wolves sped straight through, whilst deer ran and bounced past, eyes wide in fright. Bears could be heard grunting with the effort of running as they tried to keep up with boars, foxes and wild cats that seemed to be chasing each other as they hastened to distance themselves from whatever it was that had frightened them.

All ignored the travellers hiding behind the trees in their flight to get away, but what was it that was making them do this? Fleck was not looking forward to finding out the answer.

"What is happening?" said Bannel, looking around only to see squirrels jumping from branch to branch above him, whilst rabbits and martens scurried past him on the ground as they strove to get away also.

"They smell death!" said Fleck fearfully, and warily they started to walk through the forest again.

As they carried on, those animals that could not keep up with the rest began coming past them. Rats darted in amongst their feet, whilst snakes slithered their way through.

"I have never seen such a thing before," said Sleap, trying to move his feet out of the way of more snakes.

"Nor I," sighed Fleck.

As if nothing had taken place, the forest became deathly quiet. No squawks or wings beating in the air could be heard, no paws or hooves sounded pounding across the forest floor or cries of alarm from animals' frightened mouths; only the murky silence was left.

Moving slowly forward, the party's eyes were everywhere as they notched arrow to bow.

Fleck began smelling the air again. "Can you smell that?" he whispered.

"Yes, we can. Something smells rotten," answered Sleap.

A narrow river announced itself, journeying through the forest just ahead of them, winding through the trees from the Linninhorne Mountains. As the party approached it, they stopped dead in their tracks at the scene that presented itself on the other side of the river. Fleck did not know where to look first.

Mist had been with them all day, but the mist that confronted them now was of a denseness they had never encountered before. It rolled heavily over the riverbank whilst holding its cold grip over the ground behind. Trees were caught in its cold embrace as it weaved its way through them towards the river.

But it was not the dense mist that had caught their attention, but what was springing from it, crushing the very life out of the trees!

Creeping vines were rising from it, twisting around the trees in a death grip. They oozed poisonous green slime as they slid up the trees, penetrating their bark and trunks to deliver their poison into the trees' very hearts.

Then rising out of the mist came strange-looking giant pods, opening to reveal deadly spores waiting inside. Suddenly the pods exploded, releasing their spores. They shot everywhere, attaching themselves to whatever they touched.

At first, nothing seemed to happen, but then the smell that they had all smelt came to them, the smell of decay as the spores injected their deadly venom.

Trees that were already under attack from the vines now suffered the spores' venom, whilst bushes began to turn rotten before their eyes.

"She has defiled the forest with evil!" cried Fleck, as a pod shot over the river to attach itself to a nearby tree.

They watched in horror as it slowly opened to reveal its deadly contents. "Look out!" was the cry, and they all dived to the ground as the spores shot everywhere.

No sooner had they hit the ground than out of the mist appeared heads of animals of which they had never seen the like. Yellow eyes stared at them, with fang-like teeth bared in their direction, dripping with saliva.

They were no longer the animals they once were, thought Fleck; they had been turned into beasts by her evil.

The beasts hurled themselves across the narrow river, to be met by the Elfore arrows from where they fell. Two of the beasts hit the water with arrows straight through their heads, but two more lunged on top of Bannel, who had fallen awkwardly and was unable to let fly an arrow.

The beasts' fangs drove deep into him as they bit and clawed at his body. He managed to grab his dagger and drive it into the head of one of the beasts.

Sleap was up and to his aid, to see the other beast meet its death as his long, narrow sword sliced through its neck, but the damage was done. Bannel's throat had been ripped away and his face was mauled beyond recognition. He lay there with the beast Sleap had slain on top of his body, covered in blood.

Another pod shot across the river, hitting a tree behind them. Sleap dived to the ground once more as it exploded, sending its deadly spores all over them, for two to hit Levan in the face.

"Get them off you!" shouted Fleck, but no matter how he tried, Levan could not pull them out; they had latched into his skin.

Red lines started to appear, moving across his face, and it was not long before he was shouting in agony as the venom took hold. His body started to convulse as he lay there, until suddenly Levan moved no more.

"Sleap! We must get out of here!" cried Fleck. Sleap was staring at Levan and Bannel; he was not prepared to see his comrades die so horribly.

He turned to look at Fleck; his face was deathly white. "Do not worry, Fleck, you will not stop me from leaving this evil place!" But something did!

Levan's face had turned ghastly; his body twitched. He had not died but had turned into the beast that lay within him. The venom had searched for the darkness inside him and found it. Now he suddenly rose and thrust his sword straight into Sleap's back.

Sleap looked down in open shock at his stomach where Levan's sword blade had come out. Fleck gasped in disbelief. "Sleap!" Sleap dropped to the floor on his knees. Fleck looked at the cruel, disfigured face that had suddenly taken over Levan and did not hesitate; his sword took off Levan's head in an instant.

Fleck dropped to his knees at the side of Sleap, choking, "Sleap!"

"Do not concern yourself… over me, Fleck. I am going to meet my friends once more. Do just one thing for me…" he said, coughing.

"Of course I will, Sleap. What is it?"

"Make sure my wife and daughter are…" He was gone.

Another pod hit a tree to the side of Fleck; there was no time to think of what had just happened, but go! Go as fast as he could!

CHAPTER XXIV

Tarbor tied up his horse and walked into the inn for a much-needed drink. He was glad to have finally made it to Fenby to rest his aching shoulder.

He had made sure to blend in by dressing as a farmer but hoped no one would ask him anything to do with tilling the land.

He sat staring into his pot of ale, thinking of his meeting with Girvan's father. It had not been easy to tell him of his son's death, but he had done it.

He was going to tell him about the defender but thought better of it. Though he knew Girvan would have wanted him to, he decided against it. It would only get him killed, he had thought.

Instead, Tarbor spoke of a skirmish they had had and how Girvan had died protecting him, but not that it was from his own kind. He told him that he had been laid to rest with a good friend, who had also lost his life in the skirmish, looking out across the East Marchend Valley.

Girvan's father had thanked him for coming all that way to tell him about what had happened and where he could go to say goodbye.

He had been happily hammering a horseshoe into shape when Tarbor had got to his forge, but as Tarbor left, he was sitting with his head in his hands, quietly crying at the loss of his son.

Taking a drink of his ale, Tarbor looked around him. He must have arrived on a market day, he thought, with the amount of farmers that were here.

He had still come to Fenby as arranged that cold night, but his injuries and need to go to Slevenport had made him arrive much later than first thought. He was of the mind that Urchel and Idrig had already been here, to have left ages ago when he had not shown.

He managed a half-smile as he thought of them always meeting here, but it was no use sitting around waiting for them, he thought, so after feeling rested, Tarbor swallowed the rest of his ale and made to get up. It was time for him to go.

As he did so, a shout came from the door where two – so Tarbor had thought at first – farmers had just walked in, "Tarbor!" Before he could say *Shush!* there was Idrig and Urchel hugging him, glad to see he was still alive.

"What are you doing here!" laughed Idrig in fun, ordering ale before he sat down. Tarbor looked around to see if anyone was taking a second look at them before he answered.

"More to the point, what are you two still doing here?" Tarbor could not help but smile back, secretly glad they were both here.

"The journey was long and the thoughts were many, taking Brax to Slevenport. We thought that if we reported back to Stormhaven, having let you ride off, we would be in trouble, the kind we did not want. So we decided to take a chance by not returning. Instead, we went to my farm at Greenwater for a short while and after meeting up with you, we were going to Idrig's farm where his brother is," explained Urchel.

"Hmm, for letting me out of your sight, you are probably right, but it would not have been King Taliskar you would have faced," said Tarbor, getting blank looks.

"King Taliskar has gone missing from Stormhaven and nobody knows what happened to him," explained Tarbor.

"Missing? How can that be?" questioned Urchel.

"No one knows, but word has it that he is not the only one!" And Tarbor told them of what was said at Elishard.

"He is either a brave man or a fool to go back there," remarked Urchel, hearing of Kelmar's plan to rescue Queen Elina and the Princess.

"I am glad we decided not to go back to Stormhaven, if Queen Helistra is the one waiting to greet us," said Idrig, taking a slurp of his ale.

"She is, Idrig. She has all the power now. I do not like to think of what she will do with it," worried Tarbor.

"Your thoughts still say it is her who is the danger then, Tarbor?" asked Urchel.

"More so than ever, now Taliskar is no longer," replied Tarbor.

"You have not mentioned your encounter with the Tigannians and the Prince. I presume it was successful by you being here and to have travelled with them to Elishard," said Urchel with a smile. "And Girvan, he is well? Where is he?" asked Urchel further.

Smiles turned to worried frowns when they saw the look in Tarbor's eyes.

"What has happened, Tarbor?" asked Urchel, already not wanting to know the answer. Tarbor told them of Girvan's fate quietly over another drink.

"He lyes with Permellar's father, Druimar, overlooking the Eastern Valley," finished Tarbor sadly.

"There is no better place to be at rest than in the valley," said Urchel, trying to suppress his tears.

"That Wardine deserved to die!" cursed Idrig under his breath. "Will anyone else be after you, Tarbor?"

"There may well be, Idrig, when no one returns, but if they go after the Prince they will have to answer to King Stowlan this time, if they find out where the Prince is, that is," stated Tarbor.

"King Stowlan stands for Tiggannia?" asked Urchel.

"He intends to quietly build up his army to withstand any invasion that might be in the making whilst still trading with them, hoping it will keep them blinkered," answered Tarbor, "and he will be seeking out King Meldroth's support," he added.

"I do not know how he will achieve that. There are spies everywhere," wondered Urchel as he thought about it.

"Balintium and Silion farmers wielding swords does not sound right." Idrig frowned, and he slurped back his ale as they all made a move to leave the inn.

Untethering his horse, Tarbor turned to his two comrades to say goodbye. "I must leave you both. We should not be seen together, not after my killing of Wardine. You are already risking enough without being seen with me. It is as you say, Urchel, there are spies everywhere," warned Tarbor.

"You are our friend, Tarbor. It is a risk we are willing to take. We are all farmers here." Urchel pointed at Tarbor's clothes, smiling.

"Well, as long as I am not asked to milk a cow!" said Tarbor, smiling.

"Where is it that you are travelling to, that you wish to be on your own?" asked Urchel as they mounted their horses.

"Now the Prince is safe and Kelmar has decided to rescue Queen Elina and the Princess, I have decided to journey into the Great Forest to look for the one I heard: Speedwell," declared Tarbor.

Urchel nodded. "I always felt you would. You were troubled when you told us, but I could hear destiny in your voice," proclaimed Urchel.

"Then listen to me, Tarbor, if you are going to the Great Forest, we can journey to Idrig's farm in the Western Valley for Idrig to see his brother is safe, and then we three can enter the Great Forest together," said Urchel smilingly, with Idrig's approval.

Tarbor did not know what to say; they would follow a madman. He smiled to himself. "Your company would be most welcome." He smiled at their offer.

"Good, but the day is nearly done and we know just the place to rest the night," answered Urchel, for Idrig to grin.

The three horsemen rode out of Fenby in the early morning towards the Wreken Moors, having rested the night on its outskirts at a favourite lodgings of Urchel's and Idrig's.

An elderly woman of long acquaintance had looked after them. Feeding them until they thought their bellies were going to burst, to fall asleep in front of a roaring fire with a pot of ale in their hands. Tarbor knew now why they came to Fenby Market and no other.

The weather had decided to take a turn for the worse from an overcast sky as their cloaks rippled in the wind whilst rain continuously swirled around them, caught in the wind's path.

They followed the River Salleen, passing the Wreken Woods, to eventually come to the bleakness of the Wreken Moors, only for the wind to pick up.

It sent rain lashing over the heather that adorned the moors, not that they could see it properly, squinting their eyes as the wind threw the rain into their faces.

"I am glad the river shows us the way in this weather," remarked Tarbor.

"It leads us straight to the valley," said Idrig with a smile, thinking of his brother. "There are stone shelters along the way where we can rest," he added.

Now would be nice! thought Tarbor.

Onwards through the day they rode as slowly the wind and rain began to thankfully relent.

Reaching the brow of a small hill, they looked out over a sea of heather to see sheep wandering through it, ignoring them as they nibbled at the heather's shoots.

Urchel pulled up his horse and looked again. "Is that a dead sheep over there in amongst them?" He pointed.

They rode together to where he had pointed to see laying amidst the heather what remained of a sheep.

"The birds of prey have had a good day's feast by the look of that carcass," remarked Idrig, seeing all the blood and bone.

"Look over there, is that two more?" Tarbor pointed, and they rode to them.

Urchel frowned upon seeing them. "Could be wolves, but look how they have ripped them apart."

"They must have been ravenous," decided Idrig.

"Perhaps we had better keep our eyes open for them, now we can see," suggested Tarbor, smiling, and off they rode once more.

The light was starting to fade as a stone barn-like building came into view. Nestled near the river in a slight dip, it would give excellent shelter for the weary travellers.

Horses were tied and saddles removed as Idrig began making a fire from a stack of wood that was stored within the barn.

"Always a good supply here left by the farmers," said Idrig with a grin, getting the fire started.

The warmth was soon appreciated as the night closed in and clothes began to dry. Tarbor for once felt relaxed as he bit into some crusty bread the old lady had supplied them with.

"How many days will it take to get to your farm, Idrig?" Tarbor asked as he chewed away. "Perhaps two or three," said Idrig with a smile.

"I wonder what this Speedwell you seek looks like," pondered Idrig.

"He may not exist anymore," pondered Tarbor also. "Girvan said the stories that his father told him about the defenders were from a long time ago."

"Someone must exist, even if he does not. We do," reasoned Urchel, as the horses started to snort outside.

"What is ailing them? They sound frightened by something," said Urchel, frowning, and he was on his feet, going to the doorway.

"Be careful, Urchel, it could be those wolves," warned Idrig, as Urchel stepped out into the night.

Tarbor and Idrig had heard nothing when Urchel came flying through the air backwards through the doorway, with what looked like a giant dog going for his throat!

Urchel landed in a heap on the floor, somehow managing to hold the dog's snarling teeth at bay by holding its neck.

Tarbor and Idrig were up on their feet with swords in hand as the dog pinned Urchel down.

Its head suddenly turned its attention around to them, making them freeze to the spot. They had never witnessed an animal like it, if that was what it was!

Eyes of yellow glared back at them, whilst teeth like fangs dripped with saliva. Its wet grey coat covered a malformed body that throbbed with large veins pushing through its fur, whilst scars ran down its body that had healed over in horrible gatherings of yellow puss.

As suddenly as it had turned its attention to Tarbor and Idrig, it ripped into Urchel's shoulder, making him shout out in pain.

Tarbor drove the defender straight through the beast's neck, whilst Idrig found its body, to see it topple over, off Urchel.

Idrig immediately went to Urchel's aid, whilst Tarbor cautiously looked outside. The horses were in a state of panic, kicking out at the air in front of them.

There, snarling in the dark could be heard another beast, then Tarbor saw it: two yellow eyes burning in the night looking straight at him. He made ready for its attack!

Holding the defender out in front of him, he made little cutting strokes in the air as he waited for it to pounce.

It suddenly flew into the air at him and just as suddenly fell yelping to the ground, with two arrows sticking out of its head!

Tarbor stared at the dead beast in front of him. What? Where did they come from? He had no time to think. Something moved to his side; he made ready once more with his defender as three figures emerged out of the gloom.

Two had childlike faces that were smiling at his expression at seeing them holding the long bows that had just released the arrows that killed the beast.

The other figure, whose face was hidden by a hood, was holding what looked like a long walking stick and was peering at Tarbor's sword.

"Who... who are you?" Tarbor half spoke, half whispered, whilst keeping his defender pointing at them.

The hooded figure drew back his hood and revealed the face of an old man with eyes of steel blue that were looking right at him. "This is Piper and Tintwist," he said, smiling, "and I am Speedwell, King wielder!"

CHAPTER XXV

"I do not know which is worse! Driving snow or driving rain!" moaned Kraven, snapping the reins once more as he wiped his eye. Winter had supposedly just passed by and spring took its place, but on a day like today, winter was trying to hang on.

"Look at the rain as our friend, Kraven. The guards will not take much notice of us on a day such as this," said Kelmar with a smile as he watched Kraven's urging of the two horses pulling the wagon making no difference at all.

Kelmar turned his attention to look at Stormhaven stronghold's battlements looming up before them as memories flooded back to him of all those months under siege.

The two siege towers were still there outside the walls, or what was left of them. By the look of it, they had come in useful as firewood.

As they approached the gates, Kelmar heard Tarbor in the back of his mind: *Another pawn in her game has been removed. Beware of her, she is evil!*

We shall see, he thought, *we shall see.*

The huge gates were open and Kraven pulled up under the archway as two guards standing at the side door told them to stop.

"What have you there?" questioned one.

"Good day to you," greeted Kraven.

"Huh, what is good about a day like this!" scoffed the other guard.

"When you have goods like ours to deliver, the day does not matter," said Kraven, smiling.

"Traders, you are all the same. What is in your wagon?" the guard asked again.

"Why, only the finest Balintium ale you could wish to taste!" Kraven watched the two guards' expressions change.

One of the guards went to the back of the wagon and lifted the canvas sheet. He came back smiling. "Barrels of it," he said with a grin.

"Twelve, to be precise, we were told to bring it here by order of your King Taliskar," said Kraven, smiling.

The two guards looked at each other. "Have you not heard?" said one.

"Heard what?" questioned Kraven, pleading ignorance. "We are constantly on the road. We do not hear much, only what is needed and where," he added.

"Then it does not matter," said the guard, without revealing anything. "The ale will be a welcome distraction," he smiled, "go through Middle Gate above and look to your left for the storerooms," instructed the guard, waving them on, for Kraven to snap the reins and grin at Kelmar.

Kelmar looked up at the battlements. Hardly a guard showed himself as Kraven pulled into the grand courtyard and positioned the wagon near the storerooms.

Another guard appeared out of one of the doors, asking the same question as to what they had on their wagon. When Balintium ale was spoken of, he left the appropriate storeroom door open for them and disappeared to tell his comrades.

Kelmar and Kraven set about unloading the barrels of ale. Rolling them down planks off the wagon and into the storeroom.

As they were putting the last barrel into the storeroom, Kraven peeked across the grand courtyard. No guard could be seen. *Not in this weather*, he thought.

"Let us see what this secret door is all about, Kraven," said Kelmar, walking through to the back storeroom after they had stored the last barrel.

Into the corner of the storeroom they walked, to see the huge doorway that had been left open flickering in the torchlight.

Kelmar for the first time began to realise why Tarbor thought the way he did as he gazed at the doorway. How could something like that have opened if it was not magic or sorcery? And now suddenly King Taliskar was missing!

He shook his head. He was thinking like Tarbor, but here, faced with the impossible, seeing it for himself, he could begin to understand how Tarbor felt, though voices through a rock was another matter.

"Kelmar, it will soon be nightfall," whispered Kraven, open-mouthed. He had only half listened to Tarbor's ramblings, but now here it was, a doorway in the mountain!

They left the storeroom and climbed onto the wagon, all the more wary after seeing the mountain doorway.

"The servants' quarters are just over there next to the kitchen. We can rest there awhile and get ourselves dry. It is the best place to be to hear what is afoot before attempting to get Queen Elina and the little Princess," suggested Kelmar.

"Food would be good too," suggested Kraven further, suddenly feeling hungry.

"If Mrs Beeworthy is cooking then it will be," replied Kelmar smiling, as he remembered the smell of her kitchen. "I will let you do the talking. I need to keep myself to myself," added Kelmar. pulling up his hood.

Kraven pulled the wagon over and made for the servants' quarters door, with Kelmar following. A welcoming roaring fire toasted them both as soon as they walked in.

A few servants were sitting at one of three long wooden tables eating. All looked up to see who had come in, including the maid who was just clearing some empty plates from a table, Charlotte. Kelmar kept his head low. He had forgotten that Charlotte would be there too, if not attending Queen Elina.

"Greetings, travellers," she said with a smile.

"Greetings, child, we have just delivered some fine ale on this miserable day and wished to warm ourselves by your inviting fire," said Kraven, smiling back.

"Of course, sit down, both of you. Let me bring you some food."

"Thank you, that is kind of you," and without further ado, Charlotte disappeared into the kitchen.

Kelmar and Kraven sat down at the far end of one of the tables where nobody was.

Kraven nodded to the servants, smiling. "This is where to be on a day like this," he said in idle conversation to none of the servants in particular.

"The day is as dark as this place," said one of the servants, to receive a kick from under the table.

"Oh, in what way would that be?" asked Kraven, looking at Kelmar.

"Something haunts this place. I will say no more. Otherwise, I might disappear too." Without another word, all the servants got up and left, leaving the two warriors looking at each other.

Charlotte reappeared with some hot steaming food. "Ah, that looks good," Kraven said with a smile.

"Anything Mrs Bee cooks is good." Charlotte smiled back, confirming what Kelmar had said.

"Your fellow servants seemed a little edgy, child," said Kraven as Charlotte laid the food down.

"Oh, it is ever since the disappearances," she replied.

"We heard something on our travels, but disappearances, you say?" queried Kraven, thinking Charlotte looked the talkative type. He was right; Kelmar could have told him that.

Charlotte looked across to the kitchen before she sat down next to Kelmar, who kept his head over his plate as Charlotte spoke.

"Queen Helistra woke one morning to find King Taliskar was not there. He was searched for everywhere. His horse was still here, so it was presumed he must be, but he was not to be found," she explained.

"He had been drinking a lot and Queen Helistra was worried that it had caught up with him. That he was drunk and had ventured into the passageways at the back of Forest Tower, never to find his way back!" she informed them.

"That seems a reasonable assumption, if there are dangerous passageways as you have said," remarked Kraven.

"There are, but since then we have heard of prisoners disappearing from the dungeons!" she whispered.

"That is the hardship that comes with being put into dungeons. People die," put Kraven, as Cantell had.

"I thought that too, until the day when two guards came from Kelmsmere and only one was thrown into the dungeons for letting some prisoners escape, because the other one was never seen again!"

"Now, now, you be telling those stories again, young lady. He be rode away. Ignore her, she be full of gossip," chirped Mrs Beeworthy, her voice booming across the room as she walked in from the kitchen all rosy-cheeked.

Kelmar smiled inwardly at hearing her Stockdale accent once more.

"Stories of the mystery of Stormhaven, Bee," said Charlotte, sounding dramatic.

"Your mind, young girl. We have enough to be getting on with without all that," said Mrs Beeworthy, giving Charlotte a look.

"Only one put into the dungeons, though?" questioned Kraven.

"Yes, his name is Cillan. We take him food each day," said Charlotte straight away, for Kelmar to cough on some meat at hearing a name Tarbor had told him could help.

"Sounds like you be needing some of that ale you brought with you," said Mrs Beeworthy, laughing.

Kelmar held his head up and slid back his hood. "You had better get me some then, Mrs Bee, and then we can get Queen Elina out of here before she disappears too!"

Charlotte gasped, seeing the face of Kelmar right next to her as Mrs Beeworthy clasped her reddening face at seeing him.

A moment later and they were squeezing the life out of him. "Kelmar! My treasure, it is you!" Mrs Beeworthy was in raptures as Charlotte hugged him around his neck.

"Bee, Charlotte, you can let go now," he gasped.

"What of Cantell and the little Prince?" they both asked immediately.

"They are both well," replied Kelmar, without giving anything away.

"You risk much being here!" said Mrs Beeworthy after all had calmed down.

"I risk it all so as to break free our Queen and the Princess. Mrs Bee, will you help us?" asked Kelmar.

"What can we do?" asked Mrs Beeworthy, sounding worried.

"You go in and out of the royal chamber all of the time, Mrs Bee. It would be seen as normal for you to bring her down here," put Kelmar, but as he looked at her reddening face, he knew there was something amiss. "What is it, Mrs Bee?"

"I… we do not go in there as much anymore, Kelmar. Our place is down here now in the kitchen," she answered.

"Who says? Queen Helistra?" guessed Kelmar.

"Oh, no, no, she be kind and thoughtful always to us. It's just our place is here now," said Mrs Beeworthy, looking down at the floor.

Kelmar frowned. This was not like Mrs Bee; she was like a mother to Queen Elina. What was it she was not telling him?

"You could still bring her and the baby down here, Mrs Bee. We will deal with the guards," repeated Kelmar.

"What Bee is trying to say is she would if Queen Elina was still in the royal chamber," spoke up Charlotte.

"What do you mean, if she was still in the royal chamber?" asked Kelmar, looking at both of them. "Where is she then?"

"She be in the dungeons," answered Mrs Beeworthy, still looking at the floor.

"The dungeons!" exclaimed Kelmar, closing his eyes. The thought of Queen Elina down there instantly angered him.

"When I said Queen Helistra was worried about King Taliskar's drinking and thought he had had an accident in the passageways behind Forest Tower, well, what I did not tell you is that she blamed Queen Elina for luring him there to his death in one of his drunken states, so she had her put into the dungeons," explained Charlotte.

"That is a preposterous accusation! What of the Princess?" questioned Kelmar straight away.

"Queen Helistra be looking after her now in the royal chamber," answered Mrs Beeworthy, almost in tears.

Confusion weighed heavily in Mrs Beeworthy's head. In one moment she felt for Queen Elina and in the next for Queen Helistra. She did not know where she was; her feelings were all over the place. What was wrong with her? she kept asking herself.

"Now what do we do?" asked Kraven, as Kelmar tried to come to terms with Queen Elina being put into the dungeons.

At least they were still both alive, thought Kelmar, but Queen Helistra had the Princess. He could hear Tarbor now telling him, beware of her!

"I presume you have to take Queen Elina her food?" he finally asked after thinking.

"Yes, we do, Kelmar, but she has not eaten anything since being parted from Princess Amber," replied Charlotte.

"Well, it is time for her to do so. Fetch some food, Mrs Bee. I will go in your place with Charlotte and take it to Queen Elina. You will be ready to drive us out of here, Kraven, when we have rescued the Queen," ordered Kelmar.

"But what of the little Princess?" queried Kraven.

Kelmar knew they only had one chance at a rescue and that they could not be in two places at once. As soon as that chance was taken, it would alert other guards as to what they were attempting, so he had already made the difficult decision in his mind of whom they were going to rescue.

His original plan had just been ruined, thinking they would have still been together and Mrs Beeworthy could have brought them to him.

Knowing there would only be a couple of guards to deal with in the dungeons had helped make the decision for him. Forest Tower he knew would have at least six guards before getting into the royal chamber, but it was not just the lack of guards that had swayed his thoughts; Tarbor's words of warning about Queen Helistra were ringing loud and clear at this moment in his head.

So he had come to the painful decision to rescue Queen Elina from the dungeons, where if she was left, he thought, she would either die or be killed.

And though he did not like the thought of the little Princess being under the influence of Queen Helistra, he thought she had the better chance.

"She will have to remain here," he finally answered Kraven.

Mrs Beeworthy brought some covered hot food on a wooden tray and handed it to Kelmar. As she did so, she reached up to kiss Kelmar on the cheek. "Give my love to her and the little Prince when you return," she said, weeping.

"I will, Mrs Bee."

"Tell Cantell we miss him and you be minding yourself." She sighed, with tears running down her ruddy cheeks.

Kelmar gave her a smile of reassurance before disappearing with Charlotte and Kraven out into the rainy night.

Queen Helistra was in a contented mood. Earlier, her mind had watched as the broken rune staff had shown her the destruction she had caused with her casting of evil over the Plateau Forest, whilst holding Princess Amber in her arms.

Whilst embracing the visions of decay and death, she had opened the little Princess' mind so as to share them with her. Sowing the seeds of evil in her mind to grow as she grew.

As Queen Helistra had watched, decay had laid all around the little pool. Trees were rotting under the stranglehold of creepers oozing slime, whilst showers of spores had poisoned everything in their path as a poisonous mist spread over the ground, soaking into the earth. She had watched in fascination the coming of death to the forest.

She sat now where she belonged, in the royal chamber with little Princess Amber on her lap. No one was in her way – she smiled – for her to complete her quest.

"Did you see the thick mist, little one? How it caressed the ground with poison?" Queen Helistra breathed in an extra breath of satisfaction at the mere thought.

"We will go to the dungeon later to see your mother and choose our next soul giver." She laughed coldly whilst holding Princess Amber in a tight caress.

Queen Helistra stayed motionless a moment, listening. "Can I hear the beginnings of a storm, Amber?" A humming answered her. "At sea, what a spectacle that will be. Let us go and watch it," and Queen Helistra left the royal chamber, almost skipping.

Kelmar and Charlotte walked across the grand courtyard towards the dungeons. Only now did Kelmar notice his leg was aching from the journey, and he started to limp.

Reaching the dungeon door, Charlotte banged on it. Kelmar looked round; Kraven had drawn the wagon up near the stores.

A guard came to the door and looked through the grille. Seeing it was Charlotte, he opened it.

"Who is this? I do not recognise him." questioned the guard as soon as he saw Kelmar's hooded face.

"He has just arrived from Cardronia, another servant. I am showing him what he must do," replied Charlotte. The guard took a secondary glance at Kelmar and then disappeared into the guardroom.

Another guard came out of the guardroom holding a bunch of keys and escorted them down into the dungeons, not even bothering to look at Kelmar.

Torchlight lit the way down into the awful-smelling dungeons, with Kelmar keeping his face low under his hood. Gradually, the smell got worse the deeper they went down, making Kelmar remember the stench of those months being under siege.

Suddenly the guard stopped. Opening one of the cell doors, he stood back for Charlotte and Kelmar to walk in whilst he waited at the cell door.

Kelmar nearly dropped the tray when he saw the crumpled body of Queen Elina lying on the filthy floor, shackles binding her wrists and ankles.

Charlotte bent over her. "My Queen, we have brought you some food. Please try and eat some," she encouraged.

Queen Elina's head slowly rose up from the floor. Her red hair was clinging together with dirt from the cell floor and hung down raggedy over her face.

She managed to speak in a hoarse, whispery voice. "Charlotte, I cannot, I am lost," she uttered, sounding resigned to her fate as her head dropped back down.

Laying the tray down, Kelmar knelt and spoke quietly in her ear. "Then eat for me, my Queen."

At first, there was no movement from Queen Elina, then slowly her head rose. She knew that voice, but it could not be. She must be dreaming.

As she looked up and tried to focus, Kelmar put his hand over her mouth as her eyes suddenly widened. "Forgive me, my Queen. I am here to free you. Eat something whilst I deal with the guard," he said quickly, and he was up to get the keys to her shackles.

The guard was leaning on the stone wall by the cell door as Kelmar appeared from it.

"Can you not release those shackles from around her wrists to help her eat?" he pleaded, pointing, to receive a disinterested look.

"I have no time to pamper to your needs. Where is the girl?" replied the guard, looking past Kelmar into the cell. That was all Kelmar needed.

Grabbing his arm, Kelmar threw the guard through the air onto the cell floor. A dagger across the throat later and he was no more. Kelmar closed the cell door.

Queen Elina managed to sit up and let Charlotte feed her some food, to feel it go down into her aching stomach, whilst Kelmar undid her shackles.

Getting Queen Elina to her feet, Kelmar found her crying in his arms. "Come, my lady, be strong." He smiled, taking off his cloak for Charlotte to put over her whilst he donned the dead guard's uniform and helmet.

Cillan stood next to the grille of his cell door. He had watched each day as two women had brought food to Queen Elina, who he knew was in another cell.

He had witnessed the day she had been put there and had seen the cold malice written upon Queen Helistra's face when she had left with Queen Elina's child in her arms, ducking in the shadow of his cell door as her eyes had looked his way.

Why he had done that he did not know. He was doomed anyway, being in here. He would meet the same fate that must have met his friend Tarril, whom he had never seen again since they entered Stormhaven; otherwise, he would have been here with him.

Today for him was no different to any other day in this forsaken place, except this time it was one woman and a limping man who brought the food.

Suddenly there they were coming back, but what was going on here? That was not the guard; he had suddenly got a limp, just like the servant who had brought the food! Cillan instantly knew what was happening.

"Take me with you!" he called, loudly enough for Kelmar to hear him.

"I cannot, you will bring attention to us," answered Kelmar.

"You bring attention upon yourselves already!" was Cillan's response. Kelmar ignored him and carried on.

"Then let it be known that an innocent Cardronian awaits his fate here!" called Cillan after him. Kelmar stopped and turned.

Limping over to the grille, Kelmar looked to see Cillan staring at him through it. Cillan instantly recognised Kelmar as the one who had kicked him down the stairs and felt despair enter him once more. *He has only come over to smirk*, he thought.

"You are the guard from Kelmsmere," said Kelmar, recognising him.

"You have a good kick," replied Cillan, beginning to turn his back on Kelmar, giving up, but as he did so, he heard keys jangling then the cell door opening.

"Come then, Cillan the innocent," offered Kelmar.

"Thank you." Cillan smiled thankfully, unsure as to why a Tiggannian who had booted him down the stairs would help him now and how he knew his name.

Kelmar could easily see the questions on Cillan's mind. "Thank Tarbor when you see him," said Kelmar, smiling, answering both by saying Tarbor's name.

Cillan immediately went to help a grateful Charlotte by putting his arm around Queen Elina.

"Where is your comrade, Tarril?" asked Kelmar over his shoulder as they made their way out, not seeing a look from Charlotte saying, *Did you not listen!*

"He went exploring Stormhaven whilst I slept, something he always did wherever he went, but this time he never came back. This place has a darkness to it, Tiggannian, and her name is Queen Helistra," said Cillan, making Kelmar think for a moment he had let out Tarbor.

"Hold back here," ordered Kelmar as they neared the guardroom. Drawing his sword slowly, Kelmar peeked through the guardroom grille to see two guards talking to each other over a small wooden table, with one stabbing at some meat with his dagger.

Kelmar nodded to Charlotte and Cillan to move to the dungeon door with Queen Elina whilst he found the right key to open it.

Outside, a storm had moved inland from the sea on a driving wind, bringing with it more rain than ever and as Kelmar opened the dungeon door, he felt the full force of the storm as it swept across the grand courtyard, but the storm was to Kelmar's liking. No guards would want to be in this, he was thinking.

Urging Charlotte, Cillan and Queen Elina to the waiting wagon, Kelmar shut the dungeon door, leaving the two guards in the guardroom, he hoped, none the wiser for a moment longer before they missed the guard.

As luck would have it, unbeknown to Kelmar, they had told their comrade to fetch them some of the newly delivered Balintium ale when the servants had finished feeding the Tiggannian Queen, so he would not be missed for now.

Kraven had breathed a sigh of relief when they emerged from the dungeons. He was moving the wagon forward, holding the reins tightly to keep the horses in check as they stamped the ground nervously at the sound of thunder.

Reaching Kraven, Kelmar helped Charlotte and Cillan lift Queen Elina onto the back of the wagon as another bolt of lightning hit the Kavenmist Mountains, to echo over the valley, catching the paleness of Queen Elina's face; she was barely conscious.

"Thank you, Charlotte, for all your help. We will not forget what you have done, be careful," he warned her, and he moved quickly to climb up beside Kraven.

Charlotte knew what to do; she would go and tell the two dungeon guards she had been forced to help them when they were all safely gone.

She looked at Queen Elina in the back of the wagon, and stretching out her hand, she managed to grip Queen Elina's hand one last time, to see her manage a smile of thank you as yet more lightning struck.

"Ooh, did you see that, Amber?" Queen Helistra laughed as lightning seared itself across the sky, with fingers of lightning raining down onto the sea, whilst thunder boomed across its waters, but Princess Amber was frightened by the noise of the thunder and was crying.

Queen Helistra laid her down in the ceremonial room and came back to look at the storm again as lightning hit the Kavenmist Mountains, for a movement below in the courtyard to catch her eye.

There was a wagon with people in the back of it. What were they doing? They were near the dungeons. Was that that servant girl?

She watched as she reached to touch whoever it was in the back of the wagon as lightning lit up the courtyard.

Though the figure in the back of the wagon had a hood on, a shock of knotted red hair had worked itself loose and blew in the wind, to be caught in the light of the lightning, telling Queen Helistra exactly who it was!

"They dare to rescue her, she who is nothing!" exclaimed Queen Helistra, as if talking to the storm. A humming interrupted her abrupt anger, for some calmness to be restored. "It is as you say, all is in motion, nothing is going to stop us, but I think this calls for some fun!" She grinned.

Queen Helistra moved her fingers over the runes of the broken rune staff and focused herself to be ready for the next lightning strike, which did not disappoint as one shot through the dark sky down towards the earth almost instantly.

A movement of a finger over another rune saw her draw part of the lightning's power into the broken rune staff, making it glow with its intensity as it entered.

Without hesitation and with another touch of a rune, Queen Helistra redirected some of the power she had gathered in the broken rune staff towards the wagon, to release a bolt of lightning straight at it.

Charlotte did not know what hit her! She was dead before she dropped to the floor, with a hole burnt right through her body!

Kelmar stared in disbelief as another bolt tore through the wagon, straight between a petrified Cillan and Queen Elina, narrowly missing her head.

"Go, Kraven! Get us out of here!" was Kelmar's immediate cry as he looked up at Forest Tower, from where the bolts had seemed to come.

Lightning arced across the sky to light up a grinning figure leaning over the balcony, for him to see a bright light shoot from the figure straight at them.

Kraven had not needed to urge the horses on, as they jolted into life with fright, for the bolt to sear pass them and hit the inner wall.

Queen Elina could not have moved even if she had been able to; she was in total shock. She had just seen her hand maid Charlotte burnt through before her eyes.

Kelmar had ridiculed Tarbor for his beliefs of what he thought Queen Helistra to be, but not anymore. He had seen her sorcery with his own eyes as Kraven drove through Middle Gate, sliding the wagon precariously through the archway and out of Stormhaven.

Two guards watched them ride past. "I would have waited for the storm to pass, that last strike was close," said one.

"Frightened them horses, that's for sure," said the other. "Did you see someone in the back?" he added.

"Who cares when Balintium ale awaits us!" said the other, laughing.

Queen Helistra watched the wagon career out of the gates before turning to pick up the still crying Princess Amber from the ceremonial room.

Walking back to the balcony, she stroked her tiny brow. "You missed all the fun." She grinned as she looked down at the courtyard, to see that stupid woman bending over the dead body of Charlotte.

Holding the broken rune staff, she breathed in. "I thought so, not enough to feed a hair on my head!" And her cold laughter rang out into the storm.

Mrs Beeworthy sobbed over Charlotte's body. She had opened the servants' door to thankfully see the wagon pulling away, knowing that Queen Elina must be on it, but then spotted the fallen body of Charlotte.

She stroked her wet hair and looked at the burn mark in her chest. She had been hit with a bolt of lightning. Such a fate to befall someone so young, she thought. *What with her talking of them disappearing and now this happening, this place be cursed!* she was thinking as she heard laughter; laughter that sent shivers down her spine.

CHAPTER XXVI

Tarbor sat with Idrig near the rekindled fire in a daze. It was all he could do not to stare at Speedwell. Speedwell, a name put into his mind from a rock, and here he was in front of him! He was not mad after all! And what did he call him? King wielder?

Speedwell, though, was busy mixing a potion for Urchel's wounds. He had already sent a bolt of ice-blue flame into his chest to stop the poison from spreading to a wide-eyed Tarbor and Idrig.

A green goo from various herbs had started to form in the little wooden bowl he had sought from his pouch. Urchel had nearly passed out from the bolt of ice-blue flame, but it had held the poison from the beasts' bites at bay to enable Speedwell to mix the cleansing potion.

Tarbor and Idrig watched as Speedwell quickly took a small bottle out of his pouch to let a drop of its contents fall into the bowl, hearing it bubble as it met the mixture.

Then touching the contents of the bowl with the end of his rune staff, Speedwell touched one of its symbols gently with his little finger and a stir later, he had put the potion to Urchel's lips.

A look of distaste spread across Urchel's pale face. "All of it, my friend, do not hesitate," advised Speedwell.

"Forestall, will she not feel you have used your rune staff?" said Piper as she watched.

"What I have used will not disturb the balance," replied Speedwell as he made sure Urchel swallowed all of his potion, "and Piper…"

"Yes, Forestall?"

"Call me Speedwell, both of you." He smiled, to put a smile on Piper's and Tintwist's faces.

"Burn those beasts, both of you, but be careful, their blood is tainted. I do not know how harmful it could be to your skin, so do not let it touch you!" warned Speedwell to Piper and Tintwist.

They both nodded and covered their hands with cloth. Sliding two lengths of wood under one of the beasts, they lifted it up effortlessly and put it onto the fire.

Tarbor watched as the flames suddenly shot into the air as the beast caught alight in an instant. What they were or where they had come from, he had no idea, but he had no doubt he would be finding out.

Tarbor turned to see how Urchel was faring. He was lying there quietly, his eyes shut, but Tarbor could see his eyes moving under his eyelids, to tell him he was fighting it inside; he could only wait.

Tarbor looked back at Speedwell and found himself staring at the rune staff he was holding, realising that that was what Queen Helistra held all of the time, but a broken one!

"A rune staff, did I hear it called, that you hold in your hand?" he asked.

Speedwell kept his eye on Urchel as he spoke in answer. "That is right, King wielder."

"Does it always do good or can it do evil, like the broken one Queen Helistra has?" questioned Tarbor.

Speedwell turned to look at Tarbor and could see how much was plaguing his mind. "They are always meant for good, but when Helistra broke Grimstone's rune staff, it was open to corruption and now she uses it to spread her evil. That is why I am here, to retrieve its broken piece and mend it to do good again, but there is only one person who can retrieve the broken piece. That is where you can help us, King wielder," explained Speedwell.

Although he did not fully comprehend what Speedwell was telling him, Tarbor's thoughts and doubts were disappearing. He was feeling more like his old self again, except for one thing that he could not come to terms with.

"I am only too willing to help you, Speedwell." Tarbor had to pinch himself as he said his name; he only wished Girvan and Druimar were here with him. "But I need to clear something up first that is troubling me." He had to ask: "I have been told the story of these swords, that to possess one and to feel what I did, I must be the King of Waunarle, but I do not see how that is possible," queried Tarbor.

Speedwell smiled in sympathy; he could see the confusion that clouded Tarbor's warrior mind. It needed to be clear if he was to find the shield. *Time to put it right*, thought Speedwell.

"Let us sit around the fire and talk of the things that need to be said, but be careful of these two!" he warned, quickly moving to his side as Piper and Tintwist threw the other beast onto it.

The fire crackled and spat as flames shot yet again into the air. Tarbor watched as the beast's head immediately caught fire, turning its eyes yellow once more with flames shooting out of them, as if in one last gesture of defiance.

The fire began to settle, much to Idrig's relief; he thought the roof was going to catch fire! As it did, so did the small company, especially Piper and Tintwist; they loved to hear stories.

"Tell me then, King wielder, by what name are you known?" asked Speedwell, looking into Tarbor's eyes.

"Tarbor of the Cardronian horse soldiers," replied Tarbor, feeling a little nervous for some reason.

"Then, Tarbor of the Cardronian horse soldiers, tell me of your journey that brought you here and how you came to possess a defender," he prompted, for Tarbor to begin to tell Speedwell and the small company what had happened to him.

From the siege of Stormhaven to the beasts on the Wreken Moors, Tarbor did not miss out anything. At least this time, Tarbor knew his words did not fall on unbelieving ears.

"And the sword, the defender, was given to me by King Taliskar when I was made a Captain," finished Tarbor at the end.

Speedwell mulled over what Tarbor had told him. "Helistra always did like to play her games," he remembered, "giving you the defender is just one of them, but the game she seeks at Stormhaven is intended to end in death," he told them as he looked over at Urchel, to see him open his eyes. "Your friend is over the worst," he said with a smile.

Tarbor looked and smiled to see Urchel starting to sit up.

Idrig helped him and thrust a bowl of broth into his hands. "Get that down you, old friend," he said, grinning.

"I am sorry to hear of your friends' deaths. I only hope their path to the Great Forest is not in vain. She means to destroy it all," said Speedwell, with Tarbor wondering what he meant.

"A bloodshot eye, you said, when you saw her. She had used too much power and it had weakened her, to cloud her vision. That and the defender about your person combined enough for her not to be able to reach inside your mind," said Speedwell, thinking out loud.

"So she did open the mountain door! By reaching into the mind of King Taliskar! Using sorcery to open it through him!" After all this time of wondering, Tarbor now knew.

"Sorcery is a strong word to use, Tarbor. To have opened the mountain door, I prefer the word magic, but for her to destroy a forest… that is sorcery at its most evil!" remonstrated Speedwell.

"I am not sure what you are on about, Speedwell. Why do you keep talking about the forests being destroyed? What has it to do with Queen Helistra and Stormhaven?" asked a puzzled Tarbor, looking at the others.

Unfortunately, Piper and Tintwist knew what Speedwell was on about, as they looked at him, knowing what he was going to say.

"I am sorry, I have not explained. You have told me your story. Now it is my turn to tell you mine," apologised Speedwell, and he began to tell Tarbor why he was there.

"I am a Forestall, as Piper says," began Speedwell, "the Keeper of the Great Northern Forest. I have a brother, Ringwold, who looks after the well-being of the Great Eastern Plateau Forest.

"We are the only two Forestalls left. There were two others. Both were killed by Helistra, my daughter." Tarbor could not contain a gasp at hearing this, leaving him open mouthed.

He had been told to find Speedwell and here he was saying that Helistra was his daughter! Besides being a revelation in itself, how could someone who looked so young be the daughter of someone who looked so old!

Speedwell saw Tarbor's thinking. "Yes, she is my daughter, Tarbor, much to my sadness and regret, despite her youthful looks, which is something I can never comprehend… that evil can be wicked in more ways than one!

"Being a Forestall, and Helistra being my daughter, we naturally met my fellow Forestalls. My brother, of course, but also Gentian, Keeper of the Southern Plateau Forest, and Grimstone, Keeper of the Western Plateau Forest. They were of the Elfore, the children of the forest, whereas my brother and I are of man," continued Speedwell, for Tarbor to think of Girvan and Druimar again as he heard Speedwell say children of the forest.

"Helistra and Grimstone fell in love. They lived happily together and had a child, Tomin. All was well until Grimstone began teaching Tomin the ways of the forest so he could become a Forestall one day himself. That is when the evil jealousy that had hidden inside Helistra rose to the surface, and with that jealousy she killed Grimstone with the rune staff you saw in her possession, Tarbor. It is broken because in her rage she snapped it when she killed Grimstone." A stillness fell over the company at the thought of such an act.

"From then until now, she has had only one thing on her mind: to destroy all of the forests. Revenge for not being chosen to become a Forestall," revealed Speedwell.

"You mean, her jealousy of her own son led her to kill his father and now she wants to destroy the forests, because of it?" Tarbor was flabbergasted.

"That is right, Tarbor. Until the forests are no more and we are dead, she will not rest. That is why she has entered Stormhaven, for it hides an ancient power far below its battlements under the mountain thrones. The same power that spoke to you in your mind when you touched the solid rock in the archway," explained Speedwell, for Tarbor to feel a weight lifted from his mind as Speedwell spoke of the voice he had heard there.

"The dream you say you had, Tarbor, and the voice are one and the same. We know of it as the pool of life. It dwells inside a crystal chamber. The crystals give life-giving energy to the essence of life that lives within the pool. Its pure water then flows through the earth to the Great Plateau Forest to help keep the life force of the forests in harmony, but now she has tainted it. Stained it with soul blood and sent it into the heart of the Plateau Forest as poison."

Tarbor's head was reeling as he tried to understand what Speedwell had just told him. So it was a living being in a pool of crystal water that he had heard and dreamt of that had reached out to him; the impossible had just happened again!

Then Tarbor looked at Speedwell's rune staff, only now to realise where the blue flame in his dream had come from. He had just watched as Speedwell had sent a bolt of ice-blue flame into Urchel to save him; it was Speedwell!

But as one question was answered, another one appeared in his mind, tainted by soul blood, what was that?

Speedwell was answering Tarbor's question before he could ask it. "Helistra gathered many souls, before they could rest in peace, into the broken rune staff to release into the pool of life with a malevolent spell of poisoned blood. I tried to stop her, nearly losing my life, but since then she has bonded with the crystal chamber, making her malevolence stronger."

"You say King Taliskar and other poor souls have disappeared from Stormhaven?" asked Speedwell, for Tarbor to nod.

"I believe she has killed him over the pool of life with the broken rune staff and let his life force expel itself into the pool, as soul blood!" A sense of repulsion ebbed around the company at hearing this.

She has killed Taliskar with the broken rune staff! Tarbor grimaced. *Evil does not describe such an act. He has paid in more ways than one for his greed of power*, he thought.

"When Helistra killed Grimstone, there was an explosion of white light. She disappeared and Grimstone turned to stone, with the broken piece of his rune staff locked into him," continued Speedwell, picking his story back up, to wide eyes.

"The problem now was what should we do? Tomin was next in line to receive Grimstone's rune staff. Therefore, he was the only one who could retrieve the broken piece from Grimstone's stone body to mend it and make it whole again, the one thing we knew she would not let happen.

"But we realised what an impossible situation it was to do this. The well-being of the forests still needed our attention, but one of us would have to be with Tomin to protect him constantly if he was to wait by Grimstone's stone body for the moment when the broken piece locked within it would come to life for him to retrieve it, but that could only happen when Grimstone's broken rune staff was used, and it was in Helistra's hands!

"Our power is not eternal, we need to rest like anyone for it to replenish. In that time, we thought, she could suddenly emerge to use

Grimstone's broken rune staff, kill Tomin and disappear again! So we put his body to sleep and hid him from her sight with a protective shield around him," explained Speedwell, for them to hear the frustration of it all in his voice.

"Years started to go by, but thankfully nothing happened, giving us all hope that Helistra would not be able to bond with Grimstone's broken rune staff.

"Gentian in this time decided we still needed to do something. We could not just keep Tomin hidden. We needed help if keeping vigil was the only way to retrieve the broken piece, so he set about making the defenders and shields.

"He asked the Elfore blacksmiths to forge the weapons from metals he had sourced in the mountains and earth with one he had found in a rock fallen from the sky, with the intention of empowering the weapons so she could not sense Tomin behind their protective shield.

"He was then going to charge each King of the five Kingdoms of Northernland to help protect Tomin in his vigil. Two of us at a time taking it in turns to watch over him, no matter how long it took, but it did not happen.

"Gentian had empowered the defenders and shields in the crystal chamber with the essence's blessing. He had entrusted a company of Elfore to make sure they reached each King of the other Kingdoms, having already given the then King of Tiggannia his.

"Satisfied, Gentian was making his way through the mines of the Kavenmist Mountains at the back of Stormhaven to return home, but he never made it! She was waiting for him!

"Helistra rained down the Kavenmist Mountains upon him to bury his body under its weight, telling us she was learning to control the broken rune staff and using it as we feared she would: for evil!

"The company of Elfore were never to be seen again, neither were the defenders and shields, until now, that is," remarked Speedwell, looking at Tarbor.

"I think finding those defenders and shields put a wariness into Helistra as to how she should tread," reflected Speedwell as he came to the end of his story.

"Carefully, as it has turned out, to be using people like King Taliskar, manipulating them to do her work for her, using only enough of Grimstone's broken rune staff's power so as not to alert us of her presence. Hence we did not detect her and now she has struck with deadly force through the pool of life before we could react," summed up Speedwell, staring into the fire as he finally finished his story.

Tarbor could only look at Speedwell in quiet sadness for him, as they all did. This was his daughter he had been talking of, all the evil deeds she had done, and he thought he had got his troubles!

"Why did you not make more weapons?" asked Urchel, who was suddenly feeling much better.

"With Gentian and Grimstone gone, how to perform the spell of empowerment in the crystal chamber died with them. They were of the Elfore, we were not," Speedwell tried to explain.

"That was not all. When Gentian died, it caused a rift between the Elfore and man. It was my daughter that had killed them both, so they mistrusted anything to do with man. Turning their backs upon us, they branded us as outcasts.

"They left man behind. Those who lived in the Great Forest moved to settle with their brethren in the Valley of the Lakes in the Plateau Forest and to my regret we had to leave Northernland, not to return, to watch over the forests."

"My brother, Ringwold, thought we would be her next victims. By hiding Tomin we had played into Helistra's hands. With us gone, Tomin would not matter to her, and the forests would then be open to her evil."

"For a long time, we watched and waited, but that day never came. Instead, the hope that we held that she would never bond with Grimstone's broken rune staff enough to enable her to enter the crystal chamber was shattered. We were wrong to even think it." Speedwell sighed as he said it. "No, now she enjoys desecrating the forest, knowing the pain she inflicts upon us. Then it will be our turn," he brooded.

"What of these beasts that nearly killed my friend?" asked Idrig, thinking of his brother alone at the farm.

"We spotted them as we came out of the Great Forest and decided to follow them. I did not expect to see Helistra's evil so far afield. Luck was on our side for us to see them, to lead us to you, as somebody had steered our boat up the wrong river as Piper and I slept," revealed Speedwell, looking at Tintwist.

"Luckily for you, I think, Speedwell!" Tintwist smiled, looking at Tarbor's defender, to an accepted nod of Speedwell's.

"They had been caught by poisonous spores that had entered their bodies, turning them into evil beasts," explained Speedwell.

"Poisonous spores?" said Tarbor, frowning.

Speedwell spoke of the darkness that the evil would seek out once the poison had entered your body, turning you into whatever it found. Describing what would be left of the forests once the spores had injected their deadly venom.

"Everything will turn to decay. There will be nothing left, only rotting vegetation. The forests will perish before her thirst is quenched." He sighed again.

"Will she stop there? What of Northernland?" worried Urchel.

"I do not know, Urchel. There is another ancient power that dwells in the heart of the forest, one I will speak more of another time. Together, we are going to create a barrier where the two forests meet in the hope of stopping her poison there," Speedwell informed them.

"Will it work?" Urchel asked immediately.

"We will not know until the poison reaches it," replied Speedwell, making everyone feel unsettled, including himself.

"You spoke of Queen Elina of Tiggannia having twins, Tarbor?" asked Speedwell suddenly. Thinking of the Ancient One made him remember the two spirits the Ancient One had felt.

"She has, born the very day we stormed…" Tarbor stopped himself; it was not something he could be proud of. He started again. "She has… the Prince escaped Stormhaven with two loyal Tiggannians and is at Elishard Castle under the protection of King Stowlan, but the Princess is still at Stormhaven.

"Kelmar, one of the Tiggannians who escaped with the Prince, was planning to rescue the Queen and Princess as I left," informed Tarbor. A quest by a brave warrior, he thought, but a foolhardy one, having just heard Speedwell confirm his worries over Queen Helistra.

"Let us hope the stars and trees are watching over them then," worried Speedwell. Having the Princess under Helistra's wing could be a problem they had not foreseen if the Ancient One was right about their spirits.

"I have spoken more than enough of many things, but as of yet who you really must be, Tarbor," Speedwell said, smiling, "because of your uncertainty, the defender is distant to you and those doubts you harbour in your mind must be cleared away for you to find the shield that belongs to your defender. Then together we can get Tomin and with your protection I can release him from his sleep without her detecting us," he informed a slightly worried Tarbor, who was wondering as to how Speedwell was going to clear his mind.

"She planted a seed in your head a long time ago that has grown to who you have become, but in giving you that sword, she has made a mistake. Whilst playing her games, she has not realised its true power. It has put questions into your head and now we will answer the final one: who you are," said Speedwell, holding out his rune staff.

"Hold on to the rune staff, Tarbor, for a journey that will finally show you the truth," said Speedwell, beckoning. Tarbor held the rune staff where Speedwell showed him and waited, for what he did not know, whilst the others could only watch in fascination.

Nothing seemed to happen at first, when a tingling sensation suddenly swept through his body and his mind began to drift.

Everyone before him began to fade away. The fire's glow became dimmer and the barn started to dissolve into thin air, to become a swirling grey mist around his head.

Tarbor felt a breeze upon his face and watched as the grey mist passed him by whilst he stayed there, motionless.

The grey mist began to part and Tarbor found himself looking down at a rocky coastline. The sea was lapping over rocks lying on a sandy beach at the bottom of enormous cliffs, where a coastal road could be seen running along the cliff's edge.

Then out of a wood emerged a carriage pulled by two horses. He seemed to float down over the carriage to see a driver and a guard sitting on top.

Tarbor knew who the carriage belonged to; he could hear Druimar clearly telling him from that night.

Suddenly the horses veered from the coastal road in fright, but Tarbor could not see what had frightened them. They headed straight for the clifftop!

Tarbor watched as the driver tried in vain to pull them up; but they did not heed his frantic tugs on the reins. The horses, carriage and its occupants all plunged over the clifftop to plummet to their deaths, smashing on the rocks below!

Tarbor watched in dismay as they crashed into the cliffs before hitting the rocky beach, knowing it was the royal family of Waunarle.

Then out of nowhere, a hooded horse rider came into view, riding straight to where the carriage had gone over the cliff's edge. Stopping and dismounting, the hooded figure walked along the clifftop, looking over the side, but as the figure did so, it stopped to pick something up.

As Tarbor tried to look harder, he suddenly found himself floating by the hooded figure's side, to plainly see who it was and what the figure had picked up.

Tarbor felt his breath be taken away as he looked straight into dark green eyes; it was Queen Helistra! And in her hands was a tiny bundle wrapped tightly in a grey cloth; it was a baby! The child had been thrown from the carriage before it had plunged over the clifftop!

She stood there for a long moment, holding the baby out over the cliff's edge, but then brought it back into her arms, to reveal its tiny face with her finger. Tarbor looked at the baby's face and knew in that moment he was looking into his own tearful eyes! Telling him without any doubt that he was the true heir to the throne of Waunarle!

But what was she doing now? She had revealed the broken rune staff and was saying something, but he could not hear her speak as she touched the child's forehead, his head. Then she put the grey bundle that was him back down onto the ground and remounting her horse, she rode off to leave him there.

As Tarbor was still looking down at himself, another rider appeared, how soon or how much later afterwards, he was uncertain, but the tide was beginning to wash over the remains of the carriage. Tarbor did not have to strain his eyes to know who it was: Brax!

Getting off his horse, Brax had gone to the cliff's edge and was looking over at the smashed– up carriage at the bottom of the cliffs.

He was about to remount his horse when Tarbor could see Brax had spotted his tiny bundle, to pick him up and find it was a baby. He watched as Brax remounted his horse and rode away with him in his arms.

Tarbor felt himself float away from the clifftop scene and watched as the grey swirling mist began to envelope him again. No sooner had it appeared than it dispersed, for Tarbor to see he was back in the barn again, with four pair of eyes looking at him.

Tarbor looked at Speedwell, holding his rune staff in wonder at what he had just been shown. "How did you…?"

"Shall we say it is a gift I have been blessed with and leave it there, before your mind starts thinking again," he said, smiling.

"Well, what happened?" asked Tintwist first before the others could.

"I saw myself and what happened to me when I was just a baby," and Tarbor told them all of the vision that Speedwell had shown him.

"My mother saved me, and Queen Helistra made me forget who my true parents were. I have been nothing more than a plaything to her all of this time," said Tarbor, feeling used.

"So who are you really then, Tarbor?" asked Urchel. Tarbor looked at them all as he spoke the names of his mother and father for the very first time.

"My father was King Palitan of Waunarle and my mother was Queen Isabel. I am their son, Ashwell," he told them, not knowing how he knew his name, but he did and with a clear mind.

"King Ashwell, I believe," said Speedwell with a smile, pleased that his journey through time had worked without disturbing the broken rune staff as everyone gathered around Tarbor, as he still felt, like excited children slapping him on the back.

Speedwell picked up the defender whilst Tarbor was being congratulated and looked at it. Holding it out, he touched a symbol on his rune staff and then slid it slowly over both sides of the defender's blade.

By the time he had finished, the small party had stopped talking to watch what he was doing. They thought they were seeing things as the defender glimmered back at them, showing the blend of metals shimmering across its blade. No marks could be seen upon its surface as the fire reflected back its razor sharpness along its edges.

Tarbor suddenly felt an energy coming from the sword such as he had never experienced before as Speedwell gave it back to him. He stared at its blade, shining in the light of the fire. "Now you will be able to find that shield!" said Speedwell, smiling at Tarbor's open-jaw.

CHAPTER XXVII

"Stupid! You are all stupid!" Fleck kicked the door of his tree cell once again in his frustration at being locked away. He sat down on the wooden slats that formed his bed and buried his head in his hands.

Fleck had reported back the horror he had witnessed to King Vedland. Telling him of the hideous things that were happening to the forest.

He had told him of the poisonous mist that covered the ground, the creepers that were strangling the life out of the trees, the pods exploding with poisonous spores that had poisoned Levan and the evil beasts with eyes of burning poison that had ripped Bannel apart!

But the worst of all for him was to have seen Levan change into something so grotesque and take the life of his comrade Sleap!

He had told King Vedland everything he had witnessed, and how was he treated? He had thrown him into a tree cell!

"You have come back on your own! How do I know you have not killed them all?" he had accused him with mistrust.

"I heard the hurt in your voice about how my father treated you. It could be that you wanted revenge all along and made the whole story up! I saw your face change when I asked you to get proof, to prove that everything you told me was true!" Fleck had shaken his head in utter disbelief.

"So would yours if you thought you could be walking straight to your death! I came here to warn you of an evil that could be the end of the Elfore from Speedwell and the Ancient One. Witnessed their word to be true, for you to go against yours and throw me in a tree cell!" he had raged.

"You do not know what you are doing! Everyone and everything will be doomed because of your mistrust!" He had lost his temper towards King Vedland and that was more than enough for him to be where he was.

As his tree cell door shut, Fleck had pleaded with King Vedland in exasperation. "If you will not take my word as to what I have witnessed then you must send someone that you do trust. If you do not heed Speedwell's warnings, you risk the lives of all your people!"

King Vedland had thought it over. Was he letting his feelings in memory of his father get in the way? By remembering Fleck had sided with Speedwell, whose daughter had killed two of their own?

He had thought if she was ever to appear again that Speedwell and his brother, Ringwold, would be her quarry, but Speedwell was her father. Perhaps that was it; she could not kill her father, so instead she would kill everything he lived for.

Whatever the reason, he wanted tangible proof before telling his people, and Fleck had not brought any back, only himself.

King Vedland had spoken with his advisors and all agreed they could not ignore the fact that Fleck had been sent by a Forestall, no matter how they felt or what they thought of Speedwell.

So four more Elfore were sent in search of the poisoned forest, whilst all Fleck could do was kick his tree cell door.

Twenty days and counting he had been in this wretched tree cell. Even that short encounter with the poisoned forest had told Fleck of the intensity with which it was moving over the ground, and here he was, stuck up here.

Held high in a tree in a thick wooden-sided hut with no windows, wedged between two sturdy branches. A small flap at the bottom of a barred door where food was passed through was his only source of light when opened.

Fleck was sitting in silent despair when his ears picked up the walkway, which spanned between the trees outside, creaking. He heard talking and then a soft voice was speaking to him from the other side of the door.

"Fleck, can you hear me? I am Tiska. Sleap was my husband. He spoke kindly of you before he…" Fleck closed his eyes to the pain he could clearly hear, but that only made him see Sleap's face of disbelief in that fatal moment.

"I have not been allowed to speak to you, but they have finally relented. I need to know what happened to him, to hear it from you, why… why he did not come back to us." Fleck rubbed his face; what could he say without hurting her?

"I am sorry for your loss. Your husband was an honourable man, one whom I wish I could have known better. His last words were of you and his daughter." Fleck tried to sound calm as he spoke.

"What… what were they?"

Fleck closed his eyes once more, hearing her desperation for something, anything. "To make sure you were both safe." Fleck felt himself welling up inside as he listened to the tears falling from Sleap's wife.

"You still have not told me how he died," said Tiska again through her tears.

"We found an evil that manifests itself in the forest. A poison entered him that saw him die," lied Fleck, but he could not bring himself to say what really happened as he listened to more tears being shed.

"In the short time my husband knew you, he said though you were deemed an outcast, his first feelings about you told him you were an Elfore of honour. That is why he journeyed with you. If not in some awe of you knowing the Forestalls Speedwell and Ringwold," spoke Tiska quietly in memory.

"A lot of good it has done me, that is why I am in here. King Vedland does not believe what I have seen, what we all saw! Every moment you stay here puts you at risk! It is not what Sleap asked of me, but I can do nothing stuck in here," moaned an exasperated Fleck.

"The poison moves through the forest towards the lakes and when it comes it will kill everything in its path," warned Fleck, but he found he was talking to himself; Tiska was gone.

Fleck put his head in his hands once more and began seeing those last moments in his mind all over again.

Night fell and Fleck was lying in his tree cell half asleep with restless thoughts going through his mind when he thought he heard someone outside.

He sat up and instinctively looked to where the tree cell door was. Wood rubbing against wood came to his ears. Someone was sliding out the wooden bars from the metal brackets that held the tree cell door shut.

Fleck stood up as the door opened, to see a silhouette of someone in the dim torchlight that lit part of the walkway.

"Come, Fleck, follow me," said a whispering voice, and then Fleck knew it was Tiska.

"What are you doing? You will find yourself in one of these!" warned a worried Fleck.

"Believing in you, as did my husband. If this is not the place to be then we must go," she answered firmly as she led the way, keeping low over the walkway.

Fleck was not going to argue; he was glad to get out of that tree cell and smell the fresh air again, or was it?

Fleck smelt again as he tried to look through the darkness. A few torches lit the walkway and marked the path below through the trees. Their wariness of fire would pale into insignificance if they had seen what he had witnessed, he thought, as he caught an odour that made his skin crawl.

"Where are the guards?" he asked, whilst looking all around him.

"They are not worried. Who is there that would want to rescue you?" Tiska posed with irony, for Fleck to nod in agreement.

"That is true."

The scream they heard pierced the stillness of the night and confirmed what Fleck already knew: the poison was here, it had reached the lakes!

"Death is here," he whispered, making Tiska come out in goosebumps.

"Where is your daughter?" Fleck asked immediately, looking below him to see something dash past a torch.

"She sleeps in our home on the west side," replied Tiska, already feeling worried for her. "Quickly then to your home, we have no time to lose. Can we move far up here?" Fleck said with hope.

"A fair way," she answered, handing him a sword. "You might need this."

"I think you are right, thank you, and not just for the sword."

"There is no need to thank me," and Tiska moved swiftly across the walkway to the next tree.

As they moved, more screams were heard, along with shouts of panic. Growling and snarling met their ears, for Fleck to know beasts were attacking his kinfolk below them.

Onto another walkway then another, their pace quickening with the sound of frightened Elfore now coming from all directions.

Tiska suddenly stopped with a gasp at what had just emerged out of the darkness before her. A hideous creature that filled her with dread was standing there, a sword held menacingly, pointing straight at her.

Fleck saw the malformed creature's leather clothes and knew they were looking at one of the other four Elfore that had been sent by King Vedland to find the poison. They had!

Eyes of red stared from a face whose veins were pushing out against its skin as the creature swung its sword straight at Tiska!

Tiska jumped over the hand rope, turning her body in the air, avoiding the blade. Catching hold of the wooden planks that formed the floor of the walkway, she held on to them, dangling in mid-air.

It did not deter the creature. It made for Fleck, its sword raining down. Fleck met the blade and deflected it away.

Again it brought its sword to bear, this time swinging it around in a severing motion at Fleck's head. Fleck held the creature's sword at bay, locking with it to hold it off.

Pitting with the creature, strength versus strength, Fleck found himself staring into the creature's grotesque features. His concentration seeing such a hideous face waned in that moment and his foot slipped on the walkway, to send him sprawling backwards.

The creature saw its chance and held its sword ready to strike at Fleck, but Tiska managed to get its attention instead.

Gripping around a rope strut for better purchase, Tiska had managed to draw her dagger and stick it straight into the creature's foot, making it growl in anger.

Instead of red blood coming out of the wound, a thick orange blood showed itself. Fleck's instinct told him it could be poisonous and he shouted a warning. "Do not let it touch you, Tiska!" Hand over hand, Tiska pulled herself along the walkway and hung there. She was getting tired, but she had given Fleck a chance by drawing the creature's attention away from him.

He grabbed it. Getting to his feet, Fleck swung his sword up through the air, slicing the creature's sword arm clean off to fall onto the walkway, still holding its sword. Orange blood squirted out of the growling creature's remaining arm as Fleck, avoiding the orange blood, stepped to the side and brought his sword around, to slice right through the creature's throat! It fell in a crumpled heap to end up hanging halfway over the walkway.

The bouncing of the creature's body on the walkway had made Tiska lose her grip. She was holding on with one hand as she felt Fleck's grip on her wrist, to help her back up before she fell to her death.

They both sat looking at the twisted body that lay hanging over the walkway.

"What was it?" gasped Tiska, getting up.

"A poor Elfore," replied Fleck, "look at its dress."

Tiska saw the familiar leather tunic of a hunter and shuddered. "Let us be away from here," she uttered, and they were gone.

By now, pandemonium had descended and everyone was running everywhere in the panic that followed the attacks.

Beasts were rampaging their way through the settlement, biting their victims to turn them into deformed creatures who, once turned, seemed to be killing anything in sight.

Guards ran to face the beasts and as their swords cut through the hideous creatures, they were splattered in their orange blood.

The orange blood did not penetrate their skin as Fleck feared it could, but instead found its way into an open mouth, an eye or a wound, to make the guards become what they were trying to kill.

Fellow Elfore tried to help those who had been attacked without realising they were putting themselves in danger, much to the shouted cries of one Elfore as his friend who had been bitten rose before him and bit him.

So the circle of death had started to surround Fleck and Tiska as they passed overhead, unseen.

Several victims appeared on the walkways as they moved along them, slaughtered by the creature that they had killed, they assumed, when Tiska suddenly stopped.

"We can go no further up here. We have to go down to the ground," she informed Fleck, sounding anxious.

Fleck looked down at the mayhem that was happening. He nodded to her and for the first time noted her face properly.

Although worry etched her face, Fleck understood why Sleap had married her. Smooth fine looks with dark brown eyes piercing through him had quickly met his gaze.

Tiska hurried down the wooden steps that circled the tree they had reached. A beast suddenly appeared in front of her, blocking her way, showing its fang-like teeth as it snarled.

Fleck pushed straight past her and booted the beast in the throat, exposing its neck enough for him to thrust his sword straight through it, killing the beast instantly.

Down onto the forest floor they moved as two guards ran past them. Fleck shouted to get their attention. "Stop! Help us! Her daughter is in danger!"

The guards heard Fleck's plea and stopped. "We are all in danger," shouted one, keeping his wits about him by looking around.

"That Fleck the outcast was right!" commented the other as they came to join them. As they did so, the guard that had said Fleck's name became open-eyed as he stared at Fleck.

"Wait a moment? It is you! How have you escaped?" he queried.

"Does that matter right now if I am right?" Fleck said with a shrug. "Help us get Sleap's daughter. This is her mother, Tiska, but we must hurry," urged Fleck.

Recognition of whom Fleck was speaking registered straight away with the two guards, and they bowed their heads to Tiska for her loss. "We will help you," they agreed.

"Be careful of these creatures' blood. It's poisonous, it will make you become one of them," warned Fleck as they moved off.

Doors had been shut and barred to the dwellings that they ran past, with fear locked inside. More beasts showed themselves to the small party as they ran, to be met by the feel of cold steel slicing through their deformed bodies.

"Is your home much further?" asked Fleck as he followed Tiska, seeing the dwellings were becoming fewer and fewer.

No sooner had he asked than they all came to a sudden stop at the sight that had emerged out of the dark, threateningly before them: the enveloping poisonous mist! "Keep back and seek shelter," warned Fleck, immediately hiding behind the nearest tree.

All watched as pods appeared out of the deadly mist to suddenly launch themselves through the air and cling to the nearest trees, opening to shoot out their venomous spores that were held within.

Fleck felt a familiar sick feeling begin to gnaw at the pit of his stomach as creepers emerged from the mist to begin winding their way up tree trunks, tightening their grip as they slithered their way in their own oozed slime to turn the trees rotten.

Fleck watched as the deadly ground-hugging mist drifted forward, to start encircling a nearby tree that had steps going up its side. Following the steps, Fleck lost them to the night but knew they must end in a dwelling held in its branches.

He turned in worry at seeing the mist stop their progress to ask once more of Tiska where her daughter was, to see Tiska being held back for her own good by the two guards. Seeing her beside herself told him immediately she was in that dwelling he could not see.

"You must stay back here where it is safer, I will get her," ordered Fleck.

No sooner had he said it than a pod flew searchingly out of the mist and hit the tree they were sheltering behind. "Quick, look out!" And they all ran to avoid the poisonous spores that were going to shoot out from the opening pod.

It released its deadly spores to find the neck of one of the guards. He tried to pull it out, but barbs had latched themselves inside his skin and the deadly venom was injecting itself into his bloodstream.

He dropped to his knees as the poison set his blood afire. Lines of veins began to criss-cross his face.

"Kill him!" shouted Fleck at the other guard.

The guard looked at Fleck with his own painful expression at such an order. "I… I cannot. He is my friend!" he pleaded.

"Not anymore, he will become evil beyond your comprehension and will not hesitate to kill us all!" And Fleck pushed him aside to put an end to the hapless guard before he became the monster that lay inside.

Tiska was in horror; she saw in that moment what had really happened to her husband. "Is that what you did to my husband? Kill him to put him out of his misery!" she cried.

Fleck could not disguise the truth this time. "No, Levan was hit by a spore, turning him into a beast. He killed your husband and I killed him, as I have had to kill the guard. Otherwise, he would have turned upon us," explained Fleck sadly.

Tiska looked at Fleck and understood in that moment the plight he must have been going through. She wiped away her tears. She had no time to dwell upon it; her daughter was in peril!

"What is her name?" asked Fleck, eying his chances of reaching the steps before another pod exploded or a beast appeared.

"Tislea," cried Tiska hoarsely.

"If I should get hit and begin to turn, kill me!" he ordered, and he ran towards the steps.

As Fleck ran, he looked at the mist, hoping it would not penetrate his leather tunic and boots as he ran through it, hoping at the same time nothing was lurking in there. He would soon find out; it was too late now!

A pod flew past Fleck's ears and hit a tree to his side as he reached the steps. He surged up the steps for all he was worth, praying to the stars that the door would not be barred! Reaching the door, he crashed thankfully through it, falling onto the floor as he kicked it shut.

Thuds on the door followed him in and he breathed a sigh of relief; he had shut the door on the spores just in time.

His eyes met those of a young Elfore woman, looking upside down from the floor, a drawn bow in her hands, ready to fire.

"You must be Tislea!" Fleck said with a smile. *So far so good*, he thought.

"And who are you?" she asked in a high voice, holding her stance.

"I am Fleck the outcast, as I am called around here. Your mother awaits us," he informed her.

Tislea lowered her bow on hearing this. "You were with my father," she realised.

"Yes, I was. I will speak of what happened after we have got out of here and you are safe," he explained, before she could ask anything.

Seeing his boots were only damp from the mist gave Fleck further relief as he slightly opened a shutter to take a peek outside.

"What is happening out there? I did not know what to do when I found my mother was not here. I was asleep and woke to screams," said Tislea as Fleck looked.

"You did right to stay here. An evil poison is spreading through the forest. Its touch is killing the forest and Elfore alike. That is all you need to know for now, but we must go from here quickly. Have you a cloak that can help protect you?" said Fleck in one breath, to hear no answer, but when he came away from the shutter and looked at Tislea, she was wearing a long tough-looking leather cloak.

"My father's," she said proudly to Fleck's nodded approval.

After explaining about the spores, Fleck opened the door slowly. Another pod shot somewhere above his head and he slammed the door shut again. "When the spores have exploded from the pod, we run!" Tislea nodded, securing her bow over her shoulder.

Thuds on the door was their signal, and Fleck flung the door open for them to clamber down the wooden steps for all they were worth.

Fleck made for the trees where Tislea's mother was waiting anxiously. As Fleck thought they had made it, a mighty beast suddenly attacked them from the side. Fleck turned to confront it. "Keep going! Do not stop!" he shouted to Tislea as the beast reared up in front of him.

Fleck faced up to the huge beast, holding his ground as he weighed it up. Only a bear rears up like that, he thought, but its resemblance to one had long since gone.

Its claws were the first thing Fleck noticed; they looked twice as long and razor sharp. The beast's body was covered in pulsating bumps of matted fur, whilst its head was deformed beyond words. Two eyes of pure black stared at him from its misshapen head as sharp teeth, already covered in blood, bared themselves in defiance at his presence. Fleck glanced at his sword; it hardly seemed enough.

The beast suddenly dropped and lunged at Fleck. He rolled out of the way to the sound of its claws ripping through the earth at his side. Turning, they faced each other again.

A pod shot into a tree above Fleck's head as the beast charged again. Fleck threw himself across the ground, rolled and managed to reach the cover of another tree.

The pod exploded, with some of its spores hitting the tree he was hiding behind. The beast was also hit, but the spores had no effect upon it; its darkness had already been found.

The beast charged at the tree Fleck was hiding behind to make it shudder, making Fleck move out into the open once more.

Again the beast reared up, announcing its attack with a ferocious growl, but as its mouth opened, an arrow sped into it to protrude out of the back of its head, followed by another in quick succession. It fell to the ground with an earth-shuddering thump, for two of its fang-like teeth to shoot out of its mouth.

Fleck ran before another pod could release its spores and dived behind a tree. As he looked up, breathless, he was met by two shocked faces coming out from behind another tree.

Tislea let her bow drop in front of her as she looked on at the beast she had felled.

"Thank you, Tislea," called a grateful Fleck.

Making their way back, they came to the walkways again.

Fleck did not need to look down to know of the carnage that was occurring below them. The cries of the victims was enough.

"What now?" asked the guard as they made their way along a walkway.

"You must find the King and get him to go beyond the Old Ogrin Ridge to the Great Forest. He should not need convincing now," said Fleck, unable to refrain from sarcasm. "It is up to the Ancient One and Ringwold now, which is where I must go, to warn them of the speed with which this evil is moving," he added with worry.

"What of us?" asked Tiska.

"That is your choice, but if you wish, you could travel with me," he suggested, thinking their company and handiness with a bow would be more than welcome.

Tiska looked at her daughter. "We will take your path, Fleck. There is nothing here for us now, only sad memories," she confirmed, to Fleck's inward smile.

Biding the guard well, the three set off on their journey to the Ancient One, still keeping to the walkways as much as possible.

What deformed creatures they met on the walkways were dealt with by way of deadly accuracy from Tiska's and Tislea's bows until finally they descended to the forest floor, where Elfore were leaving their homes in panic at what was in their midst.

A few vital supplies were grabbed from empty dwellings and they were gone, with their eyes forever searching ahead of them for more malevolent beasts.

Fleck worried that as the poison had already reached the Valley of the Lakes, it could also be coming around the north of the Linninhorne Mountains to cut them off from reaching the Ancient One.

He would soon find out, he thought, thankful he had the bows of two huntresses at his side.

CHAPTER XXVIII

Queen Helistra walked along Stormhaven Bay, smelling the sea air blown into her face by the easterly breeze. Better than the smell of trees, she was thinking, except for dying ones, of course, she chortled to herself.

She held Princess Amber under her cloak with just her head peeking out, her little face screwing up as the sea breeze caught her breath.

The day had turned clear with the start of a new month, the month of beginning; beginning of the end, she had been smiling to herself, for the forests.

Walking past the wrecks of the invasion, Queen Helistra pondered over some information she had found out from a soldier who had just arrived from Slevenport, well, more of a conversation she had happened to overhear in the corridor that ran alongside the great hall.

There were spies everywhere throughout the Kingdoms sending her information, but she had found their reports could be misleading, especially what she had heard about Tarbor; he had been seen in four different places at the same time!

Although to back those reports up she had not heard anything about that shifty-eyed Wardine, it would come as no surprise to her if he had not been up to the task. There was one soul she would not miss!

The soldier had been talking to his comrades whilst they ate in the great hall about Brax's body arriving at Slevenport. He had seen his wooden box, but there was no mention of his escort.

That, though, was not what had caught her attention; it was who the soldier had said he had seen in Leckfell on his way to Stormhaven.

It was an old man, he had said, riding with two of his grandchildren, he had presumed. They had ridden right past him, nothing strange in that except as they passed him one of the grandchildren's hoods blew back to reveal, so he swore, that the child had pointed ears! This revelation had brought laughter from his comrades.

Humming entered her mind at this moment.

"I know, it could be him with two of his forest imps, but why would he come to Northernland? To dare to confront me again!" she scorned, for humming to strike up again.

"Yes, it has to be. He seeks out Tarbor and the shield to keep him hidden from me. A shame he did not die from the white light," she said matter-of-factly. Humming again… "I know I survived, but I had you to protect me."

Thinking of Tomin reminded her why she had been cautious in her use of its powers. Although he had been hidden, and it had left them open to attack. One wrong move by her when she was not ready and she could have been the one taken by surprise. She had always known Tomin was the only one who could retrieve the other piece of the broken rune staff from Grimstone's stone body when she used its powers, but now it did not matter, because when she used the broken rune staff to further poison the Plateau Forest, the crystal chambers power hid her from them all. She had nothing to fear.

Humming interrupted her thoughts. "Very well, I can look, but it may mean he is dead, despite his sightings, which cannot be trusted," she pointed out, sitting down with Princess Amber on an outcrop of rocks that showed itself above the sand as the humming reminded her yet again of her stupidity.

"I know, I realise that now. The defender was a mistake. If I had not played my games, nothing would have mattered, but now we have bonded with the crystal chamber, nothing does," she reminded the humming, for it to remind her. "Yes, as long as we stay at Stormhaven."

Shutting her eyes, Queen Helistra touched a symbol on the broken rune staff and reached into her mind for the trace of Tarbor that had been placed there when she entered his mind as a child, but nothing was there.

She opened her eyes and stared out to sea. "There is nothing of him. My hold has either been broken or he is dead," she informed the humming, for it not to answer. Instead, the broken rune staff started to vibrate in her lap.

"What is it? What do you feel?" Silence answered her as the broken rune staff pulsed in her hands for a long moment before replying.

"They are what! Creating a spell, what spell?"

asked Queen Helistra, feeling a little apprehensive, even though she had just proved to herself that with the crystal chamber in her power there was nothing to fear, was there?

"A spell of containment? What are you on about?" she asked, to hear answers that put her into a rage. "A barrier along the ridge? They are trying to stop us! It must be destroyed!"

Queen Helistra stood up, nearly dropping Princess Amber and the broken rune staff as she stamped in temper over the sand, shouting across the bay. "I will go and DRIVE the poison into the Ancient One myself!" she spat as the humming spoke to her with reassurance to calm her down.

Queen Helistra paced up and down along the bay as she listened to the broken rune staff before finally sitting back down upon the rocks. She breathed in the sea air to restore calmness back into her mind as she thought over what the broken rune staff had said.

The poison grows within itself as it covers and swallows the Plateau Forest. As they use their power to maintain the barrier, they must rest to sustain it, but the poison does not. It will constantly knock on their door, whilst we do not have to do anything. It will not take long for the barrier to become weak, and when it fails, the Great Forest will be awash in a swamp of death! That is when you will get your wish! We will take the energy that we will have gained from the power of the crystal chamber to confront the weakened Ancient One, destroying its being for once and for all!

The Old Ogrin Ridge sits high with the Ancient One at its heart, and when that time comes, with one final push he will fall, confirmed Queen Helistra in her mind, with a smile at the thought, nodding at the broken rune staff's wise counsel.

What then of him, if he is here to get Tomin with Tarbor? she queried, not saying her father's name, to hear the humming dismiss them.

Of course, that is all they will be able to do, help with the barrier. Not until we use the power of the crystal chamber will they be able to retrieve the broken piece, and by then it will be all too late. The Ancient One will have fallen, they will be no more and the Great Forest will be plunged into darkness! She grinned at the thought as the humming reminded her that she must keep patient.

"I know I must, my impatience blinds my judgement and gets the better of me. There are other things I can be getting on with," she said, smiling, as she tickled Princess Amber's chin.

"All is well, the Elfore will be running from their precious lakes and the Plateau Forest will soon be no more. I must bide my time and wait here where I am at my most powerful. I understand all that you have told me," she reassured the broken rune staff and herself.

As she started to leave the bay, the humming spoke to her one last time. *It is somewhere in there. Perhaps a reception would be nice,* as an idea came into her mind.

She smiled as she thought of all the trouble her so-called father was going to and that no matter what he did, it would all come to nothing!

CHAPTER XXIX

"Do you think any more beasts will attack them? I should have gone with them to Idrig's farm," worried Tarbor. He was feeling guilty at parting company with Urchel and Idrig as he rode pass the Ingle Hills, which announced they were nearing Elishard.

"They will be all right. A good fire at night will protect them," answered Speedwell as he shouted at Piper and Tintwist as they raced past once more. "Save those horses, you two!"

Tarbor hoped that they would be all right. They had parted at the stone barn, for Urchel and Idrig to go on to Idrig's farm, as was planned, to reunite with his brother, Vartig. Tarbor had told them to go to Elishard afterwards where they would be safe, and promised they would meet up again.

With the name he had had on his mind all this time riding next to him, Tarbor had no need to find Speedwell; he had found him! And now he was on a different journey altogether with Speedwell's two Manelf companions, who had made Tarbor smile when they had told him they were his bodyguards!

They had gone to Fenby, where Tarbor had purchased the horses they now rode in sight of Elishard.

Speedwell had spoken to him along the way as to where Tomin was hidden. "The Isle of Kesko is but a boat ride away from Elishard," he had said with a smile.

Tarbor looked on as Elishard came into his mind. Even though it was a spring day and the fields were beginning to turn a fresher green, the greyness that was Elishard Castle still made it feel like winter as it showed itself on the horizon, with the town wall stretching around it like a coiled snake. The only good thing was that the wind had died down as Tarbor looked upon the castle's emerging grey features.

"Inviting-looking," quipped Tintwist, as he and Piper rejoined them, to confirm Tarbor's feelings at seeing the castle.

"We will stay the night and find a boat in the morning," informed Speedwell.

"But I have not felt the shield, yet, Speedwell, to help you," said Tarbor, not really knowing how he would but worried why he had not now that his mind was clear.

"You will. Helistra, poisoning the pool of life, has not helped you. I will go on to make sure Tomin is well and wait for you to join us when you have it," said Speedwell assuredly whilst looking over his shoulder at the diminishing Ingle Hills.

"How long has he been there alone?" asked Piper.

"A long time," Speedwell replied with a smile.

They passed through a settlement of huts and workshops outside the castle town walls before entering the town wall gates via a bridge that spanned a huge ditch.

No one was taking much notice of them in the castle town; comings and goings were becoming regular at Elishard as they began to prepare themselves for what could lay ahead.

Piper and Tintwist wanted to explore; they had never seen such sights before, but Speedwell gave them a look that told them to stay where they were.

Approaching the castle drawbridge that spanned another huge ditch, Tarbor looked up at the gatehouse to spy a face he knew looking at them; it was Kelmar! He had made it! Had they rescued them both?

Inside the courtyard, they dismounted to the smiles of King Stowlan, Kraven and Cantell. "Tarbor, you are back, we never expected to see you again for many a long day," said Cantell, walking over to Tarbor.

"Nor I, Cantell, but I never got near the Great Forest, because the name I heard from the rock found me," he said with a smile.

Cantell looked at Tarbor with a frowning smile and then at the figure in a cloak of many furs that was suddenly standing right before him.

Steel-blue eyes were looking back at him from a face of age and yet he could not help but notice an underlying youthfulness about his features. Cantell knew in that moment that all he had thought of as just babbling from Tarbor was smacking him in the face, right now. Even more so when he turned to look at the two childlike faces grinning at him with bows slung across their shoulders that were nearly as long as they were, though Kelmar had come back with a face whiter than snow to dispel anything that Tarbor had said to be untrue.

"You are going to tell me this is Speedwell and two of the Elfore you talked about, Tarbor," he conceded with a grin.

"I am Speedwell, but these two are of the Manelf," spoke Speedwell, correcting him.

"Piper and Tintwist," announced Piper, with a nod of the head.

"I am pleased to meet you all," said Cantell, smiling, as King Stowlan stepped forward to greet them. "You are all welcome."

"Where is Kelmar? I saw him just now. Did you rescue Queen Elina and Princess Amber?" asked Tarbor, walking by the side of Kraven as they all went to go inside the castle.

Before Kraven could answer, Kelmar was approaching them from the gatehouse. It only took one look at Kelmar's face for Tarbor to know he had witnessed something that he would have never believed could happen; his look reminded him of how he had felt.

Kelmar was straight to the point. "I have wronged you, Tarbor. I have seen with these eyes what Queen Helistra can do. My disbelieving you, my sarcasm, I am sorry for it all. Will you accept a warrior's apology and allow me to eat humble pie?"

Tarbor looked at Kelmar's outstretched hand and saw Cantell smiling at his friend's gesture. If there was any man Tarbor had wanted on his side, it was Kelmar.

"You will not hear the last of it," Tarbor warned as he gripped Kelmar's arm with a grin.

Kelmar slapped Tarbor on his shoulder, giving him some slight discomfort. "Sorry, Tarbor, I had forgotten."

"Let me introduce you, Kelmar. This is the voice I heard, Speedwell." Tarbor smiled to see Kelmar's face as he looked at Speedwell.

"I have been told, Kelmar, that you bravely went to the rescue of Queen Elina and Princess Amber?" Speedwell enquired as they began to walk into the castle together.

"I did, with Kraven's help. I only wish it had been that successful," and Kelmar began explaining what he meant by telling them what had happened when they went to Stormhaven, with Speedwell waiting to hear what his daughter had done now.

A fire still burnt in the hall as one and all sat to tuck into the food that had been laid on a long table for them.

Tintwist sat down and went to pull off his leather hat, which was making his head itchy. "Not here, Tintwist, there are too many eyes. We need to keep our ears hidden. We cannot give ourselves away if we are to help Speedwell get Tomin," whispered Piper, to Tintwist's frustration.

"But our faces give us away, Piper," reasoned Tintwist. "Our faces reflect man, but our ears do not. They will give us away to those we cannot see but who can see us, as you nearly did when you rode off through that town!" she scolded him. "That is why we wear these," she added with a curse.

"That was not my fault! The wind blew my hood down," he pleaded.

"Because you were riding like an idiot!"

"Shh," warned Tintwist as Cantell came and sat next to them.

Cantell looked at them both, eying their childlike faces. "Tell me, Piper. Manelf. Is it as it sounds? You are of both man and elf?" quizzed Cantell, still having to manage one-handed. His arm had mended well, but it was still healing.

"We are, though we are a dying race. We have been made outcasts since the death of Grimstone," she replied, helping herself to some broth that had been brought in. Cantell had no idea whom she was on about, but got the feeling he was looking at one of the same in Speedwell.

"Your name, Tintwist, is unusual, I have never heard of a name like that before," continued Cantell, making conversation, to hear Piper groan. He did not know he had chosen the wrong person to talk to about his name.

Tintwist smiled, looking at Cantell before he spoke, for Cantell to wonder what he had let himself in for.

"Well, you are not the first to ask me about my name," he began. "My father was a craftsman in metal. He made such wonderful things," remembered Tintwist, still smiling.

"One day, he decided to try his hand at making a weapon. Well, it was more of a small dagger to use for eating. That is all. We had a blacksmith.

He did not want to take his trade. I do not know what happened, but somehow my father got his metals mixed up, resulting in the dagger he made snapping when it was used to stab some meat. The one he had made the dagger for said he had better keep to making trinkets, because he must have infused the blade with tin instead of steel the way the blade twisted and broke," explained Tintwist, going quiet for a moment as he remembered the embarrassment of it all.

"I see, so…"

"The blacksmith was not happy with him either. He told him to stop there and then," continued Tintwist, before Cantell could finish what he was going to say.

"Said he would ruin his trade making rubbish! Called him a tin twister as an insult, because that was all he was capable of. Then when I came along, they started calling me Tintwist, son of the tin twister, so the nickname has stuck."

Thinking he was finished, Cantell was just about to try and speak again. "I do have a real name. It is Lighthand, but I have always been known as Tintwist, although I do prefer Tint-wist, but it always ends up Tintwist anyway, so that is my name," he finished, smiling, with a mouthful of meat, to the chortles of everyone around the table.

Cantell wished he had never opened his mouth.

Just then, Queen Elina appeared in the hall, holding Prince Martyn lovingly in her arms, with Permellar holding little Kayla and Oneatha close behind.

All stood at the presence of Queen Elina whilst she sat down at the long table with them. "It is good to hear laughter again, please do not stop because of me." She smiled and then was almost open-mouthed when she saw Tarbor on the same table.

"Captain Tarbor, you are here," she greeted him.

"Er, yes, my lady, I am, but not as a Captain." He smiled back, not really knowing what to say.

"Cantell has told me of your heroic help in saving my son. I am forever in your debt and shall be eternally grateful to you." She smiled, for Tarbor to feel himself go hot.

"There is no need, my lady."

"But there is. You risked your life in more ways than one, as did your friend Girvan. I am only sad that he did not make it here with you, for that I am sorry."

Queen Elina turned her head towards Permellar and Oneatha. "And none of us will forget Druimar," she added, to the gratitude of them both.

"Tarbor is right, my lady, there is no need. You have lost so much yourself. Do not worry about my father. He will be busy shoeing horses ready for us to ride with him over the Great Forest one day," Permellar said with a smile.

"If there is one left!"

All eyes turned to Speedwell, who had passed the remark without realising he had done so.

"Who are you, journeyman, that speaks so?" asked Queen Elina, as she thought that the man she was looking at needed tidying up. His cloak of many furs had been discarded to reveal a linen tunic of sorts, tied in the middle by a bit of string.

Her eyes then saw the staff leaning against his side as he ate, and her face dropped; it looked like the one Queen Helistra carried! Speedwell noted her look; she was not going to like what he was going to say next, he thought.

"My name is Speedwell, Queen Elina. You have, I believe, already met my daughter, Queen Helistra," he revealed, thinking he had perhaps been a little too forthcoming as he watched Queen Elina nearly drop Prince Martyn from her arms in shock.

"You… you are the father to that sorceress!" shouted Kelmar, standing up and drawing his sword, with Kraven doing the same.

Piper and Tintwist immediately put themselves either side of Speedwell, their narrow swords drawn in opposition.

"Stop! Stop, all of you! He is here to help us!" shouted Tarbor.

"Kelmar, put your sword away. He would not be here if Tarbor did not trust him," pointed out Kelmar's mother, clutching her son's arm. "You must let him speak, let us hear what he has to say."

Kelmar looked at his mother. His mind was in conflict. He could see those lightning bolts coming from Forest Tower's balcony, striking down poor Charlotte, but his mother was right.

Though he could not believe Speedwell had just told them he was Queen Helistra's father, Tarbor would not have let him be here if he did not trust him. Tarbor's trust in Speedwell had to be his also. The time of disbelieving him was over, he thought, and with Cantell, he sheathed his sword, for tensions to ease.

"I am sorry. I did not mean to cause any of you any alarm. Your dealings with Helistra, as Kelmar has told me, have not been pleasant, Queen Elina," apologised Speedwell.

"She saw fit to throw me into the dungeons, blaming me for King Taliskar's disappearance," she chastised, letting Speedwell hear the contempt in which she held her.

Without any prompting, Queen Elina began explaining her side of the story about what had happened when she was rescued from her misery in the dungeons and of the way Queen Helistra had somehow found out about Prince Martyn escaping.

"How we survived that night, I do not know. Charlotte paid for it with her life, and my little Amber is still in her clutches," sighed Queen Elina at the end.

Speedwell looked at her in sympathy for what his daughter had put her through, but found his eyes resting on little Prince Martyn in her arms.

So this little child is one of the spirits the Ancient One has asked me to find. Born to a King and Queen in the heart of Stormhaven, could it be what he was hoping for? More worryingly, though, to Speedwell, was that if it was, as Queen Elina had just pointed out to him, his sister laid with Helistra. *Let me see*, he thought.

"Your child has been through much, may I?" Speedwell gestured that he might hold Prince Martyn. "Only to make sure she has not tainted him with her evil," added Speedwell when he saw the uncertainty upon Queen Elina's face.

Though Prince Martyn had not been in Queen Helistra's presence, Queen Elina had seen enough of her evil to be worried for her son's well-being. She looked to Cantell and Kelmar for reassurance.

Cantell looked at Speedwell and for some reason saw the moment in the Great Forest when he had laid Prince Martyn down to feel the whole of the forest go quiet, as if to soothe him, to help him on his journey, remembering how peaceful he was after doing so. "He is in safe hands, my lady," he found himself saying, with a restrained look from Kelmar.

Queen Elina stood and lifted Prince Martyn towards Speedwell. "Very well."

All eyes were upon Speedwell as he moved around the table to be handed little Prince Martyn.

Looking at Prince Martyn's sleeping face, Speedwell put two of his fingers gently across his tiny forehead and closed his eyes. Calling quietly in his mind, the soft hum of his rune staff joined him, for them to merge together.

Speedwell's presence then entered the sleeping Prince like a whisper to seek out the spirit the Ancient One had hoped was there. Speedwell already knew Helistra was not within the child; he had not screamed at his touch and not a murmur was to be had as his presence entered his being.

Speedwell's presence called softly, to feel no response; only an empty void met his call. Again he tried and as disappointment began rearing its head, Speedwell became aware of a light beginning to encircle his presence.

It grew brighter and brighter to then suddenly pulse its radiance straight into Speedwell's presence. Prince Martyn's soul had just reached out to greet him with a strength that had taken Speedwell by surprise. The circle of light then left, leaving Speedwell with a warm glow of hope.

Speedwell opened his eyes. The Ancient One was right, he thought with a smile, much to the relief of Queen Elina when she saw it.

But now the question was, had Helistra found the same in his sister? thought Speedwell.

"He is well and strong of spirit," remarked Speedwell as he handed Prince Martyn back to Queen Elina. "When did Helistra first see your daughter?" he then asked.

"On the day she was born. Mrs Bee and Charlotte told me she bent over the crib, humming a lullaby to her. Why?" replied Queen Elina.

"It is nothing, I just wondered, that is all. It seems she has not harmed either child." He smiled, hiding his concern.

Hummed a lullaby to her, he thought. A cover to possess the child's mind; that means she has not looked into her soul, but would it stay that way for long?

"What is happening? Why is your daughter doing this? And what did you mean, if there is one left, when Permellar mentioned the Great Forest?" questioned a puzzled but worried Cantell as to why Speedwell's daughter was bringing death to Northernland.

Speedwell looked at Cantell and then at all the faces looking at him, to feel the weight of what his daughter was doing play upon his mind yet again.

He began to tell them of the jealous rage she was playing out at the cost of the forests and anyone who got in her way.

"When Tarbor finds the shield to protect us from Helistra's eyes, we will be able to get my grandson, for him to retrieve the other piece. Then we can mend Grimstone's broken rune staff and end her evil," finished Speedwell, to astounded faces.

"If it is not mended, you say Northernland will also suffer?" asked King Stowlan, who had been dumbfounded before with what Tarbor had said, but this!

"If the barrier I spoke of does not hold her poison back then every Kingdom will suffer, from forest to sea, though I worry at her newfound power, the crystal chamber," said Speedwell, his brow furrowed.

"The power she has used from it has enabled her to spread her evil like a forest fire. It has made my rescue of Tomin become all the more urgent so we can return to the ridge to help make the barrier stronger, for as we speak, it is being woven into place," informed Speedwell.

"And your daughter has done all that you have said through jealousy of her own son?" gasped Permellar in disbelief, echoing the thoughts of Tarbor, Piper and Tintwist, for Speedwell to give the same sad truth in answer.

"Yes, she has."

"How will you get the broken rune staff off her to mend?" asked Queen Elina, knowing how Queen Helistra held it like a baby.

"If she stays at Stormhaven, it will be difficult. She has the constant power from the crystal chamber at her disposal, making her a daunting prospect to defeat, but having a barrier in place could push her impatience, drawing her away from Stormhaven to confront it, then she will be confronting the four of us instead," replied Speedwell in thought, trying to think it through.

"Four of us? Is that you, your brother, your grandson and me?" assumed Tarbor as he asked.

Speedwell hesitated to say what he was going to say next, but he could not hide the truth from them that he had just perceived. As soon as he had felt the spirit of Prince Martyn, Speedwell knew the child and his sister had been more than just a feeling of hope from the Ancient One. *He must have felt the strength of their presence from the very beginning and disguised his feelings to me by keeping my mind on Tomin*, thought Speedwell. That whisper from the essence must have been very loud.

"Not quite, Tarbor. You are our protector. The fourth person I am referring to is Prince Martyn, your son, Queen Elina."

Speedwell saw every face looking at him in stunned silence, whilst Queen Elina's jaw dropped at his statement.

"What are you on about? My son is the fourth one? What is he to do with anything that you have said? He is but a baby!"

Speedwell looked into Queen Elina's eyes and held them. "His spirit has been felt by the Ancient One. Your son is the future of us all," proclaimed Speedwell, to a blank look from Queen Elina.

Tarbor found himself feeling a little disappointed by not being, as he had been thinking, someone who had been called upon to confront Queen Helistra as he tried to understand what Speedwell was saying about Prince Martyn.

He must have seen something in Prince Martyn to make him think he could help defeat Queen Helistra, but Queen Elina was right, he was just a child! And what of Princess Amber? Was it because she was in Queen Helistra's grip he had not mentioned her? Is that why he had said four and not five? Tarbor spoke of his thoughts.

"Queen Elina is right, Speedwell. He is but a baby. Of what good is that against Queen Helistra? And what of Princess Amber? Is she not of the spirit you have mentioned in Prince Martyn? They are twins," he pointed out, putting Speedwell on the spot.

"The barrier that is being weaved will hold whilst he grows, to enable him to gain the power needed to defeat her," replied Speedwell to Queen Elina's open mouth. She was at a loss as to what he was saying about her son. Power to defeat his daughter?

"However, you are right, Tarbor. The Ancient One has felt Princess Amber's spirit too. My senses tell me my daughter has not looked into her soul to see what I have seen, but we can only focus on Prince Martyn. If I show any interest in the Princess, I could be putting her life in danger. That is why I speak of four," answered Speedwell, to confirm what Tarbor had thought, but it only led him to ask more questions.

"You speak of Prince Martyn joining you as a future saviour, but you have your rune staff to help you when that time comes. If her patience lasts that long, what will he have? His spirit that you speak of?" pushed Tarbor further.

Speedwell heard the same doubts that he had felt with the Ancient One, but with an understanding now as to why they needed the time for the child to grow, so he could possess what had been waiting in hope with the Ancient One for a very long time.

"You must trust in the wisdom of the Ancient One, King wielder, as I do," he replied, without revealing anything, leaving Tarbor to wonder what this Ancient One was like. He was obviously his mentor to revere him so.

"Then your trust in him will also be mine," he conceded in the end, for Kelmar to hear his own pledge in thought to Tarbor.

"Once Tomin is with us, you must journey with me into the Great Forest, where Prince Martyn can be better protected," advised Speedwell, looking at Queen Elina.

Everyone looked at each other as Queen Elina rose to her feet, Prince Martyn clutched tightly in her arms.

"You are not taking him anywhere! Your daughter already has my daughter in her clutches! I will not lose my son as well!" she warned.

"I do not intend to take him away from you. Your love for him is important. I only wish for the Ancient One to see his spirit that I felt," replied Speedwell.

"But if you take Prince Martyn into the Great Forest and she finds out, will it not make her suspicious? You said she has not looked into

Princess Amber's soul, but she will if she finds out her brother has entered the forest," put Tarbor thoughtfully, making Speedwell think.

"You are right, but she will not know his whereabouts once you have found the shield. You will be able to hide him when he enters the Great Forest, without her knowing. It will be of no surprise to her that he is in hiding. After all, his life has already been threatened for being the Prince of Tiggannia," replied Speedwell, even though Tarbor had not yet felt the shield.

Queen Elina looked at them, bemused by their talk. "There is only one thing you are forgetting. It is my son you are talking about, and he is staying here!"

And without further ado, Queen Elina stormed out of the hall with Prince Martyn. Permellar followed her, holding Kayla, with Oneatha trying to calm her down.

"I think she is upset," came the obvious comment from King Stowlan in the awkward silence that followed.

"That is my fault. I feel I have unsettled her by not explaining myself very well," said Speedwell, in understanding why she was wary of him. After all, he was the father of a sorceress! And with that thought, he moved towards the fire to find some comfort in its warmth.

As he held his hands to the warmth, into the hall walked Cillan, with open eyes when he saw Tarbor.

"Cillan! Where have you been hiding?" Tarbor smiled at seeing him.

In a way, that had been true. Cillan was keeping his distance from Permellar and Oneatha. Forgiveness had not come easily for someone who had been one of the guards that had kept them as prisoners in Kelmsmere.

"I have been taking a walk, breathing in the sea air along the cliffs," greeted Cillan, giving Tarbor a warrior's clasp of the arm as he neared him.

"Queen Elina has been telling us of her rescue from the dungeons and that you were rescued also," said Tarbor, once Cillan had sat down and found something to eat.

"Queen Helistra accused me of blindness, letting Druimar escape from under my nose, and had me thrown in there," said Cillan, visualising that day.

"And Tarril?" Cillan looked at Tarbor and shook his head. "I have not seen him since the day we entered Stormhaven. He disappeared at the same time King Taliskar did. He is gone, Tarbor," informed Cillan sadly, to see Tarbor close his eyes at hearing they had lost an old friend.

"I heard he is not the only one, Tarbor. It saddened me to hear of Girvan's loss when you saved Prince Martyn and rid the Kingdom of Wardine," said Cillan, in recognition for what he had done.

"What are you doing here anyway? The last time I saw you, you spoke of finding someone called Speedwell in the Great Forest after going after the Prince?" asked Cillan, changing the subject, not even noticing Speedwell looking at him whilst he ate.

"He had no need to, I came to him," said Speedwell with a smile, to see Cillan slowly look up at him, coughing on his food.

"You are the name Tarbor heard through the rock?" Cillan was in disbelief.

"I am Speedwell," he confirmed.

"And we are his bodyguards." Piper and Tintwist smiled, for Cillan to look around at two impish faces looking at him.

"You exist then!" said Cillan in amazement. "If Tarril were here now," he said with a smile, but with sadness in his heart. "You had better tell me what I have been missing." So whilst Cillan ate, Tarbor told him why Speedwell was there for him, to nearly choke on his food once more when he told him he was Queen Helistra's father.

Day was beginning to turn into night by the time Tarbor told Cillan how Speedwell had found Urchel, Idrig and himself on Wreken Moor, pitched against the evil beasts that nearly took Urchel's life. Then finally of how Speedwell had cleared his mind as to who he really was, so he could find the shield of Waunarle to protect Prince Martyn and Tomin.

At the end, Cillan shook his head. "So when we felt the earth shake, it was you trying to stop Queen Helistra, your daughter, from poisoning the Great Forest, not the mountains telling us it was wrong to have spilt blood beneath them, as I thought," said Cillan, trying to clarify things in his mind as to his beliefs, for Speedwell to raise his eyebrows at Cillan's profound words.

"You felt both, Cillan, although it was the Plateau Forest," Speedwell said, smiling. "Like us, the mountains only like to feel the fall of snow or rain upon their heights and the warmth of the sun."

Cillan smiled at the acknowledgement given to him from Speedwell and he turned to Tabor with many questions on his mind, but only one he wanted to ask: "I presume you will be wanting to be called King Ashwell now, or would you prefer Your Highness or my lord or King wielder, as you say Speedwell named you?" joked Cillan, for all to laugh.

"A nickname, it seems, like Tintwist." Tarbor smiled at Tintwist, to receive one back. "I think it wise at this time that although I have found my true identity as King Ashwell of Waunarle, Tarbor is who I will remain until we have seen this through," he decided.

"To us, you will always be that mixed-up Tarbor," said Cantell and Kelmar, smiling.

"I would not wish it any other way," said Tarbor with a smile.

King Stowlan slapped the side of Tarbor's arms. "Now your true test begins, fellow King." He grinned, with Kraven nodding behind him.

"Now my path is clear, I am ready to meet its challenge," he answered with a smile.

"And we will meet that challenge with you," promised Cillan, for Tarbor to grip Cillan's arm in gratitude.

Speedwell smiled at the bond he could clearly see was between them all. They would need it, he thought.

"Perhaps then as your first duty as King, you should tell Queen Elina of the importance of protecting Prince Martyn within the arms of the Great Forest and the Ancient One," suggested Speedwell, to make Tarbor immediately feel flustered.

"She will listen to you," he added, and he left the hall, smiling at Tarbor's discomfort.

Piper and Tintwist saw their chance to slip away to explore the castle, but not before a warning resounded from behind the door through which Speedwell had left. "Do not get into trouble, you two!" Speedwell's words echoed, to everyone's smiles.

"Come, I will show you around the castle," said King Stowlan, smiling, to a delighted Piper and Tintwist. Together with Kraven, they too left the hall.

"I will show you where Queen Elina rests, Tarbor," said Cantell, smiling, seeing the awkwardness Tarbor was feeling.

"King Rolfe had that same look," he said with a smile as he led Tarbor to Queen Elina's chamber, leaving Kelmar and Cillan talking around the fire.

"I mean no disrespect, Cantell. I would not dare impose upon her, not after her loss," said Tarbor, finding himself apologising to Cantell.

"I know, my friend, there is no need to reproach yourself." Cantell grinned as he led Tarbor outside to the courtyard. Tarbor felt a fool but smiled to himself, hearing Cantell call him his friend.

On one side of the courtyard was a separate oblong building, built into the castle wall, where Queen Elina was staying. Tarbor found himself standing nervously outside her chamber, guarded by two guards that looked straight through him.

Cantell left him there, wishing him well, and he knocked on the door for a servant to answer it almost immediately.

"You may go," said Queen Elina to the servant quietly, whilst giving Tarbor a cold look as he entered the room. She was holding Prince Martyn, trying to get him to sleep, when Tarbor's knocks on the door had disturbed him. Tarbor waited and said nothing.

Finally, Prince Martyn was asleep in his wooden cradle and Queen Elina gestured for Tarbor to sit down.

"Are you here to persuade me to go into the Great Forest with my son? If so, it will not work," she challenged him straight away, driving her sea blue eyes defiantly into his.

Tarbor looked back into them and wished everything was different, but if it had been, he would not be sitting here, he thought. He chided himself for even thinking that perhaps one day she might have feelings for him.

"There are forces at work here, my lady, that frighten me. You have seen it with your own eyes. In amongst it all, your children have somehow come to shine like a beacon of hope to Speedwell. If they are the future then they must be protected from Queen Helistra's evil, and that is best done in the forest. You must trust in him as I do," implored Tarbor.

"I also see a grandfather that has come to rescue his grandson for fear of him being killed by his own mother. A woman whose jealousy has turned into an evil of the like that I have never witnessed before this day, and it must be stopped, whatever is asked of us," he added, making Queen Elina see Charlotte fall down dead before her and the face of Queen Helistra smile mockingly.

"But my little Amber is in her grasp. If we are in the forest, she is all on her own. What chance will she have?" worried Queen Elina.

"She is on her own now as we speak, my lady," pointed out Tarbor, to see the tears start to flow down Queen Elina's cheeks.

"I am sorry. That was harsh of me," he apologised, "but Speedwell is right. By ignoring her, we do not put her in danger as such. It is not the first time she has taken a child to play her little games of pretending to be a mother," revealed Tarbor, to receive a tearful frown from Queen Elina.

"What do you mean, not the first time?" And Tarbor told her who he really was.

"So I must find the shield of Waunarle to help protect them both," finished Tarbor, to a disbelieving Queen Elina.

"She took you knowing you were really King Ashwell of Waunarle?" she said eventually.

"She did, my lady. Without their true King, the people of Waunarle and Cardronia have been pawns in her games of deception, to get to where she wanted, Stormhaven, but with Speedwell's help we will stop her," promised Tarbor.

"My husband always said we were just keepers, guardians of Stormhaven until the day someone would come and unlock its mysteries, but little did he know that it would be someone so evil," reflected Queen Elina.

"This shield you are to find, it is magic then, for her not to see through it?" said Queen Elina, not believing she was saying it.

"It was crafted by people in the forest called Elfore, with help from one of the Forestalls," replied Tarbor, listening to himself. He could understand why it all seemed so unreal to her ears.

"And what is a Forestall?" she asked, looking at Prince Martyn sleeping, with an impossible thought entering her head from how Speedwell had spoken.

"Speedwell says it is a title that just means a keeper of the forest. He told me he looks after the Great Forest of the North," explained Tarbor.

"Has he ever told you who he is talking about when he speaks of the Ancient One?" she queried further.

"No, he has not, my lady. I presume he is someone of great age who is likened to a King of the forests. I only know Speedwell looks upon him with great reverence," answered Tarbor.

"And we are to trust them?" she pushed.

"With our lives, my lady. He has saved mine once already."

"But where is the sense of going into a place to see someone we know nothing of, because he supposedly felt something in my children?" questioned Queen Elina.

"There is none at all, my lady, but we have seen what Queen Helistra can do. We cannot defeat her evil on our own. We must take Speedwell's advice and follow him into the Great Forest," advised Tarbor.

A long pause filled the air whilst Queen Elina thought. Still nothing made any sense to her, but she could see in Tarbor's eyes it was the only path that they could take, however unbelievable. "You had better find your shield then, King Ashwell, if you are to protect my children on this journey we are undertaking," she said, resigning herself to the unforeseen.

Getting up, she offered her hand to a smiling Tarbor. "I am still Tarbor, my lady, until the day comes when I can claim my rightful place," he said, holding her small hand and kissing it.

"I will put my trust in you then, Tarbor, as you do in Speedwell. None of it is clear to me, only that she must be defeated, and if this is what we must do, then so be it," she decided as Prince Martyn decided to stir and wake up with a whimper.

"Well, that was not long, little man," she said with a smile, and she lifted him out of his cradle.

His moaning soon subsided as he felt the comfort of his mother, for a tiny arm to fall out of his shawl. Tarbor clumsily tried to help put his arm back inside the shawl, much to Queen Elina's amusement, but as Tarbor held his tiny hand, he felt the strangest of sensations come over him, like a whispering sigh passing through his mind. He involuntarily shook, as if someone had blown cold air on the back of his neck.

Queen Elina looked at him, frowning. "I suddenly felt shivery," he said, smiling, not knowing what it was.

"The night draws on with cold in the air and I think this little one is going to be up for most of it." She smiled back and Tarbor could not help but feel a warm glow inside him as she did so.

"I will leave you in peace then, my lady," and Tarbor left, bowing, with a sigh of relief inside him that she had come around.

Queen Elina watched him go. He was a good and courageous man, she thought. She had not failed to see his look of care for her, but her heart was over the Great Forest with her husband and soon, she was thinking, *I will be near him.*

Tarbor crossed the courtyard back to the hall. He thought he would talk further with Cillan about Tarril, but when he got there the hall was empty. *It must be later than I realised*, he thought, and noted the fire still burnt well.

A chair pulled up later and Tarbor was relaxing in front of it, thinking of all the stories that had been told that day. Now it was time for deeds to be done, he thought, yawning, as he unknowingly held the hilt of the defender whilst rubbing his thumb over the top of its pommel.

With his thoughts from the storytelling still going around in his head and the warmth from the fire bringing him comfort, his eyes were soon closed, for him to fall asleep.

Cantell and Kelmar came into the hall to tell Tarbor where his bed was for the night, to find him fast asleep in the chair.

"I see he has already found his sleeping place," said Cantell with a smile on seeing him.

"His back will not be his friend in the morning," said Kelmar from experience.

"We will leave him to his dreams. The fire will keep him company," said Cantell.

"It looks like he is ready to do battle when he does," remarked Kelmar, seeing Tarbor's hand on the hilt of his sword.

"Judging by what has been said this night, we will all need to be ready for battle," replied Cantell, and they left Tarbor to his dreams.

For that is where he was; he had dropped into a deep sleep and was seeing himself drifting amongst clouds, as he had with Speedwell.

He felt himself drifting endlessly until a sudden breeze blew the clouds apart, revealing to him a bleak view of a grey sea.

No, wait, it was not the greyness of a sea but of another sea waving in the breeze, a sea of grey-green grass.

The more he looked, the more there was, spreading as far as his eye could see, with water flowing through it like veins.

Then masses of reeds showed themselves, swaying alongside the grass in dense swathes, with pools of water dotted everywhere in amongst them.

Suddenly, as if someone had pushed him in his back, he felt himself hurtling down towards the sea of grass and reeds. All he saw was a line of trees in the distance as he plummeted downwards, to hit one of the pools of water, making him jolt back awake, gasping for air out of fear of drowning.

Tarbor sat up and wiped his sweating brow; it had all felt so real. He looked around to see a servant looking at him. His sudden movement had made her more aware of him as she was clearing the long table of dishes.

"I am sorry if I startled you, a bad dream," he quickly apologised.

"That is all right, sir. A lot of us have had those recently with all that goes on." She smiled and disappeared, carrying the dishes she had cleared.

Tarbor knew immediately what the dream was telling him of, at long last. No worries in his mind this time as to what was going on, only that to him it had been long in the waiting.

He would tell Speedwell of it, but where was it he had dreamt of? The servant reappeared to clear some more pots as Tarbor got up and felt his back moan to him as he stretched.

"You work late." He smiled at the servant.

"Early, sir, the dawn is on the horizon," she stated. Tarbor frowned. Dawn? He had only just gone to sleep! The fire embers, though, told him otherwise.

Saying farewell, Tarbor left the servant to walk outside into a fresh new morning. He immediately spotted Kraven walking through the main gates and headed towards him.

"I see you are an early riser, Kraven," he greeted him with a smile.

"Not by choice, Tarbor. Speedwell and his companions, the two Manelves, wanted a boat to sail first light," he explained.

"He has gone already! But I…" There was no point, he thought, he was gone. *He certainly has faith in me to find the shield to have gone. If only I knew where it was I saw it*, he thought.

"You look as if you could do with some hot food in you," observed Kraven, seeing Tarbor looking a bit perplexed.

"I think you are right, my friend." Tarbor nodded and off they strode to the kitchen, to find Cillan already eating there.

As they sat together, Tarbor told them of his dream and of his hope that it was telling him where the shield was. Though Kraven and Cillan were still trying to come to terms with all they had heard, they did not doubt Tarbor, not after seeing Queen Helistra's evil.

"A sea of grass, well, that is easy," said Kraven with a smile after Tarbor had finished telling them.

"It is?" said Tarbor, relieved.

"You have described the salt marsh. We are not that far from it," he announced.

"I have heard of it," said Tarbor, sounding vague.

"It stretches for miles along the coast of Silion and the River Shellow. Good luck in finding your shield in amongst that vastness," he added, making Tarbor groan. His dream had not exactly been clear to him as to where it was in the salt marsh.

"No doubt you will be after a boat now," assumed Kraven, already getting to his feet.

"Thank you, Kraven." Tarbor smiled, knowing he would need one anyway so as to meet Speedwell on the Isles of Kesko, where he had told them his grandson, Tomin, was.

"I will get one whilst you finish your food," said Kraven, and he immediately left to secure one.

"Are you of good heart, Cillan, to search with me for the missing shield I have seen in my dreams? It will be good to have you by my side," said Tarbor, smiling.

Cillan swallowed a mouthful of food as he looked at Tarbor in thought. "You cannot sail a boat, can you?" he surmised with a quiet smile, for Tarbor to grin.

"Ah, you know of my weakness then, Cillan. Once, when I was young in Ardriss, but since then my skills are lacking, and somebody did tell me you were once a fisherman," admitted Tarbor.

"You heard true, it will be good to be on the open water once more in your quest." Cillan smiled in acceptance of helping Tarbor.

Tarbor nodded, smiling at Cillan, whilst hoping inside that when he found the shield he would be able to protect Tomin and Prince Martyn. Speedwell was obviously expecting it of him, but he had no idea as to how he would achieve that once he was in possession of the shield.

His hand gripped the hilt of the defender as he thought on it. He had witnessed magic and now he was a King wielder. Somehow he had to prove to a Forestall that he could perform it to protect the future of them all! The thought was a daunting one as he realised Cillan was standing waiting for him.

"Dreaming again?" He smiled, seeing Tarbor's lost look.

"Sometimes I wish that was all it was," he said, getting up and slapping Cillan on his back. "Let us hope the stars are watching over us and we can find this shield together, my friend," and the two warriors left to find Kraven.

CHAPTER XXX

"Stay still. Do not move!" whispered Fleck to Tiska and Tislea, making them hold their breath whilst perched high in a tree, where safety had been sought overnight from prowling malignant beasts.

Two such creatures were roaming below them now as they watched whilst blending in with the thick branches of the tree they had climbed.

The creatures were smelling the air, but they could only discern the smell of the forest through their putrid nostrils. They turned and scurried away in disgust, much to the relief of the three Elfore hiding above them, allowing them to breathe once more.

Ever since leaving the Valley of the Lakes, they had encountered beasts on their journey to the Ancient One. Though they had trodden carefully, there had still been enough encounters for Tiska and Tislea to only have one more arrow left between them.

The arrows they had used to strike down the beasts remained embedded within them, for fear of poisoning themselves from the orange blood that exuded from their wounds.

Down from the tree they climbed, with eyes forever searching. "How much further can it be to this ridge?" questioned Tiska, looking behind her as they began walking through the forest.

"Soon, I hope, Mother, with only one arrow left," pointed out Tislea.

"Time has passed me by more than I realised since I was last here, but I am sure we are near, though the beasts have veered us from our path," answered Fleck.

The day moved on as they did, silently with hardly a sound. The forest all around them had seemingly come to a stop in a deathly hush. No birds could be heard singing in the trees or animals nuzzling in the undergrowth, searching for food, making the three travellers even more wary of their surroundings.

The ground they were travelling upon started to become covered in ferns, died back from the winter, with new fronds trying to push their way through. Rocky outcrops started to appear here and there, some covered in thick bushes with buds starting to form, announcing like the fronds that spring had reached them.

Fleck saw an opportunity to rest at one bristling with thick bushes. "Through here," he urged the other two. They scrambled through the bushes and climbed a short distance to the top of the outcrop, where a secluded dip in the rocks was to be had.

Fleck stood at the top a moment and looked all around him until he was satisfied all was well. Sitting, he opened his pouch to take out the last of his provisions he had brought.

"This is tougher than my leather boots," remarked Tislea as she dug her teeth into her last piece of cold meat.

"My water needs replenishing," said Tiska, listening to her leather water bottle as she shook it. "I am down to my last few drops."

Fleck nodded his understanding. "If it had not been for those creatures, we would have reached the ridge by now, where water is in abundance, but no matter, we should reach the ridge by tomorrow," he assured them both, but in truth he was not sure. It had been a long time since he had trodden these parts for him to remember clearly where they were.

Fleck stood up and stretched after their rest. It was time to move on, he thought. Looking around, he nodded to Tiska and Tislea that all was clear. Down the other side of the outcrop and into the bushes they moved, when suddenly Fleck held up his arm behind him for all three of them to crouch, blending into the bushes.

As they listened, someone running through the forest came to their ears, but then what they heard next made them go tense.

There was no mistaking the guttural grunts of a beast and two more footfalls; all were chasing the first.

Fleck looked around at Tiska and Tislea. He had no need to say that someone was running for their life; they could hear for themselves well enough, as their faces of concern showed.

Fleck chanced opening the bush they were under to see if he could see who the poor soul was.

There, running through the trees, not a stone's throw from where he was watching, a terrified face ran right past him. A face of pure terror, a face that he knew; it was a Manelf! It was Ludbright! What was he doing here?

There was no time to think as to why; his trouble was right behind him in the shape of a grotesque-looking beast with two tusks snarling at his back, saliva dripping from its twisted mouth.

Fleck thought it could have once been a forest boar, but no more. Even more disconcerting was who or what was behind the boar!

Fleck recognised they were of the Manelf by their dress, but that was as far as it went. The two faces of what had been Manelf were hideous beyond words as they too chased the terror-stricken Ludbright.

Fleck did not think twice. He was out of the bushes giving chase with Tiska and Tislea hard on his heels, their blood running cold with repulsion by what they saw.

Ludbright was running on his last reserves of strength; his legs were beginning to tire. Around trees and bushes he ran, through the ferns that pulled at his tiring legs, trying to get away from the horror that was right behind him.

Fleck's fresher legs made him catch up quickly with the two deformed Manelf, but his presence was felt by them as they suddenly stopped and turned, with their swords already drawn.

As they did so, one sliced through the air with its sword, making Fleck stop in his tracks and lean out of the way of the blade. Fleck only just had time to draw his own sword as the other creature saw its chance and made to pounce upon Fleck's open guard.

All Fleck saw was Tiska following up with her blade, striking straight through the middle of the corrupted Manelf's body, sending it backwards with the force onto the ground.

It did not stop the other corrupted Manelf from attacking Fleck, but he was ready this time and parried its sword enough to push the creature away from him.

Fleck was relentless as he rained blow after blow upon the creature to eventually create an opening that saw him slice the creature from groin to shoulder, sending it reeling to the ground.

Fleck did not hesitate as he followed up to drive his sword straight through its chest, *where only the blackest of hearts sits now,* he thought as he did it.

He looked up first to see Tislea in pursuit of the beast with Tiska further behind. Wiping his blade on the deformed Manelf, he ran after them.

Tislea had not stopped; she had run past the fighting, chasing the beast. She watched in dread as suddenly Ludbright's legs buckled beneath him, sending him sprawling headlong onto the ground.

Seeing this, Tislea stopped and quickly made ready her bow, notching her arrow. The beast was onto Ludbright, jumping into the air to pounce upon his prostrate body. Ludbright closed his eyes and said goodbye. Tislea breathed once to steady her aim and let loose the last arrow!

Ludbright heard a grunt then a thud. He slowly opened his eyes; he was still alive! And there lying on the ground next to him was the beast that had been chasing him; dead, with an arrow sticking straight through its neck!

He pushed away from the creature on his bottom and looked up to see a relieved smile on a young Elfore woman running towards him. He broke down in tears.

Sitting back on top of the outcrop of rocks where they had just rested, Fleck gave Ludbright time to allow his emotions to run their course.

"What happened, Ludbright? Why are you here and not in the Great Forest?" asked Fleck, once Ludbright's tears had subsided.

"I have brought them to their deaths, because of my own foolishness," said Ludbright, looking at the ground, making the others frown. "I was curious to see the Ancient One and saw my chance when we left our settlement," he began explaining.

"We waited out the winter to make our journey to where we all lived once in harmony with the Great Forest. The tongue in the cheek under the shadow of the Kavenmist Mountains, I remember my great-grandmother affectionately calling it," he recollected.

"We thought we had time to let winter pass to make our journey easier, and told Ringwold so before he left, to his worry. He warned us not a moment more, and so when spring came, we began our journey, leaving the east wind behind us for the last time.

"That is when I made my suggestion that we should inform Ringwold we had left so he would know we were all safe, when really it was out of my own curiosity to see the Ancient One to undertake such a journey." Ludbright kept staring at the ground as he spoke. He could not look up at Fleck, Tiska and Tislea out of shame.

He wiped his nose on his sleeve and continued: "Going on my own was unthinkable, so Becup and Weaver joined me. We parted company with everyone along the Windward Pass so they could cut down to join the River Ogrin and follow it to eventually come out into the Great Forest." Ludbright paused as his story brought him to the beasts.

Fleck had closed his eyes when he heard the names of Becup and Weaver. He knew them to be kind, gentle beings, and he had just driven his sword into one of them.

Ludbright tried to hold back the tears as he remembered the snarling beasts that had attacked them. "We were making good the ground on our journey when out of nowhere, Fleck, they attacked us, those fanged beasts," he shivered, "we killed three of them before the last one ran away, but by then they had bitten Becup and Weaver. I… I was bending over their bodies thinking they had been mortally wounded when suddenly they rose before me, turning as they did into those hideous creatures." Ludbright's sorrow knew no bounds as he wept. They were his friends and he had led them here to their deaths for his own fulfilment.

"Do not blame yourself, Ludbright. Queen Helistra's evil has spread more quickly than any of us could have foretold. Who could blame you for wanting to see the Ancient One? And Ringwold would have wanted to know you were all safe," said Fleck, trying to console him.

"I should be with them. I do not deserve to be alive and yet I ran for my life," continued Ludbright, as if he had not even heard what Fleck had said.

"Three days I kept running and hiding, not knowing where I was. Then suddenly there they were in front of me, Becup and Weaver, with the fanged beast that had escaped our blades, their faces twisted, unrecognisable!

"For some reason, the stars must have been watching over me for our paths to have crossed. I owe you my life and for that I thank you," finished Ludbright, to finally look up at them, trying to smile his gratitude.

Fleck put his hand on Ludbright's shoulder in understanding, whilst Tiska handed him some cold meat. "Here, Manelf, it is tough, but it is food." Ludbright nodded his thanks to her, although at this moment he had no appetite.

"Come, we must continue our journey. We have been here long enough. The smell of their tainted blood will bring more beasts this way," warned Fleck, already moving through the outcrop's bushes.

"It does not seem right to leave them there like that," said Ludbright, looking back as the four of them set off.

"I am sorry, Ludbright, but it is best we stay away from their tainted blood," warned Fleck. Ludbright knew he was right, but it still felt wrong.

They journeyed throughout the rest of the day without further encounters and settled themselves for another night of stiff limbs above ground in two suitable trees.

The next day turned out to be the same, and Fleck was beginning to wonder if his sense of direction had completely deserted him when suddenly he stopped to listen to a sound that had been caught on the breeze. He smiled to himself, at last.

"Are we there?" asked Tiska, seeing him.

Fleck turned round and smiled. "You will see."

As they moved forward, they all began to recognise the sound Fleck had caught: the unmistakable sound of a river's rushing water.

The closer they got to its noise, the fresher the breeze that blew across their faces from the energy of the river's passage. Breathing in its freshness, they headed for an opening between the trees it had created by pushing back their low hanging branches.

Walking through them, they found themselves on the bank of a wide, fast-flowing river. "Welcome to the River Winterbourne," announced Fleck, smiling at all its glory as it sped past them, but as he turned to look at their faces, all he saw was the backs of their heads.

Although the River Winterbourne was a wonder in itself, their eyes were looking at another wonder that was dominating the skyline.

Enormous was too small a word for what they were looking at. For there, sitting majestically on a huge mound of its own making at the edge of the Old Ogrin Ridge, sat the Ancient One!

A tree like no other, its top was lost to the clouds that sailed over it, whilst branches, that were as wide as the tree was high, held themselves out in an everlasting look of embrace, as if to welcome them all from their journey.

"I… I have never seen such a sight before," said Ludbright in awe, whilst feeling the guilt inside him for the deaths of Becup and Weaver by being there.

"It is the heart of the forest that we have only ever heard of," uttered Tiska, at what she was beholding.

"You are right, Tiska. He is the beginning of all the forests," said Fleck with a smile, happy that they were there at last.

"It is the Ancient One," whispered Tislea to herself, at such a wonder.

Although you could not see them, Fleck pointed out that the long, bumpy-looking mound on the other side of the Winterbourne River, covered by years of fallen leaves enabling grass, bushes and even small trees to cover them, was some of the huge, twisted roots of the Ancient One.

Mouths did not close for a long time as they tried to take in the Ancient One's magnificence.

After filling their leather water bottles and refreshing themselves, they began walking along the bank of the River Winterbourne, weaving their way through the trees, some of which hung precariously over the river's edge. All of the time not being able to take their eyes off the splendour of the Ancient One, whose leaves and branches seemed to be waving hello to them in the breeze.

Then suddenly something moved on the other side of the river to catch their eye. "Beasts!" cried Tiska, seeing them running over the bumpy ground of the Ancient One's roots.

"Here already!" Fleck groaned in dismay; they were too late to warn Ringwold, he thought.

But as he thought it, they watched a figure appear in front of the Ancient One and stand on top of the mound, right in front of the charging beasts!

"What is he doing? He will be killed!" shouted Ludbright in alarm.

"No, he will not be," replied Fleck confidently. "It is Ringwold," he informed them.

The beasts charged straight at him, but as they neared Ringwold, something strange happened as they literally shuddered to a stop and were repelled through the air with what looked like steam coming off their bodies, their dead bodies!

Fleck smiled and put his arm up in the air to see Ringwold raise his in acknowledgement, waving at them. Fleck smiled. "They have put a barrier in place already, come," he beckoned, and they moved off.

"Those horrible beasts are everywhere, Fleck," remarked Ludbright as they walked, having to raise his voice as another noise began to reach their ears.

"I know, Ludbright, their numbers have increased fast," replied Fleck. "At least the Great Forest will be safe with the barrier in place," he added thoughtfully.

"Fleck," said Ludbright with a frown, thinking of what he had just seen.

"Yes, Ludbright?"

"If those beasts were stopped because of a barrier, how are we going to get through it?" he asked, a little bit concerned.

Fleck had to admit he did not know, but Ringwold would not let them come near if it meant they were to be in harm's way, he thought logically, conveying his thoughts to the others, for Ludbright to look back at him, hoping he was right.

The noise grew louder and louder until suddenly they found themselves standing on a rocky ledge, overlooking the most breathtaking view that Tiska, Tislea and Ludbright had ever seen.

They had come to the very edge of the Old Ogrin Ridge to stand at a giddying height that overlooked the vast canopy of the Great Forest, stretching out far below them.

The noise that had become thunderous to their ears was the Winterbourne River, plummeting over the edge of the ridge, to fall, it seemed, forever downwards into a vast lake. A rainbow shined from it, its colours mixing with the spray that threw itself outwards, where birds flew through it, seemingly in play.

The huge lake could be seen getting narrower at its far edge to become another river that soon lost itself to the depths of the Great Forest, and dominating it all stood the Ancient One, filling their vision with its splendour.

Only now as they looked at it all in awe, did they see how more of the Ancient One's huge roots were showing themselves, spiralling downwards towards the lake, looking as if they had pushed their way out of the solid rock face of the ridge in a grey twisted mass.

"I think the snow is melting on top of the Winterbourne Mountains by the look of the river," remarked Fleck as he looked back up the rushing Winterbourne. "I imagine the Linninhorne River is the same on the other side," he added, making the others look at him.

"What, there is another river?" questioned Ludbright in astonishment.

"Yes, it is hidden by the Ancient One. That is why the lake below was named the Lake of Tears, because the ridge looks like it is crying with the two falls," said Fleck with a smile, for the others to look once more at the wonder that had opened up before them.

Pulling themselves away from the spectacle that had taken their breath away, they returned in amongst the trees. It did not take Fleck long to find the dip in the ground that he knew led to the Ancient One.

Only when they were in the dip did Tiska, Tislea and Ludbright realise that Fleck had led them to an underground passageway, whose entrance lay between the trees.

Steps showed themselves once they had entered the passageway cut out of the solid rock beneath the earth. Down they went, following the steps to hear the thunder of the Winterbourne Waterfall vibrate in their ears.

The passageway by now was wet with spray as to their amazement they saw they were walking along a pathway directly behind the waterfall, which cascaded with a roar past them.

"Who in the name of the trees did all of this?" said Tiska, in puzzlement, as she walked behind with Tislea, finding she was holding hands with her daughter.

"Our ancestors, Tiska," answered Fleck loudly to get above the noise.

Passing the cascading water, they came to another passageway and started to climb back upwards, glad that the noise of the waterfall was slowly dying as they did so, although it had left a ringing in their ears.

Suddenly it felt warmer and a woody earthy smell met their nostrils.

"The Ancient One," said Fleck, almost whispering, for them to look in the dim light to see they had entered an archway of giant roots, some as big as the trees in the forest, curving over their heads.

Ludbright slipped looking at them and put his hand out to steady himself, to feel his whole body aglow with an energy the like of which he had never felt. He let go with a gasp.

"Ludbright, what are you doing!" said Fleck, seeing him.

"I... I am sorry, Fleck. I could not help myself, I slipped," he apologised.

"You must be careful not to interfere with the Ancient One," he warned, to hear a voice he knew only too well.

"Do not be too harsh with him, Fleck. The Ancient One will be glad of his presence. It is many a day since he felt the kindness of a Manelf," Ringwold said with a smile, for Fleck to grin back.

"It is good to see you are safe from your journey, Fleck, and that you are here also, Ludbright," greeted Ringwold, for Ludbright to smile at the warmness given to him by Ringwold, although he did not feel he deserved it.

"I see by your company you informed the Elfore of the danger that comes upon them," he added, looking at Tiska and Tislea.

"This is Tiska and her daughter, Tislea," introduced Fleck.

"We are honoured, Forestall," they both said, bowing deeply.

"The honour is mine," replied Ringwold, bowing back, and they continued to walk through the tunnel of roots until they finally emerged onto the mound next to the Ancient One.

Standing on top of the mound had made the River Linninhorne come into view; it had been hidden by the enormity of the Ancient One.

Beyond the bumpy mound of the Ancient One's roots, that seemed to stretch out forever, the Linninhorne rushed past in its race with the Winterbourne, pouring over the ridge to join their waters below in the Lake of Tears.

Ludbright could only stare in solitude, with his thoughts of Becup and Weaver. It was everything he had ever dreamt of and more, to be here, seeing what he was seeing, feeling what he was feeling, but not at the cost of his friends.

Tiska and Tislea were also staring, not at the wonders that surrounded them, but at Ringwold. They were looking at his long grey cloak and his funny cloth hat that covered his ears, but especially at the long staff he held in his hands before him, covered in strange symbols.

"I did inform King Vedland, but he was hard to convince. He would not believe me and wanted proof. He got it when the poison reached the Valley of the Lakes and we had to run for our lives," informed Fleck, to the sad looks of Ringwold.

"We came to tell you of the pace that the poison travels through the forest with beasts of evil running everywhere, but from what we have just witnessed, you have already put up a barrier," added Fleck.

"You are right, Fleck. The Ancient One felt the evil was getting nearer and so we have put a barrier of containment in place to resist her evil," answered Ringwold.

Ringwold then saw Ludbright staring blankly out towards the Linninhorne River, knowing the evil he had obviously encountered had upset him.

"Come, you must be hungry. Let us go and eat whilst you tell me of what has happened," responded Ringwold to Ludbright's look.

He led them around the huge mound, for them to look up at the Ancient One to see the countless branches that went on forever, protruding from its enormous trunk, until he beckoned them to go into an opening between the Ancient One's roots.

The smell of the earth, wood and food filled their nostrils as they sat in a hollowed part, underneath the Ancient One's roots.

A shaft of light pierced through the darkness inside, where smoke from a fire warming a large metal pot was making its way out. Ringwold added to its light by touching a symbol on his rune staff, for its top to turn into a soft white glow.

Whilst Ringwold filled wooden bowls with food for them to eat, they sat on the earthen floor, feeling a calmness gradually wash over them, as if the Ancient One was trying to soothe their troubled minds.

After they had had their fill, Ringwold asked them what had happened. "Your journeys I take it then have not gone untroubled?"

Fleck began by telling him of the horror he had witnessed deep in the Southern Plateau Forest. How the birds flew overhead, giving them the first warning, then how animals of all description were running away from the smell of death, whilst others had been tainted by the poison and knew nothing but how to kill.

Fleck did not speak of Sleap. Tiska and Tislea did not need to hear of his death again, he thought. He could already see the sadness in their eyes as he spoke.

Instead, he moved on to tell Ringwold of his imprisonment and how the same fate had befallen the Elfore. "If it were not for Tiska and Tislea, I would not be here to tell you the story," he acknowledged, for Tiska and Tislea to look at him, knowing that had been both ways, but nodding their gratitude for him saying so.

Ringwold had listened to Fleck with a saddened heart by what he had heard and then turned to Ludbright to hear his story.

Once more, Ludbright told how his friends had turned into a corruption of evil, for him to run and hide for his life. That it was only thanks to Fleck, Tiska and Tislea that he was alive.

"But my own vanity to see the Ancient One led to my friends' deaths. I should be with them, not here," he cried in guilt.

Ringwold looked at him and held his arms. "You are of the forest, Ludbright. You have been denied all these years to roam where you wish. I know you have always wished to see the Ancient One. Becup and Weaver were the same. That is why they wanted to travel with you. You were not to know of the prevalence Helistra's poison would take," finished Ringwold, hoping Ludbright would stop blaming himself.

"Fleck was of the same mind, Forestall. You are kind to be so" sighed Ludbright in gratitude for what he had said to him.

"Good, now the Manelf, Ludbright, they are definitely on their way to the tongue of Kavenmist?" asked Ringwold, to receive Ludbright's nodded confirmation.

"At least that is some good news after all you have told me. I will strengthen the protective barrier over the Ancient One's roots by what you have told me of the poisonous mist, Fleck," said Ringwold, thinking to make Ludbright remember what he was going to ask.

"How did we pass through the barrier, Forestall? I never felt anything," he asked.

"Of course not, you are not evil," said Ringwold with a smile. "The

Ancient One and I have weaved into place a spell that simply knows good from bad, one that does not outstretch our power, as it must cover the whole of the Old Ogrin Ridge from the Kavenmist to the Lesser Hardenal Mountains."

"If a beast, like those you saw, tries to attack by breaking through the barrier, it closes upon it, sensing it is evil. In that moment, it binds itself around the beast, taking the breath from its body, stopping its poisonous heart," explained Ringwold, making Ludbright swallow.

"Thank the trees I am not evil then."

"And the spores I have told you about, they have no heart," pointed out Fleck.

"They will not pass, their evil poison will still be sensed and repelled," assured Ringwold.

"For how long, though?" questioned Fleck.

"For as long as it must take," answered Ringwold, thinking of his brother.

"Speedwell will be here soon to strengthen the weave and then we will consult the Ancient One for his guidance as to what we must do next. For now, we can only wait in hope that King Vedland will make it through with his people," said Ringwold, thinking of their plight.

"His stubbornness should see him through," said Fleck, remembering his meetings with him.

"He may be stubborn, but he is still our King," Tiska reminded him.

"I am sorry. I did not mean to offend you," apologised Fleck, realising that being an outcast all of these years had put a bitterness in him he had to keep under control in front of Tiska and Tislea.

"I hope Piper and Tintwist come back safely," said Ludbright, thinking again of what had befallen his friends.

"They will, Ludbright, they will. Speedwell will watch over them and bring them back safely," reassured Ringwold, with a whisper in his mind from the Ancient One that they were not all he hoped Speedwell would bring back safely to rid them of her evil.

CHAPTER XXXI

Idrig closed his eyes to breathe in the fresh valley air he had missed all of this time and sighed. Urchel smiled at his friend and joined him, breathing it in deeply.

The sun shone overhead, making everything in the valley look bright and vibrant. Idrig had to leave all of this behind him to take Stormhaven, thought Urchel, a quest he himself was regretting, although, at this moment, whatever it was that Speedwell had given him had made him feel better than he had ever felt in his whole life.

His senses seemed to have… grown, for want of a better word. Everything was clearer to him now than it was before and as he breathed in the valley air, those newfound senses came into play as he detected something else mixed in with the freshness of the valley.

Idrig saw Urchel looking down into the valley with a wary eye. "Is something wrong, Urchel?" he asked, getting down off his horse to stretch his legs.

"I am not sure, Idrig. All looks well from here, but something lingers in the air to tell me that not all is as it seems," he answered, joining Idrig as he too got off his horse.

"You still smell those horrible beasts in your nostrils, Urchel. I doubt if that smell will ever truly go away, for either of us," he reflected as they both looked out over the valley, to smile at its beauty.

They had rounded a gap between two hills, leaving Wreken Moor behind them, to be confronted by the valley Idrig knew so well.

In the distance, the River Mid wound its way along the valley floor, with trees lining its banks as if to protect it. Beyond the river were the fresh pastures where Idrig's sheep, and lambs by now, he was thinking, would be grazing.

And somewhere down there out of sight tucked in a little copse, that gave shelter in times of windy weather, lay his farm home that he longed to see.

Idrig looked up to gaze at the far side of the valley, to see the line of trees that marked the edge of the Great Forest, and smiled, thinking of Tarbor.

"I cannot wait to see my brother, it has been too long!" he suddenly shouted in excitement, and he was up on his horse galloping down the slope of the hill before Urchel had time to blink.

Urchel smiled. There was no stopping Idrig, but as he mounted his horse he smelt the air again; something did not feel right. He hoped Idrig was right, that it was just a lingering smell, but what path had those beasts taken before they had come upon them? He hoped it had not been this way, and gave chase.

Down the slope and onto the valley floor the two horses sped, with Idrig grinning all over his face at the thought of seeing his brother Vartig once more. Past the trees that edged the River Mid they rode and through its waters at a place where Idrig knew it was at its most shallow, to come out on the other side into pastures of grass that saw sheep with their lambs grazing on its sweet taste.

That is when they came across the remains of sheep savagely torn apart and left to rot, as they had done on the moor.

Both men felt their stomachs turn at the sight of the mauled sheep as they pulled up their horses to look, for their horses to snort in fright at being pulled up next to the smell of death.

"They were here, Urchel, before we came upon them," said Idrig, grimacing.

"Either that or there are more," said Urchel, looking around as he got off his horse.

"Be careful of them, Urchel!" warned Idrig.

"Do not worry, I have no intention of touching them. They need to be burnt," replied Urchel as he smelt the air, his senses telling him they had not been there that long.

Remounting, Urchel and Idrig slowly rode through the field, spotting other carcasses left to rot. "Even the birds do not go near," observed Idrig as they rode through another field towards a clump of trees that formed the copse around Idrig's farm home.

Idrig shouted for his brother as they drew nearer. "Vartig! It is me, Idrig!" They listened for a reply; only the breeze answered.

Idrig shouted again, and again there was no answer. Only the leaves on the trees could be heard in the breeze, seemingly the only welcome they were going to get as they rode on into the silent copse.

Dismounting, Urchel and Idrig looked around as they tied their horses to a wooden fence rail. Suddenly a squawking chicken ran past them, making them jump. "Well, they still have the run of the place." Idrig smiled wryly, feeling slightly silly as he looked up at his home.

Nothing had changed; it was as he remembered it. Its small wooden structure had mellowed with time to a distinctive grey colour, its turf roof sprouting with all sorts of vegetation, but it kept that winter cold at bay, thought Idrig, as he remembered those winter nights sitting around the fire with his brother, but at this moment it was of no comfort. Where was Vartig?

"He would have heard us and been here by now," said Idrig, worried.

"Perhaps he has gone to Marchend to report about the sheep and get help," suggested Urchel.

"He may have, his horse is not here," agreed Idrig, nodding as he moved to the side of his house.

Before walking in the side door, Idrig took a glance around the back to see if any sheep were penned in that were about to give birth, but none were.

All was as it should be as Idrig walked into his home. There were the stones set in the middle of the floor to hold the fire when lit, with an empty metal pot hanging over them from a frame, waiting for some food to be warmed inside of it.

A crude table and bench loomed in one corner, whilst in the other a short ladder showed itself going up to a platform that held two wooden beds supported by some precarious-looking structure of wooden posts. Urchel looked at it with some concern. "That is not where we have to sleep, is it?" he queried.

"It is, unless Vartig returns, then the floor underneath is yours," replied Idrig, grinning.

"I think I would prefer it," was Urchel's retort.

The night drew on and with it a cold that hung in the air from being near a river. Both men sat around the centre stone fire that Idrig had sparked into life from firewood that had been sought from the back of the house, where the brothers had always kept a supply under a wooden covering.

Food from their supplies and an unlucky rabbit that Idrig had caught cooked in the metal pot as both men pondered about Vartig.

"He should be back in a few days," said Idrig as he gave the pot one last stir. "He would not want to leave the sheep too long whilst they still lamb," he added in thought as he spooned the food into two wooden bowls.

"Those we saw then must have been killed when he was gone. Your brother would not have left them there to infect the rest of the flock at this time," considered Urchel, looking at Idrig as he ate, for Idrig to look back at him with concern.

"You are right, we will burn those poor animals tomorrow and keep vigil over them," replied Idrig, heeding what Urchel was saying to him, that more beasts must be out there and not just those they had come across.

With the warm food in their stomachs and a hefty wooden bar wedged into place across the door, Idrig built up the fire before both men settled down for the night.

Neither man made it as far as the wooden beds. Instead, they relaxed next to the fire, letting its warmth draw them into sleep.

Urchel felt he had only just closed his eyes when he found Idrig shaking him awake. He sat up, blinking by the light of the fire, to see a worried look upon Idrig's face. "Something is out there," he whispered, making Urchel instantly worried himself as he stood up to listen.

Nothing at first could be heard, then the sound of leaves being trampled upon unevenly came to his ears.

A noise like a grunt suddenly echoed through the copse, making both men's blood run cold, and then, without warning, a bang like thunder sounded on the barred door!

"Do not open it, Idrig!" whispered Urchel hoarsely, his words catching in his throat.

Idrig's face had gone ghostly white. He had put the thought to the back of his mind but knew whatever was left of his brother was standing on the other side of the door.

"If it is Vartig out there and he has been bitten, he will no longer be the brother you knew, Idrig," said Urchel sadly, reflecting Idrig's thoughts.

"I know. What shall we do?" A question Idrig had already heartbreakingly answered in his mind as he looked down at his sword; he must confront his brother and kill him!

The beast that had grown out of Vartig did not have to think. It only knew one thing to do: kill!

It smelt the fear inside and with a ferocious growl smashed down the door, snapping the wooden bar as if it were not there.

Raising their arms to cover their faces, Urchel and Idrig managed to step back quickly enough to avoid the shattering door, only to freeze in shocked horror at the sight of what stood in its frame.

All resemblance to what used to be a strong but kind face had gone, to be replaced by a pulsating face of bumps and veins that was snarling back at them in the flickering firelight.

Idrig choked inside as he recognised the wide studded leather belt, the same that he wore, around the waist of his now lost brother.

The beast that had been Vartig took full advantage of Idrig and Urchel's frozen state by throwing itself at them without hesitation, taking them both with it as it lunged forward.

Idrig took the full force, whilst Urchel received an arm straight across his face as they all fell backwards over the fire, sending the metal pot clanging across the floor to hit the wall.

Idrig's sword spilled from his hand as the full weight of his brother's beast pinned him to the floor, whilst Urchel was sent flying to hit the wall with the metal pot.

Urchel shook his head. He looked on in horror as the beast held a gnarled hand across Idrig's face and bared its crooked teeth, sinking them into Idrig's neck. Blood gushed immediately to the sound of Idrig's painful cries.

Urchel was up in a rage of dismay; his friend was being mauled by something that used to be his brother! Nothing made sense! Where was his sword?

Urchel gripped the nearest thing to him: the metal pot! He ran at the beast, swinging the metal pot for all he was worth. In that moment, the beast turned to look up at Urchel with blood dripping from its mouth, to be met by the metal pot full in its face, knocking the beast to the floor, off Idrig.

Glancing at Idrig, Urchel saw his distraught face. He was in a bad way; blood oozed between his fingers as he tried to stem the flow, but without much success. Urchel knew in that moment his friend was doomed; there was no Speedwell here to help him as there had been for him.

Urchel then saw his sword on the floor and went to grab it. The beast kicked Urchel's legs from beneath him, sending him flying once more, making him miss his sword.

The beast stood up and looked down at Urchel, ready to pounce. Urchel stared up at its pustule face covered in orange and red blood, with what was left of its nose splattered across it.

Urchel made to grab his sword again, only to feel the boot of the beast come down on his arm to stop him. Twisting one way and then the other, Urchel tried to free himself. He grabbed hold of the boot pinning him down, but his efforts to move it proved useless. He was pinned there as the beast loomed over him with eyes that were as black as night, for Urchel to swear they were grinning at him in its moment of triumph.

A grin that suddenly turned to emptiness as Idrig's sword appeared from nowhere to sever the beast's head clean off!

The head bounced on the floor next to Urchel and as the body began to fall, relieving the weight from his arm, he managed to roll out of the way, to hear the body crash onto the floor to his side.

Idrig fell to the floor beside the body of his dead brother, distraught at what he had just done, having to kill him to save his friend. But the evil inside him had turned his brother into something unrecognisable, and soon he would be the same as he felt a tightness in his chest telling him it was on its way.

Urchel bent over him with tears in his eyes, seeing his old friend covered in his own blood, knowing his life was ebbing away and what he would turn into.

Idrig grabbed Urchel's tunic with a bloody hand and spoke, coughing up blood. "You know what you must do, my friend… do not let me become like my brother. End it, I beg you…" Coughing, Idrig let go.

Urchel could only answer sobbing as his friend closed his pain-ridden eyes for the last time. "You will not suffer, my friend, as did your brother," he promised.

The stillness of the copse returned once more as Urchel picked up his sword and stood over his good friend, with his hands shaking at what he must do.

Twice now he had witnessed this horrible evil, and still he could not believe such things were happening. *Must I do this?* he was asking himself as Idrig's eyes suddenly flew open, making Urchel catch his breath.

Even though the fire had been reduced to embers and the stars were few in the night sky, Urchel could clearly see they were blood-red. As he stared at them in horror, they started to turn black. Reacting in terror, Urchel sliced straight through Idrig's neck and then drove his blade into Idrig's heart. Letting go of his sword, Urchel watched as orange blood started to ooze from around its blade.

It was more than Urchel could take, and he turned to run away from what he had just done. Through the copse and over the fields he ran, falling along the way, until finally out of breath he fell into the River Mid.

The river's cold waters washed over him as he knelt there crying for the loss of his friend. As his tears mixed with the cold flowing water, he wished the water would wash away the dread he was feeling inside. Instead, he suddenly felt a pain in his hands. He panicked; had he been poisoned? All that blood everywhere?

Urchel looked at his hands and saw the burn marks across them. In the horror he had just been through, he had not even noticed how hot the handle of the metal pot was.

CHAPTER XXXII

The single sail billowed in the fresh westerly wind, pushing out like a proud chest as Cillan steered the small boat through the choppy waters of the Northern Sea. With Tarbor's knowledge of sailing limited, to say the least, he was thankful that Cillan had agreed to sail the small boat with his know– how of how to handle a craft from his days as a fisherman.

Tarbor looked out at the coastline of the Kingdom of Silion that could be seen stretching alongside them as they headed for the mouth of the River Shellow, with the coastline of Balintium staying with them throughout their relatively short journey, on the other side.

"You say your knowledge of the salt marsh is little and yet you dreamt of it," pondered Cillan as he watched the sail flap in the wind.

"It is as strange to me, Cillan. There is a lot I have to try and understand as being normal now," replied Tarbor, keeping his eye on the Silion coast.

"Once you have found the shield, I hope your understanding of magic will be better than your knowledge of sailing," jibed Cillan.

Tarbor grinned at Cillan's jibe, but the fact was he had no idea of what he must do or how to go about creating a shield of protection once he had found the shield, only that Speedwell seemed to have every faith in him, which was more than he had in himself at this moment.

The wind favoured them well for this part of their journey as it took their small boat onwards towards the mouth of the River Shellow.

As it did so, the coastline began changing on both sides, showing the sea broken by swathes of grass waving in the wind. Only as more and more came into view did Tarbor begin to realise the enormity of his task in trying to retrieve the shield. Kraven was right. *There is a lot*, he thought, feeling slightly worried.

"Well, where shall we head for? The Silion or the Balintium side?" asked Cillan, seeing Tarbor's quandary written upon his face. Tarbor turned to his dream in his mind, but it had been vague in its vision to him.

"I am not sure, Cillan. A line of trees showed themselves in the background then I fell into a pool of water," he answered.

"Well, that has narrowed it down a bit!" scoffed Cillan. It was obvious why he did; that was all you could see lining the back of the salt marsh on both sides, trees!

Tarbor made up his mind as they entered the River Shellow. "Go down one of these channels of water, Cillan, on the Silion side," he decided. He had to start somewhere, he thought, perhaps something would come to him, he hoped.

Cillan pulled down the sail as he entered one such channel and set about the oars, whilst Tarbor stood up precariously to look over the swathes of tall grass.

The grasses started to give way to reeds in a mixture of the two at first, before the reeds began to dominate the further they headed in, making Cillan give up on the oars as the channel they were in grew narrower.

"Time to get wet," said Cillan, wedging the small boat into some reeds. Pushing an oar down the side of the boat between the reeds, Cillan gauged how deep the water was.

"Could be up to our waists in these," he warned. "The tide is in, we could wait until it goes out," he suggested to Tarbor's shake of the head.

"We will go through them," answered Tarbor. He did not want to wait around.

Their first footings found them holding onto the tall, swaying reeds as the water came waist– high, as Cillan had said it would, but gradually the reeds became thick enough to hold them knee– deep as they waded further in.

Birds flew out before them, squawking their annoyance at being disturbed as they trudged their way through to eventually come out into a landscape of tough-looking grass that was bisected with channels of water swelled by the tide.

Tarbor looked across this rugged landscape, searching for pools of water. The only ones that met his eyes were where the channels of water had been widened by the incoming tide. He decided to look further inland downriver.

As the day wore on, so the channels of water began to recede, for mud to start taking over, but by now the landscape had changed to one of shorter grass dotted with shrubs and pools!

Tarbor kept glancing at the backdrop of trees that stretched the length of the salt marsh as they walked amongst the pools, but no pattern would emerge in his head.

Cillan stared at the network of pools before him. "Well, I think there are a few pools here to choose from," he remarked, "which one will it be that holds the shield? If we are on the right side of the river, that is," he added.

Tarbor just did not know; he was fiddling with the hilt of the defender in his irritation at not being able to interpret his vision properly when Cillan suddenly threw him down behind a shrub, to hit the ground with a squelch. He was about to take it out on Cillan when he saw him hold a finger to his mouth and then point towards the trees.

A disturbance of birds from the nearest trees had made Cillan look up to see horsemen moving in amongst them; one astride a white horse that had shown itself clearly to him had given them away, his first instinct being to drop behind the shrub, taking Tarbor with him.

"Who are they? Silions? Have they seen us?" whispered Tarbor, seeing them now.

"I do not think so. Note the full helmets they wear, Cardronian," replied Cillan, sure of himself.

"She has sent them to finish what Wardine could not. Now I know the shield must be here," said Tarbor without any doubts.

"There is not much daylight left, Tarbor. We would do well to rest in those trees when they have passed," suggested Cillan.

"A cold night awaits us then," said Tarbor, knowing a fire was out of the question with those horsemen looking for them.

Waiting until the first shadows of dark had started to descend before they moved, Tarbor and Cillan made their way to the trees.

A dense growth of bushes had conveniently placed itself at the edge of the trees for the two warriors to scramble into, giving them ample cover. Managing to sit down in amongst the bushes' woody undergrowth, Tarbor and Cillan pulled their cloaks around them in an attempt to coax some warmth into their bodies in preparation for the long night ahead.

Conversation was absent between them as the stars lit up the night sky and a cool breeze rustled the bushes around them, to make for a night of uneasy rest.

Tarbor drifted in and out of sleep with nothing but pools plaguing his mind, until suddenly there he was once more, floating in the sky.

Something felt different this time, though, as he drifted in amongst the clouds. He could feel it; he was not alone floating there. There was something, a presence, guiding him in his quest for the shield.

The clouds opened and there below him swayed the sea of grey-blue grass once more, followed by the dense swathes of reeds.

Tarbor could not discern any words as a whisper made him focus on some pools that had suddenly appeared right below him, with one in particular engraving its shape into his mind.

Tarbor then looked up to clearly see a group of trees shining back at him, only for his dream to suddenly come to an abrupt end, leaving him wide awake and puzzled once more.

Dawn had just broken and Tarbor felt a fresh sense of being at knowing what pool to look for this time, but had been left puzzled that he would find it near some shining trees. What sort of trees were they?

Peering through the bushes for any sign of the horsemen, Tarbor shook a drowsy Cillan awake.

"Again?" queried Cillan, listening to Tarbor explain his dream as they walked along the trees' edges, keeping out of sight.

"Yes, Cillan, again, but clearer, although I had the most strangest of feelings, as if someone was there with me, helping," said Tarbor, looking around him.

"So you know where the pool is this time?" put Cillan.

"Once I find the trees that shine," he answered, for Cillan to give him a look. He did not doubt Tarbor, but sometimes, he thought, he sounded ridiculous.

Keeping themselves concealed within the backdrop of trees that was now arcing to their right, Tarbor and Cillan made their way along their edge, looking for the trees in Tarbor's dream, whilst keeping a wary eye open for any sign of the horsemen.

As they searched, the weather decided to give them a taste of spring by bringing them a mixture of rain and sunshine on a fresh wind blowing in from the sea as grey-white clouds began to scuttle across the sky, to release a sudden downpour of rain.

Tarbor and Cillan watched the rain lash across the already well-weathered brown tree trunks. "Well, that has helped," remarked Cillan, seeing the rain-soaked trunks turn darker.

They stood still, watching the rain move across the salt marsh as if it was making way for the sunshine that suddenly broke through, giving rise to a rainbow that arched itself right across the salt marsh, making the trees' dark trunks glisten.

Tarbor could not believe his eyes. He had to look twice, for there where the rainbow's bright colours fell upon the trees, they were glistening in a radiant silver glow, just like his dream!

"Look, Cillan!" he exclaimed. Cillan was looking, but he was shaking his head.

"You are telling me you foresaw a rainbow in your dream that would point to the pool!" he said, dismissing it, finding it too incredible, but Tarbor was already running out across the boggy grassland to the spot.

By the time Tarbor and Cillan were only halfway there, the rainbow had gone, but Tarbor had reached a pool.

He looked in earnest at its shape, trying to visualise it in his dream, but it was nothing like it. He looked around to see there were more pools adjacent to where they were and one more, further on towards the trees that the rainbow had touched.

Tarbor chose that one to look at first as another squall of rain lashed across the salt marsh to make the ground even muddier as it sucked at their boots, making their legs feel heavier still.

Splashing through a channel of water, Tarbor squinted at the pool's reeds bending in the wind as the rain cut across the salt marsh.

Tarbor finally stood by the pool and felt his blood course through him as he looked at it; this was the one! He was sure of it; it was the pool in his dream!

He had seen the pool as a sort of face looking back at him in his dream with a blank expression that was the water. There were the two huge rocks he had seen either side of the pool that acted like ears, whilst the reeds he stood by made for a beard and there were some bushes on the far side that had seemed like hair; this was the one!

But the immediate thought of getting into the pool and searching for the shield to see if he was right was something he was not looking forward to.

A tap on his arm, though, stopped whatever he was thinking as Cillan pointed to the trees. Tarbor looked up through the rain to see four Cardronian horse soldiers on the edge of the trees looking back at them.

"They have found us," said Cillan, drawing his sword readying himself for what was going to happen next.

Tarbor did likewise, but as he drew the defender, he felt the strangest of sensations run through his hand up into his arm and through his body, to almost make him fall over.

"Are you all right, Tarbor?" worried Cillan, holding him up, to spot the pommel on the defender glowing!

"What is happening to your sword, Tarbor?" he asked, frowning. Tarbor looked at Cillan, then at the two wavy lines denoting the two rivers of Waunarle on the pommel glowing in his hand, feeling an energy flowing from it down into the blade.

He did not truly know what was happening but hazarded a guess. "The defender knows the shield is within the pool! I... I think it could be calling to it!"

Neither warrior had time to dwell upon it as they held themselves ready for the onslaught.

The Cardronian horse soldiers were ruthlessly kicking their horses straight for them through the boggy salt marsh.

Both warriors began to see the wild-eyed stares of fright in the horses' eyes; something was not right.

But nothing could have prepared the two warriors for what happened next as the pool suddenly exploded with water, for the shield of Waunarle to surge from it and land right in front of Tarbor point first!

Tarbor looked at Cillan and instinctively bent down to pick up the shield, to instantly see the crown symbol of Waunarle on its rear, glowing back at him.

As he lifted the shield up towards him, the pommel of the defender was drawn to the crown symbol and latched itself onto the glowing crown, locking itself upon it, with Tarbor just managing to get his fingers out of the way, only to drop them both onto the boggy ground!

Tarbor bent back down to pick up the defender as the first Cardronian horse soldier was almost upon him, with Girvan's words echoing in his mind; protector and defender joined as one through magic.

As he gripped the hilt of the defender, thinking of Girvan's words, it came away with a rush of air whistling around his ears and the strangest of sensations running through his body.

Tarbor had no idea what had just happened as he rose with the defender in his hand, to catch an evil face grinning at him and a sword scything down upon his head!

Tarbor only had time to hold the defender out in front of him to stop the expected blow, but the blow never came; instead, the evil-looking horse soldier and his horse collided into something, throwing them both away from him!

The second horse soldier was swinging his sword straight at Cillan, but again he too hit something, to be rebuffed, sending his sword flying through the air and his horse falling to the side.

Cillan glanced at Tarbor. "Whatever you have done, Tarbor, it protects us!" cried Cillan as the other two horse soldiers dismounted and came charging at them with their swords in the air!

Their swords rained down to strike at them, but to no effect as an invisible shield that surrounded Tarbor and Cillan stopped their blows!

By now, all four horse soldiers were attacking the two warriors. Though the invisible shield was keeping their attacks at bay, Tarbor and Cillan were still acting on their fighting instincts by countering the incoming blows.

As one of the blows was rebuffed by the invisible shield, Tarbor found his counter going straight through the protective shield and into the horse soldier's chest, drawing orange blood!

"She has tainted them!" Tarbor shouted in dismay. It was bad enough to see horse soldiers that he had once commanded sent out to kill him once more, but to have cursed them! Cillan closed his eyes for a moment;

he had listened to Tarbor's story of the beasts and their poisonous blood, but to see it!

Now realising they could attack without being hurt themselves, Tarbor and Cillan soon put paid to the four tainted Cardronian horse soldiers, finishing them off in quick succession.

As Tarbor drove the defender into the last horse soldier's chest, he remembered that Speedwell had made sure those creatures had been burnt, because of their poisonous blood. *That is what we must do with these*, he thought as he was withdrawing the blade. *We must burn them.*

No sooner had he thought it than a pulse ran up his arm from the defender and he watched in disbelief as the defender burst into flames, to set the dead Cardronian horse soldier's chest alight! Tarbor was stunned; he had just thought of burning them and the defender had acted upon it!

"How did that happen!" said Cillan in shock.

"I was thinking of when Speedwell burnt the beasts and it just… obeyed!" answered Tarbor, still stunned.

"You had better be careful what you think of then whilst that is in your hands!" warned Cillan, looking at the burning horse soldier.

As Tarbor's mind thought that was the last of them, a rush of air told him and Cillan that the protective shield was gone.

Then, Tarbor stood over the remaining three horse soldiers, one by one, to let the thought of burning them enter his head, and watched them catch fire.

As Tarbor came to the last horse soldier, Cillan stopped him a moment. He wanted to see for himself what cold-blooded cruelty had befallen the horse soldier and risked taking off his helmet, to reveal a face of horror!

Tarbor and Cillan could only look away from his disfigurement, a face so twisted it was unrecognisable.

Thinking one last time the thought of fire, Tarbor watched the defender answer by setting alight the once proud Cardronian horse soldier.

"I cannot believe what I have just seen, Tarbor, to perceive such evil," said Cillan sadly as they walked away from the burning bodies.

Tarbor looked across the salt marsh, letting the sea breeze fill his nostrils to replace the sickening smell of the burning bodies, spotting two of the horse soldiers' horses as he did so running in and out of the trees, as if thankful for being freed of their accursed burden.

"Nor can I, Cillan, her evil knows no boundaries to do such a thing," he answered, looking back, wondering himself about what had just happened.

Not just about the fate that had befallen his once loyal horse soldiers, but about the newly found shield and the magic he had found with it that was beyond words.

Any doubts there may have been of his true identity and if he was capable of wielding magic had gone when his defender, he was finally telling himself, had joined with his shield to protect them both with an invisible force, as Speedwell said they would.

If only Girvan were here to see it, he thought sadly as he looked at the muddy shield under his arm, hoping when the time came that his newfound protection would be enough to help defeat Queen Helistra's evil.

CHAPTER XXXIII

Broken point lay further behind as the open sea began to stretch out for the two warriors in their small boat on their journey to the Isles of Kesko.

Cillan had sought some supplies in Northtop before they had set out, whilst Tarbor had kept low by guarding the boat.

Only the sail could be heard flapping in the wind as Tarbor and Cillan sat quietly looking out at the vastness of the sea whilst letting their emotions run their course as the boat cut its way through the water.

Tarbor looked down at the shield by his side. He had cleaned most of the mud from it and although the water from the pool had coated it in a layer of grime, he could still make out the blend of metal colours beneath it.

Tarbor found himself picking up a piece of sack cloth that lay in the boat and idly began rubbing part of the shield whilst reflecting on what had happened when he had found it.

Cillan saw the lost look on Tarbor's face as he checked the sail. "I would keep your mind clear whilst you are doing that, you might set the boat on fire," he mused, managing to get a smile from Tarbor.

"You are right. I do not begin to understand the workings of its powers, best I left it for now," he agreed, putting down the shield.

"What were you thinking of?" asked Cillan out of curiosity.

"Nothing really, only how the defender answered me when I thought of burning those bodies. It must have sensed the evil they held," said Tarbor thoughtfully.

"It must have," replied Cillan with a nod.

Then Tarbor gave Cillan a quizzical look as he spoke next. "Though I was thinking whilst cleaning the shield that if I commanded it to clean itself, it would have," he quipped, making Cillan laugh.

"Now you are being silly!"

"Yes, I suppose I am," said Tarbor, laughing, feeling the better for it, although he did wonder.

The day wore on with the wind holding firm to take the small boat forever towards the Isles, but as night fell, so did the wind, making for slow going in the breeze that was left. Cillan decided to help by manning the oars.

"You get some sleep, Tarbor, whilst I row. I will shake you in an hour or so when I am tired," offered Cillan.

"Make sure you do then," answered a thankful Tarbor. He was not going to argue; his eyes were shutting as it was.

The gentle sway of the boat soon saw Tarbor asleep. Dreams came to him in vivid pictures as he relived finding the shield, until his dream came to a moment where he thought one of the burning bodies had got up and was coming after him, making him wake with a start to be confronted by "Tintwist?"

Tarbor looked around him at a grey dawn that had risen over the sea, and at Cillan, who was fast asleep over the oars!

"Speedwell told us to come out to meet you to show you the way. We saw your sail on the horizon and came to get you. You were beginning to drift," explained Tintwist as he shook Cillan.

Cillan came to with a jerk. "Hmm, what! Tintwist?"

"So much for waking me!" berated Tarbor.

"I… er, thank you for greeting us, Tintwist." Cillan smiled a little awkwardly to see Piper looking at him from their boat. Tarbor nodded to Piper, to get the same look.

"You could have been lost to the sea. No one has ever come back from out there!" She chastised them both, for them not to answer.

"You found the shield then," she added, spotting it, changing her mood slightly towards them.

"Yes, it is all and much more than Speedwell told me," acknowledged Tarbor.

"Perhaps then you can now set yourselves on the correct course and follow us to the Isles?" she enquired impatiently as Tintwist jumped nimbly back into their boat.

"We will," answered Cillan, rubbing his eyes.

As if hearing the two boats were ready to sail, a wind suddenly stirred into their sails and began taking them inbound for the Isles of Kesko, with the two warriors feeling a little foolish.

They sailed towards the two most northern islands of Kesko. The main island looked like a giant foot to Tarbor, rising high to one side and slowly descending to the other end. As they sailed closer, he could see that trees covered most of its top and that birds used its rocky face to build their nests as they flew squawking at each other along the cliff's side.

The two isles they were heading for were much smaller by comparison. They were once joined, but the sea over time had carved a way through, creating a channel of water for the two boats to sail between. Only a giant rock had survived, defiantly sticking out of the water in the middle.

Passing through the channel to the other side, the waters became calmer, being sheltered from the northwesterly wind by the rocky cliffs. The smaller rocky cliffs on this side were covered in ferns, tufted grass and thorny-looking bushes, greeting the four with a sweet but pungent smell at the same time.

A lonely tree had somehow managed to take root on a narrow stretch of shore beneath a cutaway in the cliffs, enough for the two small boats to run aground on. Tying the boats to an exposed part of the trees roots, the party set off along a barely visible path that led up the side of the cutaway.

It did not take long to reach the top, where small, twisted trees had laid their claim to this part of the island. They bent one way and then another, whilst their roots interlaced with each other, spreading over the ground and then suddenly disappearing into the earth, like claws gripping their prey after a kill.

Thorny brambles seemed to relish the cover given by the trees' roots as they scrambled all around them, restricting the ferns to going between the trees. Not that the party minded walking through the ferns, as long as they did not trip over a tree root, to land headlong in the brambles!

Tarbor thought of Tomin all alone on the island as he followed Piper and Tintwist. "I do not know if I would like being here on my own," he said, speaking to no one in particular.

"Well, Tomin would not know he was," said Tintwist over his shoulder, for Tarbor to remember Tomin was in a state of sleep with a protective shield hiding his presence.

"Though Dwarves did live here once," added Tintwist.

"Dwarves. We would not know of their existence, if it were not for their thirst for mining. They disappeared from our Kingdoms a long time ago, when the earth would reveal no more," piped up Cillan, sounding not exactly happy about what they had done.

Saying no more, the party continued and eventually came out of the twisted trees to be met by a more tranquil scene. A bowl-shaped valley had opened up before them, with trees lining its sides. A rugged mixture of overgrown bushes and grass covered the ground between. Although the sun was shining, whispers of mist still rose from the trees after an earlier shower of rain, looking like horses' tails to Tarbor.

Onwards down into the valley they walked, through the overgrown floor and into the trees to one side, to see Speedwell sitting by a tree, waiting.

"You have found the shield," he said, smiling straight away as he saw it under Tarbor's arm.

"Found with wonder and sadness at what we witnessed," replied Tarbor, showing Speedwell the grimy shield.

"Tell me of it as we walk," said Speedwell as he got up.

"The shield responded to you then?" said Speedwell as he headed straight towards what looked like an opening in the rock behind the trees.

"More than I could have ever imagined," said Tarbor, and he began telling Speedwell what had happened as they entered the opening in the rock.

Tarbor stopped his account a moment as he looked at where they were. They had entered a passageway that had been cut out of the solid rock. The gouge marks could clearly be seen in the light coming from the top of Speedwell's rune staff.

"These dwarves were busy people," noted Tintwist, peering down the passageway.

"The very same ones that dug the tunnels behind Stormhaven where Cantell and Kelmar made their escape with the little Prince," informed Speedwell, "and the secret passage," he added.

"They have long since gone in their search for further riches, they never have returned," informed Speedwell further, for Cillan to scoff whilst making Tarbor become more aware of what Piper had meant by *no one had ever come back from out there.*

That is where the superstition of not crossing the sea had come from, he thought, as what Speedwell had told them of the tunnels behind Stormhaven suddenly clicked into place; of course!

"You are the wise old man of knowledge who told her of the secret passage!" he blurted out, making everyone stop and look at him as his voice echoed down the passageway.

Speedwell stopped to turn and look at Tarbor. "That was a father telling his daughter a bedtime story," he pointed out sadly. "I was not to know that one day she would use it to get to the crystal chamber."

Tarbor and the others felt the sadness of it all come from Speedwell as he remembered.

"A rainbow, you say, making the trees look silver," prompted Speedwell suddenly, carrying on once more down the passageway as if no one had spoken. Tarbor gladly took up the prompt by continuing his account as they walked further and deeper underground.

"What has she set in motion?" sighed Speedwell.

"She must have poisoned their bodies with soul blood from the pool of life," he perceived as Tarbor finished his account of finding the shield. "But you have the shield, it is a beginning," he said, stopping and raising his rune staff, which became brighter, to reveal a huge chamber.

All stood and looked at the vastness of the chamber. "The dwarves did all of this?" queried Tarbor.

"It is what they did, they mined the ore that helped to make your defender and shield, amongst other things," stated Speedwell, glimpsing at Cillan, who looked the other way.

"They stopped working here because of the danger of collapse," he added.

"Collapse?" they all asked as one.

"Yes, we are under the sea!"

Everyone looked up at the rocky ceiling to see it glistening back at them, to suddenly feel very vulnerable.

"Why is Tomin down here if it is so dangerous when there is all of the island above?" questioned Tarbor, suddenly feeling cold.

"The sea and rock help guard him from my daughter's eyes," replied Speedwell, and he moved off deeper into the chamber.

To one side of the chamber a small opening appeared, which Speedwell entered, with everyone following him to find they had entered another chamber, but smaller.

Moving to near the centre of the chamber, Speedwell stopped. "We are here," he stated to the looks of the others. There was nothing there except the grey rock floor.

"Tarbor, throw your shield of protection over all of us," Speedwell instructed him as he began sorting out some herbs and berries into a bowl from his pouch.

Tarbor looked at the others, but he was not about to question a Forestall.

Taking a deep breath to calm his nerves, Tarbor drew his defender from its sheath and held it against his shield, with the two half emblems of Waunarle touching each other. The thought of what had happened at the pool came into his mind; he had not been in control then, but now he must be.

With that thought, Tarbor decided to speak in his mind to his defender and shield. He closed his eyes to concentrate.

Defender and shield of Waunarle, I ask you to protect all within this chamber from her evil stare in the name of your King wielder.

Tarbor opened his eyes to see the others not looking at him, but at the defender and shield, whose emblems were glowing in answer as he parted them.

A rush of air seemed to come from nowhere as all felt their skin tingle and a whisper of power hum in their ears. All, that is, except Speedwell, who smiled at the relief showing on Tarbor's face.

Speedwell felt in his pouch to produce a small bottle and let a tiny drop of its liquid content fall into the prepared bowl. Touching symbols on his rune staff, he let the tip touch the prepared food in the bowl for an audible hiss to come from its contact.

Speedwell put the bowl down and began touching more symbols on his rune staff, to be joined by a soft humming in his mind as he stood there motionless.

Tarbor, Cillan, Piper and Tintwist all watched as Speedwell began humming in a continuous low droning sound that seemed to make the air vibrate within the protective shield as he touched different symbols on his rune staff.

Suddenly Speedwell stopped and swept his rune staff over the grey rock floor. A sigh of air, as if in relief at not having to do something anymore, sounded all around them and there right in front of them, the grey rock floor disappeared to reveal an old man lying on a stone slab; it was Tomin!

Tarbor, Cillan, Piper and Tintwist could only look at each other in amazement. Tomin had been concealed there all of the time, as if he were part of the chamber floor!

Speedwell laid his rune staff across Tomin's chest and began chanting as his fingers touched more symbols. Speedwell then left one hand on his rune staff and laid the other over Tomin's heart.

Moving a finger to hover over a certain symbol, he then stopped chanting and touched the symbol, for Tomin's eyes to suddenly spring open, making everyone jump.

Only then as the four onlookers watched the soft white light shine over Tomin's face did they see that his eyes were white; he was blind!

"Welcome back, grandson," said Speedwell with a smile as he looked down at his grandson's face.

"Grandfather, is that you?" questioned Tomin a little groggily.

"Who else?" said Speedwell, laughing, and helped Tomin sit up, glad that there seemed no ill effects.

"We both know who, Grandfather," replied Tomin, and gripped his grandfather's arm tightly in happiness that it was him.

Tarbor looked at Tomin and thought he was looking at Speedwell, as long grey hair with a beard showed itself to the glow of the rune staff.

He did not know what to get over, the fact that Tomin was blind or that a man who looked as old as Speedwell was calling him Grandfather!

"Who is it that is here with you?" asked Tomin, sensing the others.

"Friends who have come to our aid, Tomin. First, here is Piper and Tintwist of the Manelf," he declared, for Piper to move forward and bow as she shook Tomin's hand. He may have been blind, not able to see her bow, but he was a Forestall who deserved respect.

"It is good that you are well, Forestall," she said with a smile.

Tomin felt the small, long fingers that could shoot an arrow with deadly accuracy as he held her hand. "It is an honour for me to meet you, Piper, huntress of the Manelf."

Then Tintwist followed suit as he shook Tomin's hand. "There is no need to bow, Tintwist, an unusual name for a Manelf," he stated, catching Tintwist slightly by surprise that he knew he was bowing as Piper pulled him away before he could reply. Tomin smiled, sensing it. He had probably just missed his ears being hurt, he thought.

Cillan moved forward, announcing himself as he too bowed. "I am Cillan Tomin."

"A Cardronian by the sound of you," said Tomin, noting the accent.

"I am, from Ardriss," informed Cillan.

"Ah yes, the fishing was always good there in the coastal waters of Ardriss," remembered Tomin, getting a smile of agreement from Cillan.

Though Tomin could not see, his eyes nevertheless then looked straight at Tarbor, making him feel slightly nervous. "And this is Grandfather?"

"Tarbor, for now, Tomin. He has come to protect you, for he is a King wielder," announced Speedwell as Tarbor also bowed.

"A King wielder grandfather! How is that possible?" questioned Tomin immediately as Tarbor felt him grip his hand.

"All in good time, Tomin. First, you must have some nourishment after your sleep, then we will withdraw from this dark place and I will tell you everything that has happened," promised Speedwell.

"You mean that berry and herb goo," said Tomin, grimacing.

"You know you need to eat something before anything else. The essence of the pool will renew you," said Speedwell, bringing a smile to Tomin's face.

"Ah, the essence, you have some. She still bubbles with life?" he asked.

"There is much to tell, Tomin, after you have eaten," insisted Speedwell, saying nothing for now.

Tarbor did not expect his hand to be used as a lever as Tomin suddenly pulled himself up with it to be face to face with him.

Tomin had sensed the confusion and anxiety that had reined in Tarbor's mind at finding out he was a King wielder whilst holding his hand, sensing he was only just coming to terms with who he really was.

Even though Tomin had only just awoken, Tarbor had felt a strength in Tomin's grip that he had only felt once before: when he had shaken the hand of Speedwell.

"I am pleased to meet you, Tomin," greeted Tarbor, looking right into Tomin's white eyes to feel he was looking deep within his, as if he were making sure he was who Speedwell said he was.

"And I to meet you, Tarbor, King wielder, with stories to tell also, I warrant." He smiled.

"Too many, Tomin, I can only hope together we can rid ourselves of…" Tarbor stopped himself, realising who it was he was talking to.

"My mother, Tarbor, I know," finished Tomin for him.

"Let us get to the surface then, Grandfather, so I can feel the sun on my face once more. I trust it is shining out there?" said Tomin with a smile, disguising the worry he already felt at his grandfather's silence over the pool of life.

"When you have eaten this," said Speedwell, smiling, putting the bowl of food in Tomin's hands, "and you can release us from your protection now, Tarbor," he added.

Tarbor had forgotten about the protective shield he had put into place in his awkwardness of the moment, and with a thought, he felt a rush of air as it dispersed from around them, to still surprise him.

All emerged into the daylight. The sun was shining after another shower of rain had washed the landscape, leaving it looking fresh to the party's eyes, and to Tomin's nose it gave away the countless scents of spring that he could almost taste. He breathed them all in deeply. "The best time of year," he sighed, so glad to smell the fresh air once more.

Tintwist laid his cloak on the ground for Tomin to sit on against a tree. Feeling the breeze play across his face, Tomin was already feeling his strength return as the life-giving essence and nourishment from the herbs coursed through his body, for him to soon forget its foul taste.

"I am listening, Grandfather. What have you to tell me?" he prompted, for Speedwell to take a breath before telling him of his mother's evil.

"Your mother has returned, Tomin, with an evil malevolence that we all hoped would never happen," began Speedwell, and he proceeded to tell Tomin of the full horror of what was happening to the forests.

Tears slowly seeped from Tomin's blind eyes as his grandfather told him of the curse his mother had afflicted upon the forests. "Her evil runs deep, Tomin, and yet it has given her an ageless look," finished Speedwell sadly.

It was something Tarbor had never thought of, but now he wondered how old she really was underneath that beauty. How old they all were.

"So she waits at Stormhaven with the power of the crystal chamber in her grasp," dwelled Tomin, reflecting on what he had just been told as he wiped away the tears from his cheeks.

"The crystal chamber has enhanced the evil power she has wrought in your father's broken rune staff. She will have felt the wall of containment being put into place, but will be happy in the knowledge that we are using our energy to keep it strong whilst she uses none, knowing if we should confront her it would be weakened and the poison would break through," spoke Speedwell, repeating the same worry that the Ancient One had.

"But with the crystal chamber's power at her fingertips, it would be unwise to confront her as we are. There would only be you and my uncle against a power we know little of, whilst I waited by my father's stone to retrieve the broken piece. I do not fully possess the ways of the forest. If anything should happen to either of you, and my father's broken rune staff should still be in my mother's hands…" Tomin could think no further; he did not want to.

Tarbor, Piper and Tintwist already knew that Tomin must retrieve the broken piece, but Cillan had missed Speedwell explaining, for him to explain now.

"If the broken rune staff is used for a spell strong enough to disturb the air around it, it sends out vibrations. The broken piece will pick this up and start to resonate within the stone body that was once Grimstone's. Responding to Tomin's touch, it will release itself to him, as he was the one being taught the ways of the forest with it," explained Speedwell.

Cillan thought he was hearing things; Tomin's father had turned to stone!

"Has Queen Helistra not tried to retrieve it herself?" queried Cillan.

"It will not move to her touch. The stone body of Grimstone holds the broken piece in place, knowing she was the one who killed him and triggered the white light that made my grandson blind," answered Speedwell, for them all to look at Tomin's bowed head as he remembered that fateful day.

Only one thing was clear to Cillan, clear to them all: Queen Helistra had the upper hand.

"What hope do we have of defeating her if we are not strong enough?" put Cillan despondently.

"We wait for the hope that grows within the child," answered Speedwell, "the one for whom the Ancient One has waited all of this time. A child whose spirit I have touched and whose strength I have felt," said Speedwell, smiling, for Tomin to look up.

"A spirit, Grandfather?" he questioned straight away.

"Queen Elina of Tiggannia has bore twins, a boy and a girl. The Ancient One felt their spirits through the pool of life before Helistra arrived at Stormhaven. I felt the spirit within the boy reach out to me. He waits for us at Elishard Castle with his mother to go and see the Ancient One," said Speedwell, for Tomin to hear the hope in his voice.

"He helped me find the shield!" said Tarbor suddenly, realising that because of him touching the baby Prince, his vision of the pool had become clearer to him. *Eventually, if not at first*, he thought.

"And what of the baby girl?" queried Tomin.

"Your mother has her," said Speedwell quietly after a pause, to see the hope he had given Tomin dwindle.

"We are no further then, all will be in vain," sighed Tomin.

"She has not looked into the child's soul, I know it," said Speedwell, trying to keep Tomin's hopes up.

"She plays at being a mother, as she did with me," added Tarbor, for Tomin just to stare. It made no difference, he was thinking, it was only a matter of time before she looked, then where were they?

"You do not know that for sure, Grandfather, we are back to where we started. You do not have hope, you cling on to it," he sighed again.

"It is not a reason to give up. The child's spirit will grow within our care and Tarbor has become a King wielder, it is a beginning," said Speedwell, assuring himself if anyone once again.

"There is also something that awaits you on the main island that will help," he added, making Tomin frown.

"What something?"

"You will see," said Speedwell, not giving anything away as he set out through the trees.

Piper and Tintwist helped Tomin to his feet, with Tintwist donning his cloak just in time as another shower spread across the valley.

Tomin surprised Piper and Tintwist with his inner sight that seemed to sense everything around him by avoiding the hazards of the journey. They soon let go of his arms as he easily wound his way through the valley.

Tomin got in with Tarbor and Cillan once they had arrived at the boats.

Tarbor began watching Tomin as they sailed towards the main isle and could not help but smile as his face lit up each time he sensed something.

If it was not the breeze carrying the sea air or the cry of a bird in the sky, then it was the lap of the sea upon the boat that gave him joy.

"I can feel you smiling at me, Tarbor," he said, suddenly catching Tarbor unaware.

"I smile in envy of you, Tomin, for how you enjoy all that surrounds you," admitted Tarbor.

"I have a lot to thank my blindness for. You can join me at any time, Tarbor. Simply close your eyes," said Tomin with a smile, making Tarbor laugh.

"That would be good after what I have…" Tarbor let it stop there.

"Seen my mother do?" finished Tomin once again for him.

"I was going to say witnessed, but it is nothing compared to what you have been through," apologised Tarbor.

"My father's death will be forever etched upon my mind. These years of being hidden have not diminished the sadness I feel, but I know what has to be done. Not revenge, for that would lead to her path of evil, but to save the forests and the Kingdoms of Northernland from her evil wrath."

Tarbor said no more as Tomin turned his head and looked in the direction of the other boat. His gaze seemed to look directly at Speedwell, who met it with a smile.

He had spoken like an echo of Speedwell, thought Tarbor. *How alike they are, but what they have been through and must now endure does not bear thinking about.*

Tarbor let his thoughts turn to wondering what it was Speedwell meant to retrieve as he watched in silence the main Isle of Kesko draw nearer.

The birds nesting on the side of the cliffs came into view as the boats sailed past them to reach the southern side of the island, whilst their continuous squawking filled the air above.

As they rounded the cliffs, an inviting small pebbled shore came into view, set back in a sheltered cove, with trees cutting through the cliffs acting as a backdrop.

The two boats entered the cove's still waters for everyone to jump out on reaching the shore to haul their boats up onto the pebbles.

Tarbor stood and looked up at the trees that cut through the cliffs, noting they were sheltering a small stream that had found its way to the sea.

"Will she destroy these islands as well?" asked Tarbor as he looked at the tranquil scene.

"If we do not succeed, nothing will be left untainted," answered Speedwell, who then began making his way up a sharp slope between the trees, following the small stream.

Just as the small party reached the top of the slope and thought the going would get easier, Speedwell started to climb upwards once more towards one corner of the island.

Birds and animals seemed to surround them as they walked, seemingly keeping them company. Not that you could spot any animals easily on what was now a forest floor, or see the birds under the foliage of the trees.

They sang happily high above whilst the animals could be heard making guttural sounds as they moved through the forest floor around them.

"Is it me or are the animals attracted towards Speedwell and Tomin?" puzzled Cillan aloud.

"They are Forestalls. They feel safe and happy in their presence," answered Piper, smiling, as she listened to the birds.

"More so my grandfather than I," spoke Tomin, remembering when he was young how deer used to come up to his grandfather's hand.

Onwards they walked, threading their way through the trees, coming across one that had fallen to the ground, with toadstools taking advantage, dotted along its fallen trunk, whilst small offshoots of the fallen tree had begun to take hold along its sides, with finger-like roots pushing themselves into the forest floor.

"Look, Piper, the mother has fallen, but her children survive." Tintwist smiled to himself, to make Piper look twice at Tintwist as she heard this new side to him.

"Here we are," announced Speedwell suddenly, for Tarbor, Piper, Tintwist and Cillan to look around, whilst Tomin smelt the air to sense his surroundings.

They had dropped into a slight dip on the slope of the forest floor and stood next to a tree that filled the dip.

It was no different to the rest of the trees that surrounded it, with its branches reaching out to the other trees as if trying to hold hands. Dappled light could be seen through them dancing one way and then another as the breeze played in the leaves.

"Tintwist, will you save these old legs and climb this tree for me? You will find something wrapped in leather in a hole halfway up. There is a cloak of concealment around it to keep it hidden from Helistra's eyes, but you will be able to bring it down to me," he said, smiling, for Tintwist to immediately start climbing the tree.

"I always said he was a bit of a monkey and now he is proving me right," chortled Piper to herself as she watched Tintwist's progress up the tree.

"You can be quite a monkey yourself sometimes, Piper. That must be why he loves you," commented Speedwell, making Piper go hot whilst Tomin, Tarbor and Cillan grinned.

Tintwist soon found the hole Speedwell had said would be there halfway up the tree, lending itself for him to put his arm right into it as he stood on a branch.

As he put his hand in the hole, he had visions of a bird pecking his hand off, but that was soon waylaid as he felt the touch of the leather-covered object.

Gripping it, he pulled it out of the hole at an angle to find he had pulled out a long, narrow object, not what he expected to bring out of a hole in a tree.

It was not long before he reached the ground again, to hand the leather-wrapped object over to Speedwell.

"Thank you, Tintwist," said Speedwell, smiling. "Tarbor, will you do the honours?" Speedwell said, still smiling, for Tarbor to set another rush of air flowing around them all.

Speedwell put the leather-clad object into Tomin's hands and began humming softly. Another hum came to everyone's ears, that of Speedwell's rune staff, and together they made the enclosed air around the small party vibrate with energy.

Fingers moved across the symbols of his rune staff as the humming continued, until suddenly both stopped, and with a wave of his rune staff, Speedwell removed the spell of concealment.

As soon as it was lifted, a shocked Tomin sensed straight away what he was holding. "Where did you find it?" he asked open-mouthed as he unwrapped the leather covering.

"In a stream of no note that came away from one of the rivers in the Great Forest," answered Speedwell.

The other four had not the slightest idea what they were on about, although the length of the object was the same as…! Eyes widened and mouths fell as Tomin finally unwrapped the object.

"This is the rune staff of Gentian's that my daughter believes is buried, along with Gentian, under the weight of the Kavenmist Mountains," declared Speedwell. "When we are with the Ancient One, it will be yours, Tomin. Until then, I will keep it cloaked from her eyes," he added.

"Mine, Grandfather? I thought my father's rune staff, when made whole again, would be mine?" questioned Tomin.

"It would have been, Tomin, but I fear the evil that has possessed it will have taken its toll. When it is whole once more, it will stop the evil, but I am unsure as to whether we will be able to trust it ever again. When the time comes, if it is forever cursed, then it must be cleansed with fire for the sake of the forests and Northernland," stated Speedwell, making Tomin drop his head in sadness.

"Gentian's rune staff will respond to you, knowing you will be its rightful keeper, and it will make us all the more stronger," he added, with purpose in his voice.

Speedwell wrapped Gentian's rune staff back up and handed it to Tintwist. "I charge you and Piper with looking after Gentian's rune staff whilst we journey. You will be able to hold it with the spell of concealment upon it." He smiled to see their faces light up.

For once, Tintwist did not know what to say, accepting Gentian's rune staff with deep respect as he and Piper bowed in gratitude at being given such an important task.

"It is time to go back to Elishard and then together journey into the Great Forest, where the Ancient One is waiting for us. We have come a long way in a short space of time. Now it is time to prepare ourselves for the test that is to come," forewarned Speedwell, looking at each of the faces looking at him.

Tarbor's face was set resolutely as to what lay ahead of them all, but he could not help feeling apprehensive at the same time at the thought of facing Queen Helistra.

Without further ado, Speedwell led the way back to the boats. He needed to get back to the Ancient One, not just for the hope of the child, but to reinforce the barrier. He knew the strain of holding the barrier in place by the Ancient One and his brother would be a continuous drain on their power.

It may have only been a thought before, but now Speedwell began to worry about it. How long could they hold it for? Was time going to be on their side for the child's spirit to grow? Then there was the thought of Helistra holding the child's sister. Speedwell's footsteps quickened.

CHAPTER XXXIV

The month of growing had just passed, taking with it spring. Now it was the turn of summer and the month of the trees, not that one could be seen out here as Tarbor looked out over the bleak beauty of the Wreken Moors once more.

Elishard was long behind the now extended party as they travelled towards the Great Forest. With Cillan riding at his side, Tarbor was quietly thinking of Girvan and Druimar, knowing their final resting place was not far from where they were, as was the place they never reached, Permellar's farm.

In that same moment, he wondered how Urchel and Idrig were on the other side of the Marchend Valley. He hoped that they had been reunited with Idrig's brother and were safe there when they never appeared at the castle.

He had had plenty of time to think on their journey to the Great Forest since finding the shield; not that any of it had done him any good. Thinking how he had started out as a Captain and brought about the downfall of King Rolfe, which would forever gnaw at his conscience, only to find he was a King himself!

Let alone to find he possessed a sword and shield that held magic qualities to enable him to protect them all!

Looking behind him at his fellow travellers, Tarbor smiled to see Queen Elina peeping out of the open cover of the covered wagon being drove by Kelmar and Cantell, whilst holding baby Prince Martyn.

Tomin was sitting inside the wagon at the back, talking to his grandfather, Speedwell, who rode just behind, his eyes of steel-blue fixed in thought as he listened, whilst Piper and Tintwist rode at the rear, with Tintwist in full flow recounting the stories they would tell the others when they got back.

All of us brought together, thought Tarbor, on a journey to rid the land of an evil beyond his wildest imagination: Queen Helistra.

They had joined together at Elishard Castle, leaving behind them Oneatha, Permellar and little Kayla, much to the tug of Kelmar's heart. His mother's and Permellar's tears still made Kelmar feel sad, but his duties were to the two that were peeping over his shoulder.

Permellar was going to stay a while longer before returning to her farm in the hope that the spies would think she was Queen Elina still at Elishard, throwing them off the scent.

King Stowlan and Kraven were wished well in the building of an army, though Speedwell had advised them that whilst they were keeping a watch over their borders, they should also keep a wary eye in the direction of the Great Forest if they failed to hold the barrier. "Hold yourselves ready. No matter how time passes, do not get complacent," he had warned them.

So here they all were approaching the Eastern Valley, north of Marchend, ready to rest for another night in a stone shelter that had come into view.

"Not another night in one of those," groaned Cillan, thinking of the smell of sheep inside.

"It hides a fire from prying eyes," answered Tarbor, rubbing his new growth of beard with the thought that a fire did not stop those beasts.

Everyone settled down for another night. A cool breeze had sprung up across the moors, making the fire that Cillan had brought into life all the more welcome as Tarbor, Cillan, Cantell and Kelmar sat around it, swapping stories with each other on the events that had brought them all together.

Piper and Tintwist kept first watch outside the shelter, taking it in turn to carry the leather– wrapped rune staff of Gentian's, not daring to let it out of their sight.

Tomin rested comfortably in the back of the wagon, enjoying the smell coming from the heather on the moor whilst letting the feeling of the wooden floor beneath him help put the thought of the cold slab of rock he had slept on to the back of his mind.

Queen Elina had settled quietly in one corner of the stone shelter, with Prince Martyn fast asleep in her arms. She watched Speedwell as he stood in the doorway of the shelter watching the night sky slowly fold over the heather-covered moors, with the constant thought of his daughter making her baby girl evil under her indomitable power. It only made her all the more desperate to hear anything that might give her some hope.

"Will my daughter become as evil as yours?" The four warriors stopped talking around the fire and looked at each other over the flames as she asked the question they had all thought of on their journey.

It came out blunter than she had meant it, but Speedwell only heard a mother's genuine worry in her small voice as he turned his head towards her. "She will not become so whilst my daughter plays at being a mother," replied Speedwell.

"That may be so, but how long will that last?" worried Queen Elina.

"Whilst she controls only her mind and does not look to what is within, long enough for us to prepare," said Speedwell, trying to reassure Queen Elina with a smile.

"But the love I gave her will be lost to her evil if as you say she looks at her soul, as was yours," she added, looking at her sleeping son for comfort.

Speedwell knew that only too well. "You are right, the jealousy she formed in her mind for Tomin made any love that remained from me gone forever," agreed Speedwell sadly, seeing those happier times with his daughter now as just distant memories, no longer to be repeated, "but she will not pass that hatred on," added Speedwell, without giving his thoughts away.

It had become apparent to him, as he had spoken to Tomin, what she could do with her if she were to find out what the little Princess was destined to become.

She could use her as she had used everyone else and make her become her shield, her own barrier, knowing that if they came into conflict with each other, no Forestall would kill another, thus protecting his daughter, but as Tomin had pointed out, killing her would be her first thought!

Queen Elina only felt all the more sad; she wished she had not said anything. "Will he be the saviour of us all, our hope?" she asked quietly, stopping Speedwell from having any more unpleasant thoughts.

"If the Ancient One is of the belief, then yes he is," he assured her.

"I am in anticipation of my meeting with the Ancient One," she remarked, for Speedwell to hear something in her voice to tell him she was holding on to that one bit of hope.

"I think your anticipation will be rewarded in more ways than one," he replied.

The night passed without incident and the early-morning light saw the party riding towards the Eastern Valley of Marchend, with Speedwell wishing he had not had his conversation with Queen Elina that night, as the thought of his daughter holding the little Princess high in the air, laughing, would not leave his mind.

Piper thankfully stopped those visions as she suddenly drew up next to him. "We are in need of supplies before we enter the Great Forest, Speedwell. Our food is getting low," she advised.

"The forest will provide enough for us all," replied Speedwell.

"That is true, but fresh food would help us on our way," said Piper with a smile.

Speedwell looked at her face and smiled back. "You Manelves and your insatiable appetites," he said, smiling. "Very well, tell Cillan what is needed. He is best suited to go to Marchend whilst we circle around. Tell him we will be waiting by the River Mid for his return," replied Speedwell, for Piper to ride off and tell Cillan.

"Keep your eyes and ears open, Cillan!" shouted Tarbor as he watched Cillan ride off in the direction of Marchend, to see an arm raised in acknowledgement.

Tarbor watched Cillan disappear into the tapestry of the Eastern Valley that showed itself to him as he rode to the valley's edge.

He let his eyes wander across the valley and began to wonder what awaited them in the Great Forest as they came to rest on the distance boundary of the forest's trees on the other side.

Cillan rode down a dirt track between fields that were covered in various crops. One field after another seemed to have different things growing in them; no two fields looked the same.

He soon started passing farmers too busy tending their crops to be bothered looking up to see who was riding past.

In fields between the crops, sheep and cows grazed on the lush grassland of the valley as he passed a large pond with geese cackling at him. *One of those would be nice*, he thought.

Then there it was, the Balintium half of Marchend, its roofs looking a jumbled mess on the skyline, and as if knowing he was on his way, there was an old lady on the outskirts of the town selling vegetables.

Some haggling later, which was needed with what money he had, saw Cillan throw a sackful of vegetables over his horse.

Cillan decided to walk with his horse in what turned out to be a bustling town this side of the River Talmin. A stall selling bread caught his eye. Another selling fish; and two more purchases were made.

Everything was here, he thought, from vegetables to… Cillan's eyes grew brighter as he spotted an inn on the other side of the street, to bring out a sigh in him. Now, when he thought about it, he had not really had a drink since leaving Kelmsmere. He could hardly tie his horse up fast enough!

Sitting on a crude bench in the corner of the inn, Cillan leaned back, nursing a pot of ale. He smelt the top and then proceeded to gulp half of it down. "Ahh!" He felt better now.

Cillan took in the people around him as he took another swallow. He soon noticed that all seemed to be talking in nervous whispers, with eyes wide with worry. He trained his ears towards two farmers talking, whilst looking the other way.

"There is no such thing, I tell you," said one.

"From the forest, I heard. I told you long ago why we never go in there. Them monsters are waiting for us!" said the other.

"Listen to yourself, you sound daft! Anyway, that was ages ago. There has been nothing since," dismissed the first farmer.

Cillan kept listening for more from the two farmers whilst he drank his ale.

"We need soldiers guarding our farms! Not the river border between this town; it has always been as one," remarked the worried farmer.

"Nothing has been the same since they invaded Tiggannia," remarked the other. "The stories coming from there are harder to believe than the monster that imprisoned soldier says killed his friend, that it was his friend's brother!"

Cillan nearly spat his mouthful of ale across the table. Urchel!

"His days as a deserter will be numbered when the soldiers from Stormhaven get here, then perhaps these stories of monsters will die with him," finished the doubter of the two farmers as together they drank the remains of their ale and left.

Cillan was up and out of the inn door behind them. He may have walked into the town, but out of it he was going as fast as he could astride his horse. He must tell the others what he had heard.

Tarbor was enjoying the dappled shade given by the trees along the River Mid where they had stopped. He could smell the water of the river running past and the fragrance given out by the riverside wood. A breeze stirred the leaves of the trees, bringing it all together as he lay there next to Tomin with his eyes shut.

"Well, what do your senses tell you now?" enquired Tomin, smiling.

"That I should close my eyes more often!" Both of them laughed.

The laughter stopped at the sound of water being splashed by a horse crossing the river. "Cillan is back," said Tarbor, opening his eyes to see a stern expression on the face of Cillan as he dismounted.

"They said soldiers were coming for him from Stormhaven," finished Cillan after he had explained what he had overheard in the inn.

"You are sure they were not just two drunken farmers embroidering rumours?" queried Tarbor.

"I heard them clear enough. Brothers, they said!" insisted Cillan.

"That is why they were not at Elishard Castle," groaned Tarbor, looking at Speedwell. He did not have to speak; Speedwell knew he wanted to rescue Urchel.

"It is a risk you take if you are caught. Our quest will be lacking without your newfound skills," put Speedwell in warning to Tarbor.

"It is a risk I must take. Urchel may not know much, but it could be enough to put harm the Princess' way if Queen Helistra questions him. I cannot let that happen," said Tarbor quietly so Queen Elina could not hear him from the wagon, feeling that it was his fault in the first place that Urchel had followed him onto his unknown path. He was his friend also; he could not let him pay with his life like Girvan and Druimar had.

"How do you expect to free Urchel looking like that?" queried Kelmar, who had joined them with Cantell.

"With a few minor adjustments to my uniform, I can go as a Cardronian soldier come from Stormhaven," he suggested.

"And I still have mine. One soldier turning up for a prisoner is not a plan," pointed out Cillan, to the smile of Tarbor.

"Very well, I would like to say I have not got the power to stop you, but I have," said Speedwell, for Tarbor and Cillan to look at him, "but I am not going to use it, so go and be careful. We will wait here for your return," agreed a worried Speedwell in letting them go.

It did not take long for them both to put on their Cardronian uniforms and be on their way to Marchend, but not before Speedwell had given them a parchment of paper.

"Take this, it should see you past the border and release Urchel into your custody," he beckoned, for Tarbor to look at it, with Cillan stealing a glance. Smiling, Tarbor thanked him.

Speedwell watched them go, asking the stars and spirits to watch over them as Cantell came to stand by his side.

"What will happen if they are caught and Queen Helistra finds out Prince Martyn is with you?" he asked, as if reading the thoughts Speedwell was having.

"It will alter things, it will force her hand. She will know that they must be killed sooner rather than later, taking what time we needed away from us to prepare," replied Speedwell grimly.

The day had moved on, with the long shadows from the sinking sun beginning to throw themselves across the valley. Riding down the same track Cillan had ridden earlier, the two warriors soon arrived at the outskirts of Marchend.

"We will cross the south bridge, it is the nearest to the Cardronian jail," said Tarbor as they slowed to a trot, remembering his previous times here with the Cardronian army.

There was only the two bridges that joined the two halves of Marchend together; one at the north end, built out of solid stone, and one at the south, constructed out of wood, still waiting to be replaced by one built of stone.

The town itself had been built well to the north of the River Mid so that only the River Talmin dissected the town in two rather than four, with Cardronia to the west and Balintium to the east.

Townsfolk freely travelled over the bridges for their work, to buy goods or to see friends; that is, until the invasion!

Though the bridges were still used by the townsfolk in the daytime, by night they were deserted. The invasion had put a wedge between the two Kingdoms and trust had become hard to come by. Old friendships had been put to the test and the once free-flowing bridges were now guarded on both sides, with each Kingdom suspicious of the other.

Tarbor and Cillan rode through the quiet streets with only the odd soldier passing them by, to stare but say nothing.

Finally, Tarbor and Cillan reached the southern bridge to be greeted by two guards posted there under a flickering torchlight.

"Stop! Where do you think you are going!" challenged one, to realise as he had said it that they wore the uniforms of Cardronia. Before Tarbor or Cillan could answer, the guard had waved them through.

"Well, that was easy," said Cillan with a smile as they crossed the wooden bridge.

"I do not think he wanted any trouble by stopping Cardronian soldiers going into their own Kingdom." Tarbor smiled back.

Only the horses' hooves could be heard over the wooden bridge, echoing into the night air, whilst the River Talmin slipped silently underneath it with hardly a ripple.

Two more guards were waiting for them as they neared the Cardronian side of the bridge.

"Halt! What brings you this way through Marchend?" queried one guard.

"It is the quickest way from Stormhaven," replied Tarbor, to see the two guards look at each other. "Did you expect us to ride all the way around? Is there not peace between us and Balintium for us to do so?" he chided.

"From Stormhaven, you say. You have come for the prisoner?" asked the guard, a little bit flustered.

"If you mean the deserter and traitor, then yes," answered Tarbor.

Although flustered, the guard stood his ground. "You have proof?"

Tarbor reached inside his uniform to take out the tightly rolled parchment Speedwell had given him; he handed it down to the guard.

As soon as the guard saw the writing, his eyes widened, seeing how the writing flowed across the parchment. *No ordinary hand has written this*, he thought as he read its contents:

You are holding a sergeant who has deserted the Waunarle army by the name of Urchel, a traitor to the Alliance. He is to be handed over to my guards to be dealt with at Stormhaven.

Queen Helistra

The guard quickly rolled the parchment back up and handed it back to Tarbor, standing back without saying another word, for them to pass.

Queen Helistra's name on the parchment was more than enough for the guard. The poor soul who was in jail had only death awaiting him, he had thought; monsters were the least of his worries.

"Her fame has spread," chirped Cillan as they rode through the streets on the Cardronian side, which were proving to be just as quiet, not that Tarbor minded as he smiled at Cillan whilst trying to remember which way to go for the jail.

More streets and turns finally brought them to where Tarbor had been searching for: the town meeting hall.

It was a large building that sat on its own, with the street running up to it and passing it either side before joining up again. Four sturdy-looking wooden pillars held part of the upper building up at the front, making the building look like a pair of creatures poised to attack.

A door set back between the pillars showed itself, with no one guarding it.

"That is where he will be," confirmed Tarbor, for Cillan to frown.

"What, in that place? It hardly looks like a jail."

"Do not worry, it is. You are too used to castle dungeons," smiled Tarbor, for Cillan to give him a look; he did not need reminding.

Dismounting, they tied their horses to the iron rings fixed in the wall at one side of the meeting hall and approached the door; all was quiet.

"It is like a ghost town. No one seems to be here," remarked Cillan.

"All the better for us if we have to deal with anyone," replied Tarbor, and he opened the door.

They walked into a long room with two guards sat slumped in chairs around an empty fireplace, with another leaning back in his chair with his feet on a table. All looked half asleep and bored.

Tarbor looked around to see a set of stairs disappearing through the floor above them on their left and another set on their right.

To the left of the fireplace was a solitary door, which Tarbor knew would lead to the cells.

The guard with his feet on the table took them off and sat up as soon as he saw them, to reveal he only had one arm.

"Cardronian guards, can I guess what you have come for?" he said with a smile as the other two guards got to their feet and stood behind him.

"We have come from Stormhaven to take the deserter back named Urchel," replied Tarbor.

"Ah, Stormhaven," the guard repeated, rubbing the stump of his arm, making Tarbor look at him twice. "I presume you have proof of this?" he questioned, eying them both. Tarbor produced the parchment once more and handed it to him.

Awkwardly opening it out, the guard read it. "She does not mix her words," he said with a nod, giving it back as two more guards appeared, coming down the stairs from above. "I imagine you need to rest before taking him back, the night draws on," he suggested.

"That would be good, but before we do, can we see the prisoner?" said Tarbor, smiling.

The guard did not question why and immediately reached for his ring of keys on his waist. "Of course, I do not blame you for being careful. Since the siege, you cannot trust anyone," he stated, getting up to open the solitary door.

He nodded to one of the guards to bring a torch for Tarbor and Cillan to see by as the guard led the way down some stone steps into pitch-blackness.

The steps stopped and a passageway showed itself with cell doors on one side of it. The guard with one arm opened one of the cell doors to reveal an empty cell in the torchlight, with nothing in it except a wooden bed. Tarbor and Cillan looked at the guard with a horrible feeling in their stomachs.

"This is as good a place as any to rest yourself, Captain Tarbor!" spat the guard, looking straight at Tarbor, as both he and Cillan suddenly felt swords sticking in their backs from the other guards behind them.

We have walked straight into it, groaned Tarbor in his mind, for him to look at the guard again.

"I once served under you. I thought you to be a good man, until you sent me to the front and I got this for my troubles!" The guard punched the stump of his arm grudgingly.

Tarbor now realised who he was; the day they had attacked the stronghold, he had sent a soldier to the front for still being drunk, this soldier.

"Whoever wrote your parchment is very good, by the way, and that beard becomes you." He grinned as Tarbor felt the defender being taken from him before being pushed into the cell and having the cell door slammed shut upon him.

Cillan closed his eyes as he was pushed into the next cell. What had been smiled at only a moment ago had become his nightmare once again.

"You do not remember me, do you, Captain Tarbor? But I remember you! What were your words? *See if your taste for blood is the same as your taste for ale!* Well, let us see if you will like the taste of death that awaits you when the real guards come for Sergeant Urchel! What a treat Queen Helistra is going to have when she sees you as well," he said, smirking, to leave Tarbor and Cillan in total darkness.

As the one-armed guard reached the steps, laughing, he heard Tarbor's voice call to him from within his cell. "I remember you, Tayell. I remember all my men."

It caught Tayell a bit by surprise that he had remembered, but it was far too late for him now.

CHAPTER XXXV

"They should have been back by now," said Cantell, looking from behind a tree down the dirt track in the light of a three-quarter moon.

"Perhaps they have thought it best to wait until daybreak to bring him out. It would look less suspicious," he suggested.

"I am not so sure, my daughter's name upon the parchment would have made them relieved to be rid of someone they probably did not want in their midst in the first place. No, something is wrong," felt Speedwell. "I should not have let him go. There are far more pressing matters at hand," he reproached himself.

"You would not have stopped him, Speedwell. He still feels for the loss of his friend Girvan. He was not about to lose another," spoke up Piper.

"As friends alone then, we should go and bring them all back. I for one owe him my life, and more besides," volunteered Kelmar, remembering how he had been towards Tarbor.

"I will help you," added Piper, feeling that if she had not asked for the supplies in the first place, none of this would have happened.

"What if you are caught as well and do not come back?" asked Queen Elina, worried that if they did not come back then the fate of her baby girl was sealed, but even as she asked it, she knew that if Tarbor remained captured, it probably already was.

"Then we must go to the Ancient One without them, as we can now if we choose to," answered Speedwell.

"Sometimes sacrifices have to be made," spoke Tomin, "as I should know," he added.

"Well, not this time!" interrupted Tintwist. "Will you hold on to Gentian's rune staff for us, please, Speedwell, whilst we rescue them?" asked Tintwist, looking at Piper. "You did not think I would let you go without me, did you?" He grinned, to receive a smile from her.

"It looks as if our minds have been made up for us," conceded Speedwell, "until your return only then." Speedwell smiled, holding out his hand to receive Gentian's rune staff. "Just one thing, though, do you know where the jail is?"

"I think I can help out there," said Cantell with a smile.

Kelmar, Piper and Tintwist set off to Marchend, riding down the south side of the valley with a warning from Speedwell echoing in their ears: *Remember, if you are not back by daybreak, we will be gone!*

With the three-quarter moon lighting their way, their plan was to cross the River Talmin then the River Mid, so as to come in on the Cardronian side of Marchend, avoiding the Balintium side altogether; easier said than done.

Unlike the River Mid, the River Talmin was wide, and not as shallow. Its appearance out of the Great Forest was as a rush of water over a rocky terrain before settling into a full-flowing river further down in the valley.

As the River Talmin loomed, glinting in the moonlight before them, the three comrades followed its course, hoping to find a narrower stretch to cross.

Trees dotted its banks at first, with bushes knitting them together that began to slowly open up, revealing reeds lining the river's inner sides.

Bushes rather than trees began lending themselves more to the river's banks and then there, showing itself in the moonlight, a narrow bend appeared in the river's course, with a drop in the bank to the river's edge.

"Cattle cross here," said Kelmar, seeing muddy hoof marks in the slope. That was good enough for him, and holding on tightly to his reins, he urged his horse into the river. Piper and Tintwist followed suit and were soon in the river's flow behind him.

The river suddenly dropped in the middle, forcing the horses to swim for a while before finding the river's bed to walk on again.

Kelmar and Piper thankfully made it to the other side, but when they turned round to look for Tintwist, they found they were only looking at his horse!

They caught sight of a pair of flailing arms moving rapidly away from them in the river's flow into the darkness!

"Tintwist!" shouted Piper, and she dug her heels into the horse's side whilst Kelmar caught hold of Tintwist's horse before following.

Piper caught up with Tintwist's shouts, trying to think how to help him whilst cursing at his laziness at never learning how to swim in all the time they had lived near the sea.

Managing to avoid a few trees that dotted the bank in front of her, Piper rode on, looking for a chance to get Tintwist out of there, and quickly, but how? she thought, trying to think.

She pulled up sharply, straining her eyes and ears to look at the river, but saw or heard nothing, then suddenly she heard shouts; it was Kelmar!

Riding back, she came to his and Tintwist's riderless horses. "Here, Piper! Down here!" Running down to the riverbank between some trees, she found Kelmar. He pointed to the end of a broken branch hanging in the water and there holding on to it for dear life was Tintwist.

Her laughter was of relief, and close to tears, for she had always loved him but had never really shown him that she did. If she had lost him without saying… she thought no more and jumped into the water to grab him.

"I was trying to get a better grip on the reins and the next minute I was in the river," a sodden Tintwist tried to explain as they rode on after being rescued.

"We are supposed to be rescuing Tarbor, Cillan and Urchel, not you! Perhaps now you will take to learning how to swim!" chastised Piper, making Tintwist go quiet and Kelmar smile.

They now travelled west, following the River Mid, until they saw the distant lights of Marchend were no more, before crossing its shallow waters, much to the relief of Tintwist.

Forever keeping their eyes out for soldiers, they rode as near as they dare to the outskirts of the town, until finally a thicket emerged which enabled them to tie and hide their horses.

Three figures then ran stealthily into the shadows of the nearest building.

"What sort of building are we looking for?" whispered Tintwist at the back of the other two.

"Cantell told me that when he and King Rolfe came here, it was a building on its own with four columns holding up the front of it, their town meeting hall," Kelmar informed them, after peeping around the corner to see it was all clear.

Running across the street to the cover of two houses, they dived between them as they heard horses' hooves.

Staying pressed against one of the buildings, they watched as four horse soldiers passed by at a trot. "The streets are quiet, but there are bound to be more soldiers. Let me walk on ahead whilst you keep to the shadows. I can pass as a town dweller then I will be more able to search for the town meeting hall, rather than darting in and out of the shadows," suggested Kelmar.

"Very well, but be careful," agreed Piper, taking her bow from her back in readiness, with Tintwist doing the same.

Kelmar walked out of the shadows down the street, keeping his eyes about him, gesturing to Piper and Tintwist that all was clear.

Street after street was negotiated as Kelmar looked up passing streets, hoping to see the town meeting hall.

Where is this place? he was thinking, when suddenly two soldiers appeared from around a corner in front of him. Without thinking, he quickly put his hand behind his back, pointing in warning for Piper and Tintwist to hide.

One of the soldiers spotted Kelmar doing this and wondered what he was up to. "What are you doing?" he questioned Kelmar.

"Nothing at all," said Kelmar with a smile, "just scratching my back," and he brought his hand back round in front of him.

"What are you doing here anyway? Most people are away to their beds at this late hour," asked the soldier, suspicious of Kelmar.

"I was late from my day in the fields," he answered as the soldier's comrade drew his sword to disappear down the very alley Piper and Tintwist had hidden in.

"I do not know why you are being like this. I am one of you," objected Kelmar, for the soldier to draw his sword and hold it to Kelmar's neck.

"Not with that accent, you are not!"

The soldier called out to his comrade when he did not reappear straight away. The only answer he got was an arrow straight through his neck, for him to hit the ground with a thud, sending his sword spinning through the air.

Kelmar had heard nothing as he turned to see Piper lower her bow.

Moments later, the bodies, along with the fallen swords, had been hidden in an outhouse that was perched against the side of a house where Piper and Tintwist had been hiding. With the arrow retrieved and a cover of dirt to hide the blood spilt, they were on their way again.

"That was not very pleasant," remarked Tintwist.

"Killing never is, Tintwist," replied Kelmar.

"No, not them, in there! Where we have just hidden them, it smelt awful!" Kelmar just looked at Piper with a shake of the head.

"No time to falter now, it will only be a matter of time before someone reports them missing," said Kelmar, looking down the street where the two soldiers had come from, to smile. "There it is!" he exclaimed, and they ran quickly to hide in the shadows once more to get a better look.

The soldiers had led them onto one of the streets that led straight to one side of the town meeting hall. "That is the place, see the columns," said Kelmar, seeing them lit up in the torchlight that burnt outside the building.

"I see the guards outside," answered Piper. "How many more do you think there are inside?" she posed.

"It does not matter. We must deal with them all if we are to rescue our friends," replied Kelmar.

"Is that their horses tied up outside?" wondered Tintwist as they eyed the place over.

"They may well be. There is only one way we will find out," answered Kelmar, and he began leading the way through the shadows to get nearer to the front of the meeting hall.

Finding a wall of a nearby house to hide behind, Kelmar watched as Piper and Tintwist weighed up their targets.

Notching their arrows after snatching a glance to see where the two guards were positioned, Piper looked at Tintwist. "If we can hit rabbits at that distance, then this will be no trouble." She smiled to Tintwist's nod.

Together, they spun into the open with their strings taut on their bows and let loose their arrows. The two guards were knocked off their feet as the arrows found their mark.

Running across the street, they were suddenly confronted by a guard who appeared at the door, having heard the noise of the fallen guards, only to be met by an arrow in his chest, to keel over onto the ground.

Bursting through the door, Kelmar met two more guards brandishing their swords head-on. One block and a scythe later saw one guard topple to the floor as he drove the other guard backwards with his attacks.

Seeing his comrades being killed, Tayell was on his feet, trying to unlock the solitary door that led to the cells, cursing under his breath at only having one arm as he fumbled with the keys in his hand.

Piper saw the one-armed guard trying to unlock the door. "He is trying to lock himself behind that door!" she shouted.

Two arrows later saw Tayell's body pinned to the door, the keys still in his hand, that is, until he coughed up blood. Then they fell to the floor in a red heap.

A cry later and Kelmar had found his mark, his sword finding the rib cage of the guard, who fell to the floor clutching his fatal wound.

Without a second thought, Kelmar pulled Tayell's hanging body off the door, letting it drop onto the floor, where Piper and Tintwist retrieved their arrows, leaving Tayell's body in a pool of blood.

Unlocking the door, Kelmar was soon unlocking the cell doors to see a relieved Tarbor, Cillan and finally a thankful Urchel.

"It is good to see you, Kelmar, Piper, and you, Tintwist. I thought you would have been far into the Great Forest by now." Tarbor smiled, squinting in the torchlight.

"If we are not back by daybreak, then Speedwell will be," informed Kelmar.

Tarbor looked down at Tayell's bloody body, his eyes pain-ridden as he lay there dying. Tarbor knelt over him, seeing Girvan in his mind as he saw all the blood. Although Tayell had given him away, he was feeling some guilt for what he had done that day.

Tayell was feeling his own regret as he lay there dying. "Forgive me… Captain…" was all that was left in him.

"Do not feel badly, Tarbor. You did what you thought was best at the time," said a tired, understanding voice from behind him, knowing who the solider was.

Tarbor stood up and looked around to see the tired, drawn-out face of Urchel looking at him. He immediately went over and hugged him. "It is good to see you again, Urchel."

"What happened at Idrig's farm?" he had to ask.

"Those beasts we encountered at the barn, Tarbor, had left their mark on Vartig. He had become an unrecognisable monster. Idrig saved my life, but in doing so put an end to his," recounted Urchel, leaving out what he had had to do.

"I left, setting fire to it all, and came here to warn everyone, but they thought me as mad, throwing me in here. Tayell recognised me and sent word to Stormhaven that he held a deserter," he finished.

"Come, Tarbor, whilst all is clear. We have more than outstayed our welcome. You can talk later," urged Kelmar, handing Tarbor his defender as Cillan dragged the last body in from outside.

"Before we go, set light to it all. It will help hide what has been done and cause a distraction," decided Tarbor.

Torches were taken from the walls inside the room and put to the chairs that they had stacked together, setting light to the dry wood. A blaze soon began, pushing out its heat into the room as the party fled the scene.

Tarbor and Cillan mounted their waiting horses, with Urchel climbing up behind Tarbor. They followed Kelmar, Piper and Tintwist, speeding down the streets to the outskirts of the town, back to where their horses awaited them.

They left behind a scene of chaos as townsfolk and soldiers alike ran into the streets after being awoken by the roaring sound of their town meeting hall on fire.

A young boy sat up in his bed. He had awoken in the night, having had a bad dream, when horses and people running outside his home caught his attention. He ventured to the door to see who it was, but only passing shadows appeared to him as he opened it.

Something caught his eye as it skidded along the ground in the breeze. He ran outside to pick it up; it was just a rolled-up piece of paper.

He was just about to throw it away in disappointment when his father's voice came from behind him. "What are you doing out here and what is that you have in your hand?" came the questions.

Even before the boy could say anything, people were running past them, shouting, "It's the town meeting hall, it's on fire!"

"Come inside where it is safe," the father urged his son, and he opened the parchment his son had found.

His eyes widened, seeing the name that was written upon it. A document for a prisoner held in the town meeting hall, and it was on fire?

"Did you see anyone when you found this?" he asked.

"No, Father, but I am sure I heard horses going that way," and the boy pointed towards the outskirts of the town.

His father thought on it and realised his son had stumbled upon whoever had set the fire. "Come, son, get dressed. We need to give this to someone!"

CHAPTER XXXVI

The crystal chamber pulsated in a scarlet red, reflecting the deathly blood-red pool of life as Queen Helistra sat on the chamber floor with her eyes closed, embracing the power being slowly harnessed into the broken rune staff. It was like a breath of fresh air to her as she felt another pulse of power enter its being.

The power that had passed through the broken rune staff before marking the end of King Taliskar had been at the point of being dangerous to them both. So much power gathered into one spell in their haste to break Speedwell's spell of containment could have resulted in their demise and that of all of Stormhaven, had they not cast it straight away.

Queen Helistra's bloodshot eye had been a warning. Now, in that realisation, she was gathering the crystal chamber's potency within the broken rune staff pulse by pulse.

The many souls that were still trapped within the broken rune staff were going to be twenty, perhaps thirty, times more potent when the time came, she had thought again as she sat there breathing in the power. Let alone the soul blood, which would be more than a match for those imbeciles, she gloated as she opened her eyes.

She smiled at little Princess Amber using her newfound skill of crawling as she scuffled all over the crystal chamber floor. "Oh, just look at your dirty knees!" She laughed at her, with the chamber echoing her words as they bounced off the crystals.

Picking her up, Queen Helistra made her way back up the steps to the throne room in the glow of the soft white light. A whisper of the mountain throne later and she was back in Forest Tower, going up to the balcony, where she liked to look out over the sea, avoiding looking at the forest.

Letting Princess Amber crawl her way around the ceremonial room, Queen Helistra sat down on the balcony seat. Resting the broken rune staff next to her, she watched as the sea lapped up onto the shore.

Her hand reached inside a hidden pocket of her dress as she did so and produced a parchment that had just come into her possession. She read it again and thought on the report she had received.

"He dares copy my hand for this Urchel." She frowned after reading it. Humming entered her mind. "Yes, he is one of those Taliskar charged with taking Brax's body to Slevenport with Tarbor, which they did, but Wardine should have dealt with them. His obvious incompetence must have shown itself. He has never returned," she said scornfully at the thought of him as the humming spoke again.

"No, they did not return either and as nothing has disturbed you then they must have found the shield. As this forgery has come from Marchend, we can assume they have Tomin and by now are in the Great Forest," she agreed, slightly annoyed.

"But we knew this could happen. We have spoken of it before. We now have the power of the crystal chamber to not worry about them," she pointed out, reassuring herself.

The humming was quiet for a moment as if thinking, before re-entering her mind. *As a friend, I do not know what you are on about, that he was rescued for what he might know.* The humming began answering her in a roundabout way.

"It was the power we used that blocked my senses when I tried to enter his mind, nothing more. I know who he is and what I gave him. You have told me enough times." Queen Helistra was beginning to get agitated by the broken rune staff not coming to the point as it hummed to her once more.

"There is more to it than just that? What do you mean?" she questioned, to hear more humming.

According to reports, the boy is with his mother at Elishard. Why? Humming.

"They have been wrong before. You cannot always trust them," she admitted in answer.

By now, Queen Helistra had picked up Princess Amber and had started to pace the ceremonial room as the humming continued.

"The essence could have spoken to him through the defender! Is that possible? But of what? Why do you not come to the point? You have obviously felt something I have not," she asked.

The broken rune staff this time made Queen Helistra stop her pacing up and down as it finally came to its conclusion, knowing Queen Helistra was not going to like what it was going to tell her as it quietly hummed in her mind.

You think they rescued this Urchel not just because of his knowledge of Tomin's existence, but because of what he knew about the boy Prince? That Tarbor had not wanted to kill him because the essence had made it known that the boy and Amber were both of the spirit, born to be!"

Queen Helistra held Princess Amber up before her and stared at her little giggling face. Her mouth had fallen open in disbelief at what the broken rune staff had just whispered to her.

"Born to be! FORESTALLS!" she yelled in anger, turning Princess Amber's giggles into tears.

A seething rage stormed over Queen Helistra and in the next moment she was dangling a bawling Princess Amber over the balcony by one leg!

The broken rune staff tried to reason with her. "DO NOT tell me what to do! THEY are to become what I should have been! NEVER!"

Trying not to make her any more angry than she already was, the broken rune staff quickly explained why she should keep her, just managing to hold her back from throwing Princess Amber from the balcony.

"To my advantage! How can that be!" growled Queen Helistra. She was fuming inside, feeling a complete fool for not sensing the child was going to be a future Forestall.

She could clearly hear herself say to Taliskar that this brat's brother was nothing to them, when all the time he was destined to be what she had always wanted to be, but was never allowed to!

She knew she had missed it in her haste to destroy the forests and something she would never admit to anyone, her wanting to be a mother again. She cursed herself for being so careless and stupid!

After what seemed forever, the broken rune staff finally brought Queen Helistra back from her rage, persuading her to listen more to what it had to say.

She put the frightened and tearful Princess Amber back down onto the floor with not too gentle a hand, feeling repulsion at her touch.

Sitting back down on the balcony seat, she waited for what the broken rune staff had to say. It re-entered her mind gently and began by telling her that as Tarbor had found his shield, so she had found hers in Princess Amber.

Once they had entered her soul, that they had both missed, the broken rune staff was quick to point out, they could quell any spirit there might be within her to become a Forestall, then she could still be groomed to her liking whilst using her as a foil when the time came to destroy them all.

Keeping her alive would give them a problem, as no Forestall would knowingly kill another. The broken rune staff stopped humming and waited.

Queen Helistra had listened to what the broken rune staff had to say, but was dubious about what she had been told.

"I understand all that you have said, but I am not yet convinced as to whether I should keep her alive or not. Will they not sense us when we enter the child to destroy her spirit? It would disturb the balance and then they would know she was no longer able to be a Forestall, making her useless to me as a shield," she reasoned.

The broken rune staff answered her doubt. "The crystal chamber will hide us as the shield has hidden Tomin, but what of her brother? If he is with Speedwell, what of him gaining a rune staff such as you?" she further asked, doubts still lingering.

The humming seemed to smile within her mind as it answered. "No, there is no other rune staff such as you." Even Queen Helistra's mood had to smile a little at the broken rune staff's answer as it hummed once more.

I know our years have been many together, to form the bond we have with each other, more time than they will ever have to hold the barrier and bond with a rune staff if one comes into being, this is true.

Queen Helistra made up her mind. "We will go to the crystal chamber and see what lyes within this child, but if it is not to my liking..." she warned, picking up the broken rune staff and with some disdain the sobbing Princess Amber to start making her way to the crystal chamber.

A stillness unlike any other descended upon the crystal chamber as Queen Helistra sat with the broken rune staff across her lap and Princess Amber between her legs.

Calming herself, Queen Helistra touched some symbols on the broken rune staff with one hand whilst putting her other hand onto Princess Amber's forehead.

Closing her eyes, she joined with the broken rune staff to let her presence float softly into the little Princess, calling out to her spirit.

A dark void met her presence. Nothing seemed to be happening, but the little Princess' body had suddenly become very still.

Then slowly a tiny light began to form, turning into a dense light that held its distance from Queen Helistra's presence. She smiled in welcome as she felt the spirit show itself, beckoning it towards her in soft tones, showing only kindness.

The dense light sent out one or two specks of light towards her out of caution and curiosity. The spirit had felt a dark shadow enter already and was wary of who this might be. Queen Helistra smiled inwardly; that was all she needed.

Without Princess Amber's spirit realising, Queen Helistra moved a finger to another symbol on the broken rune staff for it to hum to the crystal chamber. Within a heartbeat, the crystal chamber released a high-pitched whistling sound into the broken rune staff.

The shrill sound was joined by a droplet of soul blood from the broken rune staff and together they were bound by Queen Helistra into a spell of destruction.

It shot into Princess Amber, through Queen Helistra's presence, as a red bead of destruction, and she watched it hurtle its way towards the dense light.

The specks of light turned and sped, seeing the trap they had been led into, but it was too late. The red bead of destruction caught up with them and coated them in its deathly embrace before crashing into the dense light.

It immediately covered the dense light in a coat of red death, letting the deathly soul blood absorb the dense light until it was completely immersed in its deathly grip.

As the light died, an intense piercing sound smashed through the suffocated light, obliterating it, to send it into oblivion. What had been the dense light of hope in Princess Amber was now darkness.

Queen Helistra withdrew her presence and opened her eyes. She looked at little Princess Amber. Her body was stock-still as if in shock, then suddenly it lurched and she was looking at Queen Helistra with two blood-red eyes!

Queen Helistra smiled a smile of satisfaction as they slowly cleared and Princess Amber giggled once more, but Queen Helistra knew it was now a giggle of impending evil!

CHAPTER XXXVII

Tarbor had lost count of how many days they had been walking in the Great Forest, following the River Talmin.

Tintwist had not been able to contain his excitement that at last he would be seeing the Ancient One in all its glory, for Tarbor to correct him, saying, "You mean in all his glory?" to a chuckle from Tintwist.

"You will see!" he had said with a smile, leaving Tarbor puzzled.

The forest had proven to be tougher going the more they had travelled into it, with the vegetation being thick and the terrain varied, causing the party to weave its way through the forest, losing sight of the river in one moment by having to travel around or over a hill and in the next being beside it, like they were now as they rested in an opening by its waters.

Piper and Tintwist had disappeared amongst it, every so often coming back with berries, fruit or sometimes roots to eat, with the odd rabbit on the shoulder of a grinning Tintwist. At the moment whilst they rested, it was fish they were after, all to replace the ever-dwindling supplies.

Whether it was Tarbor's mind, he did not know, but the further they travelled into the forest and the denser it seemed to get, the taller the trees seemed to be, although as he rested there in the dappled shade of the trees, nothing, he was thinking, had prepared him for the nighttime under the dark canopy they gave.

It had taken a few restless nights, even with a bright fire, for his mind to ease with all the different noises the nighttime had brought with it. Speedwell had assured him it was only the creatures of the forest and the breeze in the trees, but it had still made his hair stand on end.

He was not alone in feeling that way as he looked over at Cillan and Urchel. Cillan was taking off his boots in relief, whilst Urchel was looking at the scars on his hands.

His story, which he had finally told them all, of how he had to save Idrig from becoming like his brother by ending his life was both chilling and heartbreaking at the same time. It had literally left its mark upon him; he had hardly said a word since.

It had made Tarbor see once more those grotesque creatures he had confronted on the moor and the salt marsh.

Tarbor glanced at Queen Elina. She was thankful for the rest, even though Kelmar and Cantell had helped her along as much as they could by carrying Prince Martyn between them.

He had noticed Cantell's arm was moving much better now since Speedwell had given him what looked like a similar mixture to the green goo he had given to Urchel.

Queen Elina, though, had been as quiet as Urchel since they had all found out that he had lost the roll of parchment with Speedwell's writing upon it. He wished he knew where he had lost it and cursed himself for making Queen Elina so unhappy. All they had gone through to try and safeguard the little Princess' future by rescuing Urchel could well have been for nothing.

All Queen Elina could see was Queen Helistra reading it and taking one last look at her daughter before ending her life. If it were not for her son's presence, she could have gladly ended hers for how she felt.

Unlike Tarbor, Prince Martyn seemed to be revelling in fascination at the forest. He was forever looking up at the enormous trees that towered above them all, the movement of the leaves catching his eyes. "He is at home here," remarked Speedwell, smiling at him looking, but Queen Elina said nothing.

Speedwell walked away quietly. He could do nothing to console Queen Elina. After all, it was his daughter who held hers. He could only ask the stars and spirits to watch over the little Princess.

"What I would not do for a horse right now," said Cillan, rubbing his feet after taking off his boots.

"They will be enjoying the lush grass of the valley," reflected Urchel, as Cillan's remark had stirred him into remembering where they had let the horses have their freedom. That was not all it had triggered as he looked down at his scarred hands once more.

"Who needs a horse when you can feel the earth beneath your feet?" asked Tomin with a smile, enjoying the warmth he was feeling inside him by being back in the forest. He sat leaning against a tree, feeling its vibrancy run through his body as he breathed in the forest air.

Speedwell stood by the river's side in quiet reflection as he looked up and down its bank. Piper came and stood next to him, seeing him looking, as if searching for something.

"Is everything well, Speedwell?" she asked in the end.

Speedwell kept looking whilst he answered her. "Not really, Piper. I feel I have failed in so many ways, but now is a time when I must stay strong. Now where did I leave it?" was his mixed reply.

"It has been too shallow and rocky before, but from here the river is deeper," said Speedwell to himself, with Piper wondering why he was going on about the river.

"Ah! Yes, further up here, I think," and he started to walk along the riverbank. Piper looked to where Speedwell had begun to walk to, but saw nothing but trees.

"Where are you going?" she asked, following Speedwell, to find him stopping under the huge but slender forms of some willow trees that were leaning precariously over the river.

Speedwell touched some of the symbols on his rune staff and seemed to whisper something as he waved his rune staff in front of him.

In between blinks of her eyes, a narrow sailing boat appeared in front of Piper, gently resting on the river's surface.

"Where? How did you do that!" she gasped.

"With practice," said Speedwell with a smile as he eyed the vessel.

"You had better get the others and make sure it is river worthy. It has been here awhile," advised Speedwell. Piper did not ask how long that was. She could hear Speedwell's answer in her mind; long enough.

"The wood seems fine," said Cillan, after inspecting the boat.

"I am not so sure about this sail, though," said Kelmar, after hoisting the single sail up the short mast. It looked tatty and was ripped in two places.

"I had forgotten about that. Tie it back for now. It is of no use like that," said Speedwell.

Tarbor looked inside the narrow sailing boat, noting oars tucked down the side. "Well, I can see where we come in to replace it," he remarked, looking at the others.

"It has been here since the Elfore left to go and live in the Plateau Forest. I borrow it occasionally," informed Speedwell as he climbed in at the back to face Tomin, where a wooden shaft showed itself, to steer the boat's rudder.

"The vessel will take days off our journey to the Old Ogrin Ridge," said Speedwell as all the party followed suit and got into the narrow Elfore sailing boat.

The Elfore sailing boat proved to be just the right size as they sat in two rows behind one another, facing Speedwell, behind Tomin, with Cantell and Queen Elina sitting at the front with Prince Martyn.

Oars were readied and pushed against the bank to set the Elfore sailing boat on its way as it slipped silently through the slender overhanging branches of the willow trees, the mast passing through them as if they were not there.

Out against the flow of the River Talmin they moved, with six oars dipping into its waters, three either side. Tintwist looked at the slender oar in his hands. "I am not so sure if walking would have been better," he remarked, making everyone quietly agree as they pulled against the flow.

"You will be seeing the Ancient One much more quickly," remarked Speedwell, making Tintwist pull harder.

"It has been a while since I last did this," said Tarbor as he pulled at the water, missed and fell backwards into Kelmar, who laughed.

Tintwist turned around. "Watch us, King wielder. You will soon become an oarsman." He grinned as, for the first time since Tarbor had met him, he took off his leather hat to feel the fresh breeze of the river flow through his hair. Piper smiled, doing the same. No prying eyes here, she thought, and together they began to row in harmony, cutting through the water with what seemed no effort at all.

After a few strokes, Tintwist and Piper both turned round, wondering why their rowing was not getting any lighter. All they saw were six pairs of eyes looking at them. They both instantly realised that it was the first time they had taken their leather hats off in front of them all, to reveal their telltale pointed ears.

"Is there something wrong?" challenged Tintwist.

"No, no, not at all. I did not know you grew your hair so long under those hats," lied Tarbor embarrassingly, for him to fumble with his oar.

"Try rowing then, instead of staring!" said Tintwist with a scowl, and they all set about their oars, feeling the instant atmosphere they had created.

Speedwell and Tomin could only groan inside, not daring to say anything, knowing how touchy Tintwist was about his ears.

By the third day of rowing, they had all become more competent at rowing, if not achy ones, as they made their way deeper and deeper into the Great Forest along the river.

Earlier that day, it had become wider still as they came to a divide in the river that had told Speedwell they had joined the River of Tears, with the River Salleen moving off to their right to eventually appear in Cardronia.

Cantell had started to row himself to strengthen his arm and was feeling more like his old self again. As he rested between times, he could not help but look at the valleys of trees that passed him by, that would become hills of trees then valleys again. It had been one thing to travel through it and quite another to see it all from the river.

"It is like a different world," he marvelled, as a splash of water hit his face.

"It is hard to believe she would want to corrupt something of such beauty," said Tarbor, also getting a splash of water over him.

The river had started to become much choppier as it flowed faster, causing more splashes. "The river has picked up momentum," pointed out Piper. "Is it rapids, Speedwell? If it is, we would do best by walking again. There could be rocks lying in wait to hit the boat," warned Piper.

"No, it is not rapids," was Speedwell's reply, without saying what it was.

"Well, if it is not rapids, what is it then?" asked Piper.

"Hoist the sail, Cillan," said Speedwell, ignoring Piper for the moment.

"But the sail is ripped, it is of no use," said Cillan, frowning, who nevertheless unfurled it and hoisted it up the mast.

Speedwell held his rune staff aloft and mumbled under his breath as he touched some symbols. He waved his rune staff in the air and all watched as the sail became whole again, to ripple in the breeze.

"You mean, you could have done that all this time and instead you had us all rowing our arms off!" chimed in Tintwist. "I hope there is good reason!" he challenged him, to immediately go quiet when he saw he had overstepped the mark by the look Speedwell gave him.

"I could have mended the sail at the beginning of our journey on the river, but I wanted it to be at its strongest when we arrived here, as I wanted all of you," he answered, still vague as to what could be awaiting them.

"And that is because?" probed Tarbor.

"The snow on the Kavenmist and Greater Hardenal Mountains is deep in winter and takes a long time to melt when the sun shows itself once more. It never completely melts, but with the help of the spring rain and summer sun, the melt off the mountains causes the rivers to run faster," began explaining Speedwell.

"The two main rivers from the mountains merge into the Great Lake, which is ahead of us," Speedwell paused, "and can sometimes cause whirlpools. I had hoped there would not be one, but by the feel of the river's flow, it seems there is," he finished, to everyone's dropped looks.

"Then stop this boat and let us walk around. You would risk the life of my son as well as my daughter!" chastised Queen Elina.

"The rivers from the mountains have only a few crossing places. It will take a journey of many days to walk around, more than I care to give. I would not risk the future of us all unnecessarily, but I feel if I do not help strengthen the barrier now, the malevolence of her poison could soon break through and all this will be for nothing," replied a worried Speedwell.

"Use your powers to get us through it then. How big can it be?" put Tarbor.

Speedwell had hoped to conserve his energy as much as possible for the barrier. He needed to be at his strongest to weave a spell strong enough to cast across the whole of the ridge when he got there.

He could already see, though, with the help of his rune staff, that a whirlpool of considerable size was waiting for them before they could continue up the River of Tears.

"If needs be, I will, but I must save myself as much as possible for the barrier, Tarbor. Together, we will get through it. You will see," was his eventual reply in reassurance, not that anyone was feeling it.

Tomin took over the steering; Speedwell knew he could count on his feel through the water whilst he readied himself to give the sail he had repaired the wind it would need to help sail the boat out of the whirlpool. All braced themselves for what lay ahead, not really knowing what to expect.

They entered the vastness that was the Great Lake, to hear Queen Elina give a gasp when she saw the size of the whirlpool ahead of them as they neared the far end of the lake.

The two rivers from the mountains could be seen rushing into the lake, forming the whirlpool, as the Elfore sailing boat began to get thrown about the nearer it got.

"Be ready with those oars to steady her," shouted Speedwell. "We will enter the whirlpool and let it catapult us out on the other side into the mouth of the River of Tears," he shouted further, making everyone feel uncomfortable. They did not like the sound of that, but it was too late; they had to trust Speedwell's judgement.

What have I got myself into? thought Tarbor, as he looked over his shoulder with the others to see a swirling mass of water waiting to swallow them up.

"Are you ready, Tomin?"

"I have it, Grandfather," replied Tomin, and he gripped the wooden steering shaft tightly, to feel the water below through the rudder as he steered the vessel straight at the swirling mass.

Suddenly the narrow sailing boat felt as if it had been thrown through the air as it was caught in the whirlpool's grip!

"Hard on those oars! Keep her steady!" shouted Speedwell, as Tomin held a line at the rim of the whirlpool.

Tarbor was sure he was pulling through the air half the time as they whirled around. Queen Elina closed her eyes, hanging on to Prince Martyn, and said a silent prayer to the stars above to help guide them through. She was not the only one!

Speedwell waited for Tomin to give the word, for when he felt a settled strip of water he could steer into, then he would billow the sail to help push them through, but Tomin's years of being hidden had taken the edge off his skills.

As they came to the other side to where the River of Tears continued, Tomin pushed his mind through the rudder into the water to feel for an opening, but as one came to him his reactions were too slow. He did not gauge the strength of the whirlpool enough and missed the opening, to send them hurtling around the whirlpool again, with the effect of pulling the narrow sailing boat deeper into the whirlpool!

Speedwell looked at Tomin for him to feel his gaze. "I have it this time, Grandfather," he shouted.

"Keep hard on those oars and when I shout stop, stop!" shouted Speedwell above the roaring noise of the whirlpool.

Tarbor looked at his shield between his feet as he battled with his oar, wondering if he could create a barrier that might help, but it was all he could do just to hold on to the oar, let alone reach for his shield and defender.

The narrow sailing boat seemed to pitch its way around the whirlpool. One moment it felt as if it was going to be drawn down into the vortex, the next riding out over the swirling water. All looked to Tomin as they neared the River of Tears once more.

Tomin was concentrating his senses through the rudder, feeling the currents below twist and turn at every moment, then there! There it was; a sudden break in the whirlpool that would lead them out of its grip!

"Now, Grandfather!" shouted Tomin, and he pushed at the wooden steering shaft to steer the vessel out of the whirlpool, to hear Speedwell shout at the same time, "Stop!"

Oars were pulled in quickly as Speedwell waved his rune staff across the sail, to see it nearly burst in front of his eyes with the strength of wind he had given it.

The narrow vessel reacted by thrusting them across the whirlpool, cutting through the water to reach the choppy but calmer waters of the continuing River of Tears.

A thankful party reached the nearest bank and gladly rested after their experience.

"I have never seen such a thing before," said Cantell, rubbing his arm, which was beginning to ache.

"And never wish to again," added Kelmar, remembering the storms that had hit the shores of Stormhaven, but they were nothing compared to what they had just endured.

Kelmar suddenly wished he had not thought of storms as the fallen body of Charlotte came straight into his mind.

"I trust, having put all our lives in danger, that our journey to the Ancient One is nearing an end?" questioned Queen Elina, stroking Prince Martyn's little brow, more to comfort her after their ordeal.

"Another few days should see us there," answered Speedwell, to a despondent sigh from Queen Elina.

Tarbor, though, was looking at Tintwist talking to Piper, feeling he should say something after staring at him, at them both, causing an atmosphere between them all.

They stopped talking as he walked towards them. "I would like to apologise to both of you for my ignorance in staring at you. You saved my life and I have repaid you by being rude. It was wrong of me. I hope you accept my apology," and Tarbor offered his hand.

"Tarbor speaks for us all," agreed Cantell, hearing Tarbor.

Tintwist looked around at all their faces looking at him, knowing they were not just fellow travellers but his friends; friends he could rely on. He looked at Piper and she nodded to him. "They did not mean any harm, Tintwist. They have never seen our like before," she said, smiling back at him.

"You have no need to apologise, Tarbor. I tend to overreact about my ears. We are proud of who we are. I am sorry also," apologised Tintwist, and he shook Tarbor's hand with a mischievous smile, "and anyway, what is wrong with long hair!" To which they all laughed, glad that Tintwist was back to his usual self.

All, that is, except Urchel, who took Tintwist's arm in a warrior's handshake, then Piper's as he spoke. "I also never thanked you both for saving my life not once, but twice," he acknowledged.

Tintwist and Piper nodded their heads in thanks, noting as they looked into his eyes that losing his friend Idrig had not only scarred his hands but had also scarred him deep within.

"Good, now perhaps moods will be better and we can get on with the rest of the journey," said Speedwell, giving Tintwist a look as he led the way back to the Elfore sailing boat, for Tintwist to look at Piper with a shrug.

Five more days of rowing and sailing saw the party at long last approaching the place where the two forests were joined, at its heart: the Old Ogrin Ridge.

Oars had stopped rowing as everyone looked in front of them, to be greeted by the strangest sight that Tarbor had ever seen.

The trees here on the banks of the river seemed to be reaching for the skies. Not only on the banks, but here right in front of them, where trees from either bank had joined together to make a bridge across the river.

Roots could be seen entwined with each other, forming an arch over the river, and as they approached it, their roots could be seen dangling beneath in mid-air, not quite reaching the water.

"That is the Bridge of Seasons, to welcome us," said Speedwell with a smile. "We are here at last."

The sail was lowered and they stopped rowing as they watched transfixed at the roots parting for them to sail through.

They all experienced the strangest of feelings as they slowly drifted underneath the bridge of tree roots. Fine ends of the roots appeared and reached out to touch them, catching their faces in a seemingly brushed caress of whispered welcome.

Worried at first what might happen, they all became overwhelmed by the moment. Speedwell smiled at their faces all in wonder as to what was happening to them, but more so at the little Prince, who laughed in delight as the fine roots paid him particular attention, bringing home to them all what Speedwell had said about him was true.

None more so than Queen Elina as she watched her son being stroked by the fine roots, making him laugh. All this time, she had listened to his talk of her baby son being the hope of everyone, and now she knew she was watching the proof of it all.

She looked at Speedwell in silent apology, to see him simply smile, seeing a face that at last was beginning to understand.

As they finally came out from the wonder of the Bridge of Seasons, they were captivated by even more wonders as their attention was immediately caught by the sheer scale of what appeared before them.

They had entered the biggest lake any of them had ever seen before; it was all they could do to stop their jaws from dropping at the magnificence of it all.

"This is the Lake of Tears and that is the Old Ogrin Ridge," said Speedwell with a smile, as they gazed all around them, trying to take it all in.

Towering trees of majestic beauty surrounded the huge lake that spread out before them, and there holding the lake from going any further was the Old Ogrin Ridge. A sheer cliff wall of solid rock that made their necks ache as they looked upon its imposing grandeur, but topping it all was the two waterfalls that cascaded down into the lake with a thunderous roar, with rainbows appearing halfway down out of the mist that billowed around them like clouds.

A gigantic tree could be seen between the waterfalls, sitting there as if defying the falls and the sheer cliff face.

As they drew nearer to the ridge, a strange-shaped island showed itself, sat there in the middle of the waterfalls.

Their eyes were drawn to the peculiar shapes coming from it that climbed all the way up the face of the ridge to stop beneath the gigantic tree that was perched on top of the ridge, overlooking everyone.

They all stared and stared at the tree then back at the peculiar shapes climbing up towards it.

Tarbor found Tintwist's words echoing in his mind: *You will see.*

"Those cannot be... are they?" he finally managed to say, for Speedwell to smile at his non– belief. "Yes, they are, Tarbor. They are the roots of the Ancient One who looks over us all, the heart of the forests," confirmed Speedwell, for Tarbor's mind to go blank.

Cantell, Kelmar, Cillan and Urchel just kept staring. They had all thought Tarbor slightly mad for saying he had heard a voice from a rock, and now they were looking at a tree that Speedwell had spoken of as if it were a man!

Queen Elina was flabbergasted, but why should she be surprised after what she had just witnessed? "But a tree? The Ancient One is a tree?" was all she could say, whereas Piper and Tintwist were overwhelmed with joy at finally seeing the heart of the forest, grinning all over their faces.

Tomin smiled; it had been so long since he last felt the inner warmth of the Ancient One greeting him. He could not wait until he was sitting in his presence after all this time.

Little Prince Martyn was quiet after his laughter with the tree roots in Queen Elina's arms. She looked at his little face looking up at the Ancient One. "He feels the Ancient One calling him," said Speedwell, seeing the concentration on his face.

The party rowed across the lake with their mixed feelings of quiet reverence and disbelief, making for the island. Only when they drew closer could they see that the island had been entirely made up from the Ancient One's giant roots.

Between and over the roots, greenery of every description seemed to be enjoying the roots' company. Shrubs popped up everywhere, plants thrived and moss covered the tangled roots, bathing in the constant mist of water that threw itself from the waterfalls over the island.

Leaving their adventure of the Elfore sailing boat behind them, grounded on the rocky shore that enveloped the island, the party followed Speedwell behind and through the giant tangled roots where to their surprise steps led the way up through the giant roots, to begin their climb up the Old Ogrin Ridge.

They began climbing, looking up as they did so to see that they had been hewn out of the rock face in a zig-zag pattern before them, stopping short of the Ancient One's roots on one side and the force of the Linninhorne Waterfall on the other, whose name they found out from Speedwell as other names on their long trudge upwards.

A platform appeared now and again as the steps turned, to give the party a well-earned rest. "They knew where we would need these," breathed in Tarbor, making the mistake of looking back down the sheer face on one of them, to feel his legs start to wobble.

"Elfore thinking," said Speedwell, smiling.

Tarbor took a step back and looked out to the sides. The roots of the Ancient One met his eyes to his right, as one it seemed with the ridge face, knotted over each other in a brown and grey mass.

Past the tangle of roots and the Winterbourne Waterfall that

Speedwell had pointed out, Tarbor could just make out a river that ran along the bottom of the ridge to enter the vast Lake of Tears.

"That is the Ogrin River. We could not see it when we entered the lake. It makes its way from the Windward Pass and then it disappears from the lake on its way to Thunder Gorge," informed Speedwell, "and that is the Linninhorne Waterfall," added Speedwell, before Tarbor could ask.

Piper looked at Tintwist when Speedwell spoke of the Windward Pass, so near the home they knew they would never see again.

Onwards they climbed until at last they reached the top of the ridge, emerging onto a semi-circle shape to be met by the smiling face of Ringwold.

Everyone had thought, except of course Piper and Tintwist, that Tomin was Speedwell's double, but they realised they were wrong when they saw the grey figure of Ringwold. "Well, he is Speedwell's brother," pointed out Tintwist.

"It is good to see you safe, Speedwell. I see you have returned with one whose spirit the Ancient One spoke of," said Ringwold, eyeing Prince Martyn.

"He is one of the spirits, Ringwold, without doubt, but Helistra has his sister," said Speedwell, in both sorrow and warning.

"That is not good. She will use her against us, if she has not already—!"

"This is his mother, Queen Elina," cut in Speedwell quickly, hoping Queen Elina had not heard his brother.

She had not; her attention had been taken by the Ancient One. She was looking up at the enormity of the Ancient One's giant trunk, piercing the sky before her.

"You are gifted indeed," bowed Ringwold, bringing Queen Elina's attention back and wondering what he was on about.

"May I?" asked Ringwold, the same as Speedwell, then making it obvious to Queen Elina what he was on about as he held his arms out to receive Prince Martyn.

She nodded, watching as Ringwold held Prince Martyn in one arm whilst touching symbols on his rune staff that rested against a mound behind them.

He closed his eyes and laid his hand on Prince Martyn's small brow, for her to see a smile light up his face to light up hers as Ringwold was touched in welcome by Prince Martyn's spirit.

Opening his eyes, Ringwold handed the little Prince back to Queen Elina, confirming to her what Speedwell had felt. "We have all been blessed by the presence of your son." He smiled with at last some hope in his heart as he looked at Speedwell and nodded to him.

Tarbor was watching Queen Elina tickle Prince Martyn under the chin as she went to gaze once more at the Ancient One, when he realised Ringwold was standing in front of him, looking at his shield. "So you must be the King wielder," greeted Ringwold.

"He is King Ashwell of Waunarle, or as he wishes to be called, Tarbor," introduced Speedwell.

Tarbor bowed. "It is my honour to meet you, Forestall."

"And it is mine to meet you. I fear there is much for you to do before you can rule your Kingdom that has been denied you," sympathised Ringwold, "but I am glad you are here with us, and with a defender," he acknowledged.

"And I hope I will be up to the task that is expected of me," replied Tarbor, for Ringwold not to be capable of responding as Piper and Tintwist suddenly hurled themselves at him, grinning, not able to wait anymore to greet him.

"You two!" He grinned back, hugging them. "No doubt I will hear all about your exploits," said Ringwold, smiling, glad to see them both safe.

"We have plenty to tell you, but have the others made it here, Forestall?" asked Piper straight away.

"Most have, Piper. They are living in the old Elfore settlement in the sight of the Kavenmist Mountains," answered Ringwold, with a hint of sadness in his voice.

"Most?" queried Tintwist.

"Not all made it, Tintwist. Ludbright was here with tales of beasts that had plagued him in the Plateau Forest," informed Ringwold, to the distress of Piper and Tintwist.

"Fleck, is he here? Did he warn the Elfore in time?" suddenly thought Speedwell, with so much on his mind he had nearly forgotten.

"He is here, Speedwell. He informed King Vedland. I will talk of it later, after you have spoken to the Ancient One. I know he will want to talk to you," answered Ringwold, keeping what he knew quiet for now.

Speedwell nodded, glad that Fleck had made it but worried that his brother was holding something back from him as he turned to Cantell, Kelmar, Cillan and Urchel, who had been waiting patiently to be introduced to Ringwold.

One by one, they stepped forward to be greeted by the firm hand of Ringwold on their forearm, to their surprise, in the handshake of a warrior. "It is good to see men from Northernland again. It has been too long. We will have to talk later," he promised.

"Cantell and Kelmar are who we have to thank for rescuing Prince Martyn from the clutches of Helistra," pointed out Speedwell after they had stepped forward.

"We are forever in your debt," thanked Ringwold.

"As I will always be," said Queen Elina with a smile, reappearing, making them both feel slightly embarrassed. After all, thought Cantell, they were only doing their duty to their King and Queen.

One person was left standing there smiling all along as he listened to the voice he had not heard in such a long time. Ringwold turned and looked at the smiling figure of Tomin, standing there with a broad grin on his face.

"Tomin!" cried Ringwold, and he embraced Tomin in joy. Laughter that had long since left the Ancient One's domain resounded once more as Tomin returned Ringwold's embrace.

"Grand-uncle Ringwold, it is good to be here once more in your presence," said Tomin, laughing, knowing how Ringwold hated him calling him that.

"After all this time, you tease me still. You are as bad as Tintwist. How I have missed you," said Ringwold, laughing.

"And I have missed you, Grand-uncle."

Speedwell smiled at the two of them reunited in laughter as Ringwold came over to him with Tomin.

"Before you go to sit with the Ancient One, Speedwell, and you, Tomin, you had better come with me to see what the barrier holds at bay," said Ringwold, with a sudden seriousness in his voice and manner that told them to be prepared for the worst.

Quietly, Ringwold led the way, with everyone following. Out of the dipped semi-circle, they walked to the constant noise from the waterfalls around the vast mound of the Ancient One, to stand upon it to look out over the Plateau Forest.

Standing there under the protective shadow of the Ancient One, Speedwell looked out in total dismay at the deadly shadow that had spread itself over the Plateau Forest and taken it in its deathly embrace.

He had spoken of it from his dreams and felt it through his presence, warned everyone, but now coming face to face with the reality of what his daughter had done, Speedwell felt all the dread of the forests wash over him as he looked out at the full horror of it all.

The putrefying bodies of the poisoned animals that had thrown themselves at the barrier caught Speedwell's attention first, rotting as they were in an arc around the Ancient One's roots.

"We had to re-enforce the weave around the Ancient One's roots for fear of the poisonous mist and those rotting animals soaking their poison into the earth," explained Ringwold, making Speedwell look up at the mist beyond the roots.

It hovered menacingly above the ground with what looked like tentacles protruding from it. Speedwell screwed up his eyes; what were they on top of the tentacles, waving through the air?

Speedwell soon saw they were some kind of giant pods. Some were seen to be flying through the air attaching themselves to the trees, opening out to shoot poisonous spores everywhere.

Most, though, were opening as soon as they came out of the deadly mist, shooting their poisonous spores straight at the invisible barrier.

For a moment, it looked as if they had attached themselves to the barrier, but then they were repelled, to drop onto the rotting bodies all dry and shrivelled, to wither away. "They never stop," commented Ringwold.

They were not the only things that had come out of the deadly mist. Creeping vines had wound themselves around every tree, oozing out green poisonous slime to soak into the bark of the trees whilst they slowly strangled the trees in their poisonous grip, like a snake wrapped around its prey, helping the spores that had already penetrated the trees to bring death and decay.

Speedwell looked over at the Winterbourne and Linninhorne Rivers, to see just the same was happening.

Then he saw between all the destruction going on, more animals that had become malformed beasts, standing there as if in defiance, watching them.

Speedwell nearly cried out as in amongst them he caught sight of ragged tunics hanging upon the hideous bodies of what were once Elfore.

Ringwold saw his brother catch sight of them. He had no choice now but to tell him the sad news.

"King Vedland did not heed Fleck's warning of the impending poison until it was too late. It reached the Lake of Tranquillity whilst he was still there. Many have not made it here," he explained sadly, to Speedwell's dismay.

"What of King Vedland?" asked Speedwell.

Ringwold shook his head.

Tomin's head had dropped; his laughter had turned to tears. Though blind, he was not blind to the sheer horror his mother had wrought upon the forest, as he smelt the lingering smell of death. *How could she?* he cried inside.

Queen Elina was aghast, wishing she had never questioned anything Speedwell had said, no matter how hard to believe! Though she questioned now, as she witnessed such evil, how it could be defeated, even if her son was the chosen one of hope.

Cantell, Kelmar, Cillan and Urchel could only stare in disbelief at what they were all looking at. "To think I was ready to put an end to you, Tarbor, for your mad ramblings, but this! This is insane!" said Kelmar eventually, in a hoarse whisper.

It had struck Tarbor before how a mother could be so as to kill her husband for the jealousy she felt for her own son, but he agreed with Kelmar. This was insanity, beyond anything any of them could have ever comprehended.

Piper and Tintwist broke down in floods of tears when they also saw the hideous forms of the Elfore just standing there. What evil was this that Queen Helistra could manifest so on their beloved forest?

"I will go and talk to the Ancient One quickly. There is work for me to do," said Speedwell through the stunned silence that followed, and he turned his face away from the forest of death to go inside the refuge of the Ancient One.

Normally, Speedwell found comfort in the solitude of the Ancient One, but not now after what he had just seen as the soft whispering of the Ancient One entered his mind.

I am glad the stars and spirits have watched over you, Speedwell.

The same cannot be said for you, Ancient One. The trees of the Plateau Forest are all but lost, and Speedwell sighed deeply, ashamed of the evil his daughter had brought upon the Ancient One.

Helistra's poison has lain all before it. I felt the pain from every leaf from every tree in the Plateau Forest, but our resolve must be strong and our weave of the barrier tight in this time of darkness.

Let us talk of the hope you have brought. The essence was right. His spirit is strong. I have felt it since you entered the Great Forest.

It is strong, but Helistra has his sister, though I have felt nothing of her entering the child's soul.

You will not when she enters the crystal chamber. It hides any disturbance in the air from us. The broken rune staff of Grimstone would have sensed this when the power of the crystal chamber passed through it.

Speedwell cursed himself; he should have remembered what the crystal chamber could do.

She will use her against us, Ancient One, warned Speedwell.

That may be so, we can only wait and see, but her brother is the key, the one I have long waited for.

Speedwell heard something in the whispery tones of the Ancient One to make him sit up. *But I thought the key was Tomin, Ancient One, to make the broken rune staff whole again and end all this?*

I have a confession to tell you, Speedwell. I have lied to you. Though Speedwell had felt something was amiss, he still thought he was hearing things; the Ancient One lying?

Lied about what, Ancient One?

When I said Tomin was the only one that could retrieve the broken piece of rune staff from the solid form of Grimstone's body, because he was his son, I lied, Speedwell. He never could. Helistra thought this to be true, so I let her carry on thinking it. I have used him as a deception to keep Helistra off the scent, so hiding what I truly felt about the coming of a spirit in the form of this child.

I had thought that when she broke Grimstone's rune staff and the white light took her, that it had made Grimstone's rune staff powerless. Therefore, she would not return knowing this, if in fact she had survived at all.

As the years passed by and there was nothing, I was beginning to think that breaking Grimstone's rune staff had been the ending of her, but how wrong was I!

To suddenly appear and kill Gentian under Kavenmist, having nurtured Grimstone's broken rune staff for all those years, to have turned it into a weapon of evil to do her bidding… the Ancient One paused with a sigh.

Gentian's death will always be upon my branches, bringing about as it did the rift between man and Elfore.

A moment of silence fell in which Speedwell could feel the sense of blame the Ancient One had put upon his being.

We both know she scattered Gentian's work then disappeared again, but gone with the thought that if she returned again she would have to deal with Tomin, her own son, if she was to keep Grimstone's broken rune staff in the ways of evil.

A risk I wished I had never taken, thinking that something of her maternal spirit was left inside her and by making her think she would have to kill him to achieve this, she would not carry on her evil.

Jealousy of her son is one thing, but killing him is quite another, so I thought, but my belief that there was still some goodness left inside her forgot that evil knows no boundaries, and now she has bonded with the crystal chamber!

Speedwell felt another sigh from the Ancient One. *You were not to know, Ancient One. None of us foresaw the evil that would come out of her jealousy, but the spirit is here now, as you knew it would be,* prompted Speedwell.

I felt it long ago, Speedwell, from the deepest depths of my roots to the edges of my leaves that touch the sky that a spirit was forming and would be born of man. When the essence whispered to me that there were two, my hopes soared as I felt them through her. Both are strong, but his is the stronger, for some of his spirit has spilt over into his sister, revealed the Ancient One.

Speedwell had never known of a spirit having split before, but he could feel that though the Ancient One was full of regret over Tomin, his own spirit had risen, because of the child's presence.

Now we must prepare and keep the darkness at bay whilst the child grows, whispered the Ancient One with purpose.

How long will we have for him to do so, though? questioned Speedwell.

Only as long as it takes for her to harness enough power from the crystal chamber, but I do not know how long that will be. It will be a slow process. I felt her break your spell of containment recklessly and she has used much to infest the Plateau Forest, but we can be sure that when she has enough she will come, and we must be ready, whenever it is.

She will be happy at this time in the knowledge that we will be constantly using our power to keep her evil at bay whilst hers grows.

The King wielder I trust has her no longer in his mind, able to protect the child whilst he learns the ways and we hold the barrier in place. It may seem futile now, but the less she feels, the better. He is a good man, Ancient One. His path has been mixed, but his heart and mind are as one now.

That is good. I felt Gentian's rune staff with you. You have brought it as I wished.

Yes, it is here, Ancient One.

I will tell Tomin to learn the ways of Gentian's rune staff. It will gladly help him on the path to being a Forestall. Fire will be a welcome element in the barrier joining my weave of earth, Ringwold's weave of air and yours, Speedwell, of water.

All will be needed, Ancient One, for what we are up against out there.

It is time then, Speedwell. Our work is just beginning. Tell the King wielder his duties and ask Tomin to come to me. I must explain to him my actions and ask him for his forgiveness. Then let us hope the stars and spirits are watching over us all for what lies ahead.

I will, Ancient One. Would you like the child to be brought to you?

There is no need. I have already welcomed his spirit through the fine roots of the Bridge of Seasons. Our bond is in place.

And with the Ancient One's purpose in mind, Speedwell left his domain, knowing their path ahead was going to be long and hard. He only hoped that it would not end with the forests lost forever.

PART II

THE ANCIENTS

CHAPTER XXXVIII

Twelve summers passed by in all of Northernland. Summers that increasingly held nothing but grey clouds and rain for all the Kingdoms, with the sun barely shining through to warm the land to bring on the crops that had been sown. Winters too were prolonging their stay to add to the misery of the land, though life itself throughout the Kingdoms was carrying on as normal, as if nothing was happening or had happened.

Queen Helistra had hardly been seen, ruling Cardronia from Stormhaven as she was.

Waunarle had set up a governing body, as a rightful heir to the throne had not been found. A few had objected at first, but those voices had been quietened by Queen Helistra. She had pointed out quite reasonably that there was nothing else they could do until such time as a rightful heir could be found. That although it was not what they wanted, at least the deaths of the royal family had been avenged, tenfold, laughingly pointing out that they were not the only ones without a royal family to rule them!

Tiggannians had found it hard to rebuild. Having been subjected to endless raids upon their lives, losses had been high, with homes destroyed and loved ones gone, only finding some kind of peace these last few years as the Cardronians seemed to have grown tired of it all.

Talk of King Taliskar and of all those that had disappeared at Stormhaven had long gone. Happy it seemed to let it pass by with time and, like the mountain door, remain a mystery.

Life at Stormhaven was now slow and decidedly boring for the garrison, except for Mrs Beeworthy, who seemed to be contented enough cooking, as she did for everyone in her place in the kitchen.

Neither Balintium nor Silion had had any confrontations with Cardronia, and borders that were tense before were more at ease than ever before.

Though King Stowlan had not forgotten Speedwell's words to him of keeping his eyes towards the forest, they were however becoming just words; it had been so long.

Talk of the so-called beasts of Marchend Valley had come and gone with the first winter snow; the ramblings of a madman who had met his end in the fire of the town meeting hall, it was rumoured, with a new meeting hall soon replacing the old burnt-down one.

A moonlight disappearance had seen Permellar back on her farm after her short pretence of being Queen Elina at Elishard Castle. With her daughter, Kayla, and Oneatha, she was at last living the life she had always wanted, which had been taken away from her.

Thoughts of Kelmar were never far away from her, even though he was. Often, she would think of him and Cantell out there in the Great Forest. A whispered prayer forever on her lips to the stars and trees to keep them safe, especially when she laid some flowers on her father's nearby grave.

So as time had passed by, in one way or another, it had brought a stillness upon the Kingdoms. All was quiet, except in one person's mind: Queen Helistra's. Her patience in waiting for the barrier to become weaker had long departed and she wished for the demise of the Great Forest, now!

"We have power enough to tear it apart!" ranted Queen Helistra to no one as she sat on the mountain throne twiddling with the broken rune staff set in the smooth rock arm.

"We have waited long enough! The spores have ceaselessly penetrated the barrier to begin affecting it, it is time!"

Humming answered her irritable mood. "No, there has been no sign of one when we have looked, and I know he will not have had the time to learn the ways, even if he had. We have discussed this many times. I do not want to look the fool again, that is all. Do not forget Tarbor can hide it from us if there is one," she replied to more humming.

"We will look, but you have hummed to me of the ever-weakening strength of their rune staffs when they reinforce the barrier, whilst we sit here at our most powerful. Now is the time. They will have no answer, I feel it. We must attack the barrier and finally rid ourselves of the Ancient One and the infernal forest."

The broken rune staff had been cautious, but it agreed with Queen Helistra. It had gathered enough power that it felt was needed to destroy the barrier, and a weakness had begun to show itself. A push was all that was needed. One last look it had asked for, to make double sure.

Queen Helistra twisted the broken rune staff to move the mountain throne. Gliding down the steps in the soft glow of light, she came into the crystal chamber, to be greeted by the shimmering crystals.

Sitting by the pool of death, as she now called it, with a smile, she dipped the broken rune staff into its silky red surface and closed her eyes.

As she touched symbols upon its exposed length, Queen Helistra's presence joined that of the broken rune staff in a spell of protection to the distant barrier on the Old Ogrin Ridge, a journey too far for her before, but not now.

Through the twists and turns of the underground stream her presence moved, forever through the malevolent poison of her spell, until she came to the once sister pool of life in the blackness that was now the Plateau Forest.

Her presence felt some satisfaction as it passed through the destruction of the Plateau Forest. Looking up, she saw dark skies hovering threateningly above over the once-green canopy of trees. Trees that now lay decayed everywhere, fallen prey to the spores and the grip of death from the clinging vines. No deadly mist showed itself here anymore, only a forest floor deep in the slime of rotted vegetation.

As her presence journeyed through the rotting forest, she passed malformed animals eating off the forest floor, nuzzling through the decayed trees for their food as rain began to fall, sending the putrid smell of the forest's decay up into the air.

Queen Helistra had decided to go to one of the furthest ends of the barrier to see if it was weaker there, and then make her way towards the Ancient One.

Now there before her was where the Old Ogrin Ridge met the Greater Hardenal Mountains that loomed above her presence.

Though the barrier was invisible to most eyes, it was not to the broken rune staff and Queen Helistra as their presence approached its form of line after line of white light knitted together in a continuous weave.

It soared skywards and was lost into the mountainside deep in its protection as mist circled all around the barrier, with pods rising from it to open out and shoot their poisonous spores at the barrier.

Queen Helistra watched the spores bombard the barrier to instantly attach themselves, injecting some of their deadly venom into the barrier before being spat out, to drop shrivelled-up and disappear into the mist.

Watching still, she saw a battle emerge between the injected poison and the barrier. She could see the barrier start to change colour to a pale yellow as the poison ate away at the barrier before finally being repulsed. It was enough; the poison was having a marked effect.

Turning, she made her way along the length of the barrier to its centre, the Ancient One, noting as she did so how her poison was having the same effect all the way along the barrier; there was no one point.

Once there, she kept her distance from the Ancient One so as not to be detected. She smiled to see the Ancient One battling to rid its protective weave of the poisonous spores as pod after pod exploded with spores at the Ancient One's roots.

She then grimaced as suddenly Speedwell appeared in front of the Ancient One. She knew immediately what he was going to do: restrengthen the barrier.

She watched as he knelt down, holding his rune staff. Words were coming from his mouth, which she knew was a chant of invocation. Suddenly he threw out his arms and the barrier crackled as Speedwell's spell knitted it together in white energy.

A scowl followed by a smile crossed her presence when she saw the draining effect performing the spell had on Speedwell. As he looked to be getting back up, he tottered sideways just for a moment. The strain of continuously replenishing the barrier was leaving its mark!

Suddenly she held her presence stock-still as Speedwell looked out right in her direction. He was screwing up his eyes to look, as if he had sensed something, and then he was turning, disappearing behind the Ancient One.

Queen Helistra let her presence stay a while longer as she searched the Ancient One before withdrawing. Her mind returned to her body in the crystal chamber and she nodded in anticipation.

"It all grows weaker. I saw nothing that could stop us. We will drive a wedge at its heart and put an end to it all," said Queen Helistra with a smile, seeing the Ancient One's ending in sight at last.

She left the crystal chamber in confident mood as humming entered her mind. "She will be my shield as you have said, and we will see how she reacts to know of her future. If there is anything that can return within her after all this time then it will show when we destroy the barrier. If she does not enhance its destruction then she will perish along with it."

Queen Helistra strode through the great hall to hear more humming. "You do persist. I know we have not, but I remain cautious of her. If she shows no sign and I am able to trust her then yes, we will show her the crystal chamber to learn our ways. We shall see," she answered, for the humming to cease.

Princess Amber sauntered along the inner ring wall battlements, gazing out at the sea with eyes to match its colour. Her red hair, once long until Queen Helistra had it cut short, stood on end from the sea breeze.

She often wandered around on her own. After all, there were no other children there for her to play with. Exploring had been fun once upon a time, but there were only so many times you could run around the stronghold.

The tunnels she knew were behind the ceremonial room had been blocked off as being far too dangerous for her to go into. That only left the secret passageway and the mountain doorway, but they had long since failed to be of any interest to her.

The place she really wanted to see was where her mother had gone to again. She had whispered its name once to her when she was very young and she had remembered it ever since. The crystal chamber, she had whispered, only for the eyes of Kings and Queens. *Well, one day I will be,* she thought, *I am a Princess now.*

Her eyes caught sight of a guard walking between the two battlements up towards Middle Gate, and her mischievous inner self smiled at an opportunity to be naughty. Picking up a piece of fallen stone, she promptly threw it at the guard, hitting his helmet with a clang, and ducked out of sight, giggling.

The guard looked up, knowing full well who it was, but he dare not shout anything for fear of being reported to Queen Helistra, though someone did shout; it was Queen Helistra! He carried on walking through Middle Gate and made for the soldiers' quarters.

"Amber! Are you up there, child?" Amber stood up and looked over the battlements.

"I am here, Mother. What is it?"

"Ready yourself, child, we are going on a journey." Amber could not believe her ears, a journey! She could not contain her excitement. She had only been allowed outside the walls of Stormhaven with a guard, and now they were suddenly going on a journey! She ran as fast as her legs could carry her to the waiting Queen Helistra.

"Where, Mother, where?" she gasped excitedly.

"You will see, child. It will be a journey like no other, one of destiny."

Amber looked at her mother in complete fascination. It sounded so exciting and mysterious. *One of destiny,* she thought, *what sort of journey could that be?* she wondered.

CHAPTER XXXIX

"Do not let your guard down, Martyn!" shouted Kelmar, laughing with Tarbor at Tintwist giving Prince Martyn sword lessons. That was how Martyn liked to be known, instead of Prince Martyn. It made him feel part of them more. Tintwist stopped and looked at them both.

"If you do not mind, I am trying to teach Martyn the ways of the Manelf. Your interruptions are not helping," said Tintwist, smiling at their laughter. Martyn joined in the laughter of his uncles, who had taught him too, as had all of his uncles; he had so many!

"Let us sit for a while, Uncle Tintwist. The day is nearly done." Martyn smiled and slumped gratefully to the ground next to Kelmar and Tarbor, for Tintwist to sheathe his sword in joining him.

"The skies look peculiar. I do not like the feeling I am getting seeing them like that," remarked Martyn as he lay there, looking up.

Kelmar, Tarbor and Tintwist looked up with him to see some strange streaks of grey that had shot through the white clouds passing overhead, unlike anything they had ever seen before.

"The barrier strains under her evil," stated Martyn as he seemed to draw into himself and feel the weight of its intensity pushing against it. Tarbor looked at Martyn, knowing he was feeling the struggle the barrier was going through.

Ever since a young age, he had shown he was the future of the forest with his feel for its well-being, confirming the belief the Ancient One had felt. Not once had he ever questioned why he was who he was; he had accepted it without question.

Tarbor had watched him in the presence of animals that would come up to him unafraid, letting him stroke them, just as they did for Speedwell.

His vision of what lay ahead of them when journeying through the forest had left Tarbor in wonder at times, and at other times it was unnerving. He would touch a tree and close his eyes saying, "The Ancient

One has just summoned Great-uncle Ringwold," as he referred to the Forestalls, to let go with a smile, as if it was the most natural thing in the forest for him to do.

For one so young, he seemed to pick things up naturally. A tall, thin lad with a shock of his mother's red hair, he looked ungainly, but that was far from the truth. His sword mastery alone at such a young age was astonishing to Tarbor. Picking up all their different styles of swordplay with a fluency he had not seen before.

Piper and Tislea had shown him the art of archery of their respective kind. He did not look to have the strength to pull the bow string, but he had taken to it like a duck takes to water.

Ah, water, thought Tarbor. That was one thing Martyn was wary of, but he knew why when Kelmar and Cantell recounted their story of when they had all escaped through the Kavenmist Mountains.

Stories were something that Martyn could listen to all day, and frequently did, though in the main they revolved around the cruelty of one person: Queen Helistra.

He seemed to live them as they were told, as if he was feeling it all, especially when his mother had spoken of her escape, having to leave behind the sister he had never seen. Tears would well up in his eyes.

Speaking of his mother, that was who was shouting him now, to bring Tarbor's wandering mind back. "Martyn!" shouted Queen Elina.

"Yes, Mother, I am here." A smiling Martyn jumped up to see her standing there.

"Come, food is on the table for all you fighters," she announced, and Martyn ran to her side and hugged her.

Though she smiled and hugged him back, Tarbor knew her heart still hurt for her daughter, Amber. Tarbor's feelings for her had not gone away and they had become firm friends, but that is where he had left it, knowing his place.

As they walked back through the settlement they now called home, Tarbor looked around him as he always did. How different to castle life it all was, with trees soaring up to the sky and in amongst them homes of all description resting there.

Under their majestic boughs, against their huge trunks, up above in their branches, Elfore and Manelf alike living together for the first time since their rift. Nestling as the settlement did between the towering peaks of the Kavenmist Mountains and the affectionately named valley they called the tongue in the cheek.

Only half of the Elfore had survived that fateful day to make it there, and they could only wonder how long their time was to be in the Great Forest. As for the Manelf, they would always feel the loss of their friends, especially Ludbright.

Queen Elina led the way in the ever-dwindling light to a wooden house built under one of the giant trees' boughs. Though those Elfore who lived high in the trees had survived better than those on the ground that day, no one was going to get her to live up there!

All sat around a wooden table with benches either side, once inside the house. Candles were lit, lighting up the food that lay upon the table for everyone to duly tuck in, but no one did until Queen Elina sat down, smiling at their politeness towards her.

"We are all equal here, there is no need," she said with a smile, "now eat!" The noise of enjoying the food soon filled the air.

"When will they be back from foraging?" asked Martyn, throwing some berries in his mouth as he referred to Fleck, Tiska, Cillan and Urchel, who had all gone to forage for food in the forest the day before.

"When Fleck decides it is time to do so," replied Tislea in a rather disparaging tone.

"You do not like him being with your mother, do you, Tislea?" said Cantell, coming straight to the point.

"No, it is not that. He is a good Elfore, but he is so much older than my mother," she answered, making everyone smile.

"But you all live for years!" said Tintwist laughingly, making Tislea feel embarrassed as everyone laughed with him.

"Perhaps by tomorrow or the next day, I would have thought," said Piper eventually with a smile.

"Take no notice, Tislea. Men and men elves do not understand women's feelings," sympathised Queen Elina.

"Well, I hope they come back soon. I did not like the look of those clouds and the feeling I felt," worried Martyn.

"What have you sensed then, Martyn?" asked Tarbor. Martyn looked at Tarbor before he answered. Out of all of his uncles, he always seemed to be the most concerned about his inner feelings, not that he was surprised by the stories he had told him.

"The barrier grows heavier to hold in place, Uncle Tarbor. The weight of the poison that constantly attacks, it is telling on the Ancient One and my great-uncles. Those grey streaks in the clouds are not a good sign," he answered.

"No, they are not!" came a voice from the doorway, and everyone turned around to see Speedwell standing there.

"Great-uncle Speedwell!" Martyn was up on his feet and hugging Speedwell before anyone could speak.

"Martyn, I swear you grow taller each time I see you," said Speedwell with a smile, rubbing Martyn's hair.

"What brings you here, Speedwell? We do not usually see you for another week at least," asked Tarbor, getting an uncomfortable feeling in his stomach from what Martyn had just said, to suddenly see him there.

Speedwell sat down for them all to see the seriousness of what he had to say to them by the look on his face. "I have travelled here in earnest," began Speedwell, "the Ancient One has sensed Helistra's presence spying upon us and fears she is about to strike," he revealed to everyone's dismay. They knew the time would come but had hoped it would not be so soon, as did Speedwell.

"It has become too strenuous for us to hold the barrier," he informed them, to echo Martyn's feelings. "The Ancient One feels she has sensed this and will make a move, sooner rather than later," he warned them.

"What of Great-uncle Tomin? Is he not sufficiently as one still with Gentian's rune staff, so as to blend more of the barrier with fire for a tighter weave?" asked Martyn.

Queen Elina looked at Martyn, never ceasing to be amazed that she had borne such a son with the thought that always came into her mind: *If he is like this, then what of his sister, my little Amber?* Wondering what she might have been if that Helistra had not got hold of her.

None of what Martyn was capable of thinking came as any surprise to Speedwell as he answered him. "He is as one with Gentian's rune staff, young Martyn, but more time is needed for him to master the element to be able to fully replenish all the barrier, time the Ancient One feels we do not have anymore. His time in hiding has told on his strength to perform such spells," answered Speedwell.

"With this threat hanging over our heads, the Ancient One has sent me here to bring you to him to claim what has been waiting for you within his domain," he added, for Martyn to beam all over his face and jump up in his excitement.

"A rune staff of my own!" he shouted.

"A staff, Martyn, that will become your rune staff once the ceremony of the runes has been performed upon it," pointed out Speedwell.

"When you say waiting for him in the Ancient One's domain, in what way do you mean?" instantly worried Queen Elina.

"Unbeknown to me at first, the Ancient One has been growing a staff amongst his branches for many years, long before Martyn was born, waiting in his knowledge that a chosen one was to be born of man. His deception with Tomin disguising the fact that there was one amongst his many branches," answered Speedwell, looking at Martyn as he spoke, to receive a big smile.

"In other words, he has to climb up that big tree!" queried Queen Elina.

"Er, yes," confirmed Speedwell.

"Do not worry, Mother, I love climbing trees," said Martyn, with a laugh, hugging her.

"Will the barrier hold her back if she attacks, if, as you say, she has sensed the strain it is under?" questioned Cantell.

"It will hold. We will be waiting with the Ancient One if she tries," replied Speedwell, sounding assured.

"But what if Queen Helistra breaks down the barrier in any way and her evil comes through? What will we do? And what of Martyn if it happens? How will he learn the ways of a rune staff to help stop her, when Tomin has not fully mastered Gentian's after all this time?" put a worried Tarbor.

"If that happens then you must all leave with Martyn," replied Speedwell.

"For where, though? It will only be a matter of time before her evil reaches Northernland," spoke Tarbor again.

"We have thought on this and whether my daughter has the power to break through or not, she will be here facing us, not at Stormhaven in the crystal chamber. If I hold her here with the Ancient One long enough, you, Ringwold and Tomin can travel to Stormhaven to return the pool of life back to clarity. Then the pool's essence can return and breathe life back into the forests. It will give us the time we need," answered Speedwell, making it all sound so simple, but not to Tarbor.

"And the Ancient One agrees?" he asked further.

"He does, whilst we engage her she will be using her gained power. She will not be able to replenish it, because you will be there ridding the crystal chamber of her evil. It will be a start," explained Speedwell to everyone's quiet, uncertain thoughts. There were too many ifs and buts.

"I only know we will be ready for her if she attacks the barrier, and Martyn will have a rune staff," said Speedwell, getting up, curtailing any more thoughts or questions.

"Come, Martyn, first you must secure your staff before anything else," he said with a smile.

"I will come with you," said Queen Elina immediately.

"No, Queen Elina, it is best that you stay here. Martyn must do this on his own without any motherly distractions," countered Speedwell, to receive a screwed-up face, but she knew this time would come and instead of demanding as she had in the past, she hugged her son tightly.

"Be safe, Martyn. The trees and stars, I know, will watch over you," she cried.

"I will, Mother. I will be back before you know it. My time has come to help the forests, it is my destiny," he answered, hugging her back.

"I know it is, but you are still my little boy," she cried further.

"I will be by his side, Queen Elina. My time to protect Martyn as a King wielder has arrived, it seems," said Tarbor, to a smile from Martyn.

"Well, he will not be going anywhere without me," said Cantell, also standing by Martyn's side. "Tarbor is not the only protector," he added, looking at Speedwell, to receive a nod of acknowledgement of his duty towards his Prince and a hug from Martyn.

"I cannot ask for more. I know now he will be in safe hands until his return." She smiled at them both, wiping away a tear.

"I will be here, my lady, to watch over you," said Kelmar with a smile, for her to hold his arm.

Speedwell saw Piper and Tintwist looking at him. "Yes, very well, you are my protectors," he conceded, making them grin.

"I will go and find my mother to tell her what is happening," said Tislea, for all to be settled.

"Good, then let us be on our way," said Speedwell, with a disguised worry in his heart. He had spoken assuredly in front of them all that they could defend the barrier against his daughter, but in truth he did not know.

CHAPTER XL

Martyn breathed in the rich earthy smell of the Ancient One. He had been in his domain before but had kept his times few and far between, not wanting to disturb the Ancient One, knowing he needed all of his being focused on the barrier. Not that the sight of the putrid Plateau Forest had helped Martyn when he had come.

The soft, whispery tones of the Ancient One entered his mind and he smiled at his calming presence.

The time has come sooner than I wished, young Martyn, for you to find your staff. Are you ready to climb my branches?

I am ready, Ancient One, but how will I know which branch to choose to become my staff? You have so many.

You will know, though there are many upon my boughs, there is only one that will call out and become as one with you.

Will it rest high in your branches?

You are full of questions to which you already know the answers in your soul, young Martyn. When you find the one, bring it to me for the ceremony of the runes. Then you can enhance the ways that have always been within you.

Martyn felt his heart soar, the ceremony of the runes when his staff would become what it was meant to be: a rune staff!

Will I be powerful enough to help cure the ill that has been done, Ancient One? A silence followed before Martyn heard the Ancient One whisper a sombre warning in his mind.

In time, young Martyn, and with our help, but that is what has always been against us. The spirit that holds true within you is strong in its bonding with the forest. It will allow you to learn quickly, but Helistra has the help of the crystal chamber. Her bonding with its power as yet is unknown to us. We will hold her at bay for as long as we have strength in our limbs for you to evolve with your staff.

I will not let you down, Ancient One.

The Ancient One felt Martyn's heart and soul speak within his words. *I know you will not. Now go, find your staff!*

Martyn left the Ancient One's domain to stand next to Speedwell and Ringwold, who were looking out at the horror of what was left of the Plateau Forest, watching for any sign of Queen Helistra.

"Do you think she is out there?" asked Martyn as he grimaced at the devastation before him.

"I do not feel anything, but we must be on our guard from now on," answered Speedwell in warning.

"What are you doing here anyway? Is there not something you should be finding?" said Speedwell, looking at Ringwold with a smile, for them both to receive a hug.

As he walked over the Ancient One's mound, Martyn was wished well by Tomin, Tarbor, Cantell, Piper and Tintwist in turn.

"There will be no need for you to see, Martyn. Your spirit will guide you," said Tomin as they hugged.

"I would come with you with a shield of protection, but I have been told that nothing must come between you and what you seek," said Tarbor, though he knew Martyn would be at home up in the Ancient One's branches.

Cantell looked up at the enormity of the Ancient One and blew out his cheeks. "Be careful, Martyn, be aware of your footing as you climb," he advised as he looked.

"You worry too much, Uncle. I will not be alone, the Ancient One will be with me." Martyn smiled back.

Looking out over the Great Forest to send him on his way, Martyn proceeded to a low-lying bough of the Ancient One, hanging close to the edge of the Linninhorne River.

Low it might have been, but to reach the bough, Martyn needed the helping hands of Piper and Tintwist to hoist him up onto the branch.

"I wish I was climbing with you," said Tintwist with a sigh as he let go of Martyn.

"When I have found my staff, I will ask the Ancient One." Martyn smiled, to see Tintwist grin.

"Do not forget about me," said Piper, with a smile.

"I never would, Aunty Piper," said Martyn with a grin, and he began making his way up the Ancient One's branches, for a snigger to be heard from Tintwist.

"We will climb the Ancient One together, Aunty," he quipped, knowing she could never get used to being called Aunty. To receive a stare from Piper he expected for Tintwist to snigger again.

A wave to them all later and Martyn had disappeared from their sight into the dense foliage.

Slowly, the sound of the Linninhorne River melted away from Martyn's hearing to be replaced by the soft, whispering tones of the Ancient One's leaves fluttering in the breeze.

Every time Martyn clung to a branch, he felt a whisper run through his body, telling him he was not alone. He stopped every now and again as a view of the Great Forest showed itself as a picture through the foliage.

Steadily, he pulled himself up through the mass of branches that met his grasp, finding he was getting closer to the Ancient One's trunk as the branches grew less thick for him to climb.

He looked up, only to see more and more branches awaiting him. Even though he was only young, his arms and legs were beginning to ache. What had started out for him as fun was beginning to get serious as he began to realise the task that he had been set.

Martyn lost all sense of time as he pulled himself up through another mass of branches. He suddenly found himself shrouded in what had to be a cloud, making him feel colder. He climbed a little bit quicker to get away from its clinging sensation, to come out into the sunlight, bursting through the Ancient One's branches.

A spread of branches presented themselves that Martyn could lie upon, and he gladly took the opportunity to lay across them for a rest.

As he rested, Martyn let his eyes wander over and through the Ancient One's branches. To his right, he saw the sun shining, with blue skies and white clouds, but as he kept looking, those streaks of dark cloud that he had seen before came into sight.

Turning to his left, he could see what was causing them as forbidding grey-black skies met his gaze, reflecting the lingering death that lay below them.

Martyn turned his gaze away to suddenly feel the breeze getting stronger as he lay there, bending the branches more so under its presence.

As he watched the branches beginning to sway around in the breeze, Martyn caught sight of two upright branches on a bough not far above him.

A sensation of realisation began to wash over him as he looked at one of the branches. Grasping the branches he was laying on, Martyn closed his eyes and began feeling a tingling in his fingers as he focused his mind upon the branch.

He let his spirit flow freely through the Ancient One and saw the trueness of the wood that the branch held within its bark, to immediately know it was the one that would become his staff! Martyn smiled a broad smile without opening his eyes; he had found it!

Martyn let his spirit dwell there a little bit longer; enjoying the feeling of strength he was getting from the very fibre of the branch's being.

As he lay there, feeling the calling of the branch, the rocking motion of the branches started to have an effect upon his tired limbs. Tiredness suddenly overtook him without him realising. Just a moment longer, he thought, then he would secure it.

Daylight was on its last rounds as Piper handed round a bowl of food to everyone. They were all sitting in the archway formed by the Ancient One's roots, feeling safe in their protection, except for Speedwell, who was keeping a wary eye over the putrid Plateau Forest.

"Do you think Martyn has found a staff?" asked Piper as she gave a bowl of food to Ringwold, reminding him of when he had had to do the same, smiling his answer, "No."

"I hope he will be all right in this fading light," worried Cantell as he sat there looking out at the ever-darkening branches of the Ancient One.

"It is a challenge he will see through, I have no doubt," answered Tomin. "I am the unfortunate one not to have climbed the limbs of the Ancient One. I would have sooner done so than receive Gentian's rune staff the way I did," he reflected.

His remarks made them all look at him, except for Ringwold, bringing home to them how young he must have been when he was hidden from Queen Helistra's eyes, knowing his blindness would not have stopped him.

Ringwold and Tarbor moved from under the Ancient One's roots to join Speedwell in the dwindling light.

"You should go and get yourself something to eat, brother. You must be hungry," said Ringwold as they joined Speedwell looking out at the darkening devastation.

When Speedwell did not answer him, Ringwold saw that Speedwell was not just looking but staring; something had got his attention.

"You see something, Speedwell?" he asked as he looked with him, to notice the mist was slowly withdrawing, feeling his body suddenly turn cold.

"She is out there, Ringwold," replied Speedwell, quietly confirming the immediate feeling Ringwold had. "Bring Tomin here, Tarbor," ordered Speedwell as he and Ringwold bent down on one knee with their rune staffs planted in front of them.

Tarbor hurried to tell Tomin and the others to be back with them all in an instant.

Though the sound of the Winterbourne and Linninhorne Rivers could be heard clearly, rushing headlong over the Old Ogrin Ridge, an eerie hush had descended over the company as they peered into the ever-decreasing light.

A bolt of lightning suddenly ripped through the sky, shuddering into the ground in front of them, lighting up the Ancient One's roots and beyond as it did so. It gave them only a glimpse of who was emerging out of a dip from in amongst the decaying forest, but it was enough.

Another strike of lightning lit the scene again before them, and they all saw Queen Helistra standing there motionless.

Gone was the crimson cloak she had always worn and in its place she had adorned herself in a cloak of pure black, the black Queen of death, thought Tarbor.

What worried Speedwell and Ringwold more was who the lightning had revealed standing in front of her: the unmistakable red-haired figure of Martyn's sister, Princess Amber.

"She uses her, Speedwell, as we knew she would, but I cannot tell if it is too late, if her spirit has been cursed!" cried out Ringwold.

"We must bond together in a spell of protection and blend it into the barrier around the Ancient One, then I will reach out to Princess Amber to see what has been done," ordered Speedwell as Tomin joined them, planting Gentian's rune staff in front of him.

"Tarbor, add your shield of protection to ours! You three get away from here and tell the others what is happening!" shouted Speedwell as another strike of lightning cracked across them all.

Cantell, Piper and Tintwist quickly retreated, but as they reached the semi-circle that led down to the rock steps, Cantell stopped.

"What are you doing, Cantell? Come, we must warn the others," urged Piper.

"You two go on, I must stay here," answered Cantell, to the shocked faces of Piper and Tintwist.

"You saw who was out there! It is no place for us!" cried Tintwist.

"I am the King's protector. My place is here by him, though he is up there somewhere," said Cantell, looking up at the huge boughs that hung over them.

"But he is still a Prince!" said Tintwist lamely, understanding Cantell's duty towards Martyn, but being afraid for him. Cantell smiled at Tintwist; they had formed a firm friendship since they had known each other.

"The Forestalls are here. They will watch over him and Tarbor," added Piper, but it was to no avail. Cantell shook his head.

"You both know my place is here. I will be safe enough under the Ancient One's roots. Now go, tell Queen Elina and the others what is happening," and without further talk they embraced each other, for Cantell to watch them both climb down the rock steps.

Taking refuge under the Ancient One's roots, Cantell drew his sword and swirled it through the air one or two times. *If the worst did happen,* he thought, *I will take a few of them with me.*

Sheathing his sword, Cantell felt his arm out of habit. Time had healed it well, albeit being slightly askew. Time and that potion Speedwell had given him. He grimaced as he thought of the taste of it in his mouth. He hoped that was all he would be grimacing at, and that Martyn would appear soon as he sat down to wait for him.

Tarbor wasted no time in throwing a protective shield across the Forestalls and himself, feeling it entwine with theirs. He knelt at their side, to hear them begin chanting words of invocation as they touched symbols upon their rune staffs.

He looked as lightning lit up the scene once more. There she was, just standing there, with the Princess in front of her, looking right at him.

Queen Helistra stood and smirked at the feeble-looking Forestalls, noting the presence of Tarbor with them.

All together! How excellent, she thought as humming entered her mind. *No, the boy child is not to be seen, but after all, what use is he? He has no rune staff*, and she laughed coldly inside.

And when this day is done, he never will! All will perish and without them, he is nothing! She cursed them all in self-assuredness.

"Look at them, child. They are attempting to protect the Ancient One and themselves. Little do they know of my power!" she gloated. Princess Amber smirked with her; she had found everything about her journey with her mother exhilarating, from the moment they had set sail from Stormhaven, sailing through the Eastern Sea, in sight of the shores that were overlooked by the towering Kavenmist Mountains. To the mouth of the Windy Pass where the Plateau Forest had once stood and looked as if it was in constant shadow from the mountains; such was the blackness of its decay.

Until now; as they faced the Forestalls her mother had told her of, she told her what Mother should have been. She felt the anger her mother clearly had for being ignored, but they would not be ignoring her now, she thought.

Princess Amber looked up with wide eyes at the giant form behind the Forestalls called the Ancient One. She felt a rush of blood run through her veins as she did so, for there was what her mother really wanted to destroy!

"What now, Mother?" she asked.

"Now the fun begins, my child," said Queen Helistra with a grin, and casting a spell of further protection around them, she moved her fingers over the symbols of the broken rune staff to summon the spell she had implanted there.

Holding it over the ground in front of her, she called upon the power of the crystal chamber that had been harnessed inside the broken rune staff to join her spell, having to move back almost immediately as the desecrated earth began to rise from the ground in a spinning motion.

A tight, spiralling whirlwind began to form, ripping into the air to turn ever upwards towards the dark, threatening sky above.

Within moments, it was spinning madly, as if out of control. The binding spell Queen Helistra had cast kept it tight and powerful as it reached for those dark, forbidding clouds.

The dark clouds reacted to the pull of the whirlwind, with lightning surging from one cloud to another. A plume of cloud began to spout out towards it, until suddenly the two joined together with a crash of lightning.

The whirlwind now spun violently, with lightning arcing from it in all directions, searing through the sky and scorching the ground.

"Let them be ripped apart and thrown into oblivion!" she cursed, grinning, and with a wave of her arm she sent the spitting whirlwind hurtling towards the waiting company, as if she had cracked a whip!

"By the stars, what power has she possessed!" shouted Ringwold as he watched the whirlwind speed towards them, tearing up everything in its path, as if it were not there.

"You can feel the darkness within it!" shouted Tomin, sensing the intensity of the whirlwind as he braced himself.

"She has gone into realms of power we have never dared to, for just this reason. She is using the power of the crystal chamber and Grimstone's element of air to its fullest, but we must hold strong to protect the Ancient One, no matter what. It must not penetrate us or we are all doomed!" shouted Speedwell.

The noise coming from the whirlwind was deafening. Tarbor could only watch this spinning monster with a paralysed fear of being totally torn to shreds! He held his shield in front of him and knelt down, trying to clear his mind to hold strong the protection he had called upon.

Cantell could not believe his eyes; what in the name! He held on tightly to one of the Ancient One's roots and was certain he felt the anguish he was feeling come from it.

The whirlwind spat out lightning at every opportunity as it coursed its way towards the waiting company. Bolts of lightning hit the protected roots of the Ancient One time and time again as the whirlwind torn across them, until finally crashing into the barrier with a thunderous noise that echoed along its length.

The barrier strained under its ferocity, whilst Speedwell, Ringwold and Tomin held their rune staffs firmly against it. They grimaced as they felt the protective barrier being pounded upon by the whirlwind as it stretched and bent it to breaking point whilst the lightning blistered its weave.

Tarbor thought his arms were going to be pulled from his shoulders; such was the vibration running through him from his shield.

He had not set much stall in the past by praying to the stars and spirits as the others had, but right now he was closing his eyes, asking for their help by watching over them all!

Martyn woke with a start; he had not meant to sleep so deeply and had to be woken by the Ancient One in earnest. *Wake up! Secure the staff! She is upon us!*

Martyn immediately saw the whirlwind rising from the ground to touch the sky, twisting its way into the barrier, ripping at its very core, its tight weave trying to destroy the barrier, with lightning shooting from it in every direction.

With a sinking heart, Martyn could feel the strain the Ancient One and his Forestall uncles were under, holding the whirlwind at bay, feeling the barrier buckling under its pressure.

For the first time, he felt a feeling of trepidation come over him. What would he do if he lost any of them! A weight of what it meant suddenly fell upon his shoulders.

Feelings like that at this moment had to be discarded if he was going to secure his staff, no matter how bad, he told himself.

He looked up at the branch and focused upon it, trying to ignore the chaos that was ensuing to his side. He moved himself rapidly up to where the branch grew.

Martyn reached the bough that held the branch and sitting astride it, he pulled himself along until he reached the branch.

Holding on to it, he immediately felt its inner strength call to him. As he stood up, the Ancient One entered his mind, for him to feel the intensity of the battle that raged against the whirlwind.

You have found it, young Martyn, that is good, whispered the Ancient One, sounding calm to Martyn, which he was not.

I have, Ancient One, but what of the ceremony of the runes? Will you still be able to perform it so I will be able to fully bond with the staff? questioned Martyn immediately.

I will not whilst this persists. The whirlwind is taking all of my strength to hold it at bay.

But what shall we do, Ancient One? We will never become powerful enough to defeat her if you do not perform the ceremony!

Your worry is well founded, young Martyn, so listen to me as to what you must do if we do not hold.

Travel to the Linninhorne Mountains. Within their midst is a frozen lake. It is called the Lake of Serenity. There is where the ancient spirits lay of the Forestalls of old, the wraith.

They were the first to protect the forests when they were formed and were honoured by resting in the Linninhorne Mountains to forever look upon the forests. All that followed rest in the Valley of the Lakes.

Only I know of this place. It is unbeknown to anyone else. Call upon them. Do not be afraid, for they are your only hope if we do not hold.

The Linninhorne, thought Martyn, he would have to travel through the decaying Plateau Forest to reach them if the unthinkable happened.

But the Plateau Forest is poisoned, Ancient One?

You forget, young Martyn, you have the King wielder. He is your guardian.

Of course. Uncle Tarbor. I am sorry, Ancient One, my feelings are troubled within me. I have not felt like this before.

You are not alone, we all have our fears, understood the Ancient One.

There is something else you must do that is important.

What is that, Ancient One?

You must go to where Grimstone met his fate and retrieve the broken piece of rune staff from his stone body. Otherwise, all will be lost, no matter what is done. As long as Grimstone's rune staff remains broken, the health of the forests can never be restored.

I remember your words to me before, Ancient One, as those of uncle Speedwell, remembered Martyn. *But will it be released to me?* worried Martyn.

That has always been my belief, once your newfound staff was made complete.

Be careful then, Ancient One, the whirlwind seems to be growing in power, worried Martyn.

Do not worry over me. Worry only of yourself in the quest to rid us of this evil. I will release the branch from its binding to me for you to be on your way.

Martyn opened his eyes to look at the branch that was to become his staff, with one small concern. It was covered at the top with its own little branches and leaves!

Hold on tight, young Martyn, for you will feel the meeting of earth and sky within your staff's being as I release it to you, whispered the Ancient One, for Martyn to blink, wondering what the Ancient One meant as his presence left him.

Lightning ripped through the sky close to Martyn, making him look immediately at the whirlwind, to see it pushing against the barrier, bending it, it seemed, at will.

Holding on tight to the other nearby branch whilst holding his staff-to-be, Martyn gritted his teeth as he waited for the Ancient One to release the branch whilst telling himself all would be well and not to look down!

A strange inner feeling began to wash over Martyn as he felt the Ancient One releasing the branch. A split suddenly showed itself on his would-be staff where it joined the bough. In that same moment a bolt of lightning seared through the top of it, sending its growth of branches and leaves flying, for Martyn's hair to stand on end!

The meeting of earth and sky fused themselves together within the branch. Martyn felt the immediate effect of strength within its fibre course through his body as his chosen branch became his staff!

But no sooner had Martyn felt the elation of having his staff than he was blown clean off the bough of the Ancient One as the barrier was torn asunder!

A crack had appeared in the barrier from the immense pressure caused by the whirlwind, enough for it to rip it apart with its brutal force and then explode! A wind had followed the explosion, ripping at everything in its path, before finally fading to leave a desolated emptiness in its wake. The barrier along the Old Ogrin Ridge was no more; it had dissolved into nothing!

The lightning ceased and all was still through the darkness. Of the place Speedwell, Ringwold, Tomin and Tarbor had been defending, nothing remained, only empty decimation.

The Great Forest now lay open for the poisonous mist to pour into, with its concealed venomous spore pods and creeping vines. For the beasts that had been held back to rush forward in their eagerness to kill and poison all before them, the waiting was over. Now their evil destruction of the Great Forest could begin!

CHAPTER XLI

Tarbor's body hit the Lake of Tears with a resounding splash. Disorientated at first, he quickly realised he was struggling to keep his head above water.

He pulled at the leather straps on his shield to free his arms to enable him to swim. Luckily, he had no cloak to weigh him down, but the shield was heavy enough!

It did not help Tarbor as he attempted to swim, making for heavy going, but he could not let it go. It was his protective shield and with the others, it had helped save his life, but what of the others?

A sudden realisation that his feet were catching the bottom of the lake made Tarbor aware he had reached the lake's bank.

Grasping at whatever he could, Tarbor pulled himself out of the water and lay gasping on the ground.

Finally, Tarbor sat up and wiped his eyes. He peered out into the darkness, letting his eyes become accustomed to it as he thought on what had just happened.

The whirlwind had blown everything apart! The barrier had disintegrated. Speedwell's, Ringwold's, Tomin's and his protection had not made the slightest bit of difference. It was as if they had not even been there; such was its power!

The beasts and the poison! He thought suddenly, he must be on his guard, but what had happened to the others? Had they also been thrown clear? Worse still, what had happened to Martyn at the top of the Ancient One?

Tarbor stood there a moment as he tried to get himself together, wondering what path he should take, when his eyes caught sight of a dim light moving on the lake. What was that? A light on the water?

Something told Tarbor what it could be, and although he was feeling jaded, he dived in to swim towards the light, leaving his protectors on the bank.

Reaching the light, Tarbor instantly saw a pale face in its soft glow: Tomin! He was floating on his back with Gentian's rune staff lying on his chest.

"Tomin, can you hear me?" There was no response. Tarbor cupped his arm around him and swam back to the bank.

Though Tomin was only a wisp of a man, his body proved heavy to drag out of the lake. Tarbor's efforts were rewarded when Tomin let out a cry, but it was a cry of pain. Tarbor could not see it properly, but Tomin's shoulder was broken.

"Tomin, what happened to you?" asked Tarbor.

"She was too strong for us, Tarbor. The Ancient One, I cannot feel his presence anymore!"

cried Tomin in despair as he started to cough with the pain. Tarbor felt his anguish. All they had tried to do had failed completely.

"When the barrier exploded, my body was sent through the air," Tomin began explaining. "I hit the Ancient One with its force and broke my shoulder before I landed in the lake. Somehow, I held on to Gentian's rune staff, for it to help me keep afloat. If we had not combined our protective shields, I would not be here," he admitted, as Tarbor had thought earlier.

"But what of Speedwell, Ringwold and Martyn, Tomin? Have you felt anything of them?" asked a worried Tarbor.

"My senses are everywhere since the explosion. My strength has all but left me. I have not felt what has happened to my grandfather or Martyn, but Ringwold I know is no more," revealed Tomin with great sadness.

"What!" gasped Tarbor. "But how, Tomin, how do you know?" gasped Tarbor again, hardly able to speak.

"When I collided with the Ancient One's trunk, Ringwold also collided with it, but where I only broke my shoulder, he broke his neck. In that moment, I felt his neck snap and his life expire. Where his body lies, I do not know," explained Tomin as he let the grief he had held back for his great-uncle pour out of him.

"Come, Tomin, we cannot stay here," urged Tarbor, feeling the sadness in Tomin at Ringwold's death as he helped him up.

Picking up his shield and defender, Tarbor threw a shield of protection around them as a caution, hoping it would hold fast if they were attacked.

He also had used a lot of energy at the barrier and did not know how his strength would hold up.

Sheathing his defender, Tarbor put Tomin's good arm over his shoulders to hold on to.

"We will follow the bank towards the River of Tears," decided Tarbor, but it was going to be slow going with Tomin's broken shoulder, he worried.

It did not seem that they had been walking for that long before Tarbor heard a growling sound coming up fast from behind them. Turning, they saw two sets of yellow eyes looking at them through the darkness.

"They must have jumped off the ridge," commented Tarbor, as he let Tomin sit down to free up his sword arm to deal with the beasts. Tomin was clearly in no fit state to help him.

Over the years Tarbor had spent in the Great Forest, he had managed to hone in on his unknown skills with his defender and shield for what he was about to do next.

Drawing his defender, he held it upright in front of him and commanded it to light the night sky with white fire. Even with the shield still on his shoulder, the defender immediately radiated with white fire.

With the defender being forged from the earth, sky and mountain, he had found the blend would lend itself to this white fire with small arcs of lightning along its blade as he commanded it.

Both beasts suddenly leapt up at them, bending the shield of protection as they did. Tarbor could see swellings throbbing along their sides as he arced his defender through the protective shield, meeting their attack by slashing both beasts straight across their malformed bodies, leaving them both with gaping wounds oozing orange blood.

As they hit the ground, Tarbor followed up his decisive strike by driving his defender into them both, triggering lightning to sear through their bodies at the same time.

A moment later and they had caught fire, making their vile orange blood bubble.

Tomin smelt the vile blood as it burnt, and winced. "You have learnt much in your time with us, Tarbor," he commented as they began walking once more.

"Not nearly enough to save the Ancient One, though," was all Tarbor could say as they tried once more to make their way along the lake's bank.

Piper and Tintwist had made it to the River of Tears beyond the Bridge of Seasons in the Elfore sailing boat, when it felt the whole of the sky had torn apart.

The earth all around them suddenly shook to shake the forest's trees from root to leaf. A wind that howled past their ears followed the explosion, sending their boat headlong down the river, forcing it into the river's bank several times as it lurched side to side, with Piper and Tintwist holding on for their lives, but luckily it held firm without grounding them.

To their relief, the wind stopped and they looked at each other with pale expressions. They knew without speaking that the barrier was no more.

"Do you… do you think any of them have survived that?" said Tintwist eventually, not wanting to think it, but how else could he think when he thought everything had come to an end?

"I do not know, but we are going back. We must search for them," replied Piper. "They would have surrounded themselves with protection, and if Martyn was still in the arms of the Ancient One, he may have fallen into the lake," she suggested hopefully, to Tintwist's agreeing nod.

"But what of Cantell, what of his chances?" Tintwist worried further.

Piper could not give much hope for Cantell's chances as she thought of him up there with the Ancient One. "The Ancient One may have protected him, but his fight will be with the beasts and poison that have been waiting for this moment." She did not have to paint a picture for Tintwist; he could see how slim Cantell's chances were.

"Let us hurry, Tintwist, before her evil descends upon us," and without further talk, they took to their oars to row for all they were worth back towards the Lake of Tears in the hope of finding their friends alive.

Reaching the Bridge of Seasons, they felt the fine roots reach down and touch their faces as ever. Only this time they were trying to tell them something in the urgency of their caresses, not that Piper and Tintwist realised; to them, they felt no different as they rowed beneath them.

If darkness had not descended upon the forest, they may never have noticed, but as they rowed under the fine roots, they became aware that some of the fine roots were seen to be softly glowing ahead of them. They rowed towards them to look further.

Piper suddenly let out a gasp, pointing at them. Tintwist had to look twice; it was the shape of a body he was looking at, held in the roots' grasp.

"Who is it?" said Tintwist quietly, as they drew closer to the fine roots that held the body.

As if hearing him, some of the fine roots gently unfolded to reveal the limp body of Martyn held there.

Only then did they see what was creating the soft glow of light; not the fine roots as they had thought, but a plain staff, gently pulsing by Martyn's side.

"It is Martyn! And he has got a staff!" cried Piper in relief, but with worry in her voice when she saw how shallow his breathing was.

"Be careful. He feels fragile," warned Piper as they lifted him onto the boat.

"Thank the stars he is alive," said Tintwist, looking at Piper then Martyn as they set off on their way again, clearing the Bridge of Seasons.

"It is good we have found him, but he looks so pale," worried Piper as she looked at Martyn lying there, wondering how long they should keep searching for the others before going back to the settlement.

She did not have to wonder long, as a white light showed itself through the darkness, catching Tintwist's eye. "Look, Piper! Over there!"

Both of them knew what it was: Tarbor's defender!

Rowing as fast as their arms would let them, Piper and Tintwist made their way towards the white flame of Tarbor's defender.

Then there it was in front of them on the bank of the river, lighting up in Tarbor's hands, showing Tarbor fending off a hideous beast. Not only that; he had a Forestall with him! But he was hanging on to Tarbor; he looked injured!

Piper realised who it was. "He has Tomin, Tintwist. He is injured. Quick, we must help him!" shouted Piper.

Tintwist saw for himself yellow eyes reflecting in the light from Tarbor's defender. How many he did not know, as he and Piper readied their bows.

Steadying themselves, with strings taut, they watched for when the white flame lit up the beasts' yellow eyes again, knowing they would have to kill them before they hit Tarbor's shield of protection. Otherwise, like the beasts, their arrows would bounce harmlessly off it.

White flame met another beast as Tarbor drove his defender into its head with an unnerving crunching sound, to set it on fire and light up the other beasts.

That was enough for Piper and Tintwist as they let loose their arrows. By the time the beast had hit the ground, Piper and Tintwist had despatched four others, bringing to Tarbor's attention that help in the form of his friends had arrived.

He turned with a thankful grin to see through the glimmer two smiling faces looking at him.

"Piper! Tintwist! Am I glad to see you!" shouted Tarbor in relief.

Moving the boat nearer to the bank so they could be rescued, Piper and Tintwist held the boat as steady as they could.

"Tomin's shoulder is broken," gasped Tarbor with the effort of climbing in with Tomin, oblivious to two more beasts leaping through the air at the boat!

But someone had sensed them as ice-blue flames shot through the air to sear holes through both of the beasts, to see them fall short of the boat in a ball of blue flames.

Wide eyes all looked over the side of the boat, first to see the beasts burning on the bank and then to see a face looking up at them from the water in the blue glow. "Are you just going to stare or get me out of here?"

"Speedwell!" they all exclaimed together, and willing hands gladly pulled him into the boat to see he was holding not one but two rune staffs.

Speedwell laid them down and went straight to Martyn's side, to see he was in a deep sleep, noting that Martyn had managed to secure his staff, but his mind was elsewhere as he sat down next to Tomin.

"Grandfather, you are safe," said Tomin with a sigh. Speedwell heard Tomin's sadness, telling him he already knew his grand-uncle was no more

"I am, Tomin, but tell me what happened to my brother," he asked sadly, telling Piper and Tintwist to their dismay whose rune staff it was: Ringwold's.

Tarbor could only bow his head as he listened to Tomin's account again.

"And you found his rune staff, Grandfather," he finished, with tears in his eyes once more.

"It cried to my rune staff, Tomin, but I do not know where his…" Speedwell could not continue.

"Thankfully, I see young Martyn is safe and found his staff before the explosion," spoke Speedwell, after a silence had fallen over them all.

Piper quickly told him where they had found him. "The Bridge of Seasons; and his staff was showing you?" he repeated. "The fine roots were giving him warmth to feed his spirit through his staff," surmised Speedwell as he moved to Martyn's side and felt him.

"But the shock from the explosion and the hurt he must have felt from the Ancient One have made his spirit lock itself away within him," discerned Speedwell as he touched some symbols on his rune staff before closing his eyes and putting a hand on Martyn's chest.

He called softly to the withdrawn spirit of Martyn and waited.

All the others saw was a sudden lurch in Martyn's body as he sat bolt upright, with the pain of the Ancient One crying out from his mouth.

"She has destroyed the Ancient One, Great-uncle!" cried Martyn, who was beside himself with the pain he had felt run right through him from the Ancient One as he was blown off the branch, to remember no more.

"She has destroyed the Ancient One's domain, but not the spirit that lay within it," replied Speedwell, looking at them all with belief in his soul that the Ancient One's spirit had survived.

"But he is gone, Great-uncle Speedwell. His being is no more," sobbed Martyn.

"Only the tree, not the soul," encouraged Speedwell once more.

"You think so?" asked Martyn, wiping away his tears.

"His presence will always be with us whilst we have our rune staffs and you have your staff that I see you have found," encouraged Speedwell.

"You are right, Great-uncle. The Ancient One has blessed me. His presence is strong in its fibre," and Martyn managed a smile as he thought on it.

"Let us be on our way from here then before we see any more horrors. There is nothing more we can do except get back to the settlement and warn everyone," decided Speedwell.

"Cantell already has a head start on us," presumed Tarbor, as he had not come back with Piper and Tintwist, to catch them looking at each other.

"Is there something we should know?" Speedwell frowned, also catching their looks.

"Cantell would not leave Martyn. He hid behind the Ancient One to wait for him," admitted Tintwist.

"We must go and look for him!" implored Martyn, but Speedwell was already shaking his head.

"I only just managed to avoid the poisonous pods that are already floating over the lake when I recovered Ringwold's rune staff, and how many more beasts will there be on our trail? We are lucky to have been found by Piper and Tintwist, Martyn. I know he was doing his duty by you, but the risk is too great to go back for him in our weakened state. Let us hope the stars are watching over him," warned Speedwell as he quietly pointed out his worries.

Martyn knew his great-uncle was right, but it did not come easy to him to leave his uncle to all that evil, an uncle who had laid his life down for him.

Tarbor felt as empty as Martyn at such a decision, but he knew it would have been the same if it had been him instead of Cantell, King wielder or not.

So with heavy hearts, Tarbor, Piper and Tintwist pulled on the oars to set the Elfore sailing boat on its way.

Speedwell turned his attention to Tomin's broken shoulder, which he was holding limply by his side, to find it had come out of its socket.

"You have been lucky, Tomin. One pull and it will be back in place, but it will hurt," informed Speedwell. A pain Tomin was only too willing to accept rather than enduring what he was going through. If only the pain in his heart was that simple to mend, he thought.

A pull and a curse later saw Speedwell tying a crude sling around Tomin's neck that he had made out of a sack lying in the boat.

"Forgive me if I do not give you any of the essence's bubbles of life, Tomin. We may need them for later," apologised Speedwell, "but I have some herbs left in my pouch," he added.

Tomin thought of the foul taste his grandfather always managed to conjure up with them. "I think I have suffered enough without adding to it," he jibed, to feel Speedwell tie the sling a little bit harder around his neck.

Speedwell heard the spirit that still lingered within Tomin and half smiled to himself as he pulled the sling tighter.

"Martyn, you have not told us how you secured your staff," prompted Speedwell, thinking they all needed their spirits lifting at this dark time.

Martyn was more than glad to remember when he climbed the Ancient One's branches and the oneness he had felt as he did so.

"As the lightning struck, the earth and sky became as one within the staff when I claimed it," finished Martyn, transfixed in his recollection at the wonder of that moment, holding on to it, blocking the hurt he had felt of the Ancient One in his mind.

"To think it had twigs upon its length then, but to see and feel it now," pointed out Martyn, holding his staff proudly for Speedwell to see and Tomin to feel.

"You have chosen well, young Martyn," said Speedwell with a smile, hiding how he was feeling. Instead of his spirit being uplifted by listening to Martyn, it had sunk lower still.

Martyn's staff was of little use without the ceremony of the runes to complete it, he was thinking. There was only him and Tomin now, their energy drained after trying to defend the barrier. They would not be able to retrieve the broken piece to mend Grimstone's broken rune staff, and they needed to if they were to have any hope of ending his daughter's evil.

The Bridge of Seasons began to emerge out of the dark as Speedwell thought on it.

"I will thank the fine roots for rescuing me as we pass under them," said Martyn in thought as the fine roots reached out to greet them.

All felt their caress, but this time Speedwell and Tomin felt their sadness at the loss of the Ancient One, knowing that evil was coming their way. It felt all the more so to Speedwell and Tomin with their loss of Ringwold.

As he said thank you to the fine roots, Martyn shared their sad caress also, but he reflected back hope to them for what he knew but had not yet told his great-uncles, because of the grief that had got in the way of that hope.

Speedwell looked at Martyn as they cleared the Bridge of Seasons, half expecting to see a face of sorrow after sensing the plight of the fine roots, but instead he saw a face he had seen before, one that told him he had something on his mind and asked him as such, "Is there something troubling you, young Martyn?"

"In all our grief, Great-uncles, I have not told you of what the Ancient One whispered to me before I claimed my staff," began Martyn.

"And what is that?" asked Tomin, who could clearly hear the anticipation in Martyn's voice.

"All hope is not lost, Great-uncles. The Ancient One told me of a place where the ceremony of the runes can be performed!" revealed Martyn, to the stunned looks of Speedwell and Tomin.

This news stopped the Elfore sailing boat from going any further as Tarbor, Piper and Tintwist lifted their oars to listen.

Martyn then proceeded to tell them all what the Ancient One had told him, to begin putting back the hope that was all but lost a moment ago.

Speedwell could not help but think he never really knew the Ancient One when he thought he did as he listened to Martyn, finding he was repeating what Martyn was telling him.

"The first of our kind, the beginning? They are known as wraiths? A frozen lake high in the Linninhorne Mountains?"

By the time Martyn had finished telling them, hope had rekindled itself.

"Our path ahead has been shown to us. Ringwold's loss will not be in vain!" announced Speedwell.

"Once we reach where the rivers divide, that is where we will part. Martyn, Tarbor and I will go to where the Ancient One has pointed, to make Martyn's staff as one with him, whilst you make your way to the settlement, Tomin. Then all of you must make haste and journey to Northernland. Tell them to be ready. Ready for the evil that has been let loose," instructed Speedwell.

"We will go and seek King Stowlan at Elishard," understood Piper.

"I will have to steer the boat through lesser rivers to get there," decided Tomin, feeling his shoulder throbbing. "This arm will not take the whirlpool." Not that Piper and Tintwist minded that.

"But what of Stormhaven and the crystal chamber, Grandfather? My mother will be able to replenish her power and we have just seen what that can do," worried Tomin.

"We might have been able to test Helistra's strength before she entered Stormhaven, but in our weakened state without my brother, we are no match for her, Tomin. We can only cross that bridge when we come to it. You know as well as I do we would have achieved nothing by doing so, without retrieving the broken piece to mend Grimstone's broken rune staff first. Now the ceremony of the runes can be performed, that chance has been given back to us and then we shall see. Our journey will be a long one, but if good fortune is with us we will be in Northernland by the month of snow," explained Speedwell as he answered.

"I think it could be much colder and darker before then, Grandfather," said Tomin, still worried.

"Then hopefully we shall bring the light with us," said Speedwell with a smile, but with worry in his heart also.

With newfound vigour, oars were taken up once more, and the Elfore sailing boat sped through the waters of the River of Tears to eventually come to where the river that led to the settlement split from it.

Giving them what sparse provisions there were, Tomin, Piper and Tintwist bade them farewell.

"May the stars and spirits watch over you on your journey," called Tomin in farewell as Piper and Tintwist rowed away from the bank.

"And may they watch over you also," Speedwell called back. "Piper! Tintwist! Look after Ringwold's rune staff till we return," he added.

"We will, Speedwell," was the call back from Piper and Tintwist as the Elfore sailing boat disappeared into the darkness.

Turning, Speedwell looked at Martyn and Tarbor. "Shall we be about finding these ancient wraiths then?"

"Yes, Great-uncle," answered a determined Martyn, and he was off. Tarbor smiled with Speedwell as together they followed Martyn to head towards the west and the Greater Hardenal Mountains.

CHAPTER XLII

Queen Helistra waited until daylight before going to see what havoc her unleashed power had wreaked, letting the beasts and poisonous mist go before her to begin spreading their venom.

She walked slowly over the burnt roots of the Ancient One, caused by the constant lightning strikes, with Princess Amber behind her, staring at the poisonous spores that now invaded them.

The broken form of the Ancient One stood out clearly against the early-morning light, showing the full extent of what the whirlwind had done.

The first thing that was plain to see was how many of the Ancient One's branches had been torn away by the explosion to now lay beneath the Lake of Tears at the bottom of the ridge, or broken, hanging from the Ancient One's stricken form in mid-air.

Some had fallen on top of each other at the base of the Ancient One, a jumbled mess of splintered wood and fallen leaves.

The thick bark on the Ancient One's huge trunk had been ripped off, and where the barrier had been held together by the Ancient One, a gaping split had appeared upon its length, for the poisonous spores to take full advantage of by entering the split to drive in their poison.

"The poison will rot its heart and then it will fall," crooned Queen Helistra, revelling in the devastation she had caused.

"It will not need much, Mother," observed Princess Amber as she watched the creeping vines slither up the Ancient One's splintered trunk, oozing slime as they went.

Only the immense roots had held the once tall and proud tree in place as it leaned over the ridge. If not for them, the Ancient One would have plummeted over the Old Ogrin Ridge, such was the force of the explosion when the whirlwind cracked open the barrier.

"Come, child, it is time to go. There is no more to be done here, I must get back to Stormhaven and regain my strength," said Queen Helistra, suddenly feeling very tired. "We will make our way under the Winterborne River back to the Eastern Sea," and she ducked under a bough that had held the other branches away from the huge trunk of the Ancient One.

Just in that moment, she felt her head go slightly giddy. Humming immediately entered her. *I know the power we use is strong to control, but I am all right.*

"What is it, Mother? Do you feel unwell?" asked Princess Amber, concerned, seeing her mother had closed her eyes as she stood up from bending her head.

As she reopened them, Princess Amber let out a gasp. "Your eyes, Mother, they are red!"

"Do not worry, child. They will return to normal." The humming returned.

I know I will not be able to feel if they are still alive, but it does not matter. They are nothing without the Ancient One.

Queen Helistra and Princess Amber made their way through the archway of roots that had bent with the force that had been put upon them. Queen Helistra could not resist holding one as she passed them, in the hope of hearing the cries of pain from the Ancient One, but there was nothing. She should have known better, she thought afterwards. After all, she was not one of its beloved Forestalls.

No one would have felt anything, for the Ancient One had withdrawn into the deepest depths of its being, down into the very nerve endings where it had all began, severing roots deep in the earth to stop the poison from following.

The Ancient One's spirit could only wait in silence, praying to the stars and spirits for the day when his being could grow again, hoping against all hope that they had survived to rid them from Helistra's evil, to be able to restore the forests, but with the unbearable knowledge that Ringwold and Tomin had crashed into his trunk before being swept away by the explosion.

Feeling the blame for all that had happened, the Ancient One's spirit silently wept for them and the plight of the forests.

As Queen Helistra came away from the emptiness of the Ancient One, a malformed Elfore caught her attention further on. It was looking over the ridge below and seemed to be growling. "What is that thing up to?" she questioned, and went to where it was looking.

The noise of the Winterborne River rushing over the ridge rang in her ears as she walked through the cutaway made by – and Queen Helistra could not help but smile as she thought on it – the creature's ancestors.

Princess Amber was there first, running past Queen Helistra to peer over the ridge. The creature stepped back as Queen Helistra joined Princess Amber, though it had no true thoughts of its own, only to kill and infect others. It knew not to stand in her way.

Looking over the side, they saw the crumpled form of a man lying bloodied on a ledge below them. A movement told them he was still alive. "Climb down and fetch him to me," ordered Queen Helistra to the Elfore creature, who obeyed immediately.

Cantell had somehow survived the explosion. He had held on to one of the Ancient One's roots, only to be ripped from it before the wind that followed the explosion had dissipated, not able to hold on any longer, although it had felt as if he had been sucked out of the archway of roots rather than blown, throwing him headlong as it did along the cutaway, hitting the rocky sides before disappearing over the edge and landing luckily on the ledge.

Though the way he felt, he did not feel lucky at all, especially when he managed to open his eyes to find he was on top of the ridge, seeing two blood-red eyes staring back at him: Queen Helistra's!

Queen Helistra smiled at Cantell's look of horror at seeing her. "Let me see, which one are you? Cantell or Kelmar?" she said, recognising Cantell was a Tiggannian.

Cantell felt in no position to lie, but still did, thinking if she found he was Martyn's protector, she would know he would have been with him. "I am Kelmar."

Cantell groaned inside as he lied, hearing Tarbor in the back of his mind – *she will enter your head, it is of no use* – but then Speedwell came to him. Her bloodshot eye had stopped her from focusing.

"Hmm, so you say, and where is the child?" she quizzed.

"In the Great Forest at the settlement," he lied again, wishing he had been and not up the stricken form he could see of the Ancient One half hanging over the ridge. There was no way for him to know if Martyn was dead or alive, seeing it.

Queen Helistra looked at him suspiciously as humming entered her head. *Do not keep reminding me. I know I could have!*

Cantell looked at Princess Amber looking at him and smiled a bloody smile. "Princess Amber, it is good to see you are well. You will be glad to know your mother and brother are also well, but miss you," he informed her, to get a puzzled frown back.

"What does he mean, Mother?" she said, her gaze keeping on Cantell's face.

"He is making up stories, my child, to save his Tiggannian skin," replied Queen Helistra without hesitation.

Cantell nearly choked on his own blood; *Mother!*

Princess Amber suddenly crouched over Cantell and put her hand around the back of his neck, digging her nails in until she drew blood.

A strange moment passed, with Cantell finding himself eye-to-eye with Princess Amber, to see her looking right through him, as if she was looking into his very soul, before giving him a cold stare.

"We do not like liars!" she hissed over his face. "Let me deal with him, Mother," she pleaded, getting up.

Queen Helistra looked at Princess Amber enquiringly. "You felt something, child?"

"No, Mother, only that he is a liar! You are my mother."

Queen Helistra smiled. "Very well, do as you wish," she consented.

"Bite him!" ordered Princess Amber to the malformed Elfore, and before Cantell could cry out, the beast had bitten him in the neck, sending its venom into his body to search out the hidden darkness within him.

Cantell's last thought was one of sadness as he saw the delight on Princess Amber's face as he passed out, before starting to convulse in the throws of becoming a beast.

When his eyes opened again they were as black as night, and his body had deformed into one of grotesque evil. He was no more the Cantell who remembered those rides with Kelmar in Kelmsmere Valley, but a beast who was ready to kill and infect anyone who came near him.

"There, Mother, he will not lie again," said Princess Amber with a smile.

"You are right, child, you have done well," answered Queen Helistra, smiling, as humming entered her head. *It has all been proof enough. When we get back, I will begin showing her.*

More humming came into her mind with a thought. *Hmm, if any have survived, they will be weak. They could finish them off, but why there? Without the Ancient One, their cause is a lost one, no staff, no ceremony of the runes. I do not even need to use you again to give them any chance of retrieving it, now the poison flows.*

The humming spoke of caution to her. *You are right, we must make sure. The Ancient One was always devious and hope will always remain if they live, though there is none.*

We have come too far not to be careful. We will send these creatures to greet them, it will be a nice little surprise, agreed Queen Helistra, and she turned to the two deformed creatures.

"You two, come here," she ordered, and told them where they were to go. "Now find others and be on your way," she commanded.

"Come, child, our journey awaits us." Queen Helistra smiled in satisfaction that Princess Amber had not shown any sign of who she really was, even though that Tiggannian had tried to evoke memories within her. Memories that were no more, she concluded.

What a wonderful day it had been; the Ancient One was dead and the Great Forest would soon follow, she thought, along with that weak, pathetic rabble who had tried to hold her back. If they were not dead already then they soon would be.

Not that she was worried. The power of the crystal chamber had now shown her what it could do and once she was replenished, no one would be able to defeat her. Her dream was nearly complete.

She held out her hand for Princess Amber to hold as she began walking through the decimated trees along the ridge, whilst the Elfore beast and the monster that was once known as Cantell disappeared under the Winterbourne to head west, where they had been told.

CHAPTER XLIII

The journey back to the settlement was the quietest Piper had ever known. Even Tintwist had hardly said a word, whilst Tomin had withdrawn into himself, grieving for Ringwold.

An eerie stillness had come over the forest to match their quietness as dark skies pressed in above them, to add to the feeling they were all getting that evil was close by.

A piercing cry of a bird overhead made Piper look up, only to see it was only one of many flying in the dark skies, to get away from what was coming, she thought, remembering Fleck's account of what had happened to him.

"The evil feels so close. Do you think they have sensed it too and gone?" said Tintwist, his eyes scanning the riverbank between the trees for anything that moved.

"Our brethren and the Elfore may well have, but I think our friends, as we would have, will wait for us until they have to leave," answered Piper. "We cannot go without looking first," she added, even though she really wanted to get away from here.

They continued rowing warily up the river, one of many that came from the Kavenmist Mountains, hugging its left bank whilst watching over to their right to where the settlement should appear. They were near now, thought Piper.

Suddenly the forest began to come alive to their ears. Bushes began to rustle, twigs snapped, undergrowth trampled on, making it clear to them that animals were running through the forest.

In the next moment, it seemed as if the river was full of splashing fish as animals appeared of every kind, pouring out of the forest in panic, plunging over the riverbank into the river all around them.

Whether they were deer, fox or wild cat, all were alike in their desperation to get across the river. With eyes wide and nostrils flared, they were swimming for all they were worth to get away from what had scared them.

The Elfore sailing boat rocked in their waves, but Piper and Tintwist had no time to worry about the boat's motion as the answer to what had frightened the animals appeared before them. As they grabbed their bows, Piper shouted at Tomin, "Forestall! Look to yourself! Tomin!"

Snarling yellow-eyed beasts were jumping on top of the slowest animals, trying to make it to the river, but mixed in amongst them were clearly Elfore who had been bitten. Five grotesque faces looked straight at the sailing boat and what it held: victims!

Tomin came round to Piper's voice, though at first it was still distant in his mind, lost as he was in his own grief for his great-uncle. His senses suddenly became aware of the repugnant evil that was about to pounce upon them.

His shoulder in its sling was a hindrance, but with his good arm, Tomin took Gentian's rune staff and touched some symbols upon it. Words were said as he slid it through his hand to then twirl it around to touch two more.

Piper and Tintwist had let loose their arrows, finding the necks of two of the deformed creatures, when Tomin struck. A searing bolt of flame sizzled out of Gentian's rune staff, taking another creature's head clean off!

Again, Tomin struck, and again, heads fell, bodies seared through, as Tomin directed the bolts of flame with uncanny accuracy.

Piper and Tintwist just looked on as Tomin dealt out the bolts of flame, to leave the riverbank covered in bodies, with orange blood staining the earth.

"Row, I will keep them at bay!" shouted Tomin, for Piper and Tintwist to take to the oars. Most of the animals had made it across the river where they were. Only the slower ones remained in the water as the Elfore sailing boat made way.

The poor animals that had been bitten were instantly burnt by the bolts of flame as Tomin felt the darkness enter them, but more deformed creatures were waiting for them further along, jumping into the river to stop them from sailing any further.

Tomin dealt out more bolts of flame, but he was getting tired; the strain of what had happened at the barrier was telling on him. His bolts of flame began to splutter and die before reaching the creatures; nothing was stopping them from making for the vessel!

Piper and Tintwist let go of their oars, taking over from Tomin as soon as they saw he was tiring, firing upon the creatures with their arrows, but still they came at them, spitting saliva, eager for the kill!

Hands with pustules grabbed the sailing boat's side, threatening to pull it over into the water. Piper and Tintwist took to their narrow swords, hacking at the grotesque hands, slicing them clean off!

Not that it stopped the creatures as they still tried to get to the sailing boat with flailing bloody arms!

Tomin kept them at bay as by now he was striking out with Gentian's rune staff one-handed, whilst Piper and Tintwist kept flaying their swords at anything that moved!

One creature finally got past their frantic actions to climb in one side of the sailing boat to be followed by another on the opposite side.

Tintwist faced one whilst Piper faced the other, either side of Tomin as he battered the life out of the creatures trying to get into the boat.

The creatures moved to pounce, but as they did so they were both met with arrows straight through their heads, with enough force to send them toppling over the side of the boat. Piper and Tintwist saw with familiarity what type of arrow had dispatched them: an Elfore arrow!

Unnoticed by them in their battle to survive, Tiska and Tislea had let loose their arrows at their attackers from the river's bank before letting death sing through their bows at the other creatures holding onto the Elfore sailing boat.

In that moment of relief, Piper and Tintwist looked to see swords being swirled all around the two Elfore huntresses, protecting them as they killed their attackers.

"Do I hear saviours?" gasped Tomin thankfully, beginning to feel exhausted.

"It is Tiska and Tislea, Tomin, with the others fighting around them!" cried Piper.

"Let us get them and be away from this place then," urged Tomin.

Turning the sailing boat around as they rowed to the other side, Piper and Tintwist immediately saw Queen Elina being shepherded straight away towards the boat by Kelmar.

Her eyes were as wide as those of the petrified animals as she clambered into the boat, but it did not stop her from asking after her son when she saw he was not there.

"Where is Martyn? Is he safe? What has happened?" she cried in anguish.

"He is well, my lady. He is with Speedwell and Tarbor," replied Piper.

Relief washed over Queen Elina, but it was instantly replaced by worry. "But why are they not with you? Where are they?" she pushed.

"Let us worry about the others first, then I will tell you," answered Tomin to a resounding crash as a body fell into the boat, to stop Queen Elina from saying anything. It was Ludbright!

He had climbed a tree that had a branch overhanging the river and had decided to drop into the boat.

"Ludbright, are you all right?" shouted Tintwist.

Ludbright raised his head from his crumpled body. "The branch was higher than I thought," was his reply.

Tiska and Tislea climbed into the boat, instantly notching more arrows to protect the others, who were keeping back the creatures.

Piper and Tintwist joined them, letting loose their own arrows to find their mark.

Kelmar, Cillan, Urchel and Fleck were fighting back to back, their swords cutting through the air, scything at anything in their path.

Suddenly Tiska saw a chance for them to get aboard as the deformed creatures regrouped to charge once more.

"Now! Run! We have you covered!" shouted Tiska.

"Before we run out of arrows!" shouted Tintwist.

Cillan jumped in first, followed by Urchel. Fleck then went to turn and stumbled, for two malformed beasts to instantly spring upon him. Kelmar cut through one whilst two arrows pierced the other. Kelmar dragged him up and together they threw themselves into the boat.

Oars pushed against the riverbank and hastily hit the water, but not before Cillan had used one to smack two more beasts around the head, to send them flying.

Strength came from somewhere as oars ploughed through the water. Keeping to the far side, they rowed for their lives, with Tiska, her bow notched, keeping watch.

Tomin had raised the sail. He prayed to the stars and spirits that his strength had not totally left him as he pushed a spell of wind into the sail. The sound of it billowing put his mind at rest whilst he steered, feeling the flow of the river in his grip.

No one spoke whilst they put their minds into rowing, until Piper saw an opening that led to a narrower river. "We are there, Tomin," she called.

"I feel it," said Tomin with a smile, for all to take a deep breath. They were clear, for now.

Oars were brought in, leaving Tomin to negotiate the Elfore sailing boat along the narrower river, to eventually stop further down for the chance to rest.

Tired bodies sat a moment, thankful they had escaped the hordes of beasts and malformed monsters, covered in orange blood from the battle.

"Their orange blood is all over us," said Ludbright, squirming.

"Do not worry, Ludbright. You would already be one of them yourself if you had an open wound or you had swallowed some," said Tomin, revealing news to them all.

"But I thought Speedwell said—" began Tintwist.

"He was not sure, he was being cautious," answered Tomin before Tintwist could finish.

"Well, he might have mentioned it in all this time," chimed in Fleck.

"I think other things took precedence," Tomin reminded him.

All thanked the stars they had been lucky enough not to have been tainted so, but long since Speedwell's earlier worries about the poisonous blood, they had made sure that if they were to meet Queen Helistra's evil, they would be covered from head to foot.

As a result, all were now wearing leather clothing that fully protected their bodies, right down to their leather gloves and full leather head coverings, which they were all gladly taking off with care.

Only Piper and Tintwist had not donned theirs in the sudden onset, whilst Tomin looked as clean as he was before the battle!

The chance to carefully wash off the orange blood in the river's waters was taken. A time then came for hugs and questions as the company sat for a while, keeping a wary eye out as they did so.

Fleck told Tomin, Piper and Tintwist how the wind had brought an unearthly noise of a loud bang followed by a weird hissing sound over two weeks ago.

"Everyone left for the edge of the Great Forest. They knew what it meant, the barrier was no more. If they had done that when I tried to warn them in the Valley of the Lakes, there would have been twice the number," reflected Fleck.

Queen Elina then asked again about Martyn, what he was doing with Speedwell and Tarbor.

"They journey to the Linninhorne Mountains," answered Tomin, and he began to tell her what had happened.

All listened to what Tomin had to say, only to be saddened and worried by what they heard. To hear of the destruction of the Ancient One when the barrier had exploded and then the death of Ringwold left everyone feeling lost.

Recounting Ringwold's death, Tomin was nearly reduced to tears once more, but for Kelmar, when Tomin came to where they had left Cantell behind to his fate, it felt like a knife had entered his heart. Kelmar could only hope his old friend had somehow survived, but after what they had just been through, he doubted it.

Queen Elina had closed her eyes in sadness for Cantell, but opened them again when Tomin began speaking about Martyn.

Tomin explained how Martyn had secured his staff before the explosion and how he had been told by the Ancient One to go to the Linninhorne Mountains for the ceremony of the runes where the Ancients were.

"The Ancients? I thought there was only the Ancient One?" queried Queen Elina.

"So did I," replied Tomin, "the Ancient One kept more from us than any of us knew."

"When will they return?" asked a concerned Fleck.

"Grandfather said they would be in Northernland by winter, with

Martyn's staff complete, ready to help defeat Helistra," replied Tomin, with mixed feelings.

He was trying to sound assured that their quest would be rewarded with the means to defeat her, but he was talking about his mother. It still hurt, but Fleck's thoughts only reminded Tomin of his reply to his grandfather. "I fear winter will be long upon us before then."

"There is something else you should know, Queen Elina," continued Tomin. Queen Elina looked at Tomin's face, distantly thinking about her son going into dangers unknown, and not being able to do anything about it.

"What is that, Tomin?"

"Princess Amber was with Helistra. Speedwell was going to try and sense if she still held the spirit inside her, but it was not to be," he said to Queen Elina's sudden joy.

"You saw her there! I mean—,"

"Yes, she was there," interrupted Tomin, saving Queen Elina from embarrassment, but at the same time not telling her that she was being used as a shield.

Queen Elina felt her emotions going everywhere at the news of her little Amber, but if she had been turned evil by that Helistra, then she was no longer her little Amber. She prayed to the stars that she had not.

"Come, we cannot rest until we have warned the people of Northernland what is about to befall them," finished Tomin, making everyone get ready to journey down the river, but as he said it, his heart lay heavy with the thought that if they could not hold the horror back, what chance had the people of Northernland?

CHAPTER XLIV

"Why did the Ancient One keep it a secret, Great-uncle Speedwell?" asked Martyn as he made his way along the side of a hill through the forest behind him, with Tarbor watching his back.

"The Ancient One has known of things that were best kept secret away from listening ears, things that we could only guess at, Martyn. His roots run deep," answered Speedwell, feeling only sadness as he spoke of the Ancient One.

Martyn could hear his great-uncle's sadness but noticed from his tone that he had not changed in his belief that the Ancient One was still with them, for Martyn to look at his staff.

Tarbor was beginning to get tired after another long day of constantly watching out for beasts that might suddenly spring upon them. Unless it became necessary, he would hold back from using his protective shield to save his strength.

Another day was coming to an end, for another night to begin that Tarbor was not looking forward to.

They had decided to climb as high as they could up any negotiable tree to evade the beasts, taking Fleck's advice. "They smell our fear more than they do our scent and have no doubt, fear will abound," Fleck had told them. Tarbor did not doubt that for one moment after his encounter at the Lake of Tears.

The tall fir trees abounding them now, indicating they were getting closer to the Greater Hardenal Mountains, according to Speedwell, came as some relief to Tarbor, with their thick branches and needles to rest upon, compared to what they had attempted to rest in so far.

Tarbor gladly settled down across the thick growth of the fir tree they had climbed for the night. As he lay there, the strong smell of the fir tree came to his nostrils and he thought idly that if fear did show itself, perhaps the smell of the fir trees would cover it.

The voice of Speedwell talking to Martyn above him then caught his attention, and Tarbor began listening to what he was saying.

"The power she used from the crystal chamber must have blocked her senses not to have chased us down," spoke Speedwell in answer to Martyn's question that Tarbor had not heard.

"It is not the first time it has happened, but she will fully replenish herself once back at Stormhaven," pointed out Speedwell, making Tarbor think of Queen Helistra's bloodshot eye, how her loss of vision dulled her senses.

"She will have no need to if we do not succeed. The death mist and those poor beings that have been turned to evil will see to that. To think she is my daughter," said Speedwell with a sigh, sounding downhearted.

"We will succeed, Speedwell," called Tarbor, trying to sound more optimistic.

"And we will find the Ancients to turn my staff into a rune staff, Great-uncle, then we shall see," said Martyn, sounding confident in what the future held for them.

Speedwell's thoughts had strayed with all that had happened, making him feel at a low ebb.

Grimstone, Gentian and now his brother all gone, because of his daughter, because he had been too blind in the first place to see what Grimstone teaching Tomin was doing to her. His brother had been right all along; it was all his fault.

Now there was only himself and Tomin, who like him had only just got away with his life.

He looked at Martyn through the dwindling light and saw a boy who, though his spirit was strong, would know nothing in the ways of how to combine it with that of a rune staff. Time was needed to bond with it, if the Ancient Forestalls deemed to bless him in the ceremony of the runes, that is!

Speedwell stopped there, cursing at himself for how he was sounding, "You will have your rune staff, young Martyn, and together we shall see what she is really made of," he responded to Martyn's smile.

"If only we had been strong enough to hold her back, we could have attacked her when her power drained," reflected Tarbor.

"Not this time, Tarbor, none of us were, but we will prevail with the help of the wraiths of the Ancient Forestalls," vowed Speedwell to them both, even though he had his doubts.

Sleep finally came to Speedwell as a welcome relief to clear his unsettled mind, whilst Tarbor tried to keep his senses alert to the sounds beneath them, but tiredness from looking out all day soon caught up with him.

Martyn fell asleep easily, clutching his newfound staff, but his eyes began to constantly move under his eyelids as a vivid dream entered his sleeping mind.

A word was coming to him, whispering from somewhere, but a greyness that surrounded him blocked his vision as to where. The word echoed constantly through the greyness, drawing him on, until suddenly the greyness disappeared and he was surrounded by horrible malformed beasts!

But it was as if they could not see him as the word pulsed in his mind, for him to be suddenly standing in front of a pillar of rock!

Then there it was, the word he could hear but could not make out, coming from the pillar of rock. *Together*, it whispered, *together you will*.

Martyn suddenly woke, puzzled by what the dream had tried to tell him, finding the morning light greeting him as he did so, coming through the branches of the fir tree.

He sat there with his legs dangling over them whilst he thought about his dream, not realising Speedwell was smiling at him.

"Was it a good or bad dream you had, Martyn, for you to talk in your sleep?" he asked straight away.

"Neither really, more a strange one," and Martyn told Speedwell what he had dreamt of.

"Well, there is only one pillar of rock I can think of," said Speedwell, knowing how close they were to that fateful spot.

"Grimstone's," answered Martyn.

"Yes, Grimstone's, but until your staff is complete, you cannot retrieve the broken piece... or can you?" said Speedwell, hesitating, suddenly questioning himself as he thought of the word Martyn had heard in his dream.

Together? Together you will, I wonder, he thought. Perhaps there was more to Martyn's spirit and his staff than he had realised, more than the Ancient One had, or had he?

"You were holding your staff when you had your dream?" questioned Speedwell.

"Yes, Great-uncle. Do you think it was my staff talking to me?" Martyn suddenly felt excitement at the thought.

"Although it is not yet your rune staff, it has sensed we are near the broken piece that lyes within Grimstone's pillar of rock and is telling you through your dream that together you could retrieve the broken piece," speculated Speedwell.

"Sounds sense to me. After all, I felt a rock talk to me," interrupted Tarbor, popping his head above the branches they were on, having listened to them once more, "and there is only one way of finding out," he added, and he disappeared down the tree as quickly as he had appeared.

"Let us go there then and see," agreed Speedwell, and they were soon on the ground, travelling towards that fateful spot of long ago.

The tall, thick fir trees brushed against each other with their branches in the breeze as they moved amongst them, making Tarbor feel all the more nervous going between them, thinking there could be a beast waiting for them behind every tree.

"Shall I throw a shield around us, Speedwell? I do not feel safe in amongst these," he asked whilst looking everywhere.

"Save yourself, Tarbor. You will smell them long before we meet them," answered Speedwell, but since Tarbor had put the smell of fir trees into his head, that was all he could smell!

They came to a long valley that seemed to be going on forever to Tarbor as they walked between and under the fir trees, until suddenly Speedwell put his arm out in a gesture for them to stop.

"We are here," he whispered, crouching down, for Martyn and Tarbor to follow suit as they peeked through some branches to a scene that made their jaws drop.

A huge barren area met their prying eyes, with the tall fir trees skirting it. Behind the furthest ones loomed the Greater Hardenel Mountains, unseen until now, and there in the centre of the barren vastness stood a single pillar of rock, but it was not standing alone, for all around it were hordes of malformed creatures!

"Now you know why we have not seen any, Tarbor. We might have known she would have sent them to do her bidding," whispered Speedwell.

"I hope my mother is all right," whispered Martyn. "If these creatures are here, they are bound to be at the settlement also," he worried.

"She will be well. She has all of your uncles and aunts to watch over her," assured Tarbor, whilst hoping the same himself.

Tarbor looked at the pillar of rock in the middle of all the beasts. "How are we going to retrieve the broken piece from it with all these creatures here?" he asked.

"Perhaps we should go to the wraiths of the Ancients first. They might be gone by the time we come back," said Martyn in hope.

"I doubt it, Martyn. They are here to stay. No, we will wait until nightfall when they are asleep, then with your protection, Tarbor, plus a little spell to, shall we say, blend in with them, we will make our way to the pillar of Grimstone's," decided Speedwell.

"Evil sleeps?" half questioned Tarbor, a little surprised.

"All creatures need to sleep, Tarbor, no matter what form they take," said Speedwell with a smile.

"Let us hope they stay that way. My strength since the explosion has been sorely tested. I only hope my shield stays strong. One splash of their blood and it will be all for nothing," worried Tarbor. Unlike the others, he had not felt the need for full protective clothing when he had his defenders to protect him.

"And I do not have my protective headwear and gloves," realised Martyn, as he had climbed the Ancient One without them.

"It will not penetrate your skin," said Speedwell, for Tarbor to frown.

"I thought it was poisonous to the skin?" queried Tarbor.

"Their blood cannot penetrate our skins. Because it is so thick, it has to find other ways; through your mouth, or a cut, then you will turn," explained Speedwell.

"You might have said something," said Tarbor, feeling only slightly relieved at knowing it could not penetrate his skin.

"I am sorry, Tarbor. My mind has been elsewhere, I never gave it a thought," apologised Speedwell.

"The Ancient One is not the only one who keeps secrets," said Tarbor with raised eyebrows, making Speedwell smile at being likened to the Ancient One.

"No, he is not," he agreed.

They waited until late into the night, waiting for the creatures to finally go quiet, restless for the taste of blood, it seemed, before they would settle down.

"Are you ready?" prompted Speedwell, for Tarbor to quietly command the protective shield to form around them.

"That should do it," said Speedwell, coughing, as he cast a spell that had them holding their noses. "They will not smell us now."

"If we are supposed to smell like them to blend in, I think you may have overdone it, Speedwell," remarked Tarbor, also coughing.

"Shh! They will hear you," warned Martyn, only just managing not to cough himself.

Emerging from the cover of the fir trees, they slowly made their way across the barren circle that was made by Grimstone when his fate had been sealed by Queen Helistra.

The thought of what happened here poured into Speedwell's very soul as he moved between the grotesque beasts that were resting on the edge of the circle.

Most of the malformed creatures had lain down, but a few seemed to be sleeping standing up. As Tarbor passed one such creature, he gripped his drawn defender tightly, ready for if it awoke, its features in the evening light making him go cold.

Martyn went quiet. The responsibility he had felt fall on his shoulders before had suddenly returned. He gripped his staff firmly and breathed in deeply.

Closer and closer they were getting to the pillar of rock as they quietly threaded their way between the malformed creatures.

Only the sound of the protective shield around them made any noise as it softly vibrated with power, not that it would have been heard if it was making any noise, as the various noises coming from the creatures easily cloaked it.

Tarbor began wondering how long he could hold the protective shield in place, as he was already feeling the energy he needed to hold it there slowly sapping his strength away.

The fallen form of Grimstone embedded in rock finally rose before them, making Tarbor take in a breath when he saw a piece of rock sticking out on one side, covered in its own stone. It was the broken piece of Grimstone's rune staff!

His reactions suddenly had to come to the fore when he saw the eyes of a creature next to the pillar of rock open. He was onto the creature and slicing its throat before it could utter a sound. "Hurry, do whatever it is you need to do," he whispered breathlessly.

Martyn looked at Speedwell. "Do what you feel inside of you, Martyn. All will become clear," encouraged Speedwell.

At first, Martyn did not know what to do as he looked at the pillar of rock. Kneeling on one knee, Martyn slowly reached out and touched the pillar of rock, but felt nothing but coldness to his touch. *Together*, he thought, *together, the dream told you.*

Closing his eyes this time, Martyn held his staff tightly and asked it to help him reach out to the pillar of rock.

Concentrating his mind, Martyn let his free hand reach out and touch the broken piece of Grimstone's rune staff embedded in the rock. Together, Martyn and his staff focused on the broken piece as they waited, hoping something would happen; it did!

A whisper of a long-lost soul came to him, locked in the rock that had formed around him for all this time. It was Grimstone's!

Who are you that dare touch all that I have left? challenged the whisper of Grimstone, for Martyn to come out in goosebumps all over his body as he heard the voice in his mind.

I am Martyn, Forestall. I felt your presence in my dreams this last night, he answered, suddenly realising it.

You? You are the one I felt?

Yes, Forestall, you came to me in a dream whilst I held my newfound staff from the Ancient One, explained Martyn.

Martyn thought he heard a sigh when his mind spoke of the Ancient One. He carried on. I am here with Speedwell and King Ashwell of Waunarle, who holds a defender.

A long silence followed, making Martyn think Grimstone had withdrawn.

He dares come here after what his daughter did to me! came Grimstone's harsh whisper.

To help me retrieve your broken piece of rune staff and make it whole again, Forestall! spoke Martyn's mind in earnest.

I have waited here all of this time, locked within this rock, for someone to come from the Ancient One to mend what she has desecrated, hoping against all hopes it would be my son. Instead, a boy with not even a rune staff awakes me! Martyn did not like being told this, even though it was true. Lost soul of a Forestall or not, determination and pride answered back.

Together, you whispered to me, and together we stand before you to put right the wrong she has done to you. The staff I gained from the Ancient One may still be plain, but it heard your call, and once the runes are written upon it then together she shall meet her match, promised Martyn to the quietness that met him.

Martyn suddenly felt Grimstone's soul look into his mind to see his plain staff that he held, making him shiver as he felt Grimstone's soul's scrutiny.

A reasoning, much calmer whisper re-entered his mind. *The Ancient One must believe in you for you to be here. Perhaps there is something in the staff you have gained. There is a strength within it and your spirit, I can feel it.*

Then please help us, Forestall. She has already destroyed the Plateau Forest and if we do not stop her, the Great Forest will follow.

What felt like a groan at hearing this echoed in Martyn's mind. *The Plateau Forest is destroyed! Her jealousy has been surpassed by an evil I did not see. Tell me what has happened. Is my son safe? And what is this defender you speak of?* Questions Martyn tried his best to answer as quickly as he could.

Tarbor could not help but glance at Martyn all the time, whilst keeping his eyes on the creatures.

"What is he doing that is taking so long?" he asked Speedwell edgily.

"He is talking to Grimstone's spirit, I can sense it. I did not realise it was trapped in there," replied Speedwell sadly.

"Did not realise? Have you never been here?" said Tarbor, frowning.

"Not until this day," admitted Speedwell.

"Well, tell him to hurry anyway, we have been lucky so far," urged Tarbor.

"I cannot, I must keep my distance. It will only hinder Martyn. Grimstone's feelings for me are not exactly forgiving," answered Speedwell.

"Well, whilst he is talking, my strength is leaving me. I do not know how much longer I can keep the protection in place," warned Tarbor as the protective shield began to drone.

"You are not alone, Tarbor. Concentrate on the shield. Let me worry about the creatures," advised Speedwell as he looked back at Martyn, whose eyes were still shut.

Gentian had them made to help us defeat Helistra, finished Martyn, but Grimstone's soul did not hear Martyn speak of the defenders, as the shock at what it heard overtook it.

The Ancient One is no more! came the disbelieving whisper of Grimstone. *Gentian! Ringwold! My son... my son is blind! What has she done!* cried Grimstone's soul.

Look through my eyes, Forestall. Look at what surrounds us, beckoned Martyn, *you will see.*

Martyn felt Grimstone's soul reach out to look through his closed eyes and felt the instant horror it felt at seeing the malformed creatures. *It is not just the forests she has poisoned, but the people and animals too*, spoke Martyn's mind, to hear the sound of sobbing.

Grimstone's soul withdrew, leaving behind all the emotions it was going through in Martyn. To have been alone all of this time, only to be woken and shown such evil from a woman he once loved. He felt the feeling of desolation Grimstone's soul was going through at learning of the Ancient One's demise and that of his fellow keepers. Then to know that his son was blinded because of her jealousy; his sobs touched Martyn's heart.

Forgive me, Martyn. I have had nothing but bitter anger to keep me company for what she did to me, but I can see it is nothing compared to what she has done to the Ancient One and those poor creatures. I can only be thankful my son is safe, admitted Grimstone's soul in reflection.

I have seen within you what the Ancient One has seen, a saviour to stop her. Let us hope it is not too late.

Put your staff against the broken piece, Martyn. It will blend into your staff and be as yours. My broken rune staff will not feel its hidden presence whilst you journey to the Linninhorne Mountains, then you must rely on the first you have spoke of; but beware. As it releases itself, it may vent my anger that has been confined all these years within this rock. Then at long last I will be able to make my own journey to rest in the Valley of the Lakes, and for that, I thank you, Martyn.

Martyn felt relief wash over him that Grimstone's soul was going to release his broken piece of rune staff to him. He opened his eyes to see a concerned Speedwell and Tarbor.

"Well, Martyn, can you retrieve the broken piece?" questioned Speedwell straight away.

"All is well, Great-uncle, but if Grimstone's soul was laying uneasy before, it is even sadder now with my telling of the Ancient One and the Plateau Forest," informed a saddened Martyn.

"Once you retrieve the broken piece, Martyn, Grimstone's soul will be able to rest at last," sympathised Speedwell.

"His very wish as he spoke to me, Great-uncle, but it has never been if we can retrieve the broken piece, but more if Grimstone allows us to retrieve it," informed Martyn further, to see an expression of realisation upon Speedwell's face.

"Of course it is! The Ancient One had thought wrongly all of this time, but that is because of me. I did not realise Grimstone's soul was trapped in there, because I never came here to find out," he cursed himself. "Tomin will never forgive me," said Speedwell thoughtfully.

"Whichever it is, I wish you would hurry up. Holding this protective shield is beginning to tell on me," warned Tarbor.

"You will have to hold it fast a while longer, Uncle Tarbor, for when I receive the broken piece. Grimstone's anger has been held within the rock, and he has told me it will manifest itself through the broken piece when I get it," warned Martyn.

"Very well, Martyn. I will throw a spell of protection around us also," understood Speedwell, and before any more time had lapsed, another layer of protection was resonating around them, for Speedwell to nod to Martyn.

For the first time, Martyn felt his hands tremble slightly as he slowly put the end of his staff onto the protruding piece of rock and pushed it against it.

Closing his eyes once more, he let his mind blend with his staff and called to the soul of Grimstone that together they were ready.

At first, there was no response as a hush of anticipation came over them as they waited. Then slowly Martyn felt a vibration begin to run through his staff up into him.

He opened his eyes to see the protruding piece of rock beginning to change. The rock was melting away, revealing the grain and runes that were left in the broken piece of rune staff.

Suddenly a wisp of cold air brushed past them. Looking up, they all watched as Grimstone's wispy form took shape before them, to whisper one last time for them all to hear.

"Be strong, Martyn, mend what has been broken," then looking at Speedwell, Grimstone's wispy form seemed to nod in acknowledgement to him and then to Tarbor, before disappearing completely.

Looking back at the broken piece of rune staff, they watched it begin to glow as it entered into the end of Martyn's staff, to meld as one.

As the broken piece separated from the pillar of rock, an audible click was heard, for Speedwell to shout a warning: "Close your eyes!"

The blast that followed shattered the pillar of rock into a thousand pieces in a blaze of white light, sending the malformed creatures that were nearest hurtling through the air, their bodies shredded with holes.

Martyn, Speedwell and Tarbor were also sent flying through the air, to land with a thud amongst the dazed beasts at the edge of the barren clearing. Though thankfully cushioned by their shields of protection, they still had the wind knocked out of them as they lay there in a heap on the ground, for the shields of protection to fizzle out.

Martyn sat up and shook his head. He immediately felt the end of his staff, expecting it to be split where the broken piece of rune staff had entered, but it was as if nothing had happened; the staff was whole!

He looked at the bottom of his staff in the night light and could not discern the broken piece inside. "How did it not shatter?" he found himself saying out aloud.

"Grimstone willed it so," replied Speedwell, getting up.

"I would not worry about that. Worry about the shields being no more and what is around us!" cried Tarbor.

Three pair of legs soon found themselves running for their lives through the confusion of the blast whilst the beasts were still disorientated, weaving between them, despatching any that got in their way with a lethal strike from Tarbor's defender and Speedwell's rune staff. With their protection over them gone, only their skills at fighting could be depended upon now.

They were nearly at the edge of the clearing, to disappear into its skirting trees, when a pack of five snarling beasts held their ground in front of them, making Speedwell, Martyn and Tarbor stop in their tracks.

Pushing Martyn behind them, Speedwell and Tarbor faced the beasts, who instantly attacked them. The first fell onto Tarbor's outstretched defender, whilst another hit his body, to send him toppling.

Speedwell stood firm and gave one almighty sweep with his rune staff, to hit two more beasts to the ground, but the last one broke through, to confront Martyn, who held his staff in front of him to fend off the beast.

Tarbor had come out on top as he rolled with the beast, to slice its throat and get up in one movement, to look over at Martyn.

Speedwell had made sure the two beasts he had hit did not rise again as he too looked over to where Martyn was fending off the beast.

Martyn was holding the beast at bay successfully, fending off its growling jaws, but then suddenly he stumbled, falling backwards, for the beast to lunge at his fallen body!

Speedwell and Tarbor knew with dread that they were not going to get to Martyn in time, before the beast was upon him. Speedwell cast his rune staff like a spear through the air at the beast as Tarbor threw his defender, for them to somehow clatter against each other in mid-air, sending them in opposite directions!

In that moment, the beast had pinned Martyn to the ground. Martyn turned his head to avoid the saliva dripping from the beast's deformed mouth as it bared its teeth to sink into Martyn's throat!

From nowhere out of the darkness sprang a malformed creature, to suddenly dive over Martyn's prostrate body, taking the beast with it. As it hit the ground in a tangle of legs and fur, the sound of a snapping neck echoed in their ears.

The creature immediately stood up and grabbed Martyn, making for the trees. As it did so, it grunted, gesturing to a shocked Speedwell and Tarbor to follow.

Tarbor picked up his defender whilst Speedwell let his rune staff come to him as they both followed, to disappear quickly behind the cover of the fir trees, to see Martyn standing there, staring at the deformed creature.

"What? Who are you to have helped me?" he croaked in shock.

Speedwell and Tarbor stared with him but began to frown as they looked closer at the creature.

"It cannot be him, can it? He has been bitten!" said Tarbor, not believing who it could be.

"Look at the clothes, though, Tarbor, and the sword," answered Speedwell.

Martyn then started to realise who it could be himself that they were talking about, but before he could say a word, the creature held out its deformed hand for Martyn to look at.

The starlight showed him a metal ring glinting back at him on one of its gnarled fingers. They all recognised the ring that Cantell wore with pride for being the King's protector of Tiggannia.

"Uncle Cantell, is it you?" cried Martyn, for the creature that was Cantell to grunt and find Martyn hugging him despite his appearance.

"Cantell, you are in there?" Tarbor found himself saying, to another grunt.

"He is, somehow he has been deformed but not poisoned," puzzled Speedwell, "but how that has happened will have to wait. We must hurry and get away from here," he urged.

Speedwell did not have to say it twice for them to disappear into the trees.

Speedwell gave one last look before he followed, to see the creatures running around everywhere, confused by the smell of their own blood. Thankful that they now possessed the broken piece of Grimstone's rune staff and that Cantell, though malformed, was alive.

He cursed himself once more for being so feeble as to never venture back here to see if Grimstone's soul had been trapped inside the pillar of rock, but he was leaving with a hope that at this moment was shining bright in his mind.

CHAPTER XLV

Princess Amber gazed out over the balcony of Forest Tower, taking in what surrounded her more than she had ever done before. She would not normally have stayed so long looking out on a scene she knew so well, but this time it was with a different mind, one that had been awakened, but it had only made her troubled.

She watched as the waves lapped over the shore of Stormhaven Bay, with the skeleton remains of the once-invading ships stuck in their midst. Slowly moving her eyes to see that nature had all but covered the small fishing village of Haven down in the valley.

Sunlight caught her eye, breaking through in rays from grey-white clouds to light up parts of the distant Great Forest, a forest that would soon be no more from a sunlight that was becoming evermore rarer as the days passed by, but of course she knew why that was, and it had begun to trouble her.

Not that she had shown it in front of her mother, the art of deception she had learnt well. The same deception she had had to use quickly in front of her mother when she confronted the Tigannian and found she could explore his mind without her mother sensing it.

She did not know why she suddenly possessed this ability to feel and sense things in the way she did, but it had become natural to her in such a short time. She knew it had happened when her mother's whirlwind destroyed the barrier and the Ancient One. Like the waves breaking over Stormhaven Bay, she had felt something wash over her, awakening feelings she had never felt before inside.

That something she did not know of was the dense white light of her brother's spirit, too strong at his birth for him to hold alone in his tiny frame, so that some of it had safely mixed into hers without her knowing, but what was more important, without Queen Helistra knowing.

On that fateful day when Queen Helistra had cast the red bead of destruction into her as a baby, it had all but destroyed her own pure soul.

If not for her brother's soul keeping a spark of hers hidden within his, locking itself away until it could emerge again to free his sister of evil, it would have surely perished altogether.

That time came when Queen Helistra used her power to the point of her own destruction when she destroyed the barrier. Sensing her power so drained, his spirit took the chance to rid itself of the evil that had invaded his sister's body, cleansing her so her spirit could rise again. This it had done without Queen Helistra realising.

Princess Amber, though, felt only confusion having these new senses invade her body and mind. She thought of her mother replenishing her power in the secret room she now knew was called the crystal chamber.

She still waited on the promise made to her that she would see the crystal chamber, but that time had still not come, not that she would ever see it if her mother found out what had happened to her. The dungeons would be her home then, if her mother was in a good mood, that is!

Confused about her newfound senses she may have been, but there was something above all else that was bothering her, and that was when the Tigannian they had confronted told her she had a brother!

But what had disturbed her even more was when he had said she had a mother too!

She had found out he was not lying when she had dug her nails into his neck out of anger and disbelief, only to find he was speaking the truth, with her newfound senses opening his mind to her.

Not that he was truthful about his name, in that he had lied, but she had seen why; he was her brother's protector, Cantell. If he had said who he really was, Queen Helistra would have known her brother was nearby.

But if he was, she had thought at the time, then like the Forestalls, he may well be dead and she would never get to know him!

But there had been no time to ponder; she had been watching her. That was when she used her actions to disguise what she did next.

She found one of her fingers had split under her nail when she had dug them into Cantell's neck. She had used it to push her own blood into him so that it would mix with the poison from the creature she was going to set upon him to deceive Queen Helistra.

Enough blood she hoped to dilute the poison so that the darkness would not take him away altogether. Why she risked herself thinking this would work, she did not know, but this evil was wrong and she did it instinctively.

She had not been entirely sure whether it had helped him or not when he turned into a monster, but if she had tried to use her mind to see if it had, then her mother, who she had thought was her mother, could have sensed her and if not, then the broken rune staff surely would have, giving her away instantly.

So she leaned on the balcony with confusion reigning in her mind. She had found out she had a brother and the mother she thought was her mother was not, who, when asked about them, denied their existence! It only unsettled Princess Amber all the more.

Even with what she had learnt, she still felt the need to hear it from somebody, for them to tell her it was true, but who?

The devastation of the barrier and the Ancient One came into her mind, how the Forestalls had been blown clean away! Anyone in its path would surely have been killed, she thought, for her to think of her brother she had not known of once more.

But the Tiggannian had luckily lived through it and with her help, if it had worked, that is, still did, though she doubted she would ever see him again. He had been sent somewhere, but she had not heard where, with her mind the way it was.

She then thought of the beasts and poison that had been set free to destroy the Great Forest. What chance had anyone got? she thought, as she thought of what was left of the Plateau Forest.

Her mind came back to Stormhaven – it was wandering again –, but everyone that once lived here were either dead or gone, she thought. Princess Amber dropped her head onto her arms in despair and rested on the balcony. She could not think clearly.

As Princess Amber rested her head, trying to clear her mind, a strange feeling began to come over her. As she leaned there, her newfound senses were picking up something. A vision was trying to appear to her. She closed her eyes in concentration to try and see if it would open up to her.

Misty at first, a picture then slowly began forming in her mind. It was where she was, right here where she was standing! But something was not right. She was looking up at the top of Forest Tower, sheltered by the Kavenmist Mountains. She was upside down!

A pain in her leg made her reach down to rub it without her realising, to let her see that she was only a baby. The vision slowly moved upwards to show her why she felt the pain in her leg.

A gasp left her mouth when she saw what, or rather, who, was causing it. It was Queen Helistra! Holding her upside down over the balcony! Her face full of loathing and hate in her eyes!

Princess Amber pulled herself out of the vision with a cry of anguish and ran down the spiral steps of Forest Tower in dismay. Down the steps she ran, tears blurring her vision, along the linking corridor and around the corner, straight into the back of Mrs Beeworthy, who was returning to the kitchen, nearly knocking her over.

"Goodness me, child, where are you off to in such a rush?" asked Mrs Beeworthy, brushing herself down.

"Do not call me that! She calls me that!" blurted out Princess Amber.

"I am sorry, I meant Princess Amber," apologised Mrs Beeworthy straight away, to see the distraught look upon Princess Amber's face.

"What is wrong my, love? What are those tears doing on those lovely cheeks? Come, come into the kitchen with me and tell me all about it," and Mrs Beeworthy held out her hand for her to hold.

The kitchen was as inviting as ever, with the rich smell of fresh vegetables and fresh bread filling the air, mixed with the aroma from a seemingly continuous simmering cooking pot hanging over a fire.

Not that Princess Amber was taking anything in as Mrs Beeworthy guided her to the long table. "Now you be sitting there whilst I get you some broth. That will soon put you to rights. You need some meat on those bones of yours, you are so thin," remarked Mrs Beeworthy not for the first time, with her usual frame of mind that good food put everything right.

Mrs Beeworthy sat down next to Princess Amber after giving her a bowl of hot broth. She watched her tinker with it in a lost world of her own, waiting and wondering what the matter was.

She was glad of the sit-down. Her back and legs ached so nowadays. Time had moved on for her; her grey hair had turned white and her memory had lapses in it that were unexplainable.

She had lost count of how many times she would just be standing somewhere in the kitchen wondering what she was supposed to be doing next, having forgotten. Not that her memory being searched, unbeknown to her, by Queen Helistra all those years ago had helped.

Her only concern at the moment, though, was seeing little Amber so distraught. She had never seen her like this before.

"What is it then, my love, that upsets you so?" she asked once again.

"I… I cannot say, Bee. You would not understand," replied Princess Amber quietly as she toyed with the broth.

Suddenly Princess Amber clattered her wooden spoon down and looked up at Mrs Beeworthy in a strange fashion. Princess Amber almost shook her head as Mrs Beeworthy would when realising what she was supposed to do next, after standing there trying to think of what it was. It was obvious who would know if she had a mother and brother; she was looking at her!

"Bee, you have been here a long time, long before I was born," began Princess Amber, looking at Mrs Beeworthy with questions burning in her eyes.

"A long time, it is true," reflected Mrs Beeworthy, sighing.

"Tell me then, Bee, is Queen Helistra my real mother?" asked Princess Amber straight away.

The question made Mrs Beeworthy's jaw drop. Clouded images crowded her mind. "Wh…what makes you ask that, my lovely?" said Mrs Beeworthy, hesitating.

"Well, is it true?" challenged Princess Amber.

"Where you be getting those ideas from, young lady?" answered Mrs Beeworthy, getting up, suddenly feeling flustered. She needed to be peeling something to calm herself down. She may have become old and befuddled, but the day Princess Amber was born to Queen Elina had never left her, despite the many blank spaces in her memory she could not fill, though she had not spoken or heard of Queen Elina since that fateful night when Charlotte had died.

Princess Amber could see she knew; her cheeks had gone red. She decided to push her once more. "On my journey with my… Queen Helistra, we met a Tiggannian called Cantell," revealed Princess Amber, "and he said I also had a brother!" Mrs Beeworthy dropped the knife she had picked up.

She sat back down and looked at Princess Amber, with the memory of Cantell smiling at her clear in her mind.

"Cantell! He is… he is still alive! I never thought I would hear his name again," she blurted out in joy before realising what she had said, knowing that if Queen Helistra had heard her, she would be in trouble.

"He is, Bee, but what of what he was saying, that Queen Helistra is not my mother and that I have a brother?" pressed Princess Amber, needing to know, whilst not revealing what she had done to Cantell.

"It will be the end of me, little Amber, if she finds out," said Mrs Beeworthy, afraid.

Princess Amber looked at Mrs Beeworthy in understanding. These new feelings she had gained had made her feel just the same.

"She will hear nothing from me, Bee," promised Princess Amber.

Mrs Beeworthy sighed. She had kept her place in the kitchen all these years and said nothing for fear of her life, but the child needed to know the truth, she could see that.

"You are just like your mother," she beamed, stroking Princess Amber's short red hair, "except her hair was long and curled around her pretty little face," remembered Mrs Beeworthy.

"I have never been allowed to have my hair like that," reflected Princess Amber, but she smiled to hear Mrs Beeworthy begin to tell her what she needed to know, and she leaned forward on the table to listen.

Mrs Beeworthy began by telling her the story of the day her brother escaped with Cantell and Kelmar. How her father, King Rolfe, had fought Brax to the death, and how Kelmar had come back for her, but could only rescue her mother.

"That be when I lost Charlotte, your mother's hand maid. Struck by lightning, she was," remembered Mrs Beeworthy, with a tear rolling down her cheek.

Princess Amber listened with sadness to the tragedy that had befallen them all. That her father she had never known had been the King of

Tiggannia, not Cardronia as she had thought, but as she listened to Mrs Beeworthy about her mother and brother, it was with a strong feeling of belonging, a sense of togetherness, a feeling she had never had before.

"So it is true! I knew it!" she exclaimed. Yet in one way she had always known of their existence. They had been with her all of the time, deep inside her, her brother more so, but they had somehow been pushed away, by her, she thought. Suddenly she felt as if she could feel her brother's spirit, comforting her right now.

"Where they are now, I do not know. That is the last I saw of your mother, when Kelmar came for her. There were rumours that King Stowlan was hiding her, but they turned out to be false," finished Mrs Beeworthy.

"I know where they are," said Princess Amber suddenly, "they are in the Great Forest," she announced, instantly worried at what might have befallen them as she pictured once more the stricken form of the Ancient One surrounded by the poisonous mist and beasts ready to spread death.

Something was stirring in her mind as she thought of the three Forestalls who had tried to defend the Ancient One.

Forestall, a name she knew only too well, what her pretend mother had wanted to be, but had been denied, so she had said, but Princess Amber's new senses could clearly see the jealousy and hate Queen Helistra had for the Forestalls.

Suddenly she was back in her mind, hanging upside down over the balcony with that word screaming in her ears: Forestall! And it was coming from Queen Helistra's mouth!

She then realised to her shock that it was her she was screaming at! Her and her brother were both destined to become Forestalls! The very thing Queen Helistra loathed! So why was she still alive if she hated them so much? she immediately asked herself.

Was she being used to lure her brother? What should she do? What could she do?

Footsteps that were unmistakable could suddenly be heard coming down the corridor, breaking any thoughts she might have.

"Quickly, my love, you know how suspicious she be," urged Mrs Beeworthy when she heard the footsteps.

Princess Amber left quietly through the door that adjoined the servants' quarters that led onto the courtyard, but not before giving Mrs Beeworthy a big hug.

Queen Helistra put her head around the kitchen door, thinking she had heard Princess Amber talking in there, only to see that idiot woman Beeworthy peeling some vegetables with her back to her, not even noticing that she was there. It was probably her talking to herself, she thought, and she closed the door.

Mrs Beeworthy smiled to herself as she heard the door shut. All these years, she had watched Princess Amber grow up under the influence of Queen Helistra, tied to her somehow, with a darkness beginning to shroud her, making her distant, but in that short moment of talking with her she had seen the little girl that reminded her of her mother. She was Elina's little girl once more, and she carried on happily peeling.

Queen Helistra opened the door to the small room where King Taliskar had once enjoyed his odd cup of wine and slumped down in a chair. Why she had even bothered to see if the child was in there, she did not know. She had more important things on her mind.

Humming immediately entered it. "It is not something I wanted to do, but the barrier has taken more souls to destroy it than I anticipated. The crystal chamber has strengthened what we have left, but it is not enough to finish what we have started. We need more souls," she stated to the empty room.

Humming spoke once more. "The poison does multiply by itself, but the more forest the poison covers, the weaker it becomes. It needs to be fed!"

Queen Helistra tried to keep her temper. It was her own fault; she had not realised how much power it would take to destroy the Ancient One and the barrier. It had left her weaker than she wanted to be. She did not want to leave the crystal chamber, but it was a risk she was going to have to take.

A lull occurred before the humming whispered again. "Do you think that is where they will surface?" More humming. "Very well, we will go there with the child and wait. We will take our fill and return with a sacrifice or two to strengthen the soul blood as well." She smiled coldly at the thought.

Humming spoke again in caution. "They are of no consequence. Even if they have survived, their power is all but gone with the Ancient One no more, and when the Great Forest dies, so will they," she said, grinning.

"We will go immediately. The quicker we do this, the quicker their end will be," and no sooner had Queen Helistra sat down than she was on her feet again, opening the door to the small room.

CHAPTER XLVI

Permellar looked up at the sky to see only more grey forbidding clouds cross her vision. The weather had changed over the last years, but suddenly the skies these last weeks were even more threatening, with rain and lightning forever crossing the land.

Not that the pigs minded as they wallowed in the mud next to the henhouse, where she was collecting some eggs.

What harvest she had gleaned from her small farm was the poorest yet, with the ground being so sodden. The month of turning was upon the land and to Permellar it had been turning since the month of fruit, when half the apples she picked were rotten!

Two more eggs went into her basket for her two visitors that had come to visit. She knew they would like some fresh eggs with a good thick slice of bacon she had left.

Over the years, they had always come to her small farm to say hello, anything to get away from that cold, miserable castle at Elishard, *especially as I am no longer Queen there*, she thought with a smile.

As she went to go inside, Permellar cast a glance at the sky once more. *Always from over the forest*, she thought. Not for the first time, her mind wandered to Kelmar and Cantell, wondering how they were. If the skies were like this here, what were they like there?

She walked in to raucous laughter from King Stowlan and Kraven, her visitors, both laughing at the antics of Kayla, her daughter, who had grown into a playful young girl, with Oneatha joining in as she put the wooden bowls out onto the rustic table.

"Your daughter would have made a fine Princess, Permellar," chuckled King Stowlan.

"A mischievous one," she said with a smile, "now who does not want fresh eggs and bacon?"

The answer came from Kraven's stomach. "The smell of that bacon is driving my stomach mad. Hurry, Permellar, before it fades away!" Laughter surrounded the room once more as they all sat at the table, laughter that Permellar and Oneatha had missed.

Permellar put some thick slices of bacon, boiled eggs and bread on a large tray for the four Balintium soldiers, who had come as escort to King Stowlan, for Kayla to take out to them, making Kraven's stomach all the more noisy. "Uncle Kraven, you are hungry," said Kayla, laughing, as she went to the barn where they were housed.

Kayla was soon back to the sound of eating that had replaced the laughter, and joined them, tucking in heartily.

"That bacon was delicious, Permellar," remarked King Stowlan as he finished, slapping his lips.

"That is the last of it. I will have to take another pig to Marchend soon to sell. We need to stock up on provisions to see us through winter, that is, if you are not here!" chided Permellar with a smile, much to King Stowlan's amusement.

"Let us escort you there when we go tomorrow. It will be our honour," suggested King Stowlan. It did not take Permellar long to make up her mind and say yes as she thought about the weather. She did not want to leave it too long, looking at it.

Oneatha dropped the wooden bar across the door. The evening had been a pleasant one, with idle chatter of fond memories. Remembered to the warmth of an open fire that sat in the middle of the room, with its smoke gently escaping through a hole in the thatched roof, an evening that Permellar's father would have enjoyed, thought Oneatha, but eyes had grown tired, with sleep beckoning to them all.

King Stowlan and Kraven gladly opted to sleep where they sat around the fire. Kayla was already asleep with a smile on her face from the stories she had heard from King Stowlan and Kraven. Permellar checked her one last time before retiring herself, saying goodnight to Oneatha.

"I hope the sky is clear for us tomorrow," she said as they hugged.

"It will be, at least you have those two to keep you company," said Oneatha with a smile, making Permellar laugh.

"Just look at him. You would not think he ruled Balintium." Permellar grinned as the snoring started from a ruddy-faced King Stowlan.

The night settled and rain began to fall, softly at first, but increasing as the night drew on.

Whether it was the thunder or the rain that woke her, Permellar was not sure, but the scream certainly did!

The dawning grey light was barely casting itself through the shuttered window as she got up to see if she was hearing things. Moving to the window, Permellar slid the wooden bar out of its brackets and opened the small wooden shutter slowly.

Screwing her eyes up, she peered out through the narrow opening at the barn across the farmyard, where the escort were resting.

She could clearly hear the horses of the escort neighing with fright as she looked. A movement caught her eye. What was that? A hand pulling at her clothes made her jump!

"Mother, I heard something." It was Kayla, shaking with fright, who had joined her.

Without looking at her, Permellar stroked her hair. "The horses are frightened at the sound of thunder, that is all," she assured her, whilst still looking out at the barn with a feeling that something was not quite right.

Then suddenly the horses were bolting out of the barn, with a soldier astride one of them. Permellar caught a face of sheer terror as lightning lit up the scene.

Another soldier appeared, running frantically out of the barn, passing the side of the farmhouse, to be heard banging on the barred door, shouting! "Let me in! Let me in! It has mauled them!"

By now, everyone was awake. Kraven had taken the wooden bar off and let the frantic soldier in. "Bar it! Bar it again! It will kill us all!" shouted the soldier.

"What are you on about? Pull yourself together, soldier. Explain yourself," ordered King Stowlan.

"A hideous monster, sire, in the barn! It torn out my comrades' throats!" cried the soldier, who shook in fear.

Permellar heard the soldier clearly, as did Kayla, who clung on to her mother with her eyes shut.

Permellar, though, in that moment was of no use to Kayla, as her own fear gripped her when she saw what the soldier was frightened of.

Lurching out of the barn with blood dripping from its mouth was a hideous creature that made Permellar's stomach turn, but what followed it took her breath away! It was one of the soldiers who had been mauled. He was unrecognisable. His neck oozed orange blood as he stumbled out of the barn!

"King Stowlan, Kraven, look!" gasped Permellar, holding on to Kayla tightly.

King Stowlan and Kraven stared in disbelief at what they saw as lightning lit up the full horror.

After all this time, King Stowlan had been thinking that Speedwell's prophecy about what could happen was not going to, but his warning was shouting loud and clear in his head right now as he stared in fear at the grotesque creatures.

"Speedwell warned us!" he cried. "The evil has come here!"

Kraven could only see red when he saw that one of his soldiers had been mauled by this monster. He was not going to let that thing do that to his men, and with his sword drawn, he ran outside to deal with the creature.

The rain poured as Kraven ran headlong at the beast through a farmyard full of mud and puddles. The creature was ready for him, with its own sword drawn. Kraven looked at the sword, only knowing of two such swords being of similar style, those of the two Manelves, Piper and Tintwist, except this one was much longer.

Not dwelling on these thoughts, Kraven weighed in heavily on the malformed creature. He tried not to look at its distorted features in the light of the storm as he brought his sword down across the creature, only to be met by its long, narrow blade in counter, pushing Kraven off.

Then he found he had to defend himself in earnest as the creature thrust its sword at Kraven, once, twice, three times, with a power that took Kraven a little by surprise, putting him on the back foot.

Defending himself, Kraven never saw the soldier who had been bitten creep up on him on his blind side to strike out and slice him across his shoulder through his leather tunic, the pain soon telling him he was there.

An automatic reaction to the blow saw Kraven's sword pull across his body and cut through the air sideways, slicing straight through the soldier's gouged throat, only just coming back in time to meet another blow from the creature.

Kraven had no time to think of the pain or who he had just killed, albeit one of his own men. His concentration was on what lay in front of him, this grotesque thing that was matching him blow for blow in combat.

Each in turn struck out with blows, only to be countered each time until suddenly the creature slipped in the mud, losing its balance, going down on one knee. Kraven pounced straight away, coming down hard on the creature, striking its neck to release its thick orange blood.

Kraven immediately followed up his advantage by driving his sword straight through the creature's rib cage, right up to the hilt of his sword, spilling more of its orange blood, finishing it off.

Standing there, staring at what he had just killed, Kraven was joined by King Stowlan, Oneatha and the soldier, who was still shaking from what he had witnessed. Permellar had stayed at the narrow window, watching, whilst she comforted Kayla.

"Speedwell spoke of orange blood, but what sort of creature is it?" remembered King Stowlan as he questioned what the creature was.

"I do not know what it is or was, but look at the sword it used, not unlike those of Piper and Tintwist," stated Kraven.

Oneatha had her hand over her mouth as she spoke. "Perhaps it was once what Druimar spoke of, a child of the forest. Its garments are unlike anything I have ever seen," she observed, as she tried to hold back her revulsion at seeing its orange blood. "Is this the dark within us all that Speedwell spoke of?" she added, having to turn away.

"There may be more. We must get away from here to warn Elishard and Marchend of what has happened, Kraven," said King Stowlan, now understanding how the soldier was feeling.

"Tarbor spoke of beasts, but this creature is beyond that," said Kraven, looking at what it had made him do, kill one of his own men.

"You need to come to the farmhouse, Kraven, and get your shoulder seen to first," said Oneatha, starting to walk back.

"Let me see what has happened in the barn, then I will," replied Kraven, having to make sure in his mind that the other soldier was dead.

He left King Stowlan talking to the frightened soldier over the dead bodies whilst he went to the barn.

As he walked towards the barn, his shoulder reminded him that it had been wounded. Kraven ignored it. To him, it was nothing compared to the irritation he was getting from his blind eye at this moment.

Whenever it rained, it was always the same, itching constantly. It drove him mad, as it did so now. Out of habit, without thinking, with a hand covered in orange blood from killing the creature, Kraven lifted up his eye patch and rubbed his eye to relieve it from the itchiness.

He came across the mauled mess of the soldier in the barn and knelt down to look. He got a closer look than he anticipated as something reached out in his body and made him fall over the dead soldier to the ground, doubled up. Kraven would be no more; the darkness had been found!

"I am sorry for not being understanding earlier," apologised King Stowlan to the soldier as they waited for Kraven.

"You do not have to apologise, sire. I am a soldier, I should be prepared for anything," he replied.

"No one would be facing this evil," said King Stowlan, grimacing, looking away from the bodies, beginning to wonder what was taking Kraven so long.

"You must tell me your name. You are my escort and I do not even know it in my ignorance," admitted King Stowlan, looking at the soldier, but before the soldier could say anything, the sight of what resembled Kraven stumbling out of the barn stopped him open-mouthed.

The look of sheer dread on the soldier's face made King Stowlan's body go weak before he had even turned round to look at what had made him be so.

He stopped in his tracks as with cold realisation he knew this creation of evil snarling in front of him was what was left of his guardian and friend, Kraven.

With tears in his eyes, he saw that the blood on Kraven's shoulder had turned the same colour as the creature he had just slain: orange. "Kraven, my old friend, what has happened to you?" he cried. Kraven's gnarled hand grabbed his throat!

It was over in a heartbeat. In the next moment, the soldier was looking at his King lying in a bloody pool of mud with his throat ripped out!

The soldier could not move in fear. He had drawn his sword, but that was thrown aside as Kraven's evil form threw itself across him, pinning him down.

One bite into his shoulder later saw the soldier joining the deformed shell of Kraven's, to set terror in the hearts of a screaming Permellar and Oneatha, who had witnessed it all.

CHAPTER XLVII

King Brodic stretched his back after climbing down from his horse under some trees, as did his four escort, after what had been a long day in the saddle. They had left Walditch earlier that day under cold grey skies that had turned into rain for most of the day.

His thoughts were with his father, King Meldroth, as he stood there looking out over the eastern side of the Marchend Valley, eyeing the North Road, which would eventually take them to Marchend.

The long illness his father had suffered had finally claimed him, and those last moments holding his hand by his bedside were constantly with him.

His father's passing meant that he was now King of Silion, and as his first act, he had decided to travel to Elishard Castle to tell his father's old friend, King Stowlan, the sad news in person, but when he arrived there, he had found that King Stowlan had come to a small farm somewhere near here to visit some old friends of his own.

The thought of going back to Flininmouth Castle to feel its cold emptiness without his father being there was not what King Brodic wanted at that moment. He needed time and space to clear his head, so instead of returning, he had carried on to be here in Marchend's Eastern Valley to find the farm that King Stowlan was visiting, to eventually press on to Marchend itself, where he had not been since he was a little boy.

As he stood there, he recollected the last time he had met King Stowlan all those years ago. He remembered quite vividly he had come to warn his father of his fear about the alliance army, which had taken Stormhaven and had Tiggannia on its knees, that it could well invade their Kingdoms in search of total power. That they must both form a bigger army to defend themselves if the time ever came.

His father had taken his advice, though in itself a risk, to invite invasion by merely preparing themselves, but the fact was nothing had happened since then. Peace had prevailed. It was quieter now than it was before Stormhaven was taken, proving sufficiently to him and his father that the alliances' only quest was to avenge the deaths of the royal family of Waunarle as promised.

However, King Stowlan had spoken further at the time of darker days that would come through the evilness of Queen Helistra, that it was her thirst for power that they had to watch. That she was the one behind the disappearance of King Taliskar and not Queen Elina seeking revenge for the death of her husband, King Rolfe.

King Brodic remembered when his father had asked King Stowlan if he had any proof of this. That he had simply answered, well, no! But he believed in the person who had told him, a Forestall he had called him, a guardian that had come from the Great Forest called Speedwell, who claimed to be Queen Helistra's father!

He remembered his father had stood there in open-eyed bewilderment, not knowing where to look first, looking at King Stowlan and then at him, trying to understand what in the name of the sea he was going on about.

"What are you talking about, Stowlan?" he had asked, and before they had time to draw breath, King Stowlan was telling them what this Forestall had told him.

By the time he had finished, they were both utterly confused, as was King Stowlan at the time when he was telling them, if the truth be known.

The Great Forest was in danger of being poisoned, he had said, if some sort of magical barrier failed to keep it at bay. If that happened, then beasts would rise from its destruction and with the poison bring death to all of Northernland, whilst Queen Helistra sat on the mountain throne of Tiggannia, looking forever innocent.

He had called her a sorceress, that she had opened a door of solid rock in the Kavenmist Mountains for the alliance army to launch a surprise attack, adding that the son of King Palitan, the true King of Waunarle, lived and had become a King wielder with an ancient sword called a defender!

That did it. He could see his father now, shaking his head, pretending to understand King Stowlan's concern, but with no idea as to what he had rambled on about. All his father could do was to promise him that he would keep a wary eye on Silion's border with Tiggannia and another along their boundary with the Great Forest, whilst quietly reinforcing their army.

"I swear age has caught up with him. I have never heard such realms of fantasy before. A storyteller has surely entered his life," his father had said afterwards. He had agreed, although it had bothered him at the time that his trusted right-hand man, Kraven, who he knew to be a man of honour and who did not suffer fools gladly, had spoken in defence of his King that he had spoken the truth, because he was there when this Forestall had spoken.

Stories had abounded throughout the Kingdoms during those times, not least about Queen Elina's rescue, for her to only disappear herself and never be seen again, let alone the story that had come from Marchend, where he was eventually heading, about someone who had seen a beast and had then been burnt to death in a fire!

That was a long time ago now and had all but been forgotten. Just like the easterly breezes that come and go, leaving behind no trace that they had ever once been there, he thought.

King Brodic held his head back to let one such breeze play on his face, hoping that as it passed by, it would take his sadness away with it, to leave no trace of how he felt.

"Sire," interrupted one of his escorts upon his melancholy mood.

"Yes, what is it?"

"A horse, sire, with no rider," pointed out the soldier.

Looking to where he was pointing, King Brodic saw a horse walking slowly along the North Road towards them with its head bowed low; it looked exhausted.

"The animal looks in distress. I see no saddle upon it to have had a rider, but let us go to its aid," he ordered, and mounting their horses, they rode towards the horse.

As they approached the riderless horse, it collapsed in front of them. Jumping off his horse, King Brodic knelt by the sickened horse to see what ailed it.

Sweat poured off the poor animal; its eyes looked unfocused and hollow. King Brodic laid his hand on its chest, to feel a racing heartbeat.

"Something has frightened this poor animal for it to be like this," said King Brodic, frowning, as he stroked the horse's forehead to try and comfort it, but in that moment the distressed horse let out one last tired snort of breath; it was no more. King Brodic felt its heart finally stop and rose to his feet.

"Sire, this horse belonged to a royal guard of King Stowlan's," pointed out one of his escort.

King Brodic looked at the guard who had spoken. "What makes you assume that?" he queried of him.

"It is a grey, sire, and its mane is plaited. Only the Balintium guard ride such horses," answered the guard.

King Brodic looked at the dead horse and nodded. "Something is not right for it to be here in such a state with no saddle. The farm King Stowlan visits must be near here. This poor animal tells us so. We will ride on to it. He may be in some danger. Be on your guard!" warned King Brodic, and leaving the dead horse where it had died, they quickly rode on.

The River Mid flowed full and fast alongside them as they rode along the muddy North Road. Trees began swaying in the eastern wind that had suddenly gusted into life along its banks.

They passed a ruined cattle shed, overshadowed by a hill. King Brodic thought he saw two stone graves in the field near to where it had once stood, but was not sure.

Trees appeared on both sides of the road as they pressed on into what became a wood, with the rain deciding to fall more heavily.

Rocky outcrops could be seen as they rode on, mixing with the trees, having punched their way through the earth long ago.

Suddenly King Brodic pulled up his horse in front of one of them. There at the side of the road, sprawled across one of the outcrops, bathed in his own blood, was the body of a soldier. King Brodic only had to look once to see it was the body of a Balintium royal guard.

Dismounting his horse, King Brodic went over to the guard's lifeless body and lifted up the dead guard's head, revealing a blood-splattered face where he had hit the rocks, with a deep wound on the side of his head, telling King Brodic that it had been his end.

He laid the guard back down onto the ground; there was nothing he could do.

"It seems we have found the saddle-less horse's rider. He was unlucky to have met his end here. The horse must have thrown him off. We will come back to bury him after we find King Stowlan," he ordered, and once more they took to the road.

Grey clouds bringing more rain made the day seem even shorter to the riders as the light began to fade as they rode on through the wood.

Finally, they emerged from the wood to be confronted by fields of grass that, if only they could see them in this gloomy light, stretched as far as the eye could see.

Cows mooed at them for interrupting their rest as they lay there at the edge of the wood, sheltering from the rain, whilst the River Mid wandered off into the distance to the southern side of the valley.

Onwards they rode until there through the ever-dimming light loomed a darkened shape of a farmhouse sitting further along the road.

It was not long before King Brodic and his escort were dismounting outside the farmhouse. Deathly silence greeted them, making King Brodic wary straight away.

Swords were immediately drawn when they saw the door had been smashed off its hinges.

Stepping carefully, they searched the farmhouse to find the door was not the only thing to have been smashed, but nobody was to be found. A shout from one of his guards outside had King Brodic running with the trepidation in his voice: "Sire!"

Round the side of the farmhouse he ran, to see the guard pointing at three bodies lying in the farmyard mud!

Though the light was fading, King Brodic could see the bodies were a mangled mess, mutilated beyond comprehension.

He stole himself to take a closer look. Crouching down, he instantly recognised that one of the bodies was the bloody remains of what was once his father's friend King Stowlan. He grimaced when he saw King Stowlan's neck; it had been ripped away!

Standing back up, he took an involuntary step back in repulsion as he saw all the orange blood covering the other two mauled bodies! Orange blood? He frowned.

King Brodic could not comprehend what he was looking at, except they were mindless horrific killings of which he had never seen the like.

Who could have done such a thing? he was asking himself, as the silence was broken by an ear-piercing yell of agony resounding from the barn, making King Brodic's blood run cold.

One of his guards had gone searching in the barn to see if anyone was in there; evidently there was!

King Brodic moved towards the barn doors slowly with his three other guards, his sword ready for anything that might move whilst trying to think who might be in there, waiting for them.

His earlier thought of a beast in Marchend suddenly flashed back into his mind as they closed in on the barn.

They did not have to reach the barn doors to find out what was inside, as the creature that had attacked his guard suddenly sprang out of the barn in front of them and began savaging one of his guards.

The word *beast* did not begin to cover what King Brodic was looking at as he witnessed the hideous monster rip his guard apart, leaving him in a pool of blood before he had time to react.

King Brodic felt all the blood in his body drain away as the monster squared up to him, nearly dropping his sword as its pulsating face looked right at him!

It was not the bumps all over it that had made him nearly drop his sword, or the twisted bloody grin that met his eyes, but the patch that covered one of its eyes as his mind went into shock, not believing who this unrecognisable creature could be!

King Stowlan was a mauled mess on the muddy ground behind him, because his trusted friend had killed him, Kraven! Or what was left of him. How?

His thoughts had no time to evolve as the monster that had taken over Kraven brought down its sword heavily upon King Brodic's head. He parried it, but the force of the blow sent him to the muddy ground.

One of his guards came immediately to his defence, striking at the creature's side, to draw orange blood!

King Brodic's attention had been so drawn to the creature in front of him that he had not even noticed that his other guard was in full battle with another hideous creature that made King Brodic gasp again.

The tattered muddy garments that the creature wore were the same as those of the guard they had found in the wood and the same as lay in the mud next to King Stowlan: those of the royal guard of Balintium!

King Brodic scrambled to his feet, feeling panic-stricken by all that he was seeing in front of his eyes, only to see the guard who had come to his aid dealt a decisive blow as the monster sliced his head clean off!

King Brodic thought that things could not get any worse, but as he thought it, the guard who had been checking the barn, who he thought was dead, suddenly came stumbling out of the barn!

His grotesqueness was that of the creatures before him, and as King Brodic found himself facing up to another onslaught of blows, the deformed guard began helping the once Balintium royal guard by attacking his own comrade!

King Brodic did not know how he kept defending himself. Blow after blow rained down upon him as he fought off the creature that was once Kraven. Then out of the corner of his eye, he saw his last guard finally overcome.

He had fought valiantly, taking the life of the creature that was once the Balintium royal guard with a last brave thrust of his sword, to see the creature fall to the ground, but even as the orange blood tainted his blade, he had felt the blade of his once comrade in arms slice through his body.

For all its ugliness, the creature that had taken over Kraven seemed to smile at seeing this and stopped attacking King Brodic, to let the guard join him in putting an end to King Brodic.

King Brodic tried to retaliate, but it was useless. As the attacks came fast and furious, he could only parry the blows one after another as they rained down upon him.

They pushed him forever backwards, forcing him out onto the North Road until finally tiredness saw him fall to his knees, dropping his sword.

The two creatures stopped and seemed to take great satisfaction at having their victim powerless before them.

The deformed guard stood back with what looked like a grotesque grin, to allow the monster of Kraven's the satisfaction of slaying King Brodic.

King Brodic bowed his head in defeat as Kraven's monster raised its sword to deal the death blow.

Closing his eyes, King Brodic waited to join his father over the Great Forest as a last thought came into his head. What evil was it that had done this? To clearly hear King Stowlan say, *Queen Helistra is a sorceress*, but what did it matter anymore? He was a dead man.

But instead of a death blow, King Brodic suddenly felt an intense rush of heat over his head, singeing his hair!

Then the smell of burnt flesh came to his nostrils, followed by the sound of two thumps next to him, making the ground tremble.

He slowly opened his eyes, feeling his singed hair, to see the smouldering bodies of the two creatures lying dead before him.

Standing up, he saw they both had gaping holes of burnt flesh right through their deformed chests!

King Brodic quickly looked around, trying to see what in the name of his father had done this.

He did not have to wait long as out of the gloom walked a strange-looking figure holding a wooden staff. King Brodic was not surprised he had a staff to help him, judging by how old he looked, the closer he got.

Then, one by one, more figures emerged behind the old man. King Brodic screwed up his eyes to see if he could see who they might be, but hoods hid their heads and their dress did not give them away as to their Kingdom.

As they drew closer, he noted four of them had bows slung across their backs, the longest bows he had ever seen, not that they showed as much on the two taller figures of the four.

They came and stood in front of King Brodic, for him to see they were all dressed the same, in leather tunics that covered them from head to foot.

A hood was pulled back and King Brodic could only stare as a shock of red hair fell around a small face that was looking at him.

"Are you all right, Prince Brodic? Your hair still smoulders," said Queen Elina, slightly smiling at his appearance.

"Queen Elina! I thought you were dead!" exclaimed King Brodic.

"As you can see, I am not," she answered, looking down at the smouldering bodies.

"I am sorry. I did not mean for it to sound like that," he apologised.

"There is no need to apologise. I can see you have met the evil we are up against," she said, turning away from the bodies.

"As did King Stowlan. His body, what is left of it, is lying back there, and this creature I believe was once Kraven. It wears an eye patch," informed King Brodic to her shocked face, making her look back at the bodies.

She was not the only one to look, as suddenly another hood was pushed back to reveal a face that King Brodic recognised from long ago, to look closer at the bodies. It was a worried-looking Kelmar.

"What of my mother? Permellar and little Kayla?" he asked straight away as he looked.

"I do not know, Kelmar. When we got here, the door was smashed and we were attacked by these," he answered.

Kelmar was up and gone in an instant with Queen Elina and two others to search for them.

"We?" asked another tall figure, who along with everyone else had now pulled his hood back, to make King Brodic stare even more. Fleck smiled at King Brodic's looks; it reminded him of the ones he had from his own kind as an outcast.

King Brodic's eyes were blinking rapidly, trying to take in who he was looking at. The day had already turned into one he would never forget, and now he was looking at faces of which he had never seen the like, with pointed ears! Where had these people come from? A phrase King Stowlan had used came into his mind: children of the forest.

Fleck answered the question he could easily see was on King Brodic's mind. "We are Elfore from the Great Plateau Forest. I am Fleck, this is Tiska and her daughter, Tislea," introduced Fleck.

"And we are Manelf, also from the Great Plateau Forest," said Tintwist with a smile. "This is Piper, that is Ludbright and I am Tintwist," said Tintwist, smiling, who for once was not worried about being stared at.

King Brodic remained speechless as he nodded to each one of them. "You said we?" questioned Fleck once more, for King Brodic to realise his rudeness at staring by answering Fleck, explaining why he was there and what had happened.

"I am the only one left alive and would not have been if not for…"

finished King Brodic, looking at them all, for them to turn as one to look at the old man he had first seen.

King Brodic also looked, and as he did so, the old man moved one of his fingers on the staff he held, making the top of the staff glow softly to give them light.

He could now see under the soft glow that it was no ordinary staff the old man held, but one with symbols carved down its length, making King Brodic realise that what King Stowlan had told his father was not all make-believe; he was surrounded by whom he had talked of.

His mind was going through what King Stowlan had said: sorceress, beasts, children of the forest and an old man?

"Speedwell?" he suddenly uttered, with the name half catching in his throat.

Tomin smiled at the confused voice he was hearing. "No, I am Tomin. Speedwell is my grandfather," he stated, much to the smiles of everyone at the look on King Brodic's face.

"You… you did this?" King Brodic pointed at the seared bodies.

"I am afraid I did. It saddens me to do so for they were once like us, until her evil touched them. I can only be thankful that I am blind so as not to see what my mother has done to them, though in my soul I know," replied Tomin painfully, making King Brodic nearly choke.

"You are blind! And your mother…!" King Brodic could not help but blurt out the words at what he was hearing. He looked more closely at Tomin to see his unfocused eyes. A blind man had saved him and his mother is? It cannot be!

Tomin ignored King Brodic's outburst; his mind was elsewhere. "My actions could have alerted her of our presence," he worried.

Shouts from the farmyard stopped any more worries or answers that might be had as Kelmar's voice desperately shouted for his mother, Permellar and Kayla.

"Mother, it is me, Kelmar! Permellar! Kayla, where are you? Can you hear me?" All stood still listening, nothing.

Everyone began searching as they joined Kelmar in the farmyard.

King Brodic saw a tearful Queen Elina standing over the mauled body of King Stowlan in the light of a lit torch.

Farm buildings and outer buildings were searched, only to find what remained of the other unfortunate guards.

"We cannot find them, Kelmar, only the bloody remains of the guards," reported Tintwist.

Kelmar hung his head in despair. "They may have escaped to Marchend," he said hopefully.

Suddenly a noise came to their ears, but it was only the pigs grunting inside their shelter.

"They smell the evil that is here," commented Cillan.

"And I can smell them," said Tintwist, holding his nose.

"And what is wrong with the smell of a pig?" came a voice from behind them, to see a dishevelled Oneatha, Permellar and Kayla stepping out of the pig shelter, with Fleck, who was the one to speak, smiling behind them.

"They were hiding in the pig shelter, still thinking it was unsafe down a hole covered by a board, but they could not get out anyway, because the pigs were lying on top of it," explained Fleck.

"What, and you heard them?" asked Cillan.

"These ears are not just to make us look good." Fleck laughed, to grins as Kelmar rushed to hug them all in relief at them being safe.

Tears of joy and laughter resounded as they moved into the farmhouse, hugging each other.

"You are alive, my son," cried Oneatha, once inside.

"Of course I am, Mother," he said, smiling, as he hugged her tight in one arm whilst hugging Permellar and Kayla in the other.

"I never thought I would see you again," cried Permellar.

"I am not that easy to get rid of," he said with a grin, just managing to choke back his emotions, not telling her that he had felt the same.

Permellar looked around at her broken home and then at all the different faces in the torchlight. Ruin and hope all in the same room, she thought, to clearly hear her father telling her those bedtime stories that once upon a time had been lost to her, but not anymore. Now she was seeing the stories in front of her. How he would have loved this, she thought, but then she noticed there were some faces missing!

"Where is Prince Martyn? He must be as tall as you by now," she asked, looking at Queen Elina, "and Cantell, where is he? Tarbor and Speedwell?" she asked further, after looking again.

"Martyn, Speedwell and Tarbor are journeying to a mountain far away, to perform a ceremony that will empower a staff Martyn now has to finally rid us of Queen Helistra," answered Tomin, with no emotion in his voice as he spoke of his mother.

Permellar was not sure what Tomin was on about as she looked at Queen Elina. "It is true. If all goes well, they should be in Northernland by the month of snow," she confirmed, but Permellar could hear only worry in her voice.

"And what of Cantell?" she asked, gripping Kelmar's arm in fear of his answer.

"We do not know if he is alive or not, Permellar. He was not with us at the settlement where we were. All we know is that where he was, there was an explosion and Speedwell lost his brother, Ringwold. We waited, but there was no sign of him. In the end, we had to fight our way out to get here," explained Kelmar, bowing his head.

Permellar saw the pain on Kelmar's face, telling her he had all but lost hope that Cantell was still alive, for her tears to flow.

"But our troubles have been your troubles by what we have come across here. What happened?" asked Kelmar.

Permellar wiped away her tears to explain. "It was awful, poor King Stowlan," she began, and she told them all of the horrific scenes they had witnessed.

"If they had not decided to gorge themselves on the bodies, I know we would not be standing here. It gave us time to make for the bolthole we have always had, in case of trouble, underneath the pig shelter. I remembered Speedwell saying how they could smell fear upon us, so I thought the smell of the pigs would disguise the fear we all had, but when we finally realised it was you calling, we could not get out for the weight of them over the board," finished Permellar, to the sound of a chuckle from Tintwist as he thought of the pigs laying there, a chuckle that soon subsided with a look from Piper.

"The sooner we warn Marchend, the better. Otherwise, they will be ill prepared for what is coming their way," spoke Kelmar worriedly.

"They will never be prepared for the evil that is coming, Kelmar," said Tomin to nodded agreement.

"I certainly was not," admitted King Brodic.

"I was with my father when King Stowlan tried to warn us of what was waiting out there and what we must do, but we thought his mind was wandering, the more he spoke, that such things could only be made up," further admitted King Brodic.

"As I did of Tarbor," remembered Kelmar.

"If my father were alive, he would still not have believed what I have witnessed this night, but I am glad he is not here to see his old friend lying out there like that. The stars willing, they will see each other again over the Great Forest," he added sadly.

"King Meldroth is gone from us," said Queen Elina in sorrow at hearing this.

"In the month of stars, my lady, in his sleep. That is why I am here. I was going to tell King Stowlan personally, but..." There was no need to say any more.

"You must warn your people, King Brodic, and the people of Balintium what is about to happen. Your army must be ready, as that of Balintium's, for what is to come. I presume when King Stowlan warned you of what you must do, it was to increase your army. I hope you took that part seriously?" queried Kelmar.

"We did, though these last years have seen nothing but peace in Northernland," answered King Brodic.

"A peace as you have seen that will soon be no more, and this is only the beginning of what Queen Helistra has planned," warned Kelmar.

"What do you mean?" asked King Brodic, not liking the sound of what Kelmar was implying.

"She means to destroy everything! All of Northernland!"

A silence followed from King Brodic at the thought of such a thing happening, before he spoke again.

"Though I am their King, I think I will be hard pressed to make them believe me," worried King Brodic.

"Not when you take our friends the Elfore and Manelf with you, with one of the deformed bodies as proof. Then they will see who they really are and what she has made them become," answered Kelmar to King Brodic's doubt.

"The same must be said for you also, Kelmar, if they are to believe you in Marchend," pointed out Fleck.

"That is true, Fleck. I am witness to that," said Urchel, remembering the ridicule he received when he told his story of what had happened to Idrig and was thrown into jail.

Kelmar nodded, remembering when the soldier called Tayell recognised Tarbor when they went to rescue Urchel.

"Yes, we have been there before. Very well, you, Fleck, Tintwist and Cillan will come with me to Marchend. Everyone else will go with King Brodic to Flininmouth," decided Kelmar.

All agreed with Kelmar, though long looks passed between the company that had become more than just friends as a fire was lit and they rested where they could for the night.

"You had better take this with you, Piper," said Tintwist, handing over the wrapped rune staff of Ringwold's to her. Piper wanted to say so much to Tintwist, but instead she silently accepted the rune staff from him.

"I will take good care of it until your return." She smiled back as she received it.

"We will not be parted for long. We are only going to warn them after all," he assured her with his usual smile.

"Yes, you are, so do not do anything silly," she warned him with worry in her heart.

Fleck watched them with a smile; it was obvious how much they cared for each other. He had always known it living with them. He would watch him, he thought.

Fleck looked at Tiska in the same way Tintwist looked at Piper. He had grown a fondness for her over all of this time, but he had kept himself at a distance, knowing that Tislea disapproved. He understood her feelings for her father; Sleap had been a good Elfore.

Tiska patrolled outside with Tislea, having taken first watch, pleased that they would still be together, although Tiska hoped that the stars and trees would be watching over Fleck on his journey to Marchend.

Kelmar sat quietly with his mother, Queen Elina, Permellar and Kayla, who was fast asleep. He watched King Brodic look from Tomin to Ludbright to Urchel and then to Cillan as they all told him their stories of what had happened to them.

"He will never get any rest," said Permellar with a smile, happy that Kelmar was here once more, but unhappy that they were to part again so soon. It had been so long. "Will it be years again before I see you this time?" she said with a certain irony.

Kelmar looked round at her. "No, once we have warned Marchend, we will journey to Flininmouth to meet up again. We need to be together to help Prince Martyn, Speedwell and Tarbor when they return to defeat Queen Helistra," replied Kelmar determinedly.

"I know you will, but what of the other villages and towns along the borders of the Great Forest? Do they not need to be warned as well?" said Permellar, worriedly.

"We cannot help them all. Tomin has sensed an evil force forever moving west towards Marchend."

"The one you have encountered here must have wandered off. Tomin thinks the more people there are, the more monsters there are for them to create and sweep through Northernland. That is why we must warn Marchend first," finished Kelmar, to a shiver at the thought from Permellar and Oneatha.

Kelmar settled down, losing himself in the flames of the fire as he stared at it, with thoughts wandering in and out of his head.

The fire was reminding him to burn the bodies before they left, except for the two they would take with them on their respective journeys, hoping they would not be too late in their warning to Marchend.

But one thought dominated all others as he lay there, that of his old friend Cantell, that he was lost to them forever and that they would all be if they failed.

CHAPTER XLVIII

Sad eyes looked out from the Lesser Hardenal Mountains over what was once the West Plateau Forest. What was left was shrouded in mist, hiding the devastation the poison had wreaked.

Once-proud trees that had reached for the sky hung in grotesque forms, slowly rotting in decay, with branches hanging from them like deformed limbs.

Obscured by the mist, other trees had succumbed to the creepers' deathly touch and had fallen to the ground, lying as they did in the wet, sodden mush that was once the forest floor. No pods or creepers could be seen spreading their venom anymore. *No need*, thought Speedwell in sadness as he looked on, *they have done their evil work.*

The four had journeyed through Thunder Gorge and over the Lesser Hardenal Mountains to finally come across the fate that had befallen the Plateau Forest. A long, arduous journey that had seen them having to climb and descend the steep sides of the Greater Hardenal Mountains to cross the Ogrin River.

Fallen rocks from the mountains had made a jumbled bridge of stepping stones at the bottom of Thunder Gorge over the Ogrin River, but with the conditions that had met them, they had been more than treacherous.

Rain had lashed down from the dark grey clouds looming overhead, helped by the never– ending wind that hurtled down the gorge, whilst lightning traced its bony fingers all around them, all brought together, it seemed, to try and throw them into the swollen river.

That was how it had felt to Martyn in one heart-stopping moment as a gust of wind-lashed rain had caught him unawares, making him slip down one of the huge rocks. Lightning had cracked all around him and Martyn saw in its light the hideous face of Cantell as his gnarled hand gripped his arm, hauling him back up onto the rock. Martyn shook his head as he remembered that moment, his ears still ringing from the sound of the thunder.

Pulling their cloaks tightly around them, Speedwell, Martyn, Tarbor and the deformed Cantell made their way slowly down the remainder of the Lesser Hardenal Mountains, careful to keep their feet on the precarious scree they had come across at the bottom.

The unearthly silence that met their ears after the clatter of the loose stones sent a coldness through the four as they began walking over the sodden mush of what was left of the Plateau Forest.

No birds were chirping, no animals scampering through the undergrowth, no leaves rustling in the breeze; just the eerie stillness of a dying forest.

Only a creak could be heard every so often, echoing in the mist, as if a tree was crying out in pain with the poison that had overwhelmed it, spreading as it had throughout its being.

Eyes flitted from one side to another as the four walked through the mire, making their own sound as their leather boots oozed in the slime that was once the forest floor.

"Are you sure we do not want any protection, Speedwell?" queried Tarbor, looking down at his feet. "This mush we tread in does not look good," he said worriedly, thinking it was still poisonous.

"What strength we have left we need to save as much as possible for the journey ahead. The poison has done its job, the forest is in decay, its potency has long since worn away and will not harm us through our leather boots," reassured Speedwell sadly, but Tarbor still felt edgy; there was something more out there, more than just the decaying forest.

He was not the only one, although Cantell had been saved in part by the intervention of Princess Amber when she blocked the poison. That part of his being that had been twisted had become more aware of the evil presence of those who had been turned, and he smelt it now.

He tapped Prince Martyn on the shoulder and as he did so, he saw a boy lost in sadness at the destruction of the forest.

Cantell tried to talk, but only grunts came out. He pointed to his malformed eyes and ears, then pointed all around them in warning. They all understood what he was trying to tell them.

"There may be something out there, Cantell, something that thrives on what is left. If there is, we may not be able to avoid it, well, not until we reach the river…" Speedwell paused in thought.

"The river?" pushed Tarbor, at Speedwell's hesitancy.

"If it is not clogged with all that surrounds us, there is a river that joins a small lake where the Elfore used to fish. There may be a boat left on its banks that we could row to the Linninhorne Mountains," suggested Speedwell.

A thought had crossed Speedwell's mind, that his daughter's malevolent spell would corrupt the rivers too. With the barrier gone, he had visions of it flowing into Northernland, and no matter what they did, they would be too late to save Northernland's people.

But he had dismissed the thought. He had seen the look on his daughter's face as his presence lay in the pool of life, the cruelty written across it as she relished the feeling of power. Relinquish that by poisoning the very waters she would need herself, let alone the monsters her evil had created that were doing her bidding? *I do not think so*, he had concluded.

On hearing of a boat, Tarbor could only think of his aching arms from the last time, but one look at Cantell's deformed face told him it was better than walking in amongst this death. "Let us head that way then, Speedwell," he quickly agreed.

The grey day wore on to the sound of their trudging feet through the mire. By now, they were all looking around with wide eyes. Speedwell had felt something lurking as soon as they had overlooked the Plateau Forest from the mountains, but had not dwelt on it. They had to cross the plateau to get to the Linninhorne Mountains, evil or no evil.

He could see that Martyn's, Tarbor's and Cantell's senses were all on alert. They needed to be, he thought.

Martyn's had come back to him after weeping inside at the devastation he saw, whilst Tarbor's, Speedwell noted, had grown much stronger since he had first felt the pool of life's essence speak to him.

He realised that Cantell would be able to detect the presence of other creatures, with his daughter's evil touching him, through his smell, but could not help but wonder how it had not touched the darkness it sought.

Night came and they rested as best they could. Back to back they sat, wrapped within themselves on a sparse patch of stony ground they had luckily found at the top of a hill.

Though, like the others, with his strength not fully returned, Tarbor was not going to take any chances if his feelings were anything to go by as he threw a ring of protection around them all for the night as Speedwell touched some symbols on his rune staff to create some warmth from the glow that began emanating from its top.

The night passed by quietly with heads falling in and out of troubled sleep. Tarbor woke with a jolt and at first thought it was still nighttime, but as his vision cleared, he could see daylight shimmering through a constant movement in front of his eyes.

He rubbed his eyes and looked again. His shield of protection felt weak but had held as he saw it was covered in crawling insects of all descriptions!

They were moving constantly, searching, thought Tarbor, to get inside. What in the name!" he exclaimed.

"The glow from my rune staff has attracted the little creatures that we hardly ever see but are always there," replied Speedwell, looking at them.

"But these are tainted by the poison, Great-uncle. Do not let your shield down, Uncle Tarbor!" warned Martyn.

"I am trying not to, Martyn. I do not like those things at the best of times, and these look like they are ready to eat us alive!" remarked Tarbor.

As they focused more on the insects, they could see the erratic behaviour they were showing. Some were trying to bore their way through the shield of protection as others scrambled over them, whilst others just ate whatever got in their way.

Suddenly thuds hit the protective shield, knocking insects out of the way to reveal hideous– looking spiders who instantly tried to push through the shield. Spiders that had grown into unrecognisable malignant creatures.

"I do not like the look of those," said Tarbor, grimacing.

"The food chain moves on. Let us see what is next," said Speedwell, making the others feel wary at his remark.

Then the pit of their stomachs tightened, knowing whatever it was they had felt before was here, moving slowly towards them. The malignant spiders suddenly stopped attacking the protective shield and moved aside, to reveal the malice that was waiting there.

Eyes of red were staring at them through scaled skins that were covered with pustules, throbbing to the beat of their poisoned hearts!

Three giant snakes were facing them, coiled, ready to strike, forever sending out their forked tongues from their grotesque features, as if licking their deformed mouths in anticipation of the kill.

Every now and then hissing a warning as they showed their razor-sharp fangs dripping with venom, ready to sink into their flesh.

A spider dared move across the sight of one and was instantly pounced upon, fangs driven through it, crushing it to a pulp, with orange blood oozing out of its jaws in its twisted grip.

Tarbor looked at the red eyes and could not help but think of Queen Helistra with her bloodshot eye. "Does she see us through their eyes?" he found himself saying.

"They want to crush us in their grip and sink those fangs of death into us, Tarbor. Beyond that, there is nothing," replied Speedwell.

"Is that all?" chided Tarbor.

"Well, I have enough strength to give them a farewell gift if you are struggling to hold the shield," prompted Speedwell, for them all to stand up.

"If those things attack us, then I will be," he agreed.

"Are you ready then?"

"Ready!"

Speedwell touched some symbols on his rune staff and whispered a spell three times over. Holding his rune staff up, he waved it through the air three times. "That should do it. Now, Tarbor!"

Tarbor cut his defender through the air as he spoke in his mind: *Cease, shield. Awaken, white fire!*

The protective shield had barely dispersed before three waves of blue fire scorched through the air from Speedwell's rune staff, straight at the three snakes' heads, setting them on fire, for them to hiss wildly before their heads exploded in a cloud of black dust!

Insects and spiders alike were caught in the searing heat from the blue flame, then the explosions, but not all, as a swarm of flying insects turned on the four.

"Run!" shouted Speedwell as he sent more waves of blue flame through the air at the swarm, turning them into instant flying blue flames, to drop into the mire.

Tarbor lashed out at two spiders jumping through the air at him, slicing one in half with the defender whilst searing the other in white fire.

Martyn expertly twirled his staff, sending another through the air, whilst Cantell merely ran behind them, treading on several spiders as he did so, squashing them flat to the murky ground.

They ran until exhaustion stopped them from doing so, having to take in deep lungfuls of air, but that only set them all coughing, such was the foul taste in their mouths from the decaying forest, all, that is, except Cantell.

"That was close!" gasped Tarbor as the white fire of his defender fizzled out, with no strength to keep it alive.

"I think I got most of them, but let us keep at a brisk pace," said Speedwell, immediately getting into his stride as he checked behind him.

"If we can in this!" moaned Tarbor, feeling the ooze trying to hold his tired legs back.

"There are still more out there, Great-uncle," warned Martyn, feeling the slow, slimy movements of the hideous snakes through his staff. Tarbor and Cantell could feel them too, but at least they knew what they were dealing with now.

Through the desolate Plateau Forest they walked, forever keeping vigil above and below until night cast its shadow once more.

"We are not far from the river now, I am sure," said Speedwell in the soft glow of his rune staff.

"Let us keep going until we find it then, Speedwell. We do not want more insects attracted to your light by staying still," prompted Tarbor.

Just as their legs were asking when they were going to rest from walking in this sticky ooze, the sound of flowing water came to their ears.

"We are here," confirmed Speedwell to the sound of the river, for two thankful sighs and a grunt to answer him!

Speedwell waved his rune staff in front of him, making it glow more, enabling them to see further ahead. A river covered in a slimy brown scum met their eyes. "By the stars, Speedwell, look at it!" gasped Tarbor, the river seeming to gurgle back at him as he spoke.

Then it occurred to Tarbor what Speedwell had dismissed in his mind earlier.

"If the rivers have been poisoned then we are too late. The people of Northernland will already be doomed!" he groaned.

"That would mean she would be poisoning herself if she tainted the waters as well, and the beasts who do her evil work. No, the strength of her spell she has cast is for the forests only, the very thing she feels has been denied to her," pointed out Speedwell assuredly, although worry did not leave Tarbor's mind.

It was then that suddenly Speedwell heard a call in his mind through his rune staff from the river, a call he knew only too well, to make him smile.

"Besides, there are forces here that are ready to fight it if she does," he added, making Tarbor frown.

"What forces could be left in all of this? Except those we hope to find?" queried Tarbor, for Martyn to suddenly shout as he felt it too.

"The essences, Great-uncle, the essences live!" exclaimed Martyn, feeling an inner strength coming from the river flowing through his staff.

"The essences? They have survived her poison!" Tarbor could not believe it. The pools of life were the first to be poisoned; he could still hear the cries of fear in his mind.

Speedwell did not answer. Instead, he moved forward and put the end of his rune staff into the river.

Closing his eyes, he breathed slowly in concentration. Tiny, gargled, bubbly sounds began coming to him through his rune staff. He moved his head sideways, as if to listen more closely, and then there they were, two little voices in harmony he knew so well. Glad to sense him, but with worry in their bubbles.

We are here, Speedwell. We have been waiting deep in the earth amongst the rocks for when we can flow to make the forests whole once more, but we felt the tear in the Ancient One's roots. It shook the ground asunder, they whispered in sadness.

But what are you doing here? they asked.

We travel to the Linninhorne Mountains where we have found there exists the first of the Forestalls who can perform the ceremony of the runes, he informed the essences.

There was a silence before the essences answered as they took this in. *Are you telling us that a staff was sought before the Ancient One's being was no more for you to travel so?* they queried in hope.

The spirit the Ancient One waited for is here with it now, he informed them.

Then be quick, Speedwell. We have felt the vibrations of power coming from the crystal chamber run through the earth! came their warning.

We will, and then together we will cleanse the evil my daughter has wrought.

Here then Speedwell, to help you in your quest. We sense your body is weak for such a journey. Take these with you to help you on your way, and Speedwell felt their tiny bubbles of life attach themselves to his rune staff.

Thank you, sisters. I am forever in your debt, and not wanting to be there any longer than they needed to be, the little bubbly voices were gone with a last plea to Speedwell through the river's waters. *Hurry Speedwell, hurry!*

Speedwell opened his eyes and looked up to the stars in thankfulness that the essences were still alive.

Lifting his rune staff carefully out of the river, Speedwell laid it down to find the little bottle in his pouch to gather the life-giving bubbles into.

He looked at the others, smiling as he did so. "The essences have survived and hold deep in the earth. They have given us their life-giving strength to see our journey through."

"I did not feel their presence, but will Helistra have sensed them?" said Tarbor, worriedly.

After safely bottling most of the bubbles, Speedwell left some out to begin mixing a potion with them whilst being thoughtful in his answer. "None of us felt their presence, because of the evil that surrounds us and our weakened state that has dulled our senses," he began, "and in that she will be like us, Tarbor, in a weakened state from the power she has used, but the evil that she has surrounded herself in has all but consumed her, to make her blind to her true senses that she was blessed with when she was a little girl, such is the malice that has overtaken her," finished Speedwell, sadly remembering his daughter in happier days.

"But it will not be just her power she has to replenish. That will not be enough to replace what she had to use against the Ancient One," added Speedwell worryingly.

"What do you mean, Great-uncle, more souls?" asked Martyn, realising what his great-uncle was saying.

"Yes, Martyn, exactly that. If they attack Marchend, she will be amongst them, for those she has turned to give her what she needs to take back to the crystal chamber," he realised with dread. "I only hope the others have made it in time to warn Marchend to defend themselves," said Speedwell with a sigh as he finished mixing the potion for them all with a touch from his rune staff.

"Then we had better find this boat and get to the wraiths of the Ancients," urged Tarbor.

"And this will give us the strength to do so," and Speedwell handed the wooden bowl containing the potion to Martyn first.

Though the taste was foul, Martyn was thankful to feel the life-giving bubbles burst with energy within him.

An empty bowl later saw the four set about their journey once more, with renewed urgency in their strides.

CHAPTER XLIX

Two horses, four riders and a stubborn donkey made their way through the cold sleet that had relentlessly pursued them from the East. Since early morning, when Kelmar, Cillan, Fleck and Tintwist had parted company at Permellar's small farm, the rain clouds had taken on a colder, greyer hew, to deliver the driving sleet upon them.

Tintwist was glad to be sitting in front of Fleck. It gave him some protection, whilst Fleck took the full force of the sleet on his back. It had turned out to be Tintwist's good fortune that there were only two horses left to be had at the farm that they could ride to Marchend.

"Are you sure you do not want to swap places, Tintwist?" shouted Fleck, managing a smile of sorts through the drenching sleet.

"It is not far now, Fleck. I can see the outskirts of the town," replied Tintwist, keeping low, with a grin.

"I am glad you can see through this," shouted Fleck again, screwing up his eyes, trying to see for himself.

Kelmar and Cillan rode the other horse, with Cillan having drawn the short straw, having to hold the rope of the donkey with the deformed body of Kraven on its back.

Every so often, it would stop dead in its tracks with a hee-haw of complaint, to nearly pull Cillan off his shared horse, as it did now.

"How many more times!" cried an annoyed Cillan as he felt his arm being almost pulled out of its socket once more.

"None, hopefully, Cillan. We are there," shouted Kelmar, seeing the outskirts of Marchend as Tintwist had.

All looked towards the first buildings that were trying to show themselves through the sleet as they approached the outskirts of the town.

Buildings that would normally stand out with their distinctive white paint, bristling with townsfolk all around them, selling their wares, but not today, not on a day like this. Just as the fields they had travelled through had been empty, with not a farmer in sight. Even the cows and sheep were huddled together out of sight in their stone shelters that were dotted throughout the valley.

The only sign of anyone being there was the smoke coming from the rooftops to tell them that fires had been lit, for cold hands to be warmed by.

The first day of the month of snow had truly announced itself, heralding in the beginning of winter, for all to stay in by the warmth of their fires.

We have come in time, thought Kelmar thankfully, noting the smoke whilst catching sight of one of the townsfolk scurrying from one building to another, braving the sleet.

"It does not seem but five minutes since we were last here, Cillan," said Kelmar, remembering Cillan's rescue.

"Do not let Tintwist hear you, Kelmar, or he will remind you who it really was that rescued me again," warned Cillan with a smile over Kelmar's wet shoulder. Kelmar nodded in agreement.

"At least the weather was better and you did not have this donkey in tow!" added Cillan, feeling the donkey pull back on his arm once more.

"Which way to the Mayor's house, Cillan?" asked Kelmar as they entered the empty town.

"On the north side, Kelmar, near the barracks," replied Cillan, trying to remember exactly where.

Onwards they trudged, through the empty streets that were awash with mud. A man opened his door and looked at them, to shut it again almost immediately.

A little boy suddenly ran out of another doorway in front of them, laughing, with his arms in the air, revelling at running through the muddy streets, for his father to appear close behind him, cursing, having to grab his mischievous little boy to take him back into the warmth of their home, barely noticing the two horses that were almost upon them.

Kelmar was beginning to realise how big the town was as they rode through its northern part when Cillan tapped him on the shoulder, having spotted the street they needed for the Mayor's house. "Up here, Kelmar, past the barracks, to the end," he remembered.

Riding past the barracks, Kelmar noticed two Balintium soldiers on guard at the gateway, looking thoroughly miserable to say the least. Even though they wore their cloaks and stood in the shelter of the gateway, they were still soaked through.

Kelmar stopped to speak to them. "Who is in charge here?" he questioned.

Without looking up, one of the soldiers answered, "Captain Ettard, why? Who wants to know?" asked the soldier, who then looked up.

"Tell him Kelmar, Captain of the Tiggannian guard of Stormhaven," replied Kelmar, making the eyes of the soldier widen and the other soldier to suddenly take notice. "I see you have heard of me," said Kelmar with a smile, feeling good to hear himself say his title again.

Hands went to swords, but were soon stopped as Fleck and Tintwist jumped down from their horse, holding daggers to the two guards' bodies, whilst at the same time pulling down their hoods to reveal themselves.

Faces could be seen to drop as the cold sleet stung the two guards; disbelieving features at the sight of Fleck and Tintwist.

"Tell your Captain Ettard to come to the Mayor's house, immediately!" shouted Kelmar as an order, smiling as the two soldiers literally ran from the point of the held daggers to go and tell their Captain.

"I do not think they will be long. The ears did the trick," said Tintwist with a smile, as he and Fleck pulled their hoods back up as they remounted.

Onwards they rode, past the barracks and around the corner to finally face a large house at the end of the street that sat on its own by the River Talmin. "That is it," confirmed Cillan.

Kelmar looked up at the house as he got down from his shared horse. "The Mayor has done well for himself," noted Kelmar, as he and Cillan walked up to the front door.

Two guards were sitting in a small entrance hall out of the sleet as Kelmar and Cillan burst through the door, to catch them totally unawares. Before they had time to think, Kelmar and Cillan had their swords pointing at their chests.

"We are here to see the Mayor on a matter of life and death. Where is he?" demanded Kelmar. Two hands immediately pointed to the door in front of Kelmar, for Kelmar to nod and point with his sword at the door to let the two guards know he wanted them to go in first.

They entered a large room to find no other guards in there, only the Mayor lounging in a chair with his boots up on a table and a warming fire at his back, smoking a pipe. He was soon on his feet when he saw Kelmar and Cillan storm in, pushing the two guards in front of them.

"You are the Mayor?" asked Kelmar, with a certain amount of sarcasm in his voice as he looked at a man who obviously only thought about himself.

"I am the Mayor, Mayor Wellbury of Balintium, Marchend," answered Mayor Wellbury straight away, before thinking he should be the one asking who this was!

"What? Wait! Should it not be you telling me who you are, coming into my office in such a manner!" he demanded.

Kelmar smiled and nodded, putting away his sword, as did Cillan, whilst eyeing Mayor Wellbury once more.

A man of wealth by the look of his dress, he thought, *a clever man too, no doubt, and looking at his hands he has never done a manual day's work in his life.*

"You are right, Mayor Wellbury. I have been rude, forgive me, but there is no time for manners, for what I have to tell you is of the utmost urgency. It means life or death for all of Marchend," replied Kelmar in earnest, making Mayor Wellbury sit down again with a frown upon his face, whilst the two guards were keeping their distance at the back of the room by Cillan's stare.

"What, what are you on about? You come barging in here! I should have you arrested! Who are you and what do you mean, life or death for all of Marchend?" came a barrage of uncertainty from Mayor Wellbury as he looked at Kelmar's stern face.

"I am Kelmar, Captain of the Tiggannian guard of Stormhaven, and this is Cillan of the Cardronian guards," said Kelmar, introducing himself and Cillan to a jaw-dropped Mayor.

"Kelmar? I have heard that name, but you are—!" Kelmar put his hand up for Mayor Wellbury to be quiet. There was only one explanation needed now.

"What I am going to tell you, you will find hard to believe, but you must believe me. Your life depends upon it, and all those of Marchend," began Kelmar to an already disbelieving Mayor, that this man was Kelmar, the one who had escaped with the baby Prince and was never seen again!

"There is an evil heading for Marchend from the Great Forest in the form of hideous monsters that will poison this town and tear it apart!" warned Kelmar straight away. "You must be prepared to defend Marchend for your lives!" But the response he got from the Mayor and the two guards was not what he wanted to hear.

At first, they looked at each other and then started laughing. "Not another, oh! Beware of the monsters coming out of the woods! Those stories have been around since the first stone was laid to build Marchend. There are no such things," ridiculed Mayor Wellbury.

Kelmar knew what he had to say would be met with doubt, as it had been with Tarbor, but unlike then he had the proof of what he was saying. He called to Fleck and Tintwist to come in with the body of Kraven.

They appeared, carrying his covered body into the room, their hoods still covering their heads from the sleet.

Mayor Wellbury's laughter soon turned into annoyance seeing the two hooded figures lay a large bundle down, creating puddles of water all over his wooden floor as they did so. "Who! What is this? Look at my floor!" he shouted, standing up once more.

"This, as you put it, is what will be coming here to poison and kill whatever gets in its way. Then it will be blood on your floor, not water!" said Kelmar scathingly, in annoyance as Kraven's deformed body was uncovered.

The shocked silence in the room at what had been uncovered was almost palpable. King Brodic's face had been pale, thought Kelmar, but Mayor Wellbury's face had turned white, and it looked as if he wanted to be sick.

Mayor Wellbury could not move; what was it he was looking at? He had never seen anything so grotesque in his life. Kelmar was right; it was making him feel sick as he looked at the creature's disfigured face that was covered in horrible lumps, with skin so stretched, it showed veins pushing out underneath. He held his breath as he continued to look with half-opened eyes.

He could see how the teeth were like those of a beast, with the bottom row overlapping the top, forcing themselves against the lips of a cruel, twisted mouth.

Mayor Wellbury saw the gaping gash right across one of its leather-covered arms, but instead of red congealed blood filling the wound, it was orange.

Then he looked at the one part of its body he had not wanted to look at but had seen as soon as the body was revealed: the gaping hole of burnt flesh that went right through its body. What had done that?

It was only now that he finally took in what the creature was wearing, to disturb him to his very core; it was dressed in the clothes of the Balintium army!

"Wh… where did you find t… this creature?" asked Mayor Wellbury, with fear in his every word as he began to understand with trepidation what he was looking at.

"A small farm not far from here in the Eastern Valley," replied Kelmar. "That is why you need to be ready," warned Kelmar again.

"There were more poor creatures like him there, but we burnt them, all that is except for one other, which King Brodic has taken to Flininmouth so that like you, the people of Silion can see what is coming to their Kingdom, so they can prepare themselves," explained Kelmar briefly.

"King Brodic?" asked Mayor Wellbury, thinking he had misheard.

"Yes, King Brodic. He was on his way to meet King Stowlan, who he had found out was visiting an old friend at a farm, to tell him that his father, King Meldroth, had died, but when he arrived at the farm, he found King Stowlan was dead, his throat ripped out, killed by what is left of the man who lies before you, Kraven, King Stowlan's trusted right-hand man," finished Kelmar to a stunned Mayor Wellbury.

The sound of running feet broke the stunned silence as Captain Ettard and six soldiers came rushing into the house.

Brandishing their swords, they immediately put Kelmar, Cillan, Fleck and Tintwist up against one of the room's walls.

"Say the word, Wellbury, and we will run them through!" shouted Captain Ettard.

When there was no answer, Captain Ettard looked at Mayor Wellbury to see a horrified face looking at the floor. Following his look, Captain Ettard nearly dropped his sword at the sight of Kraven's deformed body lying there.

"Who or what is that?"

"Put your swords away, Ettard. That was once King Stowlan's right-hand man, Kraven," replied Mayor Wellbury, hardly able to speak.

"Kraven? Never! This thing cannot be him!" exclaimed Captain Ettard, and without saying anything else, Captain Ettard was kneeling over the body of a man he had known since he was a boy, the boy with the wooden sword.

His eyes took in the same horror as Mayor Wellbury, only he was looking for the one thing Kraven always had, because of him, a patch over the eye he had blinded, and there it was on an unrecognisable face.

He stood up, closing his eyes a moment as he recognised the scruffy leather uniform that Kraven always wore. He never felt comfortable in anything else, he thought.

But what are these? he was asking himself as he looked with a frown at the hole of burnt flesh and then at the deep wound on Kraven's arm. Bending down, he went to touch the congealed orange blood.

"I would not do that if you have any sores or cuts on your fingers!" warned Kelmar, making Captain Ettard pull his hand away immediately. "Though he is dead, his blood may still carry the poison it holds into you, for if it does, you will become like him," warned Kelmar further.

"That or to be bitten by one. There is not an Elfore, Manelf or animal that has not been tainted so," spoke Fleck, who, with Tintwist, uncovered his head to gasps.

"Do not forget to tell them what will follow, the poisonous mist, creepers and spores," added Tintwist, to the open-mouthed stares they were getting.

"I think dealing with these creatures is all we need to occupy our minds at the moment, Tintwist," acknowledged Kelmar.

"Ah, you have not met my companions from the Great Forest," said Kelmar with a smile, seeing the looks they were getting.

"This is Fleck of the Elfore and Tintwist of the Manelf. Their people have already suffered greatly from these evil creatures and flee for their lives even as we speak. They are here with me to warn you all of what comes this way. You must be prepared to fight, fight for your lives or be turned into what you see before you, a monster that was once like you or me, our friend Kraven," finished Kelmar, pointing at Kraven's body.

"What must we do?" asked Mayor Wellbury finally, still trying to take in everything.

"Where do you cross the River Mid now it is swollen to get into Marchend? I have seen no bridges," asked Kelmar back.

"That is because there are none. Rope ferries are used this time of year," answered Captain Ettard, still looking down at what was left of his old friend as he spoke. "The eastern ferry rests further down the valley on this side and the western ferry sits just below Marchend on the Cardronian side."

"Then send urgent word to your counterpart in Cardronia that he must defend that crossing with every man he can muster, whilst you stop them on this side," urged Kelmar. "Bring him here to see our lost friend if he does not believe you."

"They can swim, Kelmar, even if we stop them crossing on the ferries," pointed out Fleck.

"I know, Fleck, but you saw how the Mid flows. It could be to our advantage," replied Kelmar.

Fleck nodded. It could be, he thought, but he did not share Kelmar's optimism.

After some hesitancy and a last look at Kraven's body, Mayor Wellbury donned his cloak. "I will tell the Mayor of this myself," and with his two guards he was gone.

The sleet had thankfully stopped, but the easterly wind still held firm as Kelmar, with Fleck, Captain Ettard and the rest of the soldiers, headed for the garrison. They had left Cillan and Tintwist with Kraven's body in case the Cardronian Mayor of Marchend needed proof, then he would have to deal with Tintwist also, thought Kelmar with a wry smile.

"I cannot believe Kraven has killed King Stowlan," spoke Captain Ettard, after Kelmar had told him what had happened at Permellar's farm.

"It was not the Kraven we knew, but the beast that holds itself within us all, brought out by the poison that invaded his being," answered Kelmar, remembering Speedwell's words.

"You have only glimpsed at what has been set in motion, Captain Ettard. I only hope our comrades find the cure in time," said Kelmar, for want of a better word, as he thought of Speedwell, Prince Martyn and Tarbor on their journey to the Linninhorne Mountains.

Captain Ettard just looked at him with one question: "Which is?"

"A means to kill Queen Helistra," answered Kelmar, to receive even more shock looks from Captain Ettard.

"You cannot mean that. She has done nothing but keep her promise—"

"To rid Northernland of a murdering King!" interrupted an angry Kelmar. "That would seem so, such has her craft been in manipulating people. King Taliskar found that out with his life and she blamed Queen Elina!" Kelmar had to stop himself; it was not this man's fault.

"You will see, but hopefully before it is too late for all of us. For now, what we have at hand is more than enough to contend with," said Kelmar, calming down as they arrived at the garrison.

A firm hand on Kelmar's arm stopped him from moving any further. One look at Fleck's face told him Marchend's worst nightmare was about to become real as Fleck confirmed his fears. "They are here, Kelmar!"

"Are you sure, Fleck?"

"I can smell them!"

"Summon the garrison, Captain Ettard. Hurry!" shouted Kelmar, beginning to run down the street.

"So much for getting to Flininmouth," said Fleck, right behind him, his sword already drawn, followed by four of the soldiers.

"If we are quick enough, we can hold them at the ferry whilst they catch up," urged Kelmar, but what loomed right in front of them told Kelmar differently, stopping them in their tracks.

Yellow eyes stared at them in defiance down the street from four snarling hideous beasts. Fleck saw Sleap, Bannel and Levan in his mind's eye as the beasts prepared to attack. The same beasts he had seen that fateful day; wolves made into monsters!

But then suddenly they were joined by three sword-wielding creatures that both Fleck and Kelmar knew were once Elfore.

"I must be losing my sense of smell for them to be all the way up here," said Fleck, slightly annoyed with himself for not sensing they were so close.

"Why would they be right up here anyway?" Fleck wondered out loud.

"Perhaps to go where we have just been, to kill the Mayor. You know what they say, kill the head," was all Kelmar could think of.

"But how would they know where he lived?" posed Fleck. Kelmar had one disquieting thought come to him that someone was here already, watching.

A clatter of swords cut short any more thoughts, making him look round to see two of the soldiers taking flight at the sight of the snarling beasts.

Kelmar looked at the two soldiers that had stayed, seeing the fear in their eyes as he and Fleck donned their leather hoods over their heads, not helping the two soldiers whatsoever.

"There is no running away from this evil. You must kill or be killed!" he challenged them, for Kelmar to see them grit their teeth and hold their swords tighter in answer.

Without another thought, Kelmar led the way, running headlong at the monsters with his sword swirling through the air, slicing through the first hideous wolf straight across its throat as it jumped up at him.

Fleck met two of the deformed Elfore head-on, with sparks igniting from their clash of swords whilst the two Balintium soldiers killed another malignant wolf between them.

Kelmar found himself having to parry the third Elfore creature's sword as it rained blow after blow down upon him.

A lunge from another malignant wolf saw it fell one of the soldiers, biting deep into his neck and twisting its pustule head to tear the soldier's throat out.

Seeing his comrade die in such a way inflamed the other soldier and he jumped onto the beast, driving his sword through its throbbing head, releasing as he did so thick orange blood all over his hands, hands that had cuts all over them from clumsily falling over the day before.

Fleck and Kelmar battled on, not noticing, with Fleck smashing the hilt of his sword into one of the deformed Elfore's faces, sending it reeling onto the ground, enabling him to deal with the other.

He knew how the Elfore fought and could see the pattern of swordsmanship they had all learnt, but Fleck had Speedwell's knowledge too. With a parry and turn of his body, in the blink of an eye, Fleck had driven his sword into the side of the deformed Elfore, bringing it to its knees. Pulling out his sword quickly, he despatched the creature by taking its head off!

The one he had sent reeling picked itself up to charge at Fleck from behind, but as Fleck's sword finished slicing through the first creature's neck, he turned with it, bringing it upwards, to drive his sword straight up through the creature's throat and out of the back of its head!

Only then did Fleck see the Balintium soldier convulsing on the muddy street, but before he could put him out of his misery, the last malignant wolf had taken advantage of his lack of concentration by jumping up at him, to send him sprawling onto the muddy ground, to lose his sword as he fell.

Kelmar all this time had fought blow for blow, looking for a weak spot in the deformed Elfore's defence. Only luck found its mark as Kelmar caught the back of its gnarled hand, making the creature look at it in anger. Kelmar seized on the moment and wielded his sword, slicing through its arm. As it growled in anger, Kelmar brought his sword back across the creature's face to send it reeling backwards with an orange stripe painted upon it, leaving its deformed chest open for his sword to be thrust straight through it.

Turning, Kelmar saw two things: Fleck grappling on the muddy ground with a malignant wolf on top of him trying to tear his face off and one of the Balintium soldiers that had obviously been poisoned ready to strike, standing over Fleck with his sword raised.

Kelmar hurled himself at the soldier, knocking him to the ground, with both of them ending up in a heap. The poisoned soldier was far too slow as Kelmar reacted by reaching for his dagger in his boot to drive it into the soldier's neck.

He then looked back at Fleck, who had his head sideways to avoid the malignant wolf's snapping jaws that he was holding at bay only a breath away from his hooded face, but even before Kelmar tried to move and help Fleck, an arrow suddenly appeared right between the malignant wolf's eyes.

Fleck gladly pushed it off, wiping away the saliva that had dripped onto his hood.

Getting up, he smiled to see Tintwist and Cillan running down the street. "I think you owe me, Fleck," called Tintwist.

"I had it under control," said Fleck, smiling.

"Of course you did," said Tintwist, grinning back.

No sooner were they reunited than ear-piercing screams were heard coming from somewhere in the town.

"Oh, no!" cursed Kelmar, just as Captain Ettard and the garrison of sixty soldiers came running down the street.

As they caught up with the four comrades, all eyes looked at the carnage spread across the muddy street.

"This is what you are up against! See what the poison does to you!" shouted Kelmar whilst retrieving his dagger from the fallen soldier he had had to kill, letting more orange blood ooze from the fatal wound.

Kelmar turned to Captain Ettard to see by his expression that he was querying the hoods they wore, as his soldiers looked on in horror at what was once their comrades lying there and at the grotesque-looking creatures that were laid on the ground all around them.

Although it was obvious there were openings in the hoods for their eyes and mouths that the poison could enter, their hoods had become part of them, making them feel safer.

It was far too late anyway for Captain Ettard and his men, thought Kelmar. If he did tell him how they were there to try and stop any of the monsters' poisonous orange blood from penetrating their skin, as he had thought in the first place, he could see them all running away!

"They are just an added protection of our own," was all Kelmar told him as he questioned how many soldiers Captain Ettard had with him. "Is this all you have?"

"It is. The same is to be said for the Cardronian side too. It is all we have needed. There were more here when the Alliance first invaded your Kingdom, times were more nervy then, talk of invasion, but…"

"But nothing ever happened," finished Kelmar.

"No, nothing ever did," agreed Captain Ettard with a shrug of his shoulders.

"That is because she was too busy plotting our downfall," piped in Tintwist.

"Very well, leave fifteen of your men with me and then hurry to stop any more from coming across the river," ordered Kelmar, just as more screams penetrated the air, making Captain Ettard react immediately.

Kelmar saw townsfolk running through the streets, coming out of their homes to see what was happening, with faces full of concern.

They watched as the company of soldiers passed them by, pointing in bewilderment at the sight of the hooded figures in front of the soldiers, but the sound of screaming soon made them run back into their homes as Kelmar picked up the pace.

A corner was reached and as they turned it, their eyes were met with what they had dreaded would be awaiting them.

Townsfolk were running for their lives with beasts in pursuit. Some had already met their fate lying in their own blood, whilst others were writhing on the ground, having clearly been bitten.

Then they could see doors being smashed off their hinges by a deformed Elfore, to let some sort of small misshapen beasts run into the townsfolk's homes to the immediate sound of screams and yells, for the deformed Elfore to continue whilst slaying anyone that got in its path.

"What in the name of the stars are those?" exclaimed Tintwist, as he put a poor writhing townsfolk out of his misery with a swish of his sword. "They are everywhere. Some look like they were once rats!" he added with a grimace.

"Whatever they were, they have already found their way across the Mid despite how it flows. They are ideal to bite their victims and turn them, no need for a large force, though they must be near," observed Kelmar as he watched a bitten townsfolk come out of his home to chase down one of his fellow dwellers.

"And so they turn on each other," added Fleck sadly as he too watched, seeing the same fate befalling these people as had his.

"We will soon join them if we are not careful, by standing here," warned Kelmar.

No sooner had he said it than the small beasts smelt the fear coming from the soldiers and turned on them. Suddenly, before they knew what was happening, they were surrounded by small misshapen rodents and bitten townsfolk.

Swords sliced through their malignant flesh, but one by one, the bewildered soldiers, who could not believe what was attacking them, began to fall from their bites.

If that was not enough, then the sight of their comrades writhing on the ground to then suddenly pounce upon them was too much for most of the soldiers, who were left standing as Kelmar found himself shouting the same warning as before, "Kill them or be killed!"

But it was still left in the main to Kelmar, Fleck, Tintwist and Cillan to deal with the beasts as they came at them unrelentingly. That was when Cillan felt the sting of being bitten himself!

His sword had just stopped a soldier from becoming a monster from a bitten townsfolk, but as Cillan was withdrawing his sword, one of the small beasts jumped onto the falling body, using it as a springboard to leap through the air and land on the hooded face of Cillan, to sink its razor-sharp teeth into Cillan's eye!

Kelmar saw it land on Cillan's face, shuddering when Cillan screamed in pain. His sword instantly severed the beast in two, inches from Cillan's face, but the damage was done. Cillan fell to his knees on the muddy ground, clutching his blood-soaked eye in pained realisation that his end had come.

Fleck and Tintwist immediately stood either side of Cillan, fending off anything that came near as Kelmar knelt with him.

"We have come a long way together, my friend," croaked Cillan in pained reflection. Kelmar could hardly look as blood seeped through Cillan's fingers.

"You have kicked me, saved me and now you must free me from this curse. Do not hesitate, my friend," said Cillan, smiling, as he held Kelmar's shoulder in one last moment of friendship.

"We will meet again, old friend, over the Great Forest," cried Kelmar, and without wanting to think what he was about to do, he drove his dagger into Cillan's heart, with tears running down his face.

With anger flowing through their veins at the loss of their friend, they could do no more than leave Cillan's body there amongst the rest, which by now littered the muddy street, to chase the remaining creatures.

"We must kill that monster!" yelled Kelmar, wiping away his tears as he ran after the deformed Elfore that was smashing the doors down. Fleck and Tintwist followed with four soldiers that had survived the attack.

They chased the deformed Elfore round the corner into another street, only to come across the same horror they had just battled through, with townsfolk running and screaming everywhere.

More small misshapen beasts ran through doors smashed down by another grotesque creature, who was now helping the one they had been chasing.

"I'll deal with this one. You finish that one! You four kill anything that gets in your way!" shouted Kelmar, and he was gone.

Fleck and Tintwist did not need telling twice as they ran after the second deformed Elfore, whilst the four soldiers moved up the middle of the street with wild-eyed stares at the horror they were encountering as they sliced through more beasts that tried to bite their ankles.

Kelmar ran headlong after the first creature, his feelings in a rage, when it suddenly stopped and turned from smashing doors to wait for Kelmar, with a snarl on its hideous face.

The deformed creature waited until the last moment before sweeping its sword across the path of the incoming Kelmar, but Kelmar had anticipated its actions, timing himself to jump over the sweep of the creature's sword, and bringing both of his hands onto the hilt of his sword, he drove it straight through the monster's head.

They fell together, crashing to the ground, with Kelmar merely rolling off to spring to his feet. Pulling his sword out of its head, Kelmar looked up to see if Fleck and Tintwist had caught up with the other creature whilst he wiped his blade on the body.

He had no need to see as he heard the cries from the deformed Elfore that Fleck and Tintwist had brought about by slicing through its legs. Its growls of pained anger could be heard throughout the street but came to a sudden stop as Tintwist finished it off by slashing its throat whilst Fleck skewered its head.

Kelmar needed to talk; there were too many cries of pain and terror to be heard. Joining forces with the soldiers once more, Kelmar, Fleck and Tintwist stood back to back, hacking at anything that came near whilst Kelmar spoke.

"More must have swum across than we realised before Captain Ettard got there. They are infecting the townsfolk quicker than we can kill them. We need a holding point where we can hold them back," decided Kelmar despondently.

"What about the bridges? We could hold them there," suggested Tintwist.

"But what of the Cardronian side? The same thing could be happening there," pointed out Fleck.

"They only have to cross one river this side, if they were to then they would have to negotiate the River Talmin also," reasoned Kelmar, remembering when he rescued Tarbor, Cillan and Urchel, as did Tintwist, seeing himself holding on to the tree branch!

"We will have it watched and chance our luck, but the bridges are as good a place as any. It will force them into a narrow corridor that we can defend better. Let us find Captain Ettard and tell him we are withdrawing to them," decided Kelmar, to Tintwist's suggestion.

As the company sliced their way through the town, Kelmar's frustration grew at how quickly the town was becoming infected; too quickly!

What was seen to have started in only one street was spreading fast, more so to Kelmar's dismay by the bitten townsfolk.

Finally, the company came to the North Road that led to the ferry, to be met by a panting Captain Ettard coming towards them with less than half of his men.

"Are they across the river for you to be here?" questioned Kelmar immediately on seeing him.

"No, not yet," replied Captain Ettard to frowns.

"What do you mean, yet?" came Kelmar's response.

A shaken Captain Ettard began describing what had happened to them, "As soon as we got to the ferry crossing, we found horrible small beasts swimming across the river. We killed them and kept killing them. The river carried some off, but there were so many, they just kept coming!

"My soldiers were bitten by them, then they… they started turning into monsters! We had to kill our own!" Captain Ettard broke down in despair.

To have seen one of his men earlier turned into a monster was one thing, but to be in amongst it all with his men screaming all around him!

He carried on: "Then suddenly it rained arrows, and there they were, lined up deep on the other side of the river! I have never seen anything so evil in my life before! We fired back, but they did not reach, they were out of range, it was useless!" finished Captain Ettard, distraught.

"You did what you could. None of us foresaw them sending in their small corrupt rodents first," admitted Kelmar, having an unsettling thought that all of it was thought through.

"We will go to the bridges and hold them there," informed Kelmar of his decision, with a look from Captain Ettard. "I pray to the stars that we can!"

They made their way along the streets that were becoming pandemonium, with terrified townsfolk fleeing everywhere.

The northern bridge came as some relief after running the gauntlet through the town, but that soon disappeared when they saw Cardronian soldiers blocking their way, with shields and spears pointed in their direction.

Captain Ettard with Kelmar went to confront them, whilst Fleck and Tintwist tried to hold their ground with the surviving soldiers by holding back the panicking townsfolk trying to get across the bridge.

"That is far enough," shouted a soldier from the line.

"Are you mad? Have you not eyes to see what is upon us!" shouted Captain Ettard at the soldier.

"I have had my orders no one is to pass," replied the soldier, seemingly oblivious to what was really happening, though his ignorance started to turn to worry when he saw more frightened townsfolk joining those that were already there.

"Who told you to hold here?" questioned Captain Ettard.

"Mayor Vorlic, he posted us here and on the southern bridge when he heard of the skirmish," came the soldier's answer.

"Skirmish!" groaned Captain Ettard.

"We thought another band of raiders had ridden in looking for food, so we thought to stop them if they tried to escape over the bridges," defended the soldier of their actions.

Captain Ettard nodded in understanding; he had to admit that had been happening. Two or three times they had had to deal with riders suddenly appearing in the town after food, with the weather having ruined many a crop, leaving people short.

"Was Mayor Wellbury with him?" he asked further.

"No, he was not," came the reply Captain Ettard expected to hear, turning to Kelmar in annoyance.

"The coward has run!" he said accusingly, cursing under his breath.

"He is the least of our worries. We can only hope they are not attacking the southern bridge whilst we are being held here," replied Kelmar, taking off his hood to get the soldier's attention. "There is no time to explain to you what evil comes this way, but these are ordinary townsfolk, not raiders, as you can plainly see! So I suggest you stand aside and let them through!" urged Kelmar, but it was not Kelmar who persuaded the soldier to let the townsfolk through.

A misshapen beast suddenly appeared. Jumping onto the bridge wall it ran along it to the screams of the townsfolk.

The soldier saw how the beast's matted fur was full of festering lumps pulsating all over its body. He watched in abject horror to see its twisted mouth open, to reveal fangs ready to sink into its next victim, seen as they were by two cold yellow eyes.

The beast made ready to jump at the screaming townsfolk, for Kelmar's reactions to be as sharp as the beast's fangs.

Snatching a spear from one of the stunned soldiers, he threw it over the heads of the townsfolk at the now airborne beast, lancing it straight through its malformed body, to take it sailing through the air, down into the chilling waters of the Talmin River.

That was enough for the soldier and his comrades to part, letting the frantic townsfolk through. They pushed and pulled their way past them, to run blindly through the streets in panic, causing their Cardronian neighbours to react just the same.

Even more so when they were told that the monsters they thought of as myth and legend were right behind them, killing anything in sight!

The Cardronian soldiers began listening nervously to the accounts told to them by their Balintium counterparts as they joined forces whilst the last of the fleeing townsfolk passed through.

Then as noisy as it had been, there was a deathly silence. The bridge had cleared for them all to see bodies lying in the muddy street beyond, beasts and townsfolk alike.

As they kept listening to their counterparts, they watched whilst two hooded figures went around the bodies making sure they were dead!

Fleck and Tintwist walked back to the bridge, having despatched anything that moved. "They seem to have stopped for now," observed Fleck as he and Tintwist took off their hoods to the gasp of the soldiers.

There was no time for niceties or explanations as Kelmar told the Cardronian soldier to get the rest of his soldiers from their garrison and make sure the southern bridge was reinforced as well as this one for what was to come.

"Send someone to watch over the west ferry crossing of the Mid also," he ordered. The soldier did not question Kelmar; he had seen enough and was gone.

The lull did not last long as they stood together waiting for the appearance of more hideous beasts.

They announced their renewed approach with more screams coming from those townsfolk who had tried to hide from them, but fell to their evil.

Kelmar felt the tension rise around him as he stared at what was heading their way from the street they had run from.

Townsfolk with poison in their veins appeared to be standing in front of what Fleck had fought after rescuing Tislea: a giant grotesque monster of a bear!

Kelmar could see movement to its side and behind, but could not make out what they were, but what appeared next he could; deformed Elfore with bows ready to let loose their deadly arrows.

A double row of interlocking shields were brought to bear, with spears threaded through them. The bridge was not of a great size, taking only ten men to fill its width, but Kelmar worried how long they could defend it with what they now faced against them, hoping those reinforcements would be there soon.

Arrows were notched from the half a dozen archers that held themselves ready behind the shields of their comrades to wait for the inevitable.

"We will meet over the lakes when this is done," said Tintwist with a smile, looking at the others whilst notching his arrow, thankful that Piper was not there.

"If outcasts are welcome." Fleck laughed, more to himself.

Kelmar said nothing as he waited for the onslaught. He was thinking of Cantell's and Ringwold's sacrifices that had already been made, with Cillan's fresh in his mind, whilst all of their hopes rested on Prince Martyn.

The tension intensified at the sight of the oncoming townsfolk, whose features had turned into twisted forms of what they once were, but this was no time to have any feelings, as suddenly arrows whistled death through the air.

Tintwist and the archers let loose their arrows in reply, trying to hit the malformed bear. Two hit their target, embedding in its hump, whilst the rest found the poisoned townsfolk that partially hid it, but it was nowhere near enough to stop it.

Retaliation was swift from the deformed Elfore, letting loose more arrows to find their mark, killing three of the archers.

Before they knew it, the remaining archers had spent all of their arrows and now stood waiting with their swords.

Tintwist found his mark one last time as the poisoned townsfolk ran headlong at the wall of soldiers, to hurl themselves at the shields, impaling themselves upon the spears.

The townsfolk's deformed bodies impaled on their spears brought chaos to the line and minds of the soldiers, causing it to buckle enough for the malformed bear to charge straight through it, sending all that were in its way flying through the air.

The deformed Elfore waded in, throwing their swords at the fallen soldiers whilst beasts lay prey to anything that moved, not that Captain Ettard could, he was pinned down and fell victim to the beasts as they tore at his body!

The malformed bear turned back to pounce once more, but was met by Fleck's blade through one of its legs, making it turn on him with eyes that were as black as death.

Tintwist had barely got to his feet after the charge before having to fend off two poisoned townsfolk and a beast with antlers! All the time trying to see where Kelmar was.

Fleck was diving one way then another to avoid the attacking malformed bear, bringing back his memory once more of his previous encounter. How he wished for an arrow from Tislea right now!

But the only arrow to come his way was one into his shoulder from a deformed Elfore, sending him sprawling to the ground.

Tintwist saw Fleck fall and with two strokes of his sword sent another attacker over the side of the bridge. It was then that Tintwist caught sight of Kelmar lying motionless below him on the river's bank, his feet dancing lifelessly in the flow of the river as it rushed past, whilst his head lay on a rock, covered in blood! Tintwist's heart sank, but there was nothing he could do except go to help Fleck.

Shouting at the beast, Tintwist managed to get its attention, making it hesitate as to which victim it should choose next, but it did not have to. Another shout caught its attention with immediate effect, that of Queen Helistra's!

It did not move as she rode towards the bridge, mounted on her pure white horse, her black cloak draped over her horse's back in majestic pose.

Behind her rode Princess Amber, looking blankly from her hooded cloak at Tintwist and Fleck, whilst six hooded riders sat on their horses in close attendance, giving Tintwist a bad feeling.

"Well, well what have we here? An Elfore and a Manelf helping each other, how quaint," she ridiculed, "so there are some of you left, but not for long, I fear." She smiled tauntingly.

Pulling up her horse, she looked imposingly over Fleck and Tintwist, her black cloak beginning to blend into the ever-decreasing daylight. She stared down at them mockingly as she eyed them over.

"Do my eyes deceive me? It is Fleck, Fleck the outcast! My so called father's friend!" She laughed in raptures at her find.

A humming entered her mind. *No, he is not here, but his power was weak, too weak for us to worry about. I am replenished with souls as I would want. The journey has been worth it, a few more perhaps before we go.*

More humming. *Yes, they will make good sacrifices, especially him,* and she smiled at Fleck.

Without speaking, Queen Helistra beckoned to a deformed Elfore who was standing in the background to come forward. Fleck caught his painful breath as he recognised the wide metal belt it was wearing. "King Vedland!" he said, choking.

Queen Helistra smiled as she heard the name. "What good fortune you shall have. You will be taken to Stormhaven by your King!" Her cold laughter sent shivers through them both.

Fetching a horse and cart, the deformed King Vedland sat waiting on the front of it for Fleck and Tintwist to get in, after having their hands bound.

As they climbed in, feeling helpless, they looked at the bridge they had just attempted to hold to see the bodies piled on top of each other, their red and orange blood mixing as one in death.

More deformed creatures began appearing from the direction of the south bridge, telling them that it had fallen too. "We were too late." Tintwist sighed in dejection.

Fleck did not answer; instead, closing his eyes, he snapped the shaft of the arrow that was lodged in him, gritting his teeth at the pain. When he opened them again, there was the hooded Princess Amber standing by the cart, getting Queen Helistra's full attention.

"What are you doing, child?" she asked, slightly suspicious.

"If you want him as a sacrifice, Mother, he needs to be alive. He will not survive with that in him," she answered.

"A sacrifice indeed. What gives you that idea, my child?" Queen Helistra smiled.

"He would be dead with the rest of the fodder by now," answered Princess Amber, looking up at Queen Helistra with a broad grin.

"That is true. Very well, see if anything can be done." she agreed. Smiling at what Princess Amber had said, Queen Helistra turned and rode towards a deformed Elfore who had come from the south bridge.

Princess Amber climbed into the cart, with the six hooded riders watching her every move. "This is going to hurt," she warned, and before Fleck could even think, she had pulled the arrowhead out of his shoulder, making Fleck yell in pain.

"You are strong for a scrawny girl, Princess Amber," said Tintwist, with half of him glad to see she was alive, whilst the other half was angry that she was obviously under Queen Helistra's influence.

"Thank you," she replied.

What it was she had in the bottle she produced, Fleck had no idea, only that it stung ten times more than the cold sleet upon his face that morn, when she applied it with a wad of cloth.

Princess Amber then did something that Fleck and Tintwist were not sure of, as she placed her hand over the bloody cloth onto Fleck's wound, closing her eyes.

Opening them again, she saw Fleck's puzzled look. "Just a prayer to the stars and trees, for you both," she whispered, glancing at Tintwist as she got down off the cart.

Fleck looked at Tintwist, and Tintwist looked back at Fleck with a question. *What was that about?*

There was no time for them to dwell upon it as they began to move, watching in quiet resignation as more creatures came over the north bridge.

By now, no townsfolk could be seen on the northern Cardronian side of Marchend, but they could be clearly heard as screams echoed all over the town.

Queen Helistra shouted orders to the nearest creatures as she heard the screams with a smile, her harsh voice ringing in Fleck's and Tintwist's ears: "Feast upon them and burn it to the ground! Leave nothing behind!" she cried.

Riding in front of the cart, Queen Helistra turned and gloated in great satisfaction at the faces of her captives as they passed the bodies of the Cardronian garrison. All were dead, none had made it to the bridges, not by the mark of monsters, but by a mark that Fleck and Tintwist knew only too well: a rune staff!

The cart slowly wound its way out of Marchend onto the long hill that led out of the valley heading north towards the Wreken Moors, giving Fleck and Tintwist a final look over the town, a town being consumed in flames!

It was only then as they watched the burning town that Fleck quietly asked Tintwist if he knew what had happened to Kelmar, hoping he had managed to evade capture, as he had not seen him, but his hopes were soon flattened when Tintwist told him of his fate.

"He was lying there, Fleck. When that monster charged, it must have sent him over the bridge's side. His head had hit a rock, it was covered in blood," explained Tintwist, adding to the despair they already felt.

They could do nothing more; their fate lay with Queen Helistra, as did that of all the land. She had finally shown her true self. Nothing was going to stop her now, thought Fleck, as he watched the flames lick the night sky.

His faith in Speedwell, Martyn and Tarbor had not wavered, but time was disappearing fast. He prayed they would not be too late, for what he had just witnessed had left him all but disillusioned as the cold sleet began to fall once more, adding to his gloom.

CHAPTER L

Speedwell looked into the distance, lost in thought, wondering how the others were faring. Hoping they had made it in time to warn the people of Northernland, but not to know until they had made it there themselves was worrying. There was so much uncertainty, he thought.

He watched the grey light beginning to appear, to mark another day. A light he did not want to see, for all it did was show him the death of a forest he loved so much.

They had been fortunate that night to have found an Elfore rowing boat, unfortunate perhaps that it had only been the one. Even though it was an Elfore rowing boat of larger proportions, it still made for cramped conditions for the four of them.

Looking over his shoulder, Speedwell managed a smile seeing his three travelling companions fast asleep. It had been a long night.

Tarbor was under his cloak at the back of the boat, his head resting on its rim, half covered by his shield. Martyn was sitting upright with his head buried into Cantell's deformed back, whilst Cantell was slumped over the oars, asleep. He would let them rest awhile longer; another long day was ahead of them.

Tiredness was creeping over Speedwell also as he brought his gaze back to look over the long, narrow stretch of lake they had reached. Drifting there brought back happy memories for him, forming pictures in his mind of when he had come here to fish with the Elfore, memories that were drifting with the motion of the boat, lulling him into sleep.

Splash! Speedwell jolted back to life to find he was treading water! He was splashing about in the frothy scum that made up the water of the lake! He quickly looked around him, trying to get his bearings. There was Tarbor in the lake also, and there was the boat, with Martyn waving at him frantically! What in the name of the trees had happened?

Speedwell looked to see what Martyn was waving at. The answer came in the form of another hideous giant snake that had rammed the rowing boat, to topple them unsuspectingly over into the lake. Speedwell saw it was ready to strike again, but this time it was heading straight for him!

The grotesque monster lunged through the water at Speedwell. Speedwell dropped down beneath the surface at the last moment, feeling the giant snake's slimy, scaly skin brush over his head. Coming up for air, Speedwell looked around, only to see it was turning to head straight for him again!

"Great-uncle! Grab hold of my staff!" shouted Martyn, seeing the hideous snake turn. Speedwell swam and grabbed Martyn's staff, to find himself being hauled out of the water, thanks to Cantell on the other end.

The snake hit the boat, sending Cantell backwards with Speedwell in his grasp, for Speedwell to fall on top of him. Speedwell might have found it funny under different circumstances, but for one thing, where was his rune staff? He had not got it!

He scrambled up just in time to see Tarbor lift himself up from the lake, to launch his shield through the air.

Speedwell frowned, wondering what he was doing, when his mouth fell as he realised what Tarbor had aimed at. It was at the hideous snake! But what had made him even more open-mouthed was when he saw what it had in its jaws: his rune staff!

Speedwell's heart jumped into his open mouth as a stark vision came to him of the snake snapping its jaws as Tarbor's shield hit it!

It was too late now to do anything but watch as the shield seemed to slowly turn through the air before hitting the hideous snake right in one of its blood-red eyes, with thankfully the desired effect: to cough out Speedwell's rune staff!

Speedwell breathed a sigh of relief, but not for long, as the snake hissed its anger and turned on Tarbor.

Speedwell put out his arm and summoned his rune staff to him, for it to fly out of the water straight into his hand, but before he could do anything, there was an intense pulse of air from Martyn's staff, to send the hideous snake skimming across the lake, out of sight!

"Well done, young Martyn. I think that got rid of the beast," remarked Speedwell, once Tarbor had been retrieved, along with his shield.

"It came from Grimstone's broken piece, Great-uncle. When I saw Uncle Tarbor was going to be attacked, I wished I could help him, and Grimstone's broken piece responded to me." Martyn smiled awkwardly, not really knowing how it had happened.

"You are a Forestall in the making, Martyn. You should not be surprised," said Speedwell, smiling.

"Not as surprised as I was when I hit that thing with my shield." Tarbor smiled, for Speedwell to give him a look.

"Our bodies were drained more than we realised. Even though we have had the essence's bubbles of life flow through us, we were caught out," said Speedwell, slightly annoyed with himself for being so lax.

"Let us not dwell upon it, Speedwell. We are alive. That is enough, even though we are wet!" said Tarbor, smiling, as Cantell pulled on the oars, letting Speedwell know in his own way to keep going.

"I might have given us away, Great-uncle, by my use of the broken piece," said Martyn, sounding worried.

"Do not worry, Martyn. The pulse will soon dissipate and be lost in the evil that surrounds us. She will feel nothing of its calling.

"She will not come after us whilst she is replenishing her power, and even after her fill, I do not see her doing so. She fears nothing, not since linking her power with that of the crystal chamber. No, she waits for us to come to her and take Grimstones broken rune staff from her, if we dare," contemplated Speedwell sombrely, not for the first time with these thoughts.

"Come, Speedwell, listen to yourself. First me, then you, we have done nothing but doubt ourselves since entering this decimation. We have all felt it. Was it only yesterday you felt the essences?" said Tarbor, trying to dispel Speedwell's doubts he could hear, whilst clearly seeing the pain in his eyes by all the devastation his daughter had caused.

"You are right, Tarbor. All this death around me is playing with my senses. I should know better," Speedwell chided himself.

"Once the ceremony of the runes has been performed upon Martyn's staff, together we will stop the poison and save Northernland from her evil," vowed Speedwell, snapping out of his disillusionment.

"And my sister," added Martyn, for Speedwell to look at him, half smiling.

"I know, Martyn, and your sister."

"We will need to, Great-uncle, because she is the one who saved Cantell," stated Martyn, making Speedwell and Tarbor look first at him then at Cantell. Cantell looked back at them whilst rowing, and nodded his misshapen head.

"How do you know this, Martyn? Has Cantell told you in some way?" queried Speedwell.

"No, Great-uncle, it was when I rested my head upon Cantell's back. I sensed her spirit within him mixed with mine," explained Martyn with a puzzled look.

Speedwell thought on what Martyn had just told him. "Your spirit has always been strong, Martyn. The Ancient One told me how at birth some of your spirit entered Amber. It must have helped your sister's spirit save Cantell and by doing so, has shown us Helistra does not have a hold on her!" proclaimed Speedwell.

"Good news then, Speedwell. First the essence and now Princess Amber. There is hope for us all yet!" said Tarbor with a smile.

"Hope indeed." Speedwell smiled back as Cantell drew their attention as he pointed into the distance for them to look.

Through the greyness of the day, they could see he was pointing at the beckoning beginnings of the Linninhorne Mountains.

"They say good news comes in threes, Speedwell," quipped Tarbor as he looked.

"We shall soon see, Tarbor, we shall soon see," replied Speedwell, hoping that the wraiths of the Ancient Forestalls would answer their call.

Although the Linninhorne Mountains had shown themselves, it was another long day on the river before they reached their lower reaches. Once there, two more full days of walking over their lower slopes was needed before they could finally begin their assent up a pass between the mountains.

A night in amongst some fallen boulders saw them take to broken rocks that formed the beginnings of a slippery path that led the way to the mountain range.

The further they climbed, the colder it became; a biting wind that came from nowhere accompanying them.

Onwards they climbed, between the mountains, with the cold getting harsher to their breath as the broken rocks eventually gave way to snow, making the going become slower.

It was not long before their newfound hope had turned into one of cold realisation that this was an inhospitable place that did not want them there, where the cold wind ruled, as it reminded them, by blowing icy blasts into their faces.

The snow was beginning to sink up to their knees when Speedwell waved them to a halt. "Dark will be upon us soon. We need to rest and get out of this wind," he shouted above it.

"And where would that be, Speedwell?" asked Tarbor, looking around him to see nothing but snow blown by the wind.

"We dig a hole here in the snow to shelter in," shouted Speedwell.

With a resigned look, Tarbor started to shovel a hole in the snow with his shield whilst Cantell pushed the excavated snow away. Speedwell winked at Martyn as he aimed his rune staff at the snow and touched some of its symbols.

In the next moment, he had produced a perfectly sealed round hole, big enough to crawl into, whilst Tarbor dug away with his head half lost in the snow.

Cantell tapped Tarbor on the back and grunted. Reversing out, Tarbor saw the hole and gave Speedwell a stare. "Very funny, you can finish it off now," he said, banging the snow off him, trying to bring life back into his hands.

Speedwell crawled into the hole he had made and started to make two more holes either side of it, big enough for them to rest in.

"Now I know what a rabbit feels like," commented Tarbor, to a snigger from Martyn as they all settled for the night.

Speedwell gave them light with the soft glow from his rune staff that he had wedged into the snow by his side, whilst Tarbor's shield acted as a door, wedged as it was in the opening. Not that the wind came into where they were, much to Tarbor's surprise.

Martyn wanted to talk to Cantell about his sister and how she had saved him under the nose of Helistra, but it was a waste of time, as all Cantell could do was grunt. So instead he asked his great-uncle about the ceremony of the runes, whilst Tarbor handed out what provisions there were.

"In truth, Martyn, I only know what the Ancient One told me of it. My rune staff was handed down to me, as were the others. The ceremony as far as I know has not been performed for many a long year. It will be something to behold for all of us," explained Speedwell, much to Martyn's disappointment.

"Do you know where the frozen lake lyes within these mountains to perform the ceremony?" asked Tarbor, out of curiosity.

"I only learnt of it like yourself from what was told to Martyn by the Ancient One. I have never had cause to travel over the Linninhorne Mountains before now, but it is not something we should miss," said Speedwell with a smile. "Sooner, I hope, rather than later in this cold," he added.

There was nothing else they could do but try and get some sleep whilst the wind howled outside, waiting for them to reappear from their snowy den.

Screwed-up eyes and stiff limbs crawled out of the snowy den, to look once more upon the snow-covered mountains as the wind immediately swirled around them, as if welcoming them like an old friend that had been missed.

Grey skies hung heavy over the four as Speedwell led the way, with the others making good use of his foot holes.

Half a day passed them by as they trudged through the snow, their hoods covering faces that had grown grey with snow blown by the wind, setting with the cold.

They reached the central mountains of the chain by following where the pass took them, when Speedwell saw the pass was getting narrower.

The pass then snaked its way through the mountains to reach a gap between them, where Speedwell could look out into the distance to see yet more mountain peaks rising to the sky everywhere he looked, but where was this frozen lake?

The narrow pass now wound its way downwards to eventually level out, only to begin sloping back upwards almost immediately.

"We had better start looking for more shelter," called Speedwell behind him to the others as the clouds grew greyer. Not that any shelter offered itself as they all looked to where they stood.

Mountains loomed forever upwards on their left and in front of them, whilst to their right, the pass disappeared around some craggy outcrops that towered above them all in a line, with a mountain showing itself, waiting behind them.

Snow started to fall as the light began to fade, but as they made their way up around the crags, snow could be seen blocking their way, to stop their progress.

"The snow has drifted with the wind. Another hole to be dug, I think," remarked Speedwell, already touching the symbols on his rune staff.

Out of nowhere, they heard a rumble, making them look up to see an avalanche of snow tumbling down the mountain in front of them with a roar!

Tarbor reacted quickly, thankful for the potion Speedwell had given him to enable him to throw a shield of protection around them all as they turned to run behind one of the crags, hoping it would take the brunt of the avalanche.

With a crash, the avalanche hit the rocky crag and stopped most of it, but not all as snow cascaded over the top of it to rain down on the scrambling party as they dived behind its shelter, only for Speedwell to lose his footing, accidentally releasing his spell of blue flame as he fell.

In a heap, bruised, but in one piece, glad they were not embedded deep in the avalanche, they got to their feet, with Tarbor dissipating the shield with a thought.

As they stood, eyes were drawn to a blue lined trough in the snow, made through Speedwell falling over and triggering his spell of blue flame, ploughing its way, to be finally stopped by the face of the rocky crag opposite them.

They all stared in disbelief where the blue flame had hit the rocky crag, stared at what it had uncovered, a doorway! A doorway in the rock that was open!

Tarbor felt the hairs on the back of his neck rise again, just as he had before when he witnessed the mountain door at Stormhaven.

Cantell could only grunt in amazement, whilst Martyn looked at his great-uncle, "It beckons to us, Great-uncle. Could it be… in there?" Martyn left his question hanging, wondering.

"I am not sure, Martyn. It is shelter if nothing else," answered Speedwell uncertainly as he looked at the unexpected doorway, thinking it was a strange way for fate to show its hand.

They were soon inside the mountain doorway, standing in the pitch-black, listening to the eerie sound of the wind whistling past their ears from the opening, whilst Speedwell brought light by the soft glow of his rune staff.

A narrow passageway lit up before them, showing only one person could walk along it, but instead of being of jagged rock as they had expected, it was as smooth as the groove left by Speedwell's blue flame in the snow, for Speedwell to look at the others.

"Shall we see what lyes ahead?" suggested Speedwell quietly, to a silent reply, and he led the way.

Slowly, the passageway sloped downwards, forever continuing, deep into the depths of the earth.

No one said anything as it delved deeper and deeper under the mountain, is it down here?, thought Speedwell, as the sound of their footsteps echoed along the smooth passageway.

Suddenly Speedwell stopped and touched a symbol on his rune staff, for it to glow even brighter, revealing to them they had entered a chamber.

A giant rock column stood imposingly before them, looking as if it was holding the whole of the mountain away from what they could see laying beyond it: a frozen lake! The frozen Lake of Serenity!

"We have found it, Great-uncle!" cried Martyn, hearing his words echoing around the cold chamber.

"That cannot be a lake. It looks more like a pool!" thought Tarbor, but whispering it as he looked over the frozen lake.

"I would keep those thoughts to yourself if I were you, Tarbor," cautioned Speedwell, walking towards the frozen lake and looking across it himself.

Standing at its edge, Speedwell touched some symbols on his rune staff and waved it over the frozen lake, releasing as he did so four small lanterns of glowing light, enabling them all to see the rest of the chamber as they drifted over the frozen lake.

They all watched as the floating lanterns lit up what was a huge chamber, reflecting as they floated the lake's pale blue frozen water, for Tarbor to admit it was just a bit bigger than a pool!

"Look, Great-uncle, more columns," pointed Martyn, seeing two more columns in the lantern light, one on either side of the frozen lake.

Just as the lanterns began flickering out on the opposite side of the frozen lake, Speedwell saw another column. "That makes four," said Tarbor, also seeing it.

"Well, what now?" asked Tarbor, who without realising it was holding the hilt of his defender.

"I will call to them," answered Speedwell, and he put the end of his rune staff onto the frozen lake.

Closing his eyes, Speedwell joined with his rune staff and called to the wraiths of the Ancient Forestalls, sending a hum of greeting vibrating across the frozen lake.

Speedwell waited, but felt nothing. He called again, still nothing.

"Shall I try, Great-uncle?" asked Martyn, as he felt his great-uncle have no success.

"Yes, Martyn, they may feel your staff is from the Ancient One in need of the ceremony, try," urged Speedwell.

Martyn did as Speedwell. Placing his staff onto the frozen lake, he closed his eyes, asking his staff to help him, feeling as he asked Grimstone's broken piece helping also as it pulsed across the frozen lake in greeting, but like Speedwell's, his calls were unanswered.

"Perhaps together you may rouse them?" suggested Tarbor, but when Speedwell and Martyn tried, the same thing happened: nothing.

"I will search for them with my mind," decided Speedwell, beginning to get a bit frustrated. Through his rune staff, Speedwell sent his mind searching, but all he found was an empty void.

"There was nothing but blackness," he announced as they all sat down next to the frozen lake, wondering what else they could do.

"It is as if they are ignoring us. We have travelled all this way," huffed Tarbor, who had unsheathed his defender and was fiddling with it over the surface of the frozen lake, giving Speedwell an idea.

"I could melt the lake," he put to Tarbor's raised eyebrows.

"And what good would that do?"

"Awaken them by disturbing the element that they rest with," answered Martyn, to Speedwell's nods.

Tarbor sheathed his defender and found himself looking around at the giant rock column behind him as Martyn spoke. *Is that one of them?* he thought.

Speedwell summoned the blue ice fire and touched the frozen lake with its flame.

"If this works, Speedwell, then Helistra will surely feel us this time," warned Tarbor.

"We are under the rock of this mountain, Tarbor. Have you not noticed her powers do not penetrate rock? The essences have proven that. If I am wrong, then yes, she will know we are coming for her, but by then Martyn's staff will hopefully be as one with him, if I can reach them," reasoned Speedwell, and with a touch of another symbol, he released the blue ice fire from his rune staff across the frozen Lake of Serenity.

Standing back, Speedwell watched the blue ice fire do its work as it spread to melt the whole of the frozen lake and make it glow a bright blue. Now all they could do was wait to see if it worked.

Deathly silence followed as they waited, but still nothing seemed to be happening, until suddenly what felt like a breath of cold air whispered past them, bringing even Speedwell to feel goosebumps.

They all stood still, not daring to move, as what they all thought was a murmur came from behind them, a murmur from the giant rock column!

Speedwell then felt something through his rune staff. Was it trying to say something to him? No, it was silent; it was listening to the murmur!

Then from nowhere a wisp of what looked like a feathery cloud appeared before them, buzzing around their heads, stopping at each one of their faces.

No one spoke, no one dared, as the wisp of cloud flew around them all, as if trying to weigh up who or what had awoken it.

As suddenly as it had appeared, it was gone, leaving Speedwell, Martyn, Tarbor and Cantell to look at each other.

Just as Speedwell was going to speak, a cold shudder went through him as the giant rock column behind them all began to vibrate.

For one horrible moment, they all thought it was going to collapse and bring the whole mountain down on top of them, but that was not what was happening. They had finally awoken the wraiths of the Ancient Forestalls!

They all turned around slowly to see wispy strands, like plumes of cold breath, begin to manifest themselves from the solid rock column, to waver in the air, slowly forming into the shape of a tall, thin spectre barely visible to the eye. Its drawn face loomed above Speedwell, with hollow eyes that were looking right at him!

Martyn, Tarbor and Cantell could only stare as Speedwell spoke to a wraith of the Ancients. "I am Speedwell, Keeper of the Great Forest," he announced shakily, to hear a cold whispering voice enter his mind.

I know what you are, Forestall! Why are you here in our domain, disturbing our final resting place? spoke the voice, making Speedwell feel uncomfortable. It was not going to like what he was about to say next, he thought, to hear the whispering voice answer him, *What will I not like?*

"That we have come here to ask you to perform the ceremony of the runes, because the Ancient One is no more," informed Speedwell, to feel a cold scowl go right through him and vibrations coming from the other three rock columns in the chamber.

If Speedwell wanted all of their attention, he had got it now, as the other three wraiths of the Ancient Forestalls revealed their ghost-like selves to surround them.

No more! What talk is this! hissed the first wraith of the Ancients, making Speedwell feel the sudden anger it felt.

"One of our brothers was killed with his own rune staff. It broke when the act was committed, leaving a piece in his body. What was left of the broken rune staff the murderer groomed to do her evil work, an evil that has destroyed the Plateau Forest and the Ancient One," explained Speedwell.

A cold rage swirled around the chamber from the wraiths of the Ancients, hearing of the violation of the Plateau Forest and the Ancient One. *Who is this that has struck evil at our heart? You said her!*

Speedwell swallowed. "My daughter, Helistra."

They all closed their eyes, for this time they thought the mountain was going to collapse upon them as the wraiths of the Ancients swirled around the chamber in anger, shaking fragments of rock down upon their heads and into the lake as they did so.

Your daughter! How could you let this come to pass! The first wraith's words screamed in Speedwell's mind.

Speedwell felt his whole body being slowly squeezed, forcing the air out of his lungs, as the wraiths of the Ancients suddenly surrounded him in their anger.

"She was my little girl, she could do no wrong in my eyes. I was blind," he admitted, almost gasping.

"Do not harm my great-uncle! He is a Forestall as you once were! We have travelled far to come here for your help! Do you not see the staff of pureness I have brought here in your midst from the Ancient One for you to perform the ceremony of the runes upon, to help rid the forests and lands of her wickedness!" shouted Martyn, annoyed at what they were doing to his great-uncle.

Speedwell felt the pressure on his body slacken as Martyn got their attention, whilst at the same time seeing Tarbor about to draw his defender. Speedwell shook his head for him to stop.

Who is this boy that asks for our help? spoke the first wraith of the Ancients to Speedwell, but Martyn could also hear everything the first wraith said through his staff and answered instead of Speedwell.

"I am Prince Martyn of Tiggannia and when this staff is adorned with the sacred runes, I will be a Forestall like yourselves, then I will deal with her evil," he pronounced with confidence, making the first wraith aware he was not just a boy, but a boy of the spirit that was needed to become a Forestall.

Speedwell felt their presence leave him alone as they looked to Martyn and his staff. *Your spirit is strong and pure within you,* sensed the first wraith as they examined his staff, feeling the energy it enhanced.

It is of the Ancient One. I feel the earth and sky within it, but there is something else merged inside. What is hidden for no one to see? questioned the first wraith suspiciously.

Martyn asked his staff to release the broken piece of Grimstone's rune staff for the wraiths of the Ancients to see.

"This is the broken piece of rune staff we have retrieved that has not been tainted. We must make it whole again to restore the balance of the forests," urged Martyn as the broken piece emerged out of his staff.

The wraiths of the Ancients floated the broken piece amongst them and wailed in anguish at the sight of the broken end.

Letting the broken piece float back down for Martyn to meld back into his staff, they suddenly confronted Cantell, staring at his deformity.

Cantell tried to back away to evade their looks, only to find himself backing onto the rock column. He felt their coldness as they searched his very being, leaving him feeling numb inside.

This hideous creature is your daughter's evil work too? posed the first wraith.

"Yes, it is. His name is Cantell, a man from Northernland. He was saved from total evilness by Martyn's sister, Amber, under my daughter's nose, even though she is in her clutches," answered Speedwell.

A sister to the boy! Her spirit must also be strong to have done such a deed, but if this man has suffered this way, what of the children of the forest? Speedwell's sadness welled up in him once more as he explained the evil his daughter had performed.

"The Elfore and Manelf have suffered badly from her evil. She has turned them into creatures beyond comprehension, they move upon Northernland as we speak." Speedwell dropped his head in shame as he answered, with tears close in his eyes.

The wraiths of the Ancients turned from Cantell with scowling breath at Speedwell's answer to look at Tarbor, but more so at the defender he carried. Tarbor suddenly felt it leave his sheath and watched helplessly as it floated between the wraiths of the Ancients as they examined it.

"We know the work of the children when we see it," came a cold whispering voice from the first wraith, taking Tarbor by surprise that they could talk.

"A powerful blend of their making, were you in hope that its blended power would smite her down and free you of her evil?" The first wraith of the Ancients sounded almost cynical to Tarbor in its cold, harsh voice.

"It has been a thought," answered Tarbor, feeling a bit annoyed. "And you would be the one to wield the blade?"

"That is why my uncle is called a King wielder! He has the right, for he is the King of Waunarle, King Ashwell!" interrupted Martyn, who was now feeling even more annoyed by how they were being treated. After all, Uncle Tarbor was a King, and he was to be a future Forestall!

The first wraith of the Ancient Forestalls heard and felt Martyn's emotions running through him, making the first wraith stop to think what they were doing.

The boy was right; he was the future. His spirit was plain to see. He had the proof in the staff the Ancient One had bestowed upon him, but from what they were sensing, a future of uncertainty, and here they were, wrongly venting their anger upon them when it was clear they were here in need of their help. It was not their fault.

Being woken to be told of the loss of the Ancient One and the Plateau Forest by the hand of a Forestall's daughter had clouded their senses. They could feel and see the suffering Speedwell was enduring, knowing it was his daughter that had turned to the darkness in her soul, but no matter how hard it was for them to listen to, they needed to know all that had happened without turning it to anger.

"We have not treated you with the respect that a Keeper of the forest deserves, Speedwell," said the first wraith suddenly, in quieter tones.

"Though we are only of spirit, to hear that the Ancient One is no more has torn us asunder. We were creating a barrier between you and your needs that should not be there, for that we are sorry," continued the first wraith in an apologetic whisper, much to the relief of them all.

"We will proceed with the ceremony of the runes, but we sense there is far more in the sadness of your voice that has to be told first before we do," finished the first wraith, and a silence followed as they waited for Speedwell to tell them the whole story.

Closing his eyes, Speedwell gave a nod of understanding, and as much as it hurt him to relive his daughter's evil deeds, he began telling the wraiths of the Ancient Forestalls what they had endured.

Speedwell recounted the terrible events to an ever-growing silence of sadness within the chamber as the wraiths of the Ancients listened to what had happened. By the end, all that could be heard was their grieving as they tried to take in what they had just been told.

"Your hurt is now our hurt, Speedwell. It is time to make it right," whispered the first wraith in sorrow, "but first we must rid ourselves of the evil that has come with you for fear of tainting the new staff," added the first wraith, much to the worry of Cantell.

"Do I sense the essence of life in your pouch?" asked the first wraith, to the nodded reply of Speedwell. "Then mix it, Forestall, to give him, and then be ready to release your rune staff."

Speedwell mixed the potion without questioning about his rune staff and gave it to Cantell, who felt the cleansing powers of the potion wash through him once more, to revitalise his inner being that Princess Amber had protected.

"Stand in the centre of the lake for us to rid you of your curse," ordered the first wraith of Cantell, to then evaporate back into its column of rock where the others already were, in theirs.

Cantell, who like the others had not noticed that the lake had frozen over again, moved to the centre of the frozen lake, feeling very alone as he waited there nervously in the dark, telling himself that his misshapen form would be gone forever after whatever it was they were going to do to him!

Speedwell then felt the first wraith of the Ancients beckon him to release his rune staff. Letting it go, he watched as it moved, glowing in mid-air, to stop and hover over the deformed head of Cantell before dying out, putting the chamber into darkness.

The giant columns of rock began to make a strange vibrating sound in the darkness. "What are they doing?" whispered Tarbor.

"Chanting," informed Speedwell, sensing them chanting a strange chant he did not recognise.

At first, nothing seemed to be happening, then all at once a symbol lit on Speedwell's rune staff from a streak of light that had shot from one of the giant rock columns, to join the two together in a path of light.

Then another symbol lit up, followed by two more as each of the other columns reached out to Speedwell's rune staff in a shaft of light.

Speedwell's rune staff then began to spin as the air around it swirled, caused by the rune symbols pushing against each other. Cantell looked down at his deformed body, to see the lit symbols dancing all over him.

They could only be the four symbols of the elements – air, earth, fire and water – that the wraiths of the Ancient Forestalls have brought into motion, thought Speedwell as he watched.

The wraiths within the giant columns began to make the whole of the huge chamber shudder as their chanting vibrated to reach a climax, causing the air above Cantell to swirl ever faster.

The swirling air had sent the bottom of Speedwell's rune staff whirling around over Cantell's head, whilst the top stayed where it was, with the rune staff itself spinning, having the effect of making the lit symbols appear on Cantell one moment and disappear the next.

Speedwell's rune staff whirled and spun faster still, until it was enough to make it seem as if the lit symbols were constantly shining upon Cantell, then suddenly the whole of the chamber lit up!

The elements are as one, ready to make him whole again, thought Speedwell.

Cantell, though, was feeling far from being made whole, as his skin felt as if it was on fire whilst being pulled apart; he was near to passing out!

What he could not see that Speedwell, Martyn and Tarbor could was a golden light that had started to glow between his true being and his deformed one. The evil was being drawn from his body!

Then suddenly the chanting stopped. A blinding light shot from Speedwell's rune staff onto Cantell and the chamber plunged into darkness!

Tarbor drew his defender and summoned a white flame for them to see by as they ran onto the frozen lake to Cantell's aid, but what they found made them all grin, for there walking towards them was Cantell! He was himself once more!

Tarbor took off his cloak and wrapped it around Cantell, for not only had the wraiths of the Ancients rid him of evil, they had rid him of his clothes too!

Cantell looked at them with tears and laughter in his eyes; such was his relief at being himself again. He felt as if he had been reborn. His whole body was awash with a newfound feeling of life!

Nothing was said, as all they could do was hug each other.

"I never thought we would see you again," said Tarbor, grinning, "although in some ways it was an improvement," he jibed, for laughter to ensue.

"And just as I was getting used to grunting too!" joined in Cantell to more laughter, a welcome relief from the strain they were all feeling.

"That is something we have not heard for a long time," whispered a cold voice, for them all to turn around to see the whispery spectre of the first wraith.

"Now your friend is pure of heart, it is time for the ceremony of the runes. Stand where your friend has stood with your staff, ready to become the Forestall you were destined to be," ordered the first wraith of Martyn, to disappear once more into its column of rock whilst at the same time Speedwell's rune staff began to softly glow once more.

Martyn looked at his great-uncle and uncles, his spirit lifted by the call of the first wraith of the Ancients. His time had come!

"Will you hold the broken piece for me, Great-uncle?" said Martyn with a smile, releasing Grimstone's broken piece to Speedwell.

"Are you ready to complete the bond, Martyn?" Speedwell smiled as he received it.

"I am ready, Great-uncle." Martyn breathed in to hold steady his excited nerves.

"There is one thing, Martyn."

"Yes, Great-uncle?" said Martyn worriedly, suddenly wondering what it was.

"When you are as one, you will be my equal, so no more great-uncle." Speedwell grinned to Martyn's grin.

"And that goes for us." Tarbor and Cantell grinned, both nodding.

Martyn smiled to himself as he moved to the middle of the frozen lake to stand with his staff and wait under the softly glowing rune staff of Speedwell's, which he noted was now standing upright.

Tarbor had extinguished his defender as he, Speedwell and Cantell watched with bated breath as Speedwell's rune staff that had been softly glowing slowly faded, to die out altogether again.

As softly as the light had faded, so did the wraiths of the Ancients begin chanting, with their cold tones softly humming the chant, for it to vibrate throughout the chamber.

At first, their chanting was in harmony, but then one could be heard overlaying another, then again and again until a dull droning noise vibrated around the chamber, to be joined by the humming of Speedwell's rune staff.

Small insignificant arcs of light began appearing on the four columns of rock, building in power as the chanting gained momentum.

Then suddenly streaks of light shot out from the rock columns to join up with Speedwell's rune staff, making its runes glow around the chamber whilst it started to spin over Martyn's head from their power.

Speedwell felt the power from his rune staff course through his body as he stood there watching, such was the energy coming from it.

Holding the hilt of his defender, Tarbor's whole body was tingling, whilst Cantell could only marvel at what his eyes were beholding.

Martyn stood open-mouthed, looking up at Speedwell's rune staff spinning, with light shimmering from it, as it hummed to the sound of the chanting drone of the wraiths.

A whisper came to him: *Release your staff, it is time*, and Martyn let his hand unfold from his staff, to see it stand rigid beneath Speedwell's spinning rune staff.

The chanting ceased and all that could be heard was Speedwell's rune staff humming as it spun.

Slowly, the power of Speedwell's rune staff spinning began to draw Martyn's staff up to it, until finally they touched and connected with each other, to send Martyn's staff spinning the same.

As the staffs touched, a different chant was taken up by the wraiths to begin resonating around the chamber, for Speedwell's rune staff to suddenly begin to glow at the bottom of its length, making the top of Martyn's staff glow also.

The glow began to make its way up Speedwell's rune staff, and as it did so, the glow on Martyn's staff began to make its way downwards, until finally their entire lengths had been covered, whilst all the time they had kept spinning

If Martyn's mouth was not wide enough open by now, then what happened next made it so.

The chanting ceased, the humming ceased, the glowing faded away and the staffs stopped spinning, to reveal to Martyn the transformation that had taken place!

His staff was no longer a plain wooden staff, but a rune staff whose newly adorned runes glowed before him, embossed into its length!

His new rune staff dropped away from Speedwell's rune staff for Martyn to catch it and feel its presence wash over him as it flowed through his body, bonding with him to become as one.

Speedwell's rune staff flew to him, for him to feel the new given strength that had entered it, more than he could ever remember as he released its soft glow, to see Martyn running towards them, his face beaming with joy.

Martyn looked at Speedwell and nearly cried. "It… it's my rune staff, Great… Speedwell!" remembered Martyn, crying in elation.

"The wraiths of the Ancients have blessed you, Martyn. You are now a Forestall! May the stars and trees always watch over you," said Speedwell, returning the smile.

Martyn could not help but hug Speedwell, Tarbor and Cantell as they all cried with emotion. They had come so far together. Now at last they had a chance of bringing back health to the forests and ridding them of her evil!

A cold chill made them all turn around, to see the wraiths of the Ancients looking on at them.

"Once the broken rune staff of our brother Grimstone is as one again, happiness will return to the forests and her evil work will be gone. You have given us that chance with your blessing upon Martyn in the creation of his rune staff, and for that, we thank you, wraiths of the Ancient Forestalls," thanked Speedwell, bowing deeply, with Martyn, Tarbor and Cantell following suit.

"You do not have to bow to us, Speedwell, any of you. You are all our equal," said the first wraith, making amends for how they had been treated earlier, to make Martyn smile.

"We wish you well on your journey. May the stars watch over you and your rune staffs bring back the light to the forests," wished the first wraith, and without further talk, the spectres of the wraiths were gone.

Once Martyn had the broken piece of Grimstone's rune staff safely merged into his new rune staff, the four travellers emerged from the smooth passageway into a new dawn.

One solitary shaft of sunlight momentarily hit their faces, making them blink as they stood at the opening of the rocky crag. They let the glow of its ray dance upon their faces whilst they breathed in the cold air that had met them. Then it was gone, to hide behind grey forbidding clouds. *A last ray of hope*, thought Speedwell, *as we are*.

Speedwell touched some symbols upon his rune staff to make a way for them through the snow. He could see the avalanche had blocked the passage they had travelled around the rocky crag.

"I did not think we were down there that long," said Cantell, smiling to hear his own voice once more instead of a grunt, whilst he tried to tie the makeshift tears of cloth, that they had given him, around his feet as Speedwell brought his rune staff into ice-blue flame.

"Nor I," agreed Speedwell, "you will have to tell us what happened to you and how Princess Amber stopped the poison. We thought you were dead," he admitted.

"It felt like it!" remarked Cantell as he finished with the fiddly bits of cloth and looked at Martyn's smiling face.

Martyn was in a world of his own. He was beyond daylight; he was in the sky with the stars, transformed as he was with the vibrancy of his new rune staff.

"I hope Princess Amber remains undetected of her knowledge of Martyn," said Cantell worriedly, as he looked at Martyn and thought on the moment she had saved him from that creature's venom.

"She fooled you." Tarbor smiled to the smile of Cantell.

"I am not Queen Helistra, though, Tarbor," pointed out Cantell, to Tarbor's acknowledging nod.

"What of the broken piece, Gre… Speedwell? Do you think Helistra will know we have it?" questioned Martyn, thinking on it for the first time as he felt its presence whilst revelling in his new rune staff.

"By the time we return to Northernland, those creatures that survived after the explosion will have informed her, Martyn, but only that bodies were caught within it. They would have seen nothing," said Speedwell thoughtfully.

"The rune staff that is now yours, she will not know of either, and it is best kept that way. Let her think we are still weak. When you want to hone your skills, let Tarbor throw his protective shield around you," advised Speedwell.

"I will," said Martyn, nodding.

"Until then, we must conserve as much of our newfound energy as we can for our journey and the task that lyes ahead of us all," finished Speedwell.

"After you have made a way for us to pass through the snow, though," said Cantell with a smile, for Speedwell to grin and touch a symbol on his rune staff, for a searing ice-blue bolt of flame to shoot from it.

CHAPTER LI

Holding Tomin's arm, Piper waved goodbye to the rest of the company as they disappeared out of sight, to then take Tomin back to a deserted Walditch.

Deserted, that is, after seeing the malformed body of the soldier they had brought with them and being told of the impending arrival of more like him in their village.

If that was not enough, then being told that their beloved King Stowlan had met his fate by one such creature and that they had seen Marchend on fire in the night sky tipped the scales. They were gone with whatever would see them through their journey to the walled castle town of Elishard, leaving their homes behind.

Tomin had made his decision much against the wishes of the rest of the company that he was going to wait in Walditch, with the intention of confronting his mother, Queen Helistra.

He had told them all he was going to try and stop her destruction by giving himself up, to plead with her, son to mother. After all, he was the cause of her jealousy.

All of it played on his mind. Her presence was near. He knew Marchend burning was her doing.

"Your grandfather would not want you to do this, Tomin, if he were here," a worried Queen Elina had said to him.

"No, he would not, but he is not here," he had answered resolutely, and had handed over Gentian's rune staff for King Brodic to look after.

King Brodic had felt honoured to have been given the rune staff after only knowing Tomin for a short while. "I will guard it with my life," he had sworn.

"You may have to," was Tomin's warning.

"But Speedwell will want you by his side when he returns, Tomin," Urchel had pleaded with him.

"My bonding with Gentian's rune staff is too weak to be of any help to my grandfather in defeating my mother, I can feel it. No, this is the best way I must try," he had replied, to the worry of them all, but there was nothing they could do to stop him; he was a Forestall.

"Why must you be so stubborn! It is Tomin's decision. You do not have to stay. It is a risk you do not have to take!" Ludbright had berated Piper at the same time. He was right, of course. She was taking a risk by staying with Tomin, but her thoughts were elsewhere.

When Tomin had spoken of his intentions to meet with Queen Helistra, Piper saw her chance to stay in Walditch with him to witness their meeting and then report to Elishard.

Though the chance she really saw was in the hope of seeing Kelmar, Cillan, Fleck and Tintwist, to know they were all safe, sooner rather than later, but especially Tintwist. She should have gone with him, she had told herself.

Like Tomin, she had given Ringwold's rune staff, with which Tintwist had entrusted her, to King Brodic, open-mouthed at receiving both rune staffs to look after. "If Tomin fails and the worst comes, then you must burn them. They cannot fall into her hands," she had warned King Brodic.

"Be safe, Piper," Tiska had said to her with a hug, and would have stayed with them in the hope of seeing Fleck, but her daughter came first.

Permellar had also given her a hug, with a reassuring smile. "Do not worry, Piper. Kelmar is with him," she had said with a woman's understanding of what Piper was feeling, whilst saying a prayer to the stars that Kelmar was safe also.

So Piper and Tomin walked back down the empty streets of Walditch, having travelled far enough with these thoughts on their minds, not able to travel any further.

"You risk your life, Tomin, in your gesture," said Piper as they entered the inn they had stayed at that night, to a nice warm fire.

"I am of the hope she will remember that I am her son who did not ask to become a Forestall, for her to be jealous of me. I will try and make her see that what she is doing will destroy her in the end as well," explained Tomin, troubled by these thoughts.

"Urchel was right in what he said, Tomin. Your grandfather will need you all the more with Ringwold gone from us," pointed out Piper, to see Tomin's head drop in sadness, hearing Ringwold's name.

"I know what I am doing is against all that we have fought for, but I feel mine is not to fight. Martyn is the chosen one and with his newfound staff will be the saviour of us all, once the wraiths of the Ancient Forestalls perform the ceremony of the runes. Then my mother will know of her match if I fail to seek out her heart," said Tomin, trying to reassure himself of his actions.

Piper heard Tomin's worry and love for his mother in his voice as she stared into the fire, but the glow from it only reminded her of the night sky over Marchend, making her think that it was all too late for a heart that was so black with evil.

"I hope her heart hears you, for if it does, you will have saved Princess Amber as well," Piper suddenly said thoughtfully, for Tomin to sigh and nod.

"I will tell her that I love her and pray to the stars that she does hear me, Piper, as you must tell Tintwist when you see him," added Tomin, knowing Tintwist was the real reason why Piper had stayed with him.

"Is it that obvious why I am here with you?" she apologised, feeling ashamed of herself for being so selfish.

"Not that I do not want to know of the well-being of Fleck, Kelmar and Cillan, but…" Piper left it there.

"Do not be sorry. It is only natural to worry for the ones you love," said Tomin with a smile.

Though Tomin could not see, he had always heard the love in her voice for Tintwist. "You are right, I will tell him," and she hugged him in gratitude.

"Have you found a safe place to hide when I confront her?" asked Tomin as they settled to wait.

"Do not worry, Tomin. I have seen a place that will cover me well," answered Piper, and she closed her eyes to the warmth of the fire.

The day wore on with no sign of anyone, for the night skies to return with snow as a companion as it started to fall.

A hand gripping Piper's arm stirred her from a worried slumber to hear Tomin's warning whisper. "I sense my mother approaching, Piper, with creatures by her side. Now is the time to hide!"

Piper stood and hugged Tomin tight, a hug that feared she would never see him again. "I wish you were not doing this," she cried.

"I know, but I must," said Tomin, choking, and he hugged Piper one last time. "Now go!"

Piper ran out the back way of the inn to the inn's yard, to find the snow was already starting to settle. The yard led onto a narrow back street and she peeked around the wall of the yard to see if anyone was coming before dashing down it.

Keeping hidden in the shadows at the back of some houses further along the street, Piper headed to where she was going to hide, a stone barn where horses and carts had been kept under its wooden roof; kept, that is, until they came to warn them, now it was empty.

Climbing up the wooden stairs that led to a loft, Piper laid down next to a small window opening that overlooked the main street. Laying there, she covered herself with some straw to keep herself hidden and warm whilst she waited.

It was not long before she heard the sound of horses coming up the street. Piper kept still and peered through the small opening.

Six hooded riders came into view, followed by a small figure; that of Princess Amber, realised Piper. At least she was all right, she thought.

Then a figure in a snow-flecked black cloak riding a white horse made Piper hold her breath: Queen Helistra!

If the sight of Queen Helistra made her hold her breath, then the two figures in the back of a cart following her, being driven by a hideous-looking creature, took it away; it was Fleck and Tintwist!

Piper barely stopped herself from screaming out aloud. They had been captured! But where were Kelmar and Cillan? Had they evaded capture? She could only watch with worry as they went past her, looking miserable and cold, for her heart to go with them.

They were followed by more creatures on foot, more than she could count. Her blood ran cold as she thought of what Fleck and Tintwist must have faced as she saw what had to be townsfolk, by their dress, amongst the hideous creatures.

She knew she could not draw attention to herself and suddenly felt useless by not being able to help them.

Then suddenly the column stopped, and stood there in the continuing snow, Tomin, thought Piper. There he was. He had come out of the inn to stand right in front of Queen Helistra's white horse.

She may have been well hidden, but Tomin's words were faint. Even with her good hearing, she could not hear him properly, only see his breath as he spoke.

She chided herself for not thinking it through. She could not stay here, especially now she had seen Tintwist and Fleck captured. She needed to hear what was being said.

Quietly, she got up and crept down the stairs, to disappear through the door she had entered.

Keeping low, she made her way back past the houses once more, until she reached the yard of the inn.

Stealing her way across the yard, she climbed the steps that led to the upper rooms, to tread softly across the wooden boards of the room she had entered, hoping they did not creak and give her away. Holding herself by a shuttered window, she listened to the voices she could now clearly hear below her.

"But I am the cause of your jealousy, the reason why you destroy the forests. That is why I am here, putting myself at your mercy so that you can put an end to it all," Piper could hear Tomin say in earnest.

"And what is there to gain by my doing so?" came Queen Helistra's uncaring reply.

"A son you have no need to be jealous of, who loves you, Mother," implored Tomin, letting her hear the love he had for her in his voice.

Fleck and Tintwist were looking at each other as they heard Tomin's voice. "What is he doing?" half asked Tintwist, but before Fleck could reply, a thump on the side of the cart from the deformed King Vedland told them to be quiet.

Princess Amber was nearly falling off her horse. *Her son?* she asked herself as she looked at the face of Tomin and saw he was blind.

She was still coming around to the fact that Queen Helistra was not her real mother and that she had a brother. Now this blind man, who looked old enough to be her great-grandfather, was saying he was her son!

A thought came into her head as she looked; of how deceptive the face of evil was by keeping her so beautiful, if this was her son.

"How can this old blind man be your son, Mother? Look at him, and look at you," she challenged, not helping herself.

Tomin started coughing at hearing Princess Amber call her mother. "You have chosen her as your daughter and would have me killed!" cried Tomin, trying to catch his breath.

"An accident has left him this way, but he is who he says he is," answered Queen Helistra, ignoring Tomin's outburst and leaving Princess Amber speechless.

Queen Helistra looked down at Tomin with a blank expression as humming entered her mind. "Yes, he would still make a good sacrifice, better than the other two," she said aloud, to smile at Tomin's reaction.

"But I am your son! Is there nothing left for me within you, Mother!" cried Tomin, distraught.

"I forget you are, it has been so long, but it is not you that I want, but Speedwell, your grandfather. When he is dead, then I will be at rest." She scowled, for Tomin to hear the loathing in her voice as she spoke of him.

Although Piper had heard it before in disbelief from Speedwell, she nearly choked, hearing it from Queen Helistra's own mouth, her own father!

Princess Amber went cold as she heard her. *She wants her son and her father dead! I will be in that cart with those two if she finds I am not under her influence anymore*, she thought.

"I see you stay quiet. Therefore, my informants are right. He must be alive after the explosion," discerned Queen Helistra.

"There was one loss. When you destroyed the Ancient One, we lost Uncle Ringwold. It was all we could do but run for our lives from these hideous creations of yours," said Tomin truthfully.

"Ringwold is dead! The day gets better," said Queen Helistra, grinning.

"You would have known if you had not made Father's rune staff evil!" berated Tomin, feeling anger at her coldness.

"That is true, my senses have been dulled, but it is a small price to pay for the power I have gained," she said with a smile.

"But what of Gentian's rune staff? I see it is not about you," observed Queen Helistra. "You say my rune staff failed to feel Ringwold's passing because of the evil I have made it do, but the same can be said of Gentian's rune staff, for it too has failed," stated Queen Helistra to a frowning Tomin.

"What are you on about?" said Tomin, puzzled.

"You do not know, do you?" she said, grinning. "When I spoke of an explosion, I was not on about the demise of the Ancient One, as glorious as it was. I was talking of the explosion that happened when an attempt was made to retrieve the broken piece." Queen Helistra watched Tomin's face as what she had just said sunk in.

"But I thought… Grandfather was trying… The… the broken piece?" He gasped in confusion.

"Yes, the broken piece. As they tried to retrieve it, it shattered into a thousand pieces!" Queen Helistra laughed, but her face soon became stern again.

"Only it has come to my ears that your grandfather and two others survived, escaping the blast's fury," informed Queen Helistra to a relieved, but at the same time desolate, Tomin.

They had obviously tried to retrieve the broken piece before seeking the help of the Ancients, but why? *Something must have told Grandfather to try*, thought Tomin, but without really knowing what had happened, the reality of what his mother was saying made Tomin's heart sink.

Giving himself up suddenly felt pointless. Even if he had managed to stop her poisoning the forest, all was now lost. With the broken piece shattered, her evil would be forever in their midst!

He was not the only one who realised it. Piper, Fleck and Tintwist had all closed their eyes at the news. Happy that Speedwell, Martyn and Tarbor were alive, but empty in the thought that her evil could never go away without the broken piece to mend the broken rune staff.

"You are holding back from me. What is it you thought?" pressed Queen Helistra at Tomin's hesitant response.

"Nothing, Mother," answered Tomin lamely.

Queen Helistra got down from her horse and faced Tomin. Tomin felt her breath on his face and smelt the corrupt souls she had breathed in, sensing a darker evil than he could have ever imagined coming from her.

"Very well, you give me no choice," and she called upon the broken rune staff.

"There is no need. I will tell you," intervened Tomin before she could delve into his mind.

Fleck and Tintwist waited for the inevitable; Tomin was going to tell her all.

Piper could only feel for Tomin for what he had tried to do.

"We did leave Grandfather, Tarbor and Prince Martyn, your true brother," pointed out Tomin to Princess Amber, "for them to go and retrieve the broken piece," admitted Tomin, but before he could continue, Princess Amber interrupted him.

The revelation at hearing her brother was still alive overwhelmed her with joy! Though she had found out from Mrs Beeworthy about him, Tomin pointing him out made her see a chance of finding out more without suspicion falling upon her, but she must stay calm, she told herself.

"What is he on about, Mother? He says I have a brother like that man," she pushed, playing ignorant.

She had stopped Tomin from saying any more to let him wonder who it was that had told her she had a brother, whilst at the same time giving him time to think, as to his and Princess Amber's surprise, Queen Helistra started to answer her.

"You are not my daughter, and my son is right. You do have a brother, but I have kept it from you for good reason," she declared, to at last admit it.

"At first, I thought your brother was dead. By the time I found out he was alive, I feared for you, that he would harm you if he knew of your existence. That is why I have always kept you at Stormhaven to protect you. That is all I have ever sought," explained Queen Helistra to Tomin's disbelieving ears.

"Why would he harm me if I am his sister?" asked a confused Princess Amber.

"I did not mean it to be this way, but it is because you are with me, child. He was destined to become a Forestall, that is, before I destroyed the Ancient One. Now we know he is still alive, your presence at the Ancient One's demise would have been final proof to him and my so-called father that I have groomed you in my ways. Therefore, like me, you are a threat to them," finished Queen Helistra to a quiet Princess Amber as she tried to take in what she had just been told.

Queen Helistra turned back to an expressionless Tomin, who was not giving anything away as to what he was thinking after hearing the half-lies and half-truths coming from her mouth.

Tomin did not sense the evil that possessed his mother existing in Princess Amber, and thought the only reason she had kept her by her side was what they had always thought: as a human shield!

He realised that the heart he had hoped to find in his mother was forever lost to him when he smelt her breath of corruption. With the broken piece gone, there was only one hope left to at least stop the poison flowing from the broken rune staff, and that was by her death, he told himself in sadness.

With Martyn's newfound staff and grandfathers, they would prevail, he thought. They had to! That is, if they still possessed them after the explosion!

Whatever had happened, he had to keep faith and keep it from her, but to do that he must do one thing he had never done before in his life: lie, hoping that she did not look into his mind to find out the truth.

"So are they a threat to us? Why would they think they could retrieve the broken piece when the person that was supposed to be able to is standing here in front of me?" quizzed Queen Helistra.

"Because Prince Martyn has Ringwold's rune staff," lied Tomin.

Queen Helistra could only laugh at hearing that Ringwold's rune staff was in the hands of the boy. "Ringwold's? Of what use is that to him without the Ancient One there to nurture him? No bonding, no knowledge of the ways, no power!" she scoffed, dismissing it with contempt.

"They were going to the wraiths of the Ancient Forestalls first, to ask them to perform a ceremony upon it in the hope of retrieving the broken piece," lied Tomin, again feeling his mother's open-mouthed expression.

Humming immediately entered her mind. *No, nor I!*

"What are you on about? Wraiths of the Ancient Forestalls? I have never heard of them," questioned Queen Helistra suspiciously.

"Nor had Grandfather. He only found out from the Ancient One just before you destroyed the barrier that a frozen lake existed in the

Linninhorne Mountains, where the first of the Forestalls rested. With the Ancient One gone, he saw it as our only hope to perform a ceremony that would bond Ringwold's rune staff with Prince Martyn in the hope of retrieving the broken piece, but you have told us that they have tried and failed, so it has all been in vain," explained Tomin, sounding downhearted.

Queen Helistra stared at her son as her hand twitched over the broken rune staff. Was this true? "So you were never able to retrieve the broken piece all along," she realised.

"You are not the only one that can play games of deception, Mother," taunted Tomin dangerously, making Princess Amber pull her hood down further over her face.

"It seems not, so why should I believe you now?" she challenged, drawing nearer to Tomin's face for him to sense the corruption of her soul once more.

"Because your son does not lie. We were all there when Speedwell told us," came a voice out of the darkness, making everyone turn around.

A face appeared that Fleck and Tintwist thought they would never see again, whilst Piper's ears told her it was Kelmar!

Out of a doorway stepped the bloodstained face of Kelmar, his eyes showing the pain of seeing the full aftermath of Marchend as they stared into nothing.

Coming round, he had found himself lying by the River Talmin with a headache and cold, wet feet. Stumbling his way along the bank, he had managed to find a place where he could drag himself off the riverbank, to find a town of burning death left by the monsters he had tried to keep at bay.

He had wandered through the desolation to luckily find a horse sheltering in one of the stone shelters outside the town and was riding to Elishard.

Catching up with the column as they neared Walditch, he had kept his distance, waiting for the night to fall, when they would surely rest, for him to ride on unnoticed.

Walditch was the ideal place, he had thought, with more than one way through. That was when he chanced upon the meeting to hear all.

"What a day this is turning out to be. Are you giving yourself up too, Tiggannian?" chided Queen Helistra coldly, as two deformed Elfore ran to drag him before her.

"I was not until I heard you call your son a liar. You know he cannot lie. It is not within him," bluffed Kelmar, understanding what Tomin was trying to do.

"And who are you to know him so?" she questioned.

"I am Kelmar, Captain of the Tiggannian guard of Stormhaven," he replied proudly, for Princess Amber to look at him from under her hood as she heard him say his name.

So this is the real Kelmar, who saved my mother, she thought, as Queen Helistra listened to the humming that had entered her mind.

Yes, he must have been there somewhere. The other one lied, but what he says is true. Tomin cannot lie, for the humming to warn her.

I know, I will be careful. I will find out if they are lying once I am fully replenished, but look at them. Now they know the broken piece is shattered, so are they!

She stood but a breath away from Tomin's face, for him to taste the darkness in her every word. "Well? Should I be scared of them after they have sought help from these wraiths of the Ancient Forestalls and failed? Scared of a boy with a rune staff that is useless to him? Of an old man who has already tasted defeat when I did not have the power of the crystal chamber," she was quick to point out as she stared down at Tomin, "and of a protector who has nothing to protect?" she challenged.

Tomin did not move from her corrupt breath as he replied, "You have all but won, Mother. Whatever the wraiths of the Ancient Forestalls did, it has obviously not worked, with the broken piece shattered. They may be alive, but with what to threaten you?

"You have destroyed the Ancient One, the very beginning of everything, and three of the forests Forestalls are no more. The Plateau Forest is already dead and the Great Forest will soon join it as the poison you control with the power of the crystal chamber forever flows into it.

"And now with Marchend but a cinder, fallen to your creations, Northernland will soon be no more. I do not think the word scared comes into it, Mother." spoke Tomin, recalling all she had done, only to make himself feel down as he recollected it all.

Queen Helistra's face had grown from contempt to a cold callous smile as Tomin reeled off the evil she had done.

"When you put it like that, no, it does not!" She laughed coldly as she remounted her horse. "A cart awaits you both with your friends. You will come back to Stormhaven where we will wait for what is left of them to appear. My so-called father will willingly come to sacrifice himself in your place," gloated Queen Helistra at the thought.

"What have you to gain by killing Grandfather?" implored Tomin one last time.

"You have just said it yourself, I have all, but won, when he is dead, then I will have won," she answered simply without emotion.

"And when he is dead, what will you have left? I will tell you. Nothing! Because you will have destroyed everything. There will be nothing for you to reign over, nothing to use the power you have gained. All of it will be worthless, and in the end, it will destroy you!" argued Tomin.

Queen Helistra was quiet for a moment whilst she looked into the night sky, as if for inspiration. "Ah, but you do not see what I see, there will be. Even in blackness, there is light. You see darkness all around you, but I see a new beginning, of my design!" And she grinned at the vision of her own making as she looked back at Tomin.

Tomin could only hear the ramblings of a deluded woman. What a fool he had been, trying to reach his mother, he thought. Not only was her heart evil, but she was mad as well!

"In the cart with them! We have been here long enough!" she ordered, and Tomin felt himself shoved unceremoniously into the cart with Kelmar.

The column began to move, with Tomin in the back of the cart, saddened at how he had found his mother to be. "I am sorry I was wrong to have tried to reason with her. I never thought her to be that mad with evil," he apologised, to the understanding quietness of Kelmar, Fleck and Tintwist.

"You did what you thought was best, Tomin. Anyone of us would have done the same," sympathised Kelmar.

"But by giving myself up, all I have done is condemn my grandfather to his death," added Tomin, feeling annoyed with himself.

"You have not, Tomin. Speedwell's demise has been her intention all along. She is so consumed by it, she did not see you mislead her," pointed out Kelmar quietly.

"That is only thanks to your timely intervention, Kelmar," pointed out Tomin.

"I do not think so, but let us hope all is not lost with the broken piece no more, and that they return with the means to put an end to this, one way or another," said Kelmar hopefully, to the nods of them all.

"I thought you gone, Kelmar, your head on that rock!" said Tintwist, glad to see him despite their situation.

"Tiggannian heads are harder than rock," acknowledged Kelmar with a faint smile, "this time," he added.

"At least we are alive. That is more than can be said for Cillan and the poor souls of Marchend," said Fleck in quiet reflection, for Tomin to hear their friend had also paid the price for his mother's evil, only adding to his sadness.

"He is no more?" he asked solemnly.

"He was bitten. He did not want to become one of them," said Kelmar as he looked at the creatures following them, for Tomin to hear in Kelmar's voice what he had had to do.

"We must stay strong, for whilst Martyn lives, we stand a chance," said Kelmar, trying to stay strong himself as he remembered the look in Cillan's eyes.

"Let us hope so," said Fleck with a sigh, and they all fell quiet with their own thoughts as the cart trundled along.

As they got underway, Princess Amber's head was in a spin by what she had been told by Queen Helistra.

She had lied to protect her from her own brother, who would see fit to harm her? *That cannot be true*, she thought, *his spirit has protected me all of this time!*

Would she have told her of his existence if it had not been for her son questioning her? A son she has kept alive so as to lure his grandfather to his death, her own father! Because he is a Forestall trying to save the forest and Northernland from total destruction!

As the word *Forestall* came into her mind, she remembered her vision of her hanging upside down, with those eyes of burning hatred staring at her.

Princess Amber had begun to realise why she had been kept at Stormhaven when she had spoken to Mrs Beeworthy, not because of a brother that would harm her, but because she was destined to become a future Forestall.

Now knowing her brother was alive and seeing Queen Helistra take her own son prisoner, it had become obvious to her what she was. Like her son, she shivered, she was mere bait to lure her brother to his death!

If she had not fully known it before, then Princess Amber knew it now, that Queen Helistra would not rest until they were all dead!

She could do nothing for now, she thought, as she looked back at the four sombre-looking figures in the cart, but try and watch over them whilst she waited for fate to show its hand.

With that last solemn thought, Princess Amber buried herself under her hooded cloak to ride on in quiet reflection behind Queen Helistra.

Queen Helistra felt all had fallen into place by Tomin giving himself up. Speedwell would be hers for the taking and with him, the child's brother. Then they would all die to feed the poison. What a fitting end! Forestalls killing the forest! She grinned.

Ringwold's rune staff helped by some dead spirits! How pathetic! As if any power could be greater than that of the crystal chambers. Wraiths indeed! she scorned.

With the broken piece shattered, they could not undo what she had put into place. The end is near for them all, she thought, as she glanced around to see the four dejected faces in the cart, for her eyes to rest on the bowed head of Princess Amber. She would have to be watched, she thought.

The broken rune staff had kept from humming. All was going well, but it still felt wary in its being at hearing one word: deception!

Piper finally peeked through the shuttered window to see the last of the column disappear into the darkness of the night. She wished she had never stayed behind to witness all she had seen and heard. Now Tomin and Kelmar had also been taken as prisoners, for Queen Helistra to do with as she wished, with no sign of Cillan. A bad feeling came over her as she thought about their plight. She had clearly heard the word *sacrifice*, to send her body shivering at the thought.

It made her quickly make her way back downstairs to grab some warmth before she rode to Elishard, with all she had heard and the news of their capture.

As Piper sat there warming her chilled bones, she thought of what Tomin had said about all of the evil things Queen Helistra had done, knowing he was deceiving her as he spoke, to hide the fact that Martyn had obtained a staff before the Ancient One had fallen.

She hoped that Martyn's staff had been blessed by the wraiths of the Ancient Forestalls to become a rune staff and all was not lost, but a worry had entered her mind that it still would not be powerful enough with Speedwell's to defeat Queen Helistra, for her to suddenly feel chilled again.

She leaned forward, holding out her hands to catch the warmth of the fire, and as she did so, an image of Tintwist's sad face in the cart came into her mind, to set tears in motion, that had been waiting to fall, spilling down her cheeks.

CHAPTER LII

"At least we'll see them coming," remarked Ludbright as he looked out over Elishard Castle's battlements towards the west with King Brodic, at the carpet of snow-laden fields.

"He should have been here by now. It has been too long," said King Brodic, worriedly, not hearing Ludbright.

He had hoped that King Stowlan's nephew, Galmis, would have arrived by now from Ingle. He was next in line to the throne of Balintium, with King Stowlan having no heirs. Word had been sent out, though, more than three weeks ago for him to come to Elishard, and King Brodic feared the worst, as there was no sign of him.

Especially as the only sign to have appeared was a worrying one in the form of a horror– stricken messenger from Leckfell with terrible news, telling of how his town had suffered the same fate as Marchend by invading monsters, who had torn it apart and burnt it to the ground!

Hence, Ludbright was keeping his eyes firmly fixed in the distance.

This news had triggered King Brodic to take decisive action by putting himself in charge and sending for his army to come to Elishard, feeling Elishard Castle's defences stood a better chance against the hideous monsters than at Flininmouth.

Tiska and Tislea had gone immediately on hearing the news to seek help from their fellow Elfore, who had evaded the clutches of the monsters when the barrier had fallen, knowing they would have headed for the edge of the Great Forest somewhere near Kelmsmere.

Although King Brodic was still holding out hope that Galmis would appear, he knew by hearing that Leckfell had fallen to the monsters that Ingle would surely be next, then Falfour, then Elishard!

So as the snow began to fall, the two of them both watched on anxiously; Ludbright over the western plains for any sign of monsters, whilst King Brodic kept his eye on the South Shellow Road for his army and the Elfore.

As they watched, the sound of preparations at the castle for what was feared to be on its way could be heard within the confines of the castle town walls.

It had not taken the horrific news from Leckfell to bring about the urgency with which the preparations were being made, or the tragic news that their beloved King Stowlan was dead, but rather when the garrison and townsfolk were shown the cause of King Stowlan's death, when the hideous remains of what was once a Balintium royal guard was unveiled to them!

Forges were lit as hammers hit anvils to shape swords, working as they did alongside arrow makers. Animals were being penned and firewood stacked as rocks were hauled up onto the castle walls for the catapults that were situated on the wall's dissecting turrets.

Only the south and west sides needed to be defended, as the eastern side had been built on top of the cliffs, to be guarded by the sea.

The settlement that had grown outside the castle walls was all but empty, as everyone had retreated inside.

People were arriving from nearby villages, having heard of Marchend's and Leckfell's plight, for the safety of Elishard's castle walls.

King Brodic worried how many more would come, as the town already sheltered more than enough for the food they had to go round.

Piper had arrived at Elishard only a day after King Brodic had arrived with the villagers of Walditch, with the news they had all feared, that Tomin had been taken prisoner by Queen Helistra and taken to Stormhaven.

Then she had revealed that not only was Tomin her prisoner, but Kelmar, Fleck and Tintwist also, with no sign of Cillan, for despondency to sweep through them all.

She had told them how Tomin had put himself at Queen Helistra's mercy and tried to reason with her, but she was of only one mind. She wanted Speedwell dead! And now she had the means to lure him to his fate!

Then the news of the broken piece being shattered, when Speedwell, Martyn and Tarbor had tried to retrieve it, made them feel even lower.

The only good news Piper had was that Tomin had lied about Martyn's newfound staff, saying he had Ringwold's rune staff instead, to throw her off the trail. Keeping their hopes alive that Martyn would return with a rune staff powerful enough to put an end to Queen Helistra without her suspecting anything, *but the stars help Tomin,* Piper worried, *if she finds out he has lied!*

"He is still just a boy, but I know he will save us all, and then his sister will be free from that evil woman!" Queen Elina had cried defiantly when hearing Piper.

That is when Piper had told her how Queen Helistra had spoken of Princess Amber's brother, twisting her mind to make her think that Prince Martyn wanted to harm her, because she was with her when the Ancient One was destroyed.

"I should have strangled her whilst I had the chance!" Queen Elina had sworn, forgetting about Queen Helistra's powers, and had cried in Permellar's arms.

Not that Permellar was any comfort to her, as she shed tears at the thought of what would become of Kelmar.

Kelmar's mother, Oneatha, had gone to the kitchen with Kayla as soon as she had heard of her son being taken. Like Mrs Beeworthy, she needed something to do. She was used to her son being away, but where hope had stayed in her heart whilst he was under siege, fear had taken its place at hearing Queen Helistra had him and that she may never see him again.

Kayla was glad to go with Oneatha. She had seen and heard enough at the farm that had upset her, let alone seeing her mother crying again.

So they waited at Elishard, not knowing their fate, feeling very alone and vulnerable.

Another cold night passed by, to see King Brodic, Piper, Urchel and Ludbright atop the castle battlements, peering out through the ever-falling snow.

Eyes squinted through the snowfall, for Ludbright to suddenly grip Piper's shoulder and point.

"There!" he cried, for them all to look and feel their blood run as cold as the snow that had blotted out their appearance. Monsters!

"Let us be ready then," said King Brodic calmly, and he ordered the nearest soldier to get the town gates shut, with everyone inside the confines of the castle town walls.

"Man the walls, load the catapults!" he shouted down from the castle battlements, for soldiers to run everywhere in readiness whilst the town gates were barred shut.

Archers made ready along the castle town walls whilst the catapults were loaded with rocks, covered in a thick black oil.

King Brodic wished Tomin was here with his rune staff as he watched a long column of monsters getting closer and closer, heading straight for the settlement outside the castle walls.

The monsters were not interested in trying to storm the castle walls. There was only one place they were heading for: the town gates. And the method of getting through them was held in readiness on their deformed shoulders: a giant tree trunk!

The monsters were not yet in range of the archers' arrows, but they were in range of the catapults, and King Brodic ordered them to fire.

The thick black oil was set alight and the catapults released, spitting fire rocks at the column of monsters.

With a roar, they scorched through the air to find their mark by smashing into the deformed creatures and sending them sprawling on fire onto the snow-covered ground.

"It will take more than those catapults to stop them from getting to the gates," remarked Urchel, seeing their numbers.

"Then we had better meet them there," decided King Brodic, and they left the castle battlements to run through the enclosed town.

King Brodic shouted orders as they ran to the town gates for four lines of soldiers to be positioned in front of the drawbridge, the back line to be archers, ready to fight if the castle town gates were breached.

"Make sure those battlements above the drawbridge have archers also!" he yelled at the same time.

Running up the steps of one of the turret towers that stood either side of the town gates, they reached the battlement that joined the two in time to see the monsters running across the bridge, ready to strike at the town gates.

Arrows were already raining down upon them to find their mark as Piper and Ludbright joined the Balintium archers to fire theirs, only for their victims to be replaced by more waiting monsters as the giant tree trunk crashed into the gates.

Deformed Elfore archers returned fire, to send Balintium archers plummeting from the battlements as rocks were hurled, whilst black oil was poured over the giant tree trunk and set alight, but it did not stop the gates from being rammed, even though some of the monsters were on fire themselves as they rammed the gates!

King Brodic risked a look between the battlements and saw to his dismay the amount of townsfolk that made up the hordes of monsters trying to breach the gates.

He also saw they were standing within the settlement, ready to replace any that fell on the battering ram and when the gates were breached, whilst fire rocks around them had begun to set the settlement on fire.

"Set it all alight!" he ordered, for the Balintium archers to send fire arrows into the buildings.

Growls could be heard from the monsters as the buildings around them began to blaze and the heat grew intense, but it did not deter them despite the many that fell.

King Brodic could see their smouldering malformed bodies littering the now fire-torn settlement, but there were too many to hold back, and he knew it was only a matter of time before they broke through as the gates gave a telling cracking sound to another ramming.

"We must withdraw and face them. There are too many to stop from breaking down the gates," he decided, and they left the gate's battlement, leaving the archers to kill as many as they could whilst they had arrows.

"I hope your army is not far away," said Piper as they reached the lines of soldiers.

"Nor do I, to help us out of this situation," replied King Brodic, "but if we can weaken them enough to hold them off whilst we wait…" he finished thoughtfully.

"Let us retreat into the castle then, to wait for your army. The castle gates are much stronger," suggested a nervous Ludbright.

King Brodic looked at Ludbright with understanding and shook his head. "There will not be enough soldiers in my army from Flininmouth to overcome these hordes of beasts as they stand, Ludbright."

"If we withdraw into the castle now, it will put us in a weaker position. We must inflict enough damage on them whilst we are strong enough, before retreating to the castle. Then my army will have a better chance of finishing them off when they come," explained King Brodic.

"That is, unless more of them come first," said a worried Piper.

"Then our hopes lye with Tiska and Tislea reaching the Elfore. It is a chance we have to take, but we need to buy time," replied King Brodic.

"Either way, death awaits us is what you are saying," said Ludbright solemnly, to himself.

"Well, if we are to die, let us take as many of these creatures with us as we can," said Urchel with a gritted smile, as he pulled on his leather hood and gloves before holding his sword in readiness.

Piper and Ludbright joined him as they too donned their leather hoods, for King Brodic to look at them with a slight smile on his face. They looked for all they were worth like some sort of monster themselves, he thought, as another resounding crack told him the gates were nearly broken through.

He looked at the Balintium soldiers behind him, to see both fear and grim determination written across their faces.

Behind them, he saw those who had been brave enough from both town and village wielding swords, forged from the now quiet anvils.

"Do not be of faint heart! The evil that comes through those gates must be stopped whatever the cost!" shouted King Brodic as a crash of splintering wood saw the castle town gates finally give way to the pounding of the giant tree trunk.

Archers on the castle walls fired upon the monsters that stormed through the broken gates, for the turned Elfore archers that were in amongst them to retaliate.

The bewildered face of his father came into King Brodic's mind as he held himself ready before the charging hordes. He still would not believe it, he thought.

Piper was thinking of Tintwist and whether she would ever see him again as Ludbright's skin crawled at seeing these grotesque creatures once more, whilst Urchel whispered to his lost friend, "Wait for me, Idrig, old friend. I will be with you soon."

"Archers!" cried King Brodic as they all knelt, to give a clear view for the line of archers to let loose their arrows, striking down the first of the creatures.

Two more volleys of arrows were sent, singing death, through the air into the onrushing creatures before the four first met them head-on, for their swords to ignite the snow-filled air with the clash of metal and slice through their deformed flesh.

More monsters poured through the broken gates to attack as King Brodic, Piper, Urchel and Ludbright fought toe to toe, with bodies falling everywhere.

Their bravery spurred on the soldiers as they moved forward to skewer malformed bodies on their spears, whilst severing misshapen limbs with their swords.

They were followed by the townsfolk and villagers, for carnage to ensue as arrows flew over their heads from the battlements of the castle in a never-ending rain of death.

King Brodic was hacking at anything that got near him in what became a frenzy of fighting. Piper and Ludbright were swaying one way then another to avoid the scything strokes of the deformed Elfore, who seemed to be after them in particular as Urchel killed one after another in what was becoming a blood lust.

Thick orange blood found its way into some of the wounded, for them to begin convulsing in amongst the dead bodies to add to the nightmare their comrades were already enduring.

How long it was the battle went on for like this, no one was sure, but suddenly Ludbright was reeling from a sword that had sliced through his shoulder!

Piper quickly came to his aid, despatching the creature that dealt the blow with one thrust of her sword into its malformed chest.

King Brodic saw Ludbright fall as he took another creature's head clean off. It was time they retreated, he thought, as he glanced at the dead bodies all around him. They had done enough.

He quickly looked to see the town was mostly on fire, keeping the main force of monsters back for now with the heat. Here was their chance to withdraw, he thought.

"Back inside the castle!" he shouted, forming a rear guard with those that were left standing to despatch any creatures that came onto the drawbridge, enabling Urchel and Piper to drag Ludbright back over the drawbridge.

King Brodic looked up at the castle town battlements. They were empty of Balintium archers; only deformed Elfore archers were firing from them now.

As he realised it, he felt one of their arrows tear through his leg above his knee, to send his tired body sprawling across the drawbridge!

Hands grabbed him and the next he knew, Piper and Urchel were dragging him over the drawbridge, for it to crash into the castle walls, sealing them into the castle.

"We have taken many lives," he said painfully as they leaned him against the castle wall next to a wounded archer.

"We have lost many too," replied Piper as she pulled off her hood, "but first, that needs attending to," she said, looking down at the bloody arrow sticking out of King Brodic's leg, but before anything else could be said or done, a scream came from in front of them.

It was a creature swirling its sword above its deformed head. Orange blood could be clearly seen seeping out of its shoulder as it cut through a poor member of the townsfolk who had survived the onslaught outside, who had tried to stop it.

"No, not Ludbright, we left him against that wall!" muttered Urchel, for Piper to gasp.

They stood there looking in disbelief at what had become of their comrade, to see the hate upon his twisted features where there was once laughter.

Piper snatched up the bow and an arrow from the wounded archer to send the arrow straight through Ludbright's chest, sending his malformed body backwards, to hit the snow-covered ground with a thump!

She immediately threw the bow down and ran, crying, to kneel over Ludbright's dead body, her tears falling onto the orange blood that had spilt into the snow as her body writhed with pain at what she had done. She had just saved him and now she had had to kill him!

King Brodic could only look on in painful silence whilst Urchel felt the pain Piper was going through as he remembered Idrig.

"We have done enough. My army will finish them off," said King Brodic quietly, wincing at the pain he was feeling in his leg.

"I hope they hurry before more arrive then," replied Urchel, repeating Piper's thoughts as he looked around at the women attending the wounded, whilst those who had survived the battle helped to get them out of the snow, even though they themselves were exhausted.

"They will be here," said King Brodic in pained confidence.

"Then I only hope Speedwell, Prince Martyn and Tarbor are not far behind them with the means to end this evil," added Urchel, as they both looked at Piper sobbing over the orange-stained body of what was once their friend Ludbright lying in the snow.

CHAPTER LIII

"I cannot fully remember. She had her hand around my neck. I felt her nails dig into me and in the next moment she called for the beast to bite me, because she did not like liars," explained Cantell of Princess Amber's actions that fateful day, his words echoing under the Elfore rowing boat he was carrying on his head with Speedwell and Tarbor, whilst Martyn walked ahead with the oars.

Speedwell had decided they should get the rowing boat they had left behind and take it to the north side of the mountains, where the source of the Linninhorne River could be found that would mark the beginning of their way back to Northernland.

"The rivers will be our path again to get us there quicker," he had stated.

"Rivers?" Tarbor had queried, pointing out the slight obstacle of the Ogrin Ridge that would interrupt their journey.

"Then we would have to journey on foot. We would not be able to carry this thing down those steps. Remember, the Elfore sailing boat is with Tomin, Piper and Tintwist," he had added.

"Trust me," Speedwell had said with a knowing smile that had made Tarbor feel uncomfortable. He did trust him, but that was what was making him feel uncomfortable! That and having this boat on his head!

"I think she saw into your mind and found you were speaking true," said Martyn, thinking on what Cantell had said when he met his sister.

"And in that moment, she somehow put a barrier up around your very soul to stop it from becoming evil, without my daughter realising," finished Speedwell.

"Whatever she did, I have her to thank for not letting me become a complete monster," reflected Cantell.

"I would not say that, Cantell," chirped Tarbor, for them all to snigger.

"Thank you, Tarbor. It is good to be back amongst friends again, although I would look less like an animal if I had some proper clothes," said Cantell, smiling to himself as he stumbled along in Tarbor's cloak with cloth-covered feet.

The snow-laden mountains had proven to be tough going for Cantell, even with Tarbor's shield of protection around him, and although he was coping better on the rocky ground they now travelled, he was glad to hear Speedwell call for a rest.

Lifting the rowing boat up over their heads, they rested it on the rocky ground, for Speedwell to start looking around him to get his bearings.

To the west lay the murky brown devastation of the Plateau Forest. To his south, what had seemed the endless Linninhorne Mountains they had just traversed, whilst to his east lay what was once the sacred home of the Elfore, where his daughter's never-ending flow of poison made its way to the Great Forest, the Valley of the Lakes.

Where Speedwell was looking for, though, lay just ahead of them to the north as he could sense the Linninhorne River underneath him, readying itself to emerge from the mountains, for its waters to cascade over fallen rocks before plummeting into a valley, beginning its journey to the Old Ogrin Ridge.

"We are near. I can feel the ground beneath my feet tremble. Beyond that hill is the valley where it falls into and the river begins," stated Speedwell as he sat down with the others.

"It is just as well, Speedwell. Our food is all but gone," reported Tarbor, looking in the shoulder bag they had with them at what sparse provisions were left.

"Hmm, we will be able to make up time on the river," said Speedwell thoughtfully, making Tarbor look at him suspiciously.

"The last time you said that we ended up in a whirlpool!" pointed out Tarbor, bringing back the memories to Cantell with a shudder, whilst Martyn smiled as he remembered the story being told to him.

"What, dare I ask, do you have up your sleeve this time?" he asked.

Speedwell looked out before him across the lower slopes of the Linninhorne Mountains, remembering his journeys of long ago with the Elfore, and started to tell them of his intentions to get them back to Northernland more quickly.

"I used to come across to here with the Elfore from the lakes, when they used to visit their folk where we were in the Great Forest," began Speedwell with a smile as he thought of those days.

"But the Winterbourne River is nearer to the tongue in the cheek?" queried Tarbor straight away.

"Yes, but the Winterbourne does not have an underground river," answered Speedwell to wide-eyed looks.

"For a moment, I thought you said underground river?" queried Tarbor again.

"I did, a part of the Linninhorne River splits off to disappear underground and emerge into the Lake of Tears. It will cut days off our journey," he announced to raised eyebrows.

"This underground river is wide enough to take a rowing boat then?" asked Cantell, thinking of when he was wedged in the narrow tunnel, bringing back haunting feelings of his hatred of enclosed spaces.

"Of course it is. Otherwise, I would not have suggested it. We used to do it for fun in the old days, it was an adventure," said Speedwell, smiling.

"You should be talking to Kelmar, not me. This would be his sort of thing," said Cantell, picturing the smile it would have put on his comrade's face.

"How many days quicker would it be exactly?" asked Tarbor, not liking the sound of it at all.

"Two to three weeks of walking would be cut to two to three days on the underground river with the speed it flows," answered Speedwell.

Martyn was already on his feet in anticipation. "What are we waiting for?"

"And how long ago was it you last took this journey?" queried Tarbor.

"Well, it has been a while," said Speedwell, getting up, evading Tarbor's looks but feeling his stare. "Before the rift, a few hundred years," he finally admitted.

"A few hundred years! Anything could have happened in that time. The whole thing could have collapsed!" exclaimed Tarbor, shaking his head with the thought of what Tarbor had just said, not helping Cantell at all.

"I would not risk our lives if I thought it to be that dangerous, but time is of the essence, literally," pointed out Speedwell, for them to understand, but with apprehension.

"We have our rune staffs to help us if anything gets in our way." Martyn smiled confidently, not able to stop smiling since being blessed with his own rune staff.

Tarbor looked at Cantell and Cantell looked at Tarbor. "And then we can look forward to the whirlpool again, in that this time," groaned Cantell, as he and Tarbor looked at the rowing boat.

"It will not be like the last time. It is winter now. It should be slower," said Speedwell, hoping it would help.

"Should be!" they both said, with resigned looks on their faces.

With the Elfore rowing boat hauled up onto their heads once more, they set off for the valley where the Linninhorne River began its journey.

The sound of rushing water tumbling over rocks came to their ears as they journeyed, to eventually turn into a mighty roar as the waters from the Linninhorne Mountains fell into the valley Speedwell had been heading for.

Descending slowly, having to veer their way around, they finally knew they had come into the valley as they trod in the mire of devastation once more.

They rested on fallen rocks by the freshly gouged Linninhorne River's bank before venturing onto it to start their – as far as Tarbor and Cantell were concerned – perilous journey.

"Where does the underground river show itself?" asked Tarbor, holding the rowing boat steady for Speedwell, Cantell and Martyn to climb into.

"Not far. A few miles on is where it divides," answered Speedwell, remembering.

"Can I be at the front?" asked Martyn, climbing in first.

"No, Martyn, you will be at the back. I will be at the front," answered Speedwell, to Martyn's disappointment.

Before Speedwell got into the Elfore rowing boat, he began chanting and moving his fingers across his rune staff.

"What is he doing?" asked Cantell, for Martyn to smile, being able to sense what Speedwell was performing.

"A special spell of protection for the boat."

"What for?" questioned Tarbor, immediately worried.

"If there are any obstacles in our way, then this spell will disperse them," explained Martyn, for Tarbor and Cantell to look at each other again.

Speedwell climbed in, followed by Tarbor, and brought his rune staff around him, casting an invisible spell of protection that melded into the rowing boat.

"I thought you said it was not going to be dangerous," pointed out Tarbor when Speedwell had finished.

"It should not be, but it pays to be careful," replied Speedwell, to Tarbor's inward groan.

The Elfore rowing boat was soon caught up in the river's flow, with Tarbor and Cantell taking an oar each to guide them.

"Keep to the left bank," called Speedwell, as the rowing boat began to pick up speed.

What looked to be some rocky hills at the side of the river suddenly loomed before them to divert a narrow strip of the river off into their midst, whilst the main river ran on down the valley.

They dropped down between the hills until they flattened out to flow into a narrow gorge, for Tarbor and Cantell to pull in their oars with no room to row.

Then there in front of them was a solid face of rock with a cave entrance at its base that made Tarbor and Cantell instinctively duck as they entered its mouth.

"There is plenty of room," said Martyn with a smile as they were suddenly plunged into darkness, but not for long, as Speedwell threw a soft light from his rune staff to show they had entered an underground tunnel of smooth rock.

Cantell breathed in relief at the light as the Elfore rowing boat took them down into the depths of the earth.

No one spoke as the rowing boat sped through the underground tunnel, tilting one way then another to now and again catch the sides.

The hours passed by as slowly they got used to the motion of the boat and the unnerving scraping sounds as they caught the sides of the tunnel.

Tarbor began wondering who it was that had discovered the underground river and decided to see where it went.

"Who was it that was brave enough to have found out this underground river flowed all the way to the Lake of Tears, Speedwell?" he asked out of curiosity in the end.

"Who was mad enough, you mean!" added Cantell.

"It was by chance and luck really," remembered Speedwell, "a young Elfore was fishing in the river and knew of the cave entrance, but also knew not to go near it, knowing the narrow river disappeared into blackness.

"However, curiosity got the better of him and when he came back here once more to fish, he brought a torch with him to explore the cave despite the danger he could face.

"What he had not counted on was the spring rain, for whilst he was exploring down here, wading through the water, he was unaware of the skies opening up in a spring rainstorm.

"The build-up of water was fast and furious from the Linninhorne Mountains to pour in a torrent of water into here, sweeping him off his feet to send him headlong through the water," recounted Speedwell, pausing as the boat tilted once more and then levelled out again.

"He survived to tell the story, though?" asked Cantell, held by Speedwell's story.

"He did, he was lucky. The stars and spirits certainly watched over him. Everyone thought he was dead until he walked, not back to the Valley of the Lakes, but into the tongue in cheek settlement over two weeks later," finished Speedwell.

"But how did he survive with all that water? He must have constantly been fighting for breath," asked Cantell further.

"He spoke as much, but then..." Speedwell suddenly stopped talking and called to his rune staff to glow even more.

"But what?" pushed Cantell, to see Speedwell pointing ahead.

He had no need to say anything as the underground river answered for him by suddenly throwing the soft light from his rune staff forward and outward to reveal a long chamber.

Tarbor and Cantell dropped their oars into the water to row the boat out of the main stream to the side for a rest, enabling them all to listen to the rest of the story.

"He found this to catch his breath in," said Speedwell, smiling at the timing.

"Though he was cold and wet, he was able to take refuge here whilst the waters calmed down. Then he swam his way out, finding two more such chambers before emerging exhausted but alive into the Lake of Tears," informed Speedwell.

"I would not have liked it, here alone in the dark, cold and wet. He must have been scared, not knowing if he was going to live or die," remarked Martyn, who for once was not smiling but was instead feeling a cold isolation in the chamber.

Cantell looked at him and knew, though he had been but a baby, that he was feeling that dreaded moment when he had dropped him in the pool; something which Cantell had never forgiven himself for.

"No, Martyn, nor I, but you could have asked him yourself," revealed Speedwell, for them all to frown at him.

"The young Elfore was Fleck," he announced to their astounded looks.

"Fleck!" questioned Tarbor.

"Well, he always was and still is a brave if not headstrong Elfore," remarked Speedwell, to the smiles of them all.

"Come, we have many more miles yet to travel," urged Speedwell, for Tarbor and Cantell to guide them back into the main stream of water, with Martyn glad to leave his isolated feeling behind him.

With the hours passing by and the constant swaying of the boat, tiredness grew, but the two chambers saw them snatch some much-needed sleep.

Time was lost to them as they journeyed along the underground river, passing as it did without so much as a hiccup, much to the surprise of Tarbor and Cantell, who had feared some sort of obstacle to be in their way.

"Be ready to hold on!" was the sudden shout from Speedwell, for eyes to spring open and hands to hold on to the Elfore rowing boat as it was suddenly catapulted out of the rock wall of the Old Ogrin Ridge!

Dark grey daylight, after a shock of cold soaking water, met them as they shot through the waterfall of the Linninhorne River, having catapulted out of the underground river to fall into the Lake of Tears.

The Elfore rowing boat hit the lake, to throw them headlong into the water.

Speedwell, Tarbor and Cantell managed to get themselves back to the rowing boat to hold on to it, but Martyn was floundering in the water, trying to hold on to his rune staff.

Martyn had never learnt to swim, and the reason he had never done so was happening to him now as a feeling of darkness began to come over him as soon as he felt the water pressing against his body.

A feeling that would well up from somewhere deep inside him, it had touched him in the chamber, but now it was trying to overwhelm him. It was one thing for him to look upon the water and ride its surface in a boat, but quite another to be in its depths.

The next he knew, Cantell was hauling him back into the rowing boat with Speedwell's helping hands.

As Martyn wiped his eyes, with a cough and a splutter, Tarbor then Cantell got back into the rowing boat, for Cantell to be handed back what was now a soaking cloak from Tarbor.

"Thank you, Uncle," said Martyn, coughing, forgetting Speedwell had wanted him to feel their equal now he was a Forestall, not that he felt like it at this moment.

When Cantell did not answer, Martyn looked up to see him looking upwards with Speedwell and Tarbor. He looked to see what they were looking at, and the darkness he had felt inside him instantly disappeared as his eyes fell upon what they were staring at.

All they had been through was perhaps an adventure at the time, to put a smile of hope on their faces.

They had secured the broken piece and received a blessing on Martyn's staff, had power deemed to them, the like of which they had never felt before. They had found the essences still lived and Cantell was no longer a monster, but now the reality of what they were up against was staring them in the face, bringing them back down to earth, for there above them, hanging precariously over the edge of the Old Ogrin Ridge, was what was left of the Ancient One!

Mist swirled around the giant lifeless form, whilst vines still covered the enormous trunk, squeezing their poisonous slime into the Ancient One's empty being in a suffocating dance of death.

The deadly mist was pouring down the face of Old Ogrin Ridge on either side of the two waterfalls, floating over the Ogrin River in its haste to reach the Great Forest to deliver the deadly vines and poisonous pods that lay within its midst.

Suddenly a loud crack echoed around the lake from the ridge as one of the Ancient One's huge branches finally gave way to the relentless poison, to plummet down onto the lake, onto them!

"Tarbor, a shield of protection!" shouted Speedwell as his rune staff lay in the boat, as he had just helped Martyn climb in, but in that moment, a pod had dropped into the rowing boat from out of nowhere and began opening, to release its poisonous spores!

Tarbor had grabbed his shield and was smothering the pod, to stop it from releasing them.

Martyn saw the huge branch was heading straight for them. He had done it before, he thought, and closing his eyes, he quickly called upon the help of Grimstone's broken piece of rune staff within his as he touched two symbols on his rune staff at the same time.

The next thing he knew was Speedwell falling backwards onto Tarbor and Cantell falling backwards onto him as the rowing boat launched itself across the lake, slowing to a stop near the Bridge of Seasons.

A loud splash told them that the huge branch had hit the lake, for them only to feel the resulting waves from the fallen branch, to send them drifting under the Bridge of Seasons.

After managing to sit back up, they all looked at Martyn with a thankful smile. "Well done, Martyn," thanked Speedwell, whilst Tarbor dealt with the pod he had managed to keep contained by throwing it over the side, after stabbing it with his defender and releasing white fire into it.

They watched it float away on fire as they felt the Bridge of Seasons' fine roots brush across their heads, for Martyn to instantly sense their pain.

He reached out to hold some of the fine roots in his hands that were hanging limply around them and immediately sensed the fight the majestic trees had been putting up, but it was coming to an end.

The vines were squeezing the life out of them whilst seeping their venom through their tough bark as the spores destroyed them by poisoning every fibre of their being.

Their pain and anguish brought a sudden anger to Martyn, tearing at his heart, ripping through his very soul, to make his rune staff tremble. It made him feel sick to his stomach. He could not let this pass. He must do something, if only to save the Bridge of Seasons!

Speedwell could see and sense the effect it was having on Martyn. "Do not let anger take over, Martyn," advised Speedwell, slightly worried by what he saw.

"I cannot let this happen, Speedwell! These fine roots of the Bridge of Seasons kept me safe when the Ancient One was broken! It is time to let her know we are here and ready to fight!" shouted Martyn in the end in his anger.

"I will shield you!" responded Tarbor, to which Martyn shook his head.

"No, Tarbor, we have danced around her for long enough!" replied Martyn, looking for Speedwell's approval.

Speedwell felt the fine roots for himself and instantly felt their plight, sensing as he did so Martyn's heartache that such evil had been unleashed upon them.

Martyn was right; they should do something. Whether they did or not would make no difference to Helistra, thought Speedwell. He could see her there, waiting at Stormhaven with the power of the crystal chamber at her bidding and the bargaining power of Martyn's sister, Princess Amber, at her disposal.

Speedwell looked back at Martyn. "What do you propose to do?" he asked, sensing Martyn calming down whilst receiving smiles from Tarbor and Cantell.

"Can you put some of the life-giving droplets onto my rune staff, please?" asked Martyn straight away.

Speedwell opened his pouch and took out the small bottle that held them for Martyn to hold up his rune staff so Speedwell could put the precious droplets of life onto it whilst Martyn explained his idea.

"I thought if you froze the poison then burnt it, like you did at the sister pool of life, then I could send in air after you, followed by the life-giving droplets, to cleanse the trees completely," he quickly explained, making it sound simple.

"So you want me to freeze the poison and then sear it," clarified Speedwell.

"Yes, then I will blast the spores and vines from the trees before cleansing them with the droplets," confirmed Martyn as the droplets of life soaked into his rune staff.

"You will have to be quick then, Martyn. Those spores and vines will not stop attacking," warned Speedwell.

"I will be, then together we can put a double shield of protection around them," finished Martyn.

"Very well, let us prepare," said Speedwell, nodding, and he began slowly chanting, holding his rune staff against the fine roots as he touched certain symbols upon it.

Tarbor and Cantell could only sit there in the rowing boat watching as a blue cloud began to appear around the fine roots. Then they saw his fingers move over his rune staff and heard his chanting change to a faster but softer pitch.

As he did so, Speedwell's rune staff began to glow ice-blue, freezing the fine roots to make them look like hanging crystals, whilst the blue cloud became denser and denser, to suddenly show small dark blue streaks of lighting arcing throughout its confines.

Martyn closed his eyes and felt the strength of Speedwell's spell surrounding him, giving him added confidence in what he was about to do.

Touching symbols on his rune staff, Martyn called to the broken piece of Grimstone's rune staff to help him rid the Bridge of Seasons of their poison.

Martyn felt the broken piece's immediate response to his calling, blending into his rune staff to send wave after wave of pulsating energy through it, ready to cast new breath into the trees and cleanse them of their venom.

He opened his eyes to see the whole of the Bridge of Seasons' fine roots aglow with the ice– blue crystals and the swirling blue cloud of lightning spinning tightly around Speedwell's head.

Speedwell's voice came into his mind: *Are you ready, Martyn?*

Yes, Speedwell!

Speedwell merely moved a finger to touch another symbol, for Tarbor's and Cantell's ears to go deaf as a resounding whoosh met them as the ice-blue crystals shot into the fine roots!

Then their faces felt like their skin had been pushed back by the force of the blue cloud as it exploded into a carpet of blue, dispersing all over the fine roots to then disappear behind the ice– blue crystals.

Inside the trees, the blue ice crystals and cloud of blue lightning combined to rip through them, immediately stopping any poison from spreading as it was turned into ice, then seared through to leave nothing but melted ash.

A heartbeat later, Speedwell was shouting, "Martyn!"

Martyn did not hesitate; he had been waiting for this moment to prove how strong his bond was with his rune staff ever since he had been blessed with it.

He followed Speedwell's example by laying his rune staff along some of the fine roots, and touching one of the symbols upon it, he released his spell.

A wind of such force then proceeded to unleash itself into the trees, to cast out the burnt poison. It sent melted ash spiralling out through the minute holes made by the poisonous spores. Those spores that covered the trees that had been injecting their venom shot out, froze and burnt, to explode into grey mush.

At the same time, the vines were not only being repelled but were shredded as the ejected spores exploded within them.

Grey-blue water spewed its way out of the minute holes the spores had left until there was none left, and as he sensed it, Martyn released the tiny droplets of life.

Suddenly the trees were awash with the tiny droplets of life flowing through them, cleansing them, letting them breathe new life into their beings once more, for their fibre to knit together, sealing the holes to make them whole again!

It had worked! The Bridge of Seasons was well again and the fine roots were showing it by caressing them all.

"Quick, Martyn, the shield!" called Speedwell, and Martyn immediately put his rune staff against Speedwell's to form a double spell of protection.

The sensation they all felt from the two rune staffs combining gave their bodies goosebumps as the double shield of protection threw its invisible cloak around the Bridge of Seasons.

"If she does not feel that!" remarked Cantell, blowing his cheeks in wonder at what he had just seen and felt.

"You are right!" joined in Tarbor, realising the power they had just witnessed.

Speedwell looked at Martyn with a smile for what he too had felt. "Your bond with your rune staff has become strong, Martyn. There is great power in your weave," perceived Speedwell.

"And yours, Speedwell," said Martyn with a smile, feeling better for having done something, if only a token to stop her from poisoning all of the forest.

"Now we have announced ourselves, we had better get to Stormhaven as quickly as possible," said Speedwell, worried at what she might do when she sensed what they had done.

She was his daughter, but that part of her he once knew was lost a long time ago, he thought. He did not know her anymore.

No more was needed to be said as Tarbor and Cantell took to the oars, rowing through the thankful caress of the fine roots out onto the River of Tears.

As they headed down the river, the four companions looked up to see the Bridge of Seasons' majestic trees radiating in health once more as they swayed over them, surrounded by a silver shimmer, knowing it was going to take more than a couple of spells to defeat Helistra the Black Queen.

CHAPTER LIV

Torches fought against the cold snow-filled air on top of Stormhaven's battlements as the Eastern Sea pounded restlessly at Stormhaven Bay. A lonely Cardronian guard looked out of the narrow gatehouse window, blowing into his hands to keep them warm.

His eyes drifted down the valley towards the snow-covered ruins of Haven to settle on the breaking waves. Not that he could see them clearly through the falling snow, but it did not matter. His mind was elsewhere; the sea was not the only restless one.

This was his fifth time in as many years guarding the stronghold. He just wanted to be at home in Senarth. There was nothing to do here but walk up and down.

Hardly anyone came near the place, the most frequent visitors being the merchants, mainly from Silion, with fresh supplies, and now he thought about it, he had not seen any of them for quite a while.

He thought of the stories he had heard of the place when he first came to Stormhaven. If it had not been for a few guards he had met, who were there at the invasion, telling him of the mysterious goings-on, he would have found them hard to believe. They still were.

The mountain door was testament to that. He still could not believe such a huge chunk of solid rock could have been moved by magic or sorcery as was heard tell, but whatever it was, that secret had died with King Taliskar, they had been told by Queen Helistra.

He refocused his eyes to watch the falling snow and as he did so, the smell of Mrs Beeworthy's kitchens came into his mind as he looked. She was bound to have something hot on the go, he thought.

He had had enough of standing here freezing to death. He would sneak off in a moment to the kitchens. No one would miss him, but then a movement caught his eye coming out of the valley.

Riders, he could barely see them, but then his eyes grew wide. White her horse may have been, lost to the snow, but there was no mistaking her black cloak!

"They are back! Queen Helistra returns!" he shouted down the passageways to alert his fellow guards.

Footfalls could soon be heard. The eastern winds help any of them if they were seen by Queen Helistra not to be alert at their posts.

The giant gates were already open – it was rare they were ever closed – for her to enter Stormhaven. Screwing up his eyes, the guard looked at the column of soldiers emerging out of the snow behind her.

He counted six horse soldiers, the same as went out, he thought, and there was the little Princess. Behind her was a horse and cart with one, two, three, four unfortunates, he thought to himself, followed by a large column of soldiers. He wondered why they had come here as he tried to make them out through the snow.

As the cart became clearer to his sight, he caught his breath. He looked again. Who? What was that driving the cart? And what were they following?

A memory of when he was young came into his mind as he saw them more clearly. He could hear his father telling him stories when he was a boy of monsters who lived in the forest. They had made him feel frightened, but they were just stories, he had come to realise, so what were these about to enter Stormhaven!

Shouts went up as other guards stared out at what was about to enter the gates, with open mouths and terror in their eyes.

The guard wanted to run there and then as he watched Queen Helistra ride in with a look that made him go colder than he already was, followed by the hideous-looking creatures that had death written all over them.

Queen Helistra dismounted in an empty grand courtyard. No guard had dared come near her horse to hold it whilst she did so.

She looked around her and could sense the fear in them all. So they should be afraid, she thought, amused.

By now, the courtyard was full of agitated monsters. Queen Helistra was not the only one who could smell their fear! She smiled at their obedience towards her. If she was not here, they would have already ripped them apart, she thought.

"Take them to the dungeons and put them in separate cells," she ordered to the deformed King Vedland. "Come, child, we will inform the cook there will be four more for dinner," said Queen Helistra, laughing, not helping herself.

Princess Amber followed quietly and closed her eyes. She knew what was going to happen next.

"Well? What are you waiting for!" shouted Queen Helistra to the roars of the monsters.

Hoods flew back from the six horse soldiers, revealing to the already terrified onlooking guards the grotesque features of what were once their comrades. Baring razor-like teeth through snarling, twisted mouths, they jumped down off their horses to give chase.

Following their cue, all the monsters began rampaging throughout the stronghold, for screams and yells to soon echo all around.

The guards never stood a chance. Some fought bravely, taking two or three with them, but most were torn to shreds and fed upon.

The guard in the gatehouse could think of nothing more than just running when he heard the screams; run for his life! Drawing his sword, he made for the steps that led to the archway. He was going to make for the gates and run. He knew his chances were slim, but what else was there?

He reached the archway door and peeked nervously around it, only to see one of his comrades being mauled in the archway by two monsters.

They caught sight of him looking and dropped the guard to come after him. He quickly shut the archway door, dropping the bar across it just in time to hear the annoyed growls and thumps upon the door, to suddenly hear them stop!

They are going through the opposite door of the archway to come behind me, he thought, and he chanced to reopen his.

Peeking around the door once more, he saw his comrade who had been mauled shaking on the ground. He risked running to him to see if he could help.

"Can you stand? Come, we must run for our lives!" he urged, gripping his comrade's arm whilst looking at the archway door for the monsters, but what he witnessed next left him speechless.

He looked back at his comrade as he felt him stop shaking and watched his eyes open to make him gasp. They were as black as night!

Then he saw how his face had become a mass of black and red lines pushing against his skin. The arm he was holding suddenly shot up, for a gnarled hand to grip his throat, making him drop his sword.

"What has happened to you? What are you doing?" he said, choking, as he struggled to push his comrade's gnarled hand away.

He fumbled for his dagger, shaking with fear. He had no choice but to end this madness, and sliding his dagger out of his boot, he stabbed his comrade in the throat to get him off him, leaving him there, to see orange blood run down his comrade's neck from the fatal wound.

Picking up his sword, he looked at what he had done in repulsion and sobbed. What was happening?

There was no time to think as the two monsters who had attacked his comrade suddenly appeared in the archway door he had come through.

For the first time, he noted their dress and long, thin swords they held, but that was all as they charged at him.

He quickly dropped down and rolled forward, straight between the both of them, avoiding their swords to slice through one of the monster's legs as he did so, causing it to drop to one knee.

This only made the other monster growl and turn on him with its sword ready to strike. Parrying the blow by his face, the guard immediately dropped down onto his back and pushed himself between the monster's legs, scything through its groin as he did so.

Getting up behind it, he drove his sword straight through the back of its neck, to see it fall forward onto its deformed face.

Pulling his sword out just in time, the guard parried the other monster's sword with both of his hands on the hilt to stop it penetrating the side of his chest.

He kicked the monster's leg where he had cut it, making it growl, but it was enough to take its attention away for it to slightly loosen its grip for the guard to pull away, turn and bring his sword full tilt across the monster's throat.

Then fate for the guard lent a hand as a horse came galloping into the archway. It whinnied at the smell and sight of the dead monsters, raising itself onto its back legs, kicking in the air.

Reins hung from the horse's head and the guard managed to grab them to hold on to the horse.

"Easy, my friend, easy. I am as afraid as you, but together we can both get out of here," he said, managing to stroke the horse's forehead to calm it down as it snorted the foul smelling cold air.

It was as if the horse knew exactly what he was saying as it calmed down enough for him to climb on.

In the next breath, they were galloping as fast as they could across the snow-covered valley.

Princess Amber had tried to keep her eyes closed as she followed Queen Helistra to the kitchens, only opening them once when she heard her horse whinny with fright at the mayhem that surrounded it, to see it bolt out of the courtyard through Middle Gate. *At least you will be free,* she had thought.

Queen Helistra entered the kitchens to find Mrs Beeworthy and two servant women cowering in the corner, frightened.

"Do not be frightened. They will be contented for at least a while now they have fed," she said, smirking, seeing the sheer horror on Mrs Beeworthy's face and those of the two servants.

"They will not harm you. You are needed here for the prisoners I have brought back with me. I want you to keep them well nourished for when…" She paused with a smile. "Just keep them fed," she finished.

She turned to walk out of the door, to see Princess Amber looking at her. "You disapprove, child?" she asked, with a hint of warning in her voice.

"I thought you only wanted the forests destroyed, but I was wrong," answered Princess Amber, trying to quell her emotions of how she really felt.

"Yes, you were, child," said Queen Helistra with a smile, and she left the kitchen to silence.

"What… what be happening, Amber? What… what are those horrible things?" cried Mrs Beeworthy as Princess Amber hugged her tightly, crying.

"She has brought the children of the forest here, Bee, but they are no longer who they once were. She has changed them into monsters with her evil! They are killing all the guards!" cried Princess Amber.

Mrs Beeworthy was not sure what she meant by children of the forest as she consoled a tearful Princess Amber, as much for herself as the Princess.

"Who... who be these prisoners that I have to feed?" queried Mrs Beeworthy, trying to turn her attention to the only thing she knew as the sound of feeding of another kind accompanied by growls of contentment came from the courtyard, making them all feel sick.

"Tomin, a Forestall who is her son; Fleck, an Elfore; Tintwist, a Manelf and Kelmar, Cantell's friend, who you told me also saved us," replied Princess Amber, seeing Mrs Beeworthy's face change from one of confusion at who she was on about to one of joy at hearing Kelmar's name.

"Kelmar! He is alive! The stars be praised!" she cried out.

"Not for much longer if she has her way. There will be only one fate left for them when her father and my brother confront her, perhaps for all of us," said Princess Amber, worriedly, to both the delight and puzzlement of Mrs Beeworthy.

"Little Martyn is safe as well!" she exclaimed. "But you say it be her father coming here with him to confront her? And her son is one of the prisoners?" Mrs Beeworthy frowned, trying to make sense of it all.

"Sort some food out, Bee, and we can take it to them. I will try to explain as much as I know on the way," said Princess Amber, knowing it was going to be difficult; she was not sure of everything herself!

The mountain throne felt cold and smooth to Queen Helistra's touch. It felt good to be in its powerful embrace once more. Her fingers drew around the uneven hole in the arm as she breathed in the souls of the Cardronian guards.

She smiled as she thought of the looks on their faces when she had ridden into Stormhaven. They would not be fearing anything now, as another breath told her they were no more.

She relaxed on the mountain throne with her hands resting on the broken rune staff that lay across her lap and closed her eyes.

"The end is in sight." She smiled as humming entered her mind. "Tomorrow. It has been a long journey." She sighed and waited for more humming. Normally, there was, but not this time. Instead, she felt the broken rune staff suddenly vibrate.

"What was that? What can you feel?" she asked, clutching the broken rune staff, to feel it shudder in her hands, sending it right through her body. A moment later saw another shudder and then another, pushing her body right back into the mountain throne, pressing her against the cold stone.

The shudders passed, for humming to immediately ensue. "Yes, it was his signature all over, but then I could not tell before it became mixed. Was Ringwold's in there?" she pursued, for the humming to explain what it had sensed.

"Are you sure?" For the humming to confirm what it felt. "Who is the one that is blind here," she said, cursing herself. "Not to have seen that Tomin was deceiving me by lying!"

"So there was nothing of Ringwold's to be felt and we know Tomin has used Gentian's rune staff. It was Speedwell's signature we felt, so the signature we could not recognise can only mean one thing. It was from a new rune staff!" Queen Helistra was seething at being fooled so.

"It must have been gained before we destroyed the Ancient One and proves these wraiths of the Ancient Forestalls do exist, in that he did not lie. Their power has been restored by them for us to have felt it used on the forest, but we will soon find out the truth!" And with that warning, Queen Helistra left the mountain throne room to confront Tomin.

The scene across the grand courtyard had been horrific to say the least for Mrs Beeworthy. Princess Amber had already witnessed the carnage at Marchend, but it still did not prepare her for the sight of blood dripping from the snarling mouths of the hideous creatures that were once the gentle people of the town and forest.

They entered the dungeon and let the dungeon door shut behind them, leaning on it with their hearts in their mouths, hardly able to catch their breath at what they had seen as another creature guarding the dungeons confronted them.

It saw Princess Amber and knew to leave her alone, unless it wanted to incur the wrath of Queen Helistra.

"We are here to feed the prisoners," said Princess Amber as Mrs Beeworthy held up the food for the monster to see. The monster growled at the sight of the food and turned to take them down into the dungeons, holding a torch.

Reaching a cell door, it clumsily opened it to reveal Tomin chained and sitting against the rock wall.

"We have brought you some food," said Princess Amber, handing him some, to see Tomin was smiling. Tomin held out his hand as if to receive the food, but instead he clasped Princess Amber's small hand.

"Now is the time to be strong, little one. They are on their way. Did you not feel it?" he whispered to her, and before she could reply, a voice boomed out from behind them all.

"He will not be needing that!" shouted Queen Helistra, with two hideous creatures at her side.

"You sound annoyed, Mother," said Tomin with a smile, hearing the agitation in her voice.

"You knew all along of a new staff and dared to deceive me with lies!" ranted Queen Helistra.

"And how many times have you lied to get what you want, Mother?" countered Tomin, to her scowl.

"I will not waste my time with you. Lock him back up and open up the cell of the Manelf," she ordered to the monster guard, for Princess Amber and Mrs Beeworthy to be bundled out of the cell.

Tintwist watched as his cell door was opened for Queen Helistra to walk in. He stood there cold and afraid as she stared into his face.

"You have nothing to fear, Manelf," and Tintwist started to blink as the sound of her voice became like music in his mind.

"Now tell me, Manelf, did Prince Martyn obtain a new staff from the Ancient One before I destroyed its being?" she asked, sounding like a song in Tintwist's mind.

Tintwist smiled stupidly and went to speak, but nothing came out, as there was nothing there he could recollect. Queen Helistra stared hard into his face, frowning, and asked him again. Tintwist went to talk but could not speak. Instead, he just smiled.

Queen Helistra frowned again. *A part of his mind is blocked*, she thought as she walked out of the cell. *Now who could have done that?* There was only one person she was thinking of, and she was looking right at her in the flickering torchlight.

"I thought you changed, child, but it is not the first time I have been wrong, so I have been told." The humming kept quiet.

"I see you have found hidden talents, and when did these come to light?" asked Queen Helistra menacingly whilst staring at Princess Amber, making her feel weak inside.

"I… I think it was after you destroyed the Ancient One," admitted Princess Amber, realising it was useless to pretend anymore.

"Ah, when I was at my weakest, so I did not discern you," said Queen Helistra, nodding.

"It was only when we came back to Stormhaven that I felt different. A vision of you came to me, holding me upside down over the balcony of Forest Tower with hate in your eyes," she disclosed tearfully.

"So you saw your destiny to become a Forestall like your brother," said Queen Helistra, with disdain in her voice.

"A destiny I did not know of, but now I do, I know why you have kept me in your shadow, for one reason only, to lure my brother to his death, just as your son is bait for your father!" cried Princess Amber, breaking down, for Mrs Beeworthy to comfort her.

"It could have been different, child, but it has come to pass to be that way, and now you have shown your hand," reflected Queen Helistra, making Tomin realise as he listened that somewhere inside her she still wanted to be a mother, but not with him, he thought sadly.

"You will not be in my shadow anymore, child. Lock her up in a cell," she ordered to the distraught cries of Mrs Beeworthy. "Quiet, woman, or you will be joining her!" warned Queen Helistra, to hear humming enter her mind.

Yes, a lesson must be learnt, it cannot go unpunished.

"Bring the Elfore outcast to me and replace him with her," she ordered further to the monster guarding the dungeons.

Fleck found himself being pushed out of his cell, to be replaced by a tearful Princess Amber. "I am sorry," she cried as the cell door was slammed shut on her.

"Do not be," he called as he was pushed along the dark passage of the dungeons.

Tomin had felt elation, sensing the earth pulse through him with well-being, telling him they had succeeded in their quest to find the wraiths of the Ancients to perform the ceremony. He had told Princess Amber to be strong, but hearing Fleck being taken had made him feel weak and useless, knowing what his mother was intending to do to him.

Tintwist was blinking, wondering what had just happened, when he heard the Princess crying. He gripped the iron grille of his cell door, to see Fleck being pushed down the passage, and feared the worst for his friend. He tried to call his name, but it caught in his throat as sadness suddenly welled up inside him.

Kelmar had heard everything as he stood behind the grille of his cell door, realising as he did that he was standing in the same cell as Cillan when he rescued Queen Elina.

Memories of that day had flooded back to him, but more so of the fate that had befallen him by his hand. He had felt helpless then and he felt helpless now as he watched Fleck being led away, knowing he would never see him again.

Fleck turned and saw them pressed against the grilles of their cell doors and smiled. "It has been a good journey with you, my friends," and he disappeared down the passageway, leaving darkness behind him.

Queen Helistra made her way through the great hall to the base of Forest Tower and into the mountain throne room, where she sat on the mountain throne, waiting.

Humming spoke to her. "Yes, it was hard to tell, but the boy's mastery has to be limited. We are more than ready with the power we possess. If they dare to use theirs that is for the fear of retribution when they know who we hold. Ours is the upper hand." She smiled.

The mountain throne room door opened and Fleck was pushed in, landing face down on the rock floor. Picking himself up, holding his shoulder, Fleck watched as Queen Helistra inserted the broken rune staff into an uneven hole on the mountain throne arm, a cold calculating smile slowly forming on her face.

As she touched some of its symbols, the broken rune staff turned in the hole and Fleck heard an audible click. No colours displayed themselves anymore, since the broken rune staff had harmonised with the crystal chamber. Two more clicks were heard and the mountain throne moved forward.

Fleck realised straight away that this was where King Taliskar must have disappeared, and he was about to suffer the same fate.

"Come, outcast, come and see what awaits your friends." She smiled, pointing the way with the broken rune staff.

Fleck looked into the blackness and steeled himself. He was entering the pit of evil, he thought.

He breathed in a long, deep breath of cold air and blew it out again, gathering his strength for what he knew was his end. He felt a prod in his back and stepped down onto the steps of no return.

CHAPTER LV

"How many do you make it?" asked King Brodic as he gazed out from the battlements of Elishard Castle with Piper and Urchel towards the Northern Sea.

"I make it eleven, no, twelve sails," replied Urchel, shielding his eyes from the harsh northern wind.

"At least six hundred soldiers then. It should be enough," said King Brodic, but still worried they may not be, as the monsters' numbers had begun to grow again over the last week since the battle, with a steady stream filtering into the burnt-out castle town.

The Silion force had been quicker coming by ship, something he had not thought of, as the winter seas were never the best of times to set sail, but the monsters were already making their way towards the small harbour, with bows in hand, to confront them.

"If they release fire arrows with their range, it could destroy half the ships before they have a chance to land. Why do they not lower their sails? They are too big a target," said Urchel worriedly, remembering Stormhaven Bay that fateful day.

"Look, they do so now. They have heeded your warning, Urchel," said Piper, whose face only showed the worry she had for Tintwist's well-being.

"I did not think them capable of thinking, but they obviously think our day is done to have left so few behind," remarked King Brodic as he observed how many monsters were moving to meet the ships, compared to how many were left behind.

"You cannot tell what they are thinking behind those masks of evil," remarked Urchel.

"Only who is going to be their next prey for them to kill, there is nothing else left for them," said Piper sadly as she thought of Ludbright's face.

"How many of us are left?" asked King Brodic, thoughtfully.

"Not enough if you are thinking of attacking them," put Urchel, reading King Brodic's mind.

"More have come than I had hoped, and we have sacrificed enough already," acknowledged King Brodic to the we-told-you-so looks from Piper and Urchel.

"But they think by leaving such a small force behind that we are no longer a threat," said King Brodic, repeating himself.

"But we are not. It may look a small force to you, but by the time we have fought them and made our way to the harbour, our losses would make us ineffective against those who wait for your ships," argued Piper, understanding what King Brodic was thinking.

"Unless only a few of us fight them," said King Brodic, making no sense to Piper and Urchel.

"What are you on about? Is there something you are not saying?" asked Piper, seeing the look she had come to recognise on King Brodic's face.

"A few of us could keep their attention here within the confines of the castle town walls so they cannot see below, although it is not until you reach the harbour road that you can see the harbour anyway," began King Brodic.

"Whilst we keep them occupied, we can take as many as are able through the secret passage," said King Brodic with a smile.

"What secret passage?" queried Piper straight away.

"It runs below the castle town wall and comes out beneath the second turret onto a narrow path that leads down the side of the cliffs straight to the harbour," King Brodic informed them.

"How do you know one exists?" queried Piper again.

"My father told me of many things he and King Stowlan talked about. They were great friends," he said with a smile. He could see them now, chortling together like two little boys.

"It was built as an escape route if ever… well, if ever… Well, what do you think?" he finished.

Piper looked at Urchel. "We would have the element of surprise. It worked at Stormhaven," Urchel reminded himself aloud. Only this time it was to get out, not in, he thought. Although then there was the small matter of a mountain rock door they had come through, to surprise them, as he remembered the shocked looks on the Tiggannian soldiers' faces.

"Whether there are enough of us to hold them off long enough for your soldiers to land is another question," answered Urchel further.

"It is a risk, but as you have already said, their archers could destroy half the ships with their fire arrows, preventing the rest from landing," pointed out King Brodic.

Piper blew out her cheeks. "Where is this secret passage?"

"I will muster all that are able to fight then I will show you." King Brodic smiled, already hobbling down the battlement steps.

"And you will stay here with them with that leg of yours to keep them occupied," ordered Piper, seeing King Brodic's intent on coming with them.

He went to speak, but Piper interrupted him. "You are needed here. You have already risked your life more than enough as King, and besides, you have been charged with looking after the rune staffs," she pointed out.

King Brodic went to speak again but saw the look in Piper's eyes as he felt his leg twinge. *She is right*, he thought, reluctantly, and nodded in silent agreement, for Urchel to smile for once.

"You are wise beyond your years not to argue with a woman," he remarked, for Piper to look at him.

King Brodic crouched with two Balintium archers watching safely behind the battlements as four hideous creatures prowled the castle wall battlements that overlooked the sea. He had forgotten some would come up onto them now and again to fearlessly fire arrows into the castle. They had to be dealt with if they were to proceed.

"This should get their attention, but do not miss," he ordered, to hear the archers' arrows zip from their bows at the unsuspecting creatures, with the desired effect.

Four thuds later saw the rest of the monsters running towards the castle, growling in anger and defiance, with arrows being returned in retaliation.

"I think we have it," said King Brodic with a smile, and he waved at a waiting soldier below, who disappeared into the stables.

All eyes of the company that had been mustered looked at the soldier as he entered the stables to give them the go-ahead to drop through the trapdoor, which had been uncovered from its dirt and straw, marking the beginning of the secret passage.

Holding a torch, Urchel led the way, descending through the trapdoor down some stone steps into a narrow arched passageway.

The torch fizzled and crackled as he moved along the passageway, covered as it was with cobwebs from the spiders that had taken it over.

It was not long before they reached a small, stout wooden door with two bars across it.

After borrowing a nasty-looking axe from one of the soldiers, Urchel managed to knock the wedged-in bars from their holders and open the door, to feel the northern wind trying to shut it again.

He peeked out from the door to see a short, uninviting, narrow footpath that had been cut out of the cliff face leading down onto an enclosed sheltered path between the rocks.

"Watch where you tread!" he called, seeing it covered in snow, and started to make his way along the exposed path, holding himself against the cliff face with the helping hand of the wind.

Piper stepped out behind him and told herself not to look down, to immediately see the Silion ships forever getting closer and closer to the harbour that was out of view.

Reaching the cutaway path between the rocks, they followed it downwards as it turned slowly towards the direction of the sea, to suddenly come across some steps that became wet as they descended them to an opening at the back of what turned out to be a narrow cave.

Urchel's torch reflected off the cave walls to show them glistening in its glow, telling him that the sea had been in here at high tide, for his boots to confirm it as they trod in the water that had remained.

"He never mentioned we would be going through a tidal cave," remarked Urchel over his shoulder to Piper.

"Luck is on our side then, not to have had to swim through it," she replied, as they came to the cave's opening of sand and rocks.

"Let us hope it continues," replied Urchel, as they peeked from the opening they found had come out onto a pocket of sand, with flat angled rock protruding from it, jutting out into the sea.

Arcing to their left was a headland that acted as a natural breakwater for the harbour, where the monsters had lined themselves up along its head, with archers and torch bearers waiting for the Silion ships to be in range.

To their right, the flat angled rocks continued to protrude out of the sand into the sea before stopping short of the natural inlet's harbour wall, where more monsters prowled along it, with long– abandoned houses embedded into the cliffs behind them.

A large wooden warehouse stood opposite the houses, where goods were normally stored from incoming ships, and emerging between the two was the harbour road, to complete the small harbour.

"We can deal with them on the headland and hold the rest back whilst they land," said Piper, as suddenly a wave of fiery death was sent hissing through the air at the first of the Silion ships approaching the harbour.

Two of the leading ships were soon in trouble as another hailstorm of fire arrows thudded into the ships, to set them on fire!

"It is time to snuff out their flame," said Piper with a scowl, and word was passed through the company to be ready to attack.

Donning their leather hoods, Piper and Urchel led the charge as they rushed from the cave onto the rocky headland, catching the monsters by surprise.

Half the company held themselves back at the base of the headland, ready to face the monsters that were already charging across the angled rocks from the harbour, having smelt the immediate danger that had revealed itself to them.

Piper and Urchel with the other half of the company met the first of the monsters head-on, stopping them from sending their fire arrows to the Silion ships as they scythed them down.

Retaliation was quick as the monsters further on the headland turned and fired upon them before charging themselves, leaving those at the head to keep firing.

Soon the headland was a blur of flailing arms as sword clashed against sword; the rear guard holding back the monsters from the harbour whilst the rest of the company battled their way to reach those still firing at the top of the headland.

Casualties, though, quickly mounted, and the two halves of the company soon found themselves fighting back to back as Piper tried to assess the situation.

"We will not last for much longer!" she shouted to Urchel as she sliced through the arm of another monster, making it drop its long bow, with its gnarled hand still holding it, driving her sword through its chest as it bent in pain, having lost its arm.

They feel something then, she thought absently whilst looking to see how far they had come along the headland. *About three-quarters*, she thought, as she hacked another monster through the shoulder.

"No, but look, the first of the ships are firing back at the monsters on the end of the headland," shouted back Urchel, fending off a sword just in time for Piper to help him by slashing the monster across the side of its deformed ribs.

Despite arrows being fired from the Silion ships and the heroics of the company, the monsters' numbers were telling on them.

Less than half of those defenders that came were left standing as they held a line across the headland.

Bodies littered it and floated in the water all around them as they fought desperately whilst waiting for the Silion ships to land.

Fighting side by side, toe to toe with the monsters, Piper and Urchel felt their end was near. They could not hold on much longer.

Suddenly the monster Piper was fighting was on the receiving end of an arrow, straight through its head!

At last, she thought without looking, *the Silion's have made it*, but then she glanced at the orange arrow tip as the monster dropped to the ground, to realise it was not a Silion arrow!

Then more monsters fell from arrows that could only be from one hand: that of the Elfore! Shouting could be heard from the harbour.

"It is the Elfore! Tiska and Tislea have found them!" she cried in delight and relief.

They both looked, to see swords swirling through the air on the harbour, giving those that were left on the headland renewed nervous energy to fight on.

At last, two of the Silion ships managed to land their soldiers as they dropped off the ships' sides in the water to join the Elfore in the fight.

The growls of the monsters were quenched, for both Elfore and Silion soldiers to run up the harbour road to finish off the monsters that had been kept occupied by King Brodic.

All were finally slain in an orange bloodbath, but the cost had been high.

The Elfore knelt down on one knee with their heads bowed, to grieve for their lost brethren, both the fallen and those who were lost to them by evil.

The Silion soldiers could only look on, wondering who these people were they had blindly just helped, and what in the name of the Kingdoms it was they had just put to the sword!

"Who… what are they?" a Silion soldier exclaimed as he looked at both the dead monsters and kneeling Elfore. He was soon put right by King Brodic as he walked over the drawbridge to the sight of the carnage.

"The people you have helped are the Elfore, children of the forest. These dead creatures before you were once their fellow beings, Elfore like themselves. Look well amongst them. You will see people from Balintium and Cardronia, all bitten by the evil curse that has been put upon them by Queen Helistra," pointed out King Brodic.

The soldiers could only keep staring, not able to take in what they were looking at or what their King had just told them, but those defenders of Elishard who had survived were soon telling them what they had all been through.

King Brodic limped down to the harbour, to come across the further carnage of the battle that had been fought there, managing a smile of relief when he saw Piper and Urchel walking towards him.

At their side, walking with them, were Tiska and Tislea, reunited once more.

"Our people were further in the Great Forest than we expected," spoke Tiska as they walked back to the castle.

"You made it. That is the main thing, and just in time, but not for all," stated Piper sadly, and she told them what had happened to Ludbright.

"You must not take it to heart. We have all been forced to take the lives of those we love, thanks to her evil." said Tiska, pointing out what they had all had to do to survive her cruel evil.

They walked on in silence, to come across a horse and rider standing in the middle of the road looking at them.

"King Brodic?" asked the rider as he pulled back his hood to reveal a young face looking at him, whose features were pale and drawn. A look King Brodic had grown to know well in a short space of time.

He looked twice at the face looking at him, to have it suddenly dawn on him who this young man could be. "Galmis, is that you?"

The warmth of a fire in the great hall at Elishard Castle was a welcome relief to all, away from the carnage they had endured, as they sat to listen to what Galmis had to say, to be joined by Queen Elina, Oneatha, Permellar and Kayla.

Before Galmis could begin, King Brodic told him the sad news of his uncle's death and how it had come about.

"These monsters are everywhere. I have seen them for myself before I came here, at Stormhaven and Gressby, but that means…" began Galmis, stopping as he realised the outcome of what King Brodic had just told him whilst getting everyone's attention by mentioning Stormhaven, especially Queen Elina's.

"Yes, that means you are King of Balintium, but what were you doing at Stormhaven?" pushed King Brodic, asking the question everyone wanted to ask as Galmis took off his cloak to reveal his Cardronian uniform. "And what are you doing in that?" he said with a frown.

"You never received word of my leaving Ingle?" queried Galmis, to see by King Brodic's expression that he had not.

"I sent word for you to come here, but in truth, I thought you had met your fate when you did not show, but none of that matters now. I think you need to explain to us what the future King of Balintium was doing at Stormhaven in the Cardronian army," queried King Brodic, keeping Queen Elina at bursting point, wanting to know about her daughter.

"I ran away from my life at Ingle, is the simple answer, sire," began Galmis.

"A King does not have to say sire," said King Brodic with a smile.

Galmis nodded and continued. "I ran away because I… I did not want the responsibility of being the future King. I sought adventure instead," proclaimed Galmis, making King Brodic groan and Permellar think of Kelmar.

"I made my way to Senarth and joined the Cardronian army there. Tiggannia had been under Alliance rule for five years or more by then, and I found myself posted to Stormhaven.

"At first, it was all an adventure, the unbelievable stories I heard, the place, but by my third posting there, I was, well, bored," summed up Galmis, making everyone look at him in disbelief.

"Bored? With the most evil creature in all of Northernland in your midst holding my daughter!" berated Queen Elina, not able to contain herself anymore.

"This is Queen Elina of Tiggannia, Galmis. I should have introduced everyone to you, but events have overtaken my manners," he apologised.

"The daughter she speaks of is the little girl being held by Queen Helistra at Stormhaven, Princess Amber," explained King Brodic.

"I did not know she was your daughter, my lady. I thought, well…" Galmis suddenly felt awkward, but continued.

"Nothing ever happened to her, my lady. She was left to play as we were left to our duties. Queen Helistra was hardly ever seen. She kept herself to herself and when she did appear, she was, well, strict but pleasant towards us," spoke Galmis, seeing Queen Elina staring at him, speechless.

"But then something had changed in her when I was posted there again. I was told she had been away for some time and had come back looking more withdrawn than normal. That seemed nothing new to me, but then I saw what they meant. Her eyes looked to be set deeper into her face, darker, lost in the distance…"

Galmis stopped mid-sentence, remembering that look he had seen, but they all knew what he was trying to say. The evil darkness inside her had all but taken over her soul.

"Yes, and?" King Brodic interrupted Galmis' thoughts, for him to continue.

"She journeyed once more, but when she returned this time it was with those hideous monsters and four prisoners in a cart driven by one." Galmis grimaced as he thought of the twisted face on the monster driving the cart.

"Tomin, Kelmar, Fleck and Tintwist," uttered Piper quietly, for Tiska to look at Tislea as she heard Fleck's name.

"I do not know who they were. I was too busy fighting for my life! She turned those things upon us! If it had not been for a horse finding me, I would be one of them!" cried Galmis, but he did not have to tell them that. They all knew only too well what happened if you were bitten by one.

"I rode for my life," continued Galmis, "hiding where I could to rest my horse, all the time looking out for more monsters.

"I reached Gressby under night skies. The place was deserted, but I soon saw why. There were bodies everywhere, townsfolk and monsters.

"That is when my horse reared up and I fell off. An old man had appeared out of nowhere in front of me, waving a stick, frightening my horse," said Galmis as he shook his head, remembering, suddenly sensing a stillness as he said it.

Galmis looked up at them looking at him. They were all hanging on his every word, wide-eyed, waiting for what he was going to say next. "He helped me to my feet, apologising, and said his name was Speedwell!"

Before Galmis could say another word, they were all on their feet hugging him and each other.

"He has made it! Were Prince Martyn and Tarbor with him?" asked an anxious Queen Elina.

"If you mean a warrior and a red-headed boy holding another stick, then yes," answered Galmis, to her delight.

He carried on. "When he found out who I was, he entrusted me to find you to tell you they will be waiting at Kelmsmere, but only until the month of beginning," added Galmis, warning them of Speedwell's intention to press on with or without them.

Although Speedwell had entrusted Galmis to tell them they were back in Northernland, he had not told him that they had the broken piece in their possession. It had to remain a secret, for hope and worry to show itself.

"We had better ready ourselves to join them then," said King Brodic straight away.

"Now perhaps we will be rid of her evilness, but how will they get rid of the evil she has caused over the land and forests with the broken piece of Grimstone's shattered?" said Piper with a sigh.

"It will take all of their wisdom to defeat her whilst she holds the fate of Tomin in her hands," said Urchel, reminding them all of the hold she would have over Speedwell.

"And she holds the life of my daughter over my son," said Queen Elina, worriedly.

"What of Fleck and Tintwist? What chance have they?" added Tiska, not that Piper wanted reminding of Tintwist's fate.

"My son will not let all the sacrifices that have been made already be for nothing, not whilst there is breath left in his body!" swore Oneatha defiantly, even though she knew Kelmar lay in the dungeons of Stormhaven.

Permellar looked at her as she held Kayla, seeing where Kelmar got his spirit from, but it would take more than that, she thought with worry, to get out of that place.

"The month of beginning will be an apt time to be rid of her evil," voiced Tislea, feeling Oneatha's defiance, to hopeful agreeing nods.

"There was one other travelling with them," suddenly remembered Galmis, to receive blank looks.

"Who could that be? There are no others," spoke Urchel.

"Our friends are either dead or captured," added Piper, solemnly.

"Well, he said he was the King Protector of Tiggannia, Cantell!"

CHAPTER LVI

"Do you think we can trust him? Perhaps I should have gone with him," wondered Cantell whilst resting, thankful for the find of some better clothes as he stretched out his legs in front of a roaring fire. Although in truth he would have never left Prince Martyn's side.

"Why would we not trust him, he is the future King of Balintium. He was only too happy to help us after witnessing the horror at Stormhaven, knowing we were here to put an end to it," reasoned Tarbor.

"Either way, we will be gone from here for Stormhaven if they do not emerge by the time we have said," said Speedwell, who was also enjoying the warmth of the fire as Prince Martyn watched the snow glistening from the night frost through a shuttered window of the tavern; the same tavern in Kelmsmere from where Cantell had rescued Permellar and Kayla all those years ago with Kelmar.

Cantell smiled to himself as he relaxed, wondering how his friend would react when he found he was still alive after being turned into a monster, then to have had the curse lifted by the wraiths of the Ancient Forestalls!

His journey to the tavern with Kelmar under the Kavenmist Mountains had been one he would never forget, but the journey he had been on these last weeks had been more than its equal, only to be waiting here before going back to where it had all begun. He half smiled to himself as he thought of the prospect ahead.

Not a moment too soon, though, from Galmis' account and what they had come across at Gressby, he thought.

All was quiet; only the crackle of the fire could be heard as Martyn looked out at the snow- bound square, remembering the story both Cantell and Kelmar had told him of this place. Smiling as he recounted Cillan's version at being booted down the very stairs behind him.

His eyes wandered to the lonely stump of the old oak tree that had once stood proud in the centre of the square, covered on one side by frozen snow, for Martyn's thoughts to turn to his sister as he looked upon the frozen stump.

"She will be cold and alone," he half uttered to himself in thought, and suddenly turned to Speedwell with a question on his lips. "How will we mend the broken rune staff without risking harm to my sister?" he posed.

"That thought has been constantly with me ever since we used our power to save the Bridge of Seasons," reflected Speedwell as he sat there, pondering the question.

"My daughter will not harm her, even if she finds she is no longer under her influence. Princess Amber is the means of getting to me," said Speedwell sadly, knowing his daughter wanted him dead more than anything else.

"Her hopes were denied to her when she destroyed the Ancient One, thanks to your added protection, Tarbor, and our luck to have landed in the Lake of Tears," spoke Speedwell further as he thought of the situation. "Not that my brother had any, his deserted him on that day," he added sadly.

"I will trade myself for Princess Amber's safety, then I will be close enough to put an end to her. Beyond that, I have not thought it through," he admitted, with concern in his voice at the task ahead.

"No, you have not," argued Tarbor straight away. "She will not let you take Princess Amber's place with your rune staff in hand, that could do her harm. Knowing that Martyn has a rune staff also. She will make sure neither rune staff can be used against her first, to even attempt such a trade," he reasoned, "then how will her end be possible?" he concluded.

"What of me, Speedwell? Will she not want me in such a bargain? Am I not a threat to her also now I am a Forestall?" put Martyn.

"He is right, Speedwell. She will not stop at you. I saw the evil in her eyes, it knew no bounds," warned Cantell.

"You are right, all of you," admitted Speedwell. "She cannot be trusted, and if we attack, she will kill her without a second thought," he added with a sigh.

"And there is one other thing," spoke Tarbor again, looking at Speedwell with some hesitancy, "would you be able to kill your own daughter when the time comes?" he posed, for Speedwell's mind to feel the doubt that had always been there, but knowing he had to.

"If I do not, there will be nothing left," he answered, for a silence to fall over them all at the reality of what they were up against, now they were so near.

Martyn came and sat down, to stare into the fire. He had felt such elation at the Bridge of Seasons at what they had done, but now that confidence he had gained felt useless in the situation they were in.

He held his rune staff before him, its tip on the floor, and leaned his forehead upon it as he tried to think of what they could do, for a whisper to enter his mind.

Closing his eyes, he heard the whisper speak to him once more.

He came away from his rune staff and looked at the others, catching their attention.

"My rune staff has just spoken to me," he confided in them.

"And what did it say to you?" asked Speedwell, seeing yet more despondency on Martyn's face, to know it was not good.

"That the broken piece of Grimstone's it holds has said you cannot kill her before it has been made whole once more, because the hand that has broken me must mend me!"

Speedwell groaned, he had not even considered this. "The Ancient One had hoped it would be you Martyn, as did I. Why did I not realise it had to be Helistra!" he chastised himself.

"You were not to know Speedwell. None of us were," said Martyn, knowing of the Ancient One's hopes also, to feel the same disappointment.

Tarbor could only groan along with them. "We were already in a quandary. Now how in the name of the stars are we going to get her to do that!" exclaimed Tarbor as he thought on it.

He could see her now, the Black Queen of all that is evil joining the two broken pieces of Grimstone's rune staff together to stop her poison, over their dead bodies! Which was the more likely outcome at this moment, he thought in apprehension.

"If I did not know she was the only one who could mend Grimstone's broken rune staff, then she will not, it is not much compensation, but it is all we have," said Speedwell with a sigh, feeling even more despondent. "I can see her now if she did know, laughing all the way to the crystal chamber to poison the forest again," he added.

Quietness reigned once more as they all stared at the fire, lost in empty thought, until Tarbor looked at Speedwell at what he had just said. "All the way to the crystal chamber," he repeated.

"Hmm, yes, where the pool of life is, that she has tainted," replied Speedwell, continuing to stare at the fire.

"You told me that to get into the crystal chamber, you have to put a rune staff into a hole that is in the mountain throne arm, acting like a key," he prompted, only to get blank stares.

"So could the broken piece within Martyn's rune staff be released down into the hole without bringing attention to her? Then when she puts the rest of the broken rune staff into the hole—"

"It will be mended by her own hand!" interrupted Speedwell in realisation at what Tarbor was trying to say, for them to begin talking once more in earnest as to how to achieve this, but they soon found it was not going to be easy.

"It is a risk I do not like taking, but I will stay here. You will need to focus all of your power on Martyn's rune staff to hide its presence from her. I worry, being so close to her, that if mine is present also after receiving the power from the wraiths of the Ancients, it will weaken your protection," decided Speedwell.

"We have already found she cannot penetrate stone, so the broken piece will be hidden from her sight in the mountain throne. The problem is, when Grimstone's broken rune staff is placed directly over the hole, that is when it will sense the piece is there, and it is bound to warn her not to put it into the hole. That is the time when we need to be there to force her hand," said Speedwell, thoughtfully.

"We could hide afterwards and wait for her to enter the throne room?" suggested Martyn.

"You could. Then you would be risking Princess Amber. After feeling your rune staff from the Bridge of Seasons, she will expect to see you by my side. Otherwise, she will be suspicious," pointed out Speedwell.

"No, first you go with Tarbor under the cover of darkness and put the broken piece into the mountain throne arm, then get out of there. At least if we do not come up with something in the meantime to force her hand, she will not be able to cast any more poison into the pool of life," pointed out Speedwell, to smiles and nods.

"The gates will be open. She does not fear anyone or anything. It would be a sign of weakness on her part," continued Speedwell, "then you already know the way through the mountain doorway and that the monsters will be asleep," he added, for Tarbor to give him a look as he remembered the clearing.

"Then when you are back, I can see her gladly letting me trade places with Princess Amber. I have no doubt once she has me in her power, she will not hesitate to take me to the mountain throne room to enter the crystal chamber, but as you have said, not with my rune staff, though she would want it there so as to destroy it," said Speedwell thoughtfully, trying to think it through.

"Do not forget mine also," added Martyn.

He is right, thought Speedwell, groaning to himself. It was becoming more complicated by the moment. It was only half a plan, again, but before any more could be said, a noise from outside stopped any further discussion.

Martyn quickly peered through the shutters of the tavern to see what it was.

In the next moment, he was rushing to the door to open it with a grin on his face. "Piper! Urchel!" he greeted them as they gladly walked in from the cold.

"It is good to see you both," said Speedwell with a smile, but the looks on their faces told him something was wrong.

"Not when we tell you the news we have," replied Piper, to confirm his worry, not wasting any time in explaining events since they parted.

They all listened with increasing heartache as Piper unfolded what had happened to them all, to end with Speedwell slumping down onto a chair and burying his head into his hands when he heard of what had happened to his grandson.

"All of them?" he groaned at the end.

"Yes, Speedwell. Tomin, Kelmar, Fleck and Tintwist," replied Piper, Tintwist's name catching in her throat as she said it.

"They had to be the four prisoners Galmis spoke of," realised Tarbor.

"What was Tomin thinking?" said Speedwell with a sigh.

"What of Cillan and Ludbright?" asked Tarbor, not hearing their names, already fearing what the answer was going to be.

"Cillan never came back from the burning shell of Marchend, and I had to kill Ludbright…" Piper could not go on.

"Because he had turned," finished Urchel.

Tarbor could picture the same fate had happened to Cillan.

"I was lucky then to have had Princess Amber watching out for me," thought Cantell out loud, to the immediate looks of Piper and Urchel, who had not even noticed him standing there.

"Cantell! You are alive!" they both croaked in amazement, as if not believing Galmis, and they embraced him without a second thought, tears running down their faces.

Speedwell suddenly stood back up, gripping his rune staff tightly. "Her bargaining powers have just gone up tenfold, but it alters nothing. I can only pray to the stars that she will spare their lives as well," he announced resolutely, although his immediate thought was *spare them for whom?* as he worriedly looked at Martyn.

"You say the Elfore and Silion armies are a day behind you?" he questioned Piper.

"They are, we have been travelling at night to evade the monsters, but as of yet we have not come across many since leaving Elishard," she informed him.

"They will not be far behind from what you have been telling us. You will both wait here for the Elfore and Silion armies whilst we travel on to Haven. There is something that needs to be done before we meet up again," ordered Speedwell, to Piper's and Urchel's nods, wondering what Speedwell was on about.

"Once at Haven, I will await your return with Cantell in the ruins," continued Speedwell, turning to Martyn and Tarbor, with Piper looking at Urchel.

"The time has finally arrived for us to put an end to her evil. Let us hope the stars and spirits are watching over us all," prayed Speedwell, uncertain still as to how they were going to force her hand when the time did come, if they were without their rune staffs to do so.

He looked at Martyn, hoping that what the Ancient One had felt within him would guide them now.

CHAPTER LVII

Four pair of eyes peered into the gloom of the night from the ruins of Haven. Crouched behind a ruined wall that was once part of a fisherman's cottage, Speedwell, Martyn, Tarbor and Cantell watched as a sea mist swirled through the air in front of them.

"I had forgotten how thick those things could be, a good aid for you not to be seen," remarked Cantell.

"But still you must be careful," warned Speedwell, not that Martyn and Tarbor needed telling as Tarbor let a thought pass through his mind whilst touching the hilt of his defender. A whispered reply answered in the shape of the shield of protection, throwing itself around Martyn and himself.

"If you are not back by the time the Elfore and Silion armies arrive then we will attack, even if it means what is lost to us now will be lost forever. There will be no other choice but for us to come after Helistra," warned Speedwell, gravely.

"We understand," replied Martyn and Tarbor.

"May the stars and spirits watch over you both," and with a last unspoken look between them, they disappeared into the blanket of sea mist.

"I hope she is unaware of us," said Cantell as he sat and wrapped his cloak around him in preparation for a long cold night.

He wished he was with them as Martyn's protector, but he could not hope for a better man than Tarbor to be in his place, and besides, he was no King wielder, he thought.

"She will be expecting us, but I have not felt anything as of yet, but that means nothing," said Speedwell, worriedly, wrapping his cloak around him also. "We can only wait and trust other eyes are watching over us."

The sea mist was pushed aside in swirling plumes as Tarbor and Martyn made their way up the snowy slope towards Stormhaven stronghold.

As they drew closer, the sea mist became patchy, letting them catch a glimpse here and there of Stormhaven stronghold's solid stone walls, making the torches that were crackling in the cold misty air on top of the battlements glow and fade in its shifting grip.

As he caught sight of the solid walls, memories came flooding back into Tarbor's mind of the day he had stormed those walls, making him wonder how in the name of the stars they had done it!

The gateway where the two huge gates opened into the archway suddenly showed itself to them between patches of the swirling mist.

Tarbor and Martyn squatted down, casting a wary eye to see if there was any movement, for Tarbor to point at the gateway.

Martyn looked as they warily pulled their aptly grey cloaks slowly around themselves, blending into the sea mist, wishing it was not so patchy.

Speedwell had been right about the gates being open, thought Martyn, as he suddenly saw what Tarbor was pointing at.

There, coming from the shadows of the gateway, were two short plumes of misty air. There was someone, or more likely, something, staying hidden in the gateway opening.

Staying motionless, trying to hide their breathing behind their cloaks, they heard a strange sounding snort as suddenly a head appeared from the shadows.

A head! What was left to recognise! Deformed beyond all comprehension, what was once a beautiful horse lurched fully out of the gate's shadows to show the full extent of the hideousness with which it had been cursed, and what was more, it had spotted them!

Martyn reacted by readying his rune staff, to find Tarbor's arm held firmly across him. "No, Martyn, you cannot risk it. Once you broach my shield of protection, she is bound to sense it," warned Tarbor.

His mind was in a whirl as the beast came at them. It had to be killed, but even his defender might be detected outside his protective shield, he thought.

It made Tarbor do something he had never tried before as he pushed his invisible shield of protection out further to enclose the cursed beast within its boundaries. It worked!

As the protective shield enclosed the creature within it, Tarbor saw its black eyes open wider as the tingle of the protection passed over it.

Holding his shield before him, Tarbor turned his defender into a hissing blade of white fire as he saw his chance to strike first, but the beast was quick to react as Tarbor went to strike at its malformed shoulder by rearing up in the air, kicking out its front legs to clatter down onto Tarbor's shield.

Tarbor stumbled backwards with the force of the attack, knocking Martyn to the ground in the process, but managing to stay on his feet and steady himself, ready for another attack.

The beast reared up its legs of throbbing pustules once more, flailing them through the air, but Tarbor quickly stepped aside and brought his defender down across its neck, taking off its deformed head with one powerful stroke!

It fell onto the snow, its rotten flesh seared from Tarbor's fiery blade, for its body to slump sideways.

Tarbor pulled Martyn up onto his feet whilst looking at the gateway to see if any more beasts had been alerted by the clatter of his shield.

"Your protective shield has muffled the sound," whispered Martyn, hoping he was right as he looked also.

"I hope so. Otherwise, we are done for before we start," whispered Tarbor back, keeping his eyes fixed on the gates and battlements.

They both breathed a sigh of relief when nothing else appeared as Tarbor's shield of protection resumed its protective shape around them.

"Galmis only mentioned that people were cursed here, not animals," remarked Martyn as they both moved towards the gateway slowly, having piled snow over the corpse in the hope it would not be spotted.

"Perhaps a poor unfortunate rider who sought shelter here, not knowing of the evil that was waiting inside," presumed Tarbor as they reached the gates, to peer into the gloom of the archway.

Nothing met their gaze in the archway, for them to creep around one of the huge gates to the doorway of the eastern gatehouse turret.

As he was disappearing through the doorway, Tarbor glanced at the solid rock at the end of the archway, where it had all began for him. That voice, he now knew, was the essence of the pool of life reaching out to him. *She comes, evil will reign, the land will be forever in darkness!*

She has all but achieved that, but not for much longer, he hoped, to nearly fall over three sleeping monsters as he thought it, that were sprawled out on the cold stone floor of the turret room.

Carefully, Tarbor began stepping over the first of them, with Martyn following him. Their bodies looked as if they were twitching all of the time in the flickering torchlight as suddenly one grunted and shifted its leg to the other, pinning Tarbor's foot there! Tarbor froze!

He waited then slowly started to ease his foot from between the monster's legs. He could feel the pustules on the monster's leg push and stretch against his leather leggings through the protective shield as he gradually pulled his foot out. An awareness of touch since bonding with his defender he could have gladly done without at this moment in time.

With Tarbor's foot finally emerging, they quickly disappeared down the dark passageway, thankful that the monster had stayed asleep, only to enter the next turret room to find yet more monsters asleep, but this time they were asleep on crude wooden frames acting as beds, making it easier for Tarbor and Martyn to move past them.

Once in the far passageway, Tarbor lit up his defender with the white fire, making the protective shield glow as it passed light through it onto the passageway walls. It did not take him long to find the upside-down shield like stone that would open the secret door.

Thinking of Girvan kneeling on this spot, Tarbor hoisted Martyn up towards the stone, telling him to push it firmly, twice.

An echoing clunk made Tarbor immediately look back up the dark passageway to listen if it had disturbed any of the monsters.

His fears were soon answered by a grunt and the shuffling sound of one of them getting off its wooden bed. With a thought, Tarbor extinguished his defender quickly to slide it back into its sheath.

"Quick, Martyn, push!" urged Tarbor, and together they pushed the secret doorway open in the darkness.

"Quickly, down here!" he urged Martyn again as he saw a torch appear at the far end of the passageway, framing the head of the monster in its light.

Moving quickly and as quietly as they could, they both hid in the armoury room at the end of the passageway.

They watched the torch get ever closer and with it the increasing repulsion they felt at seeing the monster's deformed face who was carrying it, stopping as soon as it discovered the secret doorway, to disappear through it.

Moving quickly back to the doorway, Tarbor and Martyn watched the monster go down the glistening stone steps as it searched for what had disturbed it.

A moment later saw Tarbor creeping up behind the monster to envelope it inside his protective shield. Feeling a tingle as the shield passed over it, the monster turned around, only to see a white hot blade burning through its deformed chest!

Noting an iron bar set in the stone that would release the secret door for when they returned, Tarbor and Martyn pushed the door to, leaving the dead monster in its own orange blood on the cold stone steps.

With Tarbor's white light from his defender lighting up the cold grey wetness of the passageway walls, they continued on their way, passing by the old wooden door that held the shield of Cardronia behind it.

He thought of Girvan once more as they did so, remembering his response to him when he spoke of the defenders of the five Kingdoms that were said to hold magic. And what had he said? It was all a myth, and here he was, holding a sword of white flame! If only he were here to see it, he thought sadly.

Then there it was in front of them, the solid rock door in the mountain that would lead them into the storerooms.

Martyn wanted to touch it as he passed through the doorway, but resisted; he did not want to give them away. "She did this through King Taliskar?" he found himself saying.

"We did not know it at the time, but yes," came Tarbor's whispered reply, feeling those goosebumps he felt then as he let darkness prevail before they entered the first storeroom to find nothing in there but a lonely torch.

As they opened the wooden door that led into the next storeroom, another lonely torch sputtering on the far wall met their gaze, but this time it revealed a floor full of sleeping monsters between barrels of ale, for Tarbor and Martyn to inwardly groan.

One by one, the sleeping monsters were negotiated as they gingerly stepped over them. Then suddenly what they thought was a mouse shot out from under Martyn's foot, making him stumble, catching a monster's arm with his leg in the process. Only a barrel of ale prevented him from falling headlong as he managed to reach out and hold on to it. The monster gave a grunt as Tarbor held his defender at its throat, waiting, but to his relief it did not rouse.

Finally, they reached the storeroom door, for Tarbor to slowly open it and peer out onto the grand courtyard, but only the cold swirling sea mist met his eyes, hiding everything from his gaze.

He stepped out of the storeroom cautiously, with his grip on his defender tightening as Martyn followed, feeling a little disappointed at not being able to see the majestic Forest Tower that he had been told of.

Coming across a door that Tarbor knew to be the servants' quarters, they quickly entered it, to feel the dying warmth of a fire and to see in its embers someone sitting in front of it!

"Who that be?" came a startled broad voice, making Tarbor and Martyn jump, even though they had seen the figure sitting there.

The voice was unmistakable, letting Tarbor know instantly who it was. "Mrs Beeworthy? What are you doing here in the dark?" he queried.

Mrs Beeworthy rose unsteadily to her feet, her heart thumping in her chest. These last days had told upon her enough, without monsters bursting in upon her in the middle of the night! So she had thought before Tarbor had spoken.

Tarbor and Martyn found themselves running to her aid, seeing her unsteady on her feet, to help her sit down again.

"That… that be nice of you. Your voice, I recognise it, but I cannot put a finger on it," she said, frowning, trying to recollect it as she calmed down, knowing she was not threatened.

Tarbor grabbed a torch from the wall and lit it from the embers, lighting up Mrs Beeworthy's ashen face, letting him see the strain written across it.

She looked, blinking in the light, at their faces. Suddenly her jaw dropped; colour came back to her cheeks and she let out a gasp, "Is it? It is! Little Martyn! Bless me. I thought I would never see the day!" And she tried to reach out to hug him through the protective shield, only to rebound back into the chair.

"I am sorry, Mrs Beeworthy. Martyn is surrounded by a shield of protection. You cannot touch him," apologised Tarbor as he watched Mrs Beeworthy's face change to one of recollection as she remembered who he was.

"You are that young Captain Tarbor. You were sent to kill Martyn, and here you be protecting him! So those stories about you were true!"

"And which stories would that be?" Tarbor smiled, seeing the glow come back into Mrs Beeworthy's cheeks.

"That you be killing that squinty-eyed Sergeant for one. Mind you, I never did trust him." Mrs Beeworthy grimaced as she thought of his face, although right now, his would be better than the grotesque things that had come to Stormhaven.

"Ah, Wardine. Yes, that is true, and if we see this day through, I will tell you the story, but for now you must get to your bed," urged Tarbor, not wanting Mrs Beeworthy to be caught up in what they were trying to do.

"Why, what you be doing? Is you here to rescue those poor people? Your sister, little Amber, be in them dungeons with them," informed Mrs Beeworthy sadly, to the shocked looks of Tarbor and Martyn.

"She has locked my sister away!" Martyn gripped his rune staff more tightly and gritted his teeth, to hold back his annoyance at hearing this.

"Keep focused, Martyn, on what we must do," warned Tarbor. "Queen Helistra must have recognised what lyes within her to have done so," he added.

"Now, Mrs Beeworthy, I suggest you go to bed and pretend you never saw us." Tarbor smiled in reassurance.

Though Mrs Beeworthy's mind was not as sharp as it once was, when she saw the strange staff Prince Martyn was holding, like Queen Helistra's, she knew they could only be here to confront her and she was in their way.

"Just be getting rid of those hideous things as well," she asked of them both, with a tear at not being able to hug little Martyn, before disappearing into the kitchen where she slept.

As soon as Mrs Beeworthy had gone, Martyn turned to Tarbor, but before he could speak, Tarbor put his finger to his mouth whilst motioning that he thought he could hear someone walking along the corridor.

Both fell quiet as they listened, but when nothing came to their ears, Martyn said what was on his mind.

"This can change things in our favour, Tarbor. With my sister being in the dungeons, she will not be under the eye of Helistra in the tower. She has played into our hands. We can rescue everyone and then she will have no one to bargain with. Then together we will have a better chance of defeating her and forcing her hand to join Grimstone's broken rune staff!" reasoned Martyn excitedly.

"I am not sure, Martyn. The quicker we are done and out of here without her knowing, the better," replied Tarbor, wanting to rescue them, but he was uncertain; they were already putting themselves at risk enough.

"But no one will be sacrificed if we rescue them," implored Martyn.

What Martyn said was common sense, thought Tarbor. It was an opportunity thrown unexpectedly their way that would put things in their favour, but he was worried that if they got caught, she would hold all the cards, and everything they had strived for would be put into jeopardy, leaving Speedwell on his own. Then what would they do?

"You are right, Martyn, it is a chance worth thinking of, but before anything, let us make sure we put the broken piece into the mountain throne arm first," decided Tarbor, to an understanding but frustrated look from Martyn.

They peeked around the door of the servants' quarters that looked out into the corridor then they were swiftly moving along its length to reach the base of Forest Tower.

They glanced through the opening to the great hall as they passed, ready to go through any door should anything show itself.

Then around the corner, there it was, bathed in light from torches set in its wall, the base of Forest Tower looking much bigger than Tarbor remembered.

Inching their way up towards the circular base, Tarbor stopped and chanced a glance, to see two monsters standing outside the mountain throne room door, looking half asleep.

"There are two, but they do not look asleep," whispered Tarbor.

"I will make sure they are," whispered Martyn back.

"What do you mean?" said Tarbor, immediately worried.

"A simple spell of serenity, it will give them peace of mind and send them into a deep sleep. She will not sense it. It is too mild a spell to even disturb the air," explained Martyn, to Tarbor's furrowed brow.

"Serenity?" questioned Tarbor, still frowning.

"Yes, before you try to say anything, I have found I have gained knowledge as well as the blessing of the runes from the first when we were there. I do not know how, but I do." Martyn shrugged, and he began to touch the symbols on his rune staff, gently watched by an apprehensive Tarbor.

Not even a whisper could be heard as Martyn waved his rune staff in the air for his spell to float around the wall, to be breathed in by the docile monsters, for its effect to have an immediate result as they collapsed to the floor with a clump!

They waited anxiously, listening to see if the noise of them falling had alerted Queen Helistra or any more monsters, but all stayed silent.

"If that was a mild spell, I would hate to see a strong one." A relieved Tarbor smiled as they propped them up against the wall to make it look as if they had fallen asleep naturally.

"I think I might need a bit more practice at that spell." Martyn smiled back and then suddenly felt something pass through him as he stood up and looked at the base of Forest Tower, to feel it yet again.

"Are you all right, Martyn?" asked Tarbor, seeing the look on his face.

"This is where my father battled with Brax and met his fate. I remember you telling me," replied Martyn in a quiet reflective voice. "I just felt its echoes," he added, for Tarbor to look at him in wonder as he felt his sadness that he had never met his father.

There was no time to dwell on these sad reflections as they stepped into the mountain throne room, to see the two polished mountain thrones glistening before them, adorned with their strange symbols.

As he looked at the symbols, Martyn thought he recognised them. Of course he did; they were the same symbols that were on his rune staff.

He twisted his rune staff around to see them. Yes, there they were, one underneath another. He wondered what would happen if he touched them in the pattern shown on the mountain throne, but other matters were at hand, as Tarbor soon reminded him.

"Martyn! This is no time to daydream if you want to rescue your sister!" Martyn smiled that Tarbor had made up his mind; they were going to rescue them!

Martyn sat on the mountain throne and raised his rune staff over the uneven hole in its arm, whilst Tarbor raised his protective shield higher, so Martyn's rune staff did not protrude.

Making sure his rune staff covered the uneven hole, Martyn closed his eyes and shut his mind to everything.

Calling silently through his rune staff, Martyn told the broken piece of Grimstone's rune staff that it was safe to release itself into the hole, where it could wait for its other part to appear.

At first, the broken piece did not seem to want to come out of the safety of Martyn's rune staff. It had waited a long time to feel freedom and had formed a strong bond with Martyn's rune staff, but it knew it had to be whole again to stop this evil.

Closing itself off so as not to trigger any of the locks that lay within the mountain throne arm, the broken piece slowly slid out of Martyn's rune staff down into the arm, to finally rest at the bottom of the hole.

"It is done," informed Martyn, already feeling the loss of the broken piece.

"Good," acknowledged Tarbor, sighing with some relief. "Now all we have to do is force Queen Helistra's hand to join the broken rune staff," he added, letting Martyn know by his worried tone that the prospect of doing so was still a daunting one. Hoping at the same time, he had made the right decision to rescue everyone. It would be to their advantage, he thought again, to convince himself.

As Tarbor started to leave the mountain throne room, he looked up at the rock ledge that held the two crowns of Tiggannia. He thought of how King Taliskar had craved this room, for its power and glory, only for it to bring about his demise.

They made their way quickly to the grand courtyard, once more through the servants' quarters, to be met by the ever-swirling sea mist.

Over to the far corner of the grand courtyard they moved, forever looking around them, expecting a monster to pounce out of the gloom at any moment, but none did.

They almost collided with the dungeon door as it suddenly emerged before them. Finding it to be open, they quickly disappeared behind it, to be met by the awful smell of the dungeons.

"Some things never change," said Tarbor, grimacing, as he peeked through the grille of the guardroom door to see two more monsters sprawled over a wooden table, and felt a twinge of apprehension pass through him.

"I do not like the feel of this, Martyn," said Tarbor, voicing his worry.

"It is as Speedwell said. They are asleep," replied Martyn, without a trace of fear in his voice. His whole being had suddenly become consumed with one thought and one thought only: to rescue his sister! A sister he had never seen or spoken to before!

Down deeper into the cold, dark dungeons they moved, Tarbor's defender giving them light, with not a torch to be seen.

They came to the first of the cell doors and squinted through the grille. They could see nothing, hear nothing. "Amber! Are you in there?" called Martyn softly, to hear his words sound ghostly through the darkness.

Another cell door produced the same result, and then another; still nothing.

Then as if they had come up against a solid rock wall, Martyn and Tarbor stopped in their tracks, sensing someone was behind them, the someone they did not want to encounter as a cold, sarcastic voice confirmed their fears. "Is this who you are looking for?"

Looking at each other, Martyn and Tarbor felt the coldness of Queen Helistra's voice pass right through them as they turned around to face her, seeing at first a soft white light penetrating the darkness, showing her cruel, dark face gloating in the moment as she held in front of her the frightened little Princess Amber.

Then, one by one, Tomin, Kelmar and Tintwist were revealed, each held by a hideous-looking creature with claw-like nails ready to rip their throats out!

"Where have you been? We have been waiting for you, wasting your time in the tower looking for your sister when she was here all the time." Queen Helistra grinned, gripping the broken rune staff and Princess Amber's arm tightly. "Or were you hoping to find me?" she quizzed, still grinning.

Martyn and Tarbor kept their minds focused at the threat they now faced so as not to give away the true reason why they had gone to Forest Tower, letting her think that was what had happened.

"I am sorry, Tarbor. This is my fault. My mind was drawn to rescuing my sister. I should have known it would not be that easy," apologised Martyn quietly.

"You do not have to be sorry. We took the risk together," whispered Tarbor back as he wondered if he would be quick enough to release his defender upon the monsters with an arc of white lightning and then take his chances with Queen Helistra.

"Thinking of something, Captain Tarbor? Or do you prefer King Ashwell, or perhaps King wielder!" Queen Helistra threw her head back in cold laughter at the mere thought of it.

"You could try, but I suggest you lay your sword and shield down. The same goes for you, child. Lay your rune staff down and back away now if you do not want any harm to come to your sister!"

Queen Helistra's eyes burnt into them both with menace as she spat out the words.

"Once we are in your grip, we will all be dead anyway," challenged Martyn, holding his rune staff ready.

"Ah, the spirit that has been talked about thrives in you, I see. Perhaps a little persuasion is needed," and she looked at the creature holding Tintwist.

Without hesitation, the creature dug its claw-like nails into Tintwist's throat, drawing blood. Tintwist cried in pain as the creature drew its own blood by clawing its deformed hand before putting it onto the bloodied neck of Tintwist, pressing home its oozing orange blood into the fresh wounds.

A last desperate look from Tintwist met their eyes before he fell onto the rock floor, convulsing. Moments later, he stood up, snarling, ready to rip them apart. Tintwist was no more!

"You see, I do not kill everyone!" And her cold laughter cut through them all as they dropped their heads in heartache at what she had done to Tintwist.

Martyn stared at Queen Helistra, his rune staff set before him. She should not have done that to his friend!

Tarbor held him back, seeing the anger that had risen up within him. Holding his shield in front of Martyn, he turned his face so Queen Helistra could not see what he was saying as he spoke in earnest to Martyn.

"Hold yourself back, Martyn! She taunts us! Remember, she has to be alive to join the broken rune staff. We have to wait for Speedwell to move. She will not kill us here. Look at her. She cannot wait to display us in front of Speedwell. Save yourself. Somehow we will force her hand," whispered Tarbor.

"Plot all you wish. The power I possess from the crystal chamber will make any attempt upon me futile and mean their certain deaths!" warned Queen Helistra at the same time.

Martyn knew Tarbor was right, but right now, he wanted to strike her down! Then he saw the frightened look on his sister's face and taking a deep breath, he lowered his rune staff.

"Do not be frightened. We will do as she asks," he called calmly to her.

Princess Amber's face lifted as she heard his voice and she tried to smile. She had been thinking how long it had seemed that she had been waiting to see and hear her brother when she knew of his existence, only now to have helped put him in danger.

"It is all my fault. I tried to help, but I did not know how evil she was until the destruction of the Ancient One." She sighed, only to feel Queen Helistra's nails dig into her arm.

"Enough of this pity! Lay down your staff!" shouted Queen Helistra, touching symbols on the broken rune staff and bringing it around to lay across Princess Amber's neck.

Martyn and Tarbor could hear the broken rune staff humming in anticipation and obeyed. Tarbor laid down his shield and defender, letting the shield of protection dissolve as he did so. Martyn followed, laying down his rune staff, but as he did so, he let his fingers slide over the symbols that matched the mountain throne symbols. He was not sure if anything would happen. Nothing did, but his instincts had told him it was worth a try.

A grinning Queen Helistra revelled in her triumph. "Throw them in the cells!" she gloated in delight; the Manelf that was Tintwist the first to grab them both and throw them into separate cells.

"Spare them, Mother. Take me instead. They are only children," pleaded Tomin as he was led away to another cell, even though he knew his fate was sealed, feeling the cynical look from her as she picked up Martyn's rune staff.

"Ringwold's rune staff, hmm. Bring those, when you have locked these other two up," she ordered the remaining monsters, pointing to Tarbor's defender and shield as she handed over a sobbing Princess Amber.

Turning, Queen Helistra looked at Martyn's rune staff as she walked away, a humming entering her mind.

"We will burn them all once we have them," she answered simply, to more humming.

"Yes, we could, but he will want to see they are alive to offer himself in their place, which we know he will, then their fates are sealed." She smiled coldly, revelling in the thought of seeing Speedwell having to watch the death of his beloved little Forestalls before meeting his own as humming entered her mind again.

"You were right, as always, that they might try something. Your vigilance was well advised. They did not sense our little friend at the mountain door. Who would have thought a mouse could have brought such rich rewards!" And her cold laughter rang out once more as she left the dungeon.

Kelmar had watched, saying nothing, as he picked himself up off the cell floor, where he had been thrown, rubbing his throbbing head.

They had waited in undying hope for their return. Friends had been lost in that hope of putting an end to her evil, and now here they all were, caught in its midst, with only Speedwell remaining, he thought despondently.

Slumping down against the cold rock wall, he felt disillusioned, feeling for the first time that hope ebbing away, seeing only one ending in sight for them all.

CHAPTER LVIII

Cries of joy seeing Cantell alive soon turned to cries of anguish for Queen Elina when Speedwell told her his news.

"Two nights ago! Captured!" burst Queen Elina, after listening to Speedwell's account of why Martyn and Tarbor were not there with him.

"The broken piece must be in the mountain throne arm. Otherwise, Helistra would have sensed it when she possessed Martyn's rune staff and that would have meant their…" He did not finish.

"Deaths!" cried Queen Elina, finishing his sentence off for him in tears.

"Yes, but I have not sensed anything. It is me that she wants and now she has more than the means to do so," he said, worriedly, as he thought of them all under her control. How many could he save? How many would she let him?

"You retrieved the broken piece after all! You did not say when we met at Kelmsmere!" exclaimed Piper, not knowing how she felt after what she had just heard.

"I am sorry, Piper, for not saying. I already had a lot of things on my mind when you told me Tomin had put himself at the mercy of my daughter, but yes, we did retrieve it. Martyn hid it within his rune staff.

"It told us that only her hand can mend Grimstone's broken rune staff, so we quickly came up with a plan to put it into the mountain throne arm so that when she goes to enter the crystal chamber, it will be joined by her own hand," explained Speedwell.

"But surely she will sense it is there before she puts the broken rune staff into the hole?" questioned Urchel.

Urchel, like Queen Elina and Piper, had felt his spirits rise in hope when Speedwell told them they had retrieved the broken piece, only to have them fall again at the news of their friends' capture.

"Only when it is directly over the hole. She cannot penetrate rock or stone. I planned to trade myself for Princess Amber so as to be in the mountain throne room when she placed Grimstone's broken rune staff over the mountain throne arm, so in that moment of surprise I could force her hand to join it," answered Speedwell, sounding rather uncertain.

"Surprise?" exclaimed Piper again. "So it would be without your rune staff to help you! Even I know she would not let you have it with you. It would pose a threat to her! Now not only is Tomin held captive with our friends, but she has Martyn and Tarbor as well! Let alone Princess Amber!" exclaimed Piper yet again.

"I confess doing it as we did, we did not think it through properly," admitted Speedwell.

"Not thought it through!" Queen Elina was beside herself, thinking about her children in the clutches of that woman.

"They will be lying in the dungeons until she displays all of them for us to see," said Cantell, not helping the situation for Queen Elina, but saying what everyone was thinking.

As Cantell spoke, they all looked from the bridge where they were standing, that once linked Haven's thriving fishing village over the River Dale, through the greyness of the morning towards Stormhaven stronghold, half expecting to see them on its battlements.

As they looked, they could see King Brodic and Galmis walking amongst the lines of the Silion army, waiting in the snow-covered valley, checking to see that they were prepared for what lay behind Stormhaven's walls, making sure their unprotected skins were covered with the simple masks and gloves that had been hastily made for them.

Next to them, Tiska and Tislea were doing the same amongst the Elfore, who had been joined by a few lucky Tiggannians that had survived by hiding in the Demeral hills, in the hope of one day ridding their Kingdom of its suffering.

Keeping themselves busy amongst the ruins of Haven, trying not to think of what was going to happen, especially to Kelmar, were Permellar, Oneatha and Kayla, all sorting out food they had managed to gather together.

"What are you going to do now?" asked Queen Elina, fearing for the lives of her children as she wiped away her tears.

"What I was always going to do, trade myself to get inside, but now things have changed I will make sure it is for Martyn and his sister, your children. It has always been me she has been after. She will be more than ready to do so," said Speedwell, assured of his actions but not of the final outcome.

"Are you sure, Speedwell? You will be lucky if she gives up anyone. She has us where she wants us," said Urchel, and although they did not want to admit it, it was exactly what the others were thinking, especially Queen Elina.

"I must try. Otherwise, it will mean their certain deaths if she finds the broken piece beforehand, and I cannot force her hand by being out here," said Speedwell, beginning to walk from the bridge.

"And if she does not, what then?" called Queen Elina after him. Speedwell stopped and looked back, for her to see the heartache in his steel-blue eyes, knowing he had forsaken his own grandson in trying to save her children.

"There can be no turning back. I will have no choice but to attack," he replied.

She could do no more than watch Speedwell move towards Stormhaven, with a prayer to the stars that her children would survive through all of this before going to where Permellar, Oneatha and Kayla were to help.

Speedwell moved through the Silion army and Elfore to stand alone halfway up the slope that led to the Stormhaven stronghold.

Holding his rune staff before him, thoughts cascaded through his mind. What he could have done, what he should have done. After all they had been through, it was as it was deemed to be, he thought, father and daughter.

The rest of the company stood behind him, further back, looking on, not knowing what to expect as an easterly breeze blew up across the valley, sending a chill through their bodies, as if in warning of what was to come.

Speedwell cleared his head of all thought, to reach out to his daughter, to hear laughter immediately enter his mind. *Ah, there you are at last, all alone I see*, came his daughter's voice, full of mockery.

Your senses fail you, daughter. I am not exactly alone, he replied in a calm voice.

You mean those pathetic beings behind you? Let me see if we cannot level things up, she said, laughing.

The next thing Speedwell saw was her army of malformed monsters emerging from the stronghold gates to stand either side of them, forming two unruly lines.

Speedwell watched as all manner of poor people and animals twisted by her evilness came through the gates, before emerging through them herself, all in her cloak of pure black, holding Princess Amber in front of her as he knew she would.

Behind her appeared two disfigured beings, holding, to his relief, his grandson, Tomin.

Speedwell's eyes grew wider as he looked more closely at the two creatures. Even through its disfigurement, it was clear one was once an Elfore, but it was the wide metal belt around its waist that caught his eye, a belt that Fleck had said was worn by King Vedland!

The other poor creature was smaller, with a hideous grin across its twisted face: a Manelf. And there was only one Manelf Speedwell knew of behind those walls; he was looking at what had become of Tintwist!

No sooner had Speedwell caught his breath at seeing Tintwist and King Vedland in their accursed states, than screams came from somewhere behind him.

He turned to see movement amidst the ruins of Haven on the other side of the river. In the next moment, a horseman appeared, cantering across the bridge, straight to King Brodic, for King Brodic to send him on to Speedwell.

"What is it?" Speedwell asked quickly.

"An army of monsters, countless hundreds of them approaching Haven!" gasped the rider, sounding out of breath, even though he was astride his horse.

"Make sure everyone is on this side of the River Dale," ordered Speedwell, and the horseman was gone.

Speedwell looked back up the slope to see a broad grin had appeared on his daughter's face.

Perhaps not so level, but in my favour, she crowed in Speedwell's mind.

This must end now, Helistra! What have these poor beings done to you? The forests are all but desecrated. What more do you want? Speedwell could not help but let his feelings get the better of him.

Helistra! You must be serious, but it is better than being called your daughter, she mocked.

You waste your time, Grandfather. I saw it in her, only darkness lays there, came Tomin's voice, adding to Speedwell's sadness, knowing he was right.

"Be quiet! Who asked you?" she said, chastising Tomin for interrupting, to answer Speedwell's emotional plea in her mind: *I may be open to suggestions.*

Speedwell knew she was playing with him, but he had to try. He pulled himself together. *I know it is me you blame for everything, so here I am offering myself to you, but first you must let them all go. They do not pose a threat to you,* he pleaded.

Hmm, all of them? Including a liar, and this would be Forestall? she questioned with a warning in her voice.

You have Prince Martyn's rune staff, and Princess Amber has never had one to cast any power against you. They would be harmless to you without one, he reasoned.

A humming interrupted any more mind talk. "Yes, then we can destroy them."

It is true I have the child's rune staff, but what of the two you have in your possession, those of Gentian and Ringwold? I will need to know they will not be used against me also, she questioned.

She is making sure there are no loose ends, unlike me, thought Speedwell.

They will be yours if you release two of your prisoners, he pushed.

A lull occurred as more humming ensued. "I agree."

"Very well, do not let it be said that I am not totally without mercy," she answered, making Tomin nearly choke. "Fetch the Tiggannian," she ordered.

Speedwell waited nervously. *All this pretence, at least two are saved and as long as I get inside Stormhaven, then I will worry about what to do next,* he thought.

Finally, a dishevelled-looking Kelmar being pushed by another creature appeared at the gates.

Here are your two prisoners in exchange for the rune staffs. Meet halfway and give them to these two, but not by your hand, old man. You stay where I can see you, she warned, stroking Princess Amber's frightened face.

I only see one prisoner you have released. Speedwell frowned.

You are blinder than he is, she said, laughing, as she nodded to the deformed King Vedland and Tintwist to let go of Tomin, much to his surprise.

"You would spare me? Why not the Princess? She cannot harm you, she is a healer," he questioned, puzzled.

"You are no longer the problem," she answered simply. "Follow them and bring back the rune staffs to me," she ordered, for Tomin and Kelmar to be pushed down the slope.

Speedwell felt wary. He could not believe she had let Tomin go. He turned around and shouted for the two rune staffs to be brought to him.

King Brodic moved to a small wagon and threw back the covering to reveal the two tied leather-bound rune staffs, finding Piper right behind him as he turned, taking them.

"I will take them, sire. You need not risk yourself," she said, holding out her arms.

"I do not think it matters in our present situation," remarked King Brodic, looking at the ruins of Haven on the other side of the river as he spoke.

Piper looked with him, to see the ruins on the other side were now full of waiting monsters, ready to charge on the word of Queen Helistra. All who had been over there had thankfully got across the bridge that was now blocked by King Brodic's army.

"We will go together. After all, we were both entrusted with them." King Brodic smiled to a nod from Piper.

"I think she has let Tomin and Kelmar go for these," remarked King Brodic, screwing his eyes up to see as they trudged up the snowy slope towards where Speedwell stood.

"She can afford to, we are trapped. Once she has Speedwell in her grasp, she will unleash the evil she has created upon us. She cannot be trusted to let us go when she has got what she has always wanted: her father. We can only hope he finishes her off before they finish us," replied

Piper to King Brodic, reminding him of the cold reality they were up against, not that he needed it.

As they reached Speedwell with the leather-bound rune staffs, they could see Tomin and Kelmar waiting ahead, with two deformed creatures hidden behind them.

"She has agreed to release Tomin and Kelmar in exchange for the rune staffs, but let King Brodic take them, Piper. You need not go," suggested Speedwell, worried what her reaction might be when she saw what was once Tintwist sneering back at her.

"I will be all right, but you know she is playing you. We are trapped," warned Piper, looking past Speedwell to where Tomin and Kelmar were waiting.

"I know we are, but there will be less for me to worry about once I am inside," said Speedwell, sounding selfish.

"As if their chances are going to be any better out here," huffed Piper. "Have you thought as to how you are going to bring about her downfall whilst saving the children, once inside, without your rune staff?" she queried, with raised eyebrows.

"I will think of something. I just need to get close to her," answered Speedwell, to another huff from Piper.

"For now, let King Brodic take the rune staffs, Piper. You stay here with me," requested Speedwell again, seeing the mood she was in, but curiosity had caught hold of Piper as to why he had asked her twice.

"No, I will be all right," she promised again, and she was gone before Speedwell or King Brodic could say another word.

As Piper and King Brodic approached the waiting party, Piper saw the wide intricate metal belt one of the creatures was wearing, immediately realising it belonged to King Vedland, or what was left of him!

Then as Piper looked at the other creature standing there, she instantly knew why Speedwell had wanted her to stay with him.

Her heart jumped into her mouth and her face fell as she looked at the unrecognisable creature standing behind Kelmar. If it had not been for the tattered clothes on its deformed back, she would not have known that the hideous monster now standing in front of her was once Tintwist.

Emotions ran high within her. Repulsion, anger and regret all fought alongside each other as she looked at him.

Repulsion was overtaken by regret as she thought of how she had always mocked him or told him off, instead of telling him that she loved him as he loved her, but anger soon replaced regret as it seethed underneath her skin to see him like this!

King Brodic held out the leather-bound rune staffs for them to take. Piper tried to keep control of her anger as she looked straight at Tintwist's grotesque face.

Bumps stuck out from a yellowing skin as glazed blood-red eyes with a slit of black looked back at her from behind a hideous bloated grin. "Tintwist!" she gasped. It was more than she could take; she had done this!

All Kelmar saw was Piper's face go white and he thought she was going to collapse, but the opposite happened before he was able to stop her.

As her breath met the cold air, she had slid her bow from her shoulder, pulled an arrow from her quiver, notched it and sent it flying through the air, straight at Queen Helistra's head! Booting Tintwist onto the snow in the process!

King Brodic gasped and launched the leather-bound rune staffs he held right round the back of King Vedland's deformed head, knocking him senseless onto the snow before he could do anything!

Kelmar pounced onto Tomin, knocking him down, knowing Queen Helistra would immediately retaliate. What was Piper doing? Queen Helistra was holding Princess Amber!

Piper's mind had snapped; she did not care. Dead or not, what did it matter! At least they would be rid of her, and she let loose yet another arrow!

Queen Helistra's eyes narrowed on seeing the woman Manelf aim arrows at her. Who did she think she was! She did no more than grab a monster near to her, to see two arrowheads penetrate right through its malformed body, to drop its dead form in front of a terrified Princess Amber.

Queen Helistra quickly touched some symbols on the broken rune staff and sent a stream of lightning bolts straight at Piper!

Speedwell, seeing all this, had no time to think but reacted on instinct as his fingers moved quickly over the symbols of his rune staff, creating a wall of thick blue ice just in time behind all six figures, stopping the barrage of white bolts aimed at Piper.

They smashed into the wall of ice, half melting, half shattering it into pieces, knocking Piper to the ground.

King Brodic hauled a dazed Piper out of the debris. Slinging the tied rune staffs over his shoulder, he picked up Piper and limped as fast as he could with his wounded leg, back towards Speedwell.

Kelmar had got to his feet with Tomin and they ran with King Brodic for their lives as another hail of lightning bolts seared through the air behind them.

This time, Speedwell sent a hail of ice-blue shards to meet them in mid-air, hitting the lightning bolts, deflecting them to the ground behind the running party, to melt harmlessly through the snow.

They ran into the ranks of Silion and Elfore as fire balls suddenly began landing everywhere. Snow and bodies flew through the air as they exploded on the ground.

Piper was not the only one to have seen red as Queen Helistra sent one fire ball after another, hurtling down on anyone and everyone whilst releasing the monsters to attack them.

The humming in her mind tried in vain to stop her using energy she had no need to use; she had the twins! *Kill them first then deal with Speedwell!* But she could only see the arrogant little Manelf in her mind, who had tried to kill her with an arrow! Her, the Queen of death itself!

Speedwell ran back, working quickly, to create a wall of protection, not only to stop the incoming fire balls, but also the monsters who were now running headlong down the slope, wielding their weapons.

Stopping, he held his rune staff before him and waved his arm in an arc, casting a spell of protection across them all in the form of an invisible wall, to then place his rune staff in the snow in front of him, chanting as he knelt to keep the wall strong.

"Grandfather, let me help!" shouted an out-of-breath Tomin as he fell by Speedwell's side with Kelmar.

Speedwell glanced sideways, managing a half-smile to see and hear his grandson once more.

"Your help will be needed at our backs, Tomin. Go to the bridge! Do not let them cross the river!" shouted Speedwell back, trying to keep his concentration as fire balls pounded his protective shield.

Tomin was up and across to King Brodic, who had knelt himself for a respite with Piper, who was slowly coming around.

Without words being spoken, Tomin took the rune staffs off King Brodic's shoulder. Unwrapping Gentian's, he immediately headed to help Galmis, where the monsters were already storming the bridge.

"Here, let me take over," offered Kelmar, seeing King Brodic was struggling.

"Thank you, Kelmar. I will go to the bridge with him." He smiled and, laying Piper down, he limped after Tomin.

Grabbing Ringwold's rune staff, Kelmar helped a still bleary-eyed Piper to her feet, putting her arm over his shoulder.

Kelmar had not even reached the ruins of Haven with Piper before he was surrounded by three tearful figures who had spotted him coming their way: Oneatha, Permellar and Kayla.

He could hardly move for their attention as he finally sat the dazed Piper down behind a broken wall to hug them all, with a worried Queen Elina looking on as she attended Piper.

"I thought I would never see you again!" cried Oneatha.

"I am here, Mother." He smiled, hugging her, although he had thought the same.

"She has let you go?" half gasped Permellar, crying in disbelief, hugging him also with Kayla.

"With Tomin, but before Speedwell could do anything else, Piper saw Tintwist and anger seized her," and Kelmar quickly told them what had happened, making Queen Elina all the more worried for her children.

"He holds a wall of protection against them now, whilst they are being held off from crossing the river behind us, which is where I must go," stated Kelmar to the looks of we have only just got you back.

"I do not know what Speedwell has planned. I only know I must help him," for them to give him one last hug as Kayla tugged his hand.

"You had better wear this, Uncle Kelmar," and she handed him a hood to protect his face. Kelmar smiled, taking the hood, and gave her an extra hug, for Permellar to cry.

As he ran to go and fight at the bridge, a voice suddenly shouted at him from behind, making him stop dead in disbelief. A voice he thought he would never hear again: "Where are you off to in a rush without me?"

Kelmar turned to see a grinning face looking at him in all the chaos that surrounded them, and cried his name: "Cantell!" It was Kelmar's turn to run and embrace this time as he choked in emotion at seeing his old friend.

"How…? When did you…?" So many questions poured into his mind at seeing him.

"It is a long story, old friend. I will tell you soon enough, but first…" Cantell grinned, his sword raised in the air.

Kelmar grinned back, and donning their hoods, they ran to help at the bridge. Although the odds were still stacked against them, Kelmar felt fresh hope run through his veins at seeing Cantell and to be finally fighting back.

Queen Helistra finally calmed down enough to stop her bombardment for a moment to hear what the humming was saying.

"What is it?" she shouted in a temper, whilst she refocused her thoughts on what spell she needed to penetrate the protective shield Speedwell had cast.

She blinked rapidly whilst looking at Princess Amber, who she had thrown to a monster to hold whilst she bombarded Speedwell.

"He is the cause of it all! I want him dead!" she shouted to a frustrated humming at her ignorance.

"No, he is not the future. They are," she agreed, feeling the humming's annoyance.

"You are right. I should have dealt with them straight away and now I have let a meaningless Manelf take my eye off our true purpose," she admitted, calming down further.

"Very well, we will let him use his power whilst ridding ourselves of these would-be Forestalls, then he will be easy prey for us to finish off," decided Queen Helistra, to more humming.

"Yes, they are twins, and even though we have the boy's rune staff, we have already been deceived once. You are right. We will take no chances. We will deal with this one first and then its brother," she agreed, to the satisfaction of the broken rune staff, but to the trepidation of Princess Amber!

"Close the gates!" shouted Queen Helistra as they walked towards Middle Gate, for the monsters in the gatehouse to leave the battle raging outside the stronghold's walls as they obeyed her command.

Speedwell felt his blood go cold, seeing Princess Amber being carried off, before the huge gates shut. It was obvious what his daughter was going to do next, sacrifice her and Martyn in the crystal chamber! She had not needed to be angered by Piper's actions to do what she had always intended to do, he thought.

But she will kill them there and then when she finds the broken piece in the mountain throne arm! he further thought in anguish.

It had all gone wrong! It was no good holding them at bay like this. He had to get in there, now!

CHAPTER LIX

Mrs Beeworthy closed the door of the servants' quarters after watching Queen Helistra drag little Amber and the old man, who had called himself her son, out through Middle Gate behind all of her hideous monsters. She leaned on the door, catching her breath at the horror of it all.

What she be doing with them? As if the poor child has not gone through enough, she thought.

Moving over to the warmth of the fire, Mrs Beeworthy sat down, trying to think. Something was happening out there. If only she could help somehow, but how? She was just a feeble old woman who only knew how to cook.

She may have been, but she knew little Amber's brother, Prince Martyn, Kelmar and that Captain Tarbor, who had all been thrown into them horrible dungeons, were the ones who could help, but they needed to be free to do anything.

Breathing in a deep breath, Mrs Beeworthy stood up. It was up to her, she thought, she would help them get out of those stinking dungeons, and she knew how she could!

Putting on her cloak, she checked the pot of broth she always had on the go in the kitchen and put some wooden bowls out, ready to take to the dungeons.

She would go to feed them as normal so the monsters in the dungeon would not suspect anything, but first she needed to get something that was hidden in the royal chamber, and with Queen Helistra gone, it was now or never!

Out into the corridor, she headed straight for Forest Tower. There were no monsters to be seen, but her heart still raced as she climbed the stone spiral steps to the door of the royal chamber.

Opening the door slowly, she peeked around it to let out a gasp of astonishment, leaving her open-mouthed as to what she was looking at.

There floating in mid-air was Martyn's rune staff! With a strange humming sound coming from it as it hovered there motionless.

That be little Martyn's staff what he came with, she thought blankly, not knowing what to make of it floating there.

She had no time to dwell upon it as she skirted around the floating staff to find what she had come for, telling herself not to let it touch her, not liking the feeling she had, hearing the humming.

At the far end of the chamber stood an old wooden chest and with what strength she had, she moved it away from the stone wall.

Now, which one is it? she thought, looking at all the stones that had been revealed from behind the chest as a small voice came into her head, making her smile as she looked.

He thought I was asleep when he put it there. She remembered Queen Elina laughing like a naughty little girl before telling her as she spotted the small stone that hid what she had come for.

A wiggle and a pull later saw her putting her hand in the hole left by the loose stone to bring out an ordinary-looking key, but it was far from that; it was a master key that opened all of the doors in the stronghold.

No one had known of its existence, only King Rolfe, and where he had got it from was a mystery. Not that it was ever needed by him; he never had a door locked, the only exception being where Mrs Beeworthy wanted to go now.

So here it had been hidden for all of these years, with only the chance sighting of its existence by a young Queen who had told of her secret to her trusted friend, this simple cook.

She reflected upon it as she looked at the key with a nervous smile. If only she had been brave enough then to have freed her from her shackles, she thought sadly, before putting it in her apron pocket.

Skirting around the floating rune staff once more, giving it one last puzzled look, she left for her kitchen.

Opening the door of the servants' quarters, with a small pot of broth and bowls on a tray, Mrs Beeworthy suddenly caught her breath, nearly dropping it all as she spotted a monster pushing someone forward through Middle Gate. Was that Kelmar? She scurried across the grand courtyard to the dungeon door as soon as they were out of sight.

The dungeon door had been left open and she breathed in nervously as she walked through it, to look through the grille of the guardroom door to see the Cardronian guard she used to know staring right back at her, with eyes as black as night.

It opened the door with a growl right in her face. "Food, I… I have brought some food for the prisoners," she stuttered, showing the tray, to receive another growl as the once Cardronian guard shoved right past her, dragging one of its deformed legs.

Down into the dank dungeons they went, to stop at a cell door halfway down. Mrs Beeworthy undid a small hatch at the side of the cell door. "Here you are, my love, you be getting this hot broth down you," she said, just managing to see it was Captain Tarbor looking back at her in the poor light thrown by the torches.

She knew the cell door would not be opened for her. They were not in shackles and were able to get to their food, not like Queen Elina, she remembered again with sadness.

Bending down, she put the tray down onto the dirty floor and poured some broth into a bowl. Putting the pot down, she reached into her apron pocket and quickly slipped the master key into the bowl, without the monster seeing her.

Not that it was taking much notice of her as it growled impatiently under one of the flickering torches.

Mrs Beeworthy carefully put the wooden bowl onto the ledge and pushed it in. "There we are. Now eat it all up whilst it be hot. It be just the key in this weather," she urged, looking into the bowl with her eyes before shutting the small hatch and moving on to the next cell, where Martyn was.

Tarbor had been pacing up and down in the cold, dark cell, wondering what was happening for Kelmar to be taken away as well.

Princess Amber and Tomin had been taken only a short while ago. It must be Speedwell trying to trade places with them, he thought, annoyed that he was in here, helpless to help him if he succeeded.

At least he was alive, he thought, unlike Fleck, who had been taken by her never to return, Kelmar had told him, and he had not been turned into a monster like poor Tintwist, he was thinking, as the sound of footsteps stopped his trail of sad thoughts.

He watched the hatch being opened and then heard the unmistakable tones of Mrs Beeworthy telling him to eat the broth she had put there for him.

Ever-faithful to the end, he thought, wondering why her eyes looked wobbly as she said, just the key in this weather. He half smiled to himself as he took the bowl.

A hot broth to warm his hands on and feed a groaning stomach were not going to be sneezed at, even if it could be his last one, he thought.

Lifting the wooden bowl to his mouth, Tarbor enjoyed the warmth it gave to him as he felt it go down his throat as he slurped it back, to suddenly feel something hit his teeth.

What has Mrs Beeworthy left in here? he thought, as whatever it was fell back into the bowl. Putting his fingers into the bowl, he immediately came across something metal in them and as he felt the object that he lifted out, he realised it was a key! Mrs Beeworthy had smuggled him a key!

Now the wobbly eyes made sense; she was trying to tell him without giving herself away!

He was soon looking through the grille to see where the guard and Mrs Beeworthy were. He could just see the guard's hideous features in the flickering torchlight near Martyn's cell door.

Putting the key into the cell door, Tarbor turned it slowly, trying to be as quiet as he could. It caught, to make his heart miss a beat. He tried again and this time he felt it turn fully.

Tarbor held himself ready and waited.

Mrs Beeworthy walked back past Tarbor's cell door, not knowing if he had taken the broth to find the key or not.

A growl of pain and a sword being drawn, to see the monster hitting the stone floor behind her, told her the answer.

Tarbor had run out of his cell, taken the torch from the wall and as the monster had turned, hearing him, Tarbor had thrust the torch straight into its hideous face. As it growled in pained anger, reaching for its face, Tarbor had drawn its sword and driven it straight into its deformed chest, for it to fall dead at his feet.

Mrs Beeworthy dropped her tray in fright, not at the sight of the dead monster, but at the sudden explosions that were booming in the valley.

"You are a brave woman, Mrs Beeworthy. Let us hope it is not too late," thanked Tarbor, already unlocking Martyn's cell door as the explosions sounded.

"I be a scared cook!" cried Mrs Beeworthy, catching her breath as a thankful Martyn appeared before her.

"Thank you, Mrs Beeworthy. We shall not forget what you have done for us." Martyn smiled, glad to get out of that horrible cell, but was immediately worried, like Tarbor, by the sound of the explosions.

"What is happening, Mrs Beeworthy? Have you seen anything?" asked Tarbor quickly.

"Little Amber and your friend, the old… her son," she corrected herself, "were dragged outside the gates with all of her horrible monsters," began Mrs Beeworthy, "then I think it was Kelmar I saw who they took a bit later," she added to Tarbor's "Yes, it was."

"Speedwell must have been trying to bargain with her to get in here, but something has gone wrong," said Tarbor, worriedly.

"We need to be near the mountain throne room in wait, but I will be of no use without my rune staff," said Martyn in earnest.

"And I my defender and shield," added Tarbor, thinking the same.

"Oh! Do you mean your staff? I saw it in the royal chamber, floating it was, in the air, made a funny sound. I stayed away from it," declared Mrs Beeworthy, with Martyn and Tarbor looking at each other.

"Come then, let us hurry. It is a start. Perhaps your defenders are in there too, Tarbor," said Martyn in hope as both of them started to run for the dungeon door, but not before giving Mrs Beeworthy a kiss on the cheek, to make her go bright red.

Opening the dungeon door, they noticed the explosions had ceased, hearing instead the fearful roar of the monsters, making Tarbor and Martyn look at each other in dread. "They attack!" cried Tarbor.

If the sound of the monsters attacking had not fully filled them with dread, then the sight of Queen Helistra with two monsters pushing a tearful Princess Amber across the grand courtyard and into the great hall did! With no thought for their own lives, they ran to her aid!

CHAPTER LX

All had seen Queen Helistra take Princess Amber back into the stronghold, knowing it would spell her end and Martyn's, but none could free themselves from the battle to help, and the huge gates had been shut!

Whilst Speedwell had held back the monsters coming down the slope from the stronghold with his wall of protection, it had enabled everyone to concentrate defending the river to stop the hordes of monsters waiting in the ruins of Haven on the other side from crossing.

Arrows were being fired and spears thrown from both sides, whilst the bridge saw the fiercest fighting as Elfore stood with Silion, holding their ground against the monsters.

Beasts swam across the River Dale's cold waters to be met by the equally cold steel of those waiting for them.

Kelmar, Cantell, Urchel and Piper were together on one side of the bridge, with Piper venting off her anger at her own stupidity for what she had done as she sliced another head clean off!

On the other side of the bridge stood King Brodic, Galmis, Tiska and Tislea, who had already let loose what arrows they had.

Behind them, Tomin sent fire into the monsters' midst, with bolts of flame searing straight through them to ignite their hideous bodies and catch those all around.

A tear-stained Queen Elina, Permellar, Oneatha and Kayla had stayed huddled together behind a ruined wall, too frightened to look.

Speedwell looked around, to see that they seemed to be holding their own at the river, but he must get to those gates, and that meant they had to defend on two fronts when he dissolved his wall of protection, for Tomin was not strong enough to take over from him for such a spell.

Speedwell stopped chanting and threw his voice powerfully in the direction of Tomin, for him to respond immediately.

"Yes, Grandfather, what is it?" he asked when at Speedwell's side, still sending flame bolts through the air.

"Be prepared for when I lower this wall of protection, Tomin. Organise enough forces to meet these hordes I hold back, and quickly!" ordered Speedwell, and Tomin was gone.

What seemed like an eternity to Speedwell, but only moments to Tomin, passed by as Elfore and Silion alike were freed to face those pounding on Speedwell's wall of protection.

Piper and Urchel joined Speedwell as he began touching symbols on his rune staff to dissolve the wall of protection.

"I am sorry, Speedwell," Piper apologised immediately, "seeing Tintwist like that upset me more deeply than I realised."

With just a look, Speedwell said nothing. He knew Piper was already upset by Tintwist's capture and had felt her agitation, but instead of holding her back, knowing her anger could surface, he had let her go. He was as much to blame, he thought.

Touching one last symbol, Speedwell waved his rune staff, for the wall to vanish, catching some monsters who were pounding upon it off guard as they fell over into the snow to find a sword awaiting them, thrust straight into the backs of their twisted necks!

Piper and Urchel had come to Speedwell's aid expecting to fight off monsters to help him get to the gates, but as soon as the protective wall was down, Speedwell was sending ice-blue shards one way then the other, straight through the bodies of the nearest monsters, clearing an immediate path for them to run into.

Speedwell did not turn around to see the ensuing battle. He only had one thing on his mind, and if he did not get there straight away he would be too late.

Piper spotted two monsters out of the corner of her eye, and they seemed to be heading straight for her when she realised who they were!

"Speedwell! Look, Tintwist and King Vedland!"

Speedwell heard the worry in Piper's voice, but he had seen them, and instead of ice-blue shards coming from his rune staff, a strange-looking thick white cloud shot out from it to wrap around them, stopping them from going any further, much to Piper's relief.

The huge gates loomed before them, and from above, out of the gatehouse's narrow arched windows, came the death whistles of arrows being fired upon them.

Speedwell reacted quickly, first throwing a shield of protection in front of them, rendering the arrows useless, then sending ice-blue flames searing through the arches, to hear the agonising roars of the monsters on fire inside the gatehouse.

Not wasting any time, Speedwell touched more symbols on his rune staff and pointed his staff at the huge gates.

Piper and Urchel could only watch as the strange symbols on the huge gates began to glow. Then, with what seemed only like a sigh, the gates sprang open to let them in!

Piper looked at Urchel as they ran in through them. "He knew how to open the gates all of the time!"

Opening the mountain throne room door, Queen Helistra immediately sat on the cold stone of the mountain throne that revealed the crystal chamber, to watch the crying Princess Amber being dragged in by two of her monsters and thrown onto the floor.

"Stop your sniffling, child! You wanted to see the crystal chamber!" teased Queen Helistra in cold laughter as she raised the broken rune staff to put it into the mountain throne arm.

Princess Amber's crying would soon stop, to be replaced by every hair on her head standing on end at what she was about to witness next.

As Queen Helistra placed the broken rune staff over the uneven hole, she suddenly felt a violent shudder of a scream course right through her body, a scream of paralysed fear that made her mouth open to release it from her body, but without making a sound.

Her arm jerked backwards to hit the back of the mountain throne, sending the broken rune staff through the air, to land behind the throne.

She sat there, not able to move, transfixed in numb realisation at what the broken rune staff had just sensed; its broken counterpart was at the bottom of the hole!

Princess Amber doubled up in fright as she felt the silent scream pass right through her, watching as Queen Helistra's face drained of blood to reveal a face of terror... that turned to disbelief... that turned to anger!

"This cannot be! It is shattered!" she yelled in her anger, making the whole of the mountain throne room vibrate.

Tarbor bumped into Martyn, who had suddenly come to a halt outside the mountain throne room door as he also felt the scream. "She has found the broken piece!" he shouted as her yell of anger shook the mountain throne room door in front of them!

One look at each other saw them bursting through the door, without thinking, to see eyes of pure hatred staring at Princess Amber.

Instantly, they saw Queen Helistra did not have Grimstone's broken rune staff in her hands and that two monsters were on the floor, holding their ears.

There was only one thing they could do as they realised how reckless they had been, bursting in like they had: grab Princess Amber and get out of there whilst luck was on their side!

Grabbing her, without looking back, they made for the spiral steps that led to the royal chamber, hoping that Martyn could release his rune staff from the binding spell that surrounded it, and quickly, or they were all dead!

What they had not seen as they ascended the spiral steps was Speedwell entering the great hall doors.

Piper, with Urchel, had gone to the aid of Martyn and Tarbor to release them from the dungeons, not knowing Mrs Beeworthy had already come to their aid.

Speedwell had felt the sudden panic from Grimstone's broken rune staff sweep through him and feared for the life of Princess Amber as he ran for the base of Forest Tower, but no sooner had he began to run than he stopped, as a figure appeared, coming from the mountain throne room.

In her cloak of black, with a face full of loathing, Queen Helistra stood at the base of Forest Tower, the regained broken rune staff shaking in her hand.

Her eyes had turned blood-red with evil and spit seeped through her gritted teeth, such was her rage at what had happened.

A sneer of a grin showed itself upon her face at the sight of her so-called father suddenly standing there before her, the man she wanted dead more than anything! This time, no humming entered her mind to stop her. All had been forgotten in the shock of finding the broken piece; only the chant of death remained!

A well of remorse swept through Speedwell; he feared he was too late to save Princess Amber as he saw his daughter, or what was left of her, standing there.

He swallowed hard and prepared himself for the day he had always dreaded, the day he would have to confront his daughter!

Queen Helistra did not hesitate as she drew on the power of the crystal chamber stored within the broken rune staff to send a fireball enclosed in a condensed ball of air to punch through any protective shield Speedwell may have, freeing the fireball to burn a hole straight through him!

It hit Speedwell with such force that it sent him hurtling through the air to hit the stone wall of the great hall behind him, but his protective shield held!

He quickly thanked the wraiths of the Ancient Forestalls in his mind for giving him the strength, even though his body had felt every stone in the wall.

They will not help you here, old man! came her cold voice inside his mind as another ball of death came Speedwell's way!

Only just reinforcing his protective shield in time, Speedwell felt as if he was being squashed into the wall as the ball of condensed air pounded into him, releasing its fireball inside to explode all over his protective shield.

Speedwell thought the fireball was not the only thing that was going to explode, as his lungs had to catch their breath as he felt the heat of the fireball through his protective shield. How much more of this could he take?

Piper and Urchel, after finding no one in the dungeons, came through the servants' quarters, crossing the linking corridor to suddenly appear in the archway of the great hall. They froze instantly at the sight of Queen Helistra.

"Get back! Run!" shouted Speedwell as Queen Helistra sent a hail of lightning bolts straight at them.

Piper leapt behind the dividing corridor wall for cover, but Urchel did not react as quickly, to feel the searing pain of a bolt go straight through his leg as he dived.

Piper grabbed his arm and half dragged him as they stumbled, making for the kitchen door, falling behind it to the gasp of Mrs Beeworthy.

"What, what be happening out there?" she cried from where she was hiding behind the kitchen table.

All Piper could say was, "Evil," as the grotesque face that she had just witnessed came into her mind.

Piper and Urchel's appearance had given Speedwell a chance to gather himself together. He saw them both dive for cover and prayed they were both alive.

He looked at his daughter, shutting his mind off to her prying eyes. She needed to be weakened of her strength from the crystal chamber. If he could drain what she had gained from that, then they would be more on equal terms. *She cannot replenish her strength for the broken piece*, he thought.

In the next moment, Speedwell had shot four spears of dense ice-blue flame at her. He sent them one behind another, equally distanced, seeing her arrogance by not throwing a shield of protection around herself.

Queen Helistra saw them coming and smiled. *Fool*, she thought; she could easily deal with these.

A flick of her wrist and she had slapped the first one out of the way nonchalantly with a wave of the broken rune staff, to hit the bottom of the spiral steps. The second shot straight through the mountain throne room door, killing the two monsters that were standing there, the third into the wall of the great hall, but as soon as she had dealt with the third one, Speedwell suddenly pushed the fourth spear of ice-blue flame twice as fast, with a touch of a symbol to catch her out; it did!

Queen Helistra felt the cold blue fire tear through her shoulder, making her scream in pain and anger.

Speedwell thought of a wounded animal at their most fearsome when hurt as he watched his daughter writhe in pain. Wounding her, he had chanced that she would use more energy, knowing her anger, but he wondered if he had put into motion his own downfall as he doubled up his protective shield, holding himself ready for her retaliation.

Martyn, Princess Amber and Tarbor almost fell into the royal chamber in their haste to get away, only to stare at Martyn's rune staff hovering in mid-air before them.

"Hurry, Martyn! Whatever it is you must do, do it and do it quickly!" shouted Tarbor as he frantically searched the chamber in his hope of finding his defender and shield.

Martyn knew that urgency was needed to release his rune staff, but he worried that he might not have mastered his abilities enough to release it as a voice came into his mind, the voice of his sister.

Holding hands with his sister to get away from Queen Helistra had triggered that part of his spirit that had flowed into her body at their birth, and it was sensing that now was the time for it to be reunited.

He looked into his long-lost sister's eyes and smiled. "I think you have been looking after something for me all of this time," he whispered. "I think I may need it for what I have to do," he added, looking at his rune staff floating there.

Princess Amber smiled back. Here at last was the brother she had never known about, hand in hand with her, face to face, the brother she had said wanted her dead. The evil witch!

She felt aglow as her spirit began to blossom whilst sensing Martyn's spirit rising within her body, ready to be reunited with him. A feeling of purpose and belonging, far more than she had ever felt before, began washing over her.

"It has kept me safe from her evil," she smiled in gratitude, "and now we are together, I can help," she pointed out, sensing his unsureness.

"What are you two doing? There is no time!" shouted Tarbor once more, seeing them smiling at each other and then hearing an almighty boom, followed by a sound like thunder that shook the very foundations of Forest Tower!

"Listen to her anger!" cried Tarbor, fearing the worst as another boom shook the chamber.

As if nothing else existed, Martyn and Princess Amber, holding hands, closed their eyes to touch forehead to forehead, for Martyn's spirit to be at last made whole.

Reunited, Martyn's spirit soared within his body, making him feel stronger than he had ever felt, whilst Princess Amber felt her body tingle with sensations she had never felt before as her spirit bloomed.

"Are you ready, sister?" said Martyn with a smile.

"I am ready, brother." Princess Amber smiled back and together they focused on Martyn's shackled rune staff.

Just at that moment, an ear-piercing scream, followed by a growl of anger, rang through the tower.

"That is a cry of pain! Someone is fighting her! It can only be Speedwell!" said Tarbor in realisation. "Hurry, we must help him!" he urged, wondering what in the name of the stars they were doing! It was nice they were together, but all that holding hands had to wait, he thought.

As the scream resounded through the tower, Martyn saw the spell around his rune staff crackle. *Speedwell is weakening her*, he thought.

"Did you see that?" he asked, without looking at his sister.

"Yes, her fighting is taking the strength from the spell," she said in realisation as well.

Then, together in spirit, they reached out to Martyn's shackled rune staff, calling out for it to come to his outstretched hand.

Princess Amber had never felt a sensation like it. It was as if part of her had pushed forward from her being to break through the binding spell and snatch the rune staff back.

Before she knew it, Martyn's rune staff had shot back into his hand and the barrier had disintegrated!

Martyn looked at his rune staff, feeling its relief at being freed. He remembered Grimstone's spirit telling him that together you will succeed. He hoped so, for now they had to face Queen Helistra!

Outside the stronghold's walls, the battle raged on, with the bodies of the fallen scattered everywhere.

Courage had shown its true colours amongst the ranks of Silion and Elfore in holding back the constant onslaught on the bridge from the monsters. It had become almost impossible with the amount of dead laying upon it.

The river's banks were not much better as they showed the struggle that had ensued, with monsters trying to cross the river, littered as they were with the dead.

Those monsters who had been held back by Speedwell's protective barrier were all but dealt with, but everywhere, the cost in lives had been high.

"Our numbers dwindle, Tomin. They are relentless! We cannot hold out here for much longer!" shouted King Brodic, skewering another hideous form with his sword as he joined Tomin, with Galmis, Tiska and Tislea on his heels.

Cantell also arrived, completely out of breath, from further up the river. "They are crossing the river further down to outflank us! We need to regroup!" he pointed out.

Tomin let loose more bolts of flame over the bridge, sensing his strength was beginning to desert him, wishing he was using it to help his grandfather instead of being here, for Tomin was feeling the fight between his mother and grandfather through Gentian's rune staff, sensing the ferocity of his mother's strikes after finding the broken piece.

He had not said anything to the others, keeping hidden the struggle that was happening.

Then suddenly his senses were sent spiralling as he felt his mother's scream. *She is in pain! Grandfather will reap her wrath!* he immediately thought, worriedly.

Cantell saw Tomin's face react to what he was feeling. "What is it, Tomin? Do you feel something?" he questioned.

"She has found the broken piece, they are fighting. I need to be in there to help Grandfather!" he answered in worry.

"And we need the safety of those thick walls to regroup," said Cantell, looking at the stronghold, "but can you get us inside the stronghold, Tomin, like Speedwell? The gates have shut behind him," asked Cantell.

Tomin turned, looking at Cantell, for Cantell to clearly see the look of disgust on Tomin's face. "I am a Forestall also, Cantell!"

Tomin touched several symbols on Gentian's rune staff whilst uttering words of incantation, to send a stream of fire across the banks either side of the bridge and onto the bridge itself, setting light to the pile of bodies upon it to create a wall of fire to hold back the monsters.

Tomin then turned to head towards the gates of Stormhaven stronghold, with King Brodic, Galmis, Tiska and Tislea forming a spearhead.

Running from all directions to their shouts came those still standing, to flank them either side, fending off any monsters that came near, with

Queen Elina, Oneatha, Permellar and Kayla joining them from the shelter of the ruins, with Kelmar guarding their backs.

As they approached the gates, Tomin thought he had perceived what could only be described as a cracking sound through Gentian's rune staff, but he had no time to dwell upon it as the gates loomed before him as another sound drowned it out completely: Grimstone's broken rune staff releasing death!

A protective shield was now surrounding a raging Queen Helistra as she sent ball after ball of condensed air to punch through Speedwell's protective shield, but this time each one was filled with hundreds of tiny dense globules of red poison.

Speedwell touched symbols on his rune staff to make it glow with ice-blue energy to deflect the poisonous balls away from him, whilst keeping his protective shield as strong as possible.

The poisonous balls flew everywhere as Speedwell deflected them. Most hit the walls of the great hall, to take on the effect of looking like the dying forests as red slime oozed down them when they exploded on impact.

Tireless in the pursuit of his death, Queen Helistra sent one after another for Speedwell to deal with.

Speedwell watched as, without intending it to happen, one deflected straight back at his daughter for her to have to deflect. This only made her become more incensed, and she increased the amount she was casting at him.

Then suddenly between the balls of poison, Queen Helistra sent a bolt of lightning at Speedwell, to catch him out as he had caught her out.

She hid the bolt of lightning behind one of the poisonous balls, and just as he was about to deflect it, she touched a symbol on the broken rune staff, to send the lightning bolt below the poisonous ball, to go straight into his protective shield, making him stumble backwards.

As the lightning bolt hit his protective shield, deflecting onto the wall behind him, it showed her a weakness within it, letting her know where to concentrate her efforts.

Concentrating on deflecting the balls of poison had seen Speedwell channel more energy into his rune staff, but by doing so he had weakened his protective shield without him realising it, and Queen Helistra was seizing on the moment.

One, two, three smaller balls of dense air packed with poisonous globules punched into the weakened spot on his protective shield where the lightning bolt had struck.

The first dented it, tearing at its weave, causing the whole of Speedwell's shield to flicker under the strain. The second followed, forcing it to tear apart, for the third to rip through it and release the poisonous globules into Speedwell!

Speedwell slammed against the stone wall once more, to instantly feel the poison enter him. Doubled up, he slid down the wall, cursing himself for his own stupidity.

This time, he had no life-giving droplets to help him. He had used them all for the ceremony of the runes and the Bridge of Seasons!

He could only freeze and burn the poison inside him, as he did at the pool of life in the forest, but that would leave him temporarily paralysed whilst it did its work, open to her attack as he lay there, but what choice had he!

Reinforcing his shield of protection, Speedwell moved his fingers shakily over his rune staff to send a bolt of ice-blue flame into his body as he sat against the stone wall looking at his triumphant daughter walking towards him with death written in her blood-red eyes.

Queen Helistra bared her teeth in a cold grin seeing Speedwell prop himself up, knowing what he must do to stop the poison reaching his heart. She watched his fingers shake as he touched some symbols on his rune staff, for it to turn ice-blue, his body jumping as a bolt of ice-blue flame entered it, rendering him motionless; he was hers!

She stooped over him, wincing at her shoulder as she did so. She had forgotten about it in her rage. How enjoyable this was going to be, she thought, as she noted the weakness still showing in the weave of his protective shield, even though he had tried to strengthen it.

"Your time is at an end, old man," she gloated, and touching symbols on the broken rune staff to draw on more power stored from the crystal chamber, she turned its end into a glowing shimmering white light. She was going to end Speedwell's life by burning a hole right through his head!

"Leave my great-uncle alone!" came a cry from behind her as she held the shimmering white light against Speedwell's weakened protective shield, to hear it hiss as it began to burn its way through.

Martyn could not call him Speedwell, a Forestall he was, but at this moment he meant much more to him, but Martyn's warning did not deter Queen Helistra. She carried on pressing the broken rune staff against Speedwell's weak protective shield!

She knew who it was, but what were he and his silly little sister without his rune staff that she had locked in a spell of binding!

But he did have his rune staff, and she was about to find that out!

Martyn thought of what he wanted to do to save Speedwell, and the bond that he had formed with his rune staff flowed through his fingers as they floated over the symbols to produce a loop of fire. In the next moment, he had thrown it over Queen Helistra, pulled it tight around her and with one pull of his arm, dragged her across the floor, pulling her over a bench, to land in the fireplace!

Martyn watched her get back to her feet, to look at him with surprise and consternation at what he had done, to the sound of a gasp from Princess Amber, who stood behind Martyn with Tarbor.

As the loop of fire crackled around Queen Helistra's shield of protection, it had lit up her blood-red eyes, but it was not her eyes that had made Princess Amber gasp. It was the wound she had received from Speedwell; it was oozing orange blood!

She has become one of her creations, she thought, though her beauty remained!

Only now did Queen Helistra come to her senses. Her rage had overshadowed everything, dulling her perception with the broken rune staff, not that the broken rune staff had been receptive after finding its broken piece!

Queen Helistra twisted the broken rune staff around the loop of fire and snapped it off, sending it hurtling back at Martyn, who dissolved the spell before it hit him.

Seeing Speedwell, after discovering that the broken piece still existed, had only triggered her anger even more. She had felt nothing of the boy retrieving his rune staff as humming came into her mind.

Shutting her mind from the others, she listened. *I have calmed down, what of you? You still sound confused.* Humming... *Yes, it was a shock to find it.* Humming again... *There is more than enough, and my shoulder will mend.* Humming... *I can see they are together and that he has an inner strength, but he does not know of the ways fully to enhance it with hers.* Humming... *Of course, why have we never seen that! I am no good to them dead! They need me alive!* Humming... *Yes, as they would wish it of me, let them use their energy and we will strike when the opportunity shows, as it did now!*

Strengthening her protective shield, Queen Helistra then sent a stream of white light straight at Speedwell's prostrate body.

Martyn's fingers had moved swiftly over his rune staff, already anticipating Queen Helistra's strike, but as he cast his spell to deflect the beam of light, Tomin suddenly appeared through the great hall doors, to throw a wall of protection across Speedwell.

His weakened state, though, showed through his spell, for as Martyn's spell deflected the white light away from Speedwell, both hit Tomin's wall of protection to explode on impact, sending Tomin flying through the air back through the great hall's doors, much to the amusement of Queen Helistra, who would have found it even more amusing had she noticed the three figures who had followed him suffering the same fate.

Having secured the gates behind them to hold the monsters at bay, Tomin had rushed to the sound of the fighting in the great hall.

Fresh supplies of arrows being found saw the rest of the company storming the battlements to rain death upon the monsters now pounding at the gates, whilst Permellar, Oneatha and Kayla had run to Middle Gate to hide in one of its turrets, but Queen Elina had not stopped with them. She had been hard on the heels of Tomin, determined to seek out her children.

Cantell and Kelmar had run after her, trying to stop her, when suddenly they found themselves hurtling across the grand courtyard!

Queen Helistra threw another beam of white light at Speedwell, for Martyn to deflect once more, but this time with a wall of reflection, to see the white light bounce straight back at her.

Hmm, he is quick of thought, thought Queen Helistra, countering her own spell to see the beam of light bounce once more before hitting the stone wall above her.

"Throw a shield of protection over me, Martyn. I will go to Speedwell," cried Princess Amber suddenly.

Martyn did not question the wiseness of her decision. He only knew she wanted to help Speedwell, and granting her wish, he threw a shield of protection over her.

Tarbor felt useless as he watched Princess Amber run to the aid of Speedwell. What could he do? He should have been the one throwing a shield of protection around Princess Amber. Where was his defender and shield when he needed them? Where had she hidden them?

Martyn took him by surprise by suddenly holding his arm. "Close your eyes and see where they are through me, Tarbor," he whispered, "then you can protect my sister whilst I deal with her," he added.

Tarbor immediately closed his eyes, picturing his defender and shield, hoping their whereabouts would come clear to him.

Queen Helistra's eyes were suddenly on Princess Amber, knowing she was going to Speedwell's aid, but she had disappeared down the adjoining corridor, out of sight. She waited for her to appear in the archway and as she sensed the moment, she sent bolts of lightning into it to meet her.

Martyn saw what she was going to do and sent spears of flame at Queen Helistra to distract her, but his distraction with Tarbor saw him being too late!

The bolts of lightning hit Princess Amber's protective shield with enough power to send her into the corridor wall, sending her sprawling onto the floor. Feeling dazed but in one piece, she looked up to see Piper calling her from the kitchen door. "Quick, hide in here!"

Queen Helistra, seeing the spears of flame coming at her, deflected them straight at Speedwell, who was starting to slowly come around.

It had taken the ice-blue flame longer to freeze and burn the poison out of his system than he had hoped, leaving him too weak to reinforce his protective shield enough, making him vulnerable to the spears of flame which were upon him!

Martyn cursed himself for not concentrating. He sensed his sister had been hit by the lightning bolts, but knew she was all right, but it had made his reactions slower again to help Speedwell.

But someone else's reactions were not, as Martyn was left speechless when Tomin reappeared to dive right in front of Speedwell to take the full force of the spears of flame!

Tomin's protective shield proved not enough to hold back all the flaming spears as the last one tore through his body, to leave him lying there in agony at the feet of Speedwell.

Martyn felt guilt rise up inside him. "Uncle Tomin!"

Tarbor heard Martyn's worry as the picture that had entered his mind became distorted, but it had been enough for him to know where his defender and shield were hidden.

Opening his eyes, he held Martyn's arm. "Do not let your emotions take over, Martyn," he warned, looking at Queen Helistra. "Look what happens when they do!"

"I know, Tarbor, only evil lyes down that path," said Martyn, nodding. "I will hold her back whilst you find your defender and shield," urged Martyn, and knowing he could best help by finding them, Tarbor immediately disappeared, to go up the spiral steps of Forest Tower.

As he passed the mountain throne room, he spotted the two monsters that had been killed by the deflected ice-blue flame, sprawled out on the steps, for him to hurry even more to get up the spiral steps.

Tarbor was out of breath by the time he entered the ceremonial room through the floor, to note the altar was already pushed aside.

Tarbor entered the pitch-blackness of the passageway behind it with a torch he had thankfully prized from its holder.

He moved cautiously down the passageway. How far along here did he need to go? For somewhere down here was the picture he had seen through Martyn.

A movement in front of him immediately told Tarbor he must be near, as in the next moment a monster suddenly lurched out of the blackness to confront him!

His torch was scythed in half by the waiting monster, stopping its sword from slicing through him!

Tarbor still had the Elfore sword and thanked the stars that he had as he parried another strike from the monster, whose deformed face flickered grotesquely in the fallen torchlight.

Moving ever backwards towards the light, from the opening of the ceremonial chamber, Tarbor managed to see the blows being levelled at him as he parried one after another from the monster.

Tarbor was becoming anxious; the longer he took, the more Martyn would be using his powers, holding Queen Helistra at bay. He needed to be there so he could protect Princess Amber whilst… no, wait! So Martyn could join with Princess Amber!

How stupid was he, just holding hands! Together, their spirits would be stronger to defeat her!

Tarbor parried another blow and suddenly heard Mrs Beeworthy in his mind: *I never did trust that squinty-eyed sergeant.*

Tarbor stopped yet another blow from the monster, but this time, he locked swords to be face to face with it.

The light coming through the opening from the ceremonial chamber showed Tarbor yellow eyes burning back at him, with razor-like teeth snarling in defiance, letting Tarbor smell its putrid breath.

Tarbor had locked swords with the monster to hold him still. His mind had been jogged by Mrs Beeworthy making him remember when he had first asked the defender to be straight and true.

Somewhere behind the monster he could sense his defender laying in wait. He hoped his bonding was strong enough to help him now as he focused his mind.

He was answered in a silent whisper as the defender appeared, sticking out of the chest of the monster, for it to fall headlong past Tarbor onto the passageway floor!

Taking his defender out of the monster, Tarbor quickly ran back down the passageway to retrieve his shield, nearly falling over it in the process, to run back down the spiral steps to the sound of lightning arcing throughout the great hall.

Martyn was holding Queen Helistra at bay by fending off the lightning she was directing at Speedwell and Tomin with a wall of protection, when Tarbor appeared behind him, his shield of protection humming in his ears.

"Success, Tarbor," he called above the arcing lightning without looking around.

"Success, Martyn."

"See if my sister can help Tomin with her healing powers, he is badly hurt. I can hold this evil witch back a bit longer," answered a worried Martyn, for Tomin and Speedwell.

"I understand your concern, Martyn, but the longer you fight her on your own, the more your power will drain, as well as hers. I have only just realised that together you will be stronger to defeat her and force her hand," said Tarbor, pointing out the obvious to Martyn.

"I know, Tarbor, and her power from the crystal chamber has to be exhausted first, but I do not want Speedwell and Tomin to be sacrificed in that quest. When you replace my protective shield with yours, get them out of sight, away from her attention, then when my sister has attended them we will finish this," he answered assuredly as he kept another strike of lightning at bay.

Tarbor did not question Martyn anymore, and with an understanding nod, he sped down the adjoining corridor to open the kitchen door, for an arrow to be pointing straight at him! "Tarbor!" cried Piper, and she let down her bow.

Tarbor wanted to smile at seeing her again, but the lightning crackling in the great hall reminded him of why he was there.

Then he saw Urchel lying on the kitchen table with a bandage around his leg, with Mrs Beeworthy hovering over him. He looked as white as a sheet.

"Is he all right?" he quickly asked.

"He be better than he was. I not be knowing how she did it with that, whatever it be, around her, but she did," piped up Mrs Beeworthy, with a bowl of broth in her hands. "He be better still when he gets this inside of him," she finished, putting a spoon of broth to Urchel's lips.

"I know your broth will fix him, Mrs Beeworthy, and there are two more that need to be fixed before we can finish what we have come to do," said Tarbor, looking at Princess Amber.

"Are you ready, Princess?" he asked, as he threw his protective shield over them both, for Princess Amber to nod as she felt Martyn's protective shield vanish.

Queen Helistra cursed, seeing Tarbor appear with Princess Amber from the corridor with the defender in his hand as she sent another arc of lightning at Tomin and Speedwell.

Why did she ever give him that wretched sword! It had all started with that, she should have melted it down, she thought irritably.

Humming interrupted her irritable mood. Shutting her mind off once more, she listened.

He does, his worries for them are a weakness which we can exploit. More humming… *Yes, whilst they are apart, we can finish him off. Then they will be easy pickings,* she agreed.

Running her fingers over the symbols of the broken rune staff as if she was going to reinforce her arc of lightning, Queen Helistra waited a moment as she glanced at Martyn, watching for the worry she knew he would show for his sister when he was at his weakest.

His eyes flitted towards his sister, and in that moment, she suddenly produced a dense ball of white light, to send it hurtling straight at the huddled group!

Martyn brought his focus back to Queen Helistra, only to see a ball of white light crackling with power heading straight for his sister, who was attending Tomin! He reinforced his wall of protection over them, but the ball of white light smashed through it before it could take effect!

All Tarbor saw was a white glow as he automatically held up his shield to protect them all, to feel his shield of protection crushed under the ball of white light's force, hit his shield and bounce onto the stone wall above them, exploding, sending them all crashing through the wall, for it to collapse all around them.

Martyn watched in horror as the whole of the great hall wall that was already weakened fell over everyone from the explosion, bringing down part of the roof with it!

What Martyn could not see was his mother, Kelmar and Cantell heading for Middle Gate as the great hall wall blew out!

Martyn felt sick inside; what had he done! Only dust and rubble remained where they all were! He had let his worried feelings take over from his concentration, and in that split moment, he had lost any help he might have had.

Suddenly Queen Helistra was walking towards him, with a knowing smile on her face.

They were too weak to stop her now, there was no movement to be felt, but she could sense they were alive, more's the pity. *But by the time they come round, I will have ripped this child's heart out. Then their spirit will be finally broken and death will come easily.* She grinned.

Martyn began backing away as he watched her fingers move over the symbols of Grimstone's broken rune staff whilst her lips moved in a chant.

He soon found himself on the steps of the mountain throne room, nearly falling over the two dead monsters. It was where he needed to be if he was going to force her hand, he thought absently, but even though he had also sensed their spirits were still alive, when there was no movement to be felt, he felt very alone. He was on his own.

The new self-assurance he had felt bonding with his lost spirit from his sister had taken a knock. He was starting to realise how much power he had used, holding her at bay; he could not afford to be lax again.

He breathed in a deep breath to calm himself down and closed his eyes, calling upon his rune staff and spirit to be strong in their time of need.

Opening his eyes, Martyn focused on his protective shield, seeing the potent energy on the end of Grimstone's broken rune staff in the form of a glimmering white light, ready to be cast his way.

It shot from the broken rune staff in a ray of blinding light, hitting his protective shield with an intenseness that shook his very being, sending him flying into the mountain throne room, to bounce off one of the mountain thrones and land face down on the rock floor!

He turned back over, shaking the buzzing out of his ears, to see the mountain throne room door in splintered pieces all around him and the two dead monsters' backs torn to shreds.

Martyn scrambled to his feet and looked around him. He could hide behind one of the mountain thrones; it offered some cover, he thought in a moment of panic. *No, Martyn, hold strong,* he chastised himself, *think!*

He checked his protective shield to find it had been weakened, but not as much as he thought it might have. He was not the only one whose power was depleting, he thought.

The wound Speedwell had inflicted on her had taken its toll. If only he could finish what Speedwell had started and drain the rest of the crystal chamber's power she had stored in Grimstone's rune staff, then he would stand more of a chance, he thought.

Martyn cast spears of flame at her advancement from around the opening, to hold her just for a moment longer.

Her smile could not have been any broader as she turned Martyn's spear flames into vapour before sending another beam of blinding light, to see Martyn disappear into the mountain throne room.

Martyn watched the ray of white light shoot through the open doorway, to hit the rock at the side of the mountain thrones.

He then immediately set about casting a spell across the open doorway, a tight weave to hold her back, like that of the barrier along the Old Ogrin Ridge, he thought, giving him the time to think on something that had come into his head.

When he had hit the mountain throne, a strange feeling had washed over him. Something seemed to awaken in his mind, as if opening a door to a thought that had been locked in there all of the time.

Finishing his spell just in time, he stood back to see Queen Helistra's evil face stare at him through the barrier.

"What is this pathetic attempt at trying to stop me?" She laughed and immediately cast lightning to arc all over its weaved surface to break it down, whilst a humming in her mind told her to be cautious. "Do not worry. We have him." She grinned.

Martyn turned away from her callous grin and looked at the symbols on the mountain thrones once more. There was something he should know about them. Why would it not come clear?

He had touched the same symbols on his rune staff in the dungeons, out of desperation, he knew, but nothing had happened, he thought.

Then he looked again, to realise that his anger at seeing Tintwist turned before his eyes had clouded his mind. He had only touched four symbols on his rune staff. There were four, but on each throne!

They could be for decoration, though, with no meaning, he thought further, but the feeling he was getting told him they were far more than just adornments.

The huge gates with their symbols came into his mind. He had not had his rune staff with him when Speedwell had opened them, but when Tomin opened them, he had, and that same feeling that had gone through him then was upon him now!

There was no more time for thinking as a last clear thought entered Martyn's mind, for him to move his fingers over each symbol methodically as Queen Helistra's lightning disintegrated his barrier.

Queen Helistra stood at the doorway facing him, with a beam across her face to match Grimstone's glowing broken rune staff.

Martyn backed away, looking at her, waiting, hoping that something was going to happen this time, as he threw a wall of protection in front of him, but nothing did.

Before any more disillusionment was allowed to gnaw at Martyn's mind, he was having to defend himself.

His wall of protection had simply shattered. His mind had been intent on the symbols upon the mountain thrones; he had not cast it properly!

Now he was holding off her halo of white fire with his shield of protection and rune staff, to stop it burning into his heart!

Queen Helistra's grin grew bigger as she felt Martyn's resistance waning under her relentless pressure. Her power was beginning to burn a hole through Martyn's shield of protection and, sensing victory, she moved in for the kill!

Her halo of white fire started to make Martyn's shield of protection shudder. His whole body was sweating under its intense heat when suddenly he felt a falter in her flow of power. It could only mean one thing, he thought: she had used all of her stored power from the crystal chamber!

A renewed confidence flowed through Martyn as he felt her power from the crystal chamber dwindle. He called upon his inner spirit to flow through his rune staff.

Symbols were quickly touched, for a spell of cold blue fire to ignite the whole of the mountain throne room with blue and white sparks as he countered her halo of white fire.

Queen Helistra cursed, but managed to hold back her annoyance as she felt the power from the crystal chamber leave the broken rune staff as she locked spells in mid-air with Martyn.

A humming came into her mind in warning. *It has given the boy fresh hope, but it is a false one. We may have faltered, but we are still stronger. He forgets the battle has given us more souls, whilst his strength still fades in his attempt at trying to get us onto the mountain throne.*

Something he has overlooked, she thought, and she waited for a telltale sign that his strength was fading.

Martyn held her there, blue against white buffeting against each other, but although her power from the crystal chamber had gone, she remained strong. He could feel it as his spell began to flicker.

He suddenly realised why. *Of course she has, the battle, the souls!* In the next moment, as he had realised this, she had blown his spell asunder, sending him flying onto one of the mountain thrones, for him to feel the heat of her spell against his heart once more! He could not move!

Sweat poured once more from Martyn's body as he gathered every part of his being to hold his shield of protection in place, but he was beginning to feel exhausted after all of his efforts. His confidence was all but gone as he felt his energy drain.

He made a last frantic search with his senses for his sister, to see if she had moved from underneath the rubble to come to his aid, but he felt nothing of her or anyone. Only the weight of the rubble that was upon them, like the weight he felt now, pressed against his heart.

Then suddenly there was Piper, with a dagger in her hand, flinging herself at Queen Helistra in a suicidal attempt at stopping her killing Martyn!

She will only hit her protective shield, thought Martyn, as he watched Queen Helistra bring up Grimstone's broken rune staff to swat her like a fly and send her crashing into the rock wall of the mountain throne room, rendering her unconscious, giving him only a breath of relief as the broken rune staff came straight back down over him.

"Is that all you have left to help you, little boy?" chided Queen Helistra, with her ever-present callous grin stretched across her face as she pressed home her halo of white fire, to see his protective shield visibly shuddering.

Martyn called upon his inner spirit and rune staff to combine in one last desperate attempt to ward off her evil as he looked at her triumphant evil face.

Her red eyes were full of loathing, and the orange blood from her wound had congealed as she twisted the broken rune staff with a sneer, letting her black cloak fall over them. *My death shroud*, thought Martyn, as his protective shield began to fragment. His end was near.

Unseen by Queen Helistra in her thirst for Martyn's death, the mountain throne runes above their heads had begun to glow.

Whereas Martyn was sweating, a sudden cold chill had entered the mountain throne room, for him to suddenly hear a voice in his mind and for Queen Helistra to turn around.

Hold strong, Forestall. I am with you!

Martyn gasped. He could not believe it, was it?

Through the mountain rock in the form of grey wispy strands came long ghost-like spiny fingers, to suddenly reach out and grip Queen Helistra's arm that held the broken rune staff, pulling it away from Martyn's chest. The wispy fingers had gone through her shield of protection, as if it was not there!

As much as she tried, Queen Helistra could not move her arm from their wispy grip, feeling her arm grow cold to its touch, unable to do anything as her halo of white fire was extinguished.

She looked on in sudden dread as the rest of the form took shape before her red eyes.

Bit by bit, grey cloud-like strands floated in the air to form a wavering spectre in front of her; it was the first wraith of the Ancient Forestalls!

"So this is the one who has turned our forests to decay and our children into monsters!" grated the first wraith in cold hisses in the face of a now petrified Queen Helistra.

Martyn got up out of the mountain throne with his heart lifted; the runes had summoned the wraiths of the Ancient Forestalls, and the first wraith had answered!

"Yes, wraith of the Ancients, it is her," answered Martyn, with relief washing over him like a waterfall.

"Sit down on your throne, witch. You look tired from all of your exertions," hissed the first wraith cynically into Queen Helistra's face, throwing her down onto the mountain throne with the uneven hole in the arm.

Queen Helistra stared wildly at the hollow-eyed spectre hovering over her, trying to speak, but she could not make a sound as the first wraith of the Ancients held her wrist and slowly forced her arm down, to put the broken rune staff into the uneven hole.

She tried to open her hand to let go of the broken rune staff, but it was as if her hand was frozen to it. Her fingers could not move.

Her body went rigid as the broken rune staff neared its broken piece. There was a scream and then nothing as the ends began to arc. The process of joining had begun, for it to mend.

Queen Helistra's body began to convulse, just as her many victims had, until it shook repeatedly.

The first wraith let go of her wrist to watch her demise, as did Martyn, with what was left of his shield of protection dissipating.

The broken rune staff suddenly began spinning in Queen Helistra's rigid hand, burning her flesh, as if in the final throws of releasing itself from her evil, before stopping dead.

Clicks were heard and the mountain throne began to move forward to reveal the steps leading down to the crystal chamber, for the broken rune staff to rise out of the mountain throne arm, its runes afire!

Its break was to be seen no more. It had melded together, making it whole again! It was no longer the broken rune staff of evil, but Grimstone's rune staff once more!

Grimstone's rune staff stopped being on fire, to be aglow, free from her evil, for Queen Helistra's body to suddenly burst into flames!

Martyn watched as flames came out of her eyes and her face began to melt. He turned his head away, he could not look any more.

Her punishment had been final, from Grimstone's rune staff, for what she had done to it, thought Martyn, as he heard her orange blood bubble with the heat.

"Martyn!" came a sudden cry from behind him, and he looked as his sister rushed into his arms with Speedwell behind her, with Tarbor helping him along, to stop dead at the sight of Queen Helistra burning.

Speedwell closed his eyes in pain. He had not wanted this. If only he had been stronger, he could have saved her. It was his little girl, his daughter, but deep down in his heart he knew there was only one way it was going to end, and he was looking at it.

"You have made it!" said Martyn, hugging his sister. "We were all buried in a mountain of rubble. If it had not been for…" Princess Amber stopped herself at the sight of the first wraith of the Ancients hovering at the side of the mountain throne, whom she had only just seen in her relief at seeing her brother alive.

But before anything could be said, a sound began to resonate from the opening that led to the crystal chamber.

"The crystals are shedding their evil!" hissed the first wraith of the Ancients.

"Quick, Tarbor, your shield!" cried Speedwell, thinking the crystals were going to explode!

"Piper, Tarbor! She is behind you!" shouted Martyn, thinking the same.

"They will not explode, merely replace themselves," assured the first wraith of the Ancients as it hovered in front of them.

The crystals began to break free from the chamber walls as the sound of splintering came to their ears, for the air to be suddenly sucked out of the mountain throne room as the crystals turned from blood-red to a blinding white light, purifying them of any evil, now Grimstone's rune staff was whole.

None could see them all falling into the pool of life, immediately cleansing it of its blood-red evil.

Linking together like a snake, they began to form one long mass of glowing power.

As the last crystal fell into the pool of life, the new crystals that had replaced them shone with power to reflect off the mass of purified crystals, sending them hurtling through its waters, destined for the Plateau Forest, to begin its healing.

For the second time, it felt like the air had been sucked out of the mountain throne room by the force of the purified crystals leaving. The ground rumbled with their power, to gradually die down as they drew further away.

A deathly silence followed and they all looked at the first wraith of the Ancient Forestalls, who they swore looked to be smiling. The reason why was that tiny specks of light were passing through him, released from Grimstone's rune staff.

"The trapped souls," whispered Speedwell, and they all watched, sensing as they did so whispered gratitude that they could now finally rest in peace.

"For them to finally rest over the Great Forest there is one more thing that needs to be done to make the process complete, now the crystal chamber is free of evil and the purified crystals are on their way to give life back to the forests," stated the first wraith, its hollow eyes looking at Speedwell.

"I understand," answered Speedwell.

"There is nothing more I can do here. I will leave you to the work you have to do," finished the first wraith.

"Our debt to you cannot be measured," thanked Speedwell.

"We are Forestalls, Speedwell, in body and in spirit we exist to help each other in time of need. There is no debt," pointed out the first wraith as its hollow eyes looked at Martyn.

"Thank you for coming. I was not sure what I was doing," admitted Martyn, and he thought he saw the first wraith smiling again.

"I felt the uncertainty within you, young Forestall. Emotions can be a blessing and a hindrance. They need to be under control when you use your gift," spoke the first wraith, reminding Martyn of what Tarbor had said to him, for Tarbor to give him a knowing look.

"You have always had the ways of the forest within you. Now you will have the time to study and learn them properly, so they will become clear to you," said the first wraith in understanding.

Its spectre then seemed to smile one last smile to them all before vanishing into thin air before their eyes.

Piper raised her aching head and looked around. "What happened to Queen Helistra?" she asked, and they all looked at the mountain throne, to see it glistening back at them. The wind from the crystal chamber had not left any trace of Queen Helistra ever being there engulfed in flames.

"She has found peace at last," said Speedwell sadly, with a sigh.

CHAPTER LXI

Joy and sadness were felt in equal measure in the aftermath of Queen Helistra's demise. It was a time for healing for all those who had survived.

Spring was the first to show the way by lifting hearts as it lifted the grey clouds that had lain heavily over the land and forests, bringing with it a fresh spring breeze to help blow them away, revealing blue skies and a golden sun, to melt what had seemed an everlasting snow, finally welcoming in the month of beginning, giving new hope to all of Northernland.

After the crystal chamber had rid itself of evil, an unerring stillness had come over the stronghold. Those on the battlements had watched as one moment the monsters were craving for blood and in the next had dropped their weapons, to stand there motionless in the snow.

King Brodic had shouted for the huge gates to be opened so he, Galmis, Tiska and Tislea could shepherd them into the grand courtyard like lost sheep, to wait there silently.

Blank expressions looking emptily into the distance met their looks from the same grotesque faces that only moments before had stared wildly at them with eyes of coloured hatred.

Amongst them, released from the thick white cloud, were Tintwist and King Vedland, with the same lost expression. Piper had run to find Tintwist, crying as she saw his lost look.

Queen Elina had cried a thousand times over her children, but no more so than when they were all reunited, hugging each other endlessly, thankful that it was all over.

She had saved a hug each for Cantell and Kelmar for saving her life, whilst they thanked the slice of luck they had that saved theirs.

Just before the great hall wall exploded, they had managed to persuade Queen Elina that it was too dangerous for her to be near there. Seeing Tomin come flying through the great hall doors to be sent sprawling themselves onto the ground had helped.

They were taking Queen Elina back towards Middle Gate when the wall did explode. They dived upon her to hit the ground, protecting her, regardless of their own lives, to take the brunt of the stone that was sent flying, but instead of stone hitting them, one of the great hall's wooden doors landed on them, saving them from the stone.

Though pounded to come out bruised, they were all in one piece to go to the aid of Speedwell, Tomin and Tarbor, who were buried under a mountain of rubble, not realising that Princess Amber was also under there, until they found her.

Princess Amber had tended to Tomin and Urchel, helping them enough to sit up in bed to enjoy Mrs Beeworthy's famous broth.

Then it had been a time to listen as one story after another was told, for her to hear in the sadness of their stories how all had lost a loved one or a friend on their long journey back to where it had all began.

To finally hear from Tarbor how the father she and her brother had never known had met his fate.

No one had gone without suffering, she thought, as she held her tearful mother, Queen Elina, in her arms.

All were there, except Speedwell; he had sat next to the pool of life with his rune staff dipped in its now shimmering glow, letting his presence move within it, to feel the powerful cleansing that had taken place when the crystals had purified it.

The red malevolence that had turned the pool of life into the pool of death was no more.

He had bathed in the little pool's cleansing, letting it wash through him, renewing his inner strength as he took his presence to the sister pool to see what effect the purified crystals were having on the Plateau Forest.

As he arrived at the sister pool, his presence marvelled at the spectacle being displayed before him. The purified crystals had formed a fountain of shimmering white crystals, letting the pool's cleansed waters cascade over them, high into the air, spraying out to cover the nearby dead forest and soak into the earth, with an extra helping hand from a spring breeze.

Speedwell watched the brown goo being eaten away that had been left by the poison's destruction. It had begun, thanks to the Ancients. He smiled.

His mind had withdrawn from the pool of life, knowing that the essences would soon return to help in the restoration of the forests.

Now his mind had turned to the monsters waiting in the grand courtyard and how the joining of Grimstone's broken rune staff had stopped the evil inside them wanting to kill, but had not returned their bodies to them, leaving them in limbo, caught between the two.

The soul blood had tainted everything, but had affected animal, man and Elfore differently to the forests. The forests had died to its touch, but they had not died. Instead, their blood had been turned and needed turning back, to see the light again, he thought.

With that thought, Speedwell had taken a clay bowl full of the cleansed water from the pool of life and Grimstone's rune staff from above the mountain throne arm where it had hovered ever since, becoming whole once more, to now stand with everyone in the grand courtyard.

The monsters sat, lay and stood looking blankly into the distance as everyone else looked at Speedwell. He looked back, seeing all their looks of hope that these poor creatures that had survived would be themselves once more, free from his daughter's evil.

All were there, except Tomin and Mrs Beeworthy.

Martyn was holding Princess Amber's hand, with Queen Elina standing next to them and Tarbor, taking him by surprise as she held his arm, for him to look at her to receive a smile of warmth, making him go hot.

Cantell smiled at seeing them both, nudging Kelmar, who also smiled, but his smile was also one of not losing Permellar who, with Kayla, was holding on to him this time and not letting go!

Oneatha felt how lucky she was to have survived to see them together again, whilst Urchel and King Brodic sat on one of the great hall stones, resting their legs, with Galmis standing behind them.

Tiska and Tislea held hands, sad in the thought that they had been too late to save Fleck, especially Tislea, who wished she had been kinder in thought about him when he was alive.

Piper stood alone in front of them all, her eyes not leaving a vacant-looking Tintwist.

Elfore and Silion stood side by side as they had in battle all around the grand courtyard as Speedwell began to speak.

"The time of healing has begun, and with this water, we will help these poor creatures rid themselves of the evil blood that has cursed them," announced Speedwell.

"Princess Amber, will you come and help me?" he asked, taking Princess Amber by surprise.

"I do not like to ask, but you already proved your blood holds the evil at bay when you helped Cantell. If you could let one drop mix with the cleansed water, I will do the rest," asked Speedwell, feeling a little awkward at asking her for her blood.

Princess Amber automatically looked at Cantell as Speedwell spoke, smiling. She had forgotten what she had done for Cantell after hearing all the sad stories. Being thrown into the dungeons had not helped, a nightmare that had made her feel even more useless than she already felt. Now suddenly she could help with just one drop of her blood!

She held her finger over the clay bowl. She did not need to cut herself; the split at the end of her finger under her nail was something she had been born with, without her realising it, until Martyn's spirit awoke her. She could open it and seal it at her command, as she did now, to let a drop of her blood fall into the cleansed water.

She stood back and watched Speedwell begin chanting as he touched some symbols on Grimstone's rune staff.

Speedwell felt the shame Grimstone's rune staff felt at what his daughter had turned it into as he held it. He could feel the determination within it, as he touched its runes, to put right the desecration it had caused, though in itself, it felt what it was doing now was never going to be enough.

He dipped Grimstone's rune staff into the clay bowl and stopped chanting, for its contents to turn a strange green colour as he touched one last symbol.

"It is ready," he announced, and he looked at Piper's anxious features, for her to bring Tintwist to him.

Piper brought the deformed figure of Tintwist with hope and trepidation inside her as Speedwell looked into Tintwist's red eyes, to see they were devoid of anything as they stared right through him.

"A drop should be enough," said Speedwell, more to himself than anyone else, and he put a drop on Tintwist's bloated lips. Standing back, he waited for something to happen, as did everyone.

At first, there was not a glimmer of movement on Tintwist's twisted features. Then suddenly his tongue was seen to lick at the single drop of liquid, as if it were a fly irritating him.

The reaction was for his deformed body to suddenly go rigid. Piper let go of his arm as his blood-red eyes rolled upwards.

A gasp came out of his mouth and he fell to the ground, convulsing. "The orange blood is being attacked," remarked Speedwell to a worried Piper.

Piper looked on in horror as Tintwist's face looked as if it had worms crawling underneath his skin, pulling it one way and then another, trying to bring the face back that everyone knew.

His body moved under his clothes in just the same way as the potion moved through stretched veins and pustules, battling to drive the evil away.

His veins began to turn back to normal as they started to flow with red blood; pustules began shrinking as the healing took hold, then suddenly his body went rigid again and he sat bolt upright, sucking in a lungful of air!

Only the sea breeze could be heard as everyone looked on as eyes of clear brown suddenly looked up at Piper to blink and smile. "What is it? Have you never seen a Manelf before!" And everyone laughed and cried at the same time; Tintwist was back! And Piper threw herself at him, crying.

One by one, all those that had been tainted were treated.

Townsfolk, Elfore, Silion, animals, they all came back with their blood and skin cleansed, their deformities shed.

A lucky few found that there were loved ones there or friends, whilst the animals ran out of the gates of Stormhaven to the Great Forest and freedom.

King Vedland came round, blinking, wondering where he was, not able to remember what had happened to him, when he saw Speedwell standing over him.

"Speedwell! Where... where am I? Where is this place? What happened?" was all King Vedland could say in his confusion in trying to remember as he saw Elfore and man together.

"You are in Stormhaven stronghold in the Kingdom of Tiggannia, Northernland. Your body was poisoned, making you become a monster, but now you are healed," replied Speedwell.

King Vedland stood up and looked at Speedwell, beginning to remember.

"Your daughter, Speedwell, Helistra, she—"

"She is dead," interrupted Speedwell, "as is Fleck, the one you called an outcast and ignored!" said Speedwell scornfully, for King Vedland to say no more but to walk away in silence.

I should not have spoken to him like that, thought Speedwell afterwards. *He is a King*, but his feelings at this moment were mixed, to say the least.

"Now it is time for you to search throughout Northernland for those others who have been unfortunate enough to have been tainted," announced Speedwell to everyone after the cleansing, "whilst we perform one last task when Tomin is well enough to travel. Then the future well-being of the forests and Northernland will be assured," stated Speedwell, looking at Martyn and Princess Amber, for her to frown at her brother, wondering what it was.

CHAPTER LXII

Two more months passed by whilst Tomin recovered, seeing spring depart and summer heralded in.

As soon as Tomin was able, Speedwell set out with the rest of the company to travel to the Old Ogrin Ridge.

They set sail from Haven on the Eastern Sea in the Elfore sailing boat that had been sailed from the River Mid by King Vedland in a humble gesture, after hearing where it was and the objections from those travelling with Speedwell that they did not want to encounter the whirlpool again!

Thanking him, Speedwell had apologised for his rudeness towards him and wished him well.

Now he was sailing under the vast shadow of the Kavenmist Mountains, knowing this was the way his daughter had come to destroy the Ancient One, but this journey, he prayed to the stars and spirits, would end in the beginning of a new dawn.

He looked at Princess Amber as he thought on it, to see she was remembering that fateful journey as she looked at him and then away again with an embarrassed smile on her face.

He smiled back at her in understanding. It had not been of her choosing; she had been under his daughter's control then.

Speedwell then looked at the familiar faces of his friends that had set sail with him.

He had spoken to them once they had set sail, for a quietness to fall over their earlier banter as they all thought on what he had told them, about the task that was going to be undertaken.

Not all were there; King Brodic had left with his army whilst it was still spring, escorting Galmis back to Elishard beforehand to take his rightful place as King before returning himself back home to Flininmouth.

Tiska and Tislea had left with a quiet King Vedland after helping him retrieve the Elfore sailing boat to join their fellow Elfore, where they would rebuild their lives in peaceful existence once more in that part of the Great Forest that had remained untainted, until the day came when they could journey back to their home in the Valley of the Lakes.

Permellar had gone back to her farm with Kayla, where they would start anew whilst waiting for the return of Kelmar, who after this journey was giving up the army to do what he should have done in the first place! Besides, he had seen enough adventure these last years to last him a lifetime!

Oneatha had decided to go with Permellar to help her get back on her feet, before returning to Kelmsmere.

Urchel had gone with them also. There was nothing more he wanted than to become a farmer again, and helping Permellar was just what he needed to set him on his way.

All had left with flasks of purified water, along with envoys sent to search high and low throughout the five Kingdoms to help heal those who had fallen foul of Queen Helistra's evil.

The Ogrin River finally showed itself, inviting them inland to the Windy Pass for memories and stories to unfold once more before they eventually arrived at the Lake of Tears.

There immediately for them all to see, resting in the lake on the far side, was the huge trunk of the Ancient One, bumping gently against the bank. It had finally fallen from the ridge.

Martyn looked away with a heavy heart but managed to smile when he saw the Bridge of Seasons still aglow with health at the neck of the lake. It had not weakened as he had feared when battling with Queen Helistra.

They made their way to the island made from the Ancient One's roots; still there despite the devastation they had been through, although, to their touch, they were empty of any life.

The long zig-zag steps of the rocky face were negotiated for them all to look out over the ridge, feeling a breeze run past them on its way to the decayed Plateau Forest, where signs could be seen that the brown sludge had dried out, awaiting the time for the healing waters to wash it away, to begin anew.

A breeze helped by the constant draught coming from the Linninhorne and Winterbourne Waterfalls that forever cascaded down into the Lake of Tears, their rainbows reaching out over the lake as if protecting it.

Martyn pointed out to Amber the shimmering white streams that could be seen within the waters of the lake, arteries of life giving renewed health that would spread from the river's banks into the forests sooner rather than later, thanks to the essences' help, who had returned to their pools of life.

"It is time for us to bring about a new beginning," announced Speedwell, as he moved into the giant hole that had been left where the Ancient One had once proudly stood.

As they all walked into the gigantic hole, more of the Ancient One's roots could be seen ripped apart, left trailing in pieces when the Ancient One had finally fallen into the lake, to remind them once more of the forests lost and why they were here.

Martyn and Tomin had always known. Amber had come to realise it, as had Tarbor. The others had thought it, but it was only a dream. Could it be possible?

They would soon be finding out, for they were here to perform a ceremony that would make Grimstone's rune staff become the new life force of the forests! The new Ancient One!

Though Speedwell had had reservations about Grimstone's rune staff, that it would be forever tainted by his daughter's evil, scarred, it had shown from its actions that it could not do enough in its remorse to make things right. Tomin, Martyn and Amber had all felt it.

Martyn had let his presence be as one with his rune staff, to see the pure light that now shone within Grimstone's rune staff to confirm it.

So here they stood facing each other, with Speedwell holding his rune staff before him. Opposite him stood Tomin, holding Gentian's, Martyn with his and opposite him Amber holding Ringwold's rune staff, all planted on the earth before them.

Amber had worried that she would be a weak link in what they were about to do, having had only a short time to bond with Ringwold's rune staff, but her spirit, which had blossomed within her, had proven to be a strong healer within Ringwold's rune staff, to be ready for what was going to be asked of it.

Speedwell put Grimstone's rune staff in the centre of them and let it go, for it to hover over the earth.

Taking a flask of the purified water, Speedwell let a few droplets of the liquid fall onto Grimstone's rune staff, to watch it slowly coat its runes.

Then he took another flask holding life-giving bubbles, given to him by the returning essences before he left Stormhaven, for them to attach themselves to each and every rune upon its length.

"Grimstone's rune staff is ready and waiting to give life back to the forests," announced Speedwell, and touching symbols on his rune staff, he began to chant.

Queen Elina, Tarbor, Cantell, Kelmar, Piper and Tintwist all watched in silence, finding themselves holding hands as suddenly Speedwell's rune staff turned blue.

Tomin then followed Speedwell's lead, for Gentian's rune staff to turn yellow.

Now Martyn for his to turn white, and then Amber for Ringwold's rune staff to turn brown.

The four rune staffs had turned into the four elements they represented, water, fire, air and earth, as they resonated together, making the earth beneath the company's feet pulsate like a heartbeat.

Then suddenly the resonating rune staffs' elemental colours shot into Grimstone's rune staff for their colours to weave together, making Grimstone's rune staff spin as they twisted around it.

It immediately felt as if the air around the company was going to lift them off their feet as Grimstone's rune staff's spinning gained momentum.

Speedwell turned and looked at Tarbor for him to unsheathe his defender. He had been told by Speedwell that it was going to be needed, as the defender was forged from a fallen star and would give strength to the elements by adding the very sky itself!

Tarbor let go of the defender as Speedwell had told him to, to see it float to Grimstone's rune staff and hold itself point first over it, to start to glow in a strange mix of colours. White, yellow, purple, silver showed themselves upon its now glowing blade, intertwining with each other in their own weave.

A pulse later saw the defender's element of sky join the four woven elements, pulsating through Grimstone's rune staff and the earth, fusing them together to form a tighter weave.

Fingers moved over rune staffs, and their chanting reached a continuous drone, increasing the intensity of the pulses travelling through the earth; pulses that they hoped were reaching far down into the earth where the severed roots of the Ancient One lay dormant, hoping that life still flowed within them.

Speedwell was feeling nothing through the pulses, but they could not hold back Grimstone's rune staff anymore. It was ready!

The ground by now was thumping with the intensity of the pulses. All the company felt an overwhelming sensation of well-being coming from the power of the woven elements coursing through Grimstone's rune staff.

The giant hole itself was aglow with the pulsating colours as Speedwell whispered in his mind to the others, *Now!*

The chanting stopped and each of their fingers touched one last symbol, to see Grimstone's rune staff suddenly stop spinning.

They were all given one last look, to see its runes aglow before it shot straight down into the earth!

Tarbor sheathed his defender that had fallen to the ground and stood back with the others, all in wonder at what they had just witnessed, but would it work? Was the Ancient One's being still there?

They sat down and waited for what seemed a lifetime for some sign, something!

Then they felt it, a tremble that became a vibration, a vibration that became a rumble, a rumble that suddenly exploded before their eyes as earth was thrown aside, for them to quickly move further back.

Jaws fell, eyes widened as there, soaring upwards in front of them, was a tree!

Its trunk roared past them, reaching for the clouds! Branches emerged, holding themselves in graceful elegance.

They found themselves rising in the air as roots coursed through the earth between the two rivers, casting aside whatever debris there was left of the old roots as they took hold.

For old they were, because they had been replaced, replaced by a reborn Ancient One!

Speedwell and Tomin were choked with emotion as their bodies felt the renewed vibrancy of the reborn Ancient One.

Martyn and Amber ran to the Ancient One's trunk, hugging it, crying.

All hugged each other in disbelief that anything like this could have happened. They had listened to Speedwell throughout their long journey together, always in hope, but for this to have happened! The Ancient One reborn!

They all stood there, staring in awe, saying nothing, but wishing that their loved ones and friends who had not made it were here with them to see it.

"Now the forests will be healed," breathed Speedwell, his heart uplifted.

Tintwist looked up at the magnificence of it all with a grin as smaller branches and leaves began to form in front of his eyes. "Well, it is the month of trees!" he quipped to the sound of joyful laughter.

Matador

For exclusive discounts on Matador titles,
sign up to our occasional newsletter at
troubador.co.uk/bookshop